P9-EEO-426

SUN-CROSS

BY BARBARA HAMBLY

Published by Ballantine Books

DRAGONSBANE

THE LADIES OF MANDRIGYN
THE WITCHES OF WENSHAR
THE DARK HAND OF MAGIC

THE SILENT TOWER
THE SILICON MAGE

The Darwath Trilogy
THE TIME OF THE DARK
THE WALLS OF AIR
THE ARMIES OF DAYLIGHT

THE RAINBOW ABYSS

THOSE WHO HUNT THE NIGHT

SEARCH THE SEVEN HILLS

SUN-CROSS

The Rainbow Abyss
The Magicians of Night

BARBARA HAMBLY

Guild America
Books

THE RAINBOW ABYSS   Copyright © 1991
by Barbara Hambly
THE MAGICIANS OF NIGHT   Copyright © 1991
by Barbara Hambly

All rights reserved under International and Pan-American
Copyright Conventions.
                    Published by arrangement with
                    Del Rey/Ballantine Books
                    201 East 50th Street
                    New York, New York 10022

Map by Shelly Shapiro

PRINTED IN THE UNITED STATES OF AMERICA

Contents

THE RAINBOW ABYSS   1
THE MAGICIANS OF NIGHT   261

The
Rainbow
Abyss

For
Mary Ann

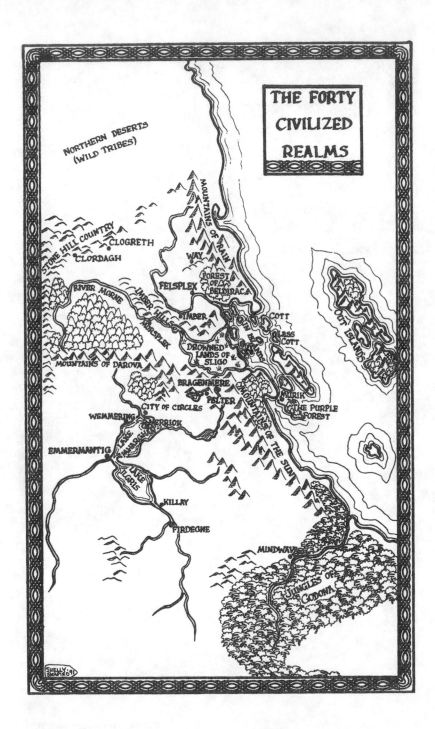

1

"It may not happen here."

"That's what they said about the Plague."

Shavus Ciarnin, Archmage of the Order of the Morkensik Wizards, flashed an irritated look at his old friend's pupil—Rhion the Brown merely pushed his spectacles a little more firmly into place on the bridge of his nose with one pudgy forefinger and returned the glare calmly. Old Jaldis the Blind brushed a tendril of milk-white hair from the tattered blanket that wrapped his thin shoulders and moved a little closer to the brown wall of chimney bricks which was the tiny attic's only source of heat. "So they did," he observed mildly. "I do not see how it *can* happen here . . . or how it could have happened at all. But this lack of understanding on my part does not alter the fact that it *has* happened there . . ."

"Don't be a fool," Ciarnin snapped irritably. His scarred, sun-darkened face seemed to darken still further, cold blue eyes appearing very light in their deep sockets. "Magic can't just cease to exist! Magic *is*! It's an element, like the light of the sun, like the air we breathe! Men could no more stop it from existing than they could keep the sun from rising by shaking their fists at it."

"To our knowledge," the blind mage replied in his curiously sweet, toneless voice.

Huddled in his threadbare cloak at his master's feet—the room only boasted two chairs—Rhion could barely recall what Jaldis' true voice had been like. He'd only heard it upon one occasion, when he was sixteen, a few months before the old king's troops had arrested Lord Henak, Jaldis' then-patron, and torn out Jaldis' tongue and eyes to keep him from witching them while they'd brought the traitor earl and his court mage to trial in the High City of Nerriok. The only reason they hadn't cut off the wizard's hands as well was because they'd feared he'd die of gangrene before judgment could be passed.

For the eleven years since his acquittal, Jaldis had spoken by means of a curved rosewood box which hung strapped to his chest, a sounding-chamber filled with intricate mechanisms of silver, reed, and gut, even as he saw—after a fashion and with head-splitting concentration—by means of a pair of massive spectacles wrought of opal, crystal, and gold. Charging the left lens with spells of seeing had been Rhion's first attempt at major magic, and he still remembered the shuddering surge of joy he'd felt when he'd seen the lattices of the crystal's inner structure shift and change, seen life stir deep in the opals' pale, fiery wells. The sense of release had been almost like the physical breaking-open of some locked core of bone deep in his chest, the realization that all those dreams, all those longings, all the strange madnesses which had whispered in his mind since childhood had been real . . .

He remembered, too, the week of vomiting and delirium which had followed, for of course he'd been far too young to attempt anything like the power needed for such spells. He'd tried desperately to keep his illness hidden—it had been his parents' first clue to their only son's abilities, and he'd come back to consciousness to the news that they had published, in all the temples of the Forty Realms, the notices of his death.

Though he'd never told Jaldis, Rhion's own extreme shortsightedness dated from the casting of those spells.

"And yet you must admit, Shavus," that thin, buzzing drone went on, "that there are places in this world where there is no air—in the depths of oceans and rivers—and no light, in caves and crevices . . . indeed, for half the turning of the day there is no light anywhere. And there are places, as we all know, where magic does not exist."

"Bah," the Archmage grunted, and the back of his cracked and much-mended chair creaked with the uneasy movement of his shoulders. The attic room above the Black Pig Inn, which had served Jaldis and Rhion as lodgings for the last two and a half years, was unheated, save for the warmth which radiated from the bricks of the kitchen chimney. On snowy midwinter evenings like this one it saved them from freezing to death, but when the turgid warmth of the low-plains summers held the city of Felsplex in its grip, the room was unspeakable. There was no fireplace in the room itself, nor any kind of candle or brazier—the landlord having an almost hysterical fear of fire—but, despite the fact that the windows were closed against the bitter cold by heavy wooden shutters, the lack of light posed little problem for wizards. Though the three men—young, middle-aged, and old—sat in complete darkness, Rhion could see the Archmage's square, ugly face and coarse shock of iron gray hair as easily as if the room were flooded with daylight. And he saw how the pale eyes shifted at the mention of such things. "Any fool knows about those."

"But this is more than the Chambers of Silence," Jaldis went on, "that lords build into the dungeons of their palaces to hold a wizard's power in check—more than the *pheelas* root that numbs our skills, more than the spells of silence, the fields of silence, that a powerful mage can weave to cripple his mageborn foes." Behind sunken and shriveled eyelids ruined muscles moved, as if his destroyed gaze could still encompass the gray-haired old ex-soldier opposite him and the short, sturdy young man at his feet. From the top of a stack of books beside his chair, Jaldis' opal spectacles seemed to review the room with a bulging, asymmetrical gaze, and the old man's hand, deft and shapely before arthritis had deformed it, stroked subconsciously at the talismans of power which festooned the rosewood soundbox like queer and glittering seaweed upon a rock.

"I am speaking of a world, a universe, where magic does not exist at all, and has not existed for many years."

"And I'm saying such a thing's preposterous," Shavus retorted.

"What you *think* you heard . . . what you *might* have seen . . ." He shook his head again, angry and dismissive, but Rhion saw the heavy, corded hand fidget uncomfortably with the snagged brown wool of his robe.

"I know what it is that I felt." Jaldis' thin face hardened with a flash of angry pride, though the monotonous voice of the soundbox did not alter. "I have opened a Dark Well and through it have seen into the Void which lies between all the infinite number of universes of which the Cosmos is made! And in that Void . . ." The sweet, shrill tones sank. "In that Void I heard a voice crying out of a world where magic had once existed, but now exists no more."

"Jaldis, old friend . . ." Shavus leaned forward placatingly, causing the ruinous chair to emit an alarming creak. "I'm not saying you didn't see it, didn't hear it. But I am asking how, if magic has ceased to exist in some other universe, someone there could make his voice heard in the Void? I've studied the Void as well, you know. I've opened Dark Wells into it, to try to glimpse something of how the Cosmos is formed . . ."

"I'm glad someone has," Rhion remarked, folding his arms around his knees and huddling a little more deeply into his faded black cloak. "The other night when Jaldis asked me to get a message to you about this was the first I'd even *heard* of the things."

"Which is as it should be," the Archmage snapped irritably. "It is not a branch of knowledge for the young—or the light-minded."

He turned back to face the blind man, bundled like a drying skeleton in cloak and quilts which all but hid the tattered brown robes of the foremost Order of Wizards in the world. His tough, seamed face softened. "Old friend, in all my studies of the Void, in all my communications across it and through it, I've never encountered a world where magic in some form didn't exist. I'm not denying that you heard something. But one piece of hearsay is damn little grounds to risk the hideous danger of crossing the Void itself, as you're asking me to do . . ."

"Not asking, Shavus," the old man said softly. "Begging. Someone must go there. Someone must help them. Don't you see that . . ."

Heavy footsteps on the narrow wooden spiral of the stairs made the whole building shudder. The Black Pig rose four floors above the common rooms and kitchens, a rickety inverted ziggurat of ever-protruding balconies and upper floors seemingly supported by a mystifying web of clotheslines and makeshift bridges over the streets and by the surrounding buildings against which it leaned. Rhion frequently wondered what would happen if any of the overcrowded tenements, taverns, countinghouses or gimcrack temples of unpronounceable foreign gods that made up the river quays quarter of Felsplex were to disappear. Beyond a doubt the entire district would come crashing down like a house of cards.

It was the landlord. Rhion recognized the tread. Pulling his cloak tighter about him, he got to his feet and navigated delicately among the few pieces of furniture which cluttered even that tiny chamber, summoning a blue-burning shred of magelight to flicker like will-o'-the-wisp above his head. The wavery gleam only served to make the room appear dingier, its moving shadows outlining with pitiless emphasis the cracks in the plaster of the walls, the stained beams from which bunches of winter mallow and stork grass hung drying, the chipped cups and water-vessels, and the precious books and scrolls arranged neatly along the table's rear edge. Darkness would have been less depressing, but Rhion had long ago learned that those who were not mageborn found wizards' ability to see without light disproportionately unnerving.

"Lady to see you," the landlord grunted, scratching his crotch.

"Are you—er—a wizard?"

Rhion was awfully tired of the question and of the dubious look that invariably accompanied it. He'd grown his beard as soon as he was old enough to do so, but the short-clipped, scruffy brown tangle evidently did nothing to dispel the boyishness of his face nor the way his wide-set blue eyes were magnified by the lenses of his spectacles. Short, unobtrusive, and of the compact, sturdy build which slips so easily into chubbiness, even without a wizard's ability to move unobserved he would have been the last person anyone noticed in a crowd.

The lady who was waiting for him in the smallest of the inn's private parlors had obviously been expecting someone a little more impressive.

He considered responding with *Are you—er—a lady?* but suppressed the impulse. He and Jaldis needed the rent. Instead he smiled genially and said, "We come in all shapes and sizes, mistress. Would you trust me more if I had horns and a tail?"

She let out an unsteady titter and her eyes, above a concealing veil of purple-embroidered silk, strayed to the hem of his robe as if she really expected to see the jointed tail of a scorpion-grim peeking out.

Inwardly, Rhion sighed. *Gold pieces to barleycorns she wants a love-potion . . .*

"And how may I serve you?" he asked, still with a smile and the reflection that asking the question in his capacity as wizard was an improvement upon doing so in the capacity of bar-boy, a position he'd occasionally filled at the Black Pig when things got bad. *If my father could see me now . . .*

She leaned forward, her little purple-gloved hands clenched upon the scrubbed oak tabletop. "There is . . . a man."

Rhion sat down on the opposite side of the table, folded his hands, and nodded encouragingly. Above the edge of the veil, her eyes were dark, enormous, and painted with green kohl and powdered gold; her cloak was lined with marten fur. From his days of loitering in the most fashionable scent shops in the City of Circles, he could price her perfume to within a few royals, and it wasn't cheap.

She went on, softly and simply as a child, "He must love me or I shall die."

"And he doesn't."

The delicate brows above those immense eyes puckered tragically. "He doesn't know I'm alive. He is fickle, frivolous . . . his affections turn on a whim. Give me something that will draw him to me, something that will make him love me . . ."

Rhion had never, personally, been able to fathom why human beings persisted in craving the love of people who didn't know they were alive, but this was far from the first time he'd encountered the phenomenon, or used the proceeds to put food on the table.

"Look," he said gently. "Are you sure he's the kind of man you want? If he's that fickle, that frivolous . . . A love-potion won't change what a person is. Only—and only temporarily—whom they want."

"That is enough," she breathed, and clasped her hands at her breast as if to contain the throbbing of her heart. Her cloak, falling back a little, showed strand upon strand of filigreed silver beads at her throat, gleaming against a ground of ribbon and featherwork like a field of summer flowers. "If only I can have the chance to win his regard, I know I can make him love me. If once I hold him in my arms, I know he will come back." She swayed forward and clutched his hand, as if fearing he would rise to his towering five-feet-five and denounce her as a strumpet. "Oh, name your price!"

They always said, *Name your price*, but Rhion had learned over the years what the going rate on love-philters was and had also learned that the rich especially would be screaming for the magistrates if the sum quoted were so much as a dequin above it.

He fetched candles from the mantelpiece, noting automatically as he passed the door of the common room the two chair bearers and the linkboy, drinking wine from boiled-leather cups beside that room's enormous hearth. Unlike the attics, the commons and the private parlors downstairs were pleasantly warm, redolent of beer and woodsmoke, sweat, onion stew, and the sawdust that strewed the floor. Judging by their clothes, the chair bearers were hired men, probably ex-slaves who'd bought themselves free and gone into business, for of course his client, no matter how rich she was, would have used hired bearers to bring her here, rather than her own household slaves.

No lady of respectable family would let her own servants know about coming to a place like the Black Pig, let alone to visit a wizard. People did visit wizards, of course, and pay for their services, in spite of the fulminations of every priest of every god in the landscape, the same way his father had visited the more expensive prostitutes and his mother had visited those skilled in the dyeing of hair. They just didn't talk about it. As he brought the tapers back to the table, he was aware of the way his client clutched her cloak about her and of the apprehension in the doelike eyes gazing at him from above the veil. She flinched when he sat down again, drawing as far from him as the high-backed chair would allow; and when he said, "Take off

your glove," her painted eyelids made as great a play as if he'd asked
her to remove her dress.

From a pocket in his robe he took a twist of paper containing the
herbal powder that was the basis of all love-philters, a supply of
which he kept made up beforehand. From another pocket he drew
the piece of red chalk he always carried and a goose-feather. He
explained, "For a love-potion to work, it has to carry the . . . the
scent, the essence, of your flesh."

"I know." Her voice sank to a whisper. "They said you . . . you
would mix it upon my naked body."

Before he could stop himself Rhion said, "Well, generally we do,
but this table's awfully hard and the fire's gone down . . ."

"I would not mind the cold." Her eyes smoldered, and Rhion bit
his tongue in exasperation, both at himself for making the joke and
at her for not realizing it *was* one.

"A hand will be fine."

She removed her glove and offered her soft little palm, scented
with attar of roses. Rhion turned her hand over and poured a quantity of the powder on the back. "If you'll keep silent now," he
remembered to say. He'd never had a client yet, male or female,
who, if not silenced beforehand, didn't feel compelled to relate the
details of the affair while he was trying to concentrate on the spells.

She let out her breath, looking a little disappointed.

He took the woman's thumb and little finger gently in his own
two hands, which rested on the table on either side of hers. Closing
his eyes, he slowed his breathing and stilled his thoughts, calling up
and focusing the power that rose from within himself like the slow
expansion of a single candle's light gradually illuminating some enormous, darkened room. This was the part of spell-weaving that he
loved and the part that made him most uneasy at times like this,
the most vulnerable in the presence of these representatives of the
mundane world for whom wizardry was a matter of rumor and
whisper and dread.

Though his eyes were shut, he could see the woman's hand still,
lying between his own. The green-gold powder sparkled against
the creamy flesh in the candles' limpid light. In time, eyes still shut, he
moved his hands, making the correct passes in the air above the

powder, drawing with the thin, glimmery air-traces that only a wizard could see the runes of binding, the symbols of oneness, that imbued the dried rose petals and shamrock leaves with the essences of the woman's well-cared-for flesh. His mind blended with the scents of the powdered sandalwood and salts, the smell of her perfume, the warmth of her hand, and the perfect shape of those cowlike brown eyes. He heard the high, delicate sweetness of her voice in his mind as a lover would hear it, finding its childish accents endearing rather than annoying, seeing in those wonderful eyes heart-touching innocence rather than—as was his private opinion—self-centered stupidity.

You must love them when you weave the spells, Jaldis had said to him years ago . . . *Seven? Six?* . . . when he had taught him the spells for the drawing of the heart. *Love them for their own sake, as a true lover does, whatever your private self may think. See charm in their imperfections, as the shadows of flowers mottle a sunlit wall. You must understand what beauty is before you can wake desire for it in another mind.*

It had taken him a long time to learn that, he recalled. Months of watching flowing water and the shadows of flowers. He still wasn't sure he understood.

Opening his eyes, he gently brushed the table before him with the goose-feather, then tipped the woman's hand so that the powder spilled off. Delicately he feathered the last residue from her skin, then with the chalk drew a small Circle of Power around the grains, and closed his eyes again. With the feather, with his fingers, with his mind, he shaped in the air above it the runes necessary for the spell, calling down the constellations of power and the clusters of invisible realities related to each archetypical sign.

The Cup, the rune of the heart, filled with clear water and utterly mutable, ruled by the Moon and the tides. The sixth rune, of caring and giving and duality, of two voices blending in harmony, and of the warmth closed in between two hands. The fifteenth, ugly and dark, the rune of obsession that chains the will and blurs the senses, sculpting reality to what one wishes it to be. And all the while the woman sat across from him, gazing with those huge, affrighted eyes, or glancing nervously back into the lights and laughter of the common room as if she feared that among the dock workers and fish-wives gathered there she'd see one of her fashionable friends, someone who'd recognize her and tell. Rhion was not a particularly strong wizard, and after ten and a half years of study he'd come to under-stand that, even if he attained the level of learning Jaldis and Shavus had, he'd probably still never have their terrible strength. But he did weave a very pretty love-spell, though he said it himself.

"Sprinkle this into his cup or his food, if you can," he said later, handing her the ensorcelled powder done up in a twist of cheap yellow paper. "If you can't get access to his food, sprinkle it on his clothing, or his bed."

"And it will bring him to me?" She raised those childlike eyes to his. Standing with her on the threshold of the common room, Rhion was uneasily conscious of the way the chair men were watching him, as if they suspected him of laying witcheries on this woman to draw her back to his bed some night against her will. "It will make him love me?"

"It will bring him to you," Rhion said wearily, pushing his spec-tacles up more firmly onto the bridge of his nose. "He will desire you for a few hours, a few days, and forget about the others in the intensity of his desire. But unless you can win his real love, his genuine affection and care—unless you can be someone that he *can* love—it won't last. It never does. There is no counterfeit for love, and over love, magic has no power."

But in her sparkling eyes he saw she wasn't listening.

Rhion climbed the stairs again feeling tired and rather old. His sense of alienation from the nonmageborn world hadn't been less-ened by an encounter with the landlord, a massive man with a stubbled chin and the broken nose of a prizefighter, who had inter-cepted him on his way through the kitchen and relieved him of half the silver royals the woman had paid. "For use of the room," he'd growled, and Rhion hadn't argued. It had been difficult enough find-ing anyone willing to rent to wizards in the first place.

Jaldis was still sitting, wrapped in cloak and blankets, in his wob-bly chair near the chimney wall. The sharp point of his chin was sunk on his breast so that his short-trimmed silver beard touched the soundbox at his chest. At the creak of Rhion's foot upon the floorboards he raised his head, his long white hair catching the wan glimmer of the witchlight that his pupil called into being among the slanting rafters overhead. The talismans dangling from the soundbox clinked and glittered faintly with the movement: pendants wrought of silver and crystal, discs of animal bone, scraps of parchment enclosed in glass or gold and the single great golden sun-cross which Shavus had made for him, symbol of the living strength of magic and its eternal renewal—objects imbued with power by all the wizards who had given him them, so that the magic which set the box's delicate chords and whistles vibrating would not fail when Jaldis' own strength became exhausted by other spells.

"Shavus is gone?"

The old man nodded. "I had hoped that I could prevail upon him to help me," he said softly, the whisper of the instrument like the sigh of harpstrings when the wind passes through. "But he sees nothing . . . nothing."

"I'm not sure my own vision of the subject is noticeably more acute." Rhion turned up the sleeves of his brown robe and those of the rough-knitted pullover he wore beneath it and began to clear the tiny coffee cups the three wizards had drunk from earlier in the evening. The dreamy velvet bitterness of the coffee and the sweet pungence of cinnamon still flavored the air, mingling with the astringent scent of the overhead herbs and the smoke that seeped from the bricks of the chimney wall. "You're saying it's possible to . . . to *cross* this Void you're talking about? To go to other . . ." He hesitated. "Other universes?"

"Not only possible," the old man murmured, "but necessary."

Rhion paused in the act of dipping wash-water from the half-empty bucket, placed near the chimney bricks to keep it from freezing, and cocked an eyebrow at his mentor. "Necessary . . . but not safe."

"No." The word was no more than a drawn-out buzz of strings, a vibrating inflection of weariness and defeat. "Not safe."

Rhion was silent, unable to picture a world so incomprehensibly separated from that which he knew.

In the ten years he had followed Jaldis, learning from him the whole tangled complex of facts and lists, spells and metaphysics, meditation and mental technique that constituted what the mundane world called "magic," Rhion had known the old man kept certain secrets, certain knowledge, to himself. In the books and scrolls Jaldis had so painfully collected over the years Rhion had found references to things he did not understand, things Jaldis sometimes explained and sometimes evaded on the grounds that his student had not been studying long enough . . .

But the night before last—when the old man had stumbled, exhausted, from the tiny chamber hidden under the eaves in which he had been closeted since the early winter sundown and had whispered to him to bring the Archmage—had been the first time that Rhion had heard of the Dark Well, the Void, or other universes besides the one he knew.

Frightened by his master's ghastly pallor and ragged breathing, Rhion had called the Archwizard's name again and again into the strongest of Jaldis' several scrying-crystals, until at last Shavus had answered. That night had been the night of the winter solstice, when all wizards were taking advantage of the additional power generated by the balance point of sun and stars to work deeper and stronger spells than were ordinarily possible, and Shavus had been less than pleased at the interruption. But he had come, with such speed that Rhion guessed he had not stopped for rest anywhere on the snow-covered roads between his house in the forest of Beldirac and the gates of Felsplex.

"Why 'necessary'?" he asked, spreading out a rough towel and setting the cups to dry. "Yes, if there's a world where magic has ceased to exist it should be investigated . . ."

"It must be investigated without delay." With sudden energy Jaldis rose to his feet, his hand finding at once the crutches which leaned against the side of his chair. In addition to blinding him and cutting out his tongue, all those years ago, the old king's soldiers had hamstrung him as well. Rhion hurried to help him, knowing he was still far from recovered from his fatigue, but leaning on the long sticks of bog-oak with their padding of leather and rags, the blind mage seemed suddenly flooded with a driven energy. Mummified in blankets, he had appeared fragile, almost tiny; standing up, he was half a head taller than his pupil. When they had first met, he had been taller still.

"*He* won't see the urgency of it, the importance of it," the blind man went on, turning to limp toward the tiny door nearly hidden in the shadows of the far wall. "But *you* must."

He paused, his crippled hand on the rough wooden latch, turning back to Rhion as if the sunken eyepits still had sight, as if the dark, haughty gaze he had once had was still his to compel, to command. "Someone must go to that world to learn *why* magic failed there. If it was something that men did . . ."

"Could they have?" Rhion felt suddenly loath to have him open that cracked plank door, dreading what might lie beyond for reasons he did not himself understand.

Some of the furious lines of concentration and will eased, leaving Jaldis' features sunken and old. "I do not know." He pushed open the door, and, limping on his crutches, hobbled through, Rhion following unwillingly, wiping the wash water from his hands, the ribbon of ghostlight trailing in their wake like will-o'-the-wisp.

This second room, no more than a triangular nook of waste space under the steeply slanting roof, had never been intended for anything but storage. During their first year of residence at the Black Pig, Rhion had spent many nights surreptitiously shifting decades' accumulation of mouse-infested junk to other sections of the attics to make of this closet an inner sanctum, a meditation chamber, a workplace of the deeper and more secret magics that comprised the true heart of the calling that was their life. It was unlighted and unbearably stuffy, and though, like their dwelling-room, ringed about with spells against the roaches and mice to be found everywhere else in the inn, it still had the dirty, musty smell of these vermin and of dry rot and smoke. From barely head-high by the door, the ceiling beams slanted sharply to the floor, forming the hypotenuse of a triangle scarcely twelve feet across the base.

In this place Jaldis—and Rhion, when he could—worked in the deepest meditations that were the foundation of the wizard's metaphysical arts, sinking the mind into silence and stretching out the senses, scrying through fire and water, crystal, and the fine-spun fabric of the wind, to study the shape and balance and pulsebeat of the world. Here in the inky silence they practiced the magics of illusion and light, not for their own sake but for what they could teach about the nature of the mind. Here Rhion meditated and studied the nature of the runes which were the foundation of the magic as the Morkensik Order practiced it; the making of the hundreds of sigils that were built of them, and the greater, more complex seals that called together from a swirling chaos of probabilities the loci of power and likelihood, bridging the gap between the will and something more. Here Rhion practiced patiently and slowly all those spells which Jaldis had taught him over the years, memorizing their forms and painstakingly exercising the slender powers that were his, until he could call trickles of water up the slanted side of a dish, bring forth illusions of flowers and jewels, make a talisman of gold which would rob poison of its virulence, or cause dustdevils to swirl all around the shut and windless room.

And in this place, Rhion saw now, Jaldis had drawn Circles of Power on the floor, circles which occupied almost the whole of that tiny chamber: circles in chalk and silver-dust, in springwater and in blood, crossed and interwoven with rings and spirals of pure, glimmering light that only wizards could see, drawn in the air above the worn and splintery floorboards or sinking down into them, visible a few inches into their depth like light submerged in water . . . stars and crescents and the sun-cross of power, all feeding the energies of air and life and the turning earth into holding the circle intact.

And in the center of that circle was darkness, a column of shadow that even Rhion's dark-sighted eyes could not pierce: a darkness which filled him with uneasy horror.

"It took me three days to call it into being." The voice of the box was no more than a thread of sweetness in the terrible silence of that tiny room. "With the strength that magic can call from the solstice's power I sent my mind deep into that Well, seeking to learn something of the nature of magic, the nature of the Cosmos that divides universe from universe in an infinity of colors and dark."

Staring into the darkness, Rhion barely heard him. It seemed to draw him, as some men are drawn with terrible vertigo to the edge of a precipice. Staring into it, he thought he saw movement there, strange iridescences as if blackness had been refracted into shuddering rainbows of something other than color, anomalous stirrings that trailed lightless fire.

Behind him, Jaldis' voice went on. "I caught glimpses of things I do not understand, of worlds whose natures and substructures are incomprehensible to me: ships that whirled flashing between stars; clouds of terrible and free-floating power, drifting eternally in the abyss. And somewhere in that chaos I heard a voice crying out, 'Magic is dead . . . magic is dead. If any can hear us there where magic thrives, magic is dead here, dead . . . magic is dead. It has been gone for two hundred years.' "

Rhion looked back at him, seeing in the soft blue glow of the witchlight the desperate tension in the old man's withered face, the mingled grief and eagerness, as if he heard again that thin voice crying. "Over and over it called, and I called back, 'I hear you! I will help you!' " His hand trembled on the crutches; his voice would have, too, had the forces of law left him with one. "I do not know whether they heard me or not."

With a sigh he turned away, as if he could no longer bear to stand so close to the place where he had heard those terrible pleas. Slowly he limped from the room, Rhion following thankfully at his heels. The witchlight drifted after them; looking back over his shoulder as he closed the door, Rhion could see that even the soft clarity of that light could not pierce the dreadful shadow held prisoned within the ensorcelled rings.

"He might have been speaking of some kind of—of field effect, the kind of thing you'd get with a spell of silence and a talismanic resonator."

"No." Jaldis shook his head as he sank once more back into his chair by the chimney wall, gathering his patched blankets about his rawboned frame. Among the rafters, the wind groaned, the whole building shuddering faintly, like a horse twitching flies from its skin. In the silence that followed, Rhion could hear the dry skitter of ice fragments, blown like sand across the tiles overhead. "He would not have spoken so, calling into the Void for help, were there any hope of help within his own world."

Below them, the inn's guests were preparing for bed. Muffled voices and the scrape of furniture came dimly through the floor, a woman's laugh. Had he concentrated, as wizards were trained to do, Rhion could have pinpointed and identified the inhabitants of every room.

"Men hate magic, Rhion," Jaldis continued very softly, his twisted hands rubbing his shoulders for warmth. The witchlight that had rippled like a sheet of blown silk in the darkness was growing small and dim—it caught a final gleam on Jaldis' sun-cross talisman, on the gold lettering of a book's worn spine and the staring, ironic crystal rounds of the spectacles still balanced beside his chair. "They hate magic and hate those of us born with the ability to work it. That woman who paid you tonight, she too will hate you in her heart, for you can do something which she cannot. If magic has perished in some other world—in an entire world, an entire universe—we must learn why. I must go on seeking, go on scrying in the Well no matter what the cost to me, to you, to anyone. I must convince Shavus to help me, to go to that world in spite of all the peril of crossing the Void.

"Don't you see?" He turned desperately toward Rhion with his sunken eyelids, his closed and scar-torn lips, wreckage left by the hatred of magic which only magic could now relieve. "If men found some way to cause this to happen, how long will it be before those in our world, in this world, learn to do so, too, and destroy magic here forever?"

2

Rhion woke with a start, from a confusion of uneasy dreams.

He was back in the Old Bridge Market in the City of Circles: a plump little dandy in a red velvet doublet whose buttons flashed with rubies and to whose carefully dressed brown curls clung the scent of cloves. Blue and yellow awnings flapped in the bright spring sunlight around the ancient bridge-temple of Bran Rhu. The air was thick with the smell of lilies and the stink of the river's sewage below. Rhion was thumbing through the old pieces of broken books piled in a used-paper seller's barrow: fragments of romances and hymnals, their illuminations faded and yellowed like dessicated leaves; scrolls of religion and philosophy with their glue cracking along the joins; old household receipt books; and the accounts of forgotten military campaigns. The lowest of kitchen slaves would come by occasionally to buy the stuff by the bagful for kindling and would look at that modishly dressed youth with curiosity and suspicion in their eyes. Rhion, even as he examined the incomprehensible glyphs of a red and green accordion-fold book from the unknown south, tried to formulate in his mind some fashionable motive—mockery, or aesthetics, or something of the kind—should one of his fashionable friends see him and laugh . . .

A shadow had fallen over him. "Are you hunting for secrets?" Jaldis asked.

And turning, Rhion saw him for the first time.

But this time—he had dreamed this scene before—Jaldis looked as he did now. His face was thin and gray under the stringy web of his beard, his white hair no thicker than spider-floss in the sunlit breeze. The threadbare blankets and worn black cloak which wrapped him parted to reveal the voice-box strapped to his breast, and its silvery drone was all the voice that Rhion heard.

No! he thought, his mind clutching at the receding shreds of the deep, musical tones which had originally framed those words. *No, he's not like that! He wasn't like that, not then! His hair and beard were still mostly brown, he still had his eyes then, dark and luminous and kind* . . .

But his mind could reconstruct neither the image of him as he had been, nor the sound of his voice.

As he had indeed done on that day of glassy sunlight and intoxicating flower-scents so many years ago, Jaldis reached into the paper seller's barrow and brought out a book.

But instead of the few pages of star lore and mathematics that it had actually been, it was a book with black covers, covered with dust and sticky with cobweb. The air around it seemed to quiver fitfully, half-visible spirals of light shuddering like a heat dance, and when Rhion opened it, what he held in his hands was not a book at all. Only darkness lay contained in those black covers, a darkness which dropped away into a hole of inky nothing between his hands. As he stared at it in horror, the Abyss exploded upward around him, like water gushing up from a spring; a darkness filled with colors that should not have been colors, gouging a hollow in air and light and in all sane things as if the world which he knew had merely been painted on paper, now touched to destroying flame. Airless beyond comprehension, cold as he had never understood cold could be, the darkness opened around him like the unfurling petals of a sable rose, dragging him down into it, swallowing him . . .

He was falling. His cry was silent.

Then he found himself in a place he had never seen before. He stood at the edge of a meadow with a forest at his back and a small hill rising before him, crowned with three ancient stones. Two had fallen and lay nearly buried in the thick, calf-deep grass; the third still reared its worn head against the azure well of the summer night. It was close to midnight, he thought—the air was laden with the peep of frogs, crinkled with the trilling of crickets, and summer constellations unrolled in a glittering banner beyond the black spikes of the surrounding pines.

The thick sweetness caught at his throat as he waded through the grass, up the hill to the stones. His feet hewed a dark swathe through the dew that glittered in the starlight, a shadowed track leading back into the coagulated gloom beneath the trees. Looking over his shoulder, he felt a kind of panic, a terror of pursuit . . . fear of being traced here, captured, taken . . . Taken where? The thought of it turned him cold but he could conjure nothing, no reason for that hideous dread.

But if he could reach the stones, he'd be safe. If he could reach them by midnight, he could escape . . .

Escape?

Jaldis. His mind groped for bearings in the disorientation of the dream. *Where's Jaldis in all this? He can't run, he's crippled. He won't be able to get away from them . . .*

Who?

The thought of capture turned him sick.

He sprang up on one fallen stone. Around him in the starlight the grass of the meadow lay like a silken lake, cut by the single dark line of his tracks. Overhead the sky was a glowing well of blue, an inverted morning-glory sewn with light. Raising his arms, he called down the power of the wheeling stars to him, calling strength and hope of flight . . .

But as he turned he saw all around him in the encircling woods the terrible glitter of silver and steel, the closing ring of eyes . . .

He jolted from sleep like a man falling from a height. His heart was pounding with panic, and for one terrible second he knew that he had not escaped. Waking had only postponed the knowledge of what would happen to him next . . . but only momentarily. They would capture him and . . . and . . .

But it was only darkness.

Only a dream.

Only a dream, Rhion thought, breathless, trying to slow his heart and still his panic. The cold killing lust of the hunters, the poisoned fog of impersonal hate . . .

But those did not fade from his mind. They grew stronger than before, and he realized that those, at least, were real.

Rhion dropped his hand from beneath the covers to where he had left his spectacles on the floor by the bed. His wizard's sight let him see as well in darkness as in light, but without his spectacles what he saw, day or night, was only a blur. The metal rims were icy against his temples and for a moment the warmth of his flesh misted the thick, curved glass. The room was freezing, for it was the last hour or two of the long winter night, when the heat of the banked fires in the kitchen far below no longer warmed the chimney. Beside him, curled tight for warmth beneath their few blankets and both their shabby cloaks, Jaldis still slept; around them, the little room was as tidy, as orderly, as it had been when they had gone to bed. On the shelf above the bed Jaldis' opal spectacles stared unwinkingly into darkness; the rosewood soundbox rested like a sleeping turtle in its sparkling nest of talismans and tangle of leather straps.

But there was danger.

And it was coming closer.

Closing his eyes, Rhion slowed the panic from his breathing and listened deeply, fully, as Jaldis had taught him years ago and as he had practiced daily in meditation, stretching his senses to the somnolent city outside.

He became immediately aware of the crunch of many booted feet, the clamor of mob rage. At the same moment the urgent tug of fear redoubled, and he understood then that it was coming to him from one of the wizard's marks he had made in the streets surrounding the inn.

In none of the Forty Realms was it considered a crime to kill a wizard. In fact the cults of the gods Bran Rhu, Agon, Kithrak, and Thismé considered such an activity an act of merit and likely to win either the god's favor or promotion to a higher plane of spiritual being, depending on the cult, and Rhion had been a wizard long enough and had talked to enough of his professional colleagues on the subject, to have a healthy wariness about settling down to sleep.

For this reason, within the first week of moving into the Black Pig Inn, Rhion had drawn wizard's marks—barely visible signs imbued with a trace of his personal power—on housewalls, fountain railings, and doorposts in a loose ring, perhaps half a mile wide with the Black Pig at its center, marks that would awaken and whisper to him if passed by a large number of people with that particular species of determined, impersonal hatred in their hearts.

It was far from a perfect warning system, of course. Wizard's marks had to be renewed periodically—Rhion's more frequently than Jaldis' would have to be, because of Rhion's lesser strength—and were by no means accurate in what stirred them to life. Time after time Rhion had been called from his meditations, from sleep, or from consultations with clients by bar fights, matrimonial disputes, and, on one occasion, by an angry mob of local fishwives out to storm the house of a particularly unpopular moneylender. At this hour of the night—or morning, for dawn was at most two hours away—it was more likely that the problem was some kind of drunken brawl.

But still, Rhion slipped from beneath the covers and, breathless with cold, hastily pulled on his robe over the knitted pullover and hose he'd worn to bed and laced up his boots. His father had been a man with a motto for every occasion—"Better to be safe than sorry," had been one of his favorites. Having seen just how sorry it was possible to become, Rhion was willing to opt for an uncomfortable safety every time.

The cold in the attic was breathtaking, and Rhion hadn't the heart to take his cloak from the top of the piles of blankets over Jaldis. Moving swiftly, his breath a trail of white behind him, he unbolted and slipped through the crazy door, pausing long enough to work the bolt back into place by magic behind him in case someone tried to break in while Jaldis was still lost in his exhausted slumber. The staircase, which rose like a flue through the inn, was warmer, and Rhion concentrated on whispering the words of a generalized sleep-spell as he hurried down the elliptical spiral of the steps, not sure whether he was getting the spell right or whether it was working. It was one he hadn't practiced lately, and half his mind was on the danger that had—he was almost certain now—shaped the fears of his dream.

In the huge kitchen, low-ceilinged, shuttered, silent, and dark but for the feeble glow of the banked embers on the hearth, Rhion pulled the landlord's heavy green cloak from its peg and slung it around his shoulders. Outside the noise was clearer—definitely armed and angry men, definitely headed this way.

He paused on the threshold, panting, to collect his thoughts. It still took him a long and meticulous time to work any kind of spell, though he practiced diligently, and Jaldis told him that speed and mental deftness would come with time. Against the rising shiver in his breast, the inner clamor of *There isn't* time *for this . . . !* he closed his eyes, calmed his breathing, and reaching out with all the senses of wizardry, realized that the mark the mob had passed was the one he'd put on the side of a little shrine of Shilmarglinda, goddess of grain, over on the corner of Sow Lane.

Clutching the landlord's cloak about him, he ducked and wove through alleyways choked with half-frozen garbage and no wider than the span of his arms. As he ran he shoved resolutely from his mind all the thousand questions trying to heave to its surface like porridge on the boil, questions like *Who's behind this?* and *Where the hell can we go? The landlord'll never bolt the door against them . . .* Instead he concentrated on forming a spell to cloak him against the notice of people who might very well know him for the wizard's apprentice. Unlike the sleep-spells at the inn, tossed hastily about him like a sower's seeds, this one had better keep him from being recognized or he stood in grave danger of having to choose between a very severe beating—if nothing worse—and some defensive action that might trigger further mob violence. In situations like this it was axiomatic that the wizard—or the wizard's friends and acquaintances—could never really win.

The mob had spilled into Suet Lane. It was nearly fifty strong, though its core of two dozen men in the dark-blue livery of some town nobleman's household bravos was being added to all the time by the kind of tavern idlers and day laborers who could always be counted upon to join an affray. Rhion recognized two of the magistrate's constables among them and a couple of lesser officials of the local Temple of Kithrak, the war-god whose cult was strong in Felsplex. One of these was yelling something about servants of evil and insulters of the names of the gods, and Rhion had a sinking certainty about whose honor this assemblage was in.

Nevertheless he fell into step with one of the local wastrels, a little female stevedore he'd seen drinking frequently in the Black Pig. Hoping his spell of Who-Me? would hold, he asked, "What's going on?"

The woman barely glanced at him. A torch in one hand, an ax-handle in the other, she appeared to be—and, by the workings of the spell, in fact was—momentarily absorbed in keeping an eye on the thickly quilted back of the liveried bravo in front of her. If later challenged to describe the man who had spoken to her, she would have been able only to arrive at a vague recollection of someone about her husband's height and build. "Gonna kill them witch scum," she grunted, and spat through gaps in her teeth into the frozen sewage underfoot.

The word she used for "kill" was *fruge*, a verb which had application only to animals, almost a technical term except that it was used so commonly. It denoted a killing which meant nothing and which demanded no explanations—a self-evident axiom. One never asked why someone would *fruge* a rat, or a cow for beef. One did it because that was what one did with rats and cows.

"Yeah?" Rhion said in the local slang, and wiped his nose on his sleeve. "What'd the bastards do this time?"

"Sold a love-potion to that whore wife of Tepack the money-lender so's she could drag her husband's partner's innocent son into bed with her." His companion nodded toward the solid core of liverymen, like a knot of lead poured into a wooden club to make of it a killing weapon. "Only sixteen, he is, and his daddy—Lord Pruul—says he's gonna *fruge* them wizards, since Tepack's not gonna let anyone say a word against his wife . . ."

But Rhion was already gone, holding the landlord's cloak-hem up out of the mud and thinking, *Real smart, Rhion. Didn't think to ask if the bint was married, did we?*

But of course the question would only have elicited a lie. Perhaps a lie that the woman herself believed. He was familiar with Lord Pruul's son, having sold that raped and innocent victim enough lover-philters and clap-cures to stock a pharmacy over the past thirty months. *Dammit, we really did need the money* . . .

He ducked into the doorway of one of the huge, gray-timbered tenement blocks that made up the neighborhood, pressed his hands to the door to work back the bolt by magic, then darted through the downstairs hall where beggars slept in rags and garbage. Cutting through the filth in the yard behind the place, he was able to reach the junction of Suet Lane, Goat Lane, and Cod Alley before the mob did, only a few hundred feet from the Black Pig. Amid the towering walls of tenement houses, wineshops, and the vast bulk of the St. Plomelgus Baths, the little square was like a deep cistern full of shadow, only the tiny brick-and-iron shrine of St. Plomelgus—a demi-god of the Thismé cult—catching the wan starlight on the iron spikes of its roof.

His hands shaking with panic, Rhion forced his mind to calm as he drew the sigils for a spell of misleading on the shrine itself, the corner of the baths, the corner timbers of a tenement house. The Lady, the Fool, the Dancer at the Heart of the World . . . runes twined together, calling into themselves and radiating forth, in their proper combination, the certainty that one turned right instead of left, that Goat Lane was in fact the street which led to the Black Pig; a line of light stretched across the mouth of Cod Alley, glowing visible for a moment, then sinking back into the air. To throw a little twist on things Rhion added a spell of argumentativeness to the governing Seals upon the shrine, then, as torchlight flickered over the stiff lead saint in her pigeon-desecrated niche and voices echoed against the high walls, he gathered his cloak around him and fled.

Jaldis was already dressed, patiently, with twisted fingers, lacing his boots. He raised his head inquiringly as Rhion fumbled the latch open with his mind from the other side.

"Lord Pruul's men," Rhion gasped, crossing immediately to the table and beginning to shove things into his pockets—packets of herbs, precious bits of bronze and gold and rare woods for the making of talismans, scrying-crystals, and bread. "That woman I sold a philter to earlier tonight was the wife of his business-partner. She used it to seduce his son, though from what I know of Pruul Junior I wonder that she needed to bother."

Jaldis slipped into the leather harness that bound the voice-box to his breast, found his spectacles without groping for them, and hooked them onto his face. The talismans on the voice-box clinked with fragile music as he erected his crutches and climbed to his feet. "My books . . ."

Rhion turned to view the row of volumes along the back of the table, the stacks on the floor beside the chimney wall, the little bin of scrolls beside his master's customary chair, and cursed. It was appalling how much impedimenta they'd picked up in two and a half years here. They'd come to Felsplex with twenty-one books of various shapes and sizes—grimoires, demonaries, herbals laboriously copied from volumes in Shavus' little library in that stone house in the forest—and in the years they'd been here they had, at great pain and expense, acquired a dozen more. Precious volumes, some of them irreplaceable. While court mage for the traitor Lord Henak, Jaldis had collected a library of nearly a hundred volumes of magic and wisdom over the years, added to what had been passed on to him by his own master. The High King's men had burned them all. Rhion had heard Jaldis say that he regretted that loss more than he did the loss of his eyes.

He cursed again, feeling already exhausted and defeated, and cast a quick glance at the window that he already knew would be their means of egress. The shouts of the mob were audible through the walls, furious and frustrated as they wandered helplessly in the maze of twisting streets. If he'd had time to cast a more elaborate spell . . .

Swiftly he tore the blanket from the bed. "It's going to be close," he warned, and crossed to the window at a run. Once the shutter was thrown back, the cold was brutal, making his eyes water and his numbed fingers ache, even with both gloves and writing-mitts on his hands. The wind had died down; the sky was iron-black above the slanting jumble of tiled roofs. Most were too steep to hold snow, but moisture had frozen on them and they'd be slick and treacherous. Rhion thought about negotiating them with forty or fifty pounds of unwieldy paper on his back, not to mention trying to guide a blind man on crutches, and shuddered.

"We can't take all of them." The words cut like a wire noose—Jaldis loved those books like children, and there were several that Rhion had not yet studied. But he knew as surely as he knew his name that if he tried it, they would both fall to their deaths. "I'm sorry. We just . . ."

A spasm of sorrow contorted the old man's face. "Then you choose." The arthritic hands passed, trembling, along the volumes on the table, touching them as he would have touched the faces of people he loved. "For they will be yours now longer than they will be mine."

"Don't say that!" Rhion spread the blanket on the bed and dove back toward the table, steeling himself against the agony of decision and thinking desperately, *That spell won't hold them long* . . . "We're going to get out of here just fine . . . Can you call fog?"

"In a moment." Jaldis remained beside the table, head bowed, hands touching this book or that as Rhion worked hurriedly around him . . . *Dammit, that one's got the Summoning of Elementals in it! I hadn't learned that yet* . . .

Shavus will have it, he told himself firmly. But the book seemed to cling to his hand like a child he was trying to abandon in the woods. *Hell, Jaldis was searching for that Book of Circles when I met him* . . .

"Jaldis . . ." With the window open the noise of the mob came to them quite clearly. It was growing louder again. They must have gotten their bearings.

"In a moment. You're leaving *these?*"

"Yes. Come *ON* . . . !" He piled the fifteen or so books that he could not possibly bear to let slip from their possession in the center of the blanket, threw in some spare clothing and food, and tied the corners, then bent and pulled from beneath the bed a long, cleated plank—the gangway, in fact, of one of the hayboats that came to the quays from upriver in spring. He'd appropriated it two years ago when he'd first mapped out this route of escape, foreseeing the possibility of just this event, even as he'd made wizard's marks that would glow at a word on the various chimneys, turrets, and crudely carved roof-tree gargoyles—designed to frighten goblins and grims, these decorated every roof in the city—along their chosen route . . .

But the thought of actually doing it still turned him queasy.

At that time he'd practiced manhandling the plank down the roof

tiles to the gap where the alley separated them from the next building. But that had been two summers ago, when the steeply sloped
tiles were dry. Black ice cracked under the soles of his boots, and
the wind froze his face, his heart hammering so hard it nearly sickened him. Eastward across the pitchy jumble of roof trees and gargoyles, his mageborn eyes could make out, like a dirty fault-scar in
the wilderness of grimy plaster and half-timbering, the line of the
river. The noise of the mob was louder, down in Cod Alley now,
certainly—there was no note in it of the baffled fury of a mob
confronted with a locked door.

Of course the landlord would let them in. His only request would
be that they not break anything downstairs. "He'll probably sell
them drinks on their way up," Rhion muttered savagely, as he struggled back through the window again.

Jaldis was still standing beside the table, head bowed and long
white hair hanging down over his face as he passed his hands lightly
across the covers of each of the rejected books in turn. For an instant, watching him, Rhion's heart constricted with grief—it was as
if the old man was memorizing one last time the touch of the bindings, the whisper of the things within that now would be destroyed.
But the building was already shaking with the pounding of fists upon
the doors, of feet upon the stairs . . .

He pulled the blanket-wrapped bundle onto his back, tangling it
with the landlord's green cloak, and girded up his robe through his
belt. "Now," he said, as gently as he could through the hammering
urgency of panic, and took Jaldis by the arm. He saw the old man's
forehead pucker with the agony of concentration as he called the
spells of sight into his opal spectacles.

"Did you call the fog?" Rhion whispered as he eased himself out
the window again, praying with all that was in him that the weight of
the books on his back wouldn't overbalance him on the slippery roof.

Jaldis, leaning out the window to take his pupil's steadying arms,
shook his head. He was using all his strength, all his attention, to
see. He could seldom operate both eyes and voice at the same time,
much less call unseasonable weather conditions like fog in winter,
even when he was rested—certainly not in the exhausted aftermath
of working with the Dark Well.

Instead he had been saying good-bye to his books. Scared as he was, Rhion could not feel anger. The *Grand Demonary* had been given Jaldis by his own old master Xiranthe, Archmage of the Morkensik Order for forty years, who had gotten it from hers—it was one of the few which had escaped the High King's men. The collection of the wizard Ymrir's personal notes had been copied nearly a hundred years ago and was the best redaction of those notes either of them knew about, the least corrupted . . .

But, Rhion thought despairingly as he started to ease his way down the steep tiles, with the old man's tall weight on one shoulder and the shifting, awkward sack of books on his back, *we surely could have used that fog.*

The flight from Felsplex was a nightmare that in later years Rhion would look back upon with a kind of wonder, amazed that he'd been scared enough even to think about trying it. Wind had started up by the time they'd crossed the gangway, blowing from the north and arctically cold. Rhion could smell sleet on it but knew that neither he nor Jaldis could spare the concentration needed to turn the storm aside. With the books overbalancing him, he didn't have the leverage to pull the gangway across after them, but had to tip it over into the deserted alley below.

Then came the slithery agony of edging along the slanted roofs, easing their way around gables and ornamental turrets, clinging to gargoyles and rain gutters slick with ice and rotten with age and neglect. For the most part, the buildings in this crowded riverside quarter were close enough together, with their projecting upper stories and jutting eaves, to make leaping over the gaps a relatively easy matter, in theory at least. But theory did not take into account the hellish cold and slippery footing, the yawning blackness of forty- and fifty-foot drops to the cobblestones below, nor the storm gusts that came whipping unexpectedly around the corners of those tall black roof trees to pluck at their clothes and claw their faces.

The coming storm had killed whatever dawnlight had been rising. Rhion hoped it would also discourage their pursuit, but he could still hear the angry voices in the streets below as the men fanned out through the whole district, torches leaping in the charcoal shadows of those twisting chasms, curses echoing against the crowding walls. One of the first things Jaldis had taught him, ten years ago— and he'd been studying it on his own even before that—was to read the weather; he could tell that the sleet wouldn't hit soon enough to drive Lord Pruul's bravos indoors. It would only soak and freeze him and Jaldis once they got clear of the town . . . if they could manage to do so without breaking their necks.

Thanks a lot, he muttered, addressing the gods Rehobag and Pnisarquas, Lords of the Storm. According to the Bereine theologians who strolled in the pillared basilicas of Nerriok, Rehobag and Pnisarquas were only aspects of the Lord Darova, the Open Sky, God of the Blue Gaze, the Lord Who Created Himself . . . a god notoriously antithetical to wizardry and all its works. *It figures.*

Rhion was trembling with exhaustion by the time they reached their goal: a tenement by the river whose five-storey bulk jutted out on pilings over the dark waters, a tenement whose inhabitants, like all those of the riverside community, routinely fished off crooked platforms that clung like swallows' nests to the building's side, connected by a thready tangle of ladder no more substantial than spiderweb and straw. As he helped the exhausted Jaldis down that suspended deathtrap of sticks and rope, Rhion thanked whatever gods listened to wizards that the river was deep enough at Felsplex not to have frozen, and that the intense cold had damped the smell of it here under the pilings where every privy in the district emptied.

There were several boats tied among the piers beneath the tenement, where a single lantern hanging from a crossbeam threw hard yellow scales of light on the oily water. Rhion's gloves had been torn to pieces by the scramble over the roofs, and his hands were so stiff they would barely close around the oars. At this season the water was low. Had it been spring, he did not think he would have had the strength to row against the current.

"I don't see any smoke," he commented after a time, as they approached the city's water gate with its thick portcullis—half-raised now like a dog's snarl—where the river ran out westwards into the flat open country beyond, dirty-white and mud-brown beneath a livid sky. Wind tore at his face, the first sleet snagging in his beard. It was, he knew, nearly impossible for even a mage of Jaldis' powers to turn a storm aside when it was this close. But he knew, too, that they'd have to try, or they'd never make the upstream market town of Imber alive.

Jaldis, sitting huddled in the boat's prow under his own cloak and Rhion's, his hood drawn up over his face, did not raise his head. White hairs flicked from beneath the edge of the hood, like snow blowing from the crest of a roof; muffled by the cloaks that covered it, the voice of the box was nearly inaudible. "That few books would not make much smoke," he said softly. "They would cast them into the kitchen stove . . . it will easily accommodate so small a number. No . . ." And he sighed, a soundless, aching breath of regret. "My great sorrow is that they will have destroyed the Well."

"The Dark Well?" Bending his aching back to the oars, Rhion tried to remember what it was about the Dark Well that had frightened him so badly, why the very name of the thing made his scalp creep. But he could remember nothing, other than standing and looking into the eldritch, shifting colors of blackness . . . that terrible hollow . . . A vague impression tugged at his mind that perhaps he had dreamed something . . .

And then it was gone.

But, grieved as he could see Jaldis was at the loss, he himself could work up very little in the way of regret.

"The Dark Well," the old man again echoed. "They will wipe out the lines that bound it, trample away the symbols that gave it power, that held it in place. It will vanish, and all its secrets with it. Those who cried out to me from its depths . . ."

"You'll be able to create another one, in time," Rhion said, manufacturing as cheerful a tone as he could. "As soon as we get to Imber and find someplace to stay . . ." He tried to recall if he'd pocketed their money in their haste to get out, and couldn't. "You'll be able to find them again, and help them."

"No, my son," Jaldis softly said, and shook his head. "No . . . If someone has found a way to destroy magic, to end it, make it cease to exist, in an entire universe—it is *we* who may need *their* help."

3

But it was to be a long time before Jaldis the Blind and his pupil found the peace and security necessary for the weaving of another Dark Well.

It took them two days to reach Imber, a good-sized market town twenty-five miles upriver from Felsplex, built around the temple complex of Ptorag, God of Grain. In most of the Forty Realms Ptorag's worship had been supplanted by that of Shilmarglinda—the north-desert deity of all the fruits of the earth—but in Imber it was still strong and the cult owned most of the vineyards lining the hill slopes above the river. Rhion, having ascertained that he *had*, in fact, dropped the little velvet pouch which Tepack the Moneylender's wife had given him—brainless trollop!—into the blanket's load of books and spare clothes, figured resignedly that if worst came to worst he could always seek employment corking and sealing bottles when the vintage was laid down toward winter's end.

"But on the other hand," he added, extending numb hands toward the small brazier of coals which the landlady of the Red Grape Inn had sent up to their miniscule—though extremely costly—chamber, "if everyone in this town is as calm about wizards as the innkeeper here, I can probably find work as an accountant. That would make my father proud." He grinned a little as he said it, his beard crackling with ice, and began gingerly unwrapping the frozen rags he'd tied around his hands. They hadn't the money to remain more than a night or two at this inn, and he'd have to sell the tiny amount of gold they kept for talismanic work in order to obtain permanent lodgings; but, for the moment, Rhion was glad to have found a warm room out of the wind, with prospects of food.

He flexed his fingers in the glow exuded by the little copper dish of coals. "Here, let me see your hands . . ." In the river-bank cave where they'd spent part of yesterday morning, sheltering from the worst of the sleet, he'd cut strips from the hem of their former landlord's cloak—which was too long for him anyway—to wrap around Jaldis' arthritic fingers and his own. He'd hauled stones up from the riverbank and had been able to call sufficient spells to them to heat them up so that their radiant warmth had kept him and his master from freezing to death, but the effort had exhausted him; Jaldis had worked for nearly two hours, drawing and redrawing the figures of power in the air, before he had been able to turn the sleet storm aside. After that the old man had collapsed and slept; when they'd pushed on later in the day and all through the next southward along the banks of the frozen stream, he had the strength to say very little.

Or perhaps, Rhion thought now, stealing a worried glance at his master's face, the delicate cords of gut and silver wire, the tiny vibrating whistles and membranes within the voice-box itself, had simply frozen fast.

Now the old man said softly, as Rhion chaffed his crippled fingers in a basin of cold water, "I am sorry, my son."

"Sorry?" Rhion looked up at him in genuine surprise. Outside the windows, the short winter day had ended in slate-colored gloom. In the kitchen directly beneath their room, the innkeeper's husband was singing a midwinter carol as he prepared supper for the Red Grape's few guests: roast lamb with rosemary for those wealthy enough to pay for it, lentils and mutton-fat for itinerant mages out of work. "*I* was the one who sold that silly woman a love-potion without asking if she was married or whom she was going to use it on." Gently he removed the two cloaks and the blanket from Jaldis' shoulders and laid them over the backs of the room's various chairs and table to dry. While it was possible to dry clothes, as it was to heat rooms, with magic, under ordinary circumstances it took far more energy than it was worth. In the long run it was cheaper to pay for coal.

For a moment he stood looking down at Jaldis' sunken cheeks and scarred eyelids, gray as fishbelly with fatigue and with long weeks indoors at the Black Pig. He remembered as from a dream how his white teeth had flashed in a smile, how his voice had boomed with laughter, the day of their first meeting on the bridge. Down to the ends of his long white braids, he had seemed to crackle with energy, with life and delight . . . with magic. And Rhion had known, as unquestioningly as if he had recognized his own face in a mirror, that that was what he wanted, and had always wanted, to be.

Quietly, he added, "I'm sorry about the books."

The hard, arthritic grip closed with its surprising strength upon his hand. "It was not your business to ask her if she would use the philter to commit adultery," Jaldis said. "No more than it is the business of a stationer to ask of a man buying paper and ink if he plans to use them to betray a friend's trust. Magic is only magic, Rhion."

The sparse white eyebrows drew down over the bridge of his nose, the thin face filled with urgency, willing him to understand. "It is neither evil nor good, it is neither health nor a sickness. It is only what it is—like a knife, or a man's life, or a new name for God. We cannot begin to judge what will be done with any of these things, for we ourselves can only hold opinions, and we cannot be sure that the information we are given on any of these is complete or correct.

"It is enough that we do no harm, as our vows enjoin us; that we do not presume to decide things for which there is no proof." The crooked, clawlike fingers tightened; as the blind face looked up into his, Rhion had the sensation that through those deformed hands the old man could feel, not only his bones and flesh and the warmth of his blood, but the soul within him, reading it like a handful of colored silk ribbons braided into some elaborate code, feeling the texture of his thoughts as he would feel the petals of a flower, the grit of granite, or the cold strength of steel.

"I am only sorry," Jaldis went on, "that having promised you the wisdom of the universe, the knowledge of balance and truth, I have caused you to leave your family and the world that would have made you comfortable, and then have given you only this: dream weaving, philter brewing, and casting horoscopes and luck-charms, the toys of magic rather than its substance. It is not magic, Rhion . . ."

Rhion was silent, remembering the soul-deep shiver he had felt when he had first understood the true name of light, the name by which fire is summoned—the true reality of what true reality is. The moment in meditation when all the component parts of the world fell suddenly together, showing that there was, in fact, sense to what happened . . . He remembered, too, all that long and gaudy parade of nobles, burghers, farmers, and slaves who had come to him and Jaldis over the past ten years, asking for what they thought was magic: medicines or luck-charms or to have their fortunes read. And every one, he reflected, had taught him a little more about what men dreamed.

"No," he said, squeezing those crippled old fingers in return. "But it sure beats working for a living."

And Jaldis laughed, sniffing through his high-bridged nose. Laughter was the one sound that it was impossible for the voice-box to make.

Acting on the advice of the innkeeper's husband, a little brown sparrow of a man whom he instinctively trusted, Rhion sought out the best of the local pawnbrokers the following day and sold the little gold and silver he and Jaldis possessed. With the proceeds, again on their landlord's advice, he found a widow who owned a garden farm a few hundred yards down the road outside Imber's gates, who had a room to rent.

"Now, I don't mind myself that you're witchylike," she said, pouring the milk bucket she carried into setting pans—Rhion had found her in the dairy behind the small, half-timbered box of the farmhouse. She turned to face him, tucking hard brown hands into the armpits of her quilted coat for warmth. She was a young woman of about Rhion's own twenty-seven years, though her face was leathery with outdoor work. Under the close-fitting cap widows wore in the low countries of the Fel Valley her braids were bright yellow; she wore a blue ribbon around her neck with a green spirit-bead upon it and a little fragment of mirror glass to scare away grims. "It's just that I don't want no trouble, see."

"We'll try to keep the orgies down to four or five a week," Rhion replied gravely, and then added, "joking . . . joking . . ." as her eyebrows dove down into a worried frown. "It's just myself and my old master; we may have clients coming from time to time but I promise you we're well behaved." *And one of these days I'll even learn to have some sense about what I say.*

She grinned, showing a gap where childbearing had cost her a tooth. "Well, as to that, if the magistrates ask why I rented to such folk, I can always say you put a Word on me, can't I? I've sold milk and greens to the wizards in the town enough to know they don't cut up children, no matter what my granny said. But, not meaning it personal, I've got a girl—three she'll be come Agonsfire Night— and I'd appreciate it if you'd stay clear of her. Just for the sake of what the neighbors say."

For God's sake, your daughter's honor is safe with me . . . "Of course," said Rhion, bowing with hand over heart.

"Are there wizards in Imber?" he asked Jaldis later, as the two men carried their meager possessions across the town square and down the cobbled lane to the western gate. The snow that had been drifting down all last night had ceased, leaving the sky overhead a high, nebulous roof of pewter. Farmers had set up their barrows under the wide arcade surrounding the market square, and housewives in yellows and greens, and the dark-dressed household slaves of the rich, were picking over bundles of beans and yams and prodding the rabbits and chickens which hung dead by their feet like grotesque tassels from hooks on the beams overhead. The square itself was a palimpsest of tracks in the churned-up snow, and now and then a mule litter or sedan chair would pass, carrying a rich man on his way to one of the town's gymnasia or baths, or a brown-robed priest of the great temple of Ptorag, archaic gold amulets flashing and temple secretaries trotting obediently in his wake.

"They are Selarnists." Jaldis' voice was incapable of expression, but by the pause before his reply and by the way he held his shoulders, he might have been identifying them as a species of roach. "A small House of them, I believe."

"Oh," Rhion said. He had met few members of the Selarnist Order of wizardry in his years of apprenticeship with Jaldis, mostly because members of the White Order, as it was called, tended to live cloistered in Houses wherever the local authorities would let them, shunning contact with politics, the public, and members of other Orders alike.

"Worthy enough mages, I suppose," the old man went on, the voice of the soundbox smooth and strong now that he had rested, the rhythm of his arms and back as he limped along steady and sure. "And their methods of teaching are, on the whole, sound." When he had taught Rhion to observe insects he had found several good things to say about the lowlier members of the grasshopper tribe as well. "But one must admit that their Order's studies have become considerably corrupted and filled with errors since first they split away from the Morkensiks, six hundred years ago."

They passed a school, thickly attended now that it was winter, boys and girls crowded eight to a bench and peering over one another's shoulders at the hornbooks they had to share. Warmth blew out of the open store front in which it was being held, pleasant on Rhion's face as he walked along under his blanketful of books. It was astounding how much easier they were to carry on the relatively level surface of the street, the packed and slippery snow underfoot notwithstanding. Jaldis, too, had insisted upon splitting the load with him, and though Rhion watched him carefully, the old man seemed strong and fit enough.

"You could do worse than go to the Selarnists for some teaching while we are here," Jaldis added as he and his pupil turned down the length of Westgate Lane, past the towering walls of the temple complex, beyond which the soft groaning of horns and of the bronze sounding-bowls could be heard, accompanying chanted prayers in languages few people understood anymore. "Though they tend to put too much emphasis on breath-control and physical orientation, they could teach you far more of the finer nuances of herbalism than I."

"If they're Selarnists they might not want to teach a Morkensik their secrets," Rhion pointed out, shifting his burden from one aching shoulder to the other. His muscles hadn't recovered yet from the scramble across the roofs or from the hours of rowing up the white-banked black silence of the river with the sleet stinging his face. "But it's worth a try. There's still a whole lot I don't understand about herbal metaphysics . . ."

"Much of it is practice, my son."

"True. But in any case, if the priests who rule this town let a whole Houseful of *them* stay here, they won't have any objections to the two of us."

And indeed, it was not the priests of Ptorag who were responsible, two days later, for having Rhion and Jaldis thrown out of town.

It was a morning warmer than the preceding week had been, warm enough that the river had begun to thaw. Clouds hung low over the hill country to the south, and a faint mist turned the air to pearl as Rhion crossed the farmyard from helping their landlady with the milking, and found Jaldis sitting at the little table under their room's wide window, arranging his books by touch.

When Rhion had first become Jaldis' student, he had known nothing of wizardry—only the desperate sense of the magic within his veins, and the insistent, terrifying, disorienting need to learn to use that ability, the need to know that he was not insane for wanting to. But he had assumed, meeting Jaldis, that magic was something one learned, like accounting. When one was done learning, one was a bookkeeper.

It had come as both a shock to him and, once the shock was over, a delight, that magic was a learning, a pursuit—that one never finished learning magic. The learning had been longer, a deep foundation against whose painstaking meticulousness he had rebelled more than once in screaming boredom: for the first year and a half he hadn't realized Jaldis had been teaching him anything. All the old man did was command the boy to do things like prepare the floors of rooms where magic was done, ritually cleansing every corner and ritually laying wards on every door, window, pot, knife, and vessel, and in betweentimes simply enjoined him to observe insects and plants, clouds and stars and rain . . . It was only after he had amassed years' worth of information, of tiny detail—until he could tell at a glance the seed of the amaranth from that of the millet—that it came to him how necessary all this information was to the weaving of spells that could change poison to harmless sap, or steer the cumuli by altering the temperature of the air beneath them.

For Jaldis, he knew, learning had never stopped. There were always new plants to study, whole new families of them from the jungles of the south or the bare rock plains of the north and west; spells that had been woven, and written, and lost again; unknown properties of gems or salts or different types of animal blood. He'd seen Jaldis bouncing up and down like a schoolboy one afternoon when they'd visited Shavus at his queer stone house in the forest of Beldirac, and the Archmage had shown off a century-old scroll containing fifty or sixty alterations to spells which strengthened or lessened their effects, depending on the position of certain stars. Rhion had spent a month copying it out—it was one of the books that had been left in the attic.

"I meant to ask you," Rhion said, untucking the folds of his robe from his wide leather belt. "Was there a reason you couldn't summon fog to cover us, when we were getting out of Felsplex? Did working with the Dark Well hurt you that much? Or was there just not enough time?"

"The Dark Well . . . tired me, yes." Jaldis half turned in his chair. "It saps power, drinks it . . ." The diffuse white light that came through the window's oiled parchment panes lent a matte yellow-gray tone to his lined face, making him look tired and ill. He'd been wearing his spectacles to accustom himself to his new surroundings; they lay now on the table beside his hand, and the air was permeated with the bittersweet pungence of lime and rue he'd burned to relieve the headache that was the result.

"That was one reason why it so grieved me that the Well was destroyed—that we had to leave it and that men, in fear, will rub out the Circles of Power which hold its darkness in place. It will be some time before I regain the strength to undertake the making of another."

The longer, the better, as far as I'm concerned, Rhion thought, a little guiltily.

"At the equinox, perhaps," Jaldis went on, turning back to the ordering of his books with crooked, groping hands. "The turning of the spring, when I can use the momentum of the forces of the stars to help me. The evening star will be in transit then, too, which should help—there are spells which call down its power at such times which I must teach you. It is imperative . . ." He broke off, and shook his head, a quick, small gesture, dismissing the preoccupation which, Rhion knew, had been gnawing at him all through their flight.

Then he looked up again, a small, closed smile flexing the scarred corners of his lips. "But as for the fog . . . I could not work two spells at once, Rhion. Not two spells as dissimilar as weather-spinning and summoning."

"Summoning?" Rhion perched one flank on the corner of the table and frowned. "Summoning what?"

"Summoning the books back to us." And his smile widened as if he could see his pupil's expression of startled, enlightened delight. "Have I never shown you the sigils to draw, the spells to weave, to convince an object that its proper place is in your possession?"

"I didn't even know such spells existed, but tell me more." He drew up another chair. Compared to the Black Pig, the room was hopelessly primitive—damply cold, so that both of them wore their cloaks and kept their blankets wrapped around them most of the time, the beds only platforms built of planks and covered with straw, and the whole place smelling of the barnyard onto which it looked. Rhion suspected from the stains on the scoured stone floor that the thatch would leak come spring. But it was clean, and the landlady was liberal in her interpretation of the word *board*.

"I thought the books were burned."

Jaldis sighed, and nodded. "And indeed, they probably were." The sweet voice was incapable of tone, but his eyebrows drew down in a faint twinge of pain, like a man who speaks of friends rumored dead in some catastrophe. Then he shook his head, gestured the thoughts aside with the two fingers still mobile upon his right hand.

"But in the event that some of them were not, in the event that they were thrown into the midden, or cast out the window, the spells I laid upon them—if my strength was sufficient at that point for any spell to work—would cause them to be found by someone who would see in them a source of income, and not an insult to whatever god he was taught to revere. And the spells—if they had worked thus far—would lead that woman or man to sell them to a dealer, perhaps, who might be journeying to Imber when the roads clear in summer, or to an antiquarian, or a seller of used paper, who would in turn, if chances so fell out, display them along with his other wares at a time when you or I or someone who knows us would be passing his shop. That is the reason I never neglect to examine the wares of old paper dealers—one reason of many. Here . . ." He reached with one stiff claw and drew the *Grimoire of Weygarth* to him, opening its crumbling leather covers to stroke the parchment within. Across the faded illuminations of the title page his finger traced a dim line of blue-white light that flickered like a live thing in the pallid gloom, then seemed to sink into the page itself, like a colored ribbon laid upon water.

"It is a spell like other sigils of summoning, but comprised of the Lost Rune, and that of the Dancer, accompanied by the words . . ."

Three shadows passed the soft brightness of the windows and Rhion touched Jaldis' wrist in warning. A moment later there was a faint, polite scratching at the rough plank door.

The man who stood on the threshold was middle-aged, the woman elderly. Both were clothed in the white wool robes, the long white cloaks, and the simple wooden beads of the Selarnist Order of wizardry. Rhion's landlady stood in the background, her skirt still tucked up from work and her muddy boots showing beneath it, her hands shoved for warmth into her sleeves.

The male wizard inclined his head. "Are you Jaldis the Blind and his pupil Rhion?"

"I'm Rhion, yes. Come in." He stepped back from the door, but neither of the two visitors made any move to follow him inside. A moment later he heard the scrape of Jaldis' chair legs on the stone, and then the almost soundless tap of crutches and rustle of robes.

"I am Chelfrednig of Imber, and this is Niane. We understand that you have come to stay in Imber."

"For a time," Rhion said, hiking his cloak a little higher over his shoulder. He mistrusted the man's tone, the cool distance of his manner. It was something he recognized, the attitude that said, *Don't blame ME for what's going to happen. It's nothing personal . . .*

"It's nothing personal . . ."

"Fine." Rhion lifted a hand amicably. "At this short an acquaintance I have nothing personal against you, either. Now that we've established that . . ."

"We understand that yesterday you sold a good-luck charm to a slave named Benno, who works at the shrine of Mhorvianne."

"He didn't tell me his name," he said, more cautious still, "but yes, I did make a talisman of good fortune for a man who came here, and by the way he dressed I figured him for a lower servant or a slave."

With a quickness that reminded Rhion irresistibly of carnival-show sleight of hand, Chelfrednig produced a round billet of elder-wood, roughly the size of a double-weight copper penny, from his sleeve and held it out. Rhion did not touch it. Upon it he recognized his own elaborately interwoven seals, spelled to attract circumstances of pleasantness and peace, of good feeling and fortunate coincidence. As he had explained to the man who had come to them yesterday, no magic could turn aside true misfortune, just as no magic could bring the thundering strokes of great luck that change a person's life—and he didn't think his first client in Imber had wanted to believe him. But as far as it went, the little emblem was good for a few extra rolls of dice, for a capricious master's change of mood when a slave had broken a dish, or for an extra jog at the memory about a pot left on the stove. And what more, Rhion thought, could you do for a slave?

With his forefinger he pushed his spectacles a little more firmly up onto the bridge of his nose, and waited.

"We of our House," Chelfrednig said sententiously, "have striven over the years to achieve a harmony with the authorities of this town, the priests of Ptorag, the local magistrates, and the Earl of Way's governor. We believe we have convinced them that those born with the powers of wizardry, if properly instructed and disciplined, are not monsters, nor are they traitors to the gods and to human-kind; that we do not hold orgies at the turning points of the universe and do not slit children's throats to make magic with their blood.

And we have done this by keeping ourselves to ourselves, and by refraining from meddling with the lives of anyone in this town."

"That's very nice," said Rhion grimly. "Who pays your rent?"

"Investments," the White Mage replied, with a dismissive gesture of one gloved hand. "But the fact remains that our living depends upon the sufferance of the local authorities. And this . . ." He took Rhion's hand in his, and placed the talisman in the plump palm. ". . . we cannot have."

Rhion heard Jaldis come up behind him; a swift glance back showed him the cold flash of daylight on the opal-and-crystal spectacles that the old man had donned.

"You cannot deny us our right," the old man said, "to make a living."

"Ah." Under a long flow of herb-scented beard, Chelfrednig's mouth flexed in a small, tolerant smile. "I had forgotten that when the Morkensiks split off from the Selarnist Order they conveniently dropped the portion of the Oath not to concern oneself in the affairs of humankind . . ."

"It was the Selarnists who split off from the Morkensiks," retorted Jaldis, with a frown of anger and what would have been a deadly edge to his voice, had it been capable of anything except a sweet, buzzing monotone. "And the Oath was and always has been, to do no harm . . ."

"Be that as it may." The Selarnist's tone was clear: *What is the point*, it asked, *of bandying words with a heretic?* "We cannot, alas, deny you what you consider to be your right to 'make a living,' as you say; but we can deny you your freedom to do so in this town. Now, you are welcome to stay in our House for a time if poverty is a problem . . ."

"So that you can tell me what I can and cannot do?" Jaldis demanded. "So that you can sequester my books, and my crystals, and the implements of my art, in your own library, for the good of the magistrates of this town?" And Rhion saw Chelfrednig's eyes shift. "Thank you," the old man went on stiffly, "but we will earn our bread in some other fashion while we are here, and study as we please."

"I am afraid," Chelfrednig said, "that that is not an option open to you either. The guilds in Imber are quite strict about wizards entering businesses or trades. Quite understandably, seeing how an unscrupulous mage—one not bound by *proper* rules—could take an unfair advantage of lesser men."

Hesitantly, the landlady said, "I'm sorry. But you see, I sell most of my greens to them, and milk . . ." Her bright, worried eyes went nervously from Jaldis' face to Rhion's, torn between her liking for them, her need for money, her sense of justice, and her fear that, as wizards, they would cause a scene of the kind she could barely guess at and draw down still more trouble upon her head.

"Right . . ." Rhion muttered furiously, and Jaldis placed a staying hand upon his shoulder from behind, and inclined his head.

"Very well," he said. "My good woman . . ." He turned his disconcertingly insectile gaze upon her, and she shrank back in spite of herself. "My sincerest apologies for the trouble we may have caused you, and . . ." With a very slight motion of his head he indicated the two Selarnists, ". . . my apologies to you on behalf of all wizardry, that these persons considered it incumbent upon themselves to interfere in your life." He turned to face Chelfrednig fully. "We shall be gone by sunset. Is that sufficient?"

"Noon would be better," the old woman with the ashstaff said, speaking for the first time, "if you want to come to shelter before night."

"That," replied Jaldis chillingly, "is our business. I bid you good day."

They were on the road again by noon. "The nerve of them!" Rhion fumed, picking his way cautiously along the most solidly frozen and least cut-up side of the main highroad that led from Imber south through the hills toward the steep-sided Valley of the Morne, and so on to the Mountains of the Sun, and to Nerriok beyond. "I mean, it's not like we were Hand-Prickers or Earth-witches selling cut-rate horoscopes and conversations with your dead ancestors on the street corners, you know! We're Morkensiks! We were the original founding line of wizardry . . . !" His foot slipped where a cartwheel earlier in the day had sliced through the snow and into the frozen clay beneath. He caught himself on the walking staff he'd cut, and put out a hand to guide Jaldis around the place.

Beyond the brown hedges and drainage cuts that hemmed in the road the fields lay empty under the silence of winter. Even this short a distance from the town walls the hedges were overgrown, the ditches silting up, and sedges prickling thick and black through the blanket of dirty snow. The road itself was narrow and unkept; for a long time the township of Imber had been disregarding the corvee laws of its titular liege, the Earl of Way. At least, thought Rhion, hunching deeper into the hood of his cloak and scanning the deserted and overgrown fields nervously, if they were attacked by bandits out here, or in the stony hills or the wilderness of the Drowned Lands that lay beyond, they had the option of fighting back without concern about future retaliation against wizardry in general.

To most people, he knew, a wizard was a wizard was a wizard— as had been the case with himself before he'd become Jaldis' pupil— a mysterious figure in a long robe who acted from unknown motives and held strange and dangerous powers. And from that standpoint, he supposed, Chelfrednig's argument was correct: his sale of potions would contradict what the Selarnists had been laboriously working to convince the town authorities was the nature of wizardry. *Though it was only their opinion of what it should be, dammit!* And thus, though he and Jaldis could have summoned lightning from the sky to blast Lord Pruul's liverymen and their volunteer helpers out of existence, or even have caused the stairs at the Black Pig to collapse under their weight long enough to have given them time to make a getaway, in the long run it would mean more trouble for other wizards they knew, who would have suffered the retaliation.

It was, in fact, the reason that Jaldis had left the house where he had lived for so many years in Nerriok—that tall, narrow house on one of the dozen tiny islands that made up the city, where Rhion had first learned the nature of magic and had first seen what it was to be a mage. When the old High King had died and his brother had briefly taken the scepter, the brother had hated wizards due to some bad financial dealings with an Ebiatic mage who, in Rhion's opinion, should have known better. As a result all mages, from respected masters of the Great Art like Jaldis down to the Figure-

Flingers throwing painted bones on the street corners, had been banished from the city and the realm, to earn what livings they could in places like the Black Pig.

The old High King's brother had died at the turning of autumn, of dysentery contracted while besieging the stronghold of a rebellious vassal in the Clogreth Hills in the west. On the night of the winter solstice, even as Jaldis had been listening in the Dark Well to the clamor of voices crying of the death of magic, the High King's daughter had been crowned in the great Temple of Darova in Nerriok, and had received the homage of all the lords of the Forty Civilized Realms.

It was, Jaldis had said quietly, time to return home.

Night fell early. Owing to the rucked and muddy condition of the winter roads and to Jaldis' lameness, the two wizards were far from the inn which even in summertime lay a good day's journey from Imber's gates. They pressed on long after it grew fully dark. Throughout the day the cloud cover had been thinning under the creeping dryness of the north wind; rags of moonlight filtering through the bare trees which pressed ever more closely about the road through the hills eventually showed Rhion the inn itself, perched on a little rise where the road up from the Drowned Lands divided to run northwards to Imber, and to Felsplex in the east.

Snow lay heavy on the bare hilltops above the road and among the trees that grew thick as a bear pelt about their feet. Against its luminous pallor, the inn's gray stone walls bulked heavy and dark. Every shutter was fastened, every door bolted; every stall in the snow-blanketed stableyard was empty and smelled of fox-mess and field mice, and the tracks of deer and rabbits were a scribbled message all about the walls: *Not at Home.*

Rhion swore fluently for a short while, then walked with what caution he could muster—a city boy born and raised, he had little woodcraft—all around the inn and its outbuildings, sniffing, listening, searching with the hyperacute senses of a wizard for the least sign of danger. But all he heard was the scurrying of mice across bare wooden floors, and the chewing of beetles in the walls. Coming nearer, he found some evidence that a small troop of horses—maybe the mounts of bandits—had occupied the stables a week or so ago, but had been gone before the fall of the snow. No smoke curled from the chimneys, no track broke the snow crust around the wood-pile outside the kitchen door.

"There was sickness, I think," Jaldis said sometime later, pressing his hands to the stones of the chimney breast in the dark and de-serted common room. "It is hard to read. So many griefs and joys, so much talk and laughter have seeped their way into the stones here. But I feel most recently bad news from somewhere, early in the autumn . . . fresh apples. They had just picked the apples, the smell of them was strong in the room. Ullana . . . Ullata . . . some name like that. Ullata is sick, they said."

He shook his head, the white strands floating around his thin face rimmed with the new-coined brightness of the fire Rhion had kindled in the hearth. The warm light turned the rosewood voice-box the color of claret, and flickered in the talismans that hung from it, dancing chips of green and gold and red. He had put his spectacles away, and wore instead, as he frequently did when he went abroad, a linen bandage over the collapsed and sunken lids of his empty eyes.

"Ullata is sick . . . and so we have to go."

Rhion looked up from adjusting massive iron firedogs meant to uphold wood enough to heat the enormous room. "Maybe Ullata was going to leave them some money." Behind the blaze, tiny in the midst of all that acreage of blackened hearth bricks, a torture cham-ber ensemble of spits, hooks, and pot-chains loured in the shadows of the huge chimney. "At least Ullata didn't get sick before they cut the winter's wood."

Nevertheless, when he straightened up again he placed his own hands to the stone of the overmantle, and sent his mind feeling its way through the tight-crossed, gritty fibers of the granite, touching the voices, the images, and the fragments of other days which per-meated the stone. The inn had stood for hundreds of years: he glimpsed a red-haired woman washing a new-born baby on the hearth and weeping bitterly, silently, as she worked; saw a young man sitting with his back to the iron firedogs, every window open into the heart-shaking magic of summer evening, greedily reading a scroll stretched between his up-cocked knees; saw an old man shelling peas and talking to a blond-haired child whose brown eyes were filled with a hungry wonder and the shadows of strange destinies. But he had not Jaldis' fineness of perception. He could not separate ancient from recent—all these people might well have been dead for centuries—nor could he make out words. Only the smells of smoke and beer and roasting meats came to him, the echoes of bawdy songs and the clink of the little iron tavern puzzles that hung silent now in a neat row from spikes driven into the chimney's stones.

The widow woman had given them bread and cheese for the journey, as well as most of Rhion's money back; there were yams, dried beans, and sweet dried apples from the trees along the inn's west wall to be found in the cellar. After a meal of these, while Jaldis sat with his opal spectacles on his nose and his scrying-crystal— a chunk of spell-woven quartz the color of bitterroot tea—between his palms, Rhion put on his cloak once more and left the inn to make another circuit of it and draw wizard's marks upon the surrounding trees.

As he came back across the moonlit stillness of the yard, he noticed a gleam like a fleck of quicksilver near the door-handle, and, looking more closely, saw that a silver nail had been driven into the heavy oak. Thoughtfully, he picked his way over the slippery drifts to the nearest of the shuttered windows. Silver nails had been driven into the sills of them all—tiny, almost like pinheads, for the metal was expensive. The inn's protection had doubtless owed more to its roaring fires and the lamps in their iron sconces which had ringed the yard and to the noise of its customers and the smells of their massed bodies and blood. But standing in the snow that lay glittering like marble all around the inn, listening to the forest silence pressing so close about its walls, Rhion remembered that in waste places at night there were more things to be feared than human prejudice and human spite.

He hated the thought of risking the only thing that stood between him and starvation. Nevertheless, he swept the crusted snow from the bench beside the door, and sat on it to draw from his pocket the little velvet bag of coins. There were seven or eight silver royals among the copper. *Minted in Felsplex*, he reflected dourly, biting one. *God knows if it's even as pure as it's stamped.* His father, one of the wealthiest bankers in the City of Circles, had always held the Felsplex municipal council's fiscal policies in utter contempt, and having seen them at medium-close range for two and a half years now Rhion couldn't blame him. However, it was all the silver they had, even if it was less pure than the buttons of some doublets Rhion had worn back when he was still his father's son.

"Alas for lost opportunities," he sighed to himself, and went to work laying small words of Ward on each silver coin. Then he buried them in the snow—with suitable, and invisible, marks over each so he could find them in the morning—in a loose ring around the inn, and drew a tenuous thread of spells from coin to coin, forming the protection of a Circle of Silver.

And thus it was that in the dead of night he was awakened by the chittering whisper of attacking grims.

4

He came awake at once out of a far deeper sleep than he'd meant to allow himself. By the dull ochre of the banked firelight he could just make out Jaldis, seated on a bench beside the shuttered window, listening with bowed head. Pulling his blankets tightly around his shoulders Rhion sat up, for it was the deep of night, and even here beside the common room fireplace the chill was like iron.

"Did the Circle hold?" He groped for his spectacles, finding them by memory, muttering a curse as the lenses misted from the warmth of his flesh.

Jaldis, still deep in his meditative listening, shook his head.

"Damn inflationist idiots on the municipal council passing off silver-washed copper . . ."

"They're going by," the voice of the box hummed. "They come from all directions, but they all go in one direction, and that is not here. They cross over the Circle on their way . . ."

Even through the heavy shutters, Rhion heard a woman scream.

He was on his feet and heading for the door almost before he could think—he and Jaldis both had been sleeping booted and clothed. He had his hands on the heavy door bolt before he remembered that grims frequently counterfeited the voices of women and children crying for help, to trick victims into opening shutters and doors and breaking what field of power the silver nails might generate. He thought the scream sounded genuine, but still . . .

"*Alseigodath, amresith,* Children of the Dusky Air . . ." he muttered, collecting the first of the demon-spells Jaldis had long ago had him memorize and hoping he could call accurately to mind the long catalogue of the names of demons and grims and the strange pain-spells that held such creatures in check. He caught up his walking staff and flung the door open as a second scream cut the air. Hearing it, he knew it was no grim that made that sound.

Calling up within him all the power that he could, he ran.

Foul with ice and half-melted snow, the road dipped beyond the inn's little hill to the thicker woods and broken jumble of ground that was the first frontier of the Drowned Lands of Sligo. In this season the pools and marshes which six hundred years ago had filled in the upper end of the Morne Valley were frozen, black cattails and the twisted stems of sunken oak and hornbeam protruding like skeleton fingers from the gray sheet of starlit ice. But with the recent thaw, even the shallow ponds were treacherous. Rhion's foot broke through what had appeared to be solid ice in the roadside ditch as he scrambled across, soaking him to the knees in freezing water.

Far off, amid the tangled bog-hummocks and leafless willows, he could see a flickering greenish light.

There were hundreds of them, thick as flies above a midden in summer. As he whispered the words of the spells within his mind he could smell them, queer and cold and bodiless; see them through their own ghastly weavings of semivisibility and shifting forms. Like the intermittent hallucinations of migraine, grims flitted through the bare boughs of maple and ash, skeletal forms with huge eyes and dangling feet, strange organs heaving luminously through transparent skin, eyes and faces and limbs, human and bestial, materializing one moment, then vanishing or becoming, hideously something else. A thing came loping out of the black underbrush beside him in the form of a huge black dog, to snap and tear at his legs with teeth suddenly solid and real; Rhion struck at it, his staff ablaze with blue-white witchfire, and the creature screamed at him with a human face and went gibbering back into the dark.

As he had suspected, they were driving the women toward the frozen sloughs.

Through snow-clotted fern and bracken, it was easy to trace the rucked hoof-tracks of her panicked horse; far off he could hear it neighing with terror. They were out on pond ice already, though, from the high ground where he stood, Rhion could see the rider fighting to rein back to safer footing. He scrambled down the scarp bank, black tangles of wild ivy and vine snagging his feet like rabbit snares under the snow, swinging his flaming staff at the grims when they came too close. Their claws raked at his face and his hands— *If they get my specs off me I'm a dead man,* he thought detachedly— shrieking like the soulless damned, while ahead of him clouds of them blew like poisoned green smoke around the frantic dark forms wheeling in the starlight.

They were far out on the ice, the horse's hooves skidding and slipping, and underfoot Rhion felt the ice buckle and crack. The Drowned Lands were a maze of fen and swamp and pond, deep even this far inland, in these sweet marshes, two days' journey from the salt marshes where the heart of the realm of Sligo had lain. By the bulrushes that fringed the gray glimmer of ice, Rhion guessed this pond was deep. Ahead of him he saw by the noxious ur-light the face of the rider, a girl of no more than seventeen, taut and scared as she tried to force her mount back into the driving swarms of eyes and claws that lay between her and the safety of the shore. Fingers like thorn-branches snagged and lifted a huge cloud of pale hair; another grim tore the long, full train of her riding skirt, and she lashed at it with her quirt, clinging to the rein as the terrified horse twisted out of control.

Then the ice cracked beneath them and they plunged, forehooves-first, into the heaving brown water beneath.

Rhion flung up his staff and cried *"ALSEIGODATH! Children of the Dark Air . . . !"* in a voice of power, the trained, booming shout completely unlike his normal light tenor, and the grims, screaming with laughter as they swirled around their struggling victims, scattered in all directions in a vicious, glittering cloud. Summoning about him the essences, the true names, of silver and fire and burning sunlight, Rhion strode forward, blazing and flashing and crying out the tale of the demon lists he had memorized over the years, the true names of as many as these flickering, amorphous things as had been gathered by wizards of the past, weaving them into a net of illusion and power and ruin.

And he tried not to show—and indeed, tried not to feel—his surprise that they did retreat, since as far as anyone could tell the power of the grims increased the more of them there were.

The girl sprang from the saddle as soon as the grims whirled back, tearing off her jacket and throwing it around the head of the terrified horse. Its forelegs were still trapped in the ice and its frantic pitching threatened to drop them through what remained; she caught the bit, trying to drag the animal free, and Rhion, still shouting the names of power and pain and light, ran to her and caught the bridle on the other side.

"*Malsleiga, Brekkat, Ykklath*—say when . . ." he panted. "*Rinancor* and *Tch'war, Flennegant the Pig-Faced* . . ."

"*Now!*"

Both hauling in unison, they pulled the terrified beast's forefeet clear, ice-water showering everywhere and soaking them both to the skin. The horse tried to bolt, demons still eddying around their heads like flaming leaves in a whirlwind, and through that hellish storm Rhion and the girl managed to drag it across the sagging floe. Only when they reached the more solid packs among the reed-beds did the wickering ring thin, swirling away like blown smoke into the darkness and melting into cruel, luminous laughter among the silent trees.

"Thank you," the girl gasped, brushing back her tangled hair with a hand that shook. Even etiolated by starshine, Rhion could see it was mingled brown and fair, the color of burned sugar, where it wasn't soaked dark with marsh water. Her cap had been torn away, but its gemmed pins remained, flashing coldly in the streaming mess like phosphorous in seaweed.

". . . *Filkedne the Black, Qu'a'htchat* . . . What the hell were you doing riding alone in the woods at night?! You could have been killed out there!"

The gratitude in those huge gray eyes turned to anger, and for a moment he thought of a very young hawk, bating against a clumsy hand. "I wanted a little exercise!" she snapped sarcastically. "And nobody had *ever* told me about grims haunting the wild places at night, so I thought I'd be *perfectly* safe!" She jerked the rein from his hand. "And since it's such a lovely night and I've had such a wonderful time so far I think I'll just . . ."

Rhion realized that his question had included an unspoken, *Are you stupid or something?* and blushed. "I'm sorry," he said quietly, catching back the girl's hand, his breath drifting in a silvery cloud around his head. "That was a stupid thing to say. What's wrong, and can I help?" The girl's face had been cut by a claw or tail-stinger—the wound was already beginning to puff. His own face was torn and welted, his robe, like the girl's dark-red riding dress, soaked and dragging with water. "I'm Rhion the Brown . . ."

"Tallisett . . . Tally . . ." She swung around at the sound of a man's voice shouting in terror, far off in the woods, the neighing of terrified horses and laughter like the sparkle of corrosive dust. The fear returning to her eyes as she looked swiftly back at him made her suddenly seem very young, despite the fact that she stood a good two inches taller than he.

"It's my sister's child," she said, trying to keep her husky young voice steady. With a sudden move, she pulled the jacket from the horse's head and drew it on, shivering at the touch of the sodden wool. "They've taken her." She caught the stirrup preparatory to mounting again.

"Wait . . ." Rhion caught her elbow, pointy and delicate in his grip. "We'll get my master."

"Why didn't you push on and take shelter in the inn, by the way?" he asked a few minutes later, as the two of them half strode, half ran up the frozen slush of the road back toward the deserted public house, their breath puffing in silver clouds with exertion, the exhausted and shivering bay gelding stumbling between them. "You do know there's an inn here . . ."

"A peddler we met this afternoon coming from Imber said it was shut up and barred. We hadn't been able to get fresh litter mules at the last inn and when we knew we couldn't get a change here, either, we decided to make camp. We lit fires all around the camp . . ."

"That doesn't always work if there's a lot of them."

Tally had tucked up her heavy skirts through her belt to run—because of her height her stride was long, though unlike so many tall girls she was not gawky, but moved as gracefully as a dancer. Heavy silver earrings swung in the tangle of her hair, gleaming coldly in the ragged blue witch-glow; her boots, the wool of her dress, and the many strands of barrel-shaped amber beads around her neck proclaimed her a rich man's child. Her hand in its buckskin glove, gripping the horse's cheekstrap, though slender, was as large as a man's.

"How many were you?"

"A dozen. One of the grooms rode with me to search. We had torches, but they fell into the snow when the horses got spooked . . . What was that you shouted at them?"

The magelight that shivered and flickered above their heads as they walked would have left her in no doubt as to what he was. But there was no apprehension in her wide, inquiring eyes. Probably, Rhion thought wryly, because no woman is ever really afraid of a man who's shorter than she is.

"Their names—or names that might have been theirs. There are lists of them, different lists for different parts of the country, lists that have been accumulated, handed down, passed on by other wizards who in one way or another have gotten some specific grim or demon in their power long enough to get it to rat on some of its fellows."

"Is that easy to do?"

"Oh, yes. They're all cowards, and half of them hate each other anyway—they feel no loyalty to anything as we understand loyalty. Since you weave spells with a thing's true name, the name of its soul, grims will generally retreat if they know you know their names. Because they don't have true bodies, you can put a *hell* of a pain-spell on a demon . . . Were you hurt?"

She shook her head. The dark blood gleamed where it was drying on her temple, and Rhion made a mental note to apply a poultice later. The uneasy feather of witchfire threw fluttering shadows over the gray trunks of the maples along the roadbed and made the snow flash like salt rime where it squeaked beneath their boots. Far off in the darkness, the dreadful slips of light still wavered, and the night was rank—to Rhion's hypertrained nostrils at least—with the nauseating ammonia muskiness of the grims' smell. Blood dripped to the snow from the horse's torn flanks and bitten hocks—they must have driven it here and there through the woods, laughing and egging one another on, delighting in its fear and in Tally's anger, trying to get it to throw her so they could chase her through the dark.

Jaldis was waiting for them in the open door of the inn, witchlight streaming out around him. As if they had discussed the matter—which they hadn't—they led the horse inside as a matter of course, and it stood, head down and shivering, while Rhion rubbed its coat dry and Jaldis listened, nodding, opal spectacles flashing weirdly in the firelight, while Tally told him of her niece's disappearance.

"What is her name?" the old man asked at length, and the girl glanced, startled, from the closed, scar-crusted mouth to the soundbox upon his chest.

But she only said, "Elucida. She's three. I still don't understand how they can have taken her. Damson—my sister—and I put a mirror over her cot and a silver chain around it in a circle . . ."

"Beyond a doubt they lured her forth in her sleep," the wizard replied, stroking the gold sun-cross talisman thoughtfully. "She crossed the silver herself, to where they could come to her. Unlike the water-goblins, they seek to frighten, not to kill, though it does not matter to them if the victim dies in the process. But goblins haunt these marshes, and if they can find a way to get her through the ice they will. My cloak, Rhion . . ."

Rhion slung a rug over the horse's back and fetched his master's cloak, while Jaldis dug in the purse at his belt and produced his scrying-crystal, whose long, irregular facets he angled to the fire's light. The reflection of the blaze, which had been built up high, glanced sharply off the brown quartz and repeated itself endlessly in the chips of crystal worked into his spectacle-lenses, and echoed in the girl Tally's worried gray eyes.

Softly, as if following his thoughts without his conscious volition, the box murmured, "Elucida, Damson's child . . . Little Elucida, daughter of daylight . . ."

Tally glanced over at Rhion, as if for help or guidance. Rhion signed to her with his fingers that all would be well. As he stepped over close to her she breathed, "We have to hurry. She was only wearing a nightdress, she'll freeze . . ." Her own clothes were steaming in the warmth of the fire, bullion embroidery sparkling faintly under the mudstains, the crisscrossed maze of ribbonwork on the sleeves discolored and sodden, save for here and there, where creases had protected and now revealed startling squares and slips of bronze and blue.

"It'll be all right," Rhion said softly. "It'll be all right."

The gesture of Jaldis' fingers, the movement of his head, were clear as a murmured, *Ah*! He made a pass or two above the crystal with his crippled hand, the tracing of runes too quick, too subliminal, for Rhion to identify them all. "Now," he said, reaching for his crutches and rising from the bench beside the fire. "Let us go."

From the inn doorway they faced out into the dark. Something swift and glowing flickered by just beyond the outstreaming bar of magelight—Rhion couldn't be sure, but he thought it was only a marsh-fae, tiny and naked and curious about all the hullabaloo. Around them, the blue-white glow of witchlight softened and dimmed until it was little brighter than the ghostly powder of starlight on the snow. "Look out across the trees, both of you," said the old mage softly. "Can you see light?"

The starlight was unsteady, the woods thick and wild, a tangle of bare black willow, of ash and maple and laurel thickets. The earthquake which six centuries ago had sunk the Drowned Lands and thrown down the walls of every city from Nerriok to Killay had left the Morne Valley a jagged ruin of fault scarps and banks, broken ground difficult to navigate even where it was not studded with potholes and ponds.

Rhion shook his head. "No."

"And now?"

Far off, a gleam of blue witchlight flickered bright among the knotted trees. "Yes . . ."

"Then come."

They found the little girl where the grims had abandoned her when they'd grown bored with driving her here and there in the haunted woods. With the self-preservative instincts of a little animal she'd crawled into a hollow log; over this log, Rhion saw as they came nearer, Jaldis with his scrying-crystal had called a glowing column of magelight, a moving rope of disembodied, unearthly brightness, whose light made the snow all around glitter as if strewn with diamonds. Rhion had brought extra blankets; Tally snatched them from his hands and fell to her knees, wrapping the half-conscious child in them, her face solemn, as if she worked to save the life of a kitten found drowning in a stream.

"She's alive . . ."

Rhion knelt in the snow beside her and felt the baby's hands and cheeks. Cold as the silken skin was, he felt blood moving beneath. Gently he called the spells of healing and warmth, and the aversion of ills. The child herself was thin and small, not pretty, but with a porcelain-doll delicacy and a soft tangle of blond-brown hair ridiculously like that of her young aunt.

"She'll be all right," he murmured, the words half-embodying the charm in themselves, both promise and invocation as his fingers traced the signs of Summer Queen and Sun, the signs of health and longevity and light, on the forehead, the cheeks, and across the energy-paths of the child's face and neck which governed lungs and skin. It seemed incredible to him, touching that skin which in its texture, its softness, and its newness was so absolutely unlike anything else of the mortal earth, that something so small could have those same paths of energy that traced the adult body, perfect in miniature, like a baby's fingernails or the veins of the tiniest leaf.

Holding the child cradled to her shoulder Tally looked across at him as they knelt side-by-side in the slush, their faces mottled by tree-latticed starlight and darkness. She drew in her breath to speak, to thank him . . . But by the soft glow of the flickering witchlight their eyes met, and silence fell between them, a silence in which Rhion was conscious of the almost-unheard sibilance of her breath, of the way her dust-colored hair stuck in dark strings to the hollows of her cheekbones, of the small, upright line of puzzlement between her brows as her eyes looked into his . . .

Clumsy with sudden haste he got to his feet. "Jaldis will . . . will be able to help if she's taken any hurt."

A moment later he realized he should probably help Tally, overburdened with the child as she was, to her feet. But she had already risen, not noticing or not thinking anything of this omission. "She's all right, I think. Thank you," she added shyly.

The two wizards walked with her back to the campsite on the southward road. Jaldis moved along behind on his crutches, the witchlight that wavered in rippling sheets all around them flashing coldly off the bulging spectacle-lenses and dancing like strange blue fire on the mud and snow of the roadbanks. Rhion and Tally, walking ahead, traded off carrying the child Elucida and leading the horse. "How did you become a wizard?" Tally asked as they passed beneath the black shadows of a grove of naked elms, and Rhion laughed and shook his head.

"Have you got till spring?"

"No, really. I mean, everybody talks about wizards as if the first thing a wizard has to do is spit on Darova's altar—and then everybody turns around and goes to wizards for spells and horoscopes and things. And the wizards I've met at . . . at my father's house . . ." She hesitated there. Rhion saw her hand steal to the amber beads she wore, which announced her to all the world as a marriageable virgin of truly substantial dowry, and wondered if somebody had told her—as his parents had repeatedly told his sister—not to reveal her father's name to chance-met strangers for fear of being carried away for ransom.

She recovered quickly and went on, "The wizards I've met at my father's house have all seemed—well, very decent, if a little strange. And you didn't have to come out to help me." She reached out, and touched the puffy red welt on the side of his face, left by a grim's stinging tail. "So I just wondered . . . Why you did it? Become a mage, I mean. Because I refuse to believe, as the philosophers say, that wizards were born without souls and have to become what they are."

Rhion sighed. "I don't know if I was born without a soul, because, if I was, I wouldn't know what really having one feels like." He glanced back over his shoulder, at Jaldis stumping sturdily along behind the exhausted horse. "But yes . . . We have to become what we are."

It was something he'd never been able to explain to anyone not mageborn. He remembered, back in the days when he was still one

of the most fashionable young dandies who hung around the perfume shops and flower boutiques, standing with several of his friends
watching a pack of children tormenting an old Earth-witch who'd
set up shop on a blanket on the steps of one of the great downtown
baths. The children had been throwing dung and rotten vegetables
at her, chanting obscene songs. Furious as the old woman was, she
had borne it in silence, and Rhion knew instinctively that she dared
not do anything that would cause the children to run to their parents
crying, *The lady hurt us* . . . And his friends had joked about why
anyone would want to be a witch in the first place.

And he, Rhion, had been silent.

Because even then he had known.

Very softly, he said, "You reach a point where you can't live a lie
anymore. Where the pain of not—not using what you *know* you
have, of not reaching out to take that power—becomes so intolerable
that you don't care what happens to you afterward. It's like sex . . ."

Oh, great! he thought in the next instant, *Go ahead and shock this
poor virgin* . . .

But the great gray eyes were not shocked.

"When I was a little boy," he went on, his voice still low, as if
he spoke to himself, "I used to see pictures in the fire. Simple things,
like my mother putting her make-up on, or my friends eating breakfast . . . One day my parents went to the shrine of St. Beldriss, and
I mentioned to my nurse that I'd seen in the fire that a wheel had
come off a cart in the narrow streets around the shrine and caused
a hell of a traffic jam and that they'd be late coming back. She beat
me." His eyebrows flinched together over the round lenses of his
spectacles. "She said that nobody saw things in the fire, that it was
just daydreams that were no good for little boys. She told me not
to say anything about it to my mother, but of course I did, and
Mother punished me for lying."

He still remembered the dark of the attic closet where he'd been
locked, the furtive, terrible scurryings of the rats he knew lurked
just behind the walls. It was not something he would ever have done
to a child of four. He remembered other things as well.

"For years I convinced myself she was right—that I had lied. And
I tried so damn hard to be good."

There was a silence, in which their feet squeaked a little in the packed snow and mud of the road. The child Elucida slept, a warm, muffled burden against Rhion's chest, beneath his patched black wool cloak. The last of the grims had faded back into the earth and trees where they lurked in daylight, and the frozen swamps, the sheets of gray ice, and the dirty piebald snow, all broken with the iron stems of naked shrub and willow, seemed to have lain locked in that sleeping enchantment since the beginnings of time.

"What were you doing traveling at this time of year, anyway?" Rhion asked after a little time, looking back across at the tall girl who strode at his side.

Tally seemed to shake herself out of some private reverie and smiled ironically across at him. "We were going to Imber to meet Damson's husband. He has property near there and interest in shipping . . . he says." She hesitated, as if debating whether to say more, her hands tucked into her armpits for warmth. A small tired line, the wry foot track of a passing thought, flicked into existence at the corner of her mouth and then as quickly fled.

"And a mistress, too?"

Her gray eyes slid sidelong at him, then away. The bitter dimple reappeared, all the comment necessary.

"And you?"

"I wanted to get away. I like to travel." They came within sight of the camp, five or six pavilions at the top of a steep bank, twenty feet high above the swerve of the road where it ran across a dilapidated stone bridge. Even in the icy night, the smell of blood, both fresh and nauseatingly stale, breathed from the round little stone hut on the nearer end of the bridge, where offerings to the guardian troll had been left. The thing's tracks were visible in the trampled snow, shambling along the bank of the marsh which the causeway spanned and so into the rocks of the glen. Lamps in the red and orange tents high on the bank turned them into glowing treasure-boxes in the bitter darkness, and Rhion could hear voices and glimpse the flash of steel by the jittery flare of torches.

He revised his estimate of the girl's social position upward. A wealthy merchant or banker could have bought those great amber beads and the silver bullion that stitched her breast and sleeves, but a camp like that meant old nobility, at least.

On the threshold of the bridge Tally halted and took her sleeping niece from Rhion's arms. Elucida murmured a little and cuddled deeper into her aunt's breast. For a moment Rhion saw Tally's face, as she turned to look down at the child, filled with a solemn tenderness, the deep, protective affection that had sent her out into the woods herself when she could have detailed grooms and liverymen to the task.

She looked up again and shrugged, her breath a misty vapor as she spoke. "When I'm married, I won't be able to journey," she said.

"Is that going to be soon?" he inquired, not nearly lightly enough.

"I suppose. Father needs an alliance, you see." Her voice was trying hard to be matter-of-fact. She glanced at Jaldis, surrounded by the nimbus of the witchfire that protected them, then back at Rhion, small and battered with his scratched face and his round-lensed spectacles and his rough ashwood walking staff gripped in one mended glove. Behind her, the lights and voices of the camp rose like a wall of color, warmth, and security within call.

"My father is the Duke of Mere," she said quietly. "So it isn't a question of what I want, really. Just when. And who."

Shaking back the filthy strings of her oak-blond hair, she turned a little too quickly and hurried across the bridge, back to her father's servants and troops. But after a step or two, almost against some inner inclination, she turned back, still holding the child cradled on one hip like a peasant woman, the rein of the exhausted horse hooked through her arm. Her face was a pale oval in the frosty gloom.

"Rhion . . . You will . . . Will you ever be coming to Bragenmere? Father . . . he's a scholar, you know. And he does invite wizards to Court."

Then as if fearing she'd said too much, she turned swiftly away and hastened across the bridge, her boots leaving deep tracks in the crusted muck of snow and dirt. For a few moments Rhion stood watching the spangled dusk of her hair and the moving white blob of the horse's off hind stocking blur with the dark of the ascending road. Then torches and colored lanterns came streaming out of the

camp and down the path to greet her and to take her back among
them again.

"Dinar of Mere may be a scholar," Jaldis' soft, artificial voice
buzzed from the freezing dark behind him, "but as for the wizards
he invites to his Court . . . ! Ebiatics trying to transmute lead into
gold and call the wind by means of silver machines; Blood-Mages
stinking like troll huts with demons and grims squeaking in their
hair like lice . . . Why, his court mage for years, when he was still
land-baron of the Prinag marshes before he overthrew the house of
the White Bragenmeres and married the old duke's daughter, was a
foul old Hand-Pricker who could barely talk for the spell-threads
laced through his lips and tongue. Go to Bragenmere indeed!"

Looking back, Rhion saw that the old man, though draped in the
heavy black cloak and surcoat that marked them both as members
of the most ancient of the Orders of Wizardry, was shivering in the
cold, all the talismans of power at his breast twinkling in the witchlight and his pale face lined with the strain of using his spectacles to
see. Rhion walked back to him and said quietly, "Let's go back to
the inn."

The witchlight faded from above their heads. They turned away,
an old cripple and a young pauper, bearded, scruffy, and insignificant
in the leaden darkness before the winter's dawn. But looking over
his shoulder, Rhion could see, on the edge of the camp, a plump
little woman in a dress scintillant with opals and featherwork come
running out to embrace Tally and the sleeping child, and lead them
toward the largest of the lighted pavilions. And he saw how Tally
turned to look out into the darkness, and it seemed to him for a
moment that their eyes met.

5

For a long time after Jaldis slept Rhion sat awake by the fire, staring into its silken heart and listening to the silence of the deserted inn.

And thinking.

You reach the point where you can't live a lie anymore, he had said. And, *I tried so damn hard to be good.*

He had never spoken to a nonwizard about wizardry like that. On the whole, those who were not mageborn—those not born with the strange sleeping fire in their veins, their hearts, the marrow of their bones—found it impossible to comprehend why those who were would subject themselves to such stringent teaching and disciplines in order to achieve a state of virtual outlawry, the state of *beldin nar*—literally, to be dead souls, whose deaths were no more a matter for vengeance than the desecration of a dog's carcass.

Yet he had said it to her, knowing she would understand.

And saying it, he had remembered afresh how much it had hurt to wonder and pretend and fake being something everyone thought he should be; to live in the subconscious hope that it wasn't true or that, if it was true, he could keep people from guessing.

On the whole, to those nonmageborn acquaintances who evinced a genuine interest in the subject—and there had been some among their patrons and clients from the court at Nerriok—he had explained his initiation into wizardry in terms of teaching, education, and eagerness to learn. To them he had recounted how he'd cooked and cleaned and run errands, fetching and carrying up and down all those long rickety stairways of the tall, narrow house in Nerriok, even in the days when they could afford a servant; made a good story of all the tedium of ritually cleansing crucibles and implements in the attic workshop, censing and sweeping the sanctum where the meditation was done, and washing the vessels before and after. That they would understand, at least in part. But never all.

All those first years he'd been reading, absorbing almost without knowing it, all the infinite, tiny gradations of lore necessary to wizardry, gradually becoming aware, through conversation with Jaldis, with Shavus, and with other mages of the Order who stayed with them of the interweavings of all things in the physical world, the metaphysical, and the strange shadowland of ghosts and faes and grims that lay between them—learning how all things were balanced and how no alteration of the fabric of the world could be made without somehow affecting the rest of the universe, sometimes in rather unexpected fashions.

After the spells of imbuing Jaldis' crystal spectacle-lenses had nearly cost him his own eyesight, Rhion had taken the concept of precautions and Limitations very seriously indeed. He had not worked a spell for a long while after that, and had been careful to make the Circles of Power and Protection absolutely correct, to study carefully the Words of Ward and Guard. Simply the study of these had taken him nearly three years of painstaking memorization, during which time he had also studied all those things that his father had never bothered to have him taught: the structure and nature of plants, and how to tell them from one another by sight and touch and smell; the names of every plant, every bird, every beast and fae and spirit and insect and stone, and how they differed from one another; and how each was its own creation, with its own secret name.

Such things were not necessary to accounting—things not only beyond a banker's ken, but beyond even one's imaginings.

And somewhere in those first few years he had learned the thing that he'd never been able to explain to even the most sympathetic of hearers: that magic was not something one did; it was something you were, ingrained in the deepest marrow of the soul. He remembered one of the local tavern girls in Nerriok, with whom he'd had a cozy, if casual, affair, asking why Jaldis hadn't quit being a wizard after he'd been blinded. "Would have made me quit quick enough, let me tell you," she'd said, shaking her tousled head.

Rhion had simply said, "He's stubborn," and had left it at that.

But the truth was that you couldn't quit, the same way he realized that it was almost impossible not to become a wizard, if you were born with the power to do so. You couldn't not be what you were.

On the whole, that was something only other mages understood. Tally . . .

The fire had sunk low; the burning log collapsed on itself with a noise like rustling silk, and Rhion fetched the poker to rearrange the blaze. The renewed flare of saffron light lent a deceptive color to Jaldis' sleeping face, an illusion of health and strength.

Jaldis. For ten and a half years, teacher and father and friend. It had taken Rhion over a year to realize that Jaldis was also one of the most prominent of the Morkensik wizards, renowned throughout the Order for the depth of his wisdom and the strength of his spells.

He had taught Rhion thoroughly, patiently, and from the ground up, riding easily through the petulance, temper-tantrums, and fits of impatience and sarcasm that the older Rhion still blushed to think about. As a rich man's son, he had been less than an ideal pupil. "What the hell does *that* have to do with magic?" had been his constant refrain—sitting by the fire, Rhion could still hear himself, like a stubborn child refusing to see what the alphabet has to do with being a poet of world renown. And Jaldis would always say gently, "Do you have anything else you're doing today?"

Personally, Rhion would have taken a stick to that plump and spoiled youth.

To philosophers, the metaphysical division of essence and accidents—of true inner nature and the chance combination of individual differences—was a matter of theoretical debate; to magicians it was the very heart of spells. It was easy, Jaldis had pointed out, to change accidents—easier still to simply change the perceptions of the beholder. But to change the essence—truly to alter a poisonous solution into harmless plant-sap, to transform the physical structure of gangrene into inert scab-tissue—required greater power. And anything above that, far more power still.

And so from metaphysics he had gone on to study the nature of power.

Jaldis had taken him to the places where the paths of power moved over the earth, deep silvery tracks pulsing invisibly in the ground: "leys" the mages called them, "witchpaths," "dragon-tracks" . . . straight lines between nodes and crossings at ancient shrines and artificial hills, marked sometimes by ponds and shrines. On these lines, spells worked more quickly, more efficaciously. Scrying was easier, particularly at certain seasons of the year. Everything related to everything, and the balances of power were constantly shifting: the pull of the moon and the tides, the waxing and waning of the days, the presence or absence in the heavens of certain stars—all these had their effects, to be learned and dealt with.

And like the earth, and the heavens over the earth, the human body was traced with leys of its own, paths that could be used to promote healing, or create illusion, or draw or repel the mind and heart. Animals, birds, insects, fish, every tree and blade of grass—all these had their paths. In his deep meditations on summer nights Rhion had often seen the faint silver threads of energy glowing along the veins of weeds and flowers, the tiny balls of seeds within their pods shining like miniscule pearls; looking into crystals, he had seen the leys shimmering there, utterly different from those of plant and animal life, but there nevertheless, whispering strange logics of their own.

All of this Jaldis had taught him, forcing him to memorize, to meditate, to strengthen his skills while building the colossal foundation of magic itself. And all the while magic was opening before him like a gigantic rose, drawing him in to deeper and ever deeper magics hidden within its heart.

He learned the runes, the twenty-six signs capable of drawing down constellations of power, clusters of coincidence, to themselves, and how these runes could be combined into sigils and seals, to affect possibility and chance. He learned the art of talisman making, how to imbue an inanimate object with a field of altered probability or to cause it to have an effect upon the mind or body or perceptions of those it touched; learned which metals, which minerals, which materials would hold power, and which would shed it like a duck's feather shedding water.

He learned Limitations and which spells were dangerous to work because of strange and unexpected effects—there were spells which would turn a man's entire body into a field of blazing good fortune, so that luck would inevitably fall his way, but which were never used because the side effect was that the man would go mad; other spells of protection that, at certain seasons of the year which could never be accurately predicted, would call upon their wielder every grim and demon for miles around, attacking and attacking in a biting cloud; or spells that transformed ugliness into astonishing physical beauty, but which brought with them unspeakable dreams.

He learned also Illusion, the wizard's stock-in-trade: how to make a man or woman believe that a cup was made of gold and gems, instead of cheap wood, and how to make them continue in that belief for hours or days; how to make them believe that the cup was filled with wine when it contained only water, and to make them not only taste the wine but get drunk on it, though it took a very clever wizard to engineer a convincing hangover the following morning; how to make a guard fall asleep, or believe that someone entering the room was a dog or a kitten, or someone else he knew and who had legitimate business there; the spells of Who-Me? and Look-Over-There that Rhion had used in dealing with the Felsplex mob.

It had all been like playing in a field of flowers.

He had learned, too, that simply knowing a spell, or having learned it once, was not enough. There were many who called themselves wizards who thought that it was, but usually these did not survive. Shavus had taught him, by the rough-and-ready expedient of chasing him around the room, beating him with a stick, that certain spells must become second nature, so that they may be cast accurately in an emergency, or when the mind is clouded with panic or sleep or—sometimes—poison or drugs.

And he had learned the Magic of Ill.

Jaldis had been unwilling for many years to teach him the spells to cause pain to another human being, spells to pierce certain portions of the brain like slivers of glass, spells to inflame the joints and the bowels with agony, spells which could, if wielded by a mighty enough mage, suffocate a man or rip his organs within him. "They are the obverse of healing spells," he had said, "the dark side of our ability to shift the small workings of the body, and they must be used only in the gravest, the direst emergencies. There have been wizards who have allowed themselves to be beaten to death, rather than work such spells upon their killers."

"Why?" Rhion had asked, remembering the wold woman sitting on her blanket, with a smear of dog turd on her cheek. He'd been in his early twenties then, and still in the stick phase of his education, nursing a dozen bruises under his robe. "I mean, if it's a choice of your life or theirs . . ."

"It isn't simply your life," Jaldis had said quietly. That had been at Shavus' house. The big old warrior-mage and the two apprentices he'd had at that time, fair-haired brother and sister from Clordhagh who bickered constantly and affectionately, had been sitting at the scrubbed oak table with them, the dark book of those spells lying on the table between. "For the mageborn, for such as we, the world is an infinity of divisions . . . it is not so for everyone. Even for us, Shavus, if you found that a fox had come into your hen-coop and killed your chickens, and if the following evening you sighted a fox in the woods, would you not *fruge* it immediately, without asking whether it was the one who had done the damage?"

"Aye," the big man growled. "If it wasn't the one had done it before, it's only a matter of time till it *does*."

"Precisely," the sweet, buzzing voice said, that was all the King's men had left him with. "And so it is with humankind, and wizards. They may use our services, but they will never truly trust us. They fear our powers over them—our powers to deceive them, if you will; our powers to make them act against their wills, or under the compulsion of illusion or threat. It takes very little to rouse them against us. Rumor of a wizard having used his powers to advance his own speculations in trade against other merchants, or to seduce a woman he wanted, is enough for all wizards in a town, or a Realm, to be driven out of their homes, deprived of their power with the *pheelas* root and executed, shot from ambush . . . Only from people's fear."

They will use our services, Rhion thought, staring into the heart of the fire on the inn's great hearth, *but they will never truly trust us . . .*

He recalled how Tally had hesitated to mention that her father was one of the richest, the most powerful, lords of the Forty Realms. Had that been because her father, as a usurper, had enemies who would not hesitate to kidnap her if they found her alone? Or had it been reflex caution against those whom every priest of every god declared excommunicate, creatures other than human?

Yet he remembered how she had turned to look out into the darkness; remembered the way their eyes had met.

Not that there was any possibility of anything existing between the Duke of Mere's daughter and himself, he hastened to add. Even had he not been a mage, even had he remained his father's douce and respectable son and inherited the biggest countinghouse in the City of Circles, he could no more have . . . His mind shied from the first phrase that sprang to it, and he hastily substituted, *have spoken seriously* . . . He could no more have spoken seriously to Tallisett of Mere than he could have spoken seriously to the High Queen of Nerriok.

And rising stiffly from his seat beside the chimney breast, he mended the fire a final time and stood for a moment listening, extending his senses out into the stillness of the woods beyond the gray stone walls for any sign, any hint of danger. Hearing none, he lay down in his blankets by the hearthstones, took off his spectacles, and fell asleep.

6

In the end, Jaldis and Rhion did not go to Nerriok after all. The morning after their hunt for the grim-harrowed child, Jaldis slept long and heavily and woke weak with fever. Their little stock of medicinal herbs had been one of the things left behind in the attic of the Black Pig; Rhion hunted patiently through the snowy thickets and roadbanks for elfdock and borage to take down the old man's fever and clear the congestion he feared was growing in his lungs. But the winter woods kept their secrets, and when he returned to the inn, well after noon, he found his teacher no better and dared not leave him again.

He was up with Jaldis, trying to work healing spells without the wherewithal to aid the physical body, for most of the following night.

"Look, I need to get you to some help," Rhion said to him, during one of the intervals in which the fever had been reduced by means of a spell which had left Rhion himself feeling ill and shaky. He took from the pouch at his belt his own scrying-crystal, a lump of yellowed quartz half the size of his fist, and held it to the wan light from the single window he'd unshuttered when daylight came. "I'm going to try to contact the Ladies of the Moon. They're the closest place we can take you."

Jaldis sighed, and his groping hand touched the voice-box long enough for it to whisper the word, ". . . corrupt . . ."

But the shake of his head was only of regret, not refusal, and Rhion settled himself into a corner of the old kitchen with his crystal to work.

He chose the kitchen hearth—which he suspected had been the main hearth of the original inn—because at that point a minor ley crossed through the building. Though he couldn't yet, like Jaldis, simply close his eyes and hear the silvery traces of energy like thin music in the air, he had had the suspicion that the inn was built upon a ley, and a brief test with a pendulum-stone confirmed it. He guessed it was the one connecting the Holy Hill beyond Imber with one of the now-inundated shrines of the ancient city of Sligo. Cradling the crystal in his hands with its largest facet angled to the pallid window-light, he slipped into meditation, and after a few minutes saw, as if reflected in a mirror from over his shoulder and a great distance away, the Gray Lady's face.

He had never met the Lady of the Drowned Lands, though he had heard of her, from Jaldis, Shavus, and travelers who had passed through the fogbound mazes of swamp and lake and cranberry bog that tangled the Valley of the Morne. She looked puzzled, to see in her scrying-mirror a stranger's face; but when Rhion explained to her who he was and that Jaldis the Blind was ill and in need at the old inn on the Imber road, she said immediately, "Of course. The Cock in Britches . . ." Her wide mouth flexed in a smile. "Once the God of Bridges, though I think the sign has a rooster on it these days. There are Marshmen who serve us living near there. I shall send them to fetch you here."

In the days before the earthquake the city of Sligo, built on a cluster of granite hills where the Morne estuary narrowed to its valley between the hills of Fel and the great granite spine of the Mountains of the Sun, had been among the richest of the Forty Realms, rivaling the inland wealth of Nerriok and ruling most of the In Islands and wide stretches of valley farmland along the great river's shores. Now all that remained of those fertile farmsteads were the marshy hay meadows and lowland pasturage for the thick-wooled, black-faced sheep, isolated oases among the sweet marshes and salt marshes, thick miles-long beds of angelica and cattail, bog-oak and willow, a thousand crisscrossing water channels where the tall reeds met, rustling overhead, and redbirds and water-goblins dwelled as if the place had been theirs from the foundations of the world. For the rest, Mhorvianne the Merciful, Goddess of Waters, had claimed her own. But whether An, the Moon as she was worshipped in Sligo of old—in Nerriok they worshipped Sioghis, Moon-God of the southern lands—was in fact merely an aspect of Mhorvianne as some said, no one these days knew.

As for the Lady of the Moon, some said she ruled the Marshmen by ancestral right, descended as she was from the Archpriestesses of the ancient shrine; some, that she held sway over them by means of her enchantments. Others claimed that she and her Ladies traded their magic for foodstuffs and wool—still others claimed they traded their bodies as well.

Crouched uneasily beside Jaldis' head in the stern of the long canoe, watching the black silhouette of the Marshman on the prow, poling with uncanny silence through the dense, fog-locked silence of the salt marsh, Rhion understood why no one could say anything for certain about the Drowned Lands. To enter here was to enter a whispering, sunken labyrinth, where the bulrushes and water weeds grew thick and the footing was uncertain—where the water was never open water, the land never dry land. Hummocks of maple, willow, and moss-dripping salt-oak loomed like matte gray ghosts through wreaths of coiling fog. Now and then, nearly obliterated by tall stands of reeds and almost indistinguishable from the root snags of dead or dying trees, the moss-clotted tips of stone spires and gables could be discerned, rising up through the brown waters, the decaying remains of the buildings sunk deep underneath.

The Marshmen themselves were a silent folk, wiry and small, impossible to track and difficult to speak to even when they consented to be seen. They used the Common Speech intelligibly enough, though with a strange, lilting inflection, but Rhion had to invoke the Spell of Tongues, the magic of hearing words mind to mind, to comprehend what they whispered to one another in their own dialect. Eyes green as angelica or the uncertain hazel which was no identifiable color—the color of the sea where it ran to the salt marsh's edge—peered watchfully from beneath loose thatches of thick brown hair at the two wizards. Often during the three-day journey, by sled across the frozen sweet marshes, and down here among the brown reed beds of the salt, Rhion had felt the sensation of those strangely colored eyes watching him from somewhere just out of sight.

It was a land of strange superstitions, Jaldis had told him, and beliefs which elsewhere had long since died out. Wrapped in the gray-green plaid of the native blankets, Rhion could see the curling line of blue tattoo marks on the boatman's hands and ears, and could count half a dozen little "dollies" woven of feathers and straw dangling from the lantern on the canoe's long prow.

"Rhion . . ." The voice of the sounding-box was soft as a single viol string, bowed in an empty room. The fog down here in the salt marshes was raw and thick, especially now that night had fallen; in spite of the blankets in which the Marshmen had wrapped him, Jaldis' breathing sounded bad.

"They will try to take the books," he murmured, as Rhion bent down close to him to hear. Rhion cast a quick glance up at the Marshman on the prow, then at the bundles of volumes stacked behind Jaldis' head: books containing the secrets of the Dark Well, the means to look behind the very curtains of Reality; scrolls of demon-spells, and the Magic of Ill.

Like twists of driftwood wrapped in rags, the cold fingers tightened urgently over Rhion's hands. "The Ladies are greedy for knowledge, stealing it where they can from other mages, other Orders. Do not let them do this . . ." The voice of the box paused, while Jaldis bent all his attention on stifling a cough, the sound of it deep and muffled with phlegm. He turned his head, feverish again and in pain, as he had been throughout the journey despite all that Rhion could do. "Do not . . . whatever they may offer. Whatever they may do."

A drift of salt air stirred the clammy fogs, shifting them like the shredded remains of a rotted gray curtain. Blurs of daffodil-yellow light wavered in the mists. Before them Rhion descried the huge, dim bulk of a domed island, dark masses of trees rising from the waters like a cliff. Below them was a floating platform, designed to rise and fall with the seasonal level of the marshes and the inundations of the tides. Just beyond the circle of the lamplight which surrounded it, marsh-faes skimmed like silver dragonflies above the mist-curled surface of the fen. Looking up at the island, Rhion could see where the long roots of trees and dangling, winter-black vines gripped the ancient blocks of hewn stone walls just visible above the waters; everything seemed thick with moss and slimy with dripping weed.

On the platform itself stood four women, dressed not in the robes of any order of wizardry, but like the Marshwomen themselves, in belted wool tunics of dull plaids or checks, or brightened by crewelwork flowers. The Gray Lady he recognized. Even if he had not seen her in the scrying-stone three days ago, he would have known at first sight of her that she was, like Jaldis, a mage.

"Welcome," she said, stepping forward. "You are most welcome to the Islands of the Moon."

When communicating through scrying-crystal, a wizard's appearance was not the same to another wizard as it was in the flesh; Rhion noted that the Lady was older than she had appeared in the crystal's depths. Certainly ten years older than he, if not more, her square, homey face was framed in heavy streams of malt-brown hair. There were blue tattoos on her ears, and her hands were knotted and strong from bread bowl, distaff, and loom. The ladies behind her were clearly as used as she to manual tasks, for they lifted Jaldis from his bed in the canoe as easily and deftly as if he had lain on a couch and carried him up the zigzagging wooden stair.

Another lady stepped forward to take the books . . . "I'll get those," Rhion said and shouldered once again the heavy sack. Deeply as he regretted the volumes left behind in Felsplex, he had become very grateful he hadn't let the impulse to take them all overcome his better judgment.

"As you will," the Gray Lady said, and he thought he detected a deep-hid flicker of ironic amusement in her hazel eyes.

Like all the Ladies' dwellings on what had been the tips of Sligo's hills, the house they had prepared for Jaldis had once been a palace, now fallen into deep decay. Vine and morning-glory from ancient gardens had run riot in centuries of neglect, and the heavy pillars, wider at the top than the bottom, were sheathed thick with cloaks of vegetation that, in several rooms, had begun to part the stones themselves. The walls of the sleeping chamber were still intact, but the windows, glazed with random bits of glass like pieces of a puzzle, were nearly obscured under a thick brown jungle of creepers, an open latticework in the leafless winter, but promising to be an impenetrable petaled curtain in summer months. Throughout the night, as he sat up with the Gray Lady at Jaldis' bedside, the faint scrape and rustle of that living cloak blended with the Lady's murmured healing-spells and the bubble of the kettle whose healing steams filled the room with the scents of elfdock and false dandelion; in the morning, their shadows made a dim harlequin of the pearly fog-light where it fell upon Jaldis' pillow.

"He should rest better now." The Lady ran her strong brown fingers through her hair, and shook out the cloudy mane of it as she and Rhion stood together in the villa's ruined porch. Through the milky fog, the glow of the community ovens, not ten yards away amid the overgrown riot of laurel and thorny bougainvillea around what had been a shrine, was no more than a saffron blur, like a yellow pinch of raveled wool, though the fragrance of baking bread hung upon the wet air like a hymn. Beneath it, Rhion smelled damp earth, water, and the sea; beyond the matted vines that enclosed the tiny chamber of the porch, the marsh was utterly silent, save for the isolated notes of stone chimes stirred by a breath of wind. It seemed to Rhion that they were cut off in that shadowy ruin—from the Forty Realms, from his life, and from the future and the past.

"You should get some rest yourself," she added. She deftly separated and braided the streams of her hair, and her hazel glance took in the grayness of his face, the blue-brown smudges of fatigue more visible when he removed his spectacles to rub his eyes. "You look all-in." Her voice was low and very sweet, like the music of a rosewood flute heard across water in the night. At times last night, Rhion had not recognized the spells she wove, but had had the impression that the voice was an integral part of them, a lullaby to soothe weary flesh, a bribe to tempt the wavering soul to remain.

"It was just that I'd been working healing-spells without the medicines to go with them," he said, shaking his head. "I didn't have much sleep on the way here. Thank you . . ." He yawned hugely. The queasiness which sometimes assailed him after he had over-stretched his powers was fading, and he felt slightly lightheaded and ravenous for sweets.

"You did well with the spells alone. I've seen men much worse in like case."

Rhion smiled a little. "I don't think that was my efforts so much as just that Jaldis is too stubborn to let illness get the better of him. I did try to find some herbs—you can usually find borage if you look long enough—but in the winter it's hard."

"Perhaps while you're here you'd like to speak to some of our healers, and see the scrolls and herbals we have in our library." She gestured out into the impenetrable wall of fog, toward what Rhion had originally taken for the dim shape of a hillock of willow and vine. Now, looking again, he saw the outline of what had been a pillared porch, a few crumbling steps, and the primrose trapezoid of an uneven window, lighted from within.

"Our library goes back to the days of Sligo's glory, though much of it was lost in the earthquake and the floods that came after. We add to it what we can."

The words, *Yeah, I was warned about that*, were on his lips, but he clipped them back. The Gray Lady was his host and might very well have saved Jaldis' life last night. Moreover, in spite of Jaldis' warnings, after a night of working at her side, of seeing her patient care and her willingness to perform even the most menial of healing chores, he found himself greatly inclined to like the woman.

"Come." She took his hand and led him to the buckled terrazzo steps. "Channa—the cook—will get you bread and honey . . . Or shall I have one of the girls bring it to you here?" For she saw him hesitate and glanced back into the slaty gloom of the house, where Jaldis lay helpless with his books piled in the corner near his bed.

"What did he mean," she asked, his hand still prisoned in those warm, rough peasant fingers, stained with silver and herbs, "when he spoke in his delirium of the Dark Well?"

Rhion had taken the voice-box from him, seeing the sudden in-tentness of the Lady's eyes, but not before the old man, clinging to it in fevered dreams, had stammered brokenly of the Well, of the Void, and of voices crying out to him from the iridescent dark. After Rhion had removed it, Jaldis had groped urgently amid the patched linen sheets, his movements more and more frantic, though he had not uttered a sound. Even in his delirium, his pride had flinched from the broken, humiliating bleatings of a mute; in ten and a half years of traveling with him, Rhion had never heard him break that silence.

Now the Lady was watching him again, with sharp interest in her face. "The most ancient scrolls in the Library make mention of something called a Well of Seeing," she continued. "It was said to 'grant sight into other worlds and other times.' Not 'other lands' . . . the glyph is very clear. 'Other worlds.' "

"I . . . I don't . . ." Rhion stammered, wanting to avoid the clear, water-colored gaze and unable to look away. "He found reference to it in some notes he'd inherited from another wizard in Felsplex. He was searching through them when the mob broke into the inn. We got out with our lives, but the notes were destroyed." The story sounded lame and thin even to him. He cursed the exhaustion that seemed suddenly to weight his tongue and clog his brain, as if the inventive portion of his mind had taken the equivalent of *pheelas* root and subsided into numbed oblivion.

The Lady leaned one broad shoulder against the marble hip of a caryatid nearly hidden within the vines beside her, and her hand, still enclosing Rhion's, had that same quality that Jaldis' sometimes did, as if through her grip she could read the bones within his flesh and plumb the shallow, sparkling shoals of his soul. "You escaped with your lives—and with the books?"

"With what we could seize." He felt a kind of confusion creeping over him, his mind distracted by the question of whether it would be worse to avoid her eyes or to try to hold that clear, tawny gaze . . . wanting to will himself to meet her eyes but obliquely aware that if he did she could read his heart. And through it all her sweet alto voice drew at his concentration as it had drawn back Jaldis' wavering will to live.

"The books, but not the notes, that so filled his fevered dreams?"

"I . . . That is . . ." He knew he should make some reply but could not frame anything even remotely believable. He felt tangled, enmeshed in his own evasions, between the strength of her hand and the strength of her gaze and the gentle, drawing sweetness of her voice. To lie seemed, not useless, but unspeakably trivial, like a child lying about the size of a fish it has seen. She waited quietly, watching him, as if they had been there together, with her watching and waiting for the truth, since the foundation stones of time were laid . . .

For an instant it seemed as if that were, in fact, the case—a moment later it flashed through his mind, *Nonsense, if we'd been here since the beginning of time we'd have felt the earthquake* . . . and somehow that gave him the last foundering grasp of logic needed for him to look away from her eyes. He found he was panting, his face clammy with sweat in the raw dampness of the morning. Desperately he fixed his thoughts on Jaldis' buzzing voice: *They are greedy for knowledge* . . . *greedy for knowledge* . . . the gentle coaxing did not seem to him like greed, but that, he understood now, was part of the spell.

He pulled his hand from her grasp and it came easily—he had to catch himself against the caryatid opposite the one she leaned upon, as if she had drawn him off balance physically as well as in his mind.

After a moment that flute-soft voice said, "I see. A thing of great power . . . a thing to be kept hidden at all costs."

Face still averted, Rhion managed to whisper, "I don't know about that."

There was silence, filled with the scents of water and fog, but he felt her mind still bent upon his, surrounded by the implacable strength of her spells.

He took a deep breath. "Please let me go."

Her fingers, firm as the fingers of the caryatids would be, but warm and vibrant, touched his brow, feeling the perspiration that wet his skin. "You work very hard for a man who claims nothing to protect." But she was teasing him now. Instead of the heart-dragging beauty of her spells, her voice was light, like a healer's magic flute playing children's songs for joy.

He looked around at her again and saw only a sturdy brown-haired woman with one braid plaited and the other still undone upon her shoulder, and a smile, half mocking, half affectionate, in her eyes. Abstractedly he identified the crewelwork flowers on her homespun gown as marigold, lobelia, thistle and iris; a thin strand of blue spirit-beads circled her throat.

"Go back and sit with him," she said gently. "I'll send someone over with bread and honey—and I promise you I won't dose it to question you further or to send you to sleep." And she smiled again at his blush. "You may sleep, if you will. No one will trouble you."

Rhion wasn't sure he could believe her on that score—he'd been badly shaken by the spells she'd cast—but as he stumbled back into the dimness of the house, he reflected that he probably didn't have much choice in the matter. He stood for a moment in the doorway of Jaldis' room, looking at the cracked black-and-white mosaic of the ancient tile floor, the frescoes of birds and dancers on the walls, faded now to cloudy shapes, like music heard too far away to distinguish the tune. His body hurt for sleep, and more than that for food, particularly sweets; he knew, too, that any circle or spell of protection he might lay around the books stacked in the corner beyond the bed would be, at this point, no more potent than the chalk scribbles around the bed itself, smudged by feet and bereft of their power.

Propped upon pillows, Jaldis lay in the narrow bed of cottonwood poles, deeply asleep, a vessel of gently steaming water on either side. For some time Rhion stood looking down at the ruined face, too exhausted to feel much beyond a tremendous sadness for which he could find no name.

In time he picked up Jaldis' cloak and mashed it into a rude pillow and, wrapping himself in his own cloak, lay down in front of the books on the floor. He slept almost at once and dreamed of starlight and witchfire and snow-clad silence, all reflected in shy gray eyes.

Jaldis mended slowly. The Gray Lady and the other Ladies of the Moon whom Rhion quickly came to know well nursed the old man by turns, not only with the healing spells and herb-lore for which they were famed throughout the eastern realms, but with a patient diligence and unstinting sympathy that, he suspected, had more to do with healing than all the medicines in the world. After that first morning, the Gray Lady made no further effort to question him regarding the Dark Well, though Rhion would generally volunteer to sit with his master at night, when his fever rose and he sometimes spoke in his dreams.

"You did rightly," Jaldis said, when Rhion told him about why he had taken the voice-box from him that night. "It is not well that the Witches of the Moon learn the secrets of the Morkensik Order." His voice was a fragile thread; his hand stroked restlessly at the silky curve of the dark red wood, toyed with the glittering flotsam of talismans among the faded quilts.

"I don't think she learned any secrets." Rhion glanced across at the books, still heaped in their corner with his discarded blankets and the empty bowl from his breakfast. In spite of the Gray Lady's assurances, he'd been a little dubious about the breakfast; much as it was his instinct to like her, he wouldn't have put it past her to dose his porridge with *pheelas* root; and several times in the course of the morning, he'd summoned a little fleck of ball lightning to the ends of his fingers, just to make sure he still could.

"But you were speaking of things you had seen—of boats with metal wings that flew through the sky, of carts that moved without horses. Of magic things without magic."

"Magic things without magic," the blind wizard echoed and his powerful chest rose and fell with his sigh. "Things that can be used by anyone, for good or ill, for whatever purposes they choose, without the training or restraint of wizardry. And the wizards themselves, born with magic in their bones, in their hearts, in their veins, even as we were born, for whom no expression of such power is possible. Wizards who are taught to forget; who, if they cannot forget, go slowly insane."

Rhion was silent, remembering his own days of slow insanity.

"They are calling to us, Rhion," that soft, mechanical drone murmured. "We must find them again, somehow. We must go and help. For their sakes, and for our own." Then the arthritic claws slipped from the silky wood, and Jaldis drifted back into his dreams.

In those days Rhion had to contend with dreams of his own.

The first time he summoned Tally's image in his scrying-crystal he told himself that it was simply to ascertain that she and her sister and her sister's baby did, in fact, reach Imber in safety. The crystal had shown him the image of Tally, very properly attired in a rust-colored gown stitched with silver and sardonyx, sitting quietly in a corner of a painted marble hall while the short, plump woman who must be her sister argued in polite hatred with a colorless young man in gray. Though the crystal, used in this fashion, was silent, he could read frigid spite and contempt in every line of the young man's slender body, while all the jewels on the plump woman's sleeve fluttered in the burning lamplight with the trembling of her stoppered rage. Tally was looking away into the noncommittal middle distance of an unwilling witness forcing herself neither to see nor hear, but her hands, all but concealed under the pheasant feathers which trimmed her oversleeves, were balled into white-knuckled fists.

After that he told himself—for a time, at least—that he only wanted to make sure that this wretchedness, whatever it was, had passed. That she was all right: That she was happy.

And sometimes she was. When riding she was, in the brown frozen landscape of the Imber hills. He could see it in her face, and in the way she laughed with her favorite maid—a tall girl like herself, but full-breasted and bold—and the chief of her honor guard, a broad-chested and rather stupid-looking young demigod who flirted with both girls and everything else moderately presentable who came his way in skirts. She was happy with her dogs, a leggy, endlessly-circling pack of red and gold bird-hunters whose ears she would comb and whose paws she would search for thorns. Alone she was happy, curled up with a silken quilt about her beside a bronze fire-dish in her bedroom, playing her porcelain flute with two dogs asleep at her feet, the huge branch of cheap kitchen candles flaring like a halo behind her head and turning her hair to a halo of treacle and gold.

But more than once he saw her, white-lipped and silent, at table with her sister and the fair young man who must be her sister's husband, while servants displayed herbed savories and frumentaries on painted platters for their approval, delicacies which Tally was clearly barely able to touch. On one such occasion, during yet another mannered, vicious quarrel, he saw her quietly leave the dining room and return to her chair a few minutes later, chalky and trembling, having clearly just vomited her heart out in the nearest ante-room. Once—though the image was unclear owing to the fact that the room they were in had long ago been ensorcelled to prevent scrying—he saw her and her sister holding one another tight, like two victims of shipwreck tossed on a single plank in rough waters, weeping by candlelight.

And with passionate despair he thought *Damn him! Damn him for doing that to you . . . !*

In time he quit watching, and put the scrying-stone away as he would have put away an addictive drug.

But like a drug it murmured to him when he was alone.

Rhion had always known that such behavior was against the ethics of wizardry and never called up her image without a pang of guilt. Among the first things that Jaldis had told him, when he had taught him to use a crystal, and later to prepare one for use, was that the powers of a scryer were not to be used for private pleasure or for private gain.

"It is not only that the evil done by one wizard redounds upon all wizards," the blind man had said, putting aside his opal spectacles and rubbing the pain from his temples. "Not only that we are not perceived as being separate individuals, good and evil, but only as wizards, without distinction and without discrimination. But spying, peeping, prying is in itself a dirty habit, and worse for a wizard who can do it so much more efficiently. What would you think, Rhion, of a mage who uses this power to look into the bathing chambers of every brothel in the city, just for the sight of women's breasts?"

Rhion, being at the time seventeen, had promptly answered, "That he's saving himself some money," and had had to wait another six months before being instructed in the scrying-crystal's use.

But it was, in fact, a conclusion that Rhion himself had come to as a tiny child, the first time he'd called a friend's image in the nursery fire and seen that friend being placed on the chamber pot by her nurse. It had embarrassed him so thoroughly he'd been very careful about calling images after that.

But abstaining now from its use didn't help. He found that quasi-knowledge of Tally—knowing what her favorite jewels were, her favorite dresses and how she braided her hair, knowing that she liked to play the flute or the mandolin when she was alone, and that she loved her little niece with the delighted affection of a child—was not the same as being her friend. All he knew was that she was in pain and that he could not help. And would never be able to help.

In his hopelessness and uncertainty, Rhion turned, as he had always turned, back to the study of magic.

The library on the Island of the Moon dated back to the days before the earthquake, a small building all but buried under thickets of laurel and vine. At least a third of its score of tiny rooms had fallen into utter desuetude, the saplings that had sprouted in the earthquake's cracks now grown to massive trees, whose roots clambered over the broken blocks like rough-scaled, gray serpents and whose branches were in many places the only roof. From these rooms the books had been moved, to crowd the other chambers, both above the ground and in the unflooded levels of the damp clay-smelling vaults below; the whole place, like the islands themselves, was a maze and a warren, shaggy with moss and choked with ancient knowledge and half-forgotten things.

Here Rhion read and studied through the rainy days of the marshlands winter and sometimes throughout the night: herb-lore and earth-lore and the deep magics of the moon and tides; the legends of the old realm of Sligo, going back two thousand years; of the islands that had sunk in the earthquake; and tales of discredited gods. Here the Lady acted as his teacher and guide, for she had been the Scribe of the place before her ascension to her current status, and if there were chambers whose thresholds he was forbidden to cross, or volumes he was forbidden to open, it was never mentioned to him.

"We add to it what we can, year by year," the Lady said, setting down two cups of egg-posset on the table near the firebasket's warming saffron glow. She shook back the loose stream of brown hair from her shoulders. "Even in the old days, it was one of the great repositories of knowledge and the beauty of letters, the joy of tales for their own sake. Many of the volumes destroyed in the floods existed nowhere else, even in their own day. And now we know of them only through notes in the ancient catalogues and a quote or two in some commentator's work."

It was late at night, and the library was silent, the black fog that pressed the irregular glass windows smothering even the glowworm spots of light from the kitchen and the nearby baths. Rhion looked up from the smooth, red-and-black bowl of the cup to the Lady's face, the strong, archaic features serene with the calm of those marble faces that clustered everywhere beneath the wild grape and wisteria or gazed half-submerged from the waters of the marsh.

"The treatises of philosophers," she went on softly, "the histories of old border-wars, tallies of spell-fragments that do not work, even . . . For who can say when we will find another fragmentary work that completes them, and broadens our knowledge of what can be done with the will, and the energies sent down to Earth by the gods?"

And who can say, Rhion thought, remembering Jaldis' warnings, *who will have access to those spells a year from now, or two years, or ten? Who can say one of the Ladies won't take it into her head to become a Hand-Pricker or a Blood-Mage and feel free to transmit whatever knowledge she gleans here to them?* He remembered what Jaldis had told him of the uses to which the Ebiatics had put the knowledge of demon-calling, when they had learned it; remembered Shavus' accounts of wizards who had not the training that the Morkensiks gave in balance and restraint.

Do no harm, Jaldis had said. But six years of brewing love-potions had taught him that the definition of "harm," even by those without thaumaturgical power, was an appallingly elastic thing.

He started to raise the posset to his lips, the sweetness of honey within it like the reminiscence of summer flowers, then hesitated, and glanced over at the Gray Lady again.

She smiled, reading the wariness in his eyes, and said, "Would you like to see me drink it first? Out of both cups, in case I'd switched them . . ."

And he grinned at the absurdity of the position. "I'll trust you."

Her wide mouth quirked, and there was a glint in her tawny eyes. "Or hadn't you heard we also have a reputation for dosing passersby with aphrodisiacs as well?"

Rhion laughed and shook his head. In the topaz glow of the brazier she had a strange beauty, the light heightening the strength of her cheekbones and catching carnelian threads in her eyelashes and hair. "*Now* you have me worried."

"That Jaldis would disapprove?"

"That I'd burn my fingers playing with fire." He raised the cup to her in a solemn toast, and sipped the sweet mull of eggs, honey, and wine within.

As the winter wore on, he found in the Gray Lady's company a respite from his thoughts of Tally, from the sense of futility that overwhelmed him at even the thought, these days, of having a non-mageborn friend. That she was fond of him he knew, as he was increasingly of her; now and then it crossed his mind to let her seduce him, but fear always held him back. He did not believe, as the garbled tales told, that the Ladies of the Moon lured lovers to their beds with spells and later sacrificed them to their Goddess at a certain season of the year; but he hadn't forgotten the spells she'd laid upon his mind to try to draw from him the secrets contained in Jaldis' books.

But her company was good. With her he practiced the art of maintaining several spells at once under conditions of duress: he would try to turn aside the acorns she hurled at him while he concentrated on holding various household objects suspended by spells in the air, and they would laugh like children when the cook's chairs, buckets, and baskets went crashing to the kitchen floor or when she scored a fair hit between his eyes. She also showed him the secret ways of the marshes, leading him across the sunken root-lines that connected the innumerable hummocks of salt-oak, cypress, and willow when the tide was low. The watery labyrinths of the Drowned Lands changed from season to season with the rains that brought down water from upcountry and from hour to hour with the rhythm of the tides. When the waters were high, the twenty or so ancient hilltops, with their ruined shrines and overgrown villas, were cut off from one another and from the hummocks that had grown up all around, rooted to the immemorial muck beneath or to the half-submerged roofs of ancient palaces. But there were times when they could cross between them on foot, picking their way carefully over the sunken trunks and roof-trees, to hunt the rare herbs of the marshes or to find skunk-cabbages by the heat of them under the snow in the sweet marshes and, later, violets by their scent.

At such times she seemed to him like a creature of the marshes herself, born of the silent waters and fog; when she spoke of the ancient days of Sligo, she spoke as if she remembered them herself, of what the ancient kings and wizards had said and done, of how they lived and how they died, as if she had been there and seen what they wore, where they stood, and whether their eyes had been brown or blue.

Some nights they would sit out, shivering in a Marshman's canoe that she handled as easily as Tally had handled her horse, watching the water-goblins play around candles set floating in bowls. "Does anyone know what they are?" Rhion asked on one such night, in the wind-breath murmur that wizards learn, scarcely louder than the lapping of the incoming tide against the boat's tanned skin. "I mean, yes, they're goblins . . . but what *are* goblins?" He pushed up his spectacles and glanced sidelong at her, seeing how the bobbing brightness of the candle intermittently gilded the end of her snub nose. "Like faes, they don't seem to have physical bodies . . . Are they a kind of fae? Do they sleep? Do they nest in the ground or in the trees, the way grims seem to do? Why do they take food, if they have no bodies to nourish? Why do they steal children and drown them? Why are they afraid of mirrors?" They'd had to cover the one on the boat's prow before the goblins would come to the candle, though the straw luck-dollies still dangled, like misshapen corpses on the gallows, from the bowsprit. "Is there any work of the ancient wizards in the library that says?"

She shook her head. "There are some that ask the same questions you ask, but none that gives an answer. Curious in itself—they are in their way much more an enigma than the grims, whose names at least can be known. The Marshmen think they fear mirrors because they can't stand the sight of their own faces, but look . . . You can see they aren't afraid of one another. And they really aren't that ugly, if you get close to them . . ."

"Well, I wouldn't want my sister to marry one."

She laughed at that, but she was right . . . outlined in the flickering candle glow the goblins were queer looking, with their huge, luminous eyes and froglike mouths, but the translucent, gelid forms did not shift, as the grims did; and if their limbs were numerous and strange, at least they remained constant.

"I think it may have something to do with the glass itself, or the quicksilver backing," the Gray Lady went on softly, as the long, thready hands reached up from the water to snatch at the flame. "You know you can put spells on fernseed and scatter it behind you to keep them from dogging your steps in the forest . . ."

"I've heard poppyseed works, too. At least, according to the scroll I read in the library last week, it can be spelled to confuse human pursuit."

"I've tried to follow them a dozen times in a boat or across the root-lines on foot—twice I've tried swimming after them. But they always vanish, and it's dangerous, swimming down underwater among the pondweed and the roots."

On the whole, Jaldis seemed to regard the spells which the Lady taught Rhion as little better than the pishogue of Earth-witches, but approved of his learning the lore of the marshes and the Moon. "To be a wizard is to learn," he said, looking up from the tray of herbs he was sorting by scent and touch. He was able to sit up now, wrapped in the thick woolen blankets the Ladies wove, beside the green bronze firebaskets in his sunny stone room. On the afternoons of rare pale sunlight he would sometimes sit outside on the crumbling terrace that fronted their house, overlooking the silken brown waters of the marsh. For weeks now they had been remaking their supply of medicines and thaumaturgical powders, Rhion hunting them in the marshes as he learned a little of the mazes of islets, Jaldis ensorcelling them to enhance their healing powers.

"Though I don't suppose," the old man added, "they let you have access to the inner rooms of the library, or the inner secrets of their power." He rubbed the bandage that covered the empty sockets of his eyes. Etsinda, the chief weaver of the island, had knitted gray mitts specially for his bent and crippled hands, easy to draw on and keeping the useless fingers covered and warm.

"I haven't been told to stay out of any room."

"I doubt they would need to tell you," Jaldis replied, with a faint smile. "You would simply never notice the doors of those rooms, though you might pass them every day; or if you did notice them, your mind would immediately become distracted by some other book or scroll, and you would forget immediately your intention to pass that threshold till another day."

Rhion blinked, startled at the subtlety of such a spell . . . but now that he thought about it, he could easily believe the Gray Lady capable of such illusion.

"Beware of her, my son," the blind man said softly. "Some of their knowledge is corrupt, and inaccurate, being gleaned from all manner of sources. But like us, they are wizards, too."

And being wizards, Rhion knew perfectly well that the Gray Lady had never given up her intention of getting hold of Jaldis' books.

On their second night in Sligo, Rhion had set out, shaking with apprehension and clutching a line of thread to guide him back to firm ground, across one of the tangled root-lines to another islet, carrying Jaldis' books once more on his back. He'd used thread to guide him because he feared to leave wizard's marks, guessing that the Lady would have a way of reading later where they had been. The ragged remains of his old landlord's cloak had been ensorcelled with every sigil of preservation and concealment he and Jaldis had had the strength to imbue, and the hollow oak where he hid the wrapped volumes he had surrounded with the subtlest of his spells of warning and guard.

As often as possible he checked this secret cache, by scrying-crystal and in person, whenever he could—at least, he thought, the Lady could not call his image in a crystal, something no mage could do except for direct communication. The islet where he had hidden the books, far up the snag-lines from the Island of the Moon, was perhaps three-quarters of a mile long and no more than fifty yards across, thickly wooded and tangled with sedges and laurel, cranberry and honeysuckle, in places treacherous with potholes where vines growing between the overarching willow-roots gave the appearance to the unwary of solid ground. Several times such potholes gave way under his feet as he crossed the root-lines at low tide, and he narrowly avoided plunging through into the shadowy waters beneath. Now and then, on his surreptitious investigations of the islet, he discovered evidence that someone had been searching that island and others around it, though the books themselves remained, as far as he could tell, undisturbed.

Then one evening during the first of the winter thaws, as he sat reading in the dark library after the failing of the short winter daylight, something—a sound, he thought at the time, though later he could not recall exactly what it had been—made him look up in time to see the Gray Lady glide noiselessly between two of the massive king-pillars. Her homespun woolen cloak hood was drawn up over her face, and, moreover, she was wreathed in a haze of spells, which would have covered her from any but the sharpest eyes. She held a book cradled in her arms; though he only glimpsed it briefly, he thought that it was the red-bound *Lesser Demonary* which had been among the books in the secret cache.

Rhion froze, stilling his breath. The Lady passed without glancing his way through a lopsided doorway and down four steps into another of the library's tiny chambers. Without so much as a rustle of robes, Rhion gathered his cloak about him and slipped out into the raw iron gloom outside.

Jaldis was deep asleep already in the big stone room with its black-and-white floors. Taking his scrying-crystal from his pocket Rhion angled a facet to the light of the room's bronze fire bowl, calling the image of the hollow oak. But the image was unclear; he seemed to see a tree that looked something like it, but the surroundings were wrong—he had only a general impression of vines and reeds, as if fog hid the place. But the night, a rare thing for winters in Sligo, was clear, with the promise of coming rain.

"Damn her!" He shoved the crystal back and was tucking his robe up into his belt as he strode from the room. "How the hell did she know where to look? If they're taking them to copy one at a time . . ."

There were half a dozen boats tied to the jetty when Rhion scrambled down the long ladder—the platform floated low on the slack tide. He took the one with the lightest draught, knowing he'd probably have to haul it over shoals and snags—he still had not acquired much of an instinct for the tides. The sluggish waters whispered around the prow as he poled away, skirting the wide beds of reeds, sedges, the silken puckers of the water's inky surface that marked submerged snags, and the moss-crusted stone spires raised like dripping skeleton fingers from the deep. Once he saw something glowing pass under his boat and felt a tentative tug at the pole—he cut down sharply at it, and the tugging ceased. There was a mirror on the bowsprit and half a dozen woven straw dollies and god-hands; Jaldis called it all superstitious nonsense, but Rhion found himself hoping his master was wrong.

There would be grims, too, on the wooded isles, lurking and whistling in the trees. For no reason, he heard Tally's low, husky voice: *Since
it's such a lovely night and I've had a wonderful time so far* . . .

And grinned.

His grin faded. As deliberately as he would turn from a painful sight,
he pushed the image of her thin, elfin face from his mind and forced
himself to pursue that line of thought no further. As soon as spring cleared
the roads, he and Jaldis would return to Nerriok, the City of Bridges.
With luck he'd never see the Duke of Mere's young daughter again.

The boat's shallow keel scraped on snags and bars as he tried to
negotiate the twisting channels through house-high beds of dripping
reeds; twice he had to pull the little craft up over root mats, his feet
sinking to his boot calves in icy ooze. *Thank God it's winter, and
night,* he thought, bending his back to the pole as he tried to force
a passage through jungles of blackened cattail. *In summer the midges
would eat you alive. You can't hold spells that make them think you're
made of garlic all day.*

At last he hit the long, sunken ford that led to the islet of the
books. He left the boat, keeping the long pole for balance, and made
his way gingerly along the dripping, snakelike strands of exposed
roots, hearing the water lap and gurgle, black and shining as obsidian
beneath his feet. These sunken hummocks, treacherous with slime,
wound for miles through this part of the marsh, the islets widening
and rising from them like knots in a string.

Even if the Ladies had seen me coming this way, he wondered, *how
the hell would they have known which islet I went to? They're all pretty
much alike. They can't have searched every tree* . . .

A flash of bluish light behind him caught his eye, and he swung
around, remembering the goblins. Clouds like stealthy assassins were
already putting pillows over the pale face of the baby moon; he
smelled the sea and rain. In the growing darkness, a lantern would
have burst upon his eyes like an explosion.

But it was only a half-dozen marsh-faes, fragile, naked sprites
darting away in every direction from something which had startled
them in a reed bed. A fox, perhaps.

But there were no birds as yet in the winter-still marshes. No
prey and no predators.

As if he had turned a page in a book and seen it written there in full, Rhion realized, *The Ladies. They're following me now.*

He could have hit himself over the head with the boat pole. *Idiot!* he cursed himself, *numbskull, dupe, goon! If the Gray Lady didn't want to be seen by you in the library, do you think you'd have been able to glimpse her, even if she walked up and hit you over the head with the silly book?* He remembered the subtleness of the Archpriestess' magic, the coercion which had operated, not through force, but through the slightest of whispered illusions.

He wondered now how he could possibly have been so sure that the book in her arms was the *Lesser Demonary*—at that distance there had been nothing but its size and shape to go on. But she'd known that, if he thought she had it, he'd run immediately to the cache to check . . .

I'll strangle the bitch.

Oh, yeah, he thought a moment later with a grin at both his own outrage and at his thoughts of vengeance. *Fat chance. You'd spend the rest of your life hopping from lily-pad to lily-pad catching flies with your tongue.*

Though there might be some advantage, he reflected, looking around him at the dripping desolation of snags and roots, *to being a frog in these circumstances.*

His mouth set in a grim smile and he turned with elaborate casualness back along the snag toward the eyots and reed beds in the whispering dark. *Well, my lady, if you want to go wading tonight, we'll go wading. I've got a pocketful of poppyseed and I'll use it just as soon as I've got you well and truly pointed in the wrong direction. We'll see who spends a soggier night.*

Balancing himself with the pole with great and gingerly care he began to work his way up the snag-line, crossing the islet where the books were hidden and angling away along another ford towards the murkiest and wettest part of the marsh.

And in very short order, as he should have known he would, he got lost.

7

Very nice, Rhion, he thought, surveying the shuddering brown waters of the marsh through a haze of wind-thrashed rain that had already rendered his spectacles opaque with spatterings. *Have we got any other clever ideas? Like maybe drowning yourself to really throw them off the track?*

He'd long ago shaken off his pursuers. With the spell-entangled poppyseed he had woven a wide pocket of disorientation, of subtle confusion, and a tendency to poor guesses and errors of judgment; in two other places he had left spell-lines of invisible brightness to tangle and turn the feet. Unfortunately, unfamiliar with the Limitations inherent in these spells and even more unfamiliar with the terrain of the marshes themselves, he was beginning to suspect that he had inadvertently stumbled back through his own spell-fields himself. He certainly seemed to have missed his way in circling back to his boat, or else the tide had begun to come in, changing the water levels around all the islets and altering or obliterating his bearing marks. It was astonishing how even six inches of water altered the appearance of a snag or root and its relationship with the shore. He'd taken as a guide mark the lights of another islet where the Priestesses of the Moon had occupied an old summer palace, but uncannily those lights seemed to have moved . . .

Then it had begun to rain. Rhion had already fallen through a pothole, soaking him to the waist in muddy water and tearing boot leather and the flesh of his calves on the splintery wood of a sub-merged branch—he had spent a panicked, agonizing half-hour in extricating himself. The cold had begun to sap his energy, making it harder still to concentrate.

And the tide was now very definitely coming in.

Emerging from the black curtains of a reed bed Rhion found that his bearing light had unaccountably shifted again. It was only when he heard laughter, thin and dry as ripping silk, seeming to drift from nowhere in the pitchy blackness all around him, that he realized that the light he had been following had been conjured by grims to lead him still further astray.

Maybe at this point drowning myself would be simpler after all.

He turned back to see grims swarming the reeds behind him like cold, glowing lice in a beggar's hair, and their pallid skeleton shapes twisted around the willow knees of the hummock he'd just quitted as he waded back to it along the submerged and slimy roots. At his approach the wraiths opened cold-burning mouths to hiss and bite, and backed away, still hissing, as he summoned a furious blaze of witchfire to the end of his boat pole and swung at them; their shrieks of laughter shivered in the streaming darkness after they had slipped out of sight into the trunks of the trees. Scrambling and slipping over the roots, Rhion reflected that coming back to the islet had done him damn little good—by the feel of the slime on the trunks the place would be chin-deep in three hours.

In the distance he thought he could hear women's voices calling out to him, but could not be sure—it might very well be the grims. Panting and shivering, he scrambled as high up the willow roots as he could, but the reed beds hemmed him in with a wall of whisper-ing black. He called out, but gusts of wind clashed in the sedges, and the rattle of rain on the waters all around him drowned out his shouts; the wind cut through his wet clothing, chilling him to the bone, and the voices faded.

Rhion had begun to feel a little frightened. He could sense deeper cold coming in on the heels of the rain, cold enough to frost hard, even this close to the sea. His clothes were soaked and his leg throbbed, and he knew he had to find shelter before morning. He did not know how deep into the marshes he was, but he guessed, from the grims' propensity for leading travelers astray, that he was miles from the nearest habitation—even if he called a bright blaze of witchlight, he wasn't sure the Ladies, if they were searching, would follow it. They, too, would be familiar with the ways of the grims.

He fished his scrying-crystal from his pocket and squinted at it in the pelting rain. Even calling witchlight over his head to create the needed reflection in its surface, he had to hold it inches from the end of his nose to see anything—a gust of wind blew rain into his eyes, and he edged around towards the lee side of the willow . . .

Beneath his feet the tangle of heather and vines gave downward with a sodden, splintery crack. Rhion yelped and clutched at the roots as he fell past them, but the whole footing caved in around him, dropping him down into blackness and freezing water. Bark tore at his palms as he grabbed the willow knees; with a hard jerk, he broke his fall, dangling by his hands in pitch blackness, the rain falling on his face and the coal-black water lapping and gurgling around his armpits and chin.

And below the water, a faint glow of blue passed through the blackness, and cold fingers closed around his ankles and pulled.

"Dammit!" Rhion yelled, genuinely frightened now. "You scum-eating . . . Celfriagnogast, dammit . . . CELFRIAGNOGAST . . ." He yelled one of the few words of power known to be effective against water-goblins, but other hands gripped his feet, tugging and scratching; he felt things pick and tear at his robe, felt stirring in the black waters all around him.

Don't panic, he thought desperately, *if you panic you can't make it work* . . .

It was perhaps one of the hardest things he'd done, to calm his mind and enter the mental state where magic can be made, to draw power from within himself, to repeat the words of power, the illusions of light and pain. The goblin fingers slacked—keeping the magic in his mind he kicked viciously at the underwater things, and felt them slither away with a few final, angry bites. His hands clawed at

the roots and vines over his head, feeling them shift and sag with
the swaying of his weight . . .

*Lady of the Moon, please don't let the grims come back to chew my
hands . . .*

Somewhere above him, distant across the water, he heard a voice
crying, "RHION!"

"*HERE!!!*" he bellowed, squirming as carefully as he could to
readjust his hold on the vines; gingerly, painfully, he pulled himself
up through the crackling, soggy mess into the air again. Rain lashed
at his face and whipped the head-high reeds all around the islet into
a churning sea of invisible movement; he flung upwards the illusion
of a ball of witchfire, climbing like a carnival rocket to burst in the
black air.

"Rhion . . . !"

"Over here, Rhion!" cried another mocking voice from somewhere in the reeds, imitating words and thoughts with the uncanny
mimicry of the Children of the Dusky Air.

"Rhion my love . . ."

"Here, my darling . . ."

"This way, beautiful princess . . ." A scattered coruscation of lights
flared, small and blue and cold, among the impenetrable sedges,
sparkling in the pelting rain.

Cursing at the grims, Rhion groped for the boat pole which he'd
let fall—it was seven feet long and hadn't dropped through the roots
into oblivion, which was more than could be said of his scrying-
crystal—and, using it to probe the muck in front of him, he waded
out through the reeds again.

The bobbing yellow glow of lanternlight swung out over the
pounded water; behind it, he made out a shallow punt and a cloaked
figure poling, bent under the downpour. Rhion flung up a bright
glow of magelight all around him—the grims hissed and shrieked
with laughter, and the figure on the prow of the punt straightened
up, slashing at the air with her open hands.

"Go!" The flute-sweet voice was no longer rosewood, but jade,
or what music would be if diamonds could be wrought to create it,
hard and sparkling and blazing with a dreadful power. "Get thee
gone, Alseigodath, Children of the Second Creation . . . Go!" And

her voice scaled up into a drawn-out cry, cold and strong and flaming with power, shaping words Rhion did not understand. Through the darkness he could see her face, knowing it for hers, though the features were unclear, reflecting a lightless glory like levin fire on silver. Her long hair swirled in the rain. The laughter in the darkness around them turned to cries of terror; Rhion felt the air thrum, as if under the beating of a holocaust of wings.

Then there was only the driving silence of the rain and the dark woman in the sodden cloak poling her boat toward him, shading her eyes to peer past the lantern's light.

"Are you all right?"

"I feel like a drowned mole, but other than that . . . Is there a way to get on one of those things without tipping you over?"

"Lie flat over the gunwales and turn . . . There!" She bent and caught a handful of sodden robe, pulling him up amidships with a soggy splash. Rhion saw that the punt was little better than a narrow raft, and already half-full of rain. Stoically, his drenched robe dragging at his every joint, he found the small bucket and began to bail while the Lady poled around the edge of the reed bed, and out across the black waters again.

It wasn't until they reached an island that promised a core of solid rock that either one spoke, except to exchange information about the water level in the punt, or instructions regarding its beaching among the clustering snags. The Lady led the way up a short path to what had been a hilltop shrine, its airy pillared walls now blocked in with rough-mortared stone. Inside, a small quantity of dry wood and sea coal were heaped upon a crude hearth; beside them lay dry blankets.

"There are a number of such places, refuges for lost travelers," the Gray Lady said, wringing out her wet hair as Rhion kindled fire on the hearth. "There are spells laid on them of summoning those who are cold and frightened—we were hoping you'd come to one eventually. Rhion, I'm sorry! I'm so sorry. We never thought you'd see us, much less . . ."

"Much less try to lead you astray in your own back garden?" He grinned up at her, shaking the rainwater out of his tangled curls. "I admit it takes a special kind of stupidity to try a trick like that." He fumbled in his pocket for his spectacles, all blotted and smeared with the greasiness of being wrapped in soaked wool—he wondered how he'd ever get them clean and dry and simply gave up on it, replacing them where they had been.

Her breath escaped her in a soft laugh, half with amusement at his self-mockery and half with relief. "We were worried about you . . ." With a simple natural modesty she gathered a blanket to her and, turning her back on him, pulled off her sodden dress and the shift underneath, letting them fall with a wet *splat* on the marble floor. While her back was turned Rhion likewise stripped off his robes, wrapping himself in a blanket and sitting down before the coin-bright newness of the fire to pick apart the torn ruin of his boot.

"Let me see that . . . We meant to trick you into moving the books to a new place—a place we'd be watching, of course—but never that you'd come to harm." She reached over to her wet clothes and disentangled her belt-pouch from the mess, drawing out several small packets of herbs wrapped securely in waxed cloth. "We didn't even know we'd been seen until we ran into your spells of misdirection . . ."

"Well, they must have been pretty good, since I walked back through them and got lost myself," Rhion sighed. "At least, I'd like to think that was what happened and not that I just got lost like any other fool who goes wading around the marshes at night . . . Ow! If that cut didn't get sufficiently washed in three hours of wading I don't know what it *would* take to get it clean . . ."

"That should hold till we get back in the morning." She bent over the bandaging of the makeshift poultice, murmuring herbwife spells; at the touch of her fingers, Rhion felt the pain lessen. Reaction was stealing over him, with the warmth of the little stone room and the fatigue that follows prolonged exertion in the cold. He leaned back against the wall and listened to the low, sweet voice as he would have listened to the rain, without trying to disentangle the spells she wove, only hearing in them the sounds of healing and of peace. He found himself wondering what her name had been and whether, if she had been born in some inland village or hill march, she would have found apprenticeship to some Earth-witch and eventually have become a village healer . . .

Or would the call of the Goddess have brought her to this place, wherever she had been born?

What would have happened to him, he wondered, had he been born a farmer's son a hundred miles from the nearest city, with no way to learn of wizardry and magic, no way to meet Jaldis. Or was it like the summoning spells on the books, he wondered. But then who was the summoner, and whom the summoned?

In the firelight, without his spectacles, her face seemed younger but very tired, the face of the girl she had been.

And if she had been born the daughter of a Duke?

Father needs an alliance . . . It isn't a question of what I want . . .

But that was something of which he could not bear to think.

She raised her head, her eyes seeming darker, like blue amber, mingled browns and russets and treacle golds. "The books would have been returned, you know," she said. There was apology in her voice.

She moved around to sit beside him, the rough stone wall poking them both in the back. "You would not even have known they'd been taken, read, the major spells copied . . ." An expression almost like pain drew at the corners of her generous mouth, and her broad brow darkened.

"The Goddess enjoins us to welcome sojourners in need, to help them. I know that what I have done is not the act of a host." She sighed, and passed a hand across her face, shaking aside the wet trail of hair from the blanket where it lay across her shoulder.

"But you have told us how you live and what became of Jaldis' other books in Felsplex. You've seen the books in our Library—old and crumbling, some of them, and some of them the only copies left of certain volumes, certain spells, certain knowledge . . . And of some books we know only their names, know only that they existed once. Paper is only paper, Rhion. Flesh is only flesh."

Profiled in the amber nimbus of the fire her face was tired, and infinitely sad. Perhaps it was that which broke the wall of his mistrust: the hunger, the sadness, and the yearning that were his own birthright of wizardry. The fire burned out of its first leaping brightness and settled down to a steady, crackling warmth, the rain's drumming eased as the sea-wind carried the somber clouds west to the stony uplands of Way, and their talk turned to other things. He had not forgotten the cold, bright power of her voice as she drove the grims away, nor the dreadful strength of the spells she had cast upon his mind—but he perceived that the power she held was only a part of her, and that at heart, within, she was very like himself.

In the warmth and pleasant weariness as they sat together he put his arm around her shoulders, and later, when she turned to him, he did not turn away.

Rhion was the Gray Lady's lover until the equinox of spring. He never did quite trust her where the books were concerned, but he liked her enormously, both as a lover and as a friend. In an odd way he felt safer, sensing that she was not a woman to weave the secrets of a man's bed and body into spells of coercion; there were magics, too, that wizards used in the bedroom which nonwizards—the tavern girls in Felsplex, or the Marshmen—found unnerving.

It would have been different, had he not known that Tally could never be his.

He knew that the Lady had had other lovers. Indeed, two of the children who sometimes accompanied the Marshfolk to the Islands had her square face and snub nose, and he had heard Channa the cook speak matter-of-factly of "the Lady's husband." But it wasn't until shortly before the equinox that he saw this man, a slender, gray-haired Marshman with a deeply lined face and twinkling eyes, when he came to the Islands to speak to her about the forthcoming spring rites.

"The chieftain of the Marshfolk is always the Lady's husband," Jaldis explained on one of the rare clear evenings when he and Rhion sat on the ruinous stone terrace along the water, observing the movement of the stars. The Moon had not yet risen—sprinkled with diamond fire, the huge arch of darkness seemed hard and shatteringly deep. "I'm told sometimes another man—or occasionally a woman—will ask to take the husband's place in the rites, but it's usually the Lady's husband . . . Have they asked you to preside over their rites at the turning of spring?"

The old man spoke without taking his concentration from the silver astrolabe he held, sighting above the lacy clouds of trees on the next island for the first appearance of the star called the Red Pilgrim. But there was, in spite of his efforts to conceal it, an edge to his voice. Across the marshes, the ducklike quacking of the first wood frogs could be heard; farther upriver, Rhion knew, in the wet meadows the sheep would be starting to lamb. The old man had only shaken his head when Rhion had told him about the Lady, but Rhion was aware these days that Jaldis was keeping a rather close eye on the hidden books. As soon as he'd been strong enough to go there himself Jaldis had marked the place with his own seals and, Rhion knew, had fallen into the habit of checking on them often.

This stung him a little, though he perfectly understood the concern. He didn't *think* the Gray Lady would—or could—use magic on him without his knowledge, but that conviction in itself, he was well aware, might have been induced by some spell more subtle than he could fathom. That she was stronger than he, he had always known.

He sighed and propped his spectacles back into place with his forefinger, keeping his attention on identifying the positions of various changeable stars. "They asked me if I'd attend, but they didn't say anything about presiding. Wouldn't the Lady herself do that?"

"Male magic and female work differently in their system," the old man replied, "as I'm sure you know. Here, see? The Pilgrim star is in twenty degrees of ascension, in the constellation of the Child." Since both of them knew that a quarrel would be based, at heart, in completely irrational feelings, neither was willing to step over the tacitly drawn lines. Thus many of their conversations had an oddly informational quality these days, something Rhion guessed would pass in time, when they left Sligo.

"Talismans of protection seem to be influenced by this position, those made while that star is in ascendance having a greater efficacy, especially against poison, though conversely poisons, too, brewed in conjunction with death-spells, have greater strength . . . Very curious."

He turned to regard his student, pinpricks of starlight twinkling deep within the bulging plates of jewels which hid what remained of his eyes. "Certainly men and women are trained in different techniques. They generally have a man to preside over the rites."

"Is it something you don't advise?"

"There is no reason why you shouldn't attend." The old man flicked back a spider-floss strand of his hair, and cocked his head like a bird. "You'll find it interesting. The principles of magic *per se* have become deeply corrupted here and mixed with what was, originally, a religious cult, as I'm sure you've seen. The equinox rites clearly have their roots in what elsewhere came to be celebrated as the Carnival of Mhorvianne—the powers evoked at the turning of the four balance-points of the celestial year they attribute to the favor of their goddess rather than to the strength of their own wizardry and the nature of the cosmos itself. But it is never an ill thing to witness the raising of power, nor the shapes taken by the human soul."

Still, it was with an irrational sense of disharmony, almost of guilt, that Rhion made his way in company with the Ladies and nearly all the folk of the marshes along the curved, gray beach of the Holy Isle at sunset of the equinox eve. Jaldis had remained behind in the main cluster of the islands, perhaps the only man in the lands of Sligo to do so, in order to work his own conjurations, calling the powers generated by the stars' balance to strengthen the spells on their medicinal herbs.

Without a word being said, Rhion knew that what Jaldis had really wanted to do was weave another Dark Well and search in its depths for the wizards who had begged their help, but he knew also that the old man was not about to do such a thing where there was a risk of having his secrets discovered, particularly by those whom he considered little better than Earth-witches. Jaldis was certainly capable of imbuing herbs with healing-spells unassisted—such was his power that he could probably have cured the plague with common grass—and, in any case, he would never have given Rhion an ultimatum of any sort.

Nevertheless, Rhion knew the old man hadn't liked being left alone.

In many ways it had been an uneasy winter.

Jaldis was right about one thing. The rituals practiced by the Ladies of the Moon were those of a religious cult rather than of wizardry, cluttered with curious practices having no apparent bearing on magic as Rhion understood it.

They were profoundly unnerving nevertheless.

The sun sank over the green-brown wall of the sweet marshes. Shadows flowed forth across the murky tangle of sawgrass and salt-oak that lay in long, uneven crescents seaward of the Holy Isle as the Marshmen began to assemble in the sacred place. The flotilla of canoes had left the Ladies' islands in the black dark long before dawn—at one time, Rhion guessed, soon after the days of the earth-quake, this islet had been the last point of land facing out over the sea. From the crumbling double circle of menhirs on the beach, twin lines of unshaped standing stones extended out into the brack brown waters of the marsh, their heads gradually vanishing beneath the surface like the Sea-God's silent armies; a cloud-streaked mauve twi-light lay upon the black, decaying shapes like a smoky shroud. When darkness was fully on them, the tapping of a drum began, and the men and women of the Marshfolk took hands, forming long winding chains that wove between the stones of circle and lines, looped far out onto the beach and into the waters and so back again, treading in the sand and the water the ancient shapes of the Holy Maze which had been passed down the years. Chill salt wind stirred their tangled hair and coarse garments, shredded the torch smoke and carried over the desolation the single, hoarse cry of a bird; Rhion, seated alone on a small boulder just above the tide line, drew his cloak about him and shivered. The lines of the dancers passed by him unseeing, though the stars that came to shine through the wispy clouds gleamed silver in their open eyes.

The dance began, and ended, and began again, now walking, now hastening, now bending down with long, shuddering ripples that passed through the lines like waves of the sea or the turning of a serpent's tail. Though torches ringed the stone circle thrust upright in the sand, the dancers carried none—as the darkness deepened their forms seemed more and more like the passing of a spirit host, lost between the realms of the living and the dead. The music was oddly random, strange knockings and dronings broken by shrill bird cries, and yet, through it all, moved a rhythm that eluded the seekings of Rhion's mathematical mind. More than ever, he had the sense of visiting a world that was half-invisible half the time, a world where things appeared to make little sense and yet moved to patterns un-guessable—where things that seemed common were lambent with power. In other parts of the Forty Realms tonight was the Carnival of Masks, the feast of Mhorvianne the Merciful, the rite of forgiveness. Here, it seemed, atonement involved something beyond a sheltered remorse.

The night drew on. The sea's whisper was hardly louder than the dragging of hundreds of feet through the heavy gray sand. Soft wind herded the clouds westward and the stars turned their courses unimpeded above the headless stones. The tide of the equinox lifted and stirred in Rhion's blood.

Beside the altar in the midst of the ring of stones and torchflame the presiding mage raised his arms to the sky—an old Hand-Pricker from up the marshes who looked ancient enough to be Jaldis' grandfather. It was close to midnight; Rhion felt it in his bones. He could feel, too, the spiral whisper of magic that floated now like a glowing mist all around the holy place. Magic rose from the dancers, from the sea, from the maze they had trodden into the sand, and from the ley that crossed through the island and plunged down the lane of stones to drown itself in the waters of the marsh; magic closed tighter and tighter about the altar-stone like the wool winding on a distaff, like the twisting ropes of a catapult's spring. In a high, shaky voice the mage was chanting the words of the raising and concentration of power, and the lines of the dancers changed their pattern and drew the circles smaller yet, giving him the power they raised.

Though Rhion had not seen her approach, the Lady stepped forward out of darkness into the bloody glare. He saw that she wore the garments of the bygone priestesses of An, red as the anemones that grew in the sweet marshes in spring, sewn with plates of pierced gold. Her face was painted white and black after the ancient fashion, framed in the smoky rivers of her hair; she wore the old diadem of the priest-queens on her head, the white moon jewel, the flowers and the bones. And to the altar her husband came, as the husbands of the Lady of Sligo had come for centuries past, naked to the waist with his silvery hair unbound and his twinkling eyes solemn.

He stretched himself upon the stone and a priest and priestess came forward—the priestess, Rhion noticed distractedly, was Channa the cook—taking knives of meteor iron that the Lady gave them, the blades glinting blue in the starlight. At a word from the Lady, the torches were quenched in the sand, but the dancers continued to turn and weave along the maze's invisible tracks in the darkness, silent as wind. Even the music had stilled, but it seemed to Rhion that he could hear, along with the hiss of their feet in the heavy sand, the beating of the blood in their veins. The old Hand-Pricker stretched forth his hands to the stars. The priest and priestess moved to either side of the man who lay upon the altar. The blades glinted as they were raised—then they bent and cut the victim's throat.

Rhion shuddered, looking away as the Lady stepped forward, her crimson gown a darkness now broken only by the white shapes of dangling bones. He'd seen that the cuts were carefully made, slitting the veins, not severing the arteries or the windpipe. Still, even allowing for the added power that the turning of the equinox midnight gave to healing magic, it would take a tremendously strong spell at this point to save the victim's life. Thin, icy wind streamed up from the salt marshes of the east, carrying to his nostrils the sweet, metallic repulsiveness of the blood; the dancers' feet swished in the sand, starlight flashing on the sweat of their faces, the curled tips of the waves, their feet weaving and re-weaving the maze between sea and earth.

A flute awakened, crying wild and sad and alone; somewhere a tiny drum trembled with a skittery beat in the torchless dark. When Rhion looked back the altar was empty. Priest and priestess, Lady and mage and victim, were gone. The air seemed to sing with the aftermath of magic, drawn from the turning of the heavens, dispersed along the leys to the four corners of the sleeping world like a shuddering silver heartbeat and called back from them again. A dark thread of blood ran down the side of the stone, gleaming black in the starlight.

But whether the Lady's husband had walked away alive, or had been carried off dead—which as he later learned frequently did happen in these rites—Rhion did not hear for many days.

Spring rains had started a few weeks previously, turning the waters of the marsh to sheets of hammered steel and transforming all the familiar channels as the water level rose. Waking early, to med-

itate on the old stone terrace or walk to the library to study, Rhion
heard among the reeds the cries of the returning birds.

One day shortly after the rite at the standing stones, Jaldis announced that enough dry weather lay ahead to permit them to take
the road once again.

"It will be good," he said simply, "to be home."

Nerriok, Rhion thought, the green City of Bridges, walled with
golden sandstone upon its island in the midst of ring after ring of
crinas, floating eyots of dredged silt and withe anchored by roots to
the bottom of Lake Mharghan and thick with trees and flowers—
corrupt, sprawling, and unbelievably colorful, with its markets heavy
with the perfumes of melons and bread and flowers, its majestic
temples and marble baths, its periodic riots among the students of
different schools of philosophy and its huge concourses of foreigners
that turned certain quarters into strange bazaars of the East or
grubby, sprawling barbarian villages . . .

The noise, the smells, and the excitement of the place came back
on him in a wave of strange nostalgia—libraries, playhouses, poetry,
music, and the meeting of minds . . .

And at the same time he thought about the shaggy green silences
of the marshes of Sligo and the faint speech of wind chimes on foggy
mornings mingling with the cawing of crows.

He pushed his spectacles more firmly up onto the bridge of his
nose, and said, "The Gray Lady has asked me to stay on here as
Scribe."

Jaldis said nothing. His bent and crippled fingers turned over and
over the seal-hair brush he'd been wielding, to write talismanic signs
on a luck-charm. The breeze off the marsh, sniffing like a little dog
across the terrace upon which Rhion had found him sitting, stirred
the cream-colored parchment under its weighting of river stones.
Cool sunlight flooded a cloud-patched sky overhead and glanced
across Jaldis' spectacles. The vines that cloaked their crumbling old
house had begun to put out leaves. Within a month the Drowned
Lands would be a jungle of whispering green.

The brush made a little silvery *tinck* as it was set down on the
pitted limestone table-top. "Perhaps you should."

Rhion shook his head. "I couldn't leave you alone."

He made his face as noncommittal as his voice. When Jaldis was wearing his spectacles it was difficult to tell whether he was using them to see or not.

"You'll have to one day, you know." The set of the old man's back, the way he tilted his head up at Rhion as if he could see, were calm and matter-of-fact. "I do not want that it should come to it, that you would begin to wish me dead."

"I won't."

Jaldis drew in his breath as if he would speak, but let it out again, and the rosewood box upon his chest only murmured, like the drawn-out trickle of the marsh winds, "Oh, my son . . ."

Rhion reached down and took his hands. In a way he knew that Jaldis was right. Unsettling as the sojourn here had been, at heart they had both known that Rhion's affair with the Lady, like his other relations with the tavern girls and flower sellers of Nerriok and Felsplex, was not something that would alter his life, or change what lay between them. Yet somewhere in the course of the winter something had changed. Learning the mazes of the marshes, studying the scrolls left by ancient wizards, meditating on the healing spells the Lady had taught him, Rhion had realized—or, more accurately, had come to believe within himself—that he could be a wizard away from Jaldis' teaching.

But now was not the time. For one thing, Jaldis needed him. In the misted silver light he could see the marks of the winter's hardship on that lined and weary face: *How could he even REACH Nerriok if I stayed behind?*

And there were other things.

"You're my teacher," he said quietly. "My friend. Ten years ago when I was going insane trying to—to crush out the fire inside me—you told me that it was possible to have that fire, to hold it and keep it, not as a secret that I had to hide but as a way I could make my living and as a glory, a joy in itself. You told me that dreams were not insanity. Just for that, if you'd done nothing for me from that moment on, I'd still owe you . . ."

"You owe me nothing!" The crippled fingers tightened fiercely over the soft, stubby ones in their grasp. "Owe—it's a filthy word! We are not permitted to marry, but we need sons and daughters,

Rhion, to whom we can pass our knowledge. To whom we can pass what we are. Not children of the blood, but children of the fire."
There was a long silence, broken by the far-off mewling of gulls.

"Ah," Rhion replied, as if he had at last understood some great piece of wisdom. "I see. So you really *enjoyed* spending all those hours getting migraines teaching me to scry through a crystal. It gave you heartfelt fulfillment, that time I lit the attic on fire back in Nerriok . . ."

The scarred ruin of Jaldis' mouth flexed, the closest he could ever come to a laugh, and he pulled his hands free of his adopted son's. "You are an impertinent boy," he said.

"Besides," Rhion added with a grin, "every time I think you've taught me all about magic, either I bollix something up and you have to remind me I need five hundred times more practice, or you pull out some obscure spell that you've forgotten to tell me about, like the come-back spells on the books. I'm not about to let you get away till I'm damn sure I've got it all, which should be in about another thirty years. So I'll just go inside and start packing . . ."

The crippled fingers, startlingly strong from eleven years of supporting his weight on the crutch handles, caught at his wrists once more. It never failed to surprise Rhion how accurate the old man's awareness was of where things were.

"You will have to leave me one day, you know," he repeated, refusing to be put off, as he had always refused to be put off by his pupil's elusive clowning. "One day you will need to seek your own path, to establish yourself. Don't give that up for the sake of looking after me."

Rhion looked about him in silence. Under a cloak of weeds, the marble pavement was pitted and broken; beyond it stood the library, the huge stone blocks of its walls being forced apart by the roots of trees. All around them, ancient marble faces peeped like ghosts from the foliage that wound this island in a flowering shroud. Gulls circled overhead, and distantly he heard a bittern's harsh cry. Chilly spots of sunlight flashed in the reed beds and on the brown waters beyond. A silence of peace lay upon the lands, and everywhere, like the murmuring of the waters, he could breathe the whispering scent of magic.

He made himself grin again, so that the lightness would carry into his voice. "When I find a path I want to tread by myself, I'll tell you." Turning quickly, he went inside.

Later he sought the Gray Lady at her loom. By the way she raised her eyes to his face when he came in he saw that she read what his answer to Jaldis had been, and thus his answer to her. Even when he had gone to seek his master on the terrace, Rhion had not been clear as to what his decision would be.

"I can't leave him," he said quietly, sitting down on the bench beside her. "Not now. Not yet. He was hurt enough by my—I don't know, deserting him, I suppose, for you, or even seeming to. It sounds silly . . ."

She smiled, shook her head, and laid the shuttle by. "All fathers want their sons to grow to manhood and walk alone," she said. "But they are all sure they know best about the direction in which their sons should walk."

Under his scrubby beard Rhion's mouth twisted at the sudden memory of his own father's constant moan about the ways of modern youth. But the thought inevitably brought back that sweaty red face trembling with anger above its tight embroidered collar. *You are dead to me as from today. My son is dead. My son is dead . . .*

And so, Rhion thought, he was.

After his ejection from the family home, he had scried for sight of his father in the fire of the cellar where he and Jaldis had been sheltering. He had seen him in tears, alone, locked in his counting room where not even Rhion's mother would find him. He had never sought for sight of him again.

"I'm sorry." He sighed, and looked up at the Gray Lady's face, then around at the little stone chamber, a round room like a dovecote built onto the back of what had been a temple, its hearth where the altar had been. Through a doorway he could see the gray pine poles and white curtains of the bed where they had lain. "I would have liked to stay longer."

Even as he said it he felt guilty, as if he had said to Jaldis, *I'd rather study with the Lady than with you. I'd rather sleep in the Lady's arms than look after a lame old man. I'd rather stay in a place where they have hundreds of books, than follow after a cripple who's down to his last dozen . . .*

And a voice still deeper within added, *I'd rather be a man than a boy*.

But right now, to Jaldis, lame and blind and set adrift, it all came to the same thing: *I'm leaving you*.

And that, he could not say.

She smiled and shook her head. "Never be sorry when the Goddess leads you somewhere by the hand. She's usually very clear about what will be best for us—it's just that sometimes we think we know more about it than She does. I will miss you, Rhion." She drew him to her and kissed him on the lips, the warm, brief kiss of friendship. Wan sunlight, falling through the open window beside the angular black skeleton of the loom, picked out the crow's-feet around her hazel eyes, and the first threads of gray at the part of her smooth-braided hair.

"We see time like wanderers in a maze," she said. "She sees it from the top. I'll have Channa put up some supplies to take on the road. But I wouldn't advise you to go to Nerriok. The queen has lately come under the influence of the priests of Agon, the Eclipsed Sun. Like most of the sun cults, they are intolerant and jealous of wizards' powers. My advice, if as you say you have done a favor for a member of the ducal house, is to go to Bragenmere instead."

They reached Bragenmere in four days. Their speed on the road was greatly assisted by the half-week of dry weather Jaldis had foreseen and by the two small donkeys and the Marshman servant the Lady had lent them for the trip. Able to carry blankets and foodstuffs as well as Jaldis' books—which Jaldis tested with spells the first night on the road, as soon as he thought Rhion was asleep, to make absolutely sure that the Gray Lady had not handled them—the two wizards were thus able to avoid spending what little cash remained to them on inns. They reached Bragenmere with enough in hand to rent two small but clean rooms—one upstairs and one down—in one of the hundreds of little courts of which that dry upland city consisted, a court which was owned, ironically enough, by the local Temple of Darova, a god whose disapproval had gotten them thrown out of more than one town in their time.

Rhion fell easily back into the role of housewife, sweeping out their new dwelling place and scouting the nearest markets and fountains. They were lucky in that, though Shuttlefly Court itself didn't possess a fountain, which was one reason the rents there were cheap, it backed onto the Laundry of Fortunate Sheets, also owned by the Temple of Darova, which operated a small banking house and a very large bordello in the neighborhood as well. The laundry master was willing to sell surplus fountain water after sundown and all the "used" they cared to carry away for bathing and dishwashing purposes. Bragenmere, perched on the high, arid knees of the Mountains of the Sun, was watered by a number of springs, two very fine stone aqueducts, and the Kairn River's sluggish marshes below the Lower Town's walls, all of which had been sufficient for its population back in the days when it had only been a trading town for the upcountry hunters and shepherds. Since the increase of the weaving trade under the patronage of the Dukes of Mere, the city, capital of this realm, had grown vastly, and as was the way of things in any city of the Forty Realms, the great public baths and temple fountains, and the water-gardens of the Duke, the nobility, and the wealthy, tended to get larger shares than any number of the poor.

The other occupants of the court were mostly weavers, with the exception of the usual two or three dramshops to be found in every court in the city, a pawnbroker, who was also subsidized by the Temple of Darova, seven free-lance prostitutes and an embroiderer who hadn't been able to afford the higher rents of Thimble Lane a dozen yards to the east. There was a school at one corner, thinly attended since most of the neighborhood children spent their days on the loom. The schoolmistress, a sturdy gray-haired woman with a voice like a war gong, descended upon Jaldis and Rhion the first day and informed them in no uncertain terms that they were not to interfere with any of her pupils, several of whom had already pelted Rhion with goat dung on his way back from the market. Three nights later the woman was back to purchase a remedy for a headache as if neither the pelting nor the confrontation had ever taken place.

Ah, what it is, Rhion thought, watching her departing back dart furtively from shadow to shadow of the cottonwood posts supporting the court's rudely thatched arcade, *to be a working mage again.*

The business of actually earning one's living by wizardry, he had long ago discovered, was transacted mostly in the first two or three

hours after sunset. It was the time when people—like Mistress Prymannie—had the impression they would not be seen. This was an
advantage as spring warmed to summer and the dust kicked up from
the unpaved court frequently made the downstairs kitchen unlivable.
There were spells that would draw down dust out of the air and
collect it in the corners, but these tended to vary so much with
weather, with the phases of the moon and the ascensions and de-
clensions of various stars that they were never really effective. In his
reading and study, Rhion was constantly on the lookout for others
that worked better and wondered if the Gray Lady would have given
him a good one if he'd thought to ask. Even in a city as relatively
friendly to wizards as Bragenmere, few people would be seen openly
going to a mage's door in the daytime.

Thus he was startled one afternoon, while sitting in the kitchen
roughing out calculations for a talisman that might work in attracting
wealth their way, by a knock on the door. Jaldis was upstairs reading,
for the light was better there and it was easier to make his spectacles
work. Rhion got to his feet and walked the length of the corridorlike
adobe room, thinking, *Not the local magistrates telling us to move on.
Please, Darova, give us a break for once. After all, we're paying our
rent* . . .

He opened the door.

Framed against the bright spring sun of the court outside, her
taffy-colored hair braided back under a virgin's stiffened gauze cap,
was Tally.

She blinked into the dimness of the kitchen, her eyes clearly not
used to the splintery blue shade under the courtyard arcade, much
less to the unmitigated gloom of the kitchen itself.

She said, "Excuse me—I have heard that you're a . . . a wizard? I
want . . . I want to purchase a potion, to win the love of a man."

8

Rhion couldn't help himself. "Is it for you?"

"Of course!" But the quickness of her reply, and the hot blush that suddenly suffused her cheeks, told their own story and the relief that went through him almost made him laugh. "That is . . ." she began, and peered suddenly into the shadows of the room. *"Rhion?"* And recognizing him, she smiled.

He thought, quite clearly, as if warning someone else against inevitable tragedy: *Don't do this.* But it was already done.

"Come in." He stepped back to let her pass, then hurried before her to the plank table—one he'd scrounged in one of the many rubbish stores of the district—to shove aside the books and papers that strewed its stained and battered surface. "Don't tell me your governess lets you come to this part of town," he added as he did so. "If I were your father, I'd sack her."

"My governess thinks I'm in the mews helping Fleance with the young hawks . . ." She gazed around her as she spoke: at the rough-hewn rafters from which every herb they could buy or gather in the Kairn Marshes hung drying; at the round little beehive of a tiled stove; at the plank shelf of dishes, the cool red-and-black-work done in the Drowned Lands. "Don't you have a crocodile?

A stuffed one, I mean, hanging from the rafters? Wizards are supposed to."

"Wizards do if they can afford them," Rhion replied with a grin. "The ones you see in spell-weavers' shops aren't stuffed but drying, and when they're properly dried you cut them up and store them for potions and mummify the skin in camphor oil, for talismanic work. But the baby crocs are tremendously expensive and you have to import them from Mindwava. Jaldis and I are still working on cheaper things like saffron seed and glass and getting a decent crucible." He leaned against the corner of the table and scratched a corner of his scruffy beard, realizing he hadn't trimmed it lately and wishing he had. She walked around the bare little room, looking at the herbs and books and cheap clay pots with their careful labels in frank wonder and delight. He remembered the grace with which she moved, surprising in a girl so tall, but he'd almost forgotten the husky, boyish alto of her voice.

"Does it have to be?" She turned back to him, her gray eyes shadowed. "A love-potion, that is. I mean, does it have to be for . . . Could someone get one that would work for two other people?"

When she had come in, Rhion had seen, as well as the smile that stopped his heart, the purplish prints of sleeplessness in the tender flesh around the eyes and the puffy spoor of last night's tears.

He sighed, wishing he didn't have to be the one to tell her. "A love-potion won't save your sister from unhappiness, Tally."

Her mouth flinched, but she didn't ask him how he knew. Perhaps she expected that, as a wizard, he simply would know.

"They don't last," he went on, as gently as he could. "Even if you were to give her husband several in succession, in time the effects would wear away. And if he hates her now, what do you think he'll feel after a few weeks, or a few months, of being impelled by his own body, by needs he doesn't understand, to make love to her?"

She was silent, digesting that. It was clearly something she hadn't thought of. Rhion remembered she was a virgin—remembered what it had been like to be seventeen.

At length she said, "I don't think . . . that is . . . He isn't indifferent. At least Damson says . . ." She hesitated, an inexperienced and well-bred girl sorting hastily through all the precepts of good breeding for what it was and was not proper to say. She took a deep breath, and plunged in. "Damson says—and I think she's right—that Esrex isn't indifferent to her. If he was, he wouldn't be trying to hurt her, he wouldn't be flaunting his mistresses the way he does. But he's very proud, and very bitter. He sees in her the daughter of the man who took the realm away from his grandfather—our grandfather, because his aunt is my mother—the man who humbled his family. And he's spiteful. Loving her could change that, couldn't it?"

The anxious look in her gray eyes, after her tomboy incisiveness and the courage she'd shown in the snowbound woods, went to his heart. Her voice was almost timid as she asked, "Are they really not permanent?"

"Love isn't permanent, Tally," Rhion said quietly. "It renews itself, from day to day—sometimes from hour to hour. And lust and longing, which create their own illusions—and illusion is what the potions really arouse—are more evanescent still. I'm sorry . . ."

She shook her head quickly, as if to say, *Not your fault,* her eyes not meeting his. For a time she leaned half-perched upon the corner of the cluttered table, head bowed beneath the drying jungle of mallows and milkwort overhead, looking down at her hands in her lap. But when she spoke again she raised her gaze to his.

"It's his pride, you see," she said. "Damson has always loved him, from the time he was sixteen and she was twenty; I think they . . . they slept together . . . in spite of the fact that he always blamed Father for the fact that he—Esrex—isn't Duke of Mere now. But he never wanted to marry her for that reason. Then he found out she was behind his family forcing him to do so—and right after that she miscarried of his son. He hasn't been near her since. But if he could just be drawn back to her, even for a little while . . . if she could just bear him a son."

Was that her wishful thinking, he wondered, or her sister's? Running an idle finger along the worn grain of the table corner on which he perched, Rhion remembered the chilly-eyed young man he'd seen in the scrying-crystal. Good-looking in his way—though Rhion had long since given up trying to decide what kind of looks drew men and women to one another—lace-gloved hands fastidiously turning bunches of expensive winter flowers, his face expressionless as a cat's.

His power over Damson had been clear in the way she'd flinch from his words, in the way her eyes would follow him when he'd stalk from the room.

"You think it would help?"

Something stiffened in her shoulders as she tucked a strand of seed-colored hair defiantly back under her cap. "It might."

And so it might, he thought. With loving and hating, one never knew. But too many people had come to him and Jaldis over the years, asking for magic to fix their lives. He knew of no spell which could not be twisted out of its purpose by fate, no potion which would for better or for worse change a human soul's inner essence. No sigil he'd made had ever altered the words that rose automatically to a person's lips when they weren't thinking.

Yet people kept acting as if someday the laws of magic would spontaneously change and spells would do all these things.

He felt suddenly very old. "Does your sister know you've come?"

Tallisett shook her head. "Damson says wizards make most of their money blackmailing the people who come to them for love-potions or potency drugs or abortions . . ."

"Damn!" Rhion smote his forehead with the heel of his hand. "So *that's* what we've been doing wrong! I *knew* there had to be a better way to make money out of this . . . Ow!" She'd come around the table in a stride and smacked him hard on the shoulder, but she was laughing as she did so.

"No," he added gently, shaking his head. "That's part of the oath of our order. Secrecy, as physicians must swear it."

Tally frowned. "But there was a wizard just a few years ago who was doing that over in Way . . ."

"So he was probably a Blood-Mage or an Ebiatic or one of the cheapjack astrologers you get on the street-corners . . ."

She shook her head, baffled, like most people completely ignorant of the differences between the orders of wizardry. "All I know is that they burned him for it, and before they burned him he confessed to having blackmailed hundreds of people. He'd get the women to sleep with him and the men to kill or beat up people who disagreed with him . . . and anyway," she added, as Rhion groaned at the retelling of those hoary rumors, those accusations which had been leveled at every wielder of magic who had ever lived, "Esrex belongs to the Cult of Agon. If he ever thought there was wizardry involved between him and Damson he'd probably stay away from her for good, out of fear of what they'd say."

"And you're willing to risk that for her without her knowledge?" He cocked an eyebrow at her, and pushed up his spectacles again. Her color heightened.

"He'd never find out . . ." But he could see that, even as she said the words, she was aware of how childish they sounded. She looked down again, for a few moments concentrating on picking precisely identical quantities of gauze undersleeve to puff out between the embroidered ribbons of her oversleeve. "She loves him, you see," she said at length, not meeting his eye. "I don't see how she could, after all the cruel things he's said to her—he really is a spiteful little prig. But she does. If she didn't . . . If she didn't need his approval the way she does . . ."

"And if we didn't all have to eat to stay alive," Rhion sighed, "think how much money we'd save at the market." Her profile, half averted, was like a line of alabaster behind the stiffened wing of her cap; the pearl that hung from the cap's point was less smooth than the forehead beneath it. He felt a certain amount of sympathy for Damson's impossible position.

The silence lengthened. Outside in the courtyard a couple of drunks were arguing in front of the Skull and Bones, and even through the weight of the adobe wall he could hear the steady beat of the looms in the chambers next door. The air smelled thickly of dust and lanolin, of the pigs foraging in the court and of acrid soap being boiled a few courts over in Lye Alley. He remembered the way Tally had jerked the wet leather of the reins from his hand, the defiant flash of her gray eyes in the gibbous reflected ghostlight of the grims. He remembered how she had charged without a second thought to seek for her sister's child.

"If I don't help you," he said, not asking it as a question, "you'll look for someone who will."

She didn't look at him but he saw her mouth flinch again.

"Tally," he sighed softly, "don't do it. Leave her free to choose her own road."

She raised her eyes then, like a child's, hoping, not that authority would relent, but that the world was in fact not constituted as it was. The stiffness went out of her back with the release of her breath. "Damn you." Her small voice was utterly without rancor, a friend's casual raillery at a friend. "Are you always right about things?"

"No," he told her sadly, for he wanted to be able to help her, wanted to free her from the grinding pressure of misery he had seen in the crystal. "But this time I'm afraid I am."

Dammit, he thought, *all those weeks in the Drowned Lands wondering if there were some way I could make her happy, and it turns out it's this.*

"There are ways to do it, yes. But really and truly, it's against our ethics to make a love-spell or any other kind of spell for someone who isn't present and consenting. Can you see why that is?"

And she nodded, not liking it, but seeing. She didn't, like many girls of that age, say, *This is different . . .* If she thought it, it was not for long.

"I'm sorry. I'm truly sorry."

"It's all right." She sighed again, and produced a crooked smile for him, manufacturing cheer in her voice as he had so recently manufactured it for Jaldis. "If she weren't so afraid of word getting back to Esrex . . . or of being blackmailed . . ." She shook her head, chasing the thought away. "He's trying very hard to curry favor with the priests of Agon, you see. Though the gods only know why anyone would want to belong to that cult. But I'll think of something."

She straightened her shoulders and smiled a little more convincingly. In that single gesture, he saw all the burnished self-confidence of one of those children of fortune who have not yet known defeat. Rhion had been acquainted with a lot of them, having gone to school with the offspring of the wealthy bankers and traders and merchant senators of the City of Circles. At one time he had been one himself. He still remembered what it had felt like.

She turned to go.

"Wait . . ." Pulling himself out of his reverie, he twisted around to grub in the debris on the table for the bits of parchment he'd purchased with the proceeds of his last toadstone. "Just a minute . . ."

Half closing his eyes, he dipped down within himself, calling forth the meditative light of magic. After a moment, he drew a standard sigil comprised of the second, ninth, and eighteenth runes—the first such seal he could think of at short notice—and threw in the Lost Rune for good measure, rolled it up in a small piece of cured lambskin, at ten or twelve dequins the square foot, and bound it with a slip of punched copper. "Carry this when you leave. It'll keep people from looking at you, or recognizing you if they do see you, provided you keep quiet and don't call attention to yourself. All right?"

She hesitated, holding it as if she feared it would somehow contaminate her soul by touch. Then she slipped it into her skirt pocket. "All right. Thank you." She meant the charm, he could tell, as he walked her the length of the shadowy room. But when he opened the door she turned back in the mottled tabby light of the arcade's thatched roof, and said, "Thank you," again, meaning something more.

Then she was gone.

He climbed the ladder to the floor above and recounted to Jaldis all that had passed, not omitting that he had called Tallisett's image in his scrying-crystal while they were in the Drowned Lands, "to make sure she and her sister got to Imber all right," and so knew the poor state of Damson's marriage.

"It's a bad business," Jaldis sighed, shaking his head. Because of the strong spring heat, worse in the upper room, he'd braided and clubbed his white hair, and his head with its narrow features and close-trimmed beard strongly resembled that of a bird, thrusting up from the loose folds of his brown cowl. Before him on the table lay his spectacles, surrounded by half a dozen fragments of flawed crystal the color of dirty water, the best they could afford.

"Not that Dinar Prinagos wasn't perfectly right to overthrow his liege lord and keep Alvus' ineffectual idiot of a son from inheriting," the old man went on, fingering each fragment in turn: reading, Rhion knew, every shear and shadow in the brittle lattices of their structure, judging how much use, if any, they would be. Every flaw meant a Limitation, or a variation of whatever spell the future talismans would hold; every shadow, a break in the energy paths of the crystal's heart which would have to be laboriously accounted for.

"There's bad blood in the White Bragenmeres, and I'm told Esrex, for all he's a fop, is a dangerous young man to cross. A Solarist, he used to be, denying all the gods and magic as well. But he switched over to the Cult of Agon when it became clear that the High Queen favored them."

The blind man shook his head, the lines of his face deepening. To a great extent he seemed to have recovered from his illness, and even the journey up from Sligo seemed to have left him little the worse. But listening to his voice as he spoke of Tally's father, Rhion found himself comparing its tone and strength with his recollections of how it had been before the flight from Felsplex—before the strain of opening and using the Dark Well. *It draws energy,* Jaldis had said . . .

Lately he had caught himself watching Jaldis closely, mentally comparing with recollections and repeatedly reassuring himself, *Yes, he looks the same . . . his movement hasn't slowed down any . . . there's been no real change* and wondering if he was just imagining that the old man seemed slower and more halt, wondering whether his hands had always looked so thin . . .

"I'm not sure which is worse," Jaldis continued, oblivious to the uneasy scrutiny. "The Solarists and their heresies or the Cult of Agon with its secrets, its spies that take every piece of information they hear back to the priests of the Veiled God. No one even knows who half its members are, though they're supposed to be legion. You were well to send the girl away, poor chit. You don't think she'll go to a Hand-Pricker, do you, or to that poisonous old Ebiatic, Mal-nuthe, over in the Shambles?"

"I don't think so," Rhion said. The window was shuttered with a pair of dried and splintery jalousie shades; sitting in the embrasure of the thick adobe wall, he was able to peer through a couple of the missing louvers into the blindingly bright sunlight of the square. With the ending of the spring rains, the lush weeds and thorn-bushes growing all around the courtyard arcade were turning brown. The mountains that towered over Bragenmere were taking on their wolf-ish summer hues: by August the sheep and cattle ranges would be coarse brown velvet, the pine trees blackish tangles in the rock clefts that marked the springs. Children too young to be working the looms were playing knucklebones in the dust, their voices rising shrilly to Rhion's ears; across the square, one of the whores lay on her balcony, a damp towel spread over her face and her hair, nearly the color of the summer hills, spread out to bleach in the sun.

"I think she understands now why it isn't a good thing to make a decision like that for someone else, no matter what *she* thinks should be done."

"We can but hope. Listen, Rhion . . ." The old man set aside his crystals and half-turned in his twig-work chair. "I have been making calculations. It is my belief that a Dark Well could be wrought in the cellar beneath the kitchen here."

Rhion tried not to shiver at the thought of Jaldis' tampering once more with the Void. "That little hole? It's so small you'd have to climb back up to the kitchen if you wanted to scratch . . ."

"Not if we removed the shelves there—they are probably rotted in any case—and cleared the wood-stores up into the kitchen." He leaned forward, the talismans dangling from the voice-box clinking with the dry silvery sound of moving wind. "Rhion, it is six weeks until the summer solstice. The solstice or the equinoxes are the only time that the wizards in that other universe—the wizards without magic—might just be able to raise enough power to reach through the Void and contact us here. Even if we can get only an image, a glimpse of their world, something to guide our search in the blackness of eternity, we will know at least in which direction to look the next time we search, and the next . . ."

Something flicked through Rhion's mind and was gone, like movement glimpsed from the tail of the eye. Something evil and cold, something . . . A dream? Night sky and standing stones . . . ?

Turning his mind from his vague fear of what danger Tally might run herself into he said, "Yes, but . . . how likely is it they'll still be calling? By the time of the solstice, it'll have been six months. That's a long time. Anything can happen in six months."

Jaldis smiled, sweet and wise in spite of the ruin of scars. "My son," he said quietly, "they may have been calling into darkness for six years. And to help them in their isolation—to learn what robbed their world of its magic, to prevent such a thing from coming to pass here, I would listen for six, or for sixty."

Not children of the blood, Jaldis had said . . . *children of the fire.* As he had been.

"I have sent for Shavus Ciarnin," the blind man went on, turning back to the table and picking up the bits of crystal, placing them one by one in a crude little painted clay pot he'd padded with bits of fleece. "We must have his help, his power, to find this world. We need his power to contact those wizards in that other universe, to tell them what they must know in order to guide us across . . ."

"*US?*" Rhion swung sharply from the window. "Wait a minute, I think that box of yours has developed a flaw, old friend. I thought I heard you say the word *us*."

"I can scarcely ask Shavus to undertake a journey I am not willing to make myself."

"The hell you can't," Rhion retorted. "That world has no magic. What's going to happen to that voice-box and those spectacles when you get there?"

"Nothing," the old man replied serenely. "The spells that imbue them and the talismans that give them power were wrought here and should hold their magic no matter what."

"You care to bet your life on that hypothesis?"

"I would," he said soberly, "if it would help."

"Look," Rhion said in subconscious imitation of his father at his most reasonable. "I'm willing to go with Shavus . . ." And he shivered as he said it. ". . . though I'm not thrilled about leaving you here alone and even less enthusiastic about traveling with the Archmage for any length of time. But I'm not going to let you go. Besides," he added more calmly, for his light, quirky voice had risen with his fears, "Shavus will need someone on this end to guide him back, if what you say is true."

"You have reason," the old man conceded. "And the less power there is there, the more there will be needed from here. But even so . . ."

From the kitchen downstairs came the swift, hard rapping of someone knocking at their door. Rhion flung open the jalousies and leaned out over the bleached gray thatch of the arcade. "COMING!" he bellowed.

We've got to stop living in slums and hovels, he thought, as he clambered down the rude pole ladder to the kitchen below. *I'm starting to lose all my manners*. His father, of course, had had a

slave—a Cotrian from the In Islands, for he did not believe north-
erners could be trained—whose sole job it was to sit in the little
alcove off the vestibule and answer the door, so there had been none
of this yelling out the windows business. He still remembered the
blue-and-white flowered tiles of the alcove's floor and the man's
matching blue tunic. *Now, if I put a wizard's mark on the door that
said, "I'm coming" in a low, polite voice* . . .

But Shavus and Jaldis had known wizards who had done things
of the kind. Aside from the difficulty of any long-distance spell of
speaking—and fifty feet *was* a long distance for such a spell—the
usual result was to fuel the fires of public uneasiness about wizards
in general and add to their reputation of uncanniness and danger.
Wizards who used their powers in such a fashion frequently found
themselves being shot with poisoned darts from ambush or having
their houses burned above their heads.

Of course, Rhion thought wryly, hurrying down the length of the
shadowy kitchen and glancing unconsciously up at the place in the
rafters where Tally had expected to see a stuffed crocodile, *wizards
who* don't *use their powers thus are just as likely to have the goon squads
after them, armed with weapons on which Spells of Silence have been
laid, so how much odds does it make?*

He opened the door, smiling as he recalled the obsequious grace
of old Minervum back home, who could make of the act a favor, a
privilege, or an insult at will . . .

A very grubby fourteen-year-old girl stood there, clad in shabby
silk obviously stolen from a much older and wealthier woman, combs
of steel and tortoiseshell gleaming at careless random in the dirty
snarl of her hair. In her arms she held a huge black book.

"My Mom says a customer brung this in," she said, with a jerk
of her head back toward the pawnshop a little further up the court.
"She says she can't sell the thing 'ceptin' for kindling paper, but you
witches might want to buy it. It's thirty dequins."

It was the *Book of Circles* that Jaldis had put a come-back spell
on, in the attic of the Black Pig.

9

"Rhion!" The sharp rattle of pebbles striking the jalousies startled him from sleep. The room was suffused with the moonstone pallor of very early morning, the window at the far end a blurred screen of silver-shot grisaille, the air tender. The voice had been human, a hissing attempt to combine a whisper with a shout, not the buzzing tones of Jaldis' box.

And indeed, all that was visible of Jaldis was a hunched twist of bone and white hair beneath the single sheet of the other cot, rising and falling with the slow, steady rhythm of sleep.

Rhion rolled hastily to his feet and, clutching his own bedsheet about him and fumbling his spectacles onto his face, hurried to the window. Outside, Shuttlefly Court was drowned in shadows still, though the sky overhead was the color of peaches, the hills beyond the roofs like something wrought of lavender glass.

Tally was down in the square, standing up in her mare's stirrups with trails of sugar-brown hair floating mermaidlike from under her cap.

"Could you really hit my window from down there?" Rhion asked softly, as—decently robed and scratching at his beard—he let her in downstairs a few moments later.

"Of course. Can't you?"

"I couldn't hit it from inside the room with the shutters closed. You shouldn't have brought your horse. You rarely see good horse-flesh in this part of the city. People will notice . . ."

"I left the charm you gave me tucked under the saddle blanket." She dropped into one of the rickety kitchen chairs and disengaged a small bag from the voluminous pocket of her green riding-habit. "I brought coffee."

"Dinar of Prinagos has just won my unqualified support against the perfidious White Bragenmeres under any circumstances, at any time, in thought, word, deed, spell, and incantation." Rhion tweaked open the bag and, holding it cradled in his hands, inhaled deeply and lovingly. Their small stock of coffee—copiously adulterated with dried acorns—was another of the things left behind in Felsplex. Beans like these they had not been able to afford since their days in Ner-riok, when they'd been patronized by nobles of the court.

"I also brought all the little doings," she added, getting up to fetch cups from the shelf while Rhion set the sack down and went to dip water into the kettle from the big—and now mostly empty—jar in the corner. "A grinder and a strainer and sugar and cinnamon . . ."

"Will you marry me?" The jest was out of his mouth before he could stop it, and she looked around swiftly, their eyes meeting, and for one flashing second it wasn't a jest.

"Forget I said that," he apologized quickly, which only made it worse. She looked away and he saw the color rise to the roots of her hair. He knew he should say something, make some other light remark to cover his own confusion and hers, but the air between them teemed with unsaid words, with possibilities unthinkable, like tinder which a spark would set ablaze.

The women he had loved had all been affairs of affection, begun in the knowledge that, as a wizard, he was legally a dead man with no position in the laws of any of the Forty Realms—unable to marry, unable to hold property, unable to enter business or trade or to sign a binding contract. And yet looking at this girl . . .

She took a deep breath after far too long, set down the cups on the table, and stammered, "Will . . . I suppose the talisman you gave me *will* keep people from noticing a full-grown horse?"

"I'm not sure," he said, gladly accepting the offer of a straight line. "It might keep them from noticing half of it but then the rest would be awfully conspicuous."

She giggled, her painful blush fading; to the relief of both, the moment passed in laughter.

"Where'd you learn to make coffee like this?" she asked a few minutes later, when he poured the inky, bittersweet liquid into the bottoms of the two red-and-black Sligo cups which were much too large for the tiny quantity to be consumed. "If wizardry ever quits paying, you really *will* be welcome in my father's service."

"What do you mean, if wizardry ever quits paying?" Rhion demanded in mock indignation. "For one thing, as you may have noticed, wizardry *doesn't* pay, and for another, making good coffee *is* wizardry. Why do you think I've been apprenticed to Jaldis for ten years? Because I like climbing over slippery roofs in the snow? No," he added, fishing in another lidded pot for yesterday's bread and putting it and the small jar of honey on the table between them. "It's just one of those things rich young men are supposed to learn, like dancing."

"I know." Tally gravely spooned enough honey onto her bread to satiate a regiment of bees. "My deportment master used to crack me over the elbow with his stick if I didn't curve my arm properly when I weighed out the sugar or added the cinnamon. My brother Syron has to put up with all that now." She held the spoon high above the bread for the sheer joy of watching that lucid amber curtain flow to its destiny. "Were you a rich young man?"

"Once upon a time." Rhion smiled, remembering the ruby doublet buttons which he'd cut off to buy the opals and gold for Jaldis' spectacles. Somewhere in the maze of courts, a rooster crowed. The mare nickered outside their door, the sound loud in the thin cool of morning. Other than that, the square was silent. Even Mistress Prymannie had not come out to unshutter her schoolroom. The rich smells of coffee and cinnamon mingled with the faintly prickly velvetiness of dust, the steamy whiff from the laundry in the next street, the odor of privies and stale cheap cooking, a strange, slubbed tapestry of fustian and silk.

"Well," Rhion went on more briskly, "did you just come to see me because your father's cook can't make a decent cup of coffee, or . . ."

"My father's cook makes a perfectly good cup of coffee and would demand that you be beheaded for treasonable utterances if he heard you say different. But," she went on, "I've figured out what to do about Damson. And she's agreed."

"I'll have to talk to her about that," he warned, and Tally nodded.

"You will." She set down her coffee, cradling the round smoothness of the cup in her hands. Something about her matter-of-factness—or perhaps the gesture of warming her hands in the steam of the cup—reminded Rhion strongly of his sister, and he felt a curious pang when he realized that he still thought of her as a girl of fifteen . . . *She must be married long ago, with children* . . .

"There's a disused pavilion at the end of the kitchen gardens of Father's palace," Tally was saying. "You can reach it through a postern in Halberd Alley. Damson will be there tonight, masked and hooded and the whole thing. I've told her you don't know who she is . . ."

"Thank God she didn't see us when we rescued her daughter."

She ducked her head shyly, then looked back at him again with her gray eyes bright. "I thought that, yes. The house is right on the palace wall. If you didn't know it was actually connected to the palace, you couldn't tell it by looking. It really could be anywhere. That should lay to rest her fears about being blackmailed or about word of it getting back to Esrex. I told her that I told you that she was a rich merchant's wife and I was her maid, so remember to treat us that way, all right?"

"Sure thing, lambchop," he leered in his slangiest street dialect, and she laughed and shoved him playfully. For all her usual gravity there was a sparkle of humor in her eyes, lurking like a wildflower in a bed of well-bred tuberoses, and he suspected she spent a good deal of her time, as he did, explaining *Joke . . . that was a joke* . . .

Regretfully, he gave her his hand. "I think you'd better be getting back. They really *will* be wondering where you are . . ."

"I told them I was going hawking in the marshes," she said, standing up and shaking out her long green skirt. "And I really am,

though it'll be awfully late by the time I get there. I told Marc—
Marc of Erralswan, the Captain of the Palace Guard, who's supposed
to be meeting me and my waiting lady Amalie there—that I had
some business to attend to in the kennels and that we'd be late.
Amalie will cover for me. She's getting the hawks and will tell them
at the mews . . ."

"You're full of tales today, aren't you?" he teased, as they passed
beneath the suspended thickets of drying herbs towards the door.
"First you're posing as your sister's maid, now you're playing cross
questions with your escort . . ."

"Well . . ." When she averted her face that way she looked like
a very dignified ten-year-old caught raiding the jam. "Didn't you do
that?"

She put her hand to her cap, a modest little thing his sister would
have called paltry. He'd seen the wealthy virgins of Bragenmere
sporting cap wings that would have lifted them out of the saddle if
they'd ridden at any speed, had some of the wearers not been a solid
half-hundredweight heavier than they should have been, that is. But
not Tally. She was too thin, if anything, with scarcely more breast
than a gawky boy. The light of the open door, strong now that the
sun was slanting down over the tiled roofs, cast a gauzy crescent
against her cheek and made the amber of her necklaces glow like
the honey that still dabbled the plates on the table behind them.

He smiled again. "All the time."

Catching his eye, Tally laughed again, brightness passing across
her face like spring sunlight in the Drowned Lands, breathtaking,
fragile, and swiftly dimmed. "I don't like to," she sighed. "There'd
be a hideous to-do if I was found out."

"To put it mildly, yes."

Across the square beyond her shoulder, boys and girls were arriving to school, loitering outside in their clumsy wool and serge clothing or chasing stray chickens in the weeds. Knowing from his own
schooldays how easily anything other than lessons will hold a child's
attention, Rhion drew about himself and the girl, and about the
mare standing with reins hitched to the cottonwood post, a thin,
numinous aura of Look-Over-There.

Tally's mouth, well-shaped without being either full or soft, tightened, the dimple beside it flexing again into a tired line. "It's just that . . . They want so much of you, you know?" Her gesture failed, half-made. "And I want . . ." She shook her head, scanning his face helplessly, not sure, in fact, what it was that she did want.

"To be alone?" The incessant grind of his father's demands seemed to echo along the corridors of his mind—learn this, help me with that, meet all the right men and be sure to be friends with their sons . . . And his mother's hands forever straightening the already-perfect set of his sleeves, her fussy disappointment in him pursuing him wherever he went.

"Sometimes." Her face softened again. "And sometimes . . ." She broke off once more, her eyes on his, and he understood, and she knew he understood. It had to do with music, some of it, and some of it with silence, but there was no clear word for what it was that she sought. His hand moved instinctively to touch hers, but he thought twice and closed his fist instead.

She turned quickly from him. "I'll come for you after dark."

And Rhion, reaching out with mind and magic, nudged the schoolmistress into a bustling fit of self-importance, so that she fussed the last of her pupils into the building and got them seated, distracting their minds from the sight of Tally mounting her mare and reining away across the court.

As Tally had promised, the pavilion near the kitchen gardens could have been any small house in the Upper City, with its modestly slanted roof of red tiles and its pale stucco bleached silver by the light of the bright spring stars. After the eternal mists of the Drowned Lands, the dry, hard brightness of the air in the Mountains of the Sun made everything seem slightly unreal, like a child's drawing; every weed stem growing along the alley walls and every pothole and broken brick in the road were distinct, even in this wan and shadowy light. The air was redolent with the flower and vegetable markets a few streets away, with the smells of the Duke's extensive stables, and with dust and garbage. Here at the back of the palace complex, the walls lacked the intricate ornamental brickwork, the tiled niches, and the marble statuary that characterized its front, and Rhion guessed as they climbed the tiled steps from the little pavilion's hall that the place had been built originally to house some married stablemaster or chief cook and his bride.

The light of the single candle in Tally's hand darted fitfully over painted rafters and bright frescoes on the walls and glinted on the spectacles hidden deep within the shadows of Jaldis' concealing hood. "Can we get ourselves seated before she comes into the room?" Rhion whispered. "That way, with luck, she won't see him standing up at all to know he's crippled."

Tally nodded. They were all cloaked and hooded like conspirators in a cheap street-corner melodrama—Jaldis had shifted his voice-box up onto his back, so that its smooth roundness, combined with a deliberately assumed crouch, gave the impression that he was hunchbacked; in place of his crutches he leaned on a long staff, and upon Rhion's arm.

"Good idea . . . Drat this mask—it won't stay tied . . ." She set her candle on a pine hall stand to tangle with the ties of her mask, and Rhion had to stop himself from reaching to help her. Under her cloak he saw she wore the plain, black frock and short petticoat of a serving-maid, her ankles slender as willow switches above sensible shoes. "There. The light's pretty low in there; I don't think there's much danger of her recognizing either of you, once you get your mask on."

She was right about that, anyway, Rhion thought when he and Jaldis entered the room. A single candle in a crude brass holder provided all the illumination—if such it could be called—available; the candle, moreover, placed not on the oak table in the center of the room but on a sideboard, where its feeble glow would leave everyone's faces in deepest shadow. "Why do they always have the lights so low they won't be recognized?" wondered Rhion aloud, helping Jaldis to his chair at one end of the table and moving the candle to the far end of the sideboard so that its light was almost directly behind him, leaving nothing visible of his face but a black shadow within his hood. "Don't they realize wizards can see in the dark?"

He took his own seat and removed his spectacles, putting on the scarlet mask he'd bought for three dequins with some of the money Tally had advanced them and pulling up his hood again. Carnival had been over a month ago—in the slop shops of the Lower Town masks were cheap this time of year. His back was to the candle, his face toward the door, which at this distance was only a muzzy line of shadow on the wall. *Good God*, he thought suddenly, *what do I do if I can't tell Tally and Damson apart at this distance . . . ?*

But the concern was set at rest a moment later, as the hall door opened and he saw two nebulous figures framed in the darkness. He'd momentarily forgotten: one form, lithe and freemoving and graceful, was a good seven inches taller than the other.

"Mistress . . ." Rhion deepened and hoarsened his voice as much as he could and half rose to his feet to bow. Jaldis, to nonmageborn eyes a black form almost invisible in the dark, merely inclined his head.

"My maid has told you what I want?" Damson groped around for the chair back in order to sit—as far as visibility went, her identity, Rhion thought, would be safe from *this* potential blackmailer, anyway. Without his spectacles, at a distance of three feet only the fact that the boiled leather mask covering her face was silvered let him know she was masked at all. He could make out the blurred shape of lips where a cut-out had been made for speech, but couldn't have taken oath whether they were long and squared, like Tally's, or round and pouty—only that they were darkened with a considerable quantity of rouge. A dark shawl the size of a bedsheet concealed her hair. She wore a cloak over her dress, and the only way he knew there was any kind of decoration on either covering was when an occasional sequin or gem would catch the candle's light and flash in the dark like a purple star.

"A philter, she said," Rhion replied. "To win the love of a man."

Damson leaned forward. Her scent was patchouli with a heavy dollop of ambergris and touches of lily and spikenard. Any wizard, trained as all were in the identification of herbs by scent, could have picked it out from among hundreds. That was another thing they never thought about. "These are his." From beneath the all-enveloping cloak she pushed a silken scarf containing a big knot of ivory-fair hair-combings, and a rolled-up linen shirt. The scarf itself was worked with a pattern of red pomegranates, the house badge of the Prinagos.

Nice disguise, Sis.

"I want him to be drawn to me, to love me . . ."

"You understand," Rhion said, "that such a philter will only work for a short time? And that afterward, because of being drawn to your bed, he may be angry with you? May even hate you?"

"No." The plump woman shook her head so that the amethysts flashed in the silk of her shawl. "He thinks he hated me before, but I made him love me. He's only a boy—I know what his needs are, better than those callow hussies . . . Better than he does himself. He needs *me*, though his pride won't let him admit it . . . And in any case, what he thinks doesn't matter. If I can bear his son, he'll not be able to have me put aside."

Tally's head turned sharply; Rhion heard the catch of her breath. "Did he say that?"

"Of course he did," Damson snapped, not looking back over her shoulder at her sister, keeping her eyes on the two wizards before her like a duellist watching circling foes. "Why do you think I agreed to this in the first place? I can't let him go—*I won't let him go!* He's mine. I'll be whatever he wants me to be—he'll see that, once I've got him back."

"If this is true," Rhion explained patiently, "it won't be because of the philter. If what you say is true, he may very well go on loving you afterward—or he may not. A spell such as the one I'll weave for you has only a limited, and a very specific, action, namely, a surge of unreasoning desire for you so powerful it would take an extremely strong-willed man to resist. But it cannot affect what he will feel about this desire, or about you, once its effect has passed."

"But it *will* bring him to my bed?"

Rhion sighed. He sometimes wondered why he bothered with the warning—they almost never listened. Inevitably they brushed it aside with, *But it WILL work, won't it?*

"Unless he's a very strong-willed man, or unless he has some kind of counterspell from a stronger wizard than I . . . Yes."

"That is enough, then." She sat back a little and there was a self-satisfied note in her crisp, high-pitched voice. "It's all that matters. I'll make him need me, once I'm past his silly pride—once he sees that he *does* need me. It's only his pride that makes him spiteful, anyway."

Rhion was silent. Loving and hating were so close, two sides of a coin whose name was Need. He wondered if Esrex' hate and cruelty had been weapons of defense rather than offense, a final bastion to protect himself, not only against the demands of the daughter of his enemy, but against his own lust for one whose family had already taken away from him all that he had. In that case the breaking of this last bastion of his personal integrity wasn't likely to make him any more pleasant . . .

But he didn't know and he couldn't know. And, as Jaldis had said, it was none of his business to judge.

For a moment he smelled sawdust and stale beer and looked again into cowlike brown eyes above a sequinned veil; and behind the woman at the Black Pig he saw clustered like a spectral regiment all those other encounters in darkened kitchens and inn parlors and the faces of every other man or woman who'd ever asked him to use his powers to get them between somebody else's sheets.

It all had so little to do with magic, with what magic actually was.

And Tally had asked for his help.

He held out his hand for hers. "As you wish, my lady."

"One other thing . . ." Her hand held back from his, as if fearing to touch. It was a very round, delicate little hand, all four stubby fingers and the thumb tightly ringed in elaborate confections of opal, ruby, and pearl whose design could have been recognized like a signature. "Another tincture, or powder, or spell that will guarantee that I conceive and bear a son."

In for a lamb, in for a sheep . . . Somebody might as well get some good out of this . . .

Again, Rhion inclined his head.

Of the two spells, the love-philter was by far the easiest. Rhion heaped the standard base-powder on Damson's scented hand, then feathered it onto the shirt which had been laid down like a table-cloth for him to work on, and around them wove the circles of power and need. The Gray Lady had taught him many variant spells of this kind, different mixes of ingredients, and he'd calculated which to use tonight to take into account the phase of the moon—which was four days past the third quarter—and the position of the rising stars. Having observed Damson in the crystal he knew what she looked like and was able to weave into the spells a specific hunger for that plump white body and no other, a thirst unquenchable save by the scent of her mouse-brown hair. Esrex was young, Tally had said, barely twenty—impecunious, unpleasant, bitter, and proud, but male and young. With them, he wove spells of luck and hope and the image of Damson in her husband Esrex' arms.

Jaldis, in silence save for a little cracked humming in his broken throat, wove the stronger geas, the more difficult one, a spell of conception, and, more importantly, to prevent miscarriage, accident, or the spontaneous shedding of the child in the first few fragile weeks. They had guessed that Damson would request such a tincture and had come prepared for it, remembering that she had miscarried at least one child already. With luck, the Duke's elder daughter would be able to keep her husband returning to her bed for several weeks. Unless the young man himself had become sterile, that should suffice.

And during the whole proceedings, Damson sat with her plump hands folded, the steel grip of her will almost palpable in the leaden gloom. She would have that young man, bring him to heel from his spiteful strayings! Now and then the jewels on her fingers would flash as they tightened, her protuberant gray eyes would shift behind the eyeholes of the silver mask. She was wondering, Rhion supposed, whether either of the wizards she'd hired would guess who she really was.

Only after Damson had gone, leaving behind her a fat pouch of coin, and Tally was leading them down the stairs to the postern gate once more, did Rhion relax, pulling the mask off and shaking the sweat out of his tousled brown curls, and putting his spectacles back on.

"That was well done," Jaldis murmured softly, his arthritic grip tight upon Rhion's sleeve. The night had turned cold, as spring nights did in these dry highlands; the smells of lotus and jasmine from the Duke's vast water gardens breathed through the window lattices, like subtle colors in the creamy dark. "As good a love-spell as any I ever cast."

"Great." Rhion sighed, and flexed the crick from his chubby fingers. "Just the reputation I always sought. The pimp's delight, provided my clients' husbands don't kill me." The memory of all those other love-spells, the sour sense of having prostituted himself, still clung like the redolent musk of Damson's perfume. "Why do they call them love-spells, anyway?" he added bitterly. "It isn't love, you know."

"Maybe because some people can't tell the difference." Tally slid back the postern bolts, and stood her candle in the near-by niche of the little gate god to open the door. "Or if they suspect there's a difference, they don't want to know."

In the candle's reflected light her gray eyes were troubled and sad. Without his spectacles, he wouldn't have been able to see her face during the conjuration, even had she not been masked; now he saw that she had been thinking about what she'd been watching. She'd gotten what she'd gone after—all of her life, he guessed, she had been Damson's champion: riding into the woods to save her child; seeking out what means she could to alleviate her heartbreak at Esrex' cruelty; and submerging her own thoughts in the necessity of fixing her sister's life. Clearly the steely self-will of Damson's words had troubled her deeply.

In her face, as she looked mutely at him in the shadows of the gateway, were questions deeper than could be asked here on the threshold of departure, the questions of a girl who has begun to realize that love was not what she thought it was, and magic was not what she thought it was . . . perhaps nothing was what she thought it was.

"Or maybe," she added, nearly inaudibly, "they think it really *is* love. Rhion . . ." There was sudden pleading in her voice for reassurance, for forgiveness, and for help against a revelation she would rather not have seen.

He couldn't answer. More than anything in the world he wanted to go somewhere quiet with her, talk to her, and share with her what he had seen of the muddled affairs of the human heart—and to have her reassurance against his own bitter confusion of mind. To get to know her.

But it was out of the question.

Their eyes held. The silence rang palpable as a tapped chime.

Then, aware that it was madness—cruelty to her and stupidity of the most suicidal kind to him—he left Jaldis leaning upon his staff, and gently taking Tally's hands, brushed her lips with his.

Her fingers crushed desperately over his, trembling and urgent, and for an instant he felt not only her body, but her spirit sway toward his, like a young almond tree in the wind's embrace. In the limpid glow of the candle, he saw tears silver her eyes; in the eyes themselves, dilate with the night, he saw the reflection of his own desire, his own knowledge that this should never be.

It should end here, he thought, with what little sanity was left to him. *In all propriety—in all sanity—we should never meet again.*

But he knew even then that they would.

Turning quickly she fled from him, brushing past Jaldis and vanishing up the stairs in a swirl of black fustian and a shuddering smoke-stream of tawny unhooded hair.

Quietly Rhion closed the postern gate behind them and used his spells to shoot the bolt on the palace side. Taking Jaldis' arm, he led the way back down the alley, making once more for their rooms in the Old Town.

If he had still been the only son of the banking house of Drethet, he thought, guiding Jaldis carefully along the wall where the pavement was unbroken and the footing better, he could have said, *Can I meet you one day in the marshes to go hawking?* He could have put on a mask of red leather and pheasant feathers and ridden in his sedan chair up to the palace on carnival night, to dance with her at least. He guessed she was a good dancer, as he himself had been once upon a time. He could have heard her voice, if nothing else; touched her hand . . . Gone to the market to buy the finest porcelain flute purchasable, or a scatterbrained red hunter pup that would please her . . .

Academically he had known when he made the decision to become Jaldis' pupil what he was giving up. His family—the love he bore for his sister and his friends—all rights under law, among them the right to marry and by implication the right to fall in love with honest women, let alone the daughters of Dukes. And his blood, the blood of a wizard born, did not question the decision.

After a long time Jaldis' sweet, thready voice, still muffled by the cloak, broke the silence. "There is enough silver in the bag she gave us," it said quietly, "to allow you to get drunk, you know."

Rhion sighed. He had never spoken to Jaldis about Tallisett, but it did not surprise him that the old man had guessed. "I'd only have to sober up again," he said resignedly. "I might as well stay . . ."

From somewhere off to their right—an alley, a doorway, a window, a balcony—came the vicious slap of a crossbow firing. Something sliced at the back of Rhion's neck, not even hurting in that first shocked second. In his grip Jaldis' body jarred and sagged, and turning his head Rhion saw, with a kind of numbed immobility of thought, a small arrow standing in his master's shoulder, blood welling forth stickily and copiously under the cloak.

Without thinking he ducked, dragging them both back as a second bolt slammed into the marbly stucco of the palace wall which had showed up their forms so clearly in the dark. Metal glinted in the shadows of a second-storey porch across the alley. In darkness that would have hidden them from other eyes, he saw a man and a woman, street-warriors, thugs by their dress, dodge back out of sight, crossbows and arrows in their hands. At the same moment half a dozen ruffians burst from the doorway beneath the balcony's shadow.

"Ambush!" Rhion yelled, and flung the first illusion he could call to mind—that hackneyed old stand-by, an exploding ball of fire—at their pursuers, and, flinging one arm bodily around Jaldis, staff and all, took to his heels.

He knew the arrow was poisoned. *Pheelas*-root would temporarily rob or weaken a wizard's power while leaving the rest of his mind clear, but it was expensive and hard to get. Most assassins contented themselves with cheaper alternatives, either a heavy soporific like toadwort or poppy or an outright, fast-acting poison like datura. If the poison didn't kill the wizard quickly, at least most of his concentration—if he were still conscious at all—would go into counteracting the deadly effects, leaving the assassins free to continue the assault with swords, ax-handles, chains, or whatever other hardware came to hand.

All this flashed through Rhion's mind in seconds as he half-dragged, half-carried Jaldis toward the refuge of the nearest alley. *I can't let them corner me . . .*

He collected his mind enough to fling behind him a spell of faulty aim and another one, a second later, of mechanical failure, though he was fairly certain the crossbows had been counterspelled . . . a suspicion which was confirmed by the bolt that splintered against the corner of the alley wall as he ducked around it.

Jaldis stumbled and slumped, and Rhion felt the last consciousness go out of the old man. He thrust him behind him into the shadows of a porch and caught up his staff, turning in time to strike aside the jab of the nearest sword. His father had never believed in weaponry training for the sons of the merchant class, and Rhion had been far too lazy, and far too much of a dandy, to oppose him in this opinion. It was Shavus the Archmage who, during his first year with Jaldis, had beaten into him the rudiments of self-defense. He swept the sword-thrust aside and reversed the staff to jab and sweep at the man coming at him from the other direction, straddling Jaldis' fallen body and trying frantically to call to mind some spell—any spell— to help him.

But it takes a trained warrior to fight unthinkingly. Backed almost to the wall, slashing with his stick at the five swords which surrounded him in a hedge of steel, Rhion could call few options to mind. A wall of fire in the circumstances wouldn't work—they were too close—and with Jaldis down an explosion of white light would not buy him enough time to get the old man on his feet and drag him away.

Desperately, he flung a spell of pain at them, the tearing and spasming of the organs of their bodies, but it took a powerful mage to do real damage in a short time. One of the men swore sharply, and he saw blood begin to trickle from the woman assassin's mouth, but her eyes hardened to an iron fury and she redoubled her attack. He'd now put them in a position of having to kill him to end the pain—and they knew it.

The Magic of Ill sapped his concentration, too. A swordblade, slicing through the longer guard of the staff, cut his arm before he could catch its wielder on the side of the head; he had to whirl to block on the other side, ducking and weaving and hoping none of them had a projectile. If he didn't have to carry Jaldis, he might just be able to escape, he thought . . . if he wasn't defending a corpse already . . .

One of the men stepped back from the fray and unshipped a weighted chain from his belt. It lashed out at Rhion like the tongue of a hellish frog, and he was only barely able to avoid having his weapon pulled from his hand. As he turned to block another sword cut, the chain snaked out like an iron whip and crashed across his ankles, dropping him to his knees. He struck back hopelessly, knowing he was finished . . .

And the assassin lunging down at him cried out suddenly and turned, cutting at the two men who had appeared, seemingly out of nowhere, in the alley behind them.

The newcomers were both big men and clearly trained to arms. The shorter of the two, a black-and-red ribbonwork doublet bulging over shoulders like a bull, drove his blade through the woman assassin's chest and shoved her aside like a straw training dummy; the other man, wearing a soldier's short crimson tunic, pulled off one of the two men bearing down on Rhion, and Rhion struck upward at the remaining one, catching him in the solar plexus with the end of his staff and sending him crashing against the wall. In the dark of the alley there was a momentary confusion of struggling shapes. Then the assailants collected their wounded and fled, vanishing around the corner or swarming over the nearest wall, leaving behind only a few splashes of blood in the dirt, vegetable parings, and mucky straw of the porch.

Rhion, still crouched gasping over Jaldis' body, realized dimly that blood was streaming from a cut on his own arm, hot against the cold of suddenly opened flesh. The back of his neck burned where the arrow barbs had slit it, and he felt sick and faint. The man in the ribbonwork doublet came swiftly to him, calling back over his shoulder "Don't bother, Marc!" to his companion, who had started to go in pursuit.

Rhion pulled his arm away from his savior's investigating hand,

and shook his head. "Jaldis . . ." he managed to say, turning his master over and feeling at the lined, slack face.

Jaldis still lived. Rhion felt quickly at the veins in his throat to make double sure, then fumbled at the arrow still in the old man's shoulder. Waves of faintness were sweeping him, his vision narrowing to a tunnel of gray at the end of which stood the arrow, like a signpost on some strange dream path rising out of the little mound of blood-soaked brown wool.

"Poison . . ."

"Easy," the big-shouldered man said, kneeling at his side.

Again Rhion shook off his help, forcing his racing heart to slow with an effort of will, collecting a spell of healing around himself. His hands were shaking as he pulled his knife from his belt and slashed Jaldis' cloak and robe to reveal the blue-veined white flesh, smeared with the dark welling of blood. Marc, the soldier, had come back, much the younger of their two rescuers, tall, handsome, and good-natured, if rather stupid-looking. He wore the crimson cloak, tunic, and gilded leather cuirass of the Duke of Bragenmere's guards, and Rhion remembered where he'd seen him before: in the crystal last winter, hunting with Tally on the Imber hills. *Marc*, Tally had said. *Marc of Erralswan.* He was carrying a small bronze lantern, and its light splashed over the porch behind them. Rhion realized for the first time that it was—by the straw and oat-grains everywhere on the pavement—the rear porch of the Duke's stables.

The older man was helping him pull aside Jaldis' gore-soaked robes. He paused at the sight of the rosewood soundbox with its tangle of talismans glittering in the lantern-glow and looked across at Rhion with surprise in his handsome, fleshy face. "You are wizards," he said.

Rhion nodded, and raised a shaky hand to straighten his spectacles. "But don't worry," he dead-panned. "Even wizards don't turn around and put curses on people who've saved their lives."

"Don't they?" The man's teeth were very white against his healthy tan when he grinned; his black hair, carefully curled and smelling of expensive pomade in spite of the sweat that dripped from its ends, still retained a milk-white narcissus or two from an aftersupper crown. "Aren't they like other men after all, then? Marc, call a couple of the guards and get these two inside. Call Ranley, too . . . my personal physician," he explained, as Marc, leaving the lantern, disappeared through a postern into the stables themselves.

He held out a warm, strong hand to Rhion, thick with jeweled rings. "I am Dinar Prinagos, Duke of Mere."

10

In his subsequent account of the ambush Rhion omitted mentioning to the Duke just what he and his master had been doing in Halberd Alley at that time of night. He said only that they had been returning from an errand in the Upper Town, and the Duke, a man of great courtesy, did not ask further. Rhion wasn't sure how much either Tally or her sister had confided in their father; but, remembering his dealings with his own father, he guessed it hadn't been much.

While the Duke listened gravely, his face crossed by the swift, purposeful shadows in the guest room's mellow lamplight, his physician—a perfectly orthodox, black-robed little representative of Alucca, God of Healing—removed the arrowhead from Jaldis' shoulder, and an assistant bound up Rhion's slashed arm.

"And you have no idea who might have wanted to slay you?" If he did not, Rhion reflected, use the word "murder"—since technically it was not murder to kill a wizard—at least the word he did use was one that applied equally to man as well as beast.

Rhion shook his head. On the guest room's narrow bed Jaldis was slowly returning to consciousness, white hair spread out over the pillow and voice-box lying under one frail hand. Though too weak to use it, he had refused to be parted from it. For years he had lived in fear of losing either it or his spectacles, mostly, Rhion suspected, because he doubted he had enough strength to create replacements. Under the bandages, his naked flesh looked almost transparent, sunk against knobby bones like damp silk draped across a pile of sticks. Though the tall windows were open upon a small garden court, the room, airy and small, smelled of herbed steams and of the medicines the physician had given to counteract the effects of the foxglove he had smelled on the arrowhead, odors which did not quite mask the smell of blood.

"Marc," the Duke said, half-turning in his chair of silvered poplarwood. The young Captain stepped over from the door where he'd stood. "Send some of your men out to the houses of Lorbiek the Blood-Mage, and Malnuthe the Black—that Ebiatic who lives in the Shambles—and May the Bone-Thrower down in the Kairnside shanties, and let them know what happened. It's frequently the case," he added to Rhion, as the young soldier departed on his errand in a dramatic swirl of crimson cloak, "that when people take it into their heads to murder wizards, they attack several at roughly the same time, wanting to make a sweep of it, you know. It's happened before, I'm sorry to say."

Rhion nodded. In their first month in Felsplex they'd gotten a warning from another Morkensik wizard in the town that a mob was out to *fruge* wizards, but nothing had come of it. As far as he knew the woman who'd given them the warning hadn't contacted either the local Hand-Pricker or the Earth-witch who operated in the same quarter.

"Believe me," the Duke went on, "I'm truly sorry such a thing came to pass in my realm. I believe—I've always believed—that, as long as they use their powers for good and as long as they don't interfere with other men's affairs, wizards have every right to live and study free of interference."

Rhion scratched at a corner of his beard. "I'd be lying if I said I didn't agree with you."

The Duke's eyes twinkled appreciatively. "You may have heard that I'm a scholar," he said. "Or a dilettante, at any rate, who'd like to be a scholar and who can now afford to surround himself with scholars . . ."

"No," Rhion said quietly. "No—'scholar,' unqualified, was the word I heard used, actually."

And to his surprise the Duke blushed with pleasure. "Well, whether it's true or not it's good of you to say so." He wore a dandy's elaborately ribboned doublet and a broad necklace of gold-work and rubies that must have cost the price of a small house, but his weapons—dagger and short sword—were by a smith whose name and price Rhion recognized at a glance, a man whose fame stemmed not from ornamentation.

"In any case," the Duke went on, "I know enough to know that learning, and the structure of the universe, rather than spells and cantrips, is the true study of wizards, and I also know that a man would be a fool to pass up the chance to taste a little of that knowledge. If any person threatens you again, or you have cause to believe yourself in danger—or if you learn who is responsible for the attack upon you tonight—let me know, and believe me, I will do for you all that I can."

Rhion nodded again. He had his own suspicions about who had been responsible for the attack, but it would hardly do to suggest to the man who had just saved their lives that his own daughter had hired assassins in order to prevent blackmail about a love-philter to get her errant husband to sleep with her—particularly if the father was the one who'd selected the husband in the first place. And besides, as he had told Tallisett, like physicians, the Morkensiks were sworn to secrecy by their vows.

So Rhion contented himself with their being carried home in a couple of sedan chairs by the Duke's slaves, escorted by Marc of Erralswan and a handful of guards.

By the time they got to Shuttlefly Court, it was close to dawn. Most of the prostitutes who hung around the Baths of Mhorvianne on Thimble Street had gone, and the mazes of little courts that made up the Old Town were silent and dark. Rhion followed Marc and the two guards who supported Jaldis up the rough ladder to the upper floor and made sure the old man was comfortable in his bed. He had amplified the physician's tinctures with spells of healing, though he could tell the man's remedies to strengthen the heart and cleanse the blood were sound. Jaldis already seemed better, though far too ill to speak.

He himself was shaking with fatigue and the chilled aftermath of shock as he descended once more to the stuffy darkness of the kitchen to see his escort to the door. His arm hurt damnably, and the remains of the poultice they'd put on the back of his neck where the arrow barbs had cut stung as if they'd laid a burning iron in the flesh. As the bearer slaves—eight big, strapping men with the brown complexions of southerners—were picking up the litter poles to go and the guards were exchanging a few final remarks with one of Rhion's fair neighbors who happened to be coming home from work at that hour, Marc of Erralswan paused in the patchy, dust-smelling darkness of the arcade and, leaning down to Rhion, whispered, "The Duke mentioned love-spells . . . Do you deal in them? There's a girl at Court, one of the Duchess' waiting maids . . . I realize you're probably tired now, but if I came back tomorrow evening do you think you could . . . ?"

After bidding him a polite good-night Rhion laughed, with genuine amusement only slightly tinged by exhausted hysteria, all the way back up the stairs.

The Duke was as good as his word. A messenger arrived the following day, his stiff politeness speaking volumes for his personal opinion of those his master chose to patronize, inquiring after Jaldis' health and asking him to dinner at the palace the following week, so that the Duke might better apologize for the ignorance of his subjects. "And might demonstrate his protection, to anyone who is interested, while he's about it," Jaldis mused, who was well enough to sit up in bed, his shoulder bandaged and a sheet over his knees.

"Well," Rhion commented, perched tailor-fashion on the other bed with the remains of his master's breakfast tray, "he also sent this." He bounced in his hand the small leather sack which had accompanied the message. It jingled with the comfortable sweetness characteristic of the nobler metals. "So you can afford to get yourself a new robe. I wonder why we didn't think of hiring assassins to beat us up before?"

"Possibly," his master returned disapprovingly, "because in most cities, passing strangers, once they knew who and what we were, would have been likelier to participate in the fray on the side of the assassins."

The dinner was an intimate one, the company comprised of the Duke, his pale, fair-haired Duchess and one of her ladies, Ranley the physician who, like his master, was genuinely interested in the metaphysical underpinnings of the visible world, Tallisett, and Syron, the Duke's thirteen-year-old son and heir. "You must excuse the absence of my older daughter and her husband," his Grace said, seating Jaldis on the spindle-legged chair at his side and himself placing the supper crown of red anemones on his brow. "Her husband, my nephew Lord Esrex, is indisposed tonight, and she has remained with him in his rooms to bear him company."

"And on the whole," Tally murmured as she passed behind Rhion on her way to her own seat beside her brother, "that's probably just as well."

Musicians played through supper, preceding each course with a trilling fanfare; afterward the talk went late. The Duchess, who despite her gracious efforts to seem interested had begun to wear the frozen-faced expression that comes of stifling yawns before the fish course was finished, departed with her lady and her son as soon as the slaves had carried out the finger bowls on the heels of the last sorbets. "My poor darling." The Duke smiled, when the crimson door curtains had fallen softly shut after them and the pad of their slippered feet had faded on the white honeycomb of the hallway tiles. "She is an educated woman and not at all prejudiced, but her tastes run very much to poetry and political philosophy, not to the mathematics of planetary movement or variations in the forms of snails and fish. And Syron, of course, isn't interested in anything he can't either ride or make come after him with a sword. I suppose at his age it's natural; all I can do is try to teach him, if not my interest in, at least my tolerance for powers and abilities he can not himself possess."

"Oh, I don't know," Rhion said. He'd had a long discussion with the boy on the subject of the general irksomeness of dancing lessons, and Syron had expressed undisguised astonishment that a wizard's apprentice had ever been subjected to anything so mundane. "He did ask me if it were possible to lay spells on a dog to drive away fleas, so it shows he's thinking."

"Is it?" Tally asked curiously. "Possible, I mean. Because my dogs suffer something cruel in the summer."

"Of course," Rhion said, "The problem is that for the spell to last more than a few days, you have to shave the dog and write the runes on its skin, and even then they don't work for more than a couple of weeks."

"Oh, the poor things!" Tally laughed, evidently picturing her own red and gold bird-hunters naked and crisscrossed with magical signs.

"Why is that?" the Duke inquired, leaning forward as a slave entered with brazier, grinder, and pot, and the room was slowly filled with the languorous scent of coffee. "I mean, how does a spell like that work and why can't it be made to work indefinitely?"

And while the Duke himself poured out the aromatic liquid into tiny cups, and Jaldis explained the problems inherent in causing fleas to believe that a certain dog was actually made of copper, Rhion's eyes met Tally's across the table in an unspoken comment on the Duke's cook's coffee, and they both had to look aside to keep from giggling.

After that, Jaldis was asked to dine at the palace fairly frequently— as often, Rhion guessed, as the Duke was not required to entertain nobles who might have objected to the presence of wizards at his board or members of the various priesthoods who most certainly would have done so. A nobleman who was seen too often in the presence of mages frequently came under suspicion of using the wizards' powers to oppress his subjects or spy upon his neighbors, just as a businessman was usually suspected of using wizardry to ruin his rivals, or a shopkeeper, to cheat his customers. And the Duke, tolerant man that he was, was still a usurper, a man who had overthrown his liege lord, no matter how many years ago it had been and how badly that liege had misgoverned. He had to be careful what people said.

But in private, he did not conceal his interest in Jaldis' company, and what had started as an intellectual patronage blossomed into genuine friendship as the summer advanced. Hardly a week went by that a messenger did not arrive at Shuttlefly Court with a gift: food from the Duke's table, game birds, fatted beef, or the sweet-fleshed orange fruits of the south; coffee; sometimes lamb and rabbit skins beautifully cured for the making of talismans, or small gifts of silver and gold.

In gratitude for this, on the last night of April, the night of Summerfire, Jaldis did what he had not done since he'd been court mage to the ill-fated Lord Henak in Wemmering—he agreed to use his magic to enliven the Duke's Summerfire masking.

To Rhion's surprise and delight, Jaldis abruptly taught him a whole new series of spells of whose very existence he had previously been ignorant, and together the two of them spent three days manufacturing and ensorcelling a powder of nitre, crushed herbs, pulverized bone, and silver, which the servants of the Duke then dusted over every tree and shrub in the palace's garden.

"What'll it do?" Tally asked, pacing at Rhion's side down the graveled path that skirted one of the garden's canals.

Rhion laughed. Morning sunlight filtered warm on their faces through the overhanging lime trees; the small lawns that lay between copses of willow and myrtle and jacaranda glittered with quick-burning dew. Tally had offered to guide him through the maze of pools to the small grotto that marked the garden's farthest corner, and on all sides they were surrounded by the bustle of the upcoming fête. Slaves were stringing garlands around the cornices of the little gazebos and shrines, pulling the ubiquitous, spiky leaves of dandelions from the miniature lawns, plucking pondweed from among the miles of waterlilies and setting up tables for buffets or platforms for musicians. Others—with a disgruntled air and suspicious care—were dusting the faintly musty-smelling powder over rosebush, laurel, and linden tree that made up the intricate knots of foliage at the crossings of the shaded paths.

"Theoretically," he said, "it'll glow. It's one of those silly, useless spells that someone came up with and handed down, something only a court wizard out to delight the heart of his patron would think up in the first place. I'll show you . . ."

Tally led the way down a twisting path that turned from the ponds, leading through a myrtle grove and around the side of an artificial hill crowned with gum trees. A tiny pavilion had been built out of one of the hill's sides, its domed roof half-covered with mounded earth which supported full-grown trees and dangling curtains of flowering vine. Doves fluttered, cooing, from beneath the eaves as they entered, and far in the back, where the marble walls gave way to rock, cool even in the summer heat, a fountain whispered its secrets to the dark.

On a bench of green porphyry and bronze that stood near the fountain's rim Rhion set down the satchel he'd been carrying, and took from it the things he'd prepared the night before: long slips of beaten silver inscribed with traced runes; three milky lumps of rose quartz the size of his thumb; candles; chalk; and half a dozen tubes of glass in which, capped with red wax, tiny rolls of parchment and leather could be seen.

"This," he said, "is a talismanic resonator—or it will be, when I've got it assembled." He knelt beside the bench, and Tally sat on the fountain's rim, pulling off her big straw gardening hat and letting her hair hang down in a big sloppy fawn-colored braid, like a child's.

"After the feast," Rhion went on, "your father's going to announce the masking. Everyone goes outside, to find the terrace dark. The maskers are assembled just below the terrace steps, and under the terrace itself, in that huge room where they keep the orange trees during the winter, is Jaldis, weaving a spell—and it's not a very complicated one—that will make this particular combination of bone and silver glow in the dark."

His hands worked while he spoke, quickly weaving the thin strapwork of ensorcelled metal into the proper patterns around the quartz. He paused, taking off his spectacles to concentrate, his mind summoning the runes, the constellations of power his master had taught him; Tally was silent, observing with grave interest. For a time there was no sound but the gentle plashing of the fountain; even the stirring in the main gardens was left far behind.

At length Rhion went on. "The trumpeters strike up a fanfare, which I'll be able to hear even this far from the terrace. Jaldis speaks the word of power, I set the talismanic resonator into life, the resonator creates a field from the original spell, and in that field the stuff will glow all night. And everyone goes home saying how clever your father is."

Tally leaned across to pick up and examine one of the glass tubes, turning the little talisman over in her long fingers. "Why the resonator? I mean, couldn't Jaldis just put a spell on the powder?"

"He could, but it wouldn't cover anywhere near all the garden, and it probably wouldn't last all night. A talismanic resonator expands the area covered by a specific spell, and can be used to lengthen its effects as well, provided it's got talismans of power to keep it going . . . these things." He took the crystal tube from her hand, and with his other fingers gestured to the other talismans—not only tubes of glass and crystal, but little round discs of bone bound in gold, or slips of carved ashwood inscribed with sigils of power.

"Resonators," Rhion continued, "draw one *hell* of a lot of power to keep up a field, even for a piddling little spell like this one." He sketched a small circle of power in silvered chalk on the flat top of the bench, closing in the strange little tangle of silver and stone. "That's why it isn't practical politics, for instance, to keep a building illuminated all night—or even a ball of witchlight burning all night—with one."

"Oh," Tally said, disappointed. "Pooh. And I thought I'd just devised a new source of illumination . . ."

"It's been tried. Also, with some spells—and light's one of them—you get pockets in the field. In a house, for instance, illuminated with a ball of witchlight and a resonator, you might get places where someone would get lost, for no reason at all, on the kitchen stairway or on the way down the hall; or places where everyone would get furiously angry at nothing; or drop and break everything they touched. Or the pocket might draw every ant in the city to it . . . or every streetwalker. You never know." He set the talismans around the initial circle of power, and was silent for a time, weaving the spirals of power to include them in the greater spell.

"Why is that?" Tally asked, when he straightened up again.

He readjusted his spectacles. "No one really knows. My guess— and Jaldis' theory—is that it's because of the impurities in the materials. A wizard's always at the mercy of the materials he has to work with. The resonator magnifies even the smallest flaws of a crystal, or the slightest traces of copper or lead in silver. Which is the reason wizards have to work with as pure materials as possible . . ."

"Is that the story, then?" a thin, rather cold voice queried from the grotto's vine-curtained entrance. Looking up, Rhion saw the slim gray shape of Lord Esrex framed against the silken light.

He had met the youthful scion of the White Bragenmeres two or three times since the first dinner with the Duke, a slender young man not much taller than himself and perhaps six years younger, always exquisitely garbed in the height of fashion, with the coldest gray eyes he had ever seen.

Rhion's feelings about him had been mixed; knowing how wretched Esrex had made Tally over the previous winter, he had been inclined to dislike him, but sensed in him also the conflict of pride and his desire for his enemy's daughter. Mingled with this had been a kind of guilt at having been instrumental in breaking that pride—probably all that Esrex had left.

The sympathy hadn't survived their initial encounter. Esrex, coldly handsome in spite of a hairline already promising to betray him, had shown to Rhion and to Jaldis nothing but an impersonal and cutting contempt, and Rhion had observed that he treated the palace slaves—and such lesser members of the court whose lineages were not equal to his—in the same fashion. Rhion had been a little curious, up to that time, about Esrex' allegiance to the egalitarian cult of Agon, but guessed that it, too, was merely a tool.

Esrex stood now with his arm possessively around the waist of the plump little Lady Damson, whose unwontedly loose-fitting gown and smug, secret sparkle told their own tale. She said nothing, only eyed Rhion warily from the pillared porch. Rhion wondered whether it was because she guessed that he might have been the wizard who had woven the love-philter—if the assassins hadn't lied and said they'd accomplished their task—or because she was afraid, if she got too close to a mage, she'd miscarry. His beard might be recognizable—his voice almost certainly would be, if she were at all observant.

In any case her bulging eyes followed her young husband apprehensively as he descended the shallow rock-cut steps into the grotto, stepping daintily in his embroidered satin slippers with their ridiculously long, curled toes.

He stopped before the bench, and stood looking down at the resonator in contempt. "Pure silver," he commented.

"I'd appreciate it if you didn't touch it," Rhion said politely, standing up and regarding the young dandy with a wary eye. "Once the spells are in place, if the circles are crossed or broken the whole thing has to be done again."

"Is that so?"

Rhion could have bitten out his tongue with annoyance the next moment, because Esrex tucked the bouquet he carried into his belt, and, his eyes holding Rhion's in deliberate challenge, slowly removed his glove, wet his forefinger with his neat little pink tongue, and drew a line exactly bisecting the circle of power and two of the talismanic spirals, all with a slow relish of one who knows he may commit outrage with impunity because he is who he is.

"It would be a shame if Uncle's fête were a failure."

"I'm sure your aunt would think so," Rhion replied steadily, holding back the desire to slap that lipless little mouth.

Tally, who had no worries about ending up *fruged* in an alley, pushed her brother-in-law aside angrily. "Esrex, what a pill you are," she said scornfully, and he turned and regarded her like an adult contemplating the fury of a child—not an easy matter considering she topped him by an inch.

"My dear cousin," he said, holding his smudged finger to the soft harlequin sunlight that came through the vines. "Are you still so naive that you haven't guessed the real reason wizards insist on pure materials? And always, you notice, silver and gold? How much silver did your father hand that blind old mendicant—if he *is* really blind— to sprinkle into his trees? He says that was what it was for, at least."

Tally opened her mouth in angry denial, but Rhion only folded his arms and said, "Oh, probably about as much as he grants you for your monthly allowance."

Esrex' face blotched up an ugly red. "He does not *grant* me anything that isn't mine by right, witch . . ."

Rhion widened his blue eyes at him, and put a hand to his heart. "Oh, I understand that. It's a tremendous shame."

The young man's hand lashed furiously out, the white kid of the glove he held slashing across Rhion's cheek with a slap like wet cloth. Rhion flinched, then bowed even more deeply. "Ah. I see. That must make it less of a shame."

The red stains on those shallow cheekbones faded, leaving him almost yellow with impotent wrath. "You are a godless little cheat," he whispered, "and your master a whore." And turning, he stalked back toward the steps where his diminutive lady stood. The long toes of his embroidered satin slippers wobbled back and forth as he walked; it was nothing for Rhion to reach out with his mind and catch one of them underneath the other. Esrex went down with an undignified squawk, striking both bony shins on the edge of the worn stone step and tearing his white silk stockings like a clumsy schoolchild. He scrambled up as swiftly as he could, shins bleeding and eyes flaming, to meet Rhion's innocent, bespectacled gaze.

For a moment they stood there in silent impasse, Esrex almost trembling with anger, Rhion with his head inclined in solemn respect. Then furiously the younger man turned away, lashing his way through the curtain of vines and striding off across the lawn in the sunlight beyond.

"That was foolish of me," Rhion said quietly. He took a rag from his pocket, and began to wipe up the violated chalk-lines. "Now I'll be stuck here for the rest of the day guarding the thing."

"Tally," Damson said in her high, rather squeaky voice, "you'd better come away."

"He won't be here tonight," Tally said, disregarding her. "The cult of Agon has their own rite tonight. That's where he'll be."

"*Tally* . . ." Damson's eyes flicked nervously from her sister to the sturdy little form in the patched brown robe. "Come with me. Please. Esrex didn't mean any harm—not really. You know how prejudiced he is, and he is under a good deal of strain."

"Are you saying his 'prejudice' is an excuse for . . ."

"Tally, *please!*"

Tally hesitated for a long moment, her fine-boned face held deliberately expressionless, and Rhion guessed that things were not as they had been between the sisters. Then with a quick graceful stride she gathered her skirts and sprang up the steps. And as the two sisters crossed the lawn outside together, Rhion heard Damson's high, clipped tones floating back on the balmy stillness: "It doesn't do for you to be unattended with such a man. You know what they say about wizards seducing young girls with love-spells . . ."

Rhion sighed and shook his head. "A love-spell," he muttered to himself, digging his chalk out of his pocket again, "under the circumstances, is about the last thing I need."

The fête itself was a dazzling success. In addition to the masking and allegorical dances, there was a carousel dance of gaily caparisoned horses in which, Rhion later heard, Marc of Erralswan distinguished himself sufficiently to win the hearts and eventually the corset ribbons of several of the young ladies of the court. At the first chime of the trumpets Rhion lighted the candles of the fire circle which activated the resonator and, in the night's windless stillness, heard, like the drift of sea-roar, the gasp of admiration and delight from the assembled guests. Coming out of the grotto a few moments later, he saw the whole of the enormous garden with every tree and leaf and grass blade outlined in a fine powder of bluish light, as if the Milky Way, stretched like a banner overhead, had been gently shaken to release a carpet of diamond dust upon the world beneath. Even the lily pads and the waxy yellow blooms upon the water were touched with light, and the glowing shapes of the trees were repeated, like the magic echo of a song, in the still sable mirrors of pool, fountain, and canal.

A beautiful spell, he thought, leaning against the mottled bark of a sycamore trunk to watch the weaving of colored lights on the far-off terrace that signaled the masque. Tally would have been standing in one of the places of honor. She would have seen that first moment when the brightness began to spread, like dye in water, to the far ends of the velvet dark.

But later, when strollers passed the lightless, leafy bulk of the grotto hill, he overheard a woman mutter what a shocking thing it was that the Duke had caused magic to be used on a night originally consecrated to the Sun God, and a man grumble, "Well, you know what they say about wizards. I only hope his Grace weighted out the silver he gave them to work the trick and made sure they used it all as they said.''

Esrex' insinuations came back to his mind a few days later as he and Jaldis were on their way up from the Old Town toward the palace on its rise, where the Duke had asked them to supper. They had spent the afternoon in the making of talismans from a crystal the Duke had sent them and the gold melted down from several of his coins, reveling in the ease with which power flowed into the unflawed materials.

"Why gold?" he asked now, as they passed through Thimble Lane where all the tailors and embroiderers were putting up their shutters in the gathering gloom and the lights of lamps made great ochre squares of warmth in the liquid blue dark. "I mean, why do certain materials—gold, silver, and gemstones—hold magic that way? What is it about them that makes them better than copper or tin?''

The old man shook his head. "To learn that," he said quietly, "is every wizard's dream. To understand, not only how magic works, but why. What it is . . .''

He sighed heavily, limping along on his crutches a half-pace ahead of Rhion, turning to lead the way up a narrow street and along an alley short cut that led to the great market square from which the main avenue to the palace rose. He wore his crystalline spectacles, but Rhion knew he wasn't using them to see with now and probably wouldn't do so all evening—they were worn as he sometimes wore a linen bandage, to conceal in politeness the ruin of his eyes from the other guests at supper. For the first several weeks in Bragenmere he had had Rhion take him up and down every street and every alleyway in the Old Town and the New, memorizing turnings, memorizing smells, learning to turn left just after the plashing of the fountain of Kithrak, if he wanted to reach the Joyful Buns Bakery, or that the slant of the ground immediately beyond the warm, steamy scents of the Pomegranate Bathhouse would lead him down twenty-five of his own limping steps to the herbalist from whom he bought ammonia and rue.

"We read the lists made by other wizards of what the metaphysical properties are of every herb, every metal, every jewel and fabric and wood and beast," he went on. "We know that, if one is making a staff for the working of magic, ash is the best wood to use and elm will disperse the power in all directions—cloud and sully it as well. We know that silver will hold impressions of spells, demons, and ghosts. We know that lead is impervious to nearly all magic, that tortoise-shell is necessary in any spell involving learning or memory but that no talisman inscribed upon it will work. We know that sigils inked with the feathers of a swan or a goose will be more powerful, and of a crow, less so, unless the spells be of mischief and chaos—we know that brushes or pens made of the feathers of a pheasant or a wren, or of grasses or reeds, are likely to produce spells less efficacious, more apt to have untoward results. We know that talismans will hold their power longer if they are wrapped in silk and stored in wood, and at that, certain kinds of wood. But why this all should be . . ." He shook his head.

"Could it have something to do with the energy tracks or the energy fields of the body?" Rhion asked. They had left the crowded tenements of the Old Town, and the walls on either side of the narrow streets were now those which enclosed the houses of the rich, pale pink or yellow sandstone ornamented with bright-colored tile or marble friezes and bas-reliefs white as meringues. Beyond the spikes which topped them and the blue or yellow tiles of the roofs, the heads of trees, willow and jacaranda and eucalyptus, reared like feathered clouds against the fading mauve of the sky. "I mean that there's something in the energy of a goose or a swan, that's more in tune with certain types of spells than a crow, for instance . . ."

"There is that theory," his master replied. "But it only leads back to the question of why. Energy travels in straight paths and collects in circles; certain types of energy are drawn to certain runes . . . but why, Rhion, *is* energy in the first place? Why is it humans who possess magic, and not the tortoises or elephants or crocodiles themselves? Or do they, and we are simply ignorant of what manner of magic it is?"

Rhion was silent. Trained as he had been in bookkeeping, he had a mathematician's delight in numbers and sometimes had a vague sense of seeing some kind of mathematical patterns in magic . . .

only to have it dissolve when he looked more closely, like faces glimpsed in shadows on water. And the questions still remained.

"It is our business to ask why," Jaldis went on quietly, "and our need. Not only to understand how to make magic work, but to understand why it works. We see its outer rules—the laws of its balance, that power must be paid for somewhere—Limitations, and the summoning of things by their true names. But we do not see its heart."

"Yet it must have one. Everywhere we see the signs that point to it—or point to something . . ."

Far off, to their left and behind them, the nightly crescendo of market carts was in full swing around the big squares, where provisions, forbidden in the daytime on account of noise and traffic in the narrow streets, were being brought in. Now and then a slave would hurry by them as they made their way along the gently sloping alley, for the night was still early. From the top of a wall, a cat's green eyes gleamed.

"That is what I sought in the Dark Well," the old man continued softly, the talismans of his voice-box rattling with the rhythm of his hobbling stride. "A glimpse of the structure of the Void and the structure of universes that drift within it, hoping that seeing, I might understand."

"And did you?"

The old man smiled a little and shook his head.

"And the universe without magic?"

"Yes . . ." The murmur of the box was no more than a drawn-out sigh. "And its very existence, perhaps, will tell me more. Perhaps it is not an uncommon thing for entire worlds to lose their magic, for the magic to draw away, to depart as light departs with the falling of the night, or water with the ebb of the tide. Since we do not know what magic *is*, any more than we know what light *is*, we cannot tell."

"But if you *had* seen," Rhion said worriedly, "if you *had* learned . . . Would you then have been able to . . . to summon and dismiss *magic? All* magic?"

Jaldis' reply was so quiet that Rhion did not know whether he had spoken with the box at all, or whether he only heard the words in his mind. "I do not know."

Emerging from the alley into a wider street, they found themselves face to face with a massive building, a gateway whose black basalt doorposts were unornamented and whose shut iron-sheathed doors were unrelieved by the smallest of decorative patterns, even the rivets pounded flush and soldered. The gray granite pylons which flanked it were windowless, bare of the marble, tile, or ornamental stone courses that made gay the houses of the neighborhood—bare even of stucco, so that the fine-hewn blocks that formed it faced the street with a hard, unblinking stare, like a skull disdaining the frivolous lingerie of flesh.

Even in the warmth of the summer evening, the place seemed to radiate cold—cold, and shadow, and the mingled smells of incense and blood.

Their way took them across the street and to the lane that led up the hill on the other side. But as Rhion and Jaldis moved onto the cobbled pavement, a man-sized slit opened in the featureless doors, and a figure draped and veiled in black stepped out and raised a black-gloved hand.

"Cross back over, witches," it said, and its voice, thin and cold and bodiless, might have been man's or woman's, a blurred harsh tone like scraped steel. "This is Agon's temple. The footfalls of devils are a pollution on the doorstep of the Veiled God."

"I'm sure they must be," Rhion replied, halting in the middle of the way. Against the black of the doors, the priest was rendered nearly invisible by the inky wool robes and the sable veils that fell from the top of a tall conical headdress to cover face, shoulders, and breast. Unlike the houses of this area, the temple had no lamps outside its door, and the whole street was very dark. Had he not been mageborn, Rhion would have been nearly unable to see anything. "And it must take up all your time, making judgment calls about who's fit to walk how close to the doors—do you have a scale? Five feet for lepers, six and a half for beggars, a yard for slaves . . . ?"

"Do not jest with the servant of the Eclipsed Sun, witch!" warned the voice. "You should be ashamed to parade the streets like whores, and the Duke should take shame for permitting it. As for lepers, beggars, and slaves, Agon has a welcome for them, as he has for all who serve him, who are not the children and spawn of illusion. Now cross back over and go on your way!"

Rhion drew in his breath to speak again but the door behind the priest opened again, and two other forms stepped out—definitely men, this time, both tall and heavily muscled in spite of the massive potbelly sported by one of them. They wore the short tunics and heavy boots of common laborers and, over their heads, close-fitting black masks that covered them down to the chins. The masks had eye slits and mouth slits, as well, for the potbellied man used his to spit on Rhion's face.

Jaldis' hand tightened hard over Rhion's arm. Rhion bowed with exaggerated respect to the priest and his two devotees. "Nice argument," he said pleasantly. "Very convincing. It tells me so much about Agon it makes me want to convert." And he and Jaldis crossed back over the street and went on their way. The priest and the two massive defenders of Agon's doorstep remained where they stood to watch them out of sight.

For a long time, Jaldis did not speak. Only when they started up the last long cobbled rise to the palace gates, ablaze with torches and gay with the crimson tunics of the guards and the yellow and purple irises that decorated their helmets, did Jaldis say, "That is why we must find that world again, Rhion. That is why someone must go there."

Rhion shivered. Part of his mind reflected that the practical upshot of all this was that he'd be moving shelves out of the cellar in the morning to make room for the drawing of the Dark Well, but part of him knew that Jaldis was right. The priests of Agon saw in wizardry what the priests of all the cults of the gods saw: a body of men and women who did not need to petition the deities for assistance, a challenge to their authority, and a living question about the way they said the world worked.

But unlike most of the other cults, which were content to thunder and jeer, the priests of Agon, if they were to hear that it was possible to do something about this situation, would bend every effort to try.

Knowing this, however, did not lift from him the nagging tug of unreasoning dread which filled him as Jaldis spoke.

"At the summer solstice," the old man said softly, "I will weave another Dark Well. I have contacted Shavus the Archmage. He will be here, he says, to help me listen, to help me cast my power through the Void, seeking out the voices that cried. And then . . ." His voice sank still further, until it was little more than the crying of the crickets or the humming of the insects in the redolent night. "Then we will see."

11

As a result of the fête of the summerfire, the Duke of Mere extended a formal offer to Jaldis the Blind of an apartment in the palace, along with his pupil and servant, Rhion, called the Brown.

And Jaldis, just as formally, thanked him and refused.

"But *why*?" Tally blurted, intercepting them in the great pillared hall of the palace as they emerged after the audience. "I know you said you were an old man, and unused to courts . . . But you can't be *that* unused to them if you knew about the silver-dust trick you used for the fête!"

And Jaldis smiled, pausing in his limping stride down the flight of shallow steps to the main floor of the long marble room, regarding her as he would have looked upon his own daughter while the next set of petitioners, like enormous butterflies in court dress of green and white, ascended past them to the bronze doors. "True, my child." His monstrous opal spectacles flashed in the diffuse light that came down through the traceried windows of marble and glass. "But I could not well have said that I declined because I knew courts too well to want to become a part of one again, not even his."

The girl, realizing she had blundered, flushed pink, a color which suited her, Rhion thought. Against the elaborate doublets and gowns of the courtiers, alive with featherwork, ribbons, and beads, the plain brown robes of the two wizards stood out like hens in a coopful of ornamental pheasants; Tally's butter-yellow gown with its embroidery of carnelian and jet must have cost the price of a good horse. She stammered, "I only thought it would be more comfortable for you here. And safer."

"And so it would be." The old man propped his crutch beneath his arm and reached out to take her hand. Looking down the length of that high-ceilinged marble room, Rhion caught a glimpse of Esrex and Damson in the shadows of the pillared space beneath the musicians' gallery and felt the young man's pale impersonal gaze like the prick of a knife in his side.

"Your father is a true friend to me and a generous one," Jaldis went on, his sweet artificial voice blending into the underwhisper of viols and flutes from the gallery. "But did I live at court, I would be under an obligation to him—how could I not be, were he my host and protector? What I gave to him last week was a gift freely and joyfully given. Though I would never feel such gifts to be a duty, still I would hesitate to put myself in a position where either of us would ever feel that it was less than spontaneous. And you know that in the celebrations for the birth of your sister's son, or when your brother enters his first warrior lists as a man, or on the occasion of your lady mother's birthday, there will be those who will expect something equal . . . or greater."

Not to mention the fact, Rhion thought dryly, *that the last time you were a court wizard, you ended up getting arrested in your patron's downfall and losing your eyes and your tongue and the use of your legs into the bargain.*

"And it is a fact," Jaldis went on, as they continued their descent toward the groups of brightly clad courtiers gossiping in the pillared hall, "that many of the great feasts of the year—the Winterfeast, the Rites of Summer, the Festival of Masks in the spring—fall upon the solstice or equinox-tides, when certain spells are possible and certain powers available, as at no other time. I know your father would not see it as a conflict, but gossip would be inevitable."

They passed beneath the shadows of the vestibule, and Esrex, rather pointedly, escorted Damson away from danger of contamination. Even upon court occasions, Rhion noticed, Damson had abandoned the corsetry that had always given her the look of a gem-encrusted sausage, and curiously the flowing eggplant-colored silk that she now wore bestowed upon her an infinitely greater dignity.

"As I told your father, my child, I hope sincerely that my choice will not make my welcome here any the poorer, or change his friendship toward us."

"I don't think it will," Tally said frankly. "Father is just and he likes you very much. I don't think he's ever—How do they phrase it? 'Ejected from his favor', I think the term is—anyone who disagreed with him. That would be like refusing to speak to someone who outran you in a race. And in any case," she added, as they came to a halt before the great outer doors, "it won't change *my* feelings toward you."

Jaldis inclined his white head, the sunlight streaming in from outside making hair and beard sparkle like snow. "Then, my child, you have indeed relieved one of my fears."

And as the red-cloaked guards in their bronze mail bowed them through, Rhion's eye met Tally's again.

As the weeks advanced toward midsummer, Rhion and Tally met more and more frequently. Sometimes Tally would angle to be seated near him when the Duke invited Jaldis to supper or find him working in the Duke's great library in the octagonal tower which overlooked the main palace square; sometimes they met when a hunting or hawking party of young courtiers would encounter the two wizards as they gathered herbs in the marsh.

Or, as often chanced, Tally would steal out of the palace at first light in the summer dawns to have breakfast with Rhion in the long adobe kitchen in Shuttlefly Court.

Those times were the best. With the deep warmth of summer evenings, Rhion would frequently stay up all night, reading or studying the plants he'd gathered, working on mathematics or sigil making, and sleep in the heat of the day. In the early mornings, when he suspected Tally might be coming to visit him, he'd call to his scrying-crystal the image of her mare; if the mare was contentedly dozing in her stall, he himself would go to bed or sally forth to do the early shopping while the teeming produce markets were still torchlit and the vegetables in the barrows wet with dew. But at least once a week—which quickly became twice, and now and then thrice—the image in the crystal would be of the rangy bay hunter trotting quietly along the streets of the Upper Town, all the little glass chips that swung from her bridle flashing softly in the pearly light; or else he'd see her standing outside the Bakery of a Thousand Joyful Buns, which stood at the foot of the palace rise, while Tally bought hot rolls.

And they would talk: of magic, of dogs; of music and mathematics, for Tally, like many musicians, had a bent that way; or she would play her flute for him softly, so as not to wake Jaldis sleeping overhead.

And after she left, to return to her dancing lessons and music lessons and dress fittings at the palace, Rhion would tell himself that these meetings had to stop before the inevitable happened. But a few mornings later she'd be back.

"They want me to get married, you know," Tally said softly one morning as the two of them sat with their backs propped on either side of the kitchen doorjamb, consuming bread and coffee and listening to the water sellers' cries in the strange, breathing coolness of summer dawn. "Father needs the alliance. He doesn't trust the White Bragenmeres, who still keep their own men-at-arms, a private army, almost. They have support among the old land-barons, the ones Father took power from when he passed laws saying they couldn't punish their serfs at their whim. And some of the priesthoods are angry at him for entertaining wizards the way he does."

Rhion said nothing. He had been awake all night; going up through the trapdoor to the flat, tiled roof, he had practiced the spells which summoned beasts by their true and secret names, calling and dismissing geckos and sand lizards and drawing down the bats which feasted on night-flying moths. Later, as the night deepened, he had slipped into long meditation, breathing the dark luminosity of the night until every whisper of sage scent from the looming mountains, every movement of the night winds, was as clear to him as song, and he could identify the position of every rat, every lizard, every chicken and pig, and every sleeper in the crowded courts that spread all around him like a lake of grubby humanity, by the colors of their dreams.

And all that calm, all that sense of wisdom and knowledge and peace that lay like shimmering light within his hand, was sponged away as if it had never been by the thought of Tally in some other man's arms.

She was tearing the roll she'd bought into smaller and smaller fragments, not eating any of it. He knew she never ate when she was upset. Trying to keep her voice steady, she went on, "It was stupid of me to think it wouldn't happen—that I'd be able to stay here, to live at Father's court, the way Damson is doing because Esrex and his family live on Father's allowance, and to think I could go on just . . . just practicing my music, and training the dogs, and . . ." She shook her head quickly and did not finish the thought.

Her voice shifted quickly over Damson's name. Rhion knew that Tally's relations with her sister had been strained since that night in the pavilion, and his altercation with Esrex had not helped matters. For many years, the younger girl had been the self-appointed protector of the older. But now that all Damson's will was bent upon Esrex—now that Tally was seeing a side of her she could not champion—she was left, Rhion guessed, feeling a little bereft.

"Every few weeks another nobleman from somewhere in the Forty Realms appears at court, and there are dances, maskings, new dresses to be fitted, the same tedious small-talk, and all my friends saying, 'Well, *he* isn't so bad.' And I can't get away. I can't think. I can't just . . . just be still. I used to be able to talk to Damson about it, but . . ." She turned her face to him, her gray eyes dry but desperately sad. "There are days when I wish I had never been born."

Don't take her in your arms, Rhion thought quite clearly, his concern for her sorrow, his helpless wish to make her life other than it was, almost drowned by the thought of that tall fragile body and the way those long limbs would fold against his. *If you take her in your arms, you're a dead man. If not now, soon . . . very soon.*

But her misery was more than he could bear.

"Father's being so good about it," she went on, her head pillowed on his shoulder and her hair a pearl-twisted smoky rope across his chest. "He doesn't want to rush me, but he truly needs a foreign alliance. And he's so . . . so *hopeful* . . . every time some good-looking peabrain or some muscle-bound martinet comes strutting around. I can just hear him thinking, *Well, is she going to like* this *one, finally?* And I just . . . I just *don't*. And Damson's worse, since she's been expecting. She keeps saying, 'Oh, when you bear your husband's child, you'll know what true happiness is . . .' until I want to slap her. I wish Jaldis had never made that silly tincture."

She wanted comfort, not love. So Rhion kissed her hair, and held her, and in time sent her on her way, then went back to his studies as well as he could.

Then in the second week of June, Shavus the Archmage came.

Rhion had been away—not with Tally, for once—most of the day. He had wandered the olive groves beyond the city walls and climbed the dry sheep pastures and the rocky mountain beyond, drenched in the hot brightness of the sun. He had observed the swooping patterns of the swallows' flight, and marked which plants grew in the rock-tanks high up the sheeptrails; in the black pockets of cool pine woods on the mountain's flank he had observed the tracks of coyote, rabbit, and deer; high up, where the grass thinned over the earth's silvery bones, he had listened to the songs of the wind. Since his stay in the Drowned Lands, a love of woodcraft for its own sake had grown in him, and he explored, observed, and practiced stillness and silence, sinking his soul into the slow baking heat and the smells of sage and dust.

He returned to the city late, though the sun had only just set; above the Old Town's crowded courts, the sky still held a fragile and lingering light. In every court, the thick blue shadows were patched with primrose squares of lamplight: clear as amber in which men and women could be seen talking, eating, and making love; or else patterned and streaked with lattices or shutters, as strange a diversity, in their way, as the stones of the stream-beds or the plants that grew beside the tanks. Everyone in the city seemed to be abroad that evening, crowding porches and balconies with skirts hiked up or tunics off, throwing dice or watching the children who ran about like dusk-intoxicated puppies through the luminous blue of the narrow lanes.

Rhion could feel the whisper of magic in the air as he turned from Thimble Lane into the court.

He checked his steps, uncertain. Between the curious disorientation of returning to the city after a day in the hills and the deep, restless beauty of the night itself, it was for a moment difficult to be sure it was magic being worked that he felt . . .

But a moment later he was sure. And looking across the court at his door, he saw the green glow of witchlight through its many cracks.

Jaldis, he thought.

And then, *But Jaldis is blind.*

A skiff of children swirled by him, shrieking with excited laughter at their game. In the tavern at the corner of the square, someone plucked a mandolin and began to sing. With his mind Rhion reached out toward the two little rooms in the long bank of the adobe tenement, singling them from the quiet talk, the giggles, the rattling of dice, and the creak of bedropes on all sides, probing deep, listening, scenting . . .

A man in the kitchen downstairs. A smell of maleness—not young, he thought—road dirt, trace whiffs of incense and old blood, and the crackling whisper of pages turning.

Jaldis' books.

And below that was the muffled murmur of voices whispering beneath the ground.

Cautiously, Rhion approached the door.

"Come in," a deep voice said from inside, before he'd reached it. "You must be Rhion the Brown."

As he pushed open the door, a tall, thin, brown-faced man, head shining bald as an egg in the witchlight above the cowl of his black wool robe, rose from where he'd been sitting at the table and held out an emaciated hand. "I am Gyzan the Archer, a friend of Shavus and, alas, not to be trusted in the same room as the magic-working below."

Rhion dropped his satchel of herbs on the table and took his hand. A huge bow of black horn reinforced with steel stood unstrung beside the cellar's rude plank door and, with it, a quiver of arrows.

The cellar door itself was shut, but through its cracks now and then flickered a ghostly, shifting light.

"What are they doing?"

"Weaving a Dark Well." He folded his arms, regarded Rhion with wise, ironic, gentle brown eyes.

Rhion had heard it said of Gyzan the Archer that if the Blood-Mages had possessed an Archmage, it would have been Gyzan. He studied him now, noting how the long brown hands were marked all over with scars like a Hand-Pricker's, the upper joints of both little fingers missing; his lips, too, and ear lobes were scarred where spell-cords had at one time been threaded through. But unlike the Hand-Prickers he was scrupulously clean, his head shaved—there were Hand-Prickers in the Lower Town that one couldn't get near for the smell of the old blood matted in their waist-length hair—and his nails cut short; unlike them, he seemed as sane as any wizard ever was.

"Shavus is going, then?" Rhion started to unpack his satchel and, as he did so, stole a glance at the cover of the book Gyzan had been reading—not one of Jaldis', after all, but a catalogue of star-spells he recognized from Shavus' library.

"So he says. Knotweed—very nice," he added, picking up a spiky stem from among the tangle of foliage. "Good for dysentery . . . And I'm going with him."

After the first moment of surprise that Shavus would have asked a non-Morkensik—even one who had been his lifelong friend—Rhion breathed a sigh of relief. He had once offered to accompany the Archwizard through the Void, but every instinct he possessed warned him that beyond it lay dangers with which he would be absolutely unable to cope.

"A curious thing, the Dark Well," the Blood-Mage went on, turning the herbs over in his scarred fingers, feeling the texture of root and blossom and leaf as he spoke. "Is it true that it shows other worlds, other universes, than our own?"

"I don't know," Rhion said warily. "I've only seen it once, and then it was quiescent, closed in on itself. But I don't know what else it could be." The Gray Lady had questioned him about it also, before they had left the Drowned Lands, and he had his suspicions about why Jaldis had begun the rites of its making on a day when he, Rhion, was away—well-founded suspicions, when he thought about them. Both the Gray Lady and the Archer were far stronger mages than he, and he wasn't quite sure what he might be likely to tell them under the influence of a really heavy drug or spell.

The Archer shrugged, long lashes veiling his eyes. Like many Blood-Mages, he'd had the eyelids and the flesh around them tattooed, giving them a bruised and slightly ominous appearance. "A reflection—a projection—of the way his own mind conceives the shape of the universe," he guessed. "Or an illusion, perhaps, designed by spirits whose very nature we can only vaguely guess."

Rhion knew the Blood-Mages believed in such spirits, wholly unlike grims and faes and the other bodiless Children of the Dark Air, and attributed their own magic to communication with them. As far as he'd ever heard, every Order except the Blood-Mages themselves and a few of the less sane Hand-Prickers described this belief as balderdash.

"But if it is what he says it is," Gyzan went on, raising his glance once more, "I consider it rather foolish of him—of them—to keep the means of its making and use so deep a secret. What if Jaldis were to fall ill while Shavus and I are on the other side of this Void they speak of? There is an unsteadiness to the aura he carries about his body; I do fear for his health. He is a very old man."

"I'd be here," Rhion pointed out, a little miffed.

Gyzan set down the stem of dragon arum he'd been examining and studied him for a very long time. In their blue-black bands of shadow his brown eyes narrowed, limpid and beautiful as a woman's—Rhion remembered uneasily the rumors that the man had second sight. But he only said, "Well . . . perhaps."

"Nonsense," Shavus blustered later, when he and Jaldis had emerged from the tiny cellar, long after Gyzan had gone up the ladder to the room above to sleep. "By looking into the Void—by looking into the darkness *outside* our universe—the Dark Well may very likely contain the clues as to what magic *is*. Its true essence, its reality. The Void seems to be filled with a magic of its own, a dreadful and powerful magic, and we'd be fools to let a Blood-Mage, or those Earth-witches in Sligo, anywhere near it."

"They're not Earth-witches," Rhion pointed out, annoyed at the Archmage's prejudice.

"Then they're the next thing to 'em, same way the Blood-Mages are only Hand-Prickers who bathe." Shavus did not bother to lower his voice. Presumably he did not express sentiments behind his friend's back that he had not also said to his face. His thick, gray hair was plastered with sweat to his massive skull, and his broad face, usually clean-shaven despite its scars, was gritty with stubble. Jaldis said nothing, only sat, bent with exhaustion, his spectacles lying on the table before him, massaging the bridge of his nose with one crippled hand. He looked, as Gyzan had said, very old, and rather unwell. Rhion came quietly around the table and rubbed the old man's shoulders and back, feeling, not tension there, but a kind of dreadful limpness.

"Besides," the Archmage added, "who's to say one of 'em won't spread the knowledge to others, the Earth-witches or some Bone-Thrower who chances by? The Gray Lady didn't seem to have any qualms about *you* making free with their library."

He tore off part of the loaf Rhion had set in front of the two of them—it was well past midnight, the court outside steeped in the silence of sleep—and sopped the bread in the honey pot. "You ask Gyzan how willing he'd be to let me have the spells to contact that 'familiar spirit' of his and see what he'd say," he went on around a sticky mouthful. "Is there a baths in this neighborhood that'd be open at this hour, my little partridge? Ah, well—the Duke likes to pretend his town's a cosmopolitan city, but when all's said you can tell you're not in Nerriok. We'll be at it again in a few hours . . ."

"Will you need my help?"

"In that gopher-hole? Only if you bring your own space with you."

Rhion found himself remembering again that Shavus knew he'd been the Gray Lady's lover and that he'd been up here fraternizing with Gyzan; he felt a kind of obscure anger stir in him. But Jaldis only reached up to grasp Rhion's hand in thanks.

Whatever Shavus' reasons, Rhion did not see the Dark Well until it was completed, two days later, the day before the summer solstice itself.

It was as he first remembered seeing it in the attic of the Black Pig. Hellishly complicated circles within circles, spirals leading out of spirals, the interlinking lines of fire-circle and water-circle, blood and smoke and silver, woven together with the intricate tracings of pure light that floated above the floor and seemed to lie, glowing, several inches beneath the surface of the hard-packed damp clay. Within those circles, like a dark and beating heart, lay the strange shuddering gate of colors, as though darkness, like light, had been refracted into a rainbow . . .

And within the colors was—nothing. Quiescent, closed upon it-self, the darkness had a brownish cloudiness that reminded him of nothing so much as an eye shut in sleep. Standing between Jaldis and Shavus, with his back to the crude ladder upon which Gyzan was forced to perch, Rhion felt the sweat start on his face, not so much from the stifling heat of the cellar as from a deep, primordial fear that the eye would open, would look at him and know him . . .

"Tomorrow night." Jaldis' voice was so weak with weariness as to be barely intelligible, the crippled hand clinging to his arm for support. "Tomorrow night, when midnight tilts the Universe to its balance point and lets its powers be turned by humankind . . . Then the wizards in that other world will have the power to make their voices heard. Then *we* shall open the Well, and search within."

"Ay," Shavus muttered, fingering the battered hilt of the sword at his waist. "But what we'll find—now, that's another tale."

Jaldis spent the rest of that day, and all of the one following, either sleeping or deep in meditation, gathering his strength for the night. Shavus and Gyzan, having a standing invitation to the Duke of Mere's palace from other years, went to pay their respects, and Rhion went with them. In part he only sought to avoid the uneas-iness that whispered in the back of his mind whenever he thought about the Dark Well—the dread, not of the terrible unknown of that Void of chaos, but of something he sensed he had once known and then forgotten. It was a dread impossible to leave behind, exacer-bated by his growing awareness of the pull of the sun-tide in his blood. But in addition to that, Tally's last visit had been four or five days ago, and he had begun to be concerned.

They found the palace in a flutter of excitement over the state visit by the Earl of the Purple Forest. This lord, who ruled the greatest of the In Islands and a whole archipelago of minor isles beyond it, was one of the most powerful in the Forty Realms: garlands were being strung in the gardens again, and among the pillars of the great entryhall. As the three wizards climbed the shallow steps and passed beneath the musicians' gallery they encountered squads of slaves with wicker tubs of flowers, trailing scent like rags of gauze in their wake, and the excited talk among the courtiers in the long pillared hall nearly drowned the floating sweetness of lyre and flute.

The Earl was seated in an ivory chair of honor beside the Duke when the three wizards were presented, a handsome, muscular man in his early forties, his red hair braided and crowned with jasmine, his mouth sensual, scornful, and hard when he forgot to smile. He expressed delight at meeting so notable a mage as Shavus Ciarnin, but, Rhion noticed, Gyzan was silent in his presence. The Duke invited them to keep the feast of solstice that night among his household. As Shavus declined gracefully, Rhion reflected again that Jaldis had been right: many of the great feasts did fall upon the occasions of solstice and equinox. Had Jaldis been a member of the Duke's suite, he could not always have had those occasions to himself.

It was only when they were descending the marbled spaces of the outer hall once more that Rhion overheard a woman saying, "Well, I'm sure he was worth waiting for—so handsome! I knew she could have no fault to find with *him* . . ."

And he realized what was going on.

The Earl of the Purple Forest had come to offer for Tally's hand.

And Tally, to judge by the Duke's relieved affability and the sheer magnificence of the decorations going up, must have accepted.

He felt as if his body were filled with broken glass. That he could not move—he could not breathe—without pain.

Why are you surprised? he thought, as the blue gloom of the vestibule closed around him like the darkness veiling the sun. *She said it, the first time you met . . . "So it isn't a question of what I want . . . just when. And who . . ."*

The red-cloaked guards opened the outer doors. Shavus and Gyzan descended the marble steps, brown robes and black like eagle and raven in the bright sun of summer, the bulky form and the gaunt. Rhion found he had stumbled to a halt among the pillars beneath the gallery, standing in the shadows like a milkweed-fae that fears the scorch of the sun.

Tally . . .

For an instant he was standing on the wharf, seeing the dust-brown hair haloed by the sunlight as the water widened between him and the ship that would take her away.

You should never have touched her. Never have taken her hand.

Of themselves his fingers had sought, in his pocket, the washed-leather bag where he kept his scrying-crystal—he let go of it in disgust. *Don't you hurt enough yet?*

The guards closed the doors, not noticing the plump, bearded little man with the flashing spectacles, who stood in the shadows of the vestibule. And he was, Rhion thought, withdrawing noiselessly to the huge square base of a drum-column where the diffuse light from the larger room behind could be caught in the crystal's facets, in-conspicuous enough, and easy to overlook.

He sat on the column base and, taking the crystal from his pocket, angled its flat purple-gray surfaces to the light.

As if she sat in a room behind him he saw her, reflected in the crystal's heart. She sat on a bench of green porphyry and bronze, shawled in green-dappled light. Water flickered darkly in the shad-ows behind her. There was no expression on her face as she stared straight ahead of her, but the red-furred hunting dog lying at her feet twisted its head around to look up at her, and pawed anxiously at her skirts. Tears crept silently from her open eyes.

"Tally?"

He paused in the shadow margin between sunlight and gloom. The vines that curtained the little pavilion's entrance had not been cut this summer and covered the space between the slender pillars like a veil of petaled green silk. The buffets, the gazebos, and the stands for the musicians were all up by the long north front of the palace, on the other side of the network of canals and linden groves. Here it was silent. The heat, though strong on Rhion's back, lacked the dense oppressiveness it would have later in the summer; the

grotto's dimness was almost chilly, the plashing of the fountain unnaturally loud.

Tally sat on the bench before it, bolt upright in her simple green
dress. The silver and amber at her throat flashed softly as she turned
her head.

For a moment she did not move, but he saw her shut her eyes
and breathe once, a thick, dragging sigh.

Then without a word, as naturally as if she had known that he
would come—and perhaps she had—as naturally as if they had been
lovers for years, she got to her feet and walked into his arms.

Though it was the longest day of the year, still it was dark by the
time Rhion got back to Shuttlefly Court.

The grotto faced east, designed to be a place of morning sunlight
and silent coolness in the long summer afternoons. It was the dog
who waked them, stealing quietly back in to lie across the feet of
the sleeping lovers, though he would have barked, Rhion knew, at
anyone's approach. Through the pillars and the gold-edged green of
the vines, the hill's shadow stretched far out over the grass, rimmed
by a line of burnished light. Against his shoulder, Tallisett's face was
peaceful in sleep. It seemed to him that he had wondered half his
life what her hair would feel like between his fingers. It was finer
than it looked for its straight thickness, soft as a child's hair.

Dear God, what have I done?

But there was nothing he possessed, or ever had possessed, that
he would not have traded for this time.

"Father needs the alliance," she said, quite some time after she
woke up. "And I can't . . . I can't tell him I won't. Because there's
no reason to—I mean, the Earl has never been anything but polite
to me, courtly and gracious. But . . ." She hesitated, struggling with
her fear that what she would say sounded silly. But at length she
blurted out, "Rhion, his *dogs* are afraid of him! We all went hunting
one morning—I could see. But he's never said a wrong word . . .
Father likes him . . ."

And she clung to him again, as if he had saved her from drowning.

Still later she said, "I didn't want this to be something that had
never happened."

Rhion nodded, his lips pressed to her hair. Their talk covered hours, a sentence or two at a time, and then long spaces where the only sound was the mingled sibilance of their breathing, the clucking of the fountain, and the occasional stir of breezes in the vines.

Gently, he pointed out, "He's going to know about it. At least, he'll know there was someone . . ."

"Do you really think he's going to give back the dowry over a little blood?"

Rhion remembered the Earl's sensual lips and cynical eye. "No," he said slowly, thinking how much of her naïveté Tally had lost even since he'd met her in the icy winter woods. To himself he added, *But he's going to hold it over you for as long as you live.*

"And so long as I'm not with child . . ."

"Don't worry." Rhion managed a faint grin. "That, at least, is something wizards know how to prevent."

"Oh, Rhion . . ."

He gathered her hands together in one of his, and held them against his chest. The dog padded over to the fountain's edge, sniffed about a little, and settled itself leggily down onto Rhion's crumpled brown robe. The rim of light on the grass drew farther and farther away, then began to fade.

It was two or three hours short of midnight when Rhion reached home, to find Shavus pacing angrily, muttering oaths, back and forth down the length of the narrow kitchen, while Jaldis sat very quiet in his chair near the cold hearth.

"God's teeth, boy, where were you?" the Archmage exploded when Rhion let himself in. "Bird-nesting? I haven't spent three days weaving spells in a hole in the ground to have you spoil things by not showing up in time!"

"But I am in time," Rhion pointed out. From long watching of the stars he knew subliminally to within a few moments when midnight was, even on ordinary nights, and Shavus knew he knew. And to a wizard, the night of the solstice was not even a matter of subconscious calculation. He could feel the tide of the sun and the stars turning, pulling at his blood and could feel the draw of magic flowing along every energy-path on the earth, in the grass, or in his body, in a glittering whisper of half-heard music in the sky.

All over the city, as he had made his way home, he had been conscious of the magic in the night. Most of the great cults were holding some kind of special rite on this, one of the major turning points of the year. He had passed procession after procession in the streets: the golden image of Darova in her glittering boat, surrounded by torchlit banners and by the shaking tinkle of sistrums; and the white-draped priestesses of Shilmarglinda with roses in their hair and their little boy dolls in their hands ready to be tossed onto the temple fires. Every tavern where the warriors who followed Kithrak forgathered blazed like a bonfire, and in even the windowless granite monolith of Agon's temple there had been the suggestion of hidden movement.

Every wizard in the city would be preparing some special ceremony, the charging of talismans or the deep scrying for some sort of knowledge, taking advantage of the additional power that moved in the air that night. Children raced excitedly about the streets, eyes bright under tousled hair, waving candy or flowers in their grubby fists. The very air seemed to crackle.

And Tally had come into his arms.

It took all Rhion's training, all the concentration disciplined into him by years of meditation, to tear his mind from the image of her rising from the bench in the grotto's darkness, walking to him . . . It took all his will not to return again and again to the memory of her lips first pressing his. Of her hair untangling from its pearled net beneath his fingers . . .

She was his.

Only for two months, part of his mind said. Only until the dowry negotiations are complete.

But a part of his soul knew that she would always be his.

And he was aware of Gyzan the Archer looking at him with a kind of pitying sadness as they descended the ladder to the black of the cellar below.

Through the odd clarity of deep meditation, Rhion watched Shavus step to the edge of the earth circle, where the great sun-cross of magic's eternal power had been drawn, and lift his scar-seamed hands. Within the woven circles, something seemed to shudder and move, the blackness deepening, clarifying, and breathing of matters unsus-

pected and better left unsuspected in the realms of mortal kind.
Panic struggled to surface in Rhion's heart as he saw the Dark Well
opening, the livid rainbow of refracted darkness parting, widening,
like the opening heart of a black crystal rose. Darkness opened into
greater darkness, abysses at whose bottom new abysses gaped. A
dream . . .

Cold wind stroked his face, and he shut his eyes. Midnight was
upon them, the power of it crying in his blood; all his will, all his
strength, he concentrated into the rite of summoning that power,
calling it from the bones of the earth, from the silver tracks of the
leys, and from the shuddering air and the turning stars. From the
four corners of the hollow earth the wizards called it, feeding it into
the crippled old man who limped forward to the edge of the chasm,
opal spectacles reflecting the hellish rainbow of darkness as he gazed
within, listening, seeking . . .

But whether it was because Rhion's concentration was distracted
by what had passed that afternoon or because Jaldis himself was
exhausted by the three days of spellweaving which had gone before—
or for some other cause that none of them knew—the power of the
solstice midnight came and went. But in the Void there was only
silence. No light, no movement stirred within that terrible chaos, to
show them in which direction the universe without magic might lie.

12

"I don't understand." The slurred drag of the voicebox was intelligible only by those who knew Jaldis well—to an outsider, Rhion thought, it would be only a seesaw of notes, like an expert musician playing a viol in an inflection to mimic human speech. The talismans of crystal and glass and the great gold sun-cross in their midst, flashed like the shattered fragments of a broken sun against the worn sheets and the hand that lay like bleached driftwood in their midst.

"They called out for help. I heard their voices at the Winterstead . . ." Jaldis sighed painfully and turned his face away. "I don't understand."

"The turn of winter was six months ago," Shavus replied, the roughness of his deep voice not quite successful in covering his concern for his friend. "God knows, a man's whole life can change in a week—in a day."

Silent at his elbow, Rhion had to agree.

"What makes you think any of them are still alive by this time?"

"If ever they existed at all," Gyzan murmured, from where he sat on the painted leather chest at the bed's foot.

"It exists." Jaldis stirred as if he would sit. Rhion, too unnerved by the grayness of his face and the ragged way he'd been breathing that morning to stand on ceremony, put out a hand and forced him gently down again.

"It exists," the old man insisted. "That I know. I heard them crying out . . ."

"I don't disbelieve you, old friend." The Archmage shook back his ragged hair, like tangled gray wool around his dark, scarred face. "But whether those people are still alive to call, let alone have enough power in 'em to reach out across the Void and guide us there . . ."

"I will find them," the old man said stubbornly. "I will. I must." And for all the weakness of his body, Rhion saw in that sunken face the indomitable determination of a dream.

"Can't you do anything for him?" he asked quietly, when he, the Archmage, and the Archer had climbed down the rough ladder to the kitchen. "Spells to give him strength, to steady his heart . . ."

"Something you can do as well as I." The big warrior grumbled the words over his shoulder as he rooted through the collection of fine porcelain bottles on the plank shelf—all gifts from the Duke— in search of brandy. Rhion picked up the nearly empty water jar and crossed the length of the kitchen to the door.

In the square outside the water seller whose beat covered this court was walking along the dense blue shade of the arcade, singing mournfully "Wa-a-a-a-ter, cool fresh wa-a-a-a-ter . . ." She eyed Rhion suspiciously but uncovered one of the buckets which dangled from her shoulder yoke and filled up his jar, then bit the halfpenny he gave her and made the little crossed square of Darova's Eye on it, in case he'd given her a pebble witched to look like a coin. Wizards were always being accused of doing that, though Rhion had never met anyone to whom it had actually happened.

"Don't be silly." He set the jar down again near the hearth in the kitchen's cool gloom. "Your spells . . ."

"My spells malarkey," Shavus retorted. "You know as well as I do, my partridge, that there's no spell can go against nature, not forever. What Jaldis needs isn't a spell, but to quit doing things like this to himself. Magic comes from the flesh as well as the will—I've seen you goin' after dates and honey and any sweet thing when you've done some bit of spell-weaving that's beyond you, same as I fall asleep like I'd been clubbed over the head, once the kick of the magic itself wears off. Jaldis can't keep goin' from spell to spell to keep himself on his feet any more than a man can keep himself goin' forever chewing cocoa leaves."

He pulled the cork from the brandy bottle with his teeth and slopped one of the red-and-black cups half-full, while Rhion heaped a little handful of charcoal in the brazier and touched it with a fire-spell even as he worked the coffee mill.

They were all tired, for they had worked the rites of the sum-moning of power for an hour or two after midnight, trying to find some sign, some clue, in the darkness of the Well. After the shortest night of the year, dawn came far too soon.

In any case, Rhion had slept very little. Fatigued as he was by the calling down of power, no sooner had his head touched the pillow than the dream of Tally lay down beside him, hair like seed-brown embroidery silk and long cool limbs like ivory. In sleep he could have tasted her lips again, but sleep, like the coy girls he'd flirted with in his youth, had played hard to get.

It had been just as well. Waking with the first slits of light through the louvers, he had heard the stertorous rasp of Jaldis' breathing and had realized that the old man had suffered something akin to a mild stroke in his sleep.

"He uses too much power as it is," Shavus grumbled, pouring another generous dollop of brandy into his coffee and taking a hand-ful of the cheese and dates Rhion had brought to the table. The dates were another gift from the Duke, like the coffee and the wine the three senior mages had drunk last night at dinner. The graceful clay bottle, stamped with the Duke's seals, still adorned the side-board and reminded Rhion that he had had no supper last night. No wonder, he thought, he was starving. "Tampering with that damn Well of his will be his death."

"Perhaps," Gyzan said, speaking for the first time, "death is the inevitable conclusion of all dreams."

In the weeks that followed, Rhion visited the cellar seldom, though he was always conscious of the Well's presence there, like something dark and terrible living in the ground beneath his feet. Even after Shavus and Gyzan had returned to Nerriok, between his own spells of healing and his pupil's, Jaldis had rallied. For all his fragility there was an odd, stubborn toughness to him; he was on his feet within days, though he moved more slowly than he had. Nevertheless Rhion was uneasy. He knew that while he himself was gone, his master would descend the perilous ladder to the cellar and open the Well, sitting for hours before it, gazing into the enigma of its abyss.

The Duke was deeply concerned to hear that his friend was ill and would dispatch a sedan chair and four bearers to Shuttlefly Court whenever he wanted the old man's company. Betweentimes, his gifts multiplied: fruits, game birds, and the light, pale wines of the high country. When Rhion came to court without Jaldis, the Duke would invariably ask after the old man and send back with Rhion some small token—a book from the library or good quality soap from the palace savonneries, or sometimes just summer flowers from the water gardens to brighten the little adobe rooms.

And Rhion was often at court. The Duke had offered both him and Jaldis free use of his library, and it would be foolish, Jaldis scolded, not to take advantage of this freedom to make notes of anything of value he might find. Thus Rhion spent much of the summer in those big marble rooms—three of them, stacked one atop the other in the stumpy octagonal tower—reading by the white, diffuse light that streamed in through the high latticed windows or browsing through the racks of ancient scrolls and shelves of books whose sheer numbers were famous throughout the Forty Realms as second only to the High King's library in Nerriok.

"And personally, I think ours is better," Tally remarked, one afternoon as she and Rhion, catalog and note tablets in hand, were engaged in one of their long paper chases through book after book, tracking down a reference by the rhetoritician Giltuus in his *Ninth Book of Analects* to spells by a wizard named Greigmeere. "The High King's library has been gone over a dozen times for orthodoxy by the priests of Darova. You can bet anything 'unfit' or 'unseemly in the sight of the gods' went for kindling years ago."

"And this hasn't?" Rhion balanced on a tall-legged stool to pull scrolls from the highest compartment of a rack between two windows: Greigmeere, according to Worgis' *Compendium*, had been a philosopher; though codex-type books had been in use for four hundred years, priests and philosophers still tended to regard them as newfangled and queer, making it far likelier that Greigmeere's writings, if they existed in the library, would be in the more ancient form. Tally, dressed in the plain green gown she wore when she was tending her dogs or hiding from court occasions, looked up at him where she held the stool steady as he sorted through the wax identification tags on the scrolls' ends.

"Well, more from pride than from intellectual merit, I think," she admitted. "I mean, the White Bragenmeres— Mother's family— always collected anything that came to hand and would never let anyone interfere with anything of theirs for whatever reason. I know Grandfather is supposed to have taken a whip to the Archimandrite of Darova when she came to him complaining his dog had bitten her—then turned around as soon as she had gone and beat the dog."

"Charming fellow." Rhion stretched out to the next compartment, nearly overbalancing himself in his effort to read the tags without climbing down and moving the stool. Tally laughed and put a hand on his calf to steady him, a touch that almost had the opposite effect; it was with great difficulty that he kept himself from springing down upon her then and there. He had found that sometimes, for hours at a time, they could be friends as they had been before, like two children playing in a garden—other moments he was consumed by consciousness of her, aware of every finger end, every pearl upon her headdress, and every eyelash, wanting nothing more from life than to crush her in his arms.

They had made love almost daily since midsummer afternoon: in the grotto at the end of the garden; in the hayloft above the Duke's stables; and in the little deserted pavilion with the painted rafters where Rhion and Jaldis had come to make spells for the saving of Damson's marriage. Of the love-philter and of Esrex and Damson, they did not speak.

Rhion was, in fact, about the court far more than anyone realized, coming silently under the cloudy aura of spells of Who-Me? and Look-Over-There. The places where he and Tally met, where they clung in passionate joy or lay drowsing in an aftermath sweet beyond words, were always hazed about by illusions which woke in chance passersby the dim sensation that there was something urgent to be done *immediately* elsewhere in the palace. The vines which covered the front of the garden grotto grew long and untended as a beggar's hair; the pavilion by the postern gate acquired a neglected air that came of not having its steps washed or its windows cleaned.

Once, while Rhion hunted for milkwort in the wolf-yellow fields above the olive groves, he heard the horns of the hunters ringing in the hills and caught a glimpse of the Duke, all in crimson, Tally in her familiar red riding dress with her dogs bounding about her, and the flame-haired Earl of the Purple Forest coursing after stag. Watching as the horses plunged out of sight into one of the thick knots of woodland that tangled these high gullies, it came over him in a sweeping rush of despair how terribly short time was. He could see, too, that Tally was right: the Earl's dogs, though too well-trained to shy when he came near, lowered their ears and moved restlessly when he was among them, cracking his whip against his boot.

Upon another occasion, he heard the horns ringing, very distantly, while he was in the Kairn Marshes, putting into practice the spells he had learned from Greigmeere's scrolls—a little-known cantrip to make a thing called a spiracle. Theoretically at least, a spiracle charged with the element of air would hold that element about it even when plunged into water; after a few tries, he found that he could, in fact, so imbue a spiracle that, with it bound around his brow, he could walk about and breathe at the bottom of the river, watching the fish slipping through the dark jungles of cattail roots. When he emerged from the water, his body dripping but his hair and beard and spectacles dry, he found Tally sitting on his clothes.

That was one of the best afternoons. The gnats, under the impression that the air was unaccountably filled with the smoke of lemon grass, hung in perplexed clouds upriver and down, the air clean of them in the thick yellow-green sunlight among the willow roots where Rhion and Tally lay. Afterward Tally insisted on trying the spiracle—a little iron circlet no bigger around than a child's bracelet, tied to a leather thong—and explored the murky greenish waters herself, breathing the bubble of trapped air which hovered around her head.

Later still, lying again on the spread-out bed of their clothing, she spoke of her upcoming marriage, the only time she had done so throughout that long summer.

"I'm saving times like this," she whispered, turning her head toward him, so that her long hair lay tangled over the worn brown robe beneath it. Out on the marsh, a fish leaped at a dragonfly, a silvery *plop* in the stillness; the air that moved above the water stirred the thick curly hair of Rhion's back and chest and thighs and murmured in the reeds which surrounded the lovers like a translucent green bed curtain, canopied with sky. "They're saying now it will be August, just before we leave for the summer palaces in the hills. Mother's been telling me to stay out of the sun so my skin will beautify and making me take baths in milk. They've been bleaching my hair and clarifying my complexion with distilled water of green pineapples, and Damson's been plying me with every kind of herb and tea and potion she knows to make me beautiful. And time is so short . . ."

She propped herself to her elbow and reached across to take his spectacles—all that he was wearing—from his face, then drew him to her, silken skin, bones like ivory spindles, beneath his hands. "This is my dowry," she murmured, holding fiercely to him, her face pressed to his shoulder. "When a noble woman marries, she has a jointure to live on, if worst comes to worst—these days are mine."

He gathered her to him, closer and closer still. His beard against her hair, he breathed. "Then we'd better make it a good one."

"I wish there was something I could do."

"Oh, Rhion." Jaldis sighed, and put his wine cup aside, to reach out and grasp his pupil's plump hand in his crippled one. The noise of the summer evening came dimly through the open door from the square: from both taverns, voices lifted in song, old ballads strangely sweet in the lapis dark and torchlight despite the rough voices that framed them. Children shrieked with laughter, whirling the big green-backed beetles they'd caught around their heads on strings to hear them buzz, and crickets creaked in the long weeds around the edge of the arcade. Two streets away the jarring rattle of the market carts rose like a clumsy staccato heartbeat to time the night's mingled sounds. On the rough wooden table between Jaldis and Rhion the supper dishes lay, and among them, like a nobleman gone slumming, stood the three-quarters-empty bottle of wine which the Duke's messenger had brought them that evening. Turning it in his hand, Rhion reflected that the Duke must have returned—he and his guest had been gone for two days, inspecting the summer-palace to which the whole court would soon move.

"I keep thinking . . ." He gestured helplessly across the ruined battlefield of plates. "I keep thinking about sailing across to Murik, the Island of the Purple Forest . . . about maybe settling there. But I don't want to leave you." It was the first time he had voiced such a choice aloud. "And I think, 'Well, he doesn't look like the kind of man who's going to get songs sung about his fidelity . . .' As long as I don't get her with child, why should he care? But *I* care. I hate the thought of her bearing his children. But that's why he's marrying her. I hate the thought of what he'll do to her."

"And what will he do to her?" his master asked softly. "She's the daughter of his ally. He can't very well take a whip to her."

Very quietly, Rhion said, "He'll make her unhappy."

Jaldis sighed and did not reply.

Rhion got to his feet and paced to the open door. For a time he stood looking out into the unearthly blue of the deepening night, his arms folded tight across his body as if to contain a bleeding wound. Above the mountains, a swollen cantaloupe-colored moon shed light brilliant enough to cast blurred shadows on every sage and juniper bush there, to silver every roof tile of the city beneath. In that drenched indigo world, the taverns stood out like tawdry carnivals; elsewhere in the square, two of the local prostitutes sat on their balcony, having a night off, their quiet-voiced conversation about hair styles and fashionable gamblers mingling with the smell of their perfume and the thick green scent of the marijuana they smoked. The day had been stifling, the last of July raging down like a furnace over the brown hills. Before the doors of their rooms, all round the arcade, men and women sat arm in arm in companionable silence, watching children playing in the dark.

Rhion whispered, "Dammit. Other people—people who aren't born to magic, who don't have it in their blood—think magic solves things. They come to us for potions, philters, talismans, amulets, and advice to solve some problem or other. But it doesn't, really. It doesn't change what we are. It doesn't change what we do."

"No," Jaldis said, from the soft glow of witchlight that haloed the table where he sat.

Rhion chuckled ironically. "Magic isn't . . . isn't magic. I keep telling myself every time I see her that it's just one more memory to hurt after she's gone. But I keep grabbing those moments, devouring them as I used to eat cookies . . . Damn, I make the best love-potions in the Forty Realms, but can I make one that'll fall me *out* of love?"

"Would you truly want to?"

His voice was nearly inaudible. "No." The witchlight flashed across the lenses of his spectacles as he turned back to the room. "No."

His hand unerring, Jaldis poured the remainder of the wine, dividing it between the two cups. Rhion shut the door, closing out the wild magic of the night, and returned to his master. As he picked up the cup, the touch of it, its graceful shape and glass-black glaze, brought back to him the still silences of the Drowned Lands, the flicker of fireflies across the blue marshes, and the marble faces dreaming in their winding sheets of vines. The Gray Lady's face came back to him, framed in the bones of the priestess' diadem and the pulse-beat tapping of the drums among the sacrificial stones. Magic.

The memories grounded him. Like *love*, *magic* was a word of many meanings: joyful or damning, hurtful or sweet, the same word describing a silly flirtation or a commitment that saved the soul.

"To magic," he said softly, raising his cup; as if he could see him do so, Jaldis returned the salute.

"To magic, then."

And draining the cup, the old man rose stiffly from his chair, collected his crutches, and limped off slowly to the ladder and so up to his bed.

Rhion gathered the dishes, dipped water from the jar, and washed them, reflecting with a twisting stab in his heart that, if the Duke had returned, it meant that the court would be getting ready to move up to the higher hills. Several of the wealthy merchants whose walled and decorated houses made up the Upper Town had left already; they would not be back until the minor festival of Shilmarglinda on the equinox of fall.

That thought brought others. He glanced across at the tiny plank door of the cellar, shut and bolted against intrusion, and wondered what Jaldis would learn at the turning of autumn when he again summoned the power of the heavens to listen into the Well. And listen he would, Rhion thought uneasily, at whatever cost to himself.

By the autumn equinox Tally will be married. This will all be over.

The autumn equinox, he realized, was less than sixty days away. It was as if something within him had been squeezed suddenly in a wire net.

And then, from upstairs, he heard the sudden, heavy crash of a stick pounding the floor. Summoning him, calling him urgently . . .

Jaldis.

He can't use the voice-box . . .

Rhion took two running strides toward the ladder and stopped, realizing belatedly that the witchlight that had illuminated the room had died. Being able to see in the dark, and being deeply preoccupied, he hadn't noticed . . .

But there was only a strange, leaden muzziness in the part of his mind that he would have used to summon the light back again. Like a limb that had been numbed, or the speech that eludes a drunkard . . .

And it came to him, whole, cold, terrifying, and with absolute clarity, what had happened and what was about to take place.

Pheelas root. In the wine.

The Duke never sent the wine.

The Duke is still out of town.

Behind him the door crashed open. Torchlight spilled into the long room like blood from a gutted beast, framing the crowding forms of men in the gray livery of the disgraced house of the White Bragenmeres—personal soldiers with weapons in their hands.

Before them, slim as a lily in unjeweled white, stood Esrex.

13

Later Rhion supposed he could have thrown something—the tin basin of dishwater, a chair, anything—at Esrex's guards to slow them down. But at the moment, he didn't think of it, and it probably would have done him more harm than good. Smashing their way down the length of the room, they caught him when he was three-quarters of the way up the ladder to the room above, tearing his hands by main force from the rungs and striking him with their spear butts when he kicked at their faces. A blow caught him over the kidneys, the pain stopping his breath; as he crumpled, retching, to the stone floor he heard them in the room above. "What the . . ." "Look under the beds . . ." "Try the chest . . ." The sound of crashing furniture, the scrape of a bedstead on the floor. Someone kicked him in the side. The room around him was a fevered harlequin of torchlight and clawing shadows. The clay earth smell of the floor choked his nostrils, and the sweat-and-leather stink of the guards.

"Where is he?"

Rhion managed to shake his head. "He went up there . . . if he's gone, I don't know . . ."

The guard kicked him again, sending him crashing against the wall. The next second he was grabbed by the front of his robe and hauled to his feet, pain stabbing him in the side so sharply that for a moment he thought one of them had put a dagger into him. The kick must have broken a rib. Two of them dragged him to the hearth, where the remains of the small supper fire still smoldered. One held him by an arm twisted behind his back while the other pokered aside the layer of ash, exposing the glowing core of embers beneath. Rhion struggled desperately as they caught his hand, forced it toward the simmering heat. "Where is he . . . ?"

"Don't waste time." Esrex turned his head a little toward them, fragile profile stained amber by the sudden renewal of the flames. "Get out and search the area. The old man's a cripple; he can't have gone far. And in any case," he added maliciously, as the guards paused, holding Rhion's hand so close to the coals that the heat of them seared the hairs on his fingers, "we don't want to burn his *right* hand. He'll need that to sign his confession."

Even in that extremity, it flashed through Rhion's mind to mention to Esrex that he was left-handed, but that, he knew, would be asking for a shovelful of coals in his palm. He was slammed back against the wall with another knife thrust of pain, but through a gray tide of sweating nausea he managed to gasp, "Confession of what?"

Guards were streaming out of the house, into the square, the alleyways around it, and across the roofs. *He's blind,* Rhion thought desperately. *Without magic to work the voice-box he's mute, a cripple* . . . A guardswoman came up from the cellar with surprising speed after she'd gone down. "Nobody down there—nothing but witchery, some kind of demon-magic . . ."

The Well would be quiescent, Rhion thought blankly—a pity. One of them might have fallen into it . . .

And much as he hated the thing, he felt a pang at its destruction. All Jaldis' work . . .

Esrex paused directly in front of him, thin and incisive as broken glass. "The confession that's going to greet his Grace when he and the Earl of the Purple Forest return to Bragenmere late tonight," he said softly. "The confession that the child my dear little cousin carries in her belly is yours."

He was already cold with shock, but still he felt as if the floor had sunk away beneath his feet. "That's impossible."

"Oh, come . . ."

Rhion started to speak, then bit his tongue, realizing that his blurted protest would have been a confession. *I've been using spells of barrenness on her to prevent that, dammit!*

"Her chamberwoman is my fellow initiate in the rites of Agon, you see," Esrex went on, apparently absorbed in smoothing the pearl-stitched kid of his glove ever more closely over his thin-fingered, childlike hands, but watching Rhion from beneath colorless lashes as he spoke. "The information one learns at the Temple is well worth what one gets under one's nails. There is no question that she has put horns on the Earl. That's all I really need to prevent that traitor Prinagos from allying himself with decent families, always supposing one could describe the Muriks as decent . . . But it will give me considerable pleasure," he went on, and looked up with a thin little smile, teeth small as rice grains in the parting of his fleshless lips, "to see you, my arrogant little warlock, pay the fullest possible penalty for rape."

Half the population of Shuttlefly Court was gathered around the door to watch Esrex's bravos manhandle Rhion out into the darkness. The torchlight showed him their faces—the tired, dirty, or unshaven faces of the weavers to whom he'd sold herbal simples, the painted faces of the whores who'd bought luck-charms and spells of barrenness from him and the snaggle-haired brown faces of the laundrywomen who'd come to him to have their fortunes read. The faces were blank and noncommittal, like the faces of people passing by a dog dying on the side of the road. Something struck his back and he heard a child's singsong giggle: "Wi-zard, wi-zard, Turn you into a li-zard . . ." and shrieks of nervous laughter from the other children in the square.

Another clear little treble crowed, "Witch, witch, Give you the itch . . ." and a rotting peach squished soggily against his sleeve. The two guards who weren't searching the neighborhood for Jaldis roped his wrists together and mounted their horses. Nobody even called out, *What'd he do?* They all knew what he'd probably done, having heard it traded back and forth in taverns all their lives: poisoned an old man to get his money, seduced an honest woman by means of spells, blackmailed a woman who came to him for help, and ruined someone—businessman, baker, farmer—by putting an Eye on their shop or stove or cattle . . .

Jaldis, dammit, get the hell out of town if you can . . . The men kicked their horses to a trot and he stumbled after them, grimly determined to keep up and wondering if he could. The pain in his side was unbelievable, turning him queasy and faint, but he knew if he fell there would be no getting up. As they disappeared around the corner into Thimble Lane he saw from the tail of his eye two of the local loiterers, pine-knot torches in hand, go curiously, cautiously into the house he and Jaldis had shared, looking to see what pickings they could find.

The horsemen avoided the main streets where farm carts would be clattering to the markets until dawn, taking instead the crisscrossing mazes of smaller alleys and back lanes, dark as pitch save for the light of the torches they bore. Rhion managed to stay on his feet through the dirt lanes of the Old Town, though the dust thrown up by the hooves nearly choked him and the pain in his side brought him close to fainting. He fell on the steep cobbled rise that led to the golden lamps and walled mansions of the Upper Town. Unable to get on his feet again, he concentrated what strength he had on keeping his head clear of the granite chunks that paved the street and not passing out. It wasn't far—at most a hundred feet—but he was nearly unconscious when they came to a stop in a granite-paved court.

"Where's the other one?" a voice demanded, and Rhion moved his head groggily, trying to see where he was. It was useless. His spectacles had been knocked off somewhere during the journey, and all he had was a blurred impression of towering dark walls. But the smell of the place was enough to tell him. Not a tree, not a fountain, not a statue broke the dark monolithic walls around him—no smell on the turgid night of water, flowers, grass, or any of the things people paid for when they bought houses in the Upper Town . . . Only stone. And far-off, the mingled scents of incense and blood.

And terrible silence, the silence of the brooding god.

The Temple of Agon.

"Got out through a roof-trap," Esrex' light, steely voice said. A slim pillar of white in the flare of the torchlight, he stood surrounded by three or four—it was difficult to tell without spectacles—pillars of shrouded black. The pearls braided into his hair gleamed dimly as he turned his head. "He won't get far; anyway, this is the one we need."

Rhion barely heard the sound of footfalls as one black figure detached itself from the group and walked to where he lay, torn flesh bleeding through the tatters of his torn robe. Looking up he saw nothing, only the pale hands protruding from beneath the cloudy black layers of veiling. But he felt the eyes. The voice was high and epicene—it could have been male or female, chilled and frigid with self-righteous spite.

"I suspect the Duke will have a different opinion of wizardry when faced with a man who used those powers to seduce his daughter."

Rhion turned over, his body hurting as if he had been beaten with clubs, to look across at where Esrex still stood. "And what about a woman who used those powers to seduce her own husband?" he asked, fighting for breath, surprised at how changed his voice sounded in his own ears—slurred like a drunkard's. He tasted blood as he spoke. "Or did you think that fit of lust you had for Damson last spring was the result of some new perfume she wore?"

The priests of Agon looked at one another for a moment, and for that moment, Esrex did not move. Then, without hurry, he walked to the nearest doorway, where a painted clay lamp burned upon a stand. Taking it, he blew it out and came back to where Rhion lay. The priest standing near-by stepped aside, and Esrex removed the lamp's top and poured the oil deliberately down over Rhion's face, hair, and the front of his robe. Then he took a torch from the nearest guard.

"Repeat that lie again," he said quietly, "and you'll discover that there are worse things than the penalty for forcing a virgin to open her legs to you by means of your spells. For myself I don't care—a true man cannot be affected by such tricks—but you have slandered a good and loyal woman for whom my love has never wavered since first I saw her face. As she will attest." And he slashed down with the torch.

Rhion twisted aside as well as he could, covering his face with his oil-soaked arms and thinking, *Nice. Got any other clever ideas . . . ?* He felt the heat of the flames, flickering inches from his cheek, tried desperately not to think about what would happen next . . . Opening his eyes after a hideously long moment he could see Esrex' feet, close enough to his face to be more or less clear to him. With bizarre irony, he saw that Esrex still wore the long-toed shoes of embroidered ivory satin he'd had on the day of their confrontation in the grotto.

"Remember," Esrex' voice said above him, "that we don't really need you alive." He handed the torch back to the guard. "Now take him away."

They put him in a sort of watching room in the temple's vaults, tying his hands to an iron ring in the wall. Three or four men were on guard there, wearing the rough tunics and baggy trousers of laborers or slaves. Masks covered their faces, but Rhion guessed, looking near-sightedly at the hard-muscled brown arms and thighs, that two of them at least were "liverymen"—household guards—of noble or wealthy families, either freedmen or slaves on a night off doing service at the beck of the priests whose followers they were. Others might have been city ditch diggers, or chair bearers—the cult of Agon welcomed men and women, children, too, of all classes, anyone who could be of use. All of these, to judge by their conversation, were ignorant, foulmouthed, and delighted to have someone helpless and in their power.

It was a hellish night. The room was smotheringly hot, the smoldering torches set all around the walls not only adding to the accumulated heat of the day but contributing smoke as well. The men joked, diced, and passed a skin of cheap wine among themselves, but never took their eyes from their prisoner. The ring in the wall was just high enough that Rhion was unable to lie down. Though his wrists had stopped bleeding, the pain and cramps in his arms and shoulders grew steadily worse until he had to set his teeth to remain silent. The reek of the smoke, of the guards, of stale wine, and of the oil that still soaked his hair and beard and clothes turned him faint and sick, and he wondered if the priests of Darova were right and there was a hell, and he'd somehow ended up there without either dying or being judged . . .

The guards sprang to their feet, bowing in obeisance. Silent as the shadow of a crow, a black-veiled priest glided in. *They must train them to walk that way,* Rhion thought distractedly. The priest said no word, but, at a sign from him, two of the guards pulled Rhion to his feet and held his arms and his head while the priest drew from his robes a steel needle and a tiny vial of some liquid with which he coated the needle's tip before stabbing it, hard and accurately, into the big veins of Rhion's neck.

Then he left again, without speaking a word.

More pheelas, Rhion thought groggily, as he sank back to the floor. Did that mean Jaldis might, by this time, be regaining some of his power to use his spectacles—if he had his spectacles with him—or his voice-box? Or had they caught him already and kicked him to death against some alley wall like men *frugeing* a rat? And anyway, where could he go? Criminals frequently sought sanctuary in the temples, but no cult offered sanctuary to wizards. Wizardry was an offense to the power of all gods. There was not one, not even Mhorvianne the Merciful, who would let the mageborn hide in the smallest fold of their robes.

He thought about Jaldis, hauling himself painfully along the smelly back streets of Bragenmere, blind and voiceless, about the gangs of drunkards who prowled the streets on summer nights, beating up anyone they saw, and about the pickpockets and thieves who haunted the alleyways, who would kill a man for his boots . . .

And Tally? What the hell had happened to Tally?

Could she really be with child?

It had to be a trap, he thought frantically. Even if she had another lover besides himself—which he knew down to the marrow of his bones she had not—the spells by which he prevented her from conceiving would have worked, no matter who she lay with. *Dammit, I know I'm not that powerful a mage, but I can at least get that spell right. It's not as if she were using a counterspell against it . . .*

And then the warm sweetness of the marshes of the Kairn River came back to him, the green, musky smell of the reeds and the silken murmur of the water, striped sunlight playing over Tally's creamy skin. *Damson's been plying me with every kind of herb and tea and potion she knows* . . .

Damson.

. . . she keeps saying, 'Oh, when you bear your husband's child you'll know what true happiness is . . .'

He remembered how, long ago, Tally had come to him to buy a philter to make Damson's life better without her sister's knowledge. It would not have taken malice—only Damson's eager good will. The wedding coming up, Damson aglow in the joy of her own pregnancy . . . the tincture Jaldis had mixed for her in the candlelit dimness of that painted room . . .

"Hey!"

Rhion looked up, startled, as a rough hand seized his hair and cracked his head back against the stone wall behind him. One of his guards stood over him, a vast blur against the torchlight, cheap wine stinking in his sweat.

"You quit that, you hear?"

"Quit what?" Rhion demanded, too startled to realize that he should simply agree and profusely apologize.

The man kicked him. "You know what, you little witch-bitch. I haven't won a pot in fifty throws and I want you to quit witching the goddam dice or I'll light that goddam beard of yours on fire, and we'll see how fast you can witch it out."

Exasperated, Rhion snapped, "Look, moron, if I had the ability at the moment to work any magic at all, why the hell would I waste my time screwing up your dice game when I could use it instead to untie these festering ropes and get myself the hell out of this mess?"

The guard struck him, hard, across the face—*definitely a chair carrier*, Rhion thought, tasting the blood as the cuts on his mouth opened up again. "Don't you get smart with me, you little . . ."

"Hell . . ." Another guard came over, bored with dicing, not drunk enough to be careless, but drunk enough to have the wicked inventiveness of drunks. He took the nearest torch from the wall and brought it down close to Rhion's face. "Let's light his beard on fire anyway. We don't got any water down here, but we all been drinkin' that wine, and maybe if he begs us real pretty we could put out the fire by . . ."

"Heads up!" another by the door called, and the man with the torch turned swiftly, putting it back in its holder in the wall as a priest entered, black clouds of veils billowing eerily around him like the smoke of a fire without light.

"Bring him."

The cell they took him to was small, hotter if anything than the watching room. But if the priest who waited for him, sitting behind the single table of spare dark wood, felt any discomfort in his long robes of black wool and the veils that shrouded his face, he gave no sign of it. By the way the guards and the other priests bowed—by the height of the headdress that supported the cloudy frame of veils—Rhion guessed this must be Mijac, Agon's High Priest in Bragenmere, though it was impossible to be sure.

Was that, he wondered with exhausted detachment, one of the strengths of the cult? That its servants served in secret, even from one another? That the masks that covered the faces of the guards in the watchroom, the veils that hid the priests, concealed them, not only from outsiders, not only from each other's witnessing, but from themselves?

He looked up at the men beside him and behind him, whose strength, he suspected, was the only thing keeping him on his feet. They might be slaves of a man, of the city, or certainly of economic realities, but their wills had once been their own. Now they had given their wills to Agon, and it was Agon who acted through them—they could spy upon their benefactors, they could betray their friends, they could torture the weak, prostitute themselves, beat a helpless old cripple to death in an alleyway, and remain, in their hearts, good people, kindly people, men and women worthy of regard, because it was, after all, the Veiled God who was acting, not them.

They shoved him forward, and he had to catch the edge of the table in his bound hands, his legs shaking under him. Without his spectacles, he wouldn't have been able to see the priest's face at this distance, anyway, but there was something unnerving about those blowing curtains of black, through which only a white blur was dimly visible, and the gleam of eyes.

A gloved black hand thrust a sheet of paper across the polished tabletop and offered him a quill. "Sign it."

He picked up the paper, his numb fingers barely able to close around the edge, and held it where he could read it, about a hand-breadth from his nose. He caught the words, *by means of potions forced her to yield to my lusts* . . . before a guard ripped it from his grasp.

"He said sign it, not read it."

"It's lies," Rhion said quietly.

Mijac's voice, behind the veils, was startlingly deep, a beautiful bass, like the deep boom of distant thunder. "What does that have to do with it?"

"Oh, I forgot," Rhion said, still holding himself up by the edge of the table, blood, lamp-oil, and sweat dripping down his matted hair and onto the paper before him. "Lies are the common coin of Agon."

Mijac reached out and wiped the droplets carefully from the document with one gloved fingertip. "As they are of wizards," he returned calmly. The veils shuddered and moved as he leaned back in his chair again. "You are the architects of lies, the artists of illusion— the thieves of matters which should be left to the gods. When a man sees a monkey running about with a man's dagger in its hand, does he stop to inquire of the animal what it intends to do with the weapon? Of course not. And when other men begin to turn to that monkey in respect, bow to it with hand on brow and ask its advice . . . then it is time for sane men to step in and correct matters. Is it true that the Lady Damson used a love-philter to bring her husband to her bed last spring?"

Rhion's arms had begun to shake with fatigue—he stiffened them desperately, feeling darkness chew on the edges of his vision, a strange, detached numbness creeping over his chest. *Don't faint now, dammit.*

"Why don't you ask her husband?"

"Lord Esrex has his uses," the priest replied in a mild tone. "He and his wife are holding the Lady Tallisett now, awaiting his Grace's return. But knowledge is always a helpful thing to have."

"Provided you get your facts straight. Who told you I was supposed to be the girl's lover?"

"The girl herself," Mijac said. "And Jaldis confirmed it before he died."

Rhion looked up quickly, his face ashen.

"They found him in an alley behind the Temple of Darova. I had given them no specific instructions—perhaps the men thought it would be easier than carrying him here. The lower orders are lazy that way. Now sign."

Sickness and grief washed him like rising tide; even his blurred myopia was darkening. His voice sounded oddly distant through the ringing in his ears. "It's a lie." Tally would never have betrayed him . . . there was no way of telling whether anything Mijac said was the truth . . .

"What is not a lie," the priest's voice came from, it seemed, farther and farther away, "is that a man can live a long time while his bones are being broken and the splinters pulled out of his flesh, so I advise you to sign before you have cause to find out how much truth I can speak . . ."

"My lord!"

Rhion's hands slipped from the table, and he felt someone catch him, supporting him as the rising darkness closed over his head. Voices came from out of that darkness, dim and muffled, like words heard underwater. He struggled to surface again, to breathe . . .

"It's the Duke! He's at the gates . . ."

A chair scraped as it was pushed back. Dimly, Rhion reflected that it was the first sound of agitated movement he'd heard from the priests of the Veiled God. "Right," Mijac said softly, and there was a momentary pause. Then, "There's no help for it. Finish him."

A huge hand gripped him under the chin and forced his head back.

"Not here, you fool—in the cellar where the blood can drain. And hurry . . ."

Rhion lashed out feebly with his bound hands, with some idea of struggling, fighting, delaying until the Duke could reach them, until he could tell him . . . Tell him what? That Tally had cuckolded his prospective ally?

But before he'd thought that far, something hard and heavy cracked over the back of his skull.

He came to lying on a stone floor, thinking, *Well, so much for that idea . . .*

Arthritis-twisted hands touched his face. In his dazed exhaustion the buzzing voice sounded no louder than a mosquito's hum. "Rhion? My son . . ."

And above him, as his mind slowly cleared and he thought, *He did lie . . .* he heard Mijac's deep, ringing tones. "We have broken no law, my lord."

Rhion opened his eyes. He was lying on the floor halfway down a dark stone hallway, through which he cloudily recalled passing on the way to Mijac's cell. A door at the far end had been opened— the movement of the tepid night air broke the stifling heat.

And surrounded by torchlight and soldiers in cloaks the color of new blood, the Duke stood framed against the heavy trapezoid of the opened doors, hands upon his hips and traveling clothes flashing with tiny mirrors and knots of gold.

"No," he said quietly. "You have broken no law, my lord Mijac. But you have disrupted my pleasure and you have done injury to my friends."

He walked forward, his gilded boots creaking faintly in the absolute hush. The priests and the masked volunteers surrounding Rhion where he lay retreated a little, leaving only Jaldis and Mijac near him.

"I met him on the rise of land before the palace gates," Jaldis murmured swiftly, beneath the voices of Duke and High Priest. "I knew he must pass by there—I listened for the sound of many horses . . ." Even without his spectacles, Rhion saw how torn and filthy the old man's brown robe was, how gutter-slime smutched his face and beard and matted the ends of his thin white hair, as if he had fallen—or been kicked—over and over into the Old Town's garbage and dust. His hands were trembling as he pulled the bonds from Rhion's wrists, the dirty orange lamplight in the hall making a hundred juddering reflections in the crystal facets of his spectacle-lenses.

"Your *friends?*" Mijac's inflection twisted irony from the word like spilled wine wrung from a rag. "No more than they have done injury to you, Lord Duke." He stepped forward, holding out the yellow paper. "You see that it is signed."

The Duke took the confession and read it through. The priests and their followers murmured in the shadows at the inner end of the hall. Gently Jaldis helped Rhion to sit up. Marc of Erralswan, like a shining bronze god in his armor, made a move as if to assist and then seemed to think better of committing himself. At that distance, five or six feet, Rhion could not see Dinar of Mere's fleshy features well enough to judge his thoughts—only a stylized blocking of light and shadow, bronze and blue and black. *Of course Mijac would sign it himself*, he thought, with a resigned weariness that made him wonder objectively if he was going to faint again. He was only surprised they'd bothered to try forcing him actually to sign in the first place. As Esrex had said, they didn't really need him to.

Without speaking, the Duke came over to where the two wizards sat, filthy, bloody, and ragged as beggars, on the polished floor, and it seemed to Rhion that Agon's faceless servants fell back a little further, leaving him and his master completely alone. For a time the Duke stood looking down on them, the old man he had befriended and to whom he had sent gifts and publicly shown his regard and the young one to whom he'd confidently given the freedom of his house. His eyes went from them to the confession in his hand, a confession of betrayal, cynicism, and rape. Then he reached down, took Rhion's left hand and turned it over in his, all streaked as it was with blood and sweat and lamp-oil. Straightening up, he looked again at the paper, clean and unstained from top to bottom. And, still without a word, he held the confession to the flame of the nearest torch.

"Bring him to the palace," he said quietly, after he had dropped the burning scrap to the floor and trodden it underfoot. "I think we need the truth."

The smell of smoke hung in the air behind them as they left the silent priests of shadow and went out into the night.

14

The horses were waiting for them in the street outside. "There is only one litter and two bearers," the Duke said, nodding toward the curtained chair and its two muscular, fair-haired slaves. "Even with his crutches, Jaldis could barely walk when he met us. Do you think you could back a horse, Rhion?"

Rhion nodded, though he had private mental reservations about his ability to get into a saddle unaided. "After being dragged up here," he said, pushing back his blood-streaked hair from his eyes, "believe me, if you just let me *walk* to your gates at my own pace, I'd be glad."

The Duke's mouth hardened and he glanced back over his shoulder at the featureless black doors which had swung shut, silent and unnoticed, behind them. The torch-blown shadows of the guards jerked and lurched over the undressed granite wall; bronze mail flickered darkly and voices rose, relieved to be out of the Temple's oppressive gloom, as Jaldis was helped into the litter. For the moment Rhion and the Duke stood in a little island of stillness in the crowd.

Now, he thought, and his stomach curled into a tight, cold ball within him. He swallowed hard.

"My lord." He reached out to touch the red leather sleeve, and the Duke looked back down at him, hearing the change in his voice.

"My lord," Rhion said, "thank you—thank you beyond words for saving us—for believing in us over Mijac . . ."

The big man sniffed. "I think I'd believe a gypsy horse coper over Mijac . . ."

Rhion shook his head, knowing there was no way out of what he had to say, and forced his eyes to meet the Duke's. "You shouldn't," he said quietly, his voice pitched low to exclude the guards. "That's what makes this all the worse. That confession is true."

The Duke regarded him in a silence which seemed to stretch out endlessly and seemed to drown even the restless snorting of the horses and the uneasy mutter of the guards. Rhion tried not to think of what the betrayal would do to this friend of Jaldis'—only what penalty Tally would have to pay for giving herself willingly to any man while her father was negotiating in good faith for her marriage.

At last he spoke. "All of it?" His voice was quiet, his face showing nothing.

"All of it," Rhion whispered, looking away. He had begun to shake all over, with exhaustion and dread and wretchedness—he had to force his voice steady. "Jaldis knew nothing. He warned me not to . . . not to betray you. Not to let my feelings for Tally get the better of me . . ."

They'll drown the child when it's born, he thought. He'd heard of that happening on those rare occasions when a woman did bear a wizard's offspring. Or Jaldis or Ranley, the court physician, could doubtless bring on a miscarriage . . .

He shut his eyes, unable to bear it, unable to bear the thought of what it would do to her.

His son. If it was Jaldis' tincture that was responsible for the failure of his spells, it would indeed be a son. Around them, the guards in their red-crested helmets fell quiet and glanced questioningly at one another, unable to hear what their master had to say to this battered and filthy little man, but aware of the forbidding stillness of the Duke's stance that kept even the stupidest of them from asking about the delay.

There was still no expression in the Duke's voice. "And is she with child?"

Still not looking up, Rhion nodded. "I think so. I don't see that Esrex could make a case for any of this if she were not." Keeping his voice level with an effort, he explained what he thought had happened, without mentioning how or from whom Damson had obtained the tincture—only that she had given it to Tally, meaning nothing more than a wedding night successful in Damson's own terms of motherhood and dynasty.

When Rhion finished, the silence was so deep he could hear a slave woman singing in the garden of some big walled house down the street and the endless rattling hum of the cicadas in the trees. He could not meet the Duke's eyes or look him in the face—even close as they stood he could have distinguished little but a blur in the fidgetting cresset glare. Overhead, the moon stood high, its whiteness shimmering on the curtains of Jaldis' litter as they stirred in a stray drift of wind.

The Duke folded his heavy arms. His voice was so quiet as to exclude even Marc or Erralswan, holding the two horses four feet away, but calm as if he were hearing the suits of strangers in his own law courts. "And you seduced her by means of a spell?"

Rhion nodded. "She . . ." he began, but could not go on. He was shivering, as if with bitterest cold.

"That is not," the Duke said, "what Jaldis told me."

Rhion looked up at him, the blood in his veins turning to dust.

"According to Jaldis," the Duke went on, "my daughter loves you very much. How much you love her I think you have just demonstrated by your willingness to shoulder the blame." And for all the quietness of his voice, his dark eyes were grim. "But half the scandals in the world are based upon sincere love, and it is scandal with which we now have to deal. Marc . . ."

At his gesture the young captain came forward with the horses.

"Come. Let's not keep Esrex waiting any longer than we have done."

Early summer dawn was just beginning to tint the sky as the cavalcade mounted the rise to the palace gates. The houses of the

Upper Town crowded close here, not the villas of the rich—not on a street which bore so much traffic—but tall blocks of expensive flats owned by the wealthier civil servants or their mistresses, built over shops that sold jewelry, spices, and silk. The alley where Jaldis had waited for the Duke's approach could have been any of a dozen near here, Rhion thought, clinging to the saddlebow of his led horse— the alley where he'd waited, listening for just this clatter of hooves on the cobble, this creaking of leather and armor, this smell of torches made up with incense to keep mosquitoes at bay. Waited and, still blind, still mute, had dragged himself out on his crutches, with the terrible, broken groans of a mute which had not passed his throat in eleven years.

Waited to save him. To save them.

No servants were about in the great court yet, save the grooms who'd slept half the night in the shelter of the colonnade awaiting the Duke's arrival from the hills. Awakened an hour earlier by the advent of the Earl of the Purple Forest and the Duke's servants and baggage horses, they came running briskly as the gates were opened once again. Overhead, the sky was losing its darkness, the late moon huge and white, a solitary lily floating upon a still lake of lilac-gray.

"My lord!" Esrex came striding rapidly down the shadow-clotted length of the pillared hall as the door guards bowed the Duke in. Rhion noted that the young man had changed into a court suit of ash-colored velvet on which rubies gleamed like splashed blood. "I have been telling the Earl of the shocking crime which has been . . ." And he stopped, seeing Jaldis at the Duke's side, leaning on his crutches with his opal spectacles flickering eerily in the long, filthy frame of his white hair. Then his eyes went to Rhion, his torn robe stained with lamp oil and blood, standing at his other hand. Up at the other end of the hall, around the two or three bronze lampstands which remained lit, a handful of courtiers self-consciously tried to pretend that staying up until the bakers were taking the bread from the ovens was their usual practice; but, in the sudden hush, the soft pat of a final card being turned was like the smack of a leather belt, and the clink of glass lace-spindles like the clatter of kitchen pans.

Lazily, the Earl of the Purple Forest rose from the pearwood couch where he had been flirting with one of Damson's maids-of-honor. He, too, had changed out of his traveling dress, though his red hair was still braided back from the journey. Opal and sardonyx gleamed on the midnight velvet of his sleeves and breast. "Really, Dinar, I think you owe me some kind of explanation about what Lord Esrex has been saying."

"Even so," the Duke said. Neither his voice nor his demeanor gave the smallest of his thoughts away. "Marc—fetch my daughter."

"She is with my wife, my lord," Esrex hastened to inform him with a mixture of officiousness and spite. His pale eyes darted uncertainly from Rhion's face to Jaldis' and back to the Duke's. "We thought it better to know where she was. If this man still holds her under his spells . . ."

"A matter you are most qualified to judge, of course," the Duke responded, and the young man's thin skin reddened with sudden anger. Then he turned and looked around him at the hall, and every head bowed quickly over fashionable needlework, lace-making, or cards, and voices rose with exaggerated brightness.

"Oh, *pounds* thinner, darling, but the way she goes on about eating vegetables, you'd think she invented them . . ." ". . . Everything—house, horses, lands, the town investments—on a single cut. The man has more guts than brains, if you ask me . . ." ". . . horse couldn't run if you lit its tail on fire . . ." A weary-looking corps of musicians in the gallery, who had been frantically discussing what part of their repertoire hadn't already been played four times since the conclusion of supper, struck up a light air on viols and flutes, as incongruous in that tense atmosphere as a fan dancer at an auto-da-fé.

The Duke raised his voice, not much, but enough to carry the length of the hall. "Good people, I bid you good night."

There was no mistaking the dismissal in his tone. The hall was cleared in five minutes, and Rhion, leaning wearily against the strapwork marble column that supported the gallery, half-smiled to himself. *If I could sell scrying-crystals that worked for anyone*, he thought wryly, *I could retire tonight on the proceeds.*

Then he thought of Tally again, and his heart seemed to die in his chest.

"Really," the Earl said, when the last reluctant gossip had collected her feather tippet, her snoring lapdogs, and her long yellow silk train and departed. "If the chit's pregnant, as Esrex claims, I'm afraid our negotiations are going to have to be . . . renegotiated. Not that I wish to spoil sport, but there is the succession to be thought of."

"How did you know it was Esrex?" Rhion stepped back to where Jaldis had unobtrusively sunk down on one of the spindle-legged couches set among the pillars which flanked the hall. In the smoky glare of a near-by lamp, the old man looked drained and gray under the coating of grime. Rhion sat down next to him, his legs still feeling weak. Between lamp-oil, blood, and the miscellaneous sewage that covered both their robes, the servants would probably have to burn the cushions, but that was something they could take up with Esrex. "And how did you know what it was about?"

"I remained to listen, of course." Jaldis raised his head from his hands, making an effort to shake off the exhaustion that all but crushed him. "After getting out through the roof trap I hid for a few minutes near the door that leads out to the midden in the back. They were hunting for me across the roofs and down the alleys, not up next to the house itself."

Rhion was aghast. "You could have been . . . !"

"I knew we had been poisoned with *pheelas* root, of course," that soft, droning voice went on. "But it did not interfere with the senses of a mage. They waited, of course, for it to take effect before coming within the theoretical range of wizard's marks . . . As soon as I heard Esrex' voice, I guessed what it was about. If one is in the habit of storing grease beside the stove, one does not have to look far for a cause when the house catches fire."

Rhion bowed his head, grief and guilt washing back over him in a sickening wave. His passion for Tally—his yielding to hers for him—had brought ridicule and shame upon the man who had just saved his life, disgrace—almost certainly banishment—on Jaldis and probably Tally as well . . . He shied from thinking about what he had brought on himself. The Duke was a just man, but he had needed that alliance with the In Islands to guard against the White Bragenmere faction at home. He had saved Rhion from the priests of Agon, but, as he had observed, scandal was scandal.

Intent and terrible, the silence deepened in the room. For the first time, Rhion understood why the very rich, in palaces this size, maintained musicians to fill up the resounding hush. The guards had left, Esrex' liverymen as well as the Duke's mailed troopers, and the huge quiet seemed to echo with the breathing of those few who remained. Once Rhion looked up to see the Earl's dark eyes turned his way, though whether he was studying the man whom Esrex had described as his rival, or merely curious about the two grubby fugitives huddled together on the couch, his eyesight was not good enough to determine.

"What can be keeping them?" Esrex muttered through his teeth. The Duke, his arms folded and his face a careful blank, did not even look at him, but Rhion could almost feel the seethe of conjecture, of anger and disappointment, of possible salvage operations, options, scenarios, and covering lies that went on behind those dark eyes.

At length, Rhion's quick hearing detected the rustle of skirts in the stairway that led from the vestibule up to the palace's private suites and the firmer tread of Marc of Erralswan's gold-stamped military boots. All eyes in the room were on the archway as shadow played suddenly across its lamplit pillars. Then the pillars framed them: the tall Captain with his bronze armor and scarlet cloak, curly dark hair falling to his shoulders; Damson in plum-black velvet that flashed with jewels; and Tally like the flame of a candle, a blurred, slender column of dull gold.

She's with child, he thought again, and shivered with wonder and dread and grief. *My child. Her child.*

A wizard's child.

A child they won't allow to live.

Without his spectacles, her face was only a blur to him as she crossed the vestibule, to sink to her knees at her father's feet. Damson remained by the door, rigid and silent—one could only guess what had passed between the sisters in the hours since Esrex had ordered his wife to lock her one-time follower and champion in her room.

"Father, I'm sorry . . ." Tally whispered, holding out her hands. "So sorry. Please, I beg you . . ."

The Duke stepped forward and took her hands, raising her, his face suddenly strained. "My child . . ."

"No." Shaking her head she stepped back quickly, as if to study his face, and, by the flash of the jewels on her rings, Rhion saw she had squeezed his hands. Though her features were a blur to him, Rhion saw how tense she stood, like a warrior ready to go into a fight—a novice warrior, into her first fight, with no confidence of victory.

"How you can dare . . ." Esrex began, but a gesture from the Duke stilled him.

"Go ahead, daughter."

She swallowed. The huge amber beads around her throat gleamed softly in the lamplight as she turned to the Earl of the Purple Forest.

"My lord, I can only beg your pardon as well. They say you are a man who understands love and lovers . . ."

If you want to call it that, Rhion thought cynically, and saw the Earl's head tilt a little, with detached interest. Esrex drew in his breath, but, at a glance from the Duke, held his peace. Tally, it was clear, was going to be given her say.

"Your pardon also I ask, Rhion the Brown . . ." She gave him his formal title, setting distance between them ". . . for this shocking misunderstanding."

She turned back to the Duke. There was a small bunch of pheasant-plumes on the back of her bodice, the ribbons that hung down from it against her skirt tipped with a crystal set in gold. Rhion could see the facets of it flash with the trembling of her knees.

The hall was utterly silent.

"As usual Esrex was only half-right," she went on, her voice very clear and steady in the hush. "Father . . . and my lord . . ." She inclined her head toward the Earl, who was watching them with folded arms and an ironic gleam in his eye. "To my shame I admit it is true that I am with child. I beg your pardon, beg it abjectly, for having fallen in love with a man other than the one you, Father, would have chosen. But I have fallen in love."

Half-turning, she stretched out her hand . . .

. . . and with only the barest perceptible hesitation, Marc of Erralswan stepped forward, took it, and put a protective arm around her waist.

"My lord," he said to the Duke, bowing his handsome head. "It is I, too, who must beg your forgiveness."

Rhion, who had risen to his feet when Tally had briefly addressed him, had just enough sense to keep his mouth shut and his eyes straight ahead. But Esrex was far too stunned to look at him. *Tally* . . . Rhion thought despairingly, his hand groping for the support of the couch. *Oh, Tally, no* . . .

Stiffly, as if she spoke with a knife-point in her back, Damson stepped forward and said, "It's true, Father." She kept her eyes averted from her husband, whose dropped jaw and twitch of startled outrage were visible even to Rhion. Her high, childlike voice sounded strained but firm. "I learned of this two days ago. I would have spoken to you of it tomorrow. Esrex," she went on, her gaze fixed determinedly upon the gold ornamentation of her father's sleeve, "said that you must be told about Tally being with child, and so bade me lock her in her room tonight. But he never told me who he thought her lover was, nor what would be done to . . . to these innocent men."

"No wizard is innocent!" Esrex sputtered, completely losing his usual aplomb and looking suddenly many years younger, pale eyes blazing like a furious boy's. "And as for . . ."

"Esrex, *be silent!*" Damson's head snapped around and for a moment their eyes locked. Something in her look, either its urgency or its deadly venom, stopped his words as if with a garrote.

Rhion sank back to the couch, his legs suddenly weak. After the first stunned moment he could see the logic—and, in fact, the brilliance—of the solution. Esrex might or might not choose to believe that the story of the love-philter was a lie. But its corollary—that the tincture to make sure she conceived, the tincture that lay at the heart of this whole hellish night—was something whose existence Damson could never let him even suspect. It was perfectly possible that Esrex, to remain on terms with the cult of Agon, would repudiate a child so conceived; it was almost certain that he would repudiate Damson. But only if the matter became public knowledge.

Tally couldn't have known it would be Marc who would be sent to fetch her, Rhion thought, with a curious, despairing detachment. *The plan must have come to her when she saw him.* One had to admit that it cut through all the problems.

Except that Tally would now marry Marc.

It was fortunate that Esrex was still staring at his wife in stupefied rage as Rhion looked away, unable to endure the sight of that slim, dull-gold form in the brawny brown clasp of the young Captain's arm.

The Duke regarded his daughter for some moments in grave silence, seeing in the set ivory face, the desperate gray eyes, the mute plea for him to understand and to help. At her side, Marc was trying to appear noble, but had the air of one who has laid everything he owns on the table and awaits the cut of the cards. Rhion wondered distractedly how Tally had talked him into this. If he failed, he would surely be banished, though it was clear that the Duke was under no illusions about what was going on. But then, Rhion's impression of Marc had always been that he was rather easily led. She probably had not told him the name of the child's true father. If he succeeded . . .

"My children." The Duke held out his hands.

Rhion closed his eyes again, shaking all over with relief and grief. He was saved—Tally was saved—their son would be allowed to live. And if Esrex had thrust the torch into his oil-soaked robes in the courtyard of the Veiled God, he thought it would have been easier to stand than this.

The rest of the scene seemed to pass over his head, an exchange of voices at some huge distance, almost meaningless.

"It is not me that has been most wronged, but our cousin and friend, the Earl of the Purple Forest . . ."

"My lord . . ." Without opening his eyes, Rhion knew that Marc had gone to kneel at the Earl's feet. That was another thing rich young men or youths of noble family like Marc were taught—how to kneel with grace and when. "I can only beg of you as a lover that you release the girl I adore from her obligation to you . . ."

It was a comedy of manners, with all the stock characters present: the handsome but impecunious young lover; the stern father; and the glamorous roué with *noblesse oblige* and a heart of hidden gold. The

Duke—and the Earl—must both have known from the start that any hope of an alliance was irreparably shattered. The rest of Marc's manly apology, of the Earl's gracious speech of agreement, of the ducal blessing upon the young lovers, and his gift to Marc of sufficient lands and estates to honor his soon-to-be-bride—undoubtedly why Marc, the son of penniless nobility, had agreed to the gamble in the first place—went unheard. Tally had seen a way out and had taken it, as she would have sprung from the roof of a burning building across a wide gap to safety.

But she would always now be another man's wife.

Of course, Rhion told himself, he had known from the start that this was how it must be. This grief he must have—he *had*—foreseen from the moment their eyes had met in the snowy, grim-haunted woods. There was no reason to feel this pain . . . no reason . . .

He lowered his head to his hand, his temples throbbing, feeling sick and cold and alone to the marrow of his bones.

After a time he felt Tally's hands on his shoulders, smelled the perfumes of her hair and gown, sweetgrass and dogs. He startled up. Esrex would see, would know . . .

But Esrex was gone.

The huge hall was empty save for Tally, Jaldis, the Duke, and himself. Gray light leaked through the window-lattices, making the whole gigantic space an echoing symphony of dove and pewter and white in which the few lamps still burning had a sleazy air. The Duke, his role in the comedy played, was regarding his daughter with grave respect tinged with deep sadness, fully aware of what she had done. Jaldis, at the other end of the couch, his head bowed upon his hands again, looked like something fished dead from a gutter.

Tally caught Rhion's face between her palms and knelt to kiss him. "Watch it . . ." He caught her wrists. "I'm covered with oil."

Something in that mundane remark served to shatter the brittle air of tragedy that hung between them. It came upon him that he really was alive, that they really were saved, that their son would be born, and that Tally's solution had been brilliant, decisive, and far better than he had ever expected. "To hell with it," he added, and crushed her tight to his chest.

It was only after a few minutes that he realized she was crying.

"Oh, Rhion, I'm sorry," she whispered, as their mouths finally parted. "I'm so sorry . . ."

"Ah!" Rhion cried, pressing a melodramatic hand to his brow. "I always knew you'd throw me over someday for some hunk of beef in a bronze breastplate . . ."

"You . . . !" She almost choked with laughter on top of her tears and, still laughing, pulled away and pummeled him on the shoulder, drawing a gasp of genuine pain . . . he'd forgotten the bruises that covered him.

"Oh!" she cried, horrified and contrite. "Oh, Rhion, I *am* sorry . . . !"

"You already said that."

And they both looked up, to see the Duke standing over them, his face grim, weary, and infinitely sad.

Hesitantly, Tally got to her feet, the front of her golden gown all blotched with grime. Her father caught her hand before she could sink once more to her knees. "No," he said gently, and touched her check.

She looked away from him, her eyes flooding again with tears of shame and remorse. In the heart of her deception, the show she was putting on for others, she had been brave. She whispered despairingly, "Father . . ."

He shook his head and removed with his thumb the tear that crept slowly over her cheekbone. "I can manage somehow without the alliance," he told her. "You haven't cost me my realm, you know. It will only mean . . . care and negotiation. And some plans which must now be postponed. The Earl is man of the world enough not to take personal offense, which is what I most greatly feared."

From what he had heard of the Earl, Rhion guessed his words had been, *Better learn now than later she's a slut,* accompanied by a casual shrug. But he kept his silence. Tally, who knew her suitor better than he, would have known perfectly well what he'd say.

The Duke's fingers moved to her lips as she began to apologize once more.

"That was very quick thinking," he went on, forcing cheer and comfort into his voice to cover his weariness and his anger at the miscarriage of all his carefully laid plans of alliance. "You forced my hand very nicely—no, I mean that as a compliment. Courage and resolution are the mark of a statesman, and the ability to use what the gods send. I'm only sorry it has to be Erralswan—not that he won't treat you well, but his family's a poor one and they have very little position . . ."

"It had to be someone," Tally said, her voice very small. "I mean, I had to find someone willing to say, *right then*, that he was my lover, that my child was his . . . And I could never . . ." Her voice faltered. "I knew I'd have to marry someone else and that I could never marry Rhion. And even without Esrex, I don't think I could have gone to the Earl pregnant by another man."

"No," the Duke said quietly. "Many women would have tried, but that he would never have forgiven." He sighed heavily, and by the expression in his eyes Rhion guessed his mind was already at work, re-shaping the possible concessions he'd have to make to the land-barons to salvage the wreck of his policies, now that he'd lost his chance of a foreign alliance.

"No," he went on. "And I expect Erralswan jumped at the chance to improve his fortunes. But if I'd known that's the way out you were going to take," he finished, with forced lightness that almost succeeded in being genuine, "believe me, I'd have sent someone of more fortune and better family up to fetch you."

Tally laughed and gulped, trying to keep back tears of relief, and the Duke turned to Rhion, who got slowly to his feet to face him, teeth gritted against the agony of his broken ribs. Cold and frightened, Tally's fingers stole around Rhion's in the concealing folds of gown and robe.

"You'll have to go away, you know."

"I know." Exhaustion, pain, and the aftermath of shock and grief were blurring into one vast, aching desolation of weariness. It would be enough, he thought, to know that his son was safe, no matter who the boy learned to call father. Enough to know that Tally was safe . . .

"I'll send you word," the Duke went on, "when the child is near to being born. I think that will be long enough to quiet tongues. But even after that, it is probably best that you do not live in Bragenmere."

It took Rhion a long moment of silence to realize that he was not being banished for good, but that he was being told that he could, eventually, re-enter the city gates. He started to speak, but the Duke raised his hand quickly, cutting off his words.

"Further than that I do not wish to know," he said. "And indeed, I cannot know. Not with what you are—not with most of the cults against such as you. I will not speak now of the decision that a scandal will force me to make, if one comes, but I warn you . . ." His eyes went from Rhion's face to his daughter's, the bitter grief in them the grief that only rulers bear. "I will make it."

Tally bowed her head, unable to meet his eye, but her hand tightened around Rhion's, and he felt it tremble.

"Until that day comes," the Duke went on, "you, Rhion, will be welcome in my city and under my roof. I trust you will remember." And before Rhion could speak he turned away; going to where Jaldis sat at the other end of the couch, he went to one knee and touched the crippled hand.

"Old friend," the Duke said softly, "half a dozen times I've offered you the hospitality of my household, to pursue your studies in quiet—and, I might add after tonight, in safety. I've banished Rhion for the time being—you understand that I had to banish him. But please understand that my offer to you—my affection for you, old friend—still stands as it has always stood. Will you come?"

Jaldis raised his head and, with the back of one twisted finger, adjusted the set of the heavy opal spectacles upon his face. He was thinking, Rhion guessed, of the elaborate preparations for the feast of Summerfire, and how they had taken him away from other matters dearer to his heart; of the constant small demands that drew energy from the great studies of magic; and of his days at the court of Lord Henak, and what had come of them.

Then he sighed, the brittle shoulders relaxing as he released what Rhion knew to be the last free years of his life. "I am an old man," he said, "and have been a wanderer for many years. Rhion my son . . ." Rhion released Tally's hand, limped stiffly to grasp the fingers his master held out to him. The surprising, powerful grip brought back to him the memories of the flight across the roofs of Felsplex, the rain in the Drowned Lands . . . a thousand memories, back to a bright morning heavy with the scent of flowers on the bridge of the City of Circles, a tall, straight old man and a young dandy in jeweled red velvet by the stalls that sold pieces of old books. *Are you hunting for secrets . . . ?*

He had certainly found them. One or two, he realized, he wished had remained beyond his ken.

"I'll be all right." He felt the old man's hand tighten over his. "I'll be back as soon as I can to see you . . ."

"And that will be soon," the Duke promised, his eyes traveling from Rhion's face to Jaldis' and on to his daughter's.

"Eleven years isn't long to study wizardry, you know," Jaldis said, straightening up a little as Tally flung herself convulsively into her father's arms. The talismans hanging from the voice-box made small, metallic music as he sat up, the golden sun-cross amulet catching a feeble glint of the dawn light. "But you have had a good start."

"Where will you go?" Tally broke away from the Duke's embrace as Rhion turned, stiff and aching—she had to catch his arm to keep him from falling when he tried to take a step. Every muscle in his body hurt without in the smallest measure detracting from the grinding pain in his side.

"First," he said a little shakily, "to have a bath. And then to get another pair of spectacles. And then," he said, sighing and putting an arm around her shoulders, "someplace where I'll never make another love-potion again as long as I live."

So it was that Rhion returned to the Drowned Lands of Sligo, to become the Scribe for the Ladies of the Moon.

And seven years slipped by with no more sound than sunlight makes upon the grass.

His son was born in April, a fat, robust baby named Kir. By that time Jaldis was settled comfortably in three small rooms on the top floor of the octagonal library tower and was looking better than Rhion had seen him in years. Of the few things stolen by neighbors from the house in Shuttlefly Court, nothing had been destroyed, and the Duke had managed to get everything back except the small quantities of gold and silver, which, to Jaldis, scarcely mattered. It was the books which had been his chief concern. Surprisingly, Prymannie the schoolmistress had kept them for him—perhaps out of gratitude for headaches cured or because, as a schoolmistress, she could not bear that books be destroyed; perhaps because, more intelligent than her neighbors, she had read the situation more clearly and was betting on a return to favor and a reward.

When Rhion saw Jaldis again, his brown robes were made of good-quality wool, warm against the sharp spring chill, his beard trimmed and his long white hair neatly cut.

"He misses you," Tally said, on one of the evenings when Rhion had come to sit beside her bed in the Erralswan apartments overlooking the palace garden, while the baby slept at her breast. "Father offered to give him a slave to look after him but he refused. He keeps house for himself well up there, but when I go up to talk to him, he usually talks about you."

"He hasn't . . ." Rhion hesitated, troubled for a moment out of his delighted contemplation of the round pink cherub curled like a puppy in the linen nest of Tally's nightdress. "He hasn't talked about something called a Dark Well, has he? Or about a world without magic?"

Tally frowned, thinking back, and shook her head. "Not to me."

Rhion returned to Bragenmere fairly frequently after that, often four or five times in the course of a summer, before the snows and rains of winter closed the roads. Though Jaldis still sometimes instructed him and though they still spent nights until dawn, talking of new learning he had found, or old learning rediscovered, in the ancient books of the palace library, Rhion gradually came to think of himself as Jaldis' former pupil instead of Jaldis' student. Among the wizards and in the countryside between Imber and the Mountains of the Sun, he came to be known as Rhion of Sligo, Scribe of the Drowned Lands.

The living on the islands was not wealthy and in some ways it was painfully primitive, but he found to his surprise that it suited him. Among the crumbling pillars and morning-glory vines of the Island library, he studied the mysteries of healing handed down from the ancient priestesses of An. The Gray Lady, with whom he remained fast friends, though they never again became lovers, instructed him further in the lore of herbs and bonesetting; all his love of human beauty and all the understanding he had gained in the workings of the body and the mind when he had made love-spells for his living flowed into this new learning.

In time he came to have a reputation as a healer in the lands round about. Three or four times his visits to Bragenmere were in response to urgent summonses from the Duke, for Damson's son Dinias, born four months before Kir, was a peaked and sickly child, unable to keep food down and susceptible to chest complaints. As for Damson herself, it appeared she had judged her husband rightly. Having broken the spiteful pride which had kept him from her, she knew indeed how to hold him at her side. Whether by obligation, by her father's wealth, by ambition, or some perverse understanding of his body's needs—or who knew, perhaps even by love, Rhion could only guess . . . but the two infants she bore after Dinias died within days.

And time drifted by.

In the Drowned Lands, time was a deceptive matter at best, the seasons passing like the slow stroke of a gigantic wing and leaving no shadow behind. In the summers Rhion studied the birds of the marshes, coots, herons, geese, and loons with their spotted backs and vacant laughter, watching their nesting and their mating and when they departed in fall. He harvested herbs, mallows, and lichens and experimented with their properties; he spent night after night with boat and lantern, watching grim and goblin and water-fae by the milky moonlight and made another spiracle charged with the element of air to wear around his head when he swam through the murky jungles of duckweed and cattail roots. He followed the goblins into their watery realms, but he never learned where they went. In the winters, he spent whole afternoons and nights listening to the whisper of the rain on the ivy that blanketed the library walls, reading the long, slow histories of the kings and priestesses of the realm of Sligo and the In Islands and the lore of the wizards who, throughout the Forty Realms, were popularly credited with the earthquake that brought its doom. He learned the deeper magics of the Ladies, and the effects of the moon's phases and the passage of certain stars upon spells and healing and the movements of birds; he learned small illusions to twist men's minds and strange little cantrips involving tangled string and braided straw.

And in the times of the spring equinox, he would sometimes preside over the rites at the half-drowned ring of stones, calling down the power of the turning stars to the victim who lay bleeding on the altar, feeling that power spread out to all corners of the earth.

They were days of peace. In his scrying-stone, almost nightly, he would summon Tally's image, or his son's—it was not the same as being with them, but at least he knew that they were happy and well. Going down to the noise and bustle of Bragenmere, visiting Shavus in his house in the Beldirac Wood, and listening to the arguments there about the latest enormities of the Selarnist or Ebiatic Orders or the insolence of the Blood-Mages and Earth-witches, he would return home to this ruinous, vine-cloaked silence, wondering if he wasn't beginning to comprehend for the first time what magic really was.

Then one winter morning in the library, while painstakingly translating an ancient scroll so black with age and decay that he had to lay spells on the crumbling linen in order to make the glyphs rise to visibility at all, he felt the scrying-crystal he carried calling to him.

Taking it from the inner pocket of his robe, he gathered his cumbrous woolen shawl about his shoulders and walked out onto the terrace, where the light would be better. It was only a few days after winter solstice and the chowder-thick fogs of the season lay like cotton wool over the estuary's watery mazes. The chipped balustrade seemed no more than a pale-gray frieze against a whitish wall, beyond which gulls could be heard dimly crying. Rhion's breath was a clouded puff of steam which fogged his spectacles in the raw cold, and the ends of his fingers, where they protruded from his woolen writing mitts, were red and numb.

"Jaldis?" He turned the faceted lump of raw amethyst over in his palm.

In the facets of the jewel, as if the old man stood behind him, reflected tiny in the smooth surface, he saw his master's face.

And he recoiled in shock. When wizards communicated by scrying-stone it was not the same as simply calling someone's image; there were differences between how a mage appeared in the lattices of the crystal and what he or she might look like in actual fact. But even so, Rhion could see that Jaldis was far from well. He seemed faded and wrung out, like a worn rag, his thin face sunken, fallen-looking behind the monstrous crystalline rounds of his spectacles. The heat of a midsummer morning years ago leaped vividly to Rhion's mind, Shavus digging through the bottles of brandy the Duke had sent them in that little kitchen on Shuttlefly Court, saying savagely, "What Jaldis needs isn't a spell, but to quit doing things like this to himself . . ."

But through the exhaustion, the old man's spirit coruscated like a sunlit fountain of triumph.

"Rhion, I've done it!" Even in his mind, now, Rhion heard the sweet, mechanical tones of the box—he could no longer bring back to mind what the old man's voice had been. "I have opened the Dark Well with the turning of the solstice of winter. I reached in, as I have reached at every solstice-tide, at the midnight of every equinox, for seven years now . . ."

He was trembling with excitement, with vindication. It might have been a trick of the light where the old man was sitting, in the small and comfortable study in the octagonal tower, but his spectacle-lenses, even, seemed to blaze with a kaleidoscope of fire.

"I reached across the Void, seeking in the darkness for the universe without magic, calling out to them . . .

"And they answered me! At midnight of the night of the solstice, *they answered*!"

15

"I spoke to them, Rhion." The mechanical voice in its rosewood box was steady, but Jaldis' crippled hands trembled where they rested on the arms of his chair. "I spoke to them, and they begged me for help. They said they had been seeking a way to project their minds into the Void for all the years since first we heard them . . ."

"Did they say what had happened to magic in their world?"

Outside, the wind groaned around the tower's eaves, driving hard little pellets of ice against the shutters. Stray drafts plucked at the lamp flames and made Jaldis' shadow tremble like a blown banner on the creamy plastered wall. For the last two days of his journey from Sligo, Rhion had been holding the storm at bay with spells, struggling over roads choked already with snow and mud and praying to Rehobag and Pnisarquas, those untrustworthy dilettante sons of the all-seeing Sky, that he could manage to keep the snow winds from blowing down the mountain passes long enough for him to reach Bragenmere's gates. It had been exactly eight years since he'd had to travel in the dead of winter, and, as he recalled, he hadn't liked it then either.

"He—Eric—his name is Eric—He said he did not know."

On the hearth, the hanging kettle boiled with a small rumbling

like the purring of a cat. Tally rose soundlessly to her feet, raked the
fire a little to one side, and tipped the water into a teapot, the
fragrance of brewing herbs rising in summery sweetness among
the room's winter smells of lamp oil and damp wool.

"That magic once existed in their world there is no question, no
doubt, he says. Document after document attests its presence and its
strength. Three hundred years ago there was a period of unrest, of
anger, and many mages and many books were burned, both by civil
authority and by angry mobs. Then two hundred years ago . . ."
The old man shook his head. "Eric says he does not know what
happened, why, or whether it was a single act, or an accumulation
of unknowable events, chance, or the moving courses of the universe.
He knows only this: that no documents of magic can be authenticated later than two hundred years ago. And beginning in that time,
magic has been regarded as no more than silliness, superstition, the
games of children, or the delusions of madmen."

"All over the world?" Rhion tried to picture it, to grasp that
deathly silence, and failed. But the thought of it turned his heart
sick.

Jaldis nodded. His twisted hands gently cradled the blue porcelain
cup Tally had set before him, seeking the warmth of the clear green
liquid inside.

"So he has said. He said that in place of magic there is a thing
called 'science' . . ." He used an alien word for it, the Spell of
Tongues carrying the term to Rhion's mind as meaning simply
'knowledge,' but with curious connotations of exactness and close-
mindedness and other things besides.

"By this science," Jaldis went on, "they have done many things
in these two hundred years: the wagons which travel without beasts
to draw them, by the burning of an inflammable liquid; the winged
ships which journey through the air; something called a telephone,
by which they speak over vast distances—anyone, not just mages;
and artificial light, which glows without burning anything but which
is the product of . . . of creating lightning at their will. But whether
this 'science,' or some element of it, arose only after magic's disappearance, or whether magic's failure was somehow connected to its
arising, Eric cannot be sure. No one can be sure."

The old man leaned forward, his pale face hollowed and gray looking in the scrim of steam curling from the cup between his hands. "But whatever the cause, they have become a world of mechanists, of bureaucrats, of slaves, working each for his own living and not looking farther than the filling of his belly every day. It is a world where magic is not only despised, but hated. There is only one ruler now in whose realm mages—those who study magic though they can no longer work it, those who seek the true secrets that lie at the heart of the universe—are honored. And against this ruler, a coalition of these other monarchs, petty and corrupt bureaucrats, ruled by wealthy merchants and narrow of soul, is gathering for war. If they succeed—if they win—then even the memory of magic will die. And then the darkness will truly triumph."

"And they want help?"

Jaldis nodded. "I have contacted Shavus," he said. "Shortly before the equinox of spring he and Gyzan will come here. They have long been preparing for this, knowing that one day I would find this world, these mages, again. Your help, too, I will need, my son. It is perilous and needs magic on both sides—the less is there, the greater it must be here, to protect them as they cross."

"But if there's no magic there at all," Tally said doubtfully, perching beside Rhion on the sheepskin-covered bench, "how can they reach out to guide our men?"

"There's magic and magic," Rhion explained quietly. "Even someone who isn't mageborn can use a scrying-crystal after a fashion, under the influence of the proper drugs. But to reach out across the Void . . . I still don't see how . . ."

"Only with the power of the solstice-tide, the sun-tide, or to a lesser extent with the momentum of the equinox's balance," the old man said, pulling one corner of the fur he wore about his shoulders more firmly around his arms. *He's too old for this*, Rhion thought, watching the careful way he moved, seeing how thin those blue-veined wrists were in the gap between gloves and soft-knitted arm warmers. *So old . . .*

"Even so it will be a great gamble, my daughter," the blind mage went on. "But it is one we must take. Shavus, Gyzan, myself . . . all of us. Or else all of this . . ." His stiff hand, its fingers barely mobile now at all, moved to take in the scrupulous neatness of the study, with its potted herbs, its small shelf of books—even, Rhion noticed with a faint smile, its tremendously expensive, half-grown crocodile drying in a glass case near the fire . . . "All that we have lived for and have accumulated over the centuries will be for nothing. It will be in danger of vanishing like frost upon the grass with the sun's rising, and our world will be left with nothing but the might of the strong against the strong, the unscrupulousness of those both clever and wicked, and the demagogues who lead the mobs."

"You don't think it's an illusion of some kind, do you?" Tally asked softly, as she and Rhion descended the narrow stair that led from Jaldis' rooms down to a discreet door hidden away in a corner of the topmost chamber of the library. "Something he's convinced himself he's heard because he's hunted so long or because he wants it so badly?"

Rhion considered this as he worked the bolt on the other side of the heavy oak door back into place with a spell. "I don't think so," he said at length. "I've dealt with people whose illnesses stemmed from that kind of self-delusion . . . he's obsessed, but he doesn't have that air."

They crossed through the high-ceilinged marble chamber with its shelves of books and racks of scrolls, the floating ball of blue witchlight over Rhion's head making the gilt bindings wink and the shadows dart and play among the lightless pendules of the hanging lamp.

"A trick, maybe, or a trap . . . ?"

"Set by whom?" Rhion asked sensibly. "And for what purpose?"

Tally shrugged, uneasy at the thought herself, and pulled closer around her shoulders the thick robe of red wool and fur which covered her court-dress of green and white—the Erralswan colors.

"You hear about the—the Great Evils, the priests of Agon call them—spirits who try to lure people into danger and wickedness, the same way grims try to lure you into getting lost in the woods." She glanced sidelong at him as they descended the wide terrazzo stairs to the floors below, as if not sure how he'd react.

"Maybe they do exist," Rhion said. "Only everyone who's been out in wild country at night has seen grims for themselves, and knows how they act. From what I understand only the priests of Agon claim to have seen the Great Evils, and then they pretty much seem to be whatever will fit Agon's purposes at the time."

Tally chuckled her agreement. "You do have a point," she said. "On the other hand, everyone has seen wizards—and still believe the lies that are told about them. And that's illusion, if you will— the altering of perception. And people don't even need magic to do it."

Rhion, wrapped against the December cold in the black cloak of the Morkensik Order, with a plaid shawl the Gray Lady had given him over that, shivered. He had passed the Temple of the Eclipsed Sun on the way up from the city gates and had seen for himself the great new hall of sable pillars that spoke of the cult's increasing riches and power. The sight of it had brought back to him, with terrifying clarity, the cold self-assurance of the High Priest Mijac's voice from behind the veils, the hideous sense he had had of seeing men who had been released from responsibility for their deeds. Artists of illusion, Mijac had called wizards . . .

And yet he sensed that his growing dread stemmed from something deeper, some rotted ghost of memory connected somehow with the Dark Well, a memory that still stirred now and then in his dreams.

They passed down through the lower two rooms of the library, each larger than the one above, and through the vast, echoing spaces of the empty scriptorium below that, and so to the library's anteroom on the ground floor of the tower, and through the great bronze doors into the colonnade that embraced the palace's vast central court. Even in its pillared shelter, gusts of wind clutched at Rhion's mantle and Tally's long fur robe, and the driven snow, scudding before the wind across the granite paving blocks of the court, swirled between the columns and wet their feet.

Sheltered by a numinous aura of Who-Me? they passed through the vestibule of the palace's marble hall. There, under the shadows of the musicians' gallery, only a few lamps burned on the clustering pillars, but beyond, a hundred lights on tall bronze stands filled the hall with silky primrose radiance, warming the tucked and pearled velvets, the shimmering featherwork and ribbons, of the courtiers' clothing to a moving rainbow of crimson, blue, and green. Pausing in the shadowy doorway that led up to the private apartments, Rhion wiped the mist from his spectacle lenses, then looked out into the hall, automatically picking out those he knew.

The Duke—and in any room he'd ever been in all eyes still went first to the Duke—looked a little older, a little more tired, than a man of fifty should. Even his son's death in a practice joust—preparing for his first tournament three years ago on the eve of what would have been his seventeenth birthday—hadn't affected Dinar of Prinagos as badly as had his wife's last summer of a fever no one had thought much of until it was too late. The big man still had his old air of power, his easy movements which dominated everyone around him, but streaks of gray had begun to appear in his thickly curled black hair under its after supper crown of hothouse roses. Damson sat beside him, corseted cruelly into a gown whose entire front seemed to be an iridescent armor of pearls, her plump, jeweled fingers nimbly flicking at the glass spindles of a lace-making pillow.

Perhaps it was losing Tally's friendship, Rhion thought, or perhaps it was her obsession with Esrex—but it seemed to him that over the years the steely quality of a single-mindedness in her had grown. Lines of will and watchfulness carved deep in the suety face now, aging it under its heavy paint. Despite her ladylike occupation, her shrewd gray eyes traveled over the room, missing nothing of what they saw.

She was currently watching Marc of Erralswan with considerable disapproval. Dressed in a very short blue velvet tunic with elaborately padded sleeves, he was flirting with one of her maids-in-waiting, their teasing intimacy telling its own tale. Rhion sighed and gritted his teeth. Marc had never, even on the night of his wedding to Tally, laid a hand on his bride of convenience; it was not to be expected that he remain celibate. *But*, Rhion thought, illogically angry for Tally's sake, *does he have to be so goddam blatant about it?* As the Duke's son-in-law and the holder of considerable wealth and estates—not to mention as a beefy champion of the tiltyards—he found his scope had considerably widened from the days when he was the captain of the ducal guard, and his hunting field hadn't been exactly narrow then.

Rhion glanced sideways at Tally and saw her face set in an attempt at unconcern. She shook her head comically and sighed, "That's our Marc . . ." But Rhion knew that it hurt her when the court ladies giggled about her behind their feathered fans.

And Esrex . . .

Esrex was almost invisible, half concealed in the shadow of a pillar, talking to someone who would have been hidden by still deeper shadows from any but mageborn eyes.

Rhion shivered. He was talking with a priest of Agon.

"Are there many of them at Court these days?" Rhion asked softly, as he and Tally moved through the small door and up the stairs. Their hands sought one another automatically—he had not seen her for nearly three months, since his last visit to Bragenmere in September. Even had he lived with her daily, he suspected he would have craved her touch. "Priests of Agon?"

"Was that who Esrex was talking to? I'm afraid so." Tally, like the rest of her family, had changed, her coltish skinniness maturing into spear-straight, graceful strength, her long features settling into serene beauty. Rhion knew that, over the years, Tally had patched up a working relationship with Damson—as two ladies of the same court must—but that never again had the sisters been friends. The isolation and the caution of leading a double life had left their mark on her—a kind of measured steadiness, sadness tinged with golden strength.

"Since the High Queen has had a shrine built to the Eclipsed Sun in the palace at Nerriok you see them more and more," she went on somberly. "Esrex is supposed to be very high in their hierarchy, though of course no one knows. And Father . . . he's had to be more careful with the cults, as you know."

That, Rhion also knew, had been the fruit of the aborted alliance with the Earl of the Purple Forest. The death of the Duke's son had destroyed the last chance of union with one of the other great Realms. With only a minor nobleman for a son-in-law Dinar of Mere had to take support where it could be found.

"With most of the priesthoods, it doesn't matter." Bars of tawny light from below crossed Tally's face as they climbed through the shadows of the columns, like two shadows themselves in the dim upper reaches of the great stair. "But they're not the same, are they?"

"No." Rhion remembered the masked men in the watchroom of the Temple, the words of the priest on the threshold: *As for lepers, and beggars, and slaves, Agon has a welcome for them, as he has for all who serve him* . . . And how many served him, he wondered, for the sake of that welcome, which relieved them of responsibility for what they did? He didn't know.

No one knew.

But he suspected that Esrex was not that kind of servant. With the lies of Agon's priests as his main source of information—lies, perhaps, that he wanted badly to believe—it might well be that Esrex was not aware of being a servant at all.

Glancing back down through an opening in the wall, he could see the ivory-fair head—losing, he could also see, its hairline's long struggle with destiny. Esrex' face, too, was prematurely lined, with petty stubbornness and will, and his eyes had a kind of restless glitter to them. Rhion knew that Esrex took drugs upon occasion, either on his own or as part of his involvement with the priests of the Eclipsed Sun, who gave them to their chosen followers; Rhion wondered what his consumption was up to these days.

"No, I'm afraid they're not."

Halfway down the gallery were the doors to the nursery wing, clear-grained red wood inlaid with patterns of silver wrought into intricate protective seals. The window shutters, Rhion knew, were silver, also—Damson had had them made—though it had been fifty years since there'd been a case of grim harrowing in Bragenmere. There were some these days who believed that silver was proof against a wizard's spells as well, but Rhion had no trouble reaching with his mind into the locks and shifting the silver pins.

A sentry dozed in the anteroom, and Rhion imperceptibly deepened the man's sleep with a whispered charm. From around the shut door of the room where the sickly Dinias slept came the drift of eucalyptus steam and the snores of a nurse. Elucida, at the age of eleven the biggest matrimonial catch in the Forty Realms, had her own suite and her own chaperon and maid. But the two sons of the Duke's younger daughter shared a smaller chamber, and there was no nurse whose dreams needed thickening as Rhion and Tally ghosted inside.

Brenat had been born when Kir was three—"Jaldis makes a good potion," Rhion had joked at the time. Standing in the doorway of the dark chamber and looking at the nightlamp's fretted red glow playing across those two double handfuls of brown curls, he felt a curious sense of unalloyed delight in these sons of his, a desire to whoop and shout, an almost uncontrollable yearning to touch . . . though he knew, as he had known the first time he had taken Tally in his arms, that it was madness.

The problem was that he could not now imagine a world that did not include his sons.

Kir's hand, clutching the hilt of the toy sword he'd fought tooth and nail to take to bed with him, was big in spite of its childish chubbiness. He would have the Duke's height when he grew up, as well as Tally's long, delicate features and gray eyes. That, Rhion thought in his moments of cynical despair, was fortunate—Marc was tall, too. Brenat's eyes were also gray. Tally, who adored the boys, sometimes spoke of another child, but they both knew they had been fools to have these.

"Will you be here to see them tomorrow?" Tally asked quietly, stepping closer to Rhion as he put his arm around her waist. She still had to bend her head just a little for him to kiss her temple.

"Oh, yes—till the storm lets up, in fact. That should be sometime tomorrow." The wind groaned along the gallery as they stepped out again, closing the door behind them. The quilted red hangings which kept the chill from the walls in winter rippled uneasily with the scurrying draughts, as if bodiless monsters raced behind them to some unknown goal.

"I'm glad. They ask after you when you're not here, you know."

In spite of himself Rhion smiled. He'd seen his boys with Marc, polite and respectful and in awe of their putative father, but on his last visit in September Kir had said something to him about, "Father chasing lightskirts all around the court," with a disapproving look in his gray eyes.

"Well," Rhion had said at the time, "it probably wouldn't do to say that to him."

Kir's mouth had hardened. "But it's wrong. He's married to Mother. And it makes her sad when the other ladies laugh. You're a wizard, Rhion. Can't you make him stop?"

Rhion had groaned. "What, you, too?" This conversation had taken place in the mews, where Rhion had gone to help Tally doctor a sick goshawk and the boys had tagged along to see what trouble they could get into in the room where the varvels and jesses were stored and the lures repaired. "Look, Kir, you might as well find out early that magic can't make people do things differently than they do. It can't change what people are like."

"Dinias says it can." The boy had picked up a long tailfeather from the floor, where Brenat sat placidly arranging straws in order of their length, and dug among the leather-scraps near the workbench for a thong to wind around it like a simple lure. "Dinias says that a wizard can cast a spell on a man that will take away his brains and make him cut up his own wife with an ax, and when he wakes up in the morning he won't remember what he did, but they'll hang him anyway." He looked hopefully up into Rhion's face for corroboration of this gory program.

" 'Fraid not." Rhion sighed, realizing that it was a tale every child in the city heard as soon as they reached school.

Kir's face fell. "Oh. Dinias said you were a wizard and didn't have a soul, but I beat him up."

"Thus changing his opinion of me and endearing yourself to his father in one—er—blow."

And Kir had said, "Hunh?" and had looked at him with the baffled exasperation of a child confronted by adult nonsense.

Thinking back on the scene Rhion sighed again, and shook his head. Tally looked at him inquiringly, the glow of the small votive-light near the nursery-door turning her lashes to ginger and leaving her eyes in shadow.

"It's just—they grow so fast," he said softly. "And I envy you the time you have with them."

She reached over and gently scratched his beard, then drew his mouth to hers. "If I were anyone else," she murmured, "I would envy myself."

But much later, as he was dressing again by the low throb of ember light that glowed from the hearth in her room, he returned to the earlier topic—something they did with subjects discussed hours, weeks, or even months previously. Wind still savaged the window shutters behind their quilted hangings, its howling sounding louder now that the small noises of servants passing in the corridors had dwindled.

"It should be quieting down by noon," Rhion said, struggling into his shabby brown robes. "Then we should have nearly a week's clear weather, enough for me to get back to the Drowned Lands before the next big storm."

She held out his spectacles to him. Without them, kneeling among the sheets, he saw her only as an upright column of shadowy gold in the firelight, wreathed in points of light—her jewels, all that she now wore. "Will the Gray Lady be angry, if you leave at the equinox?"

"Not angry," Rhion said quietly, carefully hooking the metal frames over his ears. "She'll understand. But the rites need a lot of power. If I'm not presiding, they get Cuffy Rifkin, an Earth-witch from up the marshes, to do it, and his strength isn't as great even as mine, which is only average. It puts the victim's life at greater risk. But the Gray Lady knows what I owe to Jaldis. Even at midnight of the equinox, getting Shavus and Gyzan across the Void is going to take more power than he should be trying to use these days. Maybe more than he has."

"He was very ill, the day after Winterstead." Behind the tawny halo of her hair the emblems of the house of Erralswan gleamed on the bed hangings amid a thicket of heraldic gingerbread, as if Marc's name and station covered the lovers literally as well as metaphorically. "I was afraid he'd had a stroke, or his heart had failed him. But he said no, it was only that he'd overtaxed himself . . ."

"I'll look in on him again tonight," Rhion said quietly, more worried than he cared to admit. He slung his cloak around his shoulders and the Gray Lady's plaid on top of that. "And he still won't have a slave to look after him?"

Tally shook her head. "And do you know," she said after a moment, "with what they say about the cult of Agon—about not knowing who is in it, who their spies are—sometimes I think that's just as well."

The palace bulked dark and silent as Rhion stepped out onto the ice-slick terrace, a sleeping beast with all its hues of terra cotta and peach and gold, its bronzes and its porcelains and its columns of porphyry and marble, drowned in the depths of night. Even so, Rhion chose to take the long way around from Tally's rooms, moving in silence through the barren, wind-lashed garden and surrounded once more in a cloudy haze of spells. What Damson and Esrex had had to say to one another on the day after his brush with the priests of Agon he had never found out, but he knew Esrex still sought proof that he was the father of Tally's children—sought revenge for the fool he had made of himself before the court and the priests that day. And in spite of the Duke's deep friendship for Jaldis, his fondness for Rhion and his love for his younger daughter's children, Rhion never felt quite safe in Bragenmere.

In his rooms in the octagonal tower, Jaldis was asleep. Standing in the curtained door arch of the old man's chamber, Rhion listened to the soft hiss of his breathing and reflected that he'd heard that sound almost nightly for eleven years of sharing quarters in some of the worst accommodations in the Forty Realms. And looking around at the tidy cubicle, with its warm fire and fur robes, its books neatly shelved—two more had returned to Jaldis only last year, brought by travelers who'd found them in middens or estate sales, men who'd known the Duke was a collector—its small jars of herbs, crystals, and silver powder, he felt a vast relief that the old man had found shelter at last. The years had been hard on him. He had a fragile air these days that Rhion did not like.

The thought stirred in his mind, an uneasy whisper in the darkness.

Moving soundlessly, Rhion let the thick wool curtain fall and went into the tiny study. It was pitch dark there and cold—he moved easily through it, smelling the new-cured parchment, seeing, in the dark, how every crystal, every inkpot, and every piece of chalk and wax was in place and ready for Jaldis' hands. In the far corner a ladder led to the attic above, waste space under the tower's conical roof cap. As his hand touched the rungs a hideous sense of danger seized him, the sudden, overpowering conviction that Tally and his sons were in peril, immediate and terrible, from which only he could save them and only if he got there in time . . .

It was a spell, of course. And the fact that even here, in the heart of his own rooms, Jaldis would feel such a spell was necessary troubled him deeply.

Brushing aside the phantom dreads, he ascended the ladder and opened the trap door.

It was bolted from the other side, of course—there were even spells on the bolt. Rhion remembered Jaldis' warnings, when the Gray Lady had sought to probe the secrets of the making of the Well. The key to what magic *is*, he had said. Something indeed to be protected at any cost, even at the cost of losing it entirely.

Then he stood in the dark of the loft, looking into the Well itself. It was quiet now, closed, a vague whisper of brownish shadow, a column of darkness within the scribbled circles of silver, blood, and light unpierceable even by mageborn eyes, a hidden whisper of primordial fear.

The attic had been closed for a week and, huge as it was, it smelled stuffy and cold, lingering traces of dust and incense clinging to the great wheel of the rafters overhead. Even the heat that rose from the rooms below did not warm it, and thin drafts worked bony fingers through the folds of Rhion's cloak and the robe beneath.

A world without magic, he thought. A world where all things were mechanical, sterile, even those which sounded most fantastic, like the wagons which traveled without beasts to draw them and the artificial lightning, or the flying machines. A world where beauty had been forgotten, and where the men and women born with wizardry in their blood and the gnawing conviction that other possibilities existed beyond the invisible curtain of dreams were unable to put their hand through that curtain to touch what lay on the other side.

A world that had begged for help.

A world of Jaldis' children, as Rhion was his child—a world to whom to pass his power, as he had passed it to Rhion. He would not turn aside from it.

Fear of the Dark Well—fear of what he half-remembered, of what he half-guessed—was growing in Rhion, but he forced himself to remain where he was, gazing into that darkness as Jaldis had gazed for seven years now, seeking what lay beyond.

But the Dark Well held its secrets. And in time his fear overcame him, as he felt the refracted blackness of the rainbow abyss drawing him into itself. He backed to the trap door and climbed down the ladder, bolting the door behind him.

But the thought of it pursued him into his sleep, and troubled his dreams.

16

It was carnival when Rhion came next to Bragenmere, the Feast of Mhorvianne. Ribbons and bunting decorated the tenement balconies of the Lower Town, yellow and red and green, lining the route of what had obviously been a procession. Garlands of roses, hyacinth, and cyclamen still twisted round the porch pillars of the temples in the squares and the pediments of the public baths. The remains of pink and white petals could be discerned, trampled in the muck of the brimming gutters, and the public fountains of the markets still smelled faintly of the more inexpensive varieties of wine.

"You could have knocked me over with a feather," Tally said, after their first kisses had been exchanged in the deserted shadows of the library vestibule, where even on the gray spring afternoon the slaves had already kindled the lamps. It was coming on to rain again—Rhion wondered whether Jaldis had been asked to keep the skies clear for the procession. Tally wore an unlikely geranium-hued gown whose hanging clusters of ribbons were tipped with bells, haloing her every movement in a starry glister of sound. "Father's getting married again."

"Getting married?" Rhion paused, startled and amused, in the act of cleaning his spectacle-lenses, which had gotten rather smudged in their initial embrace.

"Yes. To the heiress of Varle, who's about as old as I am. Esrex is *furious*."

"What business is it of his?" Hand in hand they ascended the long curve of the library stairs, surrounded by what Rhion—in reminiscence of a joke as old as the hills—thought of as the Nobody-Here-But-Us-Chickens Spell. Rhion had guessed from the bustle in the palace courtyard below that the library would be deserted; their footfalls echoed with small, sharp music in the tall vaults of the marble ceilings. "I mean, except that it's finally the foreign alliance he's been after all these years . . ."

"Poor father." She half-laughed at the irony of it—two marriageable daughters, each determined to have the man she wanted and not the alliance their father craved. "But it's more than that. Since Syron's death . . ." Her voice still flawed a little on the name of the young brother she had loved, "I think Esrex has gotten used to the idea that Dinias would naturally be Father's heir. And with offers coming in from all sides for Elucida's hand . . . Did you know the High Queen even sent her astrologer to take the aspects of her birth and cast a horoscope?"

"You mean, to marry Elucida to the little Prince?" Rhion's eyebrows tweaked upward—quite a fate, he thought, for that tiny fair-skinned child, sleeping in a hollow log where the grims had abandoned her. "Esrex better not count on that one. Shavus tells me the boy's sickly and suffers from convulsions. Besides, I thought the High Queen was one of Agon's initiates and didn't hold with astrologers."

"Well," Tally said, "when it comes down to it, *nobody's* supposed to go to astrologers and necromancers and people who make love-potions . . ."

"Don't look at me; I've retired."

"But all that will change," she finished simply, "if Elucida is no longer going to be sister to the Duke of Mere one day. Not to mention the White Bragenmeres being cut out of the succession entirely."

Rhion was silent, remembering Esrex' overwhelming, bitter pride.

Upon occasion, he wondered whether what really angered that young scion was the suspicion that any kinswoman of his had mingled her blood, not with a wizard, but with a banker's son.

Jaldis rose from his chair as they entered his study and hobbled to greet them, the huge, opal rounds of his spectacle-lenses flashing strangely in the witchlight that burned like marshfire above his head. Rhion frowned, seeing how bent and frail the old man looked, and wondered if he'd been working with the Dark Well since the winter solstice, probing at its shadowy secrets with whatever power of his own he could raise.

Or was it merely, he thought, that he was getting old?

"Have Shavus and Gyzan come?"

Jaldis shook his head. "They will be here late tonight." The fox-fur wrap which covered his shoulders and chest slightly muffled the voice of the box. The chamber was warm, but still the old man clung to it, and now and then Rhion saw him shiver. "Shavus said that with things as they have been, it was best . . ."

"Things?" Rhion's frown deepened. "What things?"

"You have not seen these, then?" The old man turned and limped back to the table. From the side of his eye, Rhion saw Tally's somber face and realized that the sheet of cheap yellow paper which the old man held out was not news to her.

It was a crudely block-printed handbill, labeled, *The God of Wizards*. It depicted a grossly goat-headed man in a wizard's long robe—in the print there was no attempt to show what color, or what Order, only that it was hung all over with sun-crosses, gods-eyes, and other symbols of magic—copulating with a naked woman whose mouth was open in a protesting scream. A dead baby, its throat slit, sprawled beside them.

"According to Shavus, these have been appearing in the streets of Nerriok for weeks."

Rhion's hand was shaking with anger as he set the leaflet down. *Artists of illusion* . . . "Did Shavus say anything else?"

"Only that he would speak to me more of it when he arrives tonight." The blind wizard removed his spectacles, laying them down upon the desk. Beside the leaflet, Rhion saw a scrap of paper bearing

a few lines of the Archmage's explanatory scrawl. He glimpsed Gyzan's name and remembered that the Blood-Mage had his house on
one of the capital's outlying islets. The leaflet could very well have
been found shoved under his door.

"Have you shown the Duke?"

"It only arrived today." Jaldis hobbled to the hearth and stood
there, holding out his crooked hands to the coals. "I fear it may
mean they shall have to cut short their visit to the other world . . ."

"*Cut short?*" Rhion stared at him, shocked to realize the extent
of Jaldis' obsession with the project. "What makes you think he'll
be willing to go at all?"

Jaldis turned back; by the startled ascent of his white eyebrows,
Rhion realized the old man was equally shocked that the question
would even have been raised. "Cancel our plans? I have sought
them—Eric and Paul, his helper and fellow student—for seven years.
I am not going to put the matter off over a few pieces of paper."

"It's not a few pieces of paper. It could be preparation for something, some major stroke . . ."

"Indeed it could." Jaldis limped back to him and took his arm,
his thin face in its frame of white hair as grave, as earnest as Rhion
had ever seen it. "Don't you see? It is because of this that he *must*
go. The enemies of magic are moving, my son. And what happened
in one universe could just as easily happen here."

But Rhion was uneasy as, unseen in the gallery's shadows, he
watched the feasting in the palace's great hall that night. The Duke,
when he had seen him before dinner, had apologized for not asking
Rhion or his master to the feast or the masking afterward. It was a
state occasion, and the priests of all the Great Cults would be there.
As Tally had said, since losing the possibility of foreign marriage
alliances the Duke had become more careful of the opinions of the
cults.

They were all present, seated in places of honor, from Darova's
gold-robed Archimandrite and the red-gowned Archpriestess of
Mhorvianne down to the local Solarist Holy Woman in unadorned
white who regarded the whole scene with the polite interest of an

adult at a children's party. It was not lost on Rhion that Esrex, costumed for the masking in the simple black pantaloon and white mask of a juggler, was sitting next to Mijac.

His eye traveled as it had three months ago to others he knew around the board and to the Duke, recognizable despite his red leather huntsman's costume and spiked black-and-gold mask. The way he moved, the warm charm of his manner, as much as the broad shoulders and strongly curled black hair, would have identified him had he been in rags. At his side was his new bride, blond and pretty and, as Tally had said, younger than the Duke's own daughters, costumed in a pearl-sewn gown supposed to represent a shepherdess. The plump little lady in the improbable goddess robes beside her, being gracious and kind and welcoming, was unmistakably Damson. On the Duke's other side sat Dinias, a thin pale boy in scarlet who looked as if his chest was hurting him again, and, gowned as a woman for the first time in jewel-plastered brocade and clearly embarrassed about the visible expanses of flat white chest, Elucida, promoted to womanhood on this, the feast of the Goddess of Love. As usual when she was nervous Elucida was taking refuge in her formidable erudition, and arguing theology with the Archimandrite, at whose left hand she sat.

The tables had been set in a big U around the sides of the hall to accommodate courtiers, merchants, and nobles of town and country; Rhion scanned the gaily costumed figures around them for a glimpse of Tally. She had told him Ranley the physician was coming as the God of Ocean complete with the Ocean's Twelve Daughters, and Rhion wondered where they'd found eleven other girls of Tally's height and build. They had, however—all were moving about the hall, up and down the tables as they were cleared after the final course, flirting with this man or that, absurdly gowned in identical pearls and green silk, with long green wigs like braided seaweed hanging down their backs. Rhion smiled, trying to guess which one of them was Tally.

Then his eyes passed over Esrex again, and his smile faded. Esrex, too, was watching, clearly trying to determine the same thing.

Overhead in the musician's gallery, a trumpet shrilled. A procession of young men trooped into the hall, clothed in the fantasy regalia of barbarian knights, dancing in time to the martial music and swinging their gold-hilted swords. Among them Rhion recognized his son Kir, garbed as a chieftain's squire, flourishing his weapon with a firm adeptness well beyond his years. He'd seen Brenat earlier, costumed as a baby sprite and sound asleep on what appeared to be Kithrak the war-god's cloak—at least, he thought with wry amusement, there was no doubt about *his* paternity. Where Kir got his streak of ferocity he couldn't imagine.

But looking at the boy, solemn and blazing with controlled excitement among the tall mock-warriors around him, Rhion felt the stirring of pride in his heart, a delight in his son's perfection, even at something as incomprehensible as weaponry . . .

Raising his eyes, he saw Esrex' son Dinias again, slouched at the High Table, watching with sweetmeats clutched in his sticky hand.

And it came to Rhion for the first time that Esrex sought to expose Tally's iniquity, not out of revenge for past slights or hatred for him as a wizard, but in order to discredit the boys whom the Duke favored far above his unprepossessing heir.

Better, maybe, he thought with a chill, that the Duke marry again, to father another son and put both his grandsons out of the running . . .

A hand touched his arm. He spun around, startled, and found himself looking up into the face of one of the Ocean's Twelve Daughters, whose gray eyes laughed at him from behind an explosion of green feathers. "I had to look for you five or six times before I saw you standing here," she said softly, leading him through the half-hidden doorway and toward the dark of the stair. They paused to kiss in the shadows, the down of the mask trim tickling his nose, and all considerations of the Duke and Shavus and Esrex—of wizardry and danger and the perils of the Dark Well—slipped for a time into insignificance.

"Come," she breathed. "I think by this time everyone's lost track of whether there are eleven Daughters of Ocean out there or twelve."

The last of the fireworks were blossoming like chrysanthemums against the tar-black sky when Rhion again reached the library tower.

He'd left Tally sleeping, and the sight of her closed eyelids, her face in the braid-crimped swatches of her hair relaxed as a child's, had filled him with both tenderness and guilt. *I shouldn't have left her alone in this place*, he thought, drawing his knitted pullover on over his head. And then, *Don't be absurd. Her father's the Duke, for gods' sake—Marc may be a casual husband but he wouldn't let anything happen to her, or to the children . . .*

The smell of coming rain was thick in the air—the rockets cast red and gold flares against the louring bellies of the clouds. The fragile sweetness of spring, of new grass and damp earth, breathed about him as he made his way through the darkness of the gardens, conscious of soft giggles and silken rustlings in grove and thicket as couples celebrated the coming of spring in the age-old fashion. Between the Carnival of Masks and the celebrations of the Duke's new wedding, the courtiers had already had a week and a half of continuous feasting and dancing, to culminate in tomorrow night's procession to Mhorvianne's shrine on the edge of Lake Peltcr—Rhion could only shake his head wonderingly at their stamina.

And tomorrow night, he thought, climbing the curving marble stairs—when the Sea Lady's worshipers knelt masked in her precinct, to be cleansed of their sins so that crops could grow again in the lands and when the Gray Lady's husband stretched himself on the granite altar to receive both the knife and the power of the stars— the Dark Well would open. And Shavus and Gyzan would step into the abyss.

And after that . . .

He opened the small door in the topmost of the library's rooms, and ascended the winding little stair. But even as he climbed he knew something was wrong.

No sound met his ears from the room above. No hospitable thread of firelight rimmed the tiny upper door. And as he came closer, he heard the thin drone of Jaldis' voice scraping like a cricket at the syllables of Shavus' name.

Goddess, no. He can't stand another failure—another three months of searching, of waiting . . .

And who knew what would happen in those three months?

Alone in the dark of the workroom, Jaldis sat with his brownish crystal cradled in his hand. A wan feather of blue witchlight flashing off the scrying-stone's facets prickled the rounds of his spectacles with tiny fire. Rocking back and forth with concentration he crooned, "Shavus . . . Shavus Ciarnin, Archmage . . ." over and over as he channeled all his will, all his strength, into reaching out to his friend's mind and getting him to look into his own crystal, wherever he might be.

"What happened?" Quietly Rhion brought up the other chair.

Raising his head tetchily, Jaldis snapped, "If I knew do you think I'd be doing this? I'm sorry," he added immediately, and stretched out his hand in apology. "I have been seeking word since before midnight. I scried the road between Nerriok and Bragenmere, even tried to scry Gyzan's house . . . and saw no closer than three streets away from it as usual, I might add."

"Dammit!" Rhion whispered. "It's been raining on and off, yes— the roads are muddy and the creeks swollen. But I'd have thought Shavus would have left enough time . . ."

"No," Jaldis corrected him softly. "No. When I said that I had scried that road, I mean that I have scried, to the best of my knowledge, every mile of it. And everywhere it appears passable. It is not a question of . . . simple delay."

He set down his crystal. Up until a year or so ago his hands had had enough mobility for him to cut his own fingernails—latterly Rhion or Tally had done it, but one or two of them still had the look of claws in the wavery magelight.

Rhion was silent as the implications of his words sank in. The memory returned to him, like a haunting thread of music, of the poster of the God of Wizards, and his uneasy conviction that something else was afoot. "It might still be something simple," he said hesitantly. "Illness or something that has nothing to do with . . . with their being wizards. They could have met bandits. A horse could have gone lame . . ." His voice trailed off. All those things sounded weak and unlikely. Such things happened—but they seldom happened to the Archmage of the Morkensiks or to the Blood-Mage Gyzan.

"Look," he went on after a moment. "We'll speak to the Duke, first thing in the morning. He can have men out on the road . . ."

"Indeed." With the fumbling care of the old, Jaldis removed his spectacles and laid them beside the scrying-crystal, then bowed his head so that the bridge of his nose rested against the hooked edge of his fingers. "Indeed, that . . . that is what he must do. Surely he will find them by nightfall . . ."

"Or the following day," Rhion agreed. "In rains like we've been having it takes four days, easy, to get to Nerriok. Seven or eight from the forest of Beldirac, if that's where Shavus was. If one of the bridges washed out . . ."

Without raising his head, the blind mage said, "It cannot wait four days." He spoke as simply, as steadily, as if the subject under discussion were some cantrip for his patron's entertainment, some magical toy of fires and smokes. "If he has not come by the stroke of midnight, then I must go myself."

For one long beat Rhion was silent, though it would not have been true to say that he was shocked or surprised. But it took a moment, before he could speak.

"The hell you will!"

The old man raised his head and seemed to regard him from the collapsed ruin of his eyes. "Of course I will go. Rhion, I have waited seven years to find them again. Searched seven years, solstice after solstice, equinox after equinox. The last time I waited they were gone from me, vanished . . . There is no question of waiting another three months."

Rhion was on his feet now, cold with a panic that was partly anger, partly something he did not want to look at too closely just yet. "As far as I'm concerned, there's no question of *not* waiting another three months, or six months, or as long as it takes to locate Shavus and Gyzan! You see by magic, you speak by magic . . ."

"I've told you before that it should make no difference."

"And what if it does?" He was shouting now, his quick anger covering the terrible chill of fear; the fear for Jaldis covering that other fear that his mind turned away from, refused to see even in itself . . .

If he goes you'll have to go with him.

"Holy gods, with the amount of power it takes to cross the Void, the crossing itself might kill you! You damn near had a stroke once, just working with that thing . . ."

"I will be well." The quiet serenity of his voice was unshakable, the depth of his dedication—his obsession—like a stone foundation unmovable even by the earthquake that had drowned Sligo. "I must go, Rhion. To help them, and to . . ."

"No."

The old man simply faced him, his scarred mouth with its set, drooping line as stubborn as a child's.

"And if I have to go up to that loft with a scrub-brush and wipe out the circles that are holding the Dark Well open to keep you from stepping into it and killing yourself, I'll do it."

Still Jaldis said nothing. The huge crystal spectacles on the table by his elbow seemed to stare up at Rhion's face in defiant silence.

There was something so childlike in that silence, so sure of itself, that fear-born anger swept over Rhion like a wave. "Right," he gritted between his teeth, knowing that nothing would shake Jaldis from his resolve. Turning away he picked up the broom from the corner and started for the ladder that led up to the attic trap.

From the tail of his eye, he saw Jaldis move one crippled hand.

The shock-wave that struck him took his breath away, knocking him almost off his feet and wrenching the broom from his hands. It crashed against the wall and fell clattering, its shaft snapped in two pieces. The next instant pain hit him, his vision dissolving in a swirl of grayness and flakes of falling fire. Agony clamped his head and twisted his guts like a wrenching hand. His knees turned to water and he fell, pressure crushing his chest, smothering him like burning stones. In the roaring of his ears, he thought he heard the thunder of power, the scream of black rage, blind and mute for years, a sightless revenge tearing his flesh to pieces, darkening his eyes . . .

Then he could breathe again. As he lay gasping, he was dimly conscious of the sound of something falling, the scrabble of something crawling desperately to him across the wooden floor. Crippled hands shook as they turned him over, touched his face, the bent fingers absorbing back the last of the pain while a sweet, buzzing voice said "Rhion! Oh, Rhion, forgive me . . . !"

He opened his eyes. His head still throbbed with the echo of what had felt like a vise about to split his skull and his stomach flinched with nausea. Smeared and blurred by the floor dirt on his spectacles, he saw Jaldis crouching beside him, anxiety twisting his ashen face. The horrifying vision that for a moment had flashed through his mind, the terrible sight of some nightmare entity, blind and crippled and tongueless for years of resentful inner fury, retreated into a shadow and left him feeling, not frightened of the old man who had done such a thing to him, but overwhelmed with pity. Tears tracked down from beneath the scarred eyelids, the jeweled artificial eyes, glistening in the witchlight.

"Rhion, I am sorry! So terribly sorry. I don't know what came over me . . ."

Rhion laughed shakily, knowing perfectly well that Jaldis did know, and was scorched with shame to the bottom of his soul. He closed his plump hand on the crippled one. "Not so sorry you wouldn't do that to me again if I tried to stop you, I bet."

"Rhion . . ." There was pleading in his voice. Rhion sat up, all his joints tingling with the backwash of the fevered pain, and hugged the old man close. It was like embracing a bag of sticks. Past his shoulder, he saw Jaldis' crutches lying on the floor near the table. The old man had tried to run to him, forgetting them, and falling, had crawled.

"Rhion," Jaldis said softly after a few more moments. "You may come with me—indeed, I pray that you will. But it is your own choice. The peril of crossing the Void will be great, maybe greater than either of us can survive. Eric and his friends may not be able to raise sufficient power there, even with the equinox, to guide us across. But I beg you, do not try to stop me. If I must, I will sit up guarding the Dark Well—guarding you—for the next twenty-four hours. But to be ready for the crossing, I will need rest, need sleep. Swear to me, please swear to me, that you will not try."

"Of course I swear it, Jaldis," Rhion said, deeply distressed that the old man would beg him thus—in spite of the fact, he thought wryly the next moment, that he'd just demonstrated the need for such an oath.

"If you do not choose to come, I hold you in no blame," the old man went on rapidly, his hands closing hard around Rhion's, as if willing him to understand his obsession, his need. "Truly, I leave you with my blessing. Only guard my books while I am gone, do not let strangers or curiosity seekers like the Gray Lady or Gyzan touch them . . ."

"Don't be silly," Rhion said. "I'm not letting you go without me." It was as if he had meant to say it all along.

Jaldis embraced him again, his arms surprisingly strong but his body and his narrow skull with its long streamers of white hair, fragile and delicate as a bird's against Rhion's sturdy shoulder. "My son . . ."

"Look." Rhion took off his filthy spectacles, pulled a cotton kerchief from the pocket of his robe, and wiped at the glass, peering across at his master as he did so. "It's still almost twenty-four hours until the equinox. Shavus and Gyzan could walk through that door any minute, covered with mud and cussing out their horses. Whether we're going to another universe or staying in this one . . ." He forced lightness into his voice. ". . . we're both going to need a lot of rest between now and then."

The blind man nodded. His face in the blue glow of the witchlight was wax and ashes. The magic of ill had taken from him strength he could not well spare. Rhion had forgotten, over the years, the old man's terrible power, which Jaldis had so seldom used, and had forgotten how strong the bond between master and pupil could be, and the dreadful hold of a master-spell over the student's mind. Jaldis knew, no one better, every vein and muscle and nerve of him, had seen how the fibers of his mind wove together and how memory and spirit and soul informed his flesh. His whole body hurt, and deep in his heart, buried and deliberately unseen, was the whispered knowledge that it could have been far worse.

"Sleep . . . yes," Jaldis murmured. "To rest . . . to meditate . . . Rhion, I'm trusting you not to try to stop me. I'm trusting you not to . . . to damage the Dark Well, or try to, while I sleep. I need to sleep, will need it so badly. I trust you, my son."

Trust me, Rhion thought a little bitterly, when fifteen minutes later he stood looking down at Jaldis' slumbering form, like a paralytic child's among the dark quilts of his bed. *Trust me to stand back and let you walk into danger. Trust me to enable you to get yourself killed in pursuit of your dream.*

Jaldis, he remembered, had once done the same to him. When it would have been far more sensible for him to have remained home and learned accounting from his father, Jaldis had taught him, even in pain and disorientation and new mourning for sight and voice and freedom; had helped him to pursue his own perilous dreams.

Maybe all dreams end in death, Gyzan had said.

That was the worst thing about being a wizard, he thought, as he moved around the little rooms, tidying them from habit, exhausted but unable to sleep yet, washing the supper dishes and setting the books to rights in the places where he knew Jaldis always kept them. Eventually, one saw too much. One knew too many things, and no decision was ever clear anymore.

No wonder some wizards went a little mad.

He looked across the room at the ladder which led up to the attic. His eyes strayed to the broom, its shattered pieces still lying where they had been flung by the force of Jaldis' rage. The handle was charred and splintered, but the business end could still be used. It took at least three days to weave a Dark Well's outer circles, to create that terrible flaw in the fabric of the Universe through which its dark interstices could be seen. If anything happened to it now, Jaldis would be crushed with grief, shattered with anxiety and sorrow for those young men whose voices he had heard in the Void . . .

But Jaldis would be alive.

Yet Rhion had sworn. Jaldis trusted him. And there was always the chance that Shavus would, in fact, show up at the last minute, as he had shown up so many times before.

Rhion opened the window shutters and stood looking out over the sleeping palace below him and the city—its mazes of roof tiles and arcades, balconies and squares and pillared temples—lying huddled under the scudding grimness of charcoal clouds. Deep in his bones he could feel the stirring of the equinox's approach, as he could sometimes in meditation feel the pull of the moon.

And as strong, as deep, as silent as that awareness, was the knowledge in his blood that Shavus would not come, that come tomorrow's midnight, he and Jaldis would face the darkness of the Void themselves.

17

It rained the following day. After a few hours of troubled dreams Rhion walked out through the Lower Town, where he and Tally had used to go, past the Temple of Agon with its windowless granite walls, and out to the marshes, like beaten steel under a flat silver sheet of sky. There was a shrine there, to some forgotten god, crumbled almost back to its native stones now, but built upon the invisible quicksilver track of a ley. In a corner of its old sanctuary, Rhion angled the facets of his scrying-crystal to the thin, cool light, and concentrated all his power and everything he could draw up from the ley and down from the first-stirrings of the equinox-tide into the calling of Shavus' name.

While gray rain whispered in the hollows of the broken floor and the wild herons rose crying from the reeds, he summoned every foot of the road between Nerriok and Bragenmere into the crystalline lattices of the stone's heart, scrying every footbridge, every gully, every curve of the mountain track where the rain sometimes washed stones down to block the way.

But he saw no sign of the Archmage. And the light grew broad in the sky.

All over the Forty Civilized Realms, men and women would be

drawing and heating water for ritual baths, shaking out the soot-colored cloaks of penitence, preparing to go masked to the shrines of Mhorvianne to ask that bright-haired Lady's forgiveness for the sins of a year. The Solarists, of course, serenely confident that there was no other god than the Sun in Mid-Heaven, would undoubtedly stay home tonight and play cards; the priests of Agon, behind their windowless walls, would hold their own smoky and terrible rites. In the Drowned Lands of Sligo the ancient rituals of the Moon would go forward, as they had gone forward for three thousand years, treading out the Maze in a shifting aura of blood and starlight.

And in the octagonal tower at Bragenmere . . .

Rhion shivered and blew on his cold-reddened fingers, though he knew it was not the cold that touched his flesh.

Before leaving the tower, he had made another effort to talk Jaldis out of his resolve, hoping against hope that the light of day might make the old man more amenable. Obsession, he well knew, like many things, worsens with the night.

But Jaldis had only shaken his head. "When I spoke to them—to Eric and to Paul—" And the voice of the box slid and gritted over the alien names. "—at the Solstice, I told them how to create a Dark Well, that they may see into it, and guide us through. Even that will cost them all they can raise. I cannot abandon them."

Rhion took a deep breath, knowing the words he had to say and fearing them as he had not feared the faceless soldiers of Agon. "All right," he said shakily. "I agree that someone has to go. But it doesn't have to be both of us."

Rain had wept against the shutters, the wind groaning in the rafters, hair-raisingly like the voice of something coming from the Dark Well itself. Jaldis had sat for a long time, his untouched bread and coffee before him, looking up with sightless eyes into the face of the young man who had followed him, had cared for him, and had learned from him all that he had to teach. His hand found Rhion's unerringly, as it had always done. "My son . . ." the voice of the box began, the voice that could embody no emotion, none of the feeling that tugged at the muscles of his face. Then, for a long moment, a pause.

"My son," he said again, more steadily. "Thank you—for I know how little you want to undertake this quest at all. But it cannot be. A cook knows by the smell of the broth what herbs are lacking. A farrier can tell what ails a horse by a glance at the stable muck. I have studied the nature of the Universe, the structure of magic, for sixty-five years, and Shavus has for thirty-five, even though for part of that time he was not aware what it was he learned. Even Gyzan, or the other great ones of our own order—Nessa the Serpentlady of Dun, or Erigalt of Pelter—might stare at the solution in that other universe and not realize that it was anything which pertained to magic at all. My son . . ."

His grip tightened, like a hard-polished root over the younger man's soft palm and pudgy fingers. "My son, I love you, and no more now than when you have offered to go in my stead. But yours is not a powerful enough wizardry to do what needs to be done. Maybe not even to cross the Void alive. A strange and terrible magic fills that darkness, and I do not know its strength. You simply have not the experience."

Quietly, Rhion said, "I don't want you to die."

The old man smiled. "Then I may not. It is only an hour past sunrise—there is an entire day for Shavus to reach us. And then all our fears, all our endeavors on this subject, will be for naught, and we'll laugh about them over the steam of tomorrow's coffee. But thank you. I will never forget."

Listening to the thrumming of the rain on the tower's sand-colored walls, Rhion had felt only a sinking darkness of despair. If Shavus had been delayed, the rain would delay him further. It had been too late even then to do much in the way of turning the storm aside.

And now, huddled in the sheltered corner of the old shrine under what was left of its crumbling tile roof, that despair returned, bringing panic and a hundred imagined scenarios of disaster like camp followers in its train.

Toward noon, before he left the shrine, Rhion called to the Gray Lady through the crystal and, after a few moments, saw her face in its facets, more beautiful, more ageless than in true flesh, like a crystal herself filled with hidden light.

"I don't know what I can do," Rhion concluded, having told her of Shavus' nonappearance and Jaldis' resolve to cross the Void, come what may, that night. "I can't let him go alone. He says he'll be all right, that Eric and Paul—the two wizards on the other side—will take care of him. But I can't know that."

"No," the Lady said softly. Her hazel eyes clouded, and Rhion felt a stab of guilt for laying upon her a new trouble, when, with the difference his absence could make to the power of the rites, she had sufficient worries already. "No—I understand your fears. But Jaldis is right in saying that Shavus may yet appear. He's a wily old man, and very powerful, trained in the skills of war. Neither is Gyzan to be reckoned lightly. They both know your master's resolve. If they could not come, Shavus would contrive to send word."

"To what purpose?" Rhion sighed and straightened his water-flecked spectacles with one plump forefinger. "If he tells Jaldis not to undertake the quest to this other world—which he will if he sends word at all—Jaldis will only ignore it. He is—obsessed."

"Then you must make your choice," the Lady said, and there was sadness in her eyes. "But Rhion, if you both go . . . What will become of Jaldis' books?"

"Ah . . ." Rhion looked away, unable to meet her eyes even through the crystal's tiny image. Away across the marsh, hunting horns were ringing through the drizzly mist as a party of young nobles splashed their horses through puddles, their dogs bounding happily in their wake. Rhion thought he recognized Marc of Erral-swan's bright-green doublet, close beside a lady in a yellow gown with long cascades of raven curls. He did not want to lie to the Gray Lady, but Jaldis had ordered him strictly to say that he did not know.

"Rhion," she said sharply, calling his gaze back to hers. "This is not a trick. Does he think I will wait until his back is turned and then come to steal them?"

It was, in fact, exactly what Jaldis thought, and something Rhion himself would not quite put past the Lady, much as he cared for her. So he only said, "He's made provision for them. They'll be safe—Shavus or any of the Morkensiks, will be able to get to them."

"But not corrupt and superstitious Earth-witches, not Bone-Casters who weave little spell-dollies in straw and divine the future from the flight of ducks. I must go," she said, exasperation at the opinion of her fading from her face, leaving it weary and sad. "It is noon. I must rest, and prepare. And so must you, if you will do this thing tonight."

Rhion nodded. Indeed, he thought, if the victim of the spring rite were to survive, the Lady would need all her power—even as he would need all of his, such as it was, to see the other side of the Void alive. He felt spent already from long scrying. The slow stirring of the sun-tide was rising in his veins, like the pull of the tide in his blood.

"I pray the Goddess will keep you safe."

Her image faded. Rhion got to his feet, chilled and slightly nauseated, though, as usual, the nausea changed to an overwhelming craving for sweets before he was halfway up the muddy road to the town gates. He bought half a dozen balls of steamed sweet dough wrapped in greased paper in the Old Town market, enough for himself and his sons; the rain had eased by this time, and the steam from the vendor's cart blew in soft white clouds, like rags of fog in the gray air. Most of the market stands were shutting down, farmers and their wives folding up the bright-colored awnings of orange and blue, to return to their homes to prepare for the procession tonight. Not only in his own blood could Rhion feel the coming of the equinox. It was implicit in every closed shop, in every home-hurrying slave, in the steam that leaked from every window he passed on his way back to the palace. The city and all who worshipped the orthodox gods had lapsed into the time of preparation, the time of acknowledgment of their sins from whose consequences only the gods could save them. But for the mageborn there was no salvation. As he walked by the Bull and Ring Tavern in Market Lane, a glimpse of something yellow caught his eye—he saw it was the poster of the "God of Wizards" crudely pasted to the wall beside the door.

In the rooms above the library tower, he found Jaldis asleep and no sign yet of Shavus' coming. Jaldis' books, he noticed, were gone, entrusted already under every seal of protection the blind mage could devise to the Duke's care. The old man must have told him that he was going away for a time, though of course not how or where. The secret of the Dark Well was too deep, too dangerous, to be shared, even with one whose lack of ability or thaumaturgical training would have made his knowledge harmless.

The afternoon passed like the slow gray wheel that crushes out the grain. Rhion knew he should sleep, should rest and meditate, but sought out Tally and his sons, instead. The boys were far too absorbed in the excitement of trying on their masks to have much attention to spare even for their favorite of their mother's friends. It was said to be bad luck to try on one's mask before the procession, but the boys were doing exactly what Rhion and his friends had done at their age—holding the masks to their faces with meticulous care not to touch the flesh and seeing how close they could come. In the secrecy of a loft above the mews, Rhion and Tally made love, feverishly clinging to one another amid the smells of sawdust and leather and the cinnamon of Tally's perfume, and lay locked in one anothers' arms in the huddle of cloaks and horse blankets until nearly dark.

The dark fell early, overcast and grim. After a final, inconclusive attempt to argue Jaldis out of his resolve, Rhion tried to sleep, but the slow fever of the spring-tide was flowing too strongly in him now, the awareness of the heavens' turning towards their balance point . . . and the awareness of how increasingly unlikely it was that Shavus would arrive in time.

"You are fretted," the old man said comfortingly and patted Rhion's arm. He seemed rested, stronger and livelier and with the quiet serenity of one whose mind is made up. "That is understandable . . ."

"*Fretted* is *not* how I'd describe my reaction to the prospect of throwing myself into an infinity of chaos, with nothing reaching out toward me from the other side but a bunch of half-trained wizards who can't even work magic!"

Jaldis smiled. "All will be well," he said softly. "They need my help, Rhion, if they are to defeat the enemies of magic in their world—if they are to return their world to the true paths of power. I cannot turn my back."

"We can't leave this way!" he pleaded. "Shavus could be in trouble! We have no idea what's going on in Nerriok, in Felsplex, or anywhere . . ." He thought of Esrex again and of Tally and his children—a wizard's children—floating like chips in a tailrace on the deep intrigues of court.

Jaldis' face contracted for one moment with concern, anxiety for his friend and for all the possible permutations of what would happen in this world after they left it . . . then he shook his head. "We cannot think of that," he said, and his lined face was deadly grave. "Truly, truly, we cannot. Not if we are going to call forth our entire strength, our entire concentration, to make the leap across the abysses of the Void. We can think of neither the future that we go to nor the past that we leave behind."

From the massed shadows of the pillars of the library porch Rhion watched the Procession of Masks assemble in torch smoke and drizzle. The stone-gray cloaks of the penitents gave them a look of fantastic ghosts, the cressets' glare picking out here the blue mask of a grim, there a lion head's serene golden eyes. Horns, jewels, feathered dragon manes . . . men and women alike, no matter what god or gods they worshipped. Rhion suspected that the crowd numbered a sprinkling of Solarists—certainly he thought he had seen Esrex and Damson, discreetly masked from the eyes of other gods than Mhorvianne.

"They won't miss me," Tallisett murmured, standing in the darkness at his side. On either side of the bland silver face of a marshfae her unbound hair hung in curtains of bronze-gold silk, darkened with the rain and the bath. "The boys are with Dinias, his nurse is looking after them all."

Rhion trusted the furtive and sickly heir no more than he trusted Esrex, but there was no time to think of more elaborate arrangements. Dread and tension were making it difficult for him to think at all; added to those, were his growing guilt at leaving Tally and his sons unprotected and the black premonition of disaster which had settled on his heart. "Tally . . ." he began desperately, but she touched his arm and shook her head.

Together, beneath the cloudy cloak of his spells, they made their way to the massive bronze doors, where Jaldis waited. The smoky torchlight from the court, flaring and dying between the arcade's shadows, caught in the huge rounds of his spectacles; the voice-box with its clinking talismans seemed about to overset his fragile form, like a too-heavy yoke bound upon too young a child. Propping one crutch in the hollow of his armpit he held out his hand, and said, "My son . . . daughter."

Tally pushed up her mask, stepped forward swiftly and hugged him. She had, Rhion realized, been much closer to Jaldis these last seven years than he had, looking after him and making sure he was not lonely in his little attic rooms. Then, turning, she placed her hands on Rhion's shoulders, and all he could remember were all those afternoons when she'd play her flute for him in the grotto at the end of the gardens, and the hazy glimmer of firelight in her hair.

Clutching at any straw of hope, he whispered, "Keep watch for Shavus," in a voice very unlike his own. "If he comes, send him up, please, fast . . ."

Somewhere above them, the palace clocks struck eleven, the heavy bronze note sounding leaden and dead.

"I will." She took his face between her palms and their mouths met desperately. "I love you." Her hands traveled down his shoulders, his arms, his back, as if to memorize the shape of muscle and flesh. "Always . . ."

"I'll come back . . ."

She nodded convulsively, and he knew she didn't believe him. Then she was gone, walking swiftly through the blowing curtains of rainy mist to the dark of the palace gates.

In the black loft above Jaldis' quarters, they made the conjuration, waking the Dark Well from its shadowy quiescence, watching it deepen and clear until it stretched before their feet in an abyss of sightless chaos. Past the shuddering dark rainbow of unnamable colors, Rhion sensed things about the Void which terrified him, and it took all the discipline of seventeen years to keep his concentration unwavering upon the spells they wove in concert. For Jaldis was right: they could afford to think neither of the future nor the past, neither of what strange world they would find nor of what would befall those they loved once they had stepped through the shifting colors of that dreadful gate. He became only the spells that he worked, summoning power from air and earth and aether, watching the darkness before him deepen to blackness and to something else far beyond that, something that swallowed all matter, all light, all time.

Deep in that bottomless infinity, Rhion saw a shining pinprick of gold.

He knew instinctively that what he saw was ten or twenty times as far away as it seemed, that the flickering glimmer, the tiny suncross shining like a star in the blackness, had been blown huge so that they could see it at all.

And he understood that, delayed by the gods only knew what, Shavus was not going to arrive to save him from having to do this thing.

Midnight was upon them. He felt it through the shining tracks of energy which webbed the earth and carried magic forward and back to the world's farthest corners, the balance point swinging like the fulcrum of some huge beam above their heads. Beside him, Jaldis' face was untroubled, the withered lips and throat twitching in subconscious echo of the voice that spoke the words of power, the words that would open the Void itself, from the box upon his chest.

He held out a hand and Rhion took it, his own palm icy as death. The arthritic fingers gave his a quick squeeze of thanks, the only human thought they could spare, then transferred their astonishing grip to his forearm. Rhion focused his mind away from his terror— for his life, for his past, for the nightmare dreams of the future—and formed of it a cutting crystal lightblade of concentration. Together, the two men stepped into the Dark Well.

And fell. Fell into infinity.

Later Rhion remembered very little of it except the terror, and the cold that drank at his life in a single greedy draught. Jaldis' mind and soul closed around his, a blazing column of strength that had nothing to do with the old man's frail body—the splendid obverse of the strength that had swept him aside in anger when Rhion had tried to part him from his dream. It was only that, Rhion understood even then, which kept him from dying or worse than dying. He could see the tiny red beacon of the far-off sun-cross; but, as he had feared from the start, there was nothing there to touch, no magic in it, no power to draw them through.

The drag of the abyss pulled them, the black current which had never heard the name of life, and swept them away.

Then the fragile spark seemed to gleam brighter, a flare like a tiny starburst. Something, tenuous and silvery, like a single glowing spider-strand of magic came drifting towards them across the flooding spate of darkness . . .

He was lying on something hard. His fingers moved and felt damp stone which would have been cold had there been any warmth left in his body. A confusion of voices drifted in and out of the exhausted darkness of his brain, voices crying "Eric . . . *Eric* . . . !", shouting things he didn't understand.

Eric, he thought. The wizard born to magic in a world without it—the wizard who had summoned them, brought them here.

They'd made it. They were in this world where magic no longer existed.

And, more surprisingly, he was still alive.

He was too weary for joy or exultation, almost too weary for surprise or thought of any kind. It occurred to him that he really hadn't expected to make it here.

But where and what was "here"? Unbidden, there crossed his mind, like the fragment of remembered magic, something—a dream?—some dread connected with this world, some terrible premonition that made him wonder suddenly what this world was, that they had come to . . .

Jaldis had said, *We can think neither of the future, nor of the past we leave behind* . . .

The stench of blood and incense filled his nostrils, dark forms bending over him out of darkness. He heard someone say Jaldis' name. Then he passed out.

The
Magicians
of Night

Special thanks to Donald Frew, Diana Paxson, Steven Jacobsen, and Adrian Butterfield, for letting me raid their libraries and pick their brains. Thanks also to John Hertz, Allan Rothstein, Aaron Blechman, and Betty Himes for details great and small, and especially to Lester Del Rey.

1

"I think he's coming around."

The words reached Rhion of Sligo as he hung in darkness, suspended above cold screaming infinities of lightless chaos, slipping back . . . slipping back . . .

He tried to cry out, tried to fight, unconsciousness dragging at his limbs like the darkness that lay between Universes, the darkness of the Void through which he had come. *Jaldis, help me* . . . But his numb lips and mouth would not form the syllables of his master's name. *Don't let me die* . . .

Burnt vinegar kicked his brain. He gasped as the darkness of unconsciousness stripped away like a rag; strong fingers closed around his flailing wrist. The dagger of amber light that stabbed his eyes faded to the glow of candles, a constellation of six small flames in an iron holder opposite the bed where he lay. The light of them still hurt, and he closed his eyes again. The hideous leaching of the Void's remembered cold eased. A voice asked, "Are you all right?" in a harsh, guttural alien language, and Rhion thought, with what little strength was left in him, *At least the Spell of Tongues works here.* His master Jaldis had warned him that in this strange universe magic no longer existed—he had been afraid the spell that allowed a wizard to understand speech mind to mind would no longer be effective.

"I—I don't know."

He opened his eyes. The candle flame seemed warm now, comforting in its familiarity. Around him, the room was dim, and they'd taken away his spectacles. Without them, the face of the young man seated beside him on the narrow bed was, even at this distance, blurred, but Rhion's eyesight was good enough to show him a face pale and beautiful, the pitiless beauty of a god carved in ivory, beardless, with short-cropped fair hair and a sword scar crossing one high cheekbone like the careless slip of a sculptor's chisel. Beyond that he could see only umbrous shapes, glints of silver on close-fitting black garments, and the shadow of exhaustion, strain, and some dreadful grief that informed every line of the face and the set of those wide shoulders.

"Rest easy," the beautiful young man said. "You're quite safe."

A shadow stirred in the darkness; candlelight flashed across spectacle lenses and a boy of eighteen or so, unhealthily fat, pallid, sweaty, and likewise clothed in close-fitting—in his case ill-fitting—garments of gray and black loomed beyond the young god's shoulder. "Should I tell the others, P-Paul?"

"In a moment, Baldur." The kindness in his voice, the infinite control, spoke worlds about the young mage's relationship with this boy, whoever he was, who stared at him with such eager adoration in his eyes.

Paul, Rhion thought, turning the alien name over in his mind. The two wizards whom Jaldis had contacted through the Dark Well, the two wizards who had begged him to cross the Void and help them restore magic to this magicless universe, had been called Eric and Paul.

He whispered, "Eric . . ." and the wizard Paul's control cracked, infinitesimally, his lips pressing taut and his eyes flinching away.

But a moment later his glance returned to Rhion, and he said, quite steadily, "Eric is dead. The Dark Well . . ." He hesitated, then went on as if repeating something he had memorized, his gray eyes focused resolutely on the pillow next to Rhion's head. "He said, 'We are losing him . . .' He cried out." His fingers, which still held

Rhion's wrist, began to shake and he released his grasp quickly, pressing his hands together to still them. The boy Baldur lurched forward, reaching toward those square, dark shoulders, but after all he did not quite have the courage to touch.

Like a nightmare ghost of pain, Rhion remembered the terror of feeling his own life slide away. Those eternal seconds in the Void whispered where he had tried to blot them from his consciousness— the howling abysses of all the colors of blackness, the horror of realizing that though the tiny gold emblem of the burning sun-cross flickered somewhere in the darkness to guide them, there was no magic to bring them through.

He remembered Jaldis' soul, his strength that was so much greater than the twisted fragile shell of his body, surrounding the failing core of his own being and holding him up.

Then the marshfire flicker of a sudden spurt of light, the thread of magic that had come through to bring them across at last.

"He . . . he stepped into the Dark Well, into the Void." Paul stared beyond Rhion as if he could still see into the Well that had given them a window to the Void. "And it collapsed upon him. Fell in on itself around him. He screamed—the sound seemed to come from . . . from very far off. And when we pulled him out, he was dead."

His hands had begun to shake again. Rhion whispered, "I'm sorry." But, looking up into that set, ravaged face, he doubted the young mage heard.

While Paul had been speaking, a door had opened behind him, and a harsh bar of unnaturally steady yellow light fell through. Two forms stood there—Rhion fumbled for his spectacles, resting, he now guessed more than saw, on the small table near the head of the bed where he lay. The forms clarified into a very tall man in his fifties with hollow cheeks and a burning dark glance beneath a hand-breadth of greasy black hair, and a smaller, slighter man, perhaps twenty years older, with flowing white mane and beard framing a pale, fanatic stare. The light behind them haloed them with its bizarre, motionless glare, brighter than a hundred torches. Rhion remembered Jaldis had spoken of *electricity*, artificial light that was made without magic, made for the benefit of anyone who cared to use it.

With his spectacles, Rhion was able to see a little more of the room, small and spartan and lined with more books than he'd ever seen in a private residence with the exception of the stone house of Shavus Ciarnin, Archmage of the Morkensik Order, his own Order of wizardry at home.

Paul seemed to pull himself together a little, sitting up in his leather-covered wooden chair. "These are Auguste Poincelles and Jacobus Gall, my colleagues in the effort to restore wizardry to this world," he said in his soft voice. The tall man acknowledged the first introduction with a nod, the bearded fanatic the second. "Baldur Twisselpeck . . ."

"I'm Rhion of Sligo." He saw the swift glance that passed between Poincelles and Gall behind Paul's back. "The Dark Well is gone, then?"

In his own world, where magic still existed, simply breaking the Circles of Power that held the shuddering dark of the window into the Void was sufficient to destroy it. In this world, who knew?

"Yes," Paul said, after long silence. "Yes."

"You can see the place where it was," the wizard Gall added, still standing, arms folded, in the doorway.

"We did everything we knew how to bring it back." The wizard Poincelles gestured with one long arm, like a spider against the light. "But it was useless."

Dizziness caught at Rhion as he stood up. Paul, clearly now the leader of these otherworld mages, put a steel-strong arm around him to keep him on his feet, and Gall and Poincelles fell back before them as they passed through the door and into the hall. Baldur trailed behind like a lumpish black dog at Paul's heel.

The walls of the hallway, Rhion noted automatically, were of plaster and wood, like the houses in Felsplex, impregnated with stale incense and the smoke of burned herbs—some form of nicotina, he thought. Their feet rang hollow on the oak planks of the bare floor, and he guessed, even before he turned to glimpse a wide stairway leading down, that they were on an upper floor of some good-size building. Voices murmured from below, echoing in the well of the stairs; he saw Poincelles and Gall trade another glance, but their eyes were chiefly on him, wondering at this chubby, bespectacled little man with his scruffy brown beard and his shabby brown-and-black robes, as if they could not actually believe they'd seen him come stumbling out of that column of darkness.

He wondered what they'd made of Jaldis' thick jeweled spectacles, whose magic gave his blind eyes sight, or of the wooden box of silver whistles and gut that to some degree replaced the voice that the old King's men had cut out of him with their knives, to keep him from witching them all those years ago . . .

As they had said, the Dark Well was gone.

The stars and circles of its weaving still sprawled, smudged with a confusion of hurried foot scuffs, over the worn plank floor of the upstairs room a few doors down the hall from the one in which he'd come to. The air was heavy with the cloying sweetness of dittany and the copper-sharp stink of dried blood. Baldur put out his hand and touched a switch in the wall, and glaring yellow light sprang to being in the room from a glass globe in the middle of the ceiling. Rhion blinked up at it for a moment, shading his eyes against its blaring strength, then looked at the floor again.

But there was nothing to be seen among the spirals and circles of power—dribbled candle wax, dried blood, a few dark spots where the Water Circle had been drawn, only the great ritual sun-cross they had drawn as a guide, the emblem of magic's eternal renewal scrawled upon the floor, and the prosaic air of this world dispersing the last veils of smoke.

"Well," he said shakily, putting a hand on the wall for balance to stand. "It took Jaldis three days to weave one on our side of the Void—the gods know how long it will take him here. But I don't expect he'll be well enough to for weeks—the Void's magic drained his strength very badly the last time he touched it—and after one crossing I for one am in no hurry to have him start. Is he . . . Is he all right?"

It came to him that none of them had mentioned his master; as the cloudiness and exhaustion cleared a little from his mind, he cursed himself for not asking earlier. Jaldis might need him; tampering with the Void or working with the Dark Well had always left the old man prostrated, too exhausted to work so much as a simple fire-spell, for days, sometimes weeks . . . Seven years ago, during an earlier vain attempt to contact the wizards whose voices he had heard crying out of magic's death, he had suffered a mild stroke.

But the four men surrounding him remained silent.

Cold touched him inside, an echo of cries in darkness, forever unheard.

At length Paul asked quietly, "You mean . . . Jaldis came with you after all?"

Looking up into that beautiful angel face, Rhion felt as if the floor beneath his feet had given way. "He . . . he stepped into the Void with me, yes."

No, he thought numbly, grayness beginning to creep into the edges of his sight. *Oh please, gods of magic, don't tell me he's dead . . . Jaldis my friend . . . Don't tell me I'm here on my own . . . Jaldis dead . . . no way back . . . Jaldis my friend . . .*

From what seemed to be a great distance Paul's voice came to him. "He said he was trying to get another wizard to come in his stead." His gray eyes were worried as he touched Rhion's elbow with a steadying hand. "He was blind, he said, and in need of certain magical implements to see and speak . . ."

Dear gods . . . Rhion's mind stalled on the brink of a roaring vortex of panic and despair. *Dear gods, don't do this to me.* "The other mages couldn't come." He was surprised at how steady his voice sounded, even though barely audible even to his own ears. "He and I . . . I wasn't going to let him come alone . . ."

"But you are a wizard, too, aren't you?" Baldur demanded, sudden anxiety in his watery brown eyes. "We c-can't have wasted . . ."

"Shut up, pig-dog!" Paul snapped viciously, his own face chalky in the hard yellow glare.

A thousand images swam through Rhion's mind in a single hideously elongated instant of time—Tally, his beloved, the sunlight dappling her hair as they lay together in the grotto at the end of her father the Duke's palace gardens; the laughter of his sons. Jaldis' thin mechanical voice saying *We can afford to think neither of the future nor of the past which we leave behind* . . .

So this was the end of the dream Jaldis had cherished these seven years—the dream that had sustained him, obsessed him—the dream of restoring magic to a world in which it had vanished, the dream of, perhaps, saving magic, if it came to be threatened in their own. *I'm here alone.*

No magic. And no way home.

Jaldis had never showed him how to weave a Dark Well. And though he had studied magic for seventeen of his thirty-five years, he knew that his own power was no more than average, his learning scanty in comparison to what his master's had been, what Shavus the Archmage's was, or what any of the great wizards of his own or any other of the major Orders . . .

"Come." Paul urged him gently back through the door. Blindly Rhion was aware of Baldur touching the button on the wall again, and the light vanishing as instantly as it had appeared, with a hard metallic *click. So that's electricity.*

"Lie down and sleep. We'll speak of this in the morning; we'll find some way to continue the work your friend wanted to help us do."

Rhion staggered, faintness rising through him with sudden, dizzying heat. He caught himself on the jamb of a door across the hall. Through that door the soft luminescence of candles wavered; his sight cleared again, and he saw within the half-lit darkness a tall man lying dead upon a leather divan, candles burning at his head and feet and an ornamental silver dagger unsheathed upon his breast. Rhion looked back quickly and saw beside him Paul's drawn gray face. He was not, he realized, the only one to have lost a friend tonight.

"Eric," Paul said softly. "Eric Hagen. It was he whose dream this was—the dream of bringing back magic to this world, before the enemies of magic who encircle our realm destroy us all."

Perhaps ten years older than Paul, like him Eric had been strong-featured and fair, and like him he was clad in close-fitting garments of black and gray, with buttons and buckles of gleaming silver. A little emblem of the sun-cross, red and black and white, glistened like a drop of blood on the collar of his shirt. Behind him, illuminated in the hard bar of light that fell through from the hall, hung a banner, the sun-cross wrought huge in black upon a white circle against a ground of bloody red.

The sun-cross, Rhion noticed for the first time, was reversed, so that it turned not toward light, but toward darkness.

"My name, by the way," Paul's voice said quietly, "is Captain Paul von Rath, of the Occult Bureau of the Ancestral Heritage Division of the Protection Squad. And though it is a sorry and tragic welcome, I do welcome you nevertheless, in the name of the German Reich."

Solstice

2

"As far as we can determine," Paul von Rath said, the light wind generated by their vehicle's speed flicking the fair hair like a raw-silk pennon from his forehead, "magic has not existed in our world for at least a hundred and seventy years. Whether this was the result of the actions of the men who hated it—and in our world magic has been deeply hated by both society and the church, as Jaldis told me that it is in yours—or whether it was an accident, a natural event like the fall of night, we have not been able to determine."

He sighed and turned his head, watching the endless monotony of dark pinewoods flashing past them: the low roll of moraine hills still shawled with cold blue shadows on their western sides, though the sky overhead was bright; the gray loom of granite boulders among soft green bracken or pine straw the color of dust; a landscape occasionally broken by abandoned meadows rank with weeds and murky with shallow, silted ponds; and here and there a crumbling barn.

"We only know that accounts of what can be termed actual magic became more and more sparse, and harder and harder to authenticate, until they ceased entirely. And that when we attempt to work what magicians of old claimed to be spells, we achieve nothing."

Rhion shivered, wondering what it must have been to be born with the power of wizardry—as he had been born—in a world where magic no longer existed—where such power, such longing, such dreams, could never be consummated and could never be anything but the slow oncoming of madness.

It was something he didn't like to think of at present. It was difficult enough to tell himself, as he did daily, sometimes hourly, that even the smallest of his own powers and perceptions—his ability to scry through a crystal, to channel energy into divining cards, or to deepen his senses to perceive sounds and scents and vibrations beyond the range of ordinary human awareness—would return and that they had not been permanently stripped away by the passage through the Void.

Three weeks isn't so long . . .

The first two weeks had seemed an eternity of lying feverish and weak in the great, gray granite hunting lodge called Schloss Torweg, mourning for Jaldis, sick with terror, disoriented and more alone than he had ever felt in his life.

He had been up and around for some days, but it was good now to be out in open air.

They came onto the main road through the hills. Gold morning sunlight slanted into their eyes as they drove eastward, palpable as javelins of gold. It splashed with light the tangles of wild ivy crowning the steep banks of the road cut, turned to liquid gold the buttercups in the roadside ditches, and made stars of the frail white spangles of dogwood and may. Somewhere in the woods a robin called, the sweet notes a comforting reminder of the thickets of the Drowned Lands, where for seven years he had served the Ladies of the Moon as scribe. A gray hare flickered momentarily into view at the top of the bank, but bounded away at the roaring approach of the vehicle they called a car.

Rhion had to grin at the thought of the car. It was a conveyance straight out of a fairy tale, moving, without beast to draw it, at speeds that covered in an hour the distance it would take to journey in a day—except, of course, that no talespinner he'd ever encountered in any marketplace in the Forty Civilized Realms had ever thought to describe such a marvel as being so raucously noisy or so comprehensively smelly.

Beside him, von Rath went on, "Germany is the only realm now whose rulers believe in magic, who will support wizards and then give them aid and help. And now her enemies have declared war on her and are massing on our borders, ready to attack as soon as the weather dries. It is essential that we recover magic, learn what became of it and how we can bring it back. For, if they conquer, even what belief still exists will perish and there will be nothing left— only those mechanistic bureaucracies, those believers in nothing, who seek to destroy what they cannot understand."

In the front seat the young blond titan named Horst Eisler who had been assigned as their driver by the Protection Squad— Schutzstaffel, in the harsh German tongue, shortened, as the Germans did with all long words, to SS—gazed straight ahead at the broken black cut of the pavement where it passed through the hills. Baldur, sitting beside the driver, was as usual twisted half round in his seat so that he could hang onto von Rath's every word. The driver slowed, easing the car around a place where last night's rain had washed a great slide of mud and boulders down from the twelve-foot banks that hemmed in this stretch of road; because of a car's speed and power, it required a deal more concentration to drive than a horse and, moreover, required a far better surface to drive upon.

To Rhion's right, Auguste Poincelles was arguing with Gall, who sat perched on the little jump seat that folded down from the door. "Of course Witches Hill was a place of power, a holy place!" Gall was fulminating in his shrill Viennese accent, his silver mane and beard streaming in the wind. "It lies upon a crossing of the leys, the energy-tracks that cover all the earth in a net of energy. Moreover, upon the night of the last full moon I slept among the time-runneled menhirs there, among the Dancing Stones, and a vision was visited unto me of eldritch Druids and olden warriors with the sacred swastika tattooed upon their broad breasts . . ."

Poincelles let out a crack of rude laughter. "Druids in Germany? You've been reading Bulwer-Lytton's novels again, Jacobus." He took a cigar from his pocket and lit it. Most of the people in this world were addicted to the inhaled smoke of cured tobacco leaves, and everything—cars, houses, furniture, and clothing—stank of it.

"Scoff if you like," the old wizard replied calmly, and his pale, fanatic eyes took on a faraway gleam. "I saw them, I tell you. Upon those stones they performed sacrifices that raised the power to keep the mighty armies of Rome at bay."

Poincelles laughed again, shaking back his greasy black forelock. "Ah, now when Mussolini invades us we'll know just what to do!"

Rhion sighed inwardly, not surprised at the constant bickering of the three wizards under von Rath's command. Wizards in his own world squabbled constantly. He wondered, with a stab of grief and regret, what Jaldis would have made of them.

He wondered, too, when they reached the place called of old Witches Hill, whether Jaldis would have been able to detect the ancient magic Gall claimed had been raised upon that spot.

The hill itself was clearly artificial, standing alone at one end of an overgrown meadow to the east of the long pine-cloaked ridge that backed Schloss Torweg. As they waded toward it through the knee-deep grass, Rhion studied the low, flattened mound, guessing that there had probably once been an energy-collecting chamber of some kind underneath—it was a good guess that if ley-lines did exist in this world, this was raised on one. According to Gall, Schloss Torweg had been likewise built upon a ley. Certainly the little hill upon which it stood, larger than this one but probably also artificial, had enjoyed a rather queer reputation in centuries past.

Standing among the three lumpish stones that crowned the hill— the Dancing Stones, they were called, one erect, two lying fallen and nearly covered with dew-sodden weeds—Rhion could feel no magic here at all.

And yet, he thought, that didn't mean it didn't exist. While the others moved about among the stones, Poincelles caressing the worn dolomite with his eyes half shut and Gall swinging pebbles on pendulum threads, their feet leaving dark-green swathes in the flashing diamond carpet of the dew, Rhion sat at one end of a fallen stone, breathing silence into his heart and listening. Though he was unable yet to detect the faint, silvery pulse of ley-energy through the ground, still the sweet calm of the April sunlight that warmed his face eased something within him. For the first time since his coming to this world, the hurt of losing Jaldis and the fear that he would never be able to find his way back lessened. He found himself thinking, *If magic still exists here it might give von Rath and his partners another energy source, help them in their efforts.*

Suddenly curious, he got to his feet, brushed the dirt and twigs from the hand-me-down Wehrmacht fatigue pants he wore, and turned his steps down the little hill. Pinewoods surrounded the meadow on all sides, rising to the west almost at the hill's foot behind a tangled belt of laurel and blackberry brambles. Though Rhion still sensed no buried energy as he picked his way among nests of fern, bracken, and fallen gray branches, still the cool spice of the pine scent, the sigh of the moving boughs, and the occasional coin-bright warmth of stray beads of sunlight were balm to him. The land sloped gently toward the main ridge as he walked on. There was some hope, he thought, both for himself and for this world, for magic's return . . .

"Halt!"

Startled, Rhion stopped and raised his head. A Storm Trooper in the black uniform of the Protection Squad—the SS—stood beside a boulder a few yards away. His rifle—another product of the magicless magic of this world—was leveled at Rhion's chest. Like most of the SS, this man's hair was fair, his eyes light, chill, and empty, reminding Rhion of something, of someone else . . .

"You will return to the meadow, please."

Rhion blinked at him in surprise, pushed his spectacles more firmly onto the bridge of his nose. "I'm just investigating . . ."

"You will return to the meadow." Dapplings of light strewed one sleeve of his black uniform jacket, made the silver buttons flash. Upon his left sleeve the sun-cross—the swastika—splashed black on a crimson ground, pointing backward, toward chaos, toward darkness, toward death. "This was Captain von Rath's order."

"Look," Rhion said reasonably, "I'm sure Captain von Rath didn't mean I needed protection from getting hit on the head by a falling pine cone . . ."

"It is not my business what Captain von Rath meant," the young man said without change of inflection, though his pale arrogant eyes traveled over Rhion's short, stocky form and his curly brown hair and beard with chill disapproval and suspicion. "Nor is it yours. He said you were not to be permitted to leave sight of the others. You will return, or I will take you back there myself. I assure you I will shoot you if you attempt to flee."

"You're making flight sound more and more appealing," Rhion remarked, turning back toward the meadow, and realized the next second that the guard probably took his jest literally and had his rifle cocked and ready. He was conscious of it behind him, all the way back through the trees down the slope toward the sunlight.

"I am dreadfully sorry," von Rath apologized, as the car picked its way along the rutted and potholed black pavement once again. "The young man was only following orders; he will be reprimanded for his lack of tact. But indeed, it does not do for you to wander too far alone. For one thing, you might have become lost and, having no identity papers . . . We are getting you some, of course, but these things take time."

And, seeing the expression on Rhion's face, he added gently, "The government has taken wizardry and all its workings under its protection, has given the Occult Bureau guards to make sure it is not interfered with. We are at war with forces that do not believe in wizardry, that hate our government, and that seek to destroy us. Believe me, this protection is needed."

"If you say so." Rhion settled back into the leather seat cushions and watched the landscape whisk by, the occasional silted meadows and crumbling barns among the dark trees speaking of a time when the countryside had been prosperous and well tended.

"It was the war," von Rath explained, when Rhion asked about it. "We were defeated in the war . . ."

"We were betrayed," Baldur put in, twisting around in the front seat where he sat next to the driver. "Betrayed by C-Communists and Jews who had wormed their way like maggots into the government while true men were fighting. All lost their money, except the Jews. That's why the Nazi Party appeared, with the SS as its adamantine spearhead, to save the German race from the muck into which it had been dragged and to lead it to its d-destiny."

Poincelles' dark eyes gleamed with malice. "And I suppose slitting the throats of most of its original members was a part of the Party's destiny?"

"That's a lie!" Baldur snapped, his fat cheeks mottling red. Since leaving the meadow he had been increasingly jittery, the restlessness of his weak brown eyes behind their thick glasses and of his twitchy, curiously shapely hands confirming Rhion's earlier suspicions that the boy was addicted to some kind of drug. "And anyway they were traitors to the Party and h-h-homosexuals . . ."

"All—what was it? Nearly a thousand?—of them?"

"I think now is not the time for a discussion of the Party's internal politics," von Rath said with quiet smoothness. "I doubt there is a government in the world that did not go through its formative upheavals. I trust, Rhion, that this expedition has not proved too tiring for you?"

Poincelles sneered, but settled back without argument and applied himself to fouling the air with another cigar. His fingernails, Rhion noticed not for the first time, were long and dirty and filed to points, his fingers stained yellow with nicotine. Gall, throughout the discussion, had merely stared ahead of him, perched again upon the little jump seat. Though, as far as Rhion could ascertain, neither Gall nor Baldur were actual members of the SS, both wore the close-fitting black trousers and clay-colored uniform shirts of the Order, a garb that was less than flattering to the lumbering boy. Poincelles retained civilian clothes—in this case a pair of rather loud tweed trousers and a tweed jacket, reeking of cigar smoke and old sweat.

"I'm tired, yes, but I think that will pass." Rhion turned to look up at the young Captain beside him. "The ritual of meditation we've been doing in the mornings helps; all week I've felt my strength coming back."

The gray eyes changed, losing their coldness. "Eric—Major Hagen—had used the morning ritual for years, since he was a youth at school." His soft, steady voice still echoed with the grief of loss, a grief as sharp, Rhion knew, as his own mourning for Jaldis. Was it Gyzan the Archer who had said *Perhaps the ending of all dreams is death* . . . ?

"That was what first brought us together, years ago—the dawn opening of the ways to power. I had the Crowley texts and was looking for those that had been *his* sources—I was only sixteen, and terrified that the masters at the Academy would find out I was interested in such matters. A bookseller in Brandenberg gave me Eric's name. He was living in the most awful garret while he pursued his studies . . ." He shook his head, his mouth quirking a little as he recalled the young student he had known, the haunted, conscientious little cadet he had himself been . . . "He was the only one who understood, the only one I could talk to about that which was within me—that which I knew *had* to be true."

Then he laughed a little, like a sudden flash of sun on frost-hard December earth. "I remember the winter night in that garret of his when we first contacted Jaldis. It was a few days before Christmas and freezing cold. I had to be on the train home the next morning, to a true old Prussian Christmas with every aunt and uncle and cousin I possessed. With the drugs we were using to project our minds into the Void, I still can't imagine why we didn't kill ourselves . . ."

The car slowed as it swung into the shadows of the road cut, where earlier they had edged past the washed-down rocks and mud. Now a gang of men was there, chained together and wearing shabby gray shirts and trousers, shoveling the clayey yellow mud into a sort of sledge under the rifles of four or five gray-uniformed guards. One of the guards yelled, "Get that *verfluchter* sledge the hell out of the road!" Others cuffed and shoved the corvee to obey. The men moved with the slow shakiness of borderline starvation as they set down their shovels and stumbled to comply.

The officer in charge hastened to the side of the car as it pulled to a halt. "Heil Hitler. My apologies, Captain, we'll have it clear in a minute. This road sees so little traffic . . ."

"That's hardly an excuse for blocking it!" Baldur flared, but von Rath waved him quiet.

"Quite understandable, Lieutenant."

"I—I heard about Major Hagen, sir," the officer said after a moment, touching the brim of his cap in respect. His uniform was gray instead of black, but Rhion recognized the insignia of the SS on collar and shoulder tabs; he reflected that the Reich of Germany was probably the most comprehensively protected realm he had ever seen. "A great loss to the service of the Reich, but I was afraid something of the kind would happen. The drugs you were using for those experiments . . ." He shook his head. "He should have taken a little more time. After all the men who died while he was experimenting for the right dosage, he should have been more careful. Hell," he added, nodding toward the workers, stumbling as they dragged at the sledge. "The Commandant would have sent him over as many more of these swine as he needed to make sure."

"We were under a time constraint," von Rath said politely. "Thank you, Officer . . ."

With a gravelly scraping on the rough asphalt of the road, the sledge was hauled clear. Horst put the car in gear and started to move forward slowly. The officer touched his cap again. "Ah, well, there it is. If you need any more, just let us know!"

"That troubled you." With a touch on his sleeve von Rath halted Rhion in the doorway of the library, a long room occupying much of the main lodge's eastern face, and let the others go past them along the upstairs hall to their own rooms to prepare for lunch. Only Baldur stopped and came back to trail them into the long, gloomy chamber, unwilling, Rhion suspected, to let his hero have a conversation with anyone in which he was not included.

Still shaky with shock, anger, and a vague sense of betrayal, Rhion didn't much care. "Just a little, yes."

Neither von Rath nor Baldur seemed to notice the heavy sarcasm in his voice. Baldur snuffled, wiped his nose on his crumpled sleeve, and said matter-of-factly, "I d-don't see why it should. They were just . . ."

"I did debate about whether to tell you how we arrived at the drugs under whose influence we were able to project our minds into the Void." Von Rath cut the boy off gently, seating himself at the library's long table. "I did not know what your attitude toward it would be. Further, you were sufficiently grieved over your master's death that I did not wish to burden you with the possibility of fancied guilt."

"*Fancied* guilt?"

Even at this hour of the late morning the library, facing east into the little courtyard between the wings of the grim, gray lodge, was thick with gloom. The tobacco-colored velvet curtains, which were never opened, created a dusk, thick and palpable as the smells that seemed to have accumulated over the hundred-odd years of the building's life: the odors of dust and the stale, gritty foetor of ancient wool carpets; the faint moldery atmosphere that clung to the desiccated trophy head of an antelope over the doorway; the dry breath of old paper, crumbling cloth and glue; and the beaten-in reminiscence of tobacco smoke that would never come out. The walls here were thick with books, more books than Rhion had ever imagined: Lanz and von List; Blavatsky's *Isis Unveiled* and the *Chymische Hochzeit*; Nostradamus' prophecies; the collected works of Charles Fort; and the *Library of Those Who are Blond and Defend the Rights of the Male*. They had overflowed the original mahogany shelves and stacked two deep the newer pine planks that had been erected over the ornamental paneling. Neat boxes of half-decayed scrolls and chests of parchment codices were arranged upon the floor; in those few spaces of wall not occupied by books hung fragments of Assyrian carvings and the long, fading columns of Egyptian glyphs. Rhion, used as he was to the libraries of the Duke of Mere and the Ladies of the Moon, had been staggered at the prodigality of books in this world.

Here he spent most of his afternoons, listening to Baldur, Gall, or von Rath as they read to him from these endless texts. The Spell of Tongues that permitted him to understand German worked, in essence, from mind to mind—thus he could understand what was read aloud, if the reader understood it, though the written languages were a mystery to him. And here Baldur spent most of his nights, taking notes, looking up obscure references, reading his way patiently through collections of ancient letters, centuries-old diaries, crumbling grimoires, and yellowing broadsides and scandal sheets that the SS's Occult Bureau in Berlin had sent them, searching for some scrap of knowledge, some clue that would show them how and why magic had died in this world and how it might be restored.

Baldur was sitting now, hunched over his notes, puffy, untidy, and sullen, snuffling and wiping his nose on his soiled sleeve. On Rhion's world, Lord Esrex, son-in-law of the Duke of Mere and an old enemy of Rhion's, was addicted to a drug brewed from certain leaves given to him by the priests of the dark Cult of Agon. Here a similar substance was—rather disgustingly, in Rhion's opinion—rendered to a powder that was then snorted through the nasal membranes, with the result that Baldur's sinuses always ran.

"Fancied, yes." Von Rath's well-shaped brows drew down slightly, shadowing his clear gray eyes. "The men who were used in Eric's experiments were criminals, traitors against the state, men whose crimes in any society would have rendered their lives forfeit. The SS has the management of the labor camps and the concentration camps in which they in some measure atone for their deeds by service to the state they have tried to destroy. We had to find some way of speaking through the Void, some way of renewing contact, and drugs—mescaline, psilocybin, and others—were the only things we had found that worked. We were permitted an arrangement with the commandant of the Kegenwald camp to obtain men for experiments with the correct dosage. But the men themselves would have died anyway."

There was a polite tapping at the door; von Rath looked up as one of the guards assigned to watch room duty in the old parlor at the foot of the stairs entered. "Reichsführer Himmler is on the phone for you, Captain."

"Please excuse me." Von Rath reached for the telephone on the corner of the library table, and Rhion, rising, left him in such privacy as Baldur's company afforded. Telephones were another thing straight out of tales of wonder, though in marketplace fables the means by which two people without magical powers could communicate instantaneously over distance generally involved sight as well as hearing.

Curiously, though the Spell of Tongues held good when the speaker was in his presence, Rhion could not understand an electronically transmitted voice, either over the telephone or on that totally unexpected device, the wireless radio. Last night, when he had gone down to the big drawing room downstairs for the first time to watch a cinema being shown for the benefit of the guards—

the simple and unspeakably tragic love story of a wise man for a whore—Poincelles had had to translate for him.

He turned down the hallway of the south wing, paused before the door of what had been the great master bedroom, pushed it open, and stood looking in.

The room was still empty. Yellow sunlight filled it from the wide south-facing windows; through the uncurtained panes could be seen the rude and hastily built block of the guards' barracks and, beyond, the wire fence that enclosed the entire low hill upon which the Schloss had been built. Telephones, automobiles, even the huge quantities of books available in this world hadn't staggered Rhion so much as the cheap plentifulness of wire. In his own world it was so difficult to manufacture that it was generally used only for decorative jewelry. When the gate was closed at night the wire fence was charged with enough electricity to knock a man down, and Rhion had been warned repeatedly against going anywhere near it. *Not*, he reflected wryly, remembering his experiences that morning, *that the perimeter guards would let me*.

And in the chamber itself . . .

Dust motes sparkled in the mellow sunlight. On the oak planks of the floor every trace of the Circles of Power had been eradicated.

Jaldis, dammit, he thought, grief for his master's loss mingling with exasperation and regret. *Why didn't you trust me with the secret of its making? Even though I worked for the Ladies of the Moon, you know I wouldn't have passed that secret on to them.* But Jaldis had never trusted wizards of any other Order, as far as his secrets were concerned.

"I'm sorry." Von Rath's soft voice spoke at his elbow. Rhion, leaning in the sunny doorway, glanced back to see the tall black figure in the shadows of the hall. He said nothing in reply, and there was a long moment's silence, the younger wizard looking over his shoulder into the room, empty and filled with light, where the darkness had been.

"I'm sorry," von Rath said again, and this time he was not simply apologizing for the interruption of their conversation by a telephone call from Berlin. His voice was quieter, gentle with regret. "You know, I do think that the use of drugs to create the Well probably had something to do with . . . with its collapse. With Eric's death. I am sorry . . ." He shook his head, closing his gray eyes as if doing so would erase the image from his mind.

After a moment he went on, his voice hesitant as if he were carefully choosing his words. "I swear to you, Rhion, that as soon as it is possible to . . . to risk it . . . we will weave a Dark Well again. We will get in touch with wizards on your own side of the Void, to take you back through. But you understand that it is not possible now."

"Yes." Rhion sighed almost inaudibly, leaned once more against the oak doorjamb, weary in every bone. "Yes, I understand."

"Spring is the time for war," Paul said quietly. "When the weather clears . . . I fear that the English, the French, the Dutch, the Belgians, and the Russians are only waiting for that. They will launch an attack upon us at any time now, and we cannot risk losing another one of us, should what happened to Eric happen again. Not when we have made this much progress toward returning magic to our world."

"I understand," Rhion said again.

The strong, slender hands rested for a moment on his shoulders, tightened encouragingly, as if willing him strength, like a commander willing his men to be brave in coming battle. For a moment something in that touch made Rhion think the younger wizard was about to say something else, but he did not. After a brief time, he turned away, and Rhion heard the highly polished boots retreat down the hall to his own small study, leaving Rhion alone.

In the silence, the faint chatter of the radio in the watch room downstairs seemed very loud. Outside in the yard, a Storm Trooper cracked a rude soldier's joke, and another guard guffawed. Rhion remained where he was, bone-tired and hopeless, leaning in the doorway of that sun-flooded room, remembering . . .

There HAD to have been some magic on this side, he thought, *even the tiniest fragment—there had to be magic on both sides of the Void for a crossing.*

Somehow, just for that instant, at the stroke of midnight on the night of the spring equinox, some spark of magic had been kindled in a fashion that von Rath and his colleagues still did not understand. Enough to bring him through.

His mind returned to that fact, again and again. Perhaps Eric had known . . . But Eric was dead, destroyed in the Well that he had made. If that magic could be duplicated, even for an instant . . .

If he could only find some way to remake the Dark Well and contact the wizards in his own world.

But even if Baldur had found notes of it in the library, he reflected, they'd never reveal that to him. And without someone to read the texts to him he was helpless, illiterate, as utterly dependent upon them as he was for clothing and food and—he grinned wryly at the irony—Protection.

He stared down at the bare oak planks of the floor, seeking for some remaining trace of the Circles. He only remembered from seeing the ones Jaldis had made that they were hellishly complicated—blood, earth, silver, and light interwound and woven with smaller rings, curves, and crescents of power. And even so he did not know the words that went with their making.

In any case there was nothing to be seen. Only the bare oak planks . . .

. . . *bare oak planks* . . .

What was it, he wondered suddenly, about the oak planks of the floor that touched a chord of wrongness in his mind? As wrong as the backward-turning swastikas, as wrong as the eyes of the guards in the watch room, cold and caring nothing except to follow whatever orders they were given . . .

And then he remembered coming to in darkness, sick and freezing and exhausted to the marrow of his being, wondering with what strength was left in him that he was alive at all and thinking how the *stones of the floor would have been cold if any warmth had been left in his hands.*

The stones of the floor.

His eyes went back to the oak planks, naked and worn and scuffed with a thousand scrubbings.

Von Rath lied.

His heart jolted with a lurching surge of certainty, knowing that it was true.

Von Rath lied so that I'd think there wasn't a way home. So that I'd be at their mercy. So that I'd do whatever I could to restore magic in this world, because only in restoring magic could I get myself home.

Excitement, rage, dread that he was wrong and bone-deep awareness that he was right swept through him in a confused wave, like the stab of needles and pins in a long-numbed limb coming once more to life. He began to shake, his breath coming fast with hope and blazing anger.

They drew up fake Circles here while I was unconscious, to make me believe them. Hell, they could have brought me here from another building, another place entirely, the way cars can travel . . .

They could have drugged me . . . I have only their word on how long I was out.

I have only their word on everything.

For a long time he stood there unmoving: a stout little man with his shabby, graying beard and thick-lensed spectacles, listening to von Rath's quiet voice talking to Baldur in the hall by the library door, the crunch of car tires on gravel outside, and the distant, indistinguishable murmur of the guards exchanging greetings as they walked the barbed-wire perimeter of the fence. He felt exactly as if he had been crossing a floor that he had thought to be solid, only to feel it buckle suddenly beneath him and to hear the echoes of bottomless chaos yawning under his feet.

A floor enormously wide, he thought. And no way of knowing which way to run for safety.

If I have only their word on everything . . .

What else are they lying to me about?

3

"You want me to find a *what?*" Tom Saltwood tossed the slim dossier of photographs, maps, handwritten notes, and one or two cheesily printed magazine articles back onto the desk and regarded the man who had been his commander in Spain with mingled bemusement and uncertainty. "With all due respect, Colonel Hillyard . . ."

"I know." Hillyard's mouth flicked into its wry, triangular grin. "I'll admit that's how it sounded to me."

"And to me." The third man in the nameless London office, a stooped Englishman with very bright black eyes peering from a heavily lined face, reached across to the dossier with one arthritic finger and flipped free a snapshot that hadn't been very good even before it had been blown up to eight-by-ten. Mayfair, Hillyard had introduced him to Saltwood, though Tom was pretty certain that wasn't his name.

"But some rather strange rumors have come to us from some of the more secret bureaus of the SS, and this one we've had—er—independently confirmed. We think it bears looking into."

"Not," Hillyard added, settling his lean form back in the worn brown leather of his chair and reaching briefly, almost automatically, behind him to tweak the tiniest chink out of the bow window's heavy curtains, "that it would be easier to believe if we'd had it confirmed by personal telegram from Hitler, but there it is."

Tom was silent for a moment, wondering what it was that was causing the alarm bells to go off at the back of his mind. A false note in Hillyard's voice, maybe, or the way he tilted his head when he looked across at the man he called Mayfair—the suspicion and query in his eyes. Maybe it was just time and place. What three weeks ago—when he'd gotten the enigmatically worded request to report back to London—would have been normal or at least explicable now bore a staggering load of contextual freight.

Or maybe he was just tired. Several hours spent crammed in a corner of a destroyer's gun deck with seven hundred filthy and exhausted British soldiers wasn't particularly conducive to napping, even under the best of circumstances. The steady cannonade of shell-fire and strafing hadn't helped, nor had the unencouraging sight of slate-colored water, littered with hawsers, oil slicks, fragments of mined ships, and floating bodies visible every time he turned his head to glance over the rail.

But on the whole, it was better than the hell of exhaustion and death he'd left behind him on the Dunkirk beach.

And there on the docks at Dover, among all those nice British ladies with cups of tea and elderly blue-clothed policemen saying *Step along this way now* . . . had been Colonel Hillyard, tired, un-shaven, and grimy as any of the troops, but with that old businesslike glint in his dark eyes as he'd said, "About time you showed up. I have a car." Tom had barely had time to change and shave—he'd slept on the way up.

And now they were asking him to do . . . What?

He blinked, rubbed his eyes, and picked up the photograph. The reproduction was grainy. The building in the background might have been one of those big mansions rich folks built up the Hudson from New York a hundred years ago—heavy granite walls, peaked gables, crenellated ornamental turrets on the corners and pseudo-Gothic traceries on the windows—except that, judging by the number of men in SS uniforms standing around and the little swastika flags on the hood of the car in the foreground, it was obviously somewhere in Germany. A civilian was standing near the car: a bearded, tired-looking little man of forty or so with curly hair long and unruly and steel-rimmed glasses concealing his eyes.

"His name is Sligo," Mayfair said in a voice crusty and plummy as eighty-year-old port. "Professor Rhion Sligo."

"Sounds Irish," Hillyard remarked from the depths of his armchair. "Gaelic form of Ryan, maybe." He ran a hand over his sunbrowned bald scalp. "Any Irishman working for the SS these days would be using the Gaelic form, of course."

"Perhaps," Mayfair agreed. "We have no record of anyone of that name graduating, teaching, or publishing at any university or college we have checked; but then, a false degree is as easy to assume as a false name, and both are rather common in occult circles." He sipped his tea, which a secretary had brought in a few minutes before.

Tired as he was, Tom had to smile a little at the teacups. In an American office they would have been those thick white mugs reminiscent of every cheap diner from Brooklyn to Bodega Bay. Here they were somebody's second-best Spode that had gotten too chipped for company. The office, in one of those politely anonymous terraced squares so typical of London, likewise had the air of having been donated by a Duke in reduced circumstances. It had clearly started life as somebody's parlor, with faded pink wallpaper framing a stained plaster mantel and a fireplace prosaically tiled over and occupied by an electric grate. The whole setup was straight out of Thackeray. The faded draperies were firmly shut over the bow window, the blackout curtain beyond them cutting out any possibility of a view. Now and then a car would go by outside with a soft swishing of tires, or he would hear the swift clip of hurrying shoe heels on the pavement. But few, Tom thought, would be abroad tonight.

Somewhere in the building, someone had a radio on. Tom couldn't make out the words, but he didn't need to. So many ships safely returned to Dover with their cargos of beaten, exhausted, wounded men—so many shelled to pieces or sunk by mines in the channel. And still more men trapped on the beaches, between the advancing German army and the sea.

No sign yet of an air attack on London.

No sign yet of landing barges setting out with German troops.
No sign yet.

Sitting here in this quiet, lamplit office, Tom experienced a sensation of mild surprise that he was alive at all. Twelve hours ago he would have bet money against it.

Mayfair's voice called his attention back. ". . . arrangements made, as you know, three weeks ago to transfer you from your unit in Belgium. What was important then, when the entire question was an academic one of if and when, is doubly important now in the light of an imminent invasion."

Tom looked from the bent, grizzled old man behind the desk to the lean, browned one in the dull khaki uniform, and rubbed his hand over his face, trying to be sure he was completely awake and alert for all this. "With all due respect, sir . . . a *wizard?*"

"So he claims." Mayfair produced a pipe from his jacket pocket and began the meticulous ritual of reaming, cleaning, stuffing, and experimental puffing that Tom had observed pipe smokers to treasure, probably above the actual taste of the tobacco itself. "And the SS seem to believe him enough to cherish him . . ."

"Yeah, well, they cherish Himmler's slumgullion about a master race, too."

"Perhaps. But Sligo's claim is not only that he is a wizard himself, but that he can teach wizardry to others."

Tom chuckled. "Hell—sir. Professor Marvello the Magnificent taught *me* magic in the carney when I was eighteen, but nobody from the government ever tried to hire me."

"Well." Hillyard smiled, brown eyes sparkling against a brick-red tan. "Now they have."

Saltwood was startled. "You mean just because . . ."

"No, no." Mayfair waved a dismissive hand and set his pipe down on the scarred leather blotter before him. "Although that is what you Americans call a 'dividend' for us—that you may stand a better chance of spotting a hoax. No. The reason I asked Colonel Hillyard to contact you—the reason we've arranged for you to be seconded from your regiment . . ."

What's LEFT of my regiment, Tom thought grimly, remembering the men who had fallen at the crossings of the Leutze and the

Scheldt, remembering the men who had crouched in shell holes in the sand with him, who had not gotten up again.

". . . is because you speak German like a native, because you look German, and because you've done a bit of intelligence work during the fighting in Spain. Is this correct?"

There was another folder, closed, at Mayfair's elbow on the battered mahogany of the desk; Tom glanced at it, guessing it was his and wondering exactly how much it contained.

"A whole swarm of Germans and Swedes homesteaded the bottomlands along the Missouri near our ranch when I was a kid," he explained. "My grandmother was German—she lived with us. I spoke it at home and playing with the German kids. For years I had this real hick Saxon accent—I boarded with a German family when I worked on the New York docks, and the wife said I spoke German like a pig and worked to straighten me out." He grinned a little at the memory, not adding that his landlord had also been his cell leader in the Industrial Workers of the World and that most of his practice in the language had been obtained in endless summer-night discussions on the stoop about socialist political argument.

Mayfair studied him awhile longer, taking in, Saltwood knew, the craggy bones of his face, the ridiculously baby-fine dust-colored hair, the blue eyes, broad shoulders, fair skin. His "intelligence work" in Spain had come about because he'd been the only man of their company in the Lincoln Brigade capable of passing himself off as a German. One night he'd gotten three of the local Anarchists out of rebel hands with only some very unconvincing forgeries of Gestapo i.d. Their Russian military advisor had reprimanded him strongly, for the Anarchists, though officially Republican allies, were considered not worth the risk.

"You understand," Mayfair went on after a moment, "that you'll probably be impersonating an SS Trooper for part of the time—and the Nazis are not signatories of the Geneva accords."

"Neither were the nationalists," Tom said quietly. "I went through all that in Spain."

"So I see." Mayfair sat back and picked up his pipe again, puffing at it in the usual vain effort to get the thing to go. He nodded down at the closed folder. "A volunteer in the Abraham Lincoln Brigade, later seconded to the Internationalist Front headquarters in thirty-six. You were listed as captured—"

"I escaped," Tom said. "Nobody seemed to be trying very hard to get us out."

"Ah." Mayfair took a few more draws on the pipe, then gave it up as a bad job and opened the folder, turning over the pages with an arthritic's careful deliberation. Presumably, Tom thought, it hadn't been his department. At least he had the good grace not to say, as so many did, "Well, politically we were in an awkward situation with regard to prisoners . . ."

After a moment he resumed. "You returned to America, though we don't have any record here of an official repatriation . . ."

"It wasn't under my own name."

The grizzled eyebrows took a whole ladder of parallel forehead wrinkles with them on their way up.

Saltwood shrugged. "They weren't falling over themselves to repatriate those of us who'd been antifascist enough to go to Spain and get shot at, so I figured somebody who'd been in trouble over labor unions would stand even less of a chance. So when one of my old chess-playing buddies in the Brigade took a bullet in Madrid I sort of appropriated his papers."

"I see." By the shrewd glance in his black eyes Tom wondered exactly what he *did* see. "And *were* you involved with the labor unions in the United States?"

"I was on the fringes of them, yes," Tom lied, folding his hands over the buckle of his Sam Browne belt and doing his best to look like a dumb, blue-eyed farmboy, something he had always been good at. "After Pa died and our ranch went bust, I spent a lot of time on the road. Working in the mines and the factories, you couldn't hardly help running across them." From the corner of his eye he saw Hillyard sigh and shake his head, but, after all, his old commander said nothing. Considering Tom's rowdy and violent career as an organizer in the IWW, that was probably just as well.

"Well," Mayfair grunted at length, "least said about that the better, perhaps. And you arrived in this country last September and volunteered . . . again."

Tom felt himself blush as if Mayfair had unearthed a stint with a ballet troupe in his past. After Spain he really should have known better. "Hell—begging your pardon, sir. But nobody back in my country seemed to be standing in line to do anything about Hitler . . ."

"You need hardly apologize, Sergeant Saltwood." The old man closed the folder again and looked across at him from under jutting brows. "Will you take it?"

Tom hesitated for a long time, all the topics that the old man had *not* brought up—like, *Who is this man REALLY and, for that matter, who are you?* and *Why don't you get somebody from regular Intelligence?* and *What's scared you into sending someone at a time like this?*—combining in his mind into a strong odor of rat. He'd gotten Hillyard's telegram asking him to come back to London for "family business"—a code between them from their days with the Brigade that had meant "I've got a job for you . . ."—two days before the panzers had come rolling out of the Ardennes Forest like a tidal wave of iron and fire. *At least*, he reflected wryly, *I was already packed.*

"There are, of course, a number of explanations as to what might be going on," Hillyard said, in the deep, brocaded baritone that wouldn't have disgraced an RADA performance of *King Lear*. "Sligo may very well be a confidence trickster, out to take the SS for whatever he can."

"That's not something *I'd* care to try, unless I had some way of getting out of that country real fast."

"As you say," Hillyard agreed. "But stupider things have been attempted—and have succeeded. In fact, he may know that Hitler has a blind spot where the occult is concerned. Then again, Sligo may be mad . . ."

"He's definitely mad," Mayfair put in. "According to one of our sources, he seems to suffer from a number of rather curious delusions, apparently without affecting his usefulness to the SS."

"The third explanation," Hillyard went on, "is that the occult group—composed of several genuine occultists from Paris and Vienna spiritualist and theosophist circles—is a cover for something else, some new weapon or device that is being developed, and *that* is what we're worried about."

He folded his hands on one jodhpurred knee—like Tom, he'd had a change of uniform, a wash, and a shave in that rented room in Dover, but then, he'd always managed to look neat, even when crouching in a Catalan sheep pen under Luftwaffe fire. "We still don't know how the Germans took the fortress of Eban Emael—the key to that whole section of the Maginot Line. We only know that it was impregnable and that it went without a shot being fired."

"Conversely," Mayfair added, "the occult trappings could just as easily be for Sligo's benefit as for ours or Himmler's. From all we can ascertain, the man definitely believes himself to be a wizard. Whatever he has or may have invented, he may attribute to magic, just as our system of radio directional finders grew out of an attempt to invent a death ray—something the Nazis are still working on. The Nazis may have enlisted his assistance by humoring his belief.

"In any case it makes no odds." He picked up his pipe again, and appeared to be surprised—as pipe smokers invariably were—to find that it had gone out. For a moment he sat cradling it, his dark eyes gazing out past Tom, into some middle distance of thought, and Tom saw weariness descend upon him like a double load of grain bags carried too far—the weariness of waiting and wondering, less urgent perhaps than the ground-in ache in his own flesh, but ultimately just as exhausting. At least for the past ten days his own thoughts had been absolutely concentrated on the moment: cover, spare ammo, a place in the retreating trucks. He hadn't had time, as this old man had, to consider the larger implications of that tidal wave of gray-clad men sweeping across the flat green Belgian landscape—he hadn't spent the past ten days wondering *What the hell will we do when the Germans land at Dover?* knowing that every gun, every truck, every grenade and clip of ammo the British Army possessed had been left on Dunkirk beach.

Then Mayfair sighed and straightened his shoulders again, as if reminding himself, *First things first.* "Are you interested? You'll be put ashore by submarine, probably near Hamburg; we'll give you the names of contacts in Hamburg and in Danzig as well—if you have to flee in that direction—for you to radio for instructions about when and where you'll be taken off again. You'll have a couple of German identities, with uniforms, passbooks, ration cards, maps . . . photographs of the men involved, if we can get them in time. Colonel Hillyard tells me you're a man to be trusted to do the job and not to panic if things come unstuck. At present, Sligo's group is headquartered somewhere in the wilds of Prussia near the Polish border, and you may have to make a judgment about which direction to run. But that can all be worked out later. The question is, are you willing?"

"To kill Sligo?"

Mayfair nodded, unfazed at the bald statement that the mission was, in fact, being undertaken for the purpose of murder. "If you can ascertain what they're up to, of course we'd like to know that, too. But I understand you're not a scientist. The main object is to kill Professor Sligo, at whatever cost."

Tom glanced over at Hillyard. His brain was still ringing with the alarm bells of unanswered questions, where it wasn't thick with sleepiness and exhaustion, but he guessed if he were to ask now, he wouldn't get answers anyway.

But two years of fighting in Spain, of ambushes in dry ravines and blowing up bridges and trains, of firefights in the streets of Madrid, and of the thornbush morasses of guerrilla politics had taught him that Hillyard was a man to be trusted. Hillyard met his eyes and nodded.

"I'm your man," Tom said laconically. Then he added, "God willing and the creek don't rise."

Mayfair's mouth tightened. "As you say," he agreed, and his tone was dry. Elsewhere in the building, the radio announcer's voice chittered frighteningly on.

"So what's the story?" Tom fished in the pocket of his uniform tunic for makings as he and Hillyard emerged onto the high porch and paused to let their eyes adjust. With every window in the city swathed tight in blackout curtains, the darkness was startling, darker even than open country would be, for the shadows of the buildings blocked the dim ambient glow from the dusting of stars overhead. The night was fine and warm, the moist, thick smell of new-cut grass drifting to them from the little park in the center of the square, the colder, damper breath of moss-greened pavement and last year's dead leaves rising from the sunken areaway that dropped like a dry moat

below the porch to either side of them. The freshness of the air and
the sweet, calm silence of the night cleared his head and drove back
the exhaustion that seemed to weight his bones.

Tom's match made a startling glare in the blackness. "You know
as well as I do they've got guys in regular Intelligence who know
German."

"So they do. I've booked us rooms over in Torrington Place."
Starlight gleamed on the bald curve of Hillyard's head as he led the
way down the narrow porch stairs, his gas mask swinging awkwardly
at his belt. "My guess is that Alec—Mayfair—" He corrected himself. "—couldn't get approval from Intelligence to send one of their
men. It's not his department, you know."

"It's not?" They passed the little park. Against the pale scars of
cut-up earth, Saltwood saw the low, dim bulk of a redbrick air-raid
shelter, new and raw and waiting. He remembered Madrid again,
and what he'd seen of the village of Guernica. Though the night was
warm and peaceful, he shivered.

Hillyard shook his head. "He approached me privately, asked if
there was anyone from the Brigade who'd be reliable. Most of the
native Brits, I might add, have already vanished into the F.O.'s murky
ranks—not that that affected my choice much. If he hadn't arranged
to call you back now over this, I'd still have been waiting for you
on the docks."

"I bet you meet all the ships, honey." Tom grinned and made
a smooching noise in the dark. From behind them came the sudden, full-throated rumble of a car's engine—a big eight-cylinder
American job by the sound of it—and a moment later a lightless
black shape swept gleaming past them and away into the dark.
"Whoa—somebody was sure thinking when they drew up the
blackout regs . . . What's up?"

"Well, there's been a certain amount of discussion about forming
guerrilla forces, probably based in Scotland . . ."

"You don't think England's going to surrender, then?"

"Never," Hillyard said decisively. "You've been in the fighting,
so I don't know how much you've seen of what the Luftwaffe and
the German army did to Rotterdam . . ."

"I've heard." Saltwood's voice was grim.

"It's going to be bad here," Hillyard went on, suddenly quiet, as if he sensed all those families, all those children, all those peaceful lives and day-to-day joys that lay like a vast, murmuring hive around them in the lightless city. "And it may get bad very soon. But Churchill's never going to surrender."

"And with all this going on," Saltwood said thoughtfully, dropping his cigarette butt to the sidewalk and grinding it out under his heel, "Mayfair still thinks this mad professor of theirs is important enough for me to go over to Germany *now*?"

There was long silence, broken only by the strike of the two men's boots on the sidewalk and by the occasional surge of traffic— punctuated now and then by the startled screech of brakes—a few blocks away in Gower Street. But there were few passersby. Everyone in London—everyone in England, Tom thought—would be glued to a radio tonight.

They turned a corner, Hillyard seemed to know where he was going—but then, he always did, and could see like a cat in the dark. He steered Tom carefully across the street to avoid an entanglement of sandbags and barbed wire around some large building, nearly invisible in the pitchy gloom. Once they were stopped by a coveralled civilian, a fat old white-haired man wearing a warden's armband and carrying a gas mask strapped to his belt, and asked for their papers, but when he saw their uniforms by the quick glow of his flashlight he hastily saluted and waved them on by.

At length Hillyard said, "We'll probably have a little bit of breathing space, anyway—the latest reports say the German armored divisions are already turning south to mop up France."

"Makes sense if Hitler wants to secure naval bases on the Channel."

"So it does. But if there is to be an invasion, Mayfair seems to think that whatever Sligo is doing will make the situation worse. He's been scared pretty badly."

"Yeah, but . . . a *wizard*, Bill?"

And Hillyard laughed. "Well, I didn't read the reports. That should be the Red Cow opposite." He gestured toward what appeared to be a solid and anonymous wall of dark buildings on the other side of the narrow lane. "There isn't a wireless in the hotel room. Think you can stay awake long enough for a beer?"

"I always knew you could smell beer across a street."

Together they plunged across the bumpy pavement, dark as the inside of a closet, narrowly missing being run down by something powerful and nearly silent—a Dusenberg or Bentley, Tom guessed by the throb of the engine—that passed close enough to them that the wind of it flapped their trouser legs against their calves. Having spent twenty-four hours in a shell crater on the beach listening to machine-gun bullets smacking into the sand on all sides of him, Tom didn't bother to jump, just quickened his stride enough to let the whizzing car pass.

"Here lies the body of Thomas Leander Saltwood," he quoted his own epitaph, *"who survived union goons in the West Virginia mines, special deputies in the California orchards, two years of fighting in Spain, nine months in a Spanish prison, the German invasion of Belgium, the shelling of the Dunkirk beaches, Luftwaffe strafing on the Channel, his commander's driving on the way up to London . . ."*

"Watch it, Sergeant!"

". . . only to be killed in quest of beer by a careless driver during the blackout in the streets of London. You remember that case of Chateau Lafitte you found in Madrid?"

"Ah," Hillyard said reminiscently as he reached into the stygian pit of a darkened doorway for a handle—even on the step here, Tom could now hear the hushed murmur of voices and smell the inevitable warm fustiness of beer and bodies within. "A very good year." More than the wine, Tom remembered the bombing raid that had been going on when they'd found it . . . remembered his commander casually pouring out glassfuls for them both in the ruins of the old cellar, listening to the explosions getting nearer and nearer and remarking, *That one's two, three streets away yet . . . plenty of time . . . hmm, sounds like they're dropping mines . . .* "I remember old Palou insisting on unloading the wine from his cart during that big raid. 'They are only Germans, but this . . . this is money . . .'"

"Funny what you get used to. I met Californios when I was working the Long Beach docks who wouldn't get up from the suppertable for an earthquake but who swore they'd never go east of the Rockies for fear of tornadoes—*tornadoes*, for Chrissake!"

In the broad slit of yellow light as Hillyard opened the pub door, Tom saw his commander blench. "Er—have you seen many tornadoes?"

And Tom, who'd grown up with them, only laughed.

He took a seat at a table in a corner, under a moldering trophy head some aristocrat had shot in Kenya and an enameled tin ad for Green King Ale. The pub was very quiet, the scattering of working-men and housewives there speaking softly, if at all, over their pints of ale and bitters, listening to the chatter of the radio announcer's voice.

". . . general withdrawal of all remaining forces to Dunkirk. On the Channel, the destroyer *Wakeful* was torpedoed and sunk, only a few survivors escaping to be picked up by the motor drifter *Nautilus* and the danlayer *Comfort*, themselves heavily loaded . . . the *Queen of the Channel*, with 920 men aboard, bombed and sunk, her crew and passengers picked up by the store-ship *Dorrian Rose* . . . *Harvester*, *Esk*, *Malcom* . . . the minesweeper *Brighton Belle* sunk in the Channel, her troops rescued by the *Medway Queen* . . . destroyers heavily engaged with shore batteries . . ."

They'll never make it, Tom thought, leaning back against the dark wainscot walls and letting his eyes slip closed. Hillyard had gone to get them drinks—the soft murmur of voices washed over him, men's and women's both. It was a neighborhood pub, a family pub . . . It was good beyond anything to be among normal people, decent people, not in the terror and sweat and dirt of battle, the horrible inferno of waiting under shellfire, maybe to have your life saved and maybe not . . .

The rocking of the old *Codrington* that had taken him off the beach returned to him, seemingly woven into his bones. Like the rhythmic jostle of the freight cars he'd ridden, he thought, that came back to a man even when he was lying on a stable bed again. The memory of the smell of tornado weather, the dense, waiting stillness, the livid color of the sky, waiting and watching for spouts.

Funny, he hadn't thought about that since he was fourteen, the summer the ranch had finally gone bust and the bank foreclosed on

them, sold their hard-held herd and plowed the whole concern under
for a wheat farm. That was the first time he'd ridden the rails, down
to Oklahoma, looking for work in the oil fields.

His head jerked; he realized he'd been slipping over into sleep.
He saw Hillyard still by the bar, bending forward to catch the radio
announcer's voice. He tried to remember the last time he'd been this
warm, this comfortable—tried to remember the last time he hadn't
been expecting to get blown away by the Germans in the next ten
seconds . . .

His eyes slid closed again. The smells of tobacco and beer
wreathed his thoughts, the gentle patter of voices like falling rain.
". . . expecting an announcement by the King of Belgium . . . *Abukir*
destroyed . . . *Shikari* and *Scimitar* at Dover . . . special trains to
take the men to rest camps . . ."

". . . must use his influence, now more than ever," a woman's soft
voice murmured at the next table. He'd noticed the two women
there when he'd sat down, one delicate little white-haired finch of a
lady, like a duchess in plain clothes, the other a striking redhead
with eyes the color of the sherry in her glass. Like everyone else in
the pub, they had gas masks with them, incongruous on the floor
beside their worn leather handbags and as little regarded. The redhead's voice was low and desperate as she went on, "I saw it in the
crystal. I felt his coming on the night of the equinox . . . I felt it the
first time he used the power of the leys. If he isn't found, if he isn't
stopped . . ."

"He will be, darling," the old lady's comforting tones came,
motherly and gentle through the drowsy fog of dreaming that padded Saltwood's mind like a goose-down quilt. What they were saying
made no sense, but it was good to just listen to women's voices,
after all those weeks of men, of gunfire, and of the overhead shriek
of planes.

"Trust my husband to do his part, as we do ours. We have raised
the power to keep the skies clear for the planes . . . later we can call
down the clouds over the Channel . . . Alec!" she added in surprise,
and Tom opened his eyes—or thought he opened his eyes, though
he could very well have been dreaming, he thought—surely it was a
dream that Mayfair had come into the pub, gas mask tucked under

his arm, and was stooping, hesitant with arthritis, to kiss the little duchess on the lips.

"It is all being taken care of," Mayfair said, and the red-haired woman sighed, her slim shoulders bowing suddenly, as if with exhausted relief. He added, "As the Americans say, God willing and the creek don't rise . . ."

"No beer for you, Sergeant."

Tom jerked awake, to see Hillyard standing at his elbow, a glass in either hand.

"I refuse to carry you all the way to Torrington Place."

Saltwood blinked and rubbed his eyes. The table beside his was empty.

"Sorry for the delay." Hillyard settled himself into the chair next to Tom and gave himself the lie by pushing a pint of Bass across to him. "They say they've got somewhere near seventeen thousand men landed at Dover and more coming over all the time . . . nearly all the army's within the perimeter of Dunkirk. And the German armored divisions have definitely turned south, toward Paris. That leaves the Luftwaffe to contend with, but we may get a little breathing space . . . it's my guess, in fact, that with Intelligence in a frenzy, there'll be quite a delay in your setting out on your travels. It takes time to assemble papers, arrange transport, get photographs and maps, especially if one is doing it on the sneak."

"Look," Tom said curiously, as a few cautious sips of the nut-flavored ale cleared his head a little. "Just who *is* Mayfair? What department is he in? I mean, how did he find out about Sligo in the first place, if he's not in Intelligence?"

"I didn't ask." Hillyard smiled. "Not that he'd have told me if I had. He's in Finance—an auditor. Rumors do get around, especially the weird ones—perhaps he heard it from his wife."

"His wife?" *Alec*, the little Duchess in his dream—if it had been a dream—had exclaimed. In her simple tweed skirt and strand of pearls under the neat home-knitted green cardigan the old lady had certainly been no Mata Hari. "Is she in Intelligence?"

Hillyard chuckled. "Intelligence? No—it's just that for years there's been a rumor going about that she's a witch."

Tom rolled his eyes. *"Wunderbar."*

4

"Well, Toto," Rhion sighed, misquoting to an imaginary canine companion a line from the American cinema he had watched—with a certain amount of bemusement—last week, "I'd say just offhand that we are definitely not in Kansas anymore." Over the din in the tavern the Woodsman's Horn nobody heard, which was probably just as well.

There was a piano in the corner, a relic of the tavern's more respectable days before the SS had been garrisoned at the Kegenwald labor camp. From Tally, Rhion had acquired an interest in all sorts of musical instruments, but the chief virtues of pianos seemed to be that they were capable of far more volume than any similar instrument in his own world, and that it was much easier to play them badly. Both attributes were being lavishly demonstrated at the moment by the Storm Trooper at the keyboard, and a dozen or so Troopers around him were bawling out the words to a filthy cabaret song about Jewish girls at the top of their collective lungs. The air was blue and acrid with tobacco smoke, and Rhion, sitting in a dark corner at a table with Auguste Poincelles, pushed up his glasses, rubbed his eyes, and hoped to hell this trip would be worth the headache he was going to take back with him to the Schloss.

"Ten ships, ten of them!" a weedy, middle-aged merchant at the bar was whooping triumphantly to the impassive counterman. "Our boys are blasting the damned English out of the water! We'll be in London by this time next week!"

So much, Rhion thought wearily, *for our enemies attacking us at any moment.* He wondered that he could possibly have been naïve enough to have believed von Rath's version of the progress of the war, no matter how it had started. But he had not mentioned the discrepancy to von Rath.

Beside him, Poincelles raised one dirty, pointed fingernail to the nearest barmaid. The girl slithered like a weasel from among a pawing crowd of uniformed admirers and came across the room to them, splendid haunches switching under the thin blue cotton of her dress. It was Poincelles who had proposed tonight's expedition, to discuss matters that could not easily be mentioned in the presence of Baldur, Gall, and von Rath, Rhion guessed.

He couldn't possibly have come here for the beer.

"A whiskey, Sara, if there is such a thing in this place." Poincelles glanced inquiringly at Rhion. "Professor?"

Rhion gestured with his three-quarters-full steel mug, smiled, and shook his head. The barmaid Sara regarded him with eyes black and bright as anthracite coal in a pointed, triangular face, skin pale to translucence save for the garish redness of her painted mouth.

"So this is your famous professor?" She sized him up with a professional eye and shifted the tray she held so that her breasts bulged like white silk pillows beneath the half-unbuttoned bodice of her dress. "Glad you've finally come out of seclusion in that monastery they're running out there. We've heard tell about you. Go on, have another beer, Professor. Old Pauli's good for it."

"Later." Rhion smiled gallantly. "That way I get to watch you walk across the room again."

She laughed, tossed her frizzed red head, and returned to the bar to fetch Poincelles' whiskey, deliberately undulating her hips to the noisy approbation of the group around the piano.

"Nice little piece, that," Poincelles remarked. He produced a cigar from his pocket and a lighter—a small gold box containing flint, steel, and a highly combustible liquid fuel, as good as a fire-spell,

Rhion thought, at least within arm's length and while the fuel lasted. Rhion coughed in the ensuing cloud of smoke and resigned himself to being ill for the rest of the night. "The girls here are the only decent thing about the place. That beer has no more relationship to hops than the petrol in the car does. At least the whiskey's more or less pure."

"Pure what?" Rhion demanded, coughing. Poincelles laughed, as at a witticism, and handed another cigar back over his shoulder to Horst, their SS driver-cum-bodyguard. The young man accepted it gratefully and strolled off to join the group around the piano. The other two barmaids were there already, one a honey-fair girl who reminded Rhion heart-stoppingly of Tally, the other a little black-haired minx who had only moments ago emerged from the back room with an elderly man in the gold-belted brown uniform of a local Nazi Party leader. The piano thumped tunelessly, the stout barman paused in his steady dispensing of beer to sell condoms to a couple of Storm Troopers, someone turned up the radio to better hear the latest bulletins from the war in the West, and someone else shouted, "Hey, you know what they're going to get Hitler for his birthday? Frontier posts mounted on wheels!" The noise was deafening, the smoke nauseating as a gas. Rhion sighed, closed his eyes, and wished with everything that was in him that he could simply go home.

May was fading into June. Even at this hour, light lingered in the sky, soft as the color of pigeons' eggs, and the air outside was thick with the smell of apple blossoms from the nearby farms. Now and then the wind stirred, carrying the scent of pinewoods, whose dark wall enclosed the village, as it enclosed the Schloss, the undulating sandy hills, and, it sometimes seemed to Rhion, the entire world in a whispering monotony of somber green. In the Drowned Lands, the streams would still be high, and broad lakes would hold like quicksilver the shining echo of the light.

He felt a hand touch his wrist, warm and very strong; opening his eyes in the choke of cigar smoke, he saw that Poincelles had leaned near him, vulpine face as close to his as a lover's.

He whispered, "I can help you get home."

Rhion had been expecting those words, waiting for them—waiting for them, in fact, for several weeks. And he had almost been certain that it would be Poincelles to say them. Still he felt the jolt of adrenaline in his veins, and the pounding of his heart nearly stifled him.

And the words having been said, he must, he knew, go very carefully now. He kept his face impassive, but his fingers were shaking as he moved his arm away from Poincelles' grip and turned his beer mug a judicious ninety degrees on the grimed and splintery table. Though he neither liked nor trusted the Frenchman, he needed the help of another wizard and needed it desperately.

"You never have trusted them, have you?" the French occultist went on in his deep, beautiful voice. "Captain von Rath, and Baldur, and Gall."

"Well," Rhion admitted, "I must admit I was a little put off when I found out about the enemies of the Reich who were used for the drug experiments."

Poincelles blinked, for one second actually looking surprised that this was what had bothered him. Then he quickly molded his features into an expression of disgust and anger. "Oh—oh, yes!" He waved his cigar, trailing a ribbon of blue smoke. "I was horrified, as well, completely shocked—a ghastly business. I was furious when I heard, for of course I wasn't told about any of it until it was too late." He smiled slyly and added, "They don't exactly trust me, these Nazis."

"Now, how could anyone distrust a man of such obvious virtue and probity?" Rhion made his blue eyes wide behind his glasses, and Poincelles grinned like a wolf with his stained teeth.

"Clever." He smiled, and pinched Rhion's cheek. "I like a clever boy." He cast a quick glance across the room at Horst, presently conversing crotch to crotch with the blond barmaid. Like most Storm Troopers, Horst didn't impress Rhion as being terribly bright, but it didn't pay to take chances. Lowering his voice, Poincelles went on, "They don't trust me, but they needed my help in the rituals that went into the making of the Dark Well. They needed my power. I know von Rath has told you that, with the offensive on, none of us can be risked just now to create a Dark Well so that you can locate your home again—if he intends to send you home at all, ever. Myself, I doubt it."

He laid his hand again on Rhion's wrist, the cigar smoldering between two fingers, and his dark eyes gleamed beneath the shelved hollows of his brows. "My memory for matters of ritual is excellent. I can help you create another Dark Well."

Rhion looked away, understanding now the nature of the proposition—understanding that with those words, Poincelles had in fact announced that he had no intention of helping him get home. Disappointment settled like a swallow of cold mercury in his chest as he realized the man was not to be trusted, not to be turned to for help.

He said nothing.

"For a price," Poincelles went on.

Over by the bar there were fresh howls of laughter. A Waffen SS lieutenant in the gray uniform of the Kegenwald labor camp was pitching pfennigs for an old derelict, a whiskery drunk who made his living selling papers and picking up trash, to crawl for. As the old man groped on hands and knees for the coins, the other Troopers would kick them farther and farther out of his reach, like children tormenting a crippled dog. Horst whooped "Here's a drink for free!" and poured his whiskey over the old man's head; old Johann sat up, grinning with a terrible combination of terror and fogged pleasure, with hope that this would be the worst that would happen, and lapped at the liquid running down his hair.

The barmaid Sara, who had returned with Poincelles' drink, bumped Rhion's shoulder playfully with her hip. "No sense of humor, Professor?"

His mouth quirked dryly. "I guess not."

She looked down at him and some of the brittle quality eased from her face. "Kurt will see they don't hurt him, you know," she said in a quieter voice, and nodded at the impassive barman. She shrugged her shoulders, oddly delicate above the jutting splendor of her breasts. In spite of the lines of cynicism and dissipation around her dark eyes, Rhion realized she couldn't be more than twenty-two. "It gives the boys a laugh. They don't mean any harm."

Neither, Rhion supposed as the girl strolled away, had the guards in the Temple of Agon, the faceless servants of the Veiled God, who had pretended to set his oil-soaked beard on fire when Lord Esrex had had him imprisoned there.

He looked back to meet Poincelles' narrow, speculative eyes behind a haze of putrid smoke. "What price?"

"I want you to teach me."

Rhion gave his beer mug another quarter turn. "I am teaching you," he said quietly. "I have been teaching you for over six weeks now, and aside from the fact that you now know spells that work in my world, and your technical knowledge is cleaner than it was, none of the four of you is any closer to making magic work than you were before I came. You know that."

"I know that." Poincelles leaned forward and the smell of his breath, drowned in whiskey and cigar, was like the exhalation of a month-old grave. "And I know also that you're keeping something back."

Rhion kept his eyes on the beer mug but his hands and feet turned perfectly cold.

The Frenchman chuckled throatily. "My little friend, we all keep something back." He drained his whiskey with a gulp, stood and shook back the limp swatch of hair from his forehead. Across the room Horst, engaged in buying a condom from the barman to augment the weekly barracks ration of one, hastily departed to fetch the car around. After a long moment, Rhion stood up also and followed the tall occultist shakily from the room.

If the man has to make one true statement in the entire night—which is not a bad average for Poincelles, Rhion thought as he climbed into the rear seat of the open Mercedes that waited for them in the harsh trapezoid of yellow electric light—*why does it have to be that one?*

For Poincelles was quite right. They all did keep something back.

What Poincelles had kept back in the course of the discussion was what von Rath and the others had been keeping back from the start—that the Dark Well had not, in fact, been destroyed.

Rhion had confirmed his suspicions a few weeks after the expedition to the Dancing Stones, as soon as his ability to use his scrying crystal had grown strong enough to get a clear image once more. Those weeks in between, those weeks of suspicion, of not knowing who was lying to him and when, were nothing he would care to go through again. He had known he was entirely at von Rath's mercy for food and shelter and advice in this strange world—only during

those weeks had he realized how much he'd felt comforted by the
illusion that he was among friends.

He sighed and shook his head, glancing sidelong at the tall man
beside him as the car shot with its eerie speed along the forty kilometers of woods between Kegenwald village and Schloss Torweg. He
still felt keenly the disappointment that had come over him when it
had been clear that Poincelles had no intention of telling him that
the Well still existed; the fact that the Germans were in the process
of invading his erstwhile country evidently did not mean that the
Frenchman opposed them in principle. Had that little charade tonight been for Poincelles' own purposes, he wondered, or at von
Rath's instigation, to find out if Rhion knew more about magic than
he'd taught them in the weeks since his recuperation?

In either case, it made no odds. Poincelles was not to be trusted,
and it left him in a horrible position, for he desperately needed the
help of a wizard he could trust.

For Rhion, too, was keeping something back.

He had found—or thought he had found—the thing for which the
wizards of the Occult Bureau had begged Jaldis to come here in the first
place—the trick of making magic work in this magicless world.

The problem was that without the help of another wizard, bringing
this about in order to get himself home would almost certainly kill him.

"Captain wants to see you," the guard at the gate reported when
the car pulled up and the electricity was turned off long enough for
the gate to be opened. When the SS had taken over Schloss Torweg,
in addition to erecting the fence and cutting down all the trees that
surrounded the lodge itself, it had rigged floodlights to drench the
grounds in a harsh white electrical glare. The sentry at the gate
furthermore shined the beam of an electric torch—a flashlight, they
called such things—into the back of the open car before passing it
on through, presumably, Rhion thought, to assure himself that no
"enemies of the Reich" were hidden under the lap rugs.

Von Rath was waiting for them in the library. The voices of Baldur
and Gall were audible—arguing as usual—as Rhion and Poincelles
ascended the wide, wood-paneled stairs.

"I still say that electricity must have *something* to do with the disappearance of m-magic! There is no d-documented, authenticated case of magical operancy—of the human will being converted to physical instrumentality—after the middle of the eighteenth century, and that was just when experiments with electricity were becoming p-popular. Benjamin Franklin . . ."

"Nonsense! Magic is a quality of the *vril*, the mystical power inherited by the Aryan Race from the men of Atlantis whom Manu, the last of the Atlantean Supermen, led across Europe to the secret fastnesses of Thibet. It is not electricity, but the slow race pollution by mutants and Jews after the fall of the third moon that has robbed the race of its power. In Thibet the Hidden Masters and Unknown Supermen still hold this power . . ."

"And it's in Thibet that this c-curse of electricity does not exist!"

"Nor does any way of verifying the reports one hears of magic and Hidden Masters," Poincelles added maliciously, lounging in the doorway.

Baldur looked up swiftly from a huge mass of notes, his weak, piggy eyes slitted with irritation and cocaine; Gall merely sniffed. "That is the sort of argument one would expect from a Frenchman," he remarked.

Von Rath, from the depths of his red leather armchair, raised a finger for quiet. Though the Schloss had been fitted with electricity thirty years ago, the wizards—for varying reasons—avoided using it, and the library, like the Temple of Meditations in what had been the ballroom of the north wing and the workshop above it, was illuminated by candles. They made a soft halo of his ivory-pale hair and caught sparks of molten gold in the silver buttons and collar flashes of his black uniform as he leaned forward to speak.

"You've been listening to the news, I suppose," he said, and Poincelles folded his long arms and grinned.

"Yes—it looks as if the Luftwaffe's botched the job pretty thoroughly and let the English army get clean away."

Baldur jerked to his feet furiously. "The German Air Forces are mo-more than capable of d-d-destroying those d-d-debased b-b-b . . ." Rhion knew from past outbursts that the youth's stutter was infinitely exacerbated both by anger and by cocaine, and the present combination was deadly. Poincelles' grin widened at the boy's blazing-eyed frustration and he was about to speak again when von Rath's soft, level voice cut him off.

"I've had a call from Himmler. The German Armies will invade England before the summer is out."

"Of c-course we must," Baldur declared, sitting clumsily down again and knocking a sheaf of his notes to the floor. "The destiny of the Reich demands that all of Europe be ours," he went on rather thickly as he spoke while bending over to collect them. "It is obvious that . . ."

"What is obvious," von Rath said with a quick sidelong glance at Rhion's impassive face, "is that the Jews and Communists who run the government of America from behind the scenes aren't going to permit that country to mind its own business. If we don't have England secured for our own defenses before they force the government into a declaration of war, the Americans will use it as a base to overrun us."

When Rhion did not dispute this he turned to him more fully, his gray eyes grave in the deep shadows of his brows. "Himmler was quite emphatic in his demand that we of the Occult Bureau have something to contribute to this final battle, something to tip the scales in our favor to resolve the conflict in Europe once and for all. And I believe Baldur may have arrived at a way to solve the problem of the raising of magical power."

Young Twisselpeck sniffled and wiped his nose on his sleeve, then rooted around in his notes again. Rhion settled himself on the red leather hassock beside von Rath's chair, his mind still half preoccupied with the problem of how to gain the magical assistance he needed without giving Poincelles—the only thing resembling a maverick among the group—any information that could be used against him.

"My insight into this n-new line of reasoning," Baldur began in his reedy tenor, "goes back, I think, to Major Hagen's d-death . . ."

And for one cold, sickening instant Rhion thought, *They've guessed* . . .

The boy sniffled loudly and pushed his glasses more firmly into place on his nose. "He d-died stepping into the Dark Well, you see. And it was only after that, as he was dying, that our spells reached out into the Void and got anywhere. It must have been his death that released the magic."

They haven't guessed, Rhion thought, shaken with relief. They hadn't stumbled into the keystone of his own secret.

Then he realized what conclusion Baldur *had* stumbled into.

"Now in the Grimoire of Pope Leo, and d'Ehrliffe's *Culte des Goules,* and in any number of letters and diaries, there are reports of power being raised by drawing it out of a human being at d-death. We have partial accounts of the Blue Hummingbird Society of the Aztecs, and these tally closely with what we know of the rites practiced by the Adepts of the Shining C-Crystal in the sixteenth and seventeenth centuries—"

"No!" Rhion cried sharply, almost before he was aware he was speaking.

"DON'T INTERRUPT ME!" the boy screamed passionately. "Everybody's always interrupting me! Here!" He fumbled in the notes, dropping papers all around him like a tree shedding leaves in a high wind. "There are seven references in the Vatican letters, two in the communications of the Fuger banking house, one in Nostradamus' third letter to the Viscountess de la Pore and in Bernal D-Diaz's account of—"

"I'm not arguing that you can't make magic from the energies released from the human psyche at death," Rhion retorted, aware from the corner of his eye of the interest on the candlelit faces of Poincelles and Gall. "But it's a damn dangerous thing to do and in my world there isn't a respectable wizard who'd try it . . . I take it you're not talking about using volunteers."

"Of course not!" Gall snapped indignantly. "The ancient Druids raised power from the sacrifice of prisoners of war! The spirits of the noblest of their foes . . ."

"Here!" Baldur straightened up and thrust out a mass of references with trembling hands. "Letter from Gustavus Dremmel to the Fugers, November of 1612. *'B-by reliable witnesses these Adepts have been seen, by various rites and ceremonies involving the murder of the aforesaid wo-wo-women, to empower talismans which later enabled them to find hidden treasure, to drink poisons unscathed, to draw the love of both wo-wo-women and men . . .'"*

"Well, that should interest you, at any rate," Poincelles remarked *sotto voce*, studying his pointed fingernails.

"If we c-could discover what those rites were . . ."

"Is it truly so dangerous?" Von Rath crossed his knees, his tall boots gleaming like oil in the wavering light. "You understand that we are willing to take the risk."

YOU are willing?!? Rhion almost shouted at him. But there was nothing in those grave eyes that he could shout it to.

There was long silence, von Rath waiting politely for his answer, and Rhion, struggling with shock and outrage, trying to come up with an argument against murder that the Nazi *would* credit. At length he said, "You seem to think dropping dead like Hagen did is the only thing that will happen. You've never seen a magic field go septic. I've talked to people who have. I'm telling you: Don't do it."

Down at his end of the table Jacobus Gall straightened his thin shoulders militantly and stroked his flowing silver beard. "That is nonsense. On Witches Hill, in my dreams of ancient days, I saw the ancient priests cut the throats of their tribal enemies, pouring out the sacred blood of sacrifice to bring them victory . . ."

"As you saw the Roman legions surrounded and routed by their Teutonic foes in places the maps show to have been permanently underwater since the retreat of the last glacier?" Poincelles retorted, his black eyes glinting wickedly.

"You understand none of these things."

"My friends . . ." The Frenchman raised his hands. "We've gone to a great deal of trouble to bring in an expert as a consultant, and while I've got no objections on principle to slitting a few throats, I'd say that we listen when he says something is dangerous, because he does know more about this than we do. But it's up to you—do as you please." And with that he pushed with his flat, bony shoulders against the doorframe and stood up straight, lighting a cigar as he strolled out of the room and down the electric brightness of the hall, the acrid whiff of smoke as disrespectful as the snap of fingers.

With a massive sniffle Baldur started to jerk to his feet to go after him, and von Rath waved him down again. "I agree," the young Captain said with a sigh, and rubbed the high bridge of his nose with his fingers, as if his eyes were suddenly weary even of the candlelight.

"That still doesn't give him the right . . ."

"Of course one doesn't need voluntary sacrifice!" Gall declared. "That was a different matter entirely."

"No." Von Rath lowered his hand and looked over at Rhion again. "You're right. We do not know what might happen. But we must find something, some way out of this impasse, before the Americans decide to interfere in our struggle against England and its allies. We lost Eric . . . we cannot take another risk like that."

"I'll search," Baldur promised, bending down clumsily to gather his notes again from where he'd dropped them on the floor. His hands were nervous and fidgety, his eyes flicking restlessly from von Rath's face to the shadows of the bookshelves, thick with ancient knowledge, that crowded the long room. "The ancient societies performed the rites in safety. The p-proper rites, the correct means of making the sacrifices, have to be there . . . I'll find them for you, P-Paul . . . C-Captain . . ."

"Books." Gall got to his feet contemptuously and shook back his snowy mane. "Books are the refuge of those who need such things. It is by the purification of the body and the mind that the True Adept will come to an understanding of the *vril* within him." He was still muttering as he left in Baldur's shuffling wake.

Von Rath expelled his breath in a sound of mingled amusement and exasperation, and got to his feet. "Children." He laughed, shaking his head. "All of them—jealous and quibbling and fractious. In the past six months I've acquired an enormous respect for my old nanny . . . Would you care for some cognac?" He crossed the room to a cabinet whose brass-grilled doors formed one of the few places in the wall not solidly paved in books. Rhion wondered where the Occult Bureau had collected so many; according to von Rath, Himmler, the Bureau's head, had a library of his own three times this size.

The young Captain paused with his hand on the cabinet door. "Or did you have enough of liquor among the camel drivers?"

"Camel drivers?" Rhion leaned back against the arm of the red leather chair, looking up at von Rath in the swimming halo of candlelight. Two minutes ago he'd been furious with outrage at this black-uniformed wizard's callous readiness to practice blood-sacrifice; for weeks he had lived with the knowledge that von Rath was his jailor and that the wizard was lying to him about the existence of the Dark Well and had lied from the moment Rhion had regained consciousness. But the other side of the man was genuine, as well: the quiet courtesy, the soft-voiced charm, the gentleness with which he handled Baldur's nervous worship, and the homesickness that he had made clear he understood Rhion felt.

"*And some who went into the wilderness,*" von Rath quoted, returning with two fragile glass bubbles of henna-colored liquor, "*and thirsted with the beasts of prey, merely did not want to sit around the cistern with the filthy camel drivers.* Nietzsche. A wise man and a brilliant one—I'll have Baldur read him to you sometime, if your German isn't up to it yet, as a break from the *Malleus Maleficarum*. Do you still thirst, my friend?"

"For something that hasn't obviously come out of a cistern, yes." Lacking a friend, the undeniable pleasure of the man's company was difficult to resist.

A smile of great sweetness momentarily swept the cold angel face. For a time he stood cradling the glass in his hands, his eyes like smoky opals gazing into a candlelit middle distance, his face in repose young and very sad.

"You understand what is at stake here?" he asked softly, after a long time in thought. His gaze returned to Rhion's, tiredness and old wounds in his eyes. "It is not only victory over the English, you know; not only doing what our Führer demands that we do. It is the ability to do it that will be our victory, a victory over magic's true foes—a matter less simple. It is . . . vindication. Do you understand?"

Sitting on the hassock, bespectacled and unprepossessing, Rhion looked down into his glass for a moment, unwilling to admit how much he understood. "I think so."

"Since I was a boy," the young wizard continued slowly, "I have felt—I have *known*—that there had to be something else, something other than the sterile pragmatism of Freud, of Marx, and now of this man Einstein—Jews all, incidentally, but it goes deeper than that. Something . . . I don't know. And as the years went on and I kept looking, and there was nothing . . . Just the world closing in and bleeding to death without even being aware of what it was losing or what it had lost."

He shook his head, returned to perch on the arm of his chair, and stared for a time into the depths of his glass as if to scry there where the magic had gone. "But it had died," he said, very simply, his voice almost too low to hear.

"Eric said he had felt the same thing," he went on after a time, and his eyes flinched shut for a moment in remembered pain. "Eric was the first man I ever knew who had felt it. He and I . . ." He shook his head quickly.

"Without magical operancy—without the ability to transform the will into physical being—magic remains only a legend, and the fire that consumes me—that consumed us—is no more regarded by other men than a thousand similar crank curiosities, on par with phrenology and ginseng and that mediocre bureaucratic, keyhole-listener Himmler's stupid attempts to locate the ancient races that are said to dwell in the hollow earth. And so it will remain, unless you and I can prove to them that it is . . . real."

Rhion was silent, remembering again his first meeting with Jaldis on the bridge in the City of Circles. *Are you searching for secrets?* Remembering the sensation of ice-locked bone breaking open inside him, when he had first called fire from cold wood. Remembering the aching relief of knowing he was not mad.

"How old were you," von Rath asked quietly, "when you first understood that you were a wizard?"

"Twelve," Rhion said slowly. "I mean, I didn't understand what it was then, but I knew I was different."

"I was fourteen." His voice sank almost to a whisper, as if he spoke not to another man but to the quiet, gold-haired boy he saw across all that gulf of years. "Immured in a military academy in Gross-Lichterfelde, learning parade drill and classical Latin, while outside a pound of sausage was going for a million marks . . . The fact that you had any choice in the matter makes me so envious that I could kill you."

Choice. Had there really ever been any? Tally had asked him once why he'd become a wizard, if he had known what it would mean: that he could not marry the woman he loved to desperation; that he could not admit that the children she bore were his for fear that they would be killed; and that he and Jaldis would spend most of their ten years together as outcasts, living on the love spells he concocted for sale to people who despised them. He remembered the growing fear of what he was, pain so awful he had wanted to kill himself, hollowness and fear of what he sensed was growing in his dreams, then the worse pain of knowing what it would cost him to pursue those dreams.

I tried so damn hard to be good, he had said to her.

And for Paul von Rath there hadn't even been that choice—only the disreputable shadow world of cranks and covens and charlatans, of theosophists and hollow earthers and those who sought Atlantis or Shangri-La, infinitely less thinkable for the only child of Prussian aristocrats than a career as a wizard had been for the son of the wealthiest banker in the City of Circles.

"I'm sorry" was all he could say.

Von Rath shook his head and smiled again. "No, it is I who should apologize to you for becoming maudlin in my cups. I like you, Rhion, and I truly regret that you are here in my world against your will . . . and I know it is against your will. I know you miss your own world, your loved ones. Do not think that I don't know."

Rhion was silent, remembering Tally—remembering his sons—remembering his home in the Drowned Lands—with a poignance that shook him to his bones.

Von Rath hesitated, struggling briefly with some inner decision, then said, "I promise you that as soon as the war with England is won we shall . . . we shall open another Dark Well, no matter what the risk to us, and search through it to find the wizards of your home." His voice was wistful at the thought of a world in which his dream of magic was reality. "But for the time being we must serve destiny. Yours—mine—the Reich's." He sighed softly. "Heil Hitler." His hand barely sketched the salute.

"Heil Hitler." Setting his glass down quietly, Rhion returned the gesture, then rose and stepped out into the brassy electric glare of the hall.

5

In the darkness of his attic bedroom Rhion fetched the hard wooden chair from the corner and put it beneath a certain spot in the rafters. Through the wide windows opposite the foot of his iron-framed bed shone a broad rectangle of chalky arc light from the yard below, making eerie runic shadows of the bare ceiling beams with their trailing curtains of cobweb. Through the open window he could smell the pinewoods, and the drift of smoke from the cigarette of the guard patrolling the fence; the peep of crickets and frogs and the occasional cry of a nightbird came to him like comforting echoes of a life he'd once known.

Standing on the chair, he stretched to reach the rafter, edging along it with his fingers until his hand encountered a small wash-leather bag. Thrusting this in his pocket, he climbed carefully down, moved the chair to another place, and climbed up again. This time he brought forth a packet wrapped in several sheets of the *Volkischer Beobachter*, a packet that weighed heavily in his hand.

He put the chair back in its corner. The room had been searched three times in the seven weeks he'd occupied it, the last occasion less than a week ago.

Rhion had originally asked for the small south attic room—a servant's, in some former era—because the rest of the Schloss was permeated by the smell of cigarettes. But he'd found that from its big window he could see the light that fell from the window of von Rath's study to the bare ground at the side of the lodge, and thus tell when the young Captain went to bed.

The glow was there now, a citreous smudge on the hard-packed earth below him and to his left. Von Rath must have retired there from the library after their cognac together, to meditate and to write up the endless reports demanded by the Occult Bureau of their daily experiments—with magic, with electricity, with talismans, with pendulums, with anything they or any writer before them had ever been able to think of that might possibly hold a key to the return of magic to this thaumaturgically silent world. But even as Rhion watched, the glow dimmed as von Rath snuffed the candles one by one.

He'd be asleep in an hour, Rhion thought. Resting his forehead on the sill, he closed his eyes and reached down through the ancient lodge with a trained mage's deep, half-meditative senses. He heard Gall's sonorous murmur as he recited runic mantras before retiring and the jittery crackle of parchment and pen from Baldur's room and the youth's endless muttering and sniffling. Farther down, he heard the tinny staccato of the radio in the guards' watch room at the foot of the main stairs, repeating names he did not understand: Leutze, the Scheldt, Dunkirk. A guard spoke. Newspaper rattled.

Too early. Much too early.

Turning, Rhion crossed the room to the rough plank wall behind the head of his bed. In a tin box—for there were mice in the attics—behind a loose board he kept a stash of coffee beans. He'd had a beer and a healthy jolt of cognac, and had never had much head for liquor. Eating half a dozen coffee beans made him slightly sick to his stomach, but at least he wouldn't fall asleep.

Then, sitting on the edge of the bed, he took up the newspaper-wrapped package, unfolded it, and looked at the thing that lay within it in the dark.

He thought about the nature of magic.

The thing in his hands was a metal ring, roughly the diameter of his palm, formed of strips of iron of varying thicknesses—some of meteor iron, some drawn of iron mixed with salt or with certain other impurities—all carefully pilfered over the course of the last five weeks from the supplies requisitioned from the Occult Bureau. Twisted around the iron were an equal number of strips of the purest silver obtainable, silver so pure it was soft, each strip scribbled with a hair-fine line of runes. Between the iron and the silver, five crystals were twined, in a specific shape Rhion hoped he'd calculated properly—he'd never made one of these for the purposes he planned for this and wasn't entirely sure whether his theoretical estimates would stand up in reality. He had been weeks assembling this, laboriously raising what little power he could in this world, whispering spells as he worked in the laboratory in the dead of night—hoping, as he worked, that von Rath wouldn't guess what was going on, and wondering fearfully what would happen to him if he did guess. There was still a great deal Rhion did not know about the Nazis, and he didn't want to find out.

And the making of the ring, he reflected with an odd, cold feeling behind his breastbone, was the easy part.

Since he had come to this world, Rhion had given a great deal of thought to magic: what had happened to it here; why it had failed; and how it might be brought back. As the Torweg group had found out very early, power of a sort could still be raised through the rites of their morning meditations. But it cost an enormous amount of energy to raise even the smallest power, and it was never enough to do much with, even had they been able to convert it to physical instrumentality. The power levels of this world had sunk, as water sinks back into the earth in drought, but it was still there, like the slow silvery pulse of the ley-lines that he had felt through the wheels of the car as they'd driven along the ancient road from the village back to the Schloss.

What had vanished utterly from this world was the point of conversion between power and operationality.

And that, Rhion thought, turning the iron circle over in his hand, was why he and Jaldis would have died in the Void but for Eric Hagen stepping to his death in the Dark Well.

Baldur had almost guessed it tonight. But, his mind running on the ancient cults and societies that he so endlessly studied, the efforts of past wizards to solve the problem of waning levels of power and not the conversion point between power and magic, the youth had seen only Hagen's death, and not the fact that for one second, before the Void had killed him, Hagen had been working his spells *outside the confines of this world*. For those few moments, he had been standing in the Void itself.

And there was magic in the Void.

Every mythological Fire-Bringer Rhion had ever heard of, when faced with the problem of Darkness, of Night, had had to steal fire from a source. And so, Rhion thought, must it be here. He hadn't the faintest idea how to create a Dark Well, for Jaldis, fearing Rhion's connection with the Ladies of the Moon, had never taught his student the mechanics of the multiplicity of Universes. But in his pursuit of information about water goblins, Rhion had manufactured Spiracles of Air, devices that, charged with the element of air and then bound upon his forehead, had held that element around him while he walked the muddy bottoms of the Drowned Lands' endless ponds and canals, seeking the goblins in their forests of ribbonweed and cattail root.

He was theoretically acquainted with the spells by which Spiracles of Heat could be charged to keep their wielder surrounded by warmth in bitterest cold, or Spiracles of Daylight that would permit, within their small field of brightness, the use of spells that ordinarily had power only during the hours when the sun was in the sky. Whether a Spiracle could be charged so that it would hold the essence of the Void's magic about itself he didn't know, for it had never to his knowledge been tried.

Theoretically, once he had a localized field of magic from the Spiracle, there was no reason why he had to be anywhere near the Dark Well to open a gate through the Void—all that it required was magic. Practically, of course, unless he wanted to perish in the airless cold chaos between universes, he needed the Dark Well, needed it to establish contact with the Archmage Shavus and the other Morkensik wizards so that they could draw him through the Void, back to his own world.

Not to mention the fact, he thought dryly, though his stomach was sinking with terror and dread, that he would have to be standing *in the Void* to charge the Spiracle.

And that meant the Dark Well.

That meant doing the thing that had taken Eric Hagen's life.

And that brought him back to Poincelles and the conversation in the tavern tonight.

Rhion got to his feet and prowled restlessly back to the window. In the acid glare he could see the black-uniformed sentry, rifle on shoulder, walking the perimeter of the fence. He needed help, needed another wizard to ground him, hold him anchored to this world, while he charged the Spiracle with the Void's wild magic, but the thought of putting his life in Auguste Poincelles' nicotine-yellowed hands terrified him. For all von Rath's gentle charm, it was perfectly possible that the SS Captain had put Poincelles up to making a pass at Rhion tonight in the tavern to test his intentions—to see whether he really *was* holding something back.

He didn't know, and the uncertainty, the dreadful sensation of never knowing whom to trust and whether his instincts were correct or not, was profoundly disorienting and exhausting.

"And anyhow," he muttered dourly, climbing back on the chair and replacing the Spiracle in its hiding place in the rafters, "the whole question is pretty academic until I can *find* the goddam Dark Well."

He returned to the window and checked the stars. Shortly after midnight. By the glow in the east above the spiky black of the tree-clothed hills, the moon would be rising soon, wan and cold in its last quarter. First dawn was some three hours away. From the drawer in the dresser where he kept his old brown robes Rhion fished the wristwatch von Rath had given him, and after a moment's study confirmed the timepiece's accuracy, at least as far as he understood the way time was reckoned here.

He put the watch back in the drawer. Though he recognized the ingeniousness of the mechanism he seldom wore it, chiefly from annoyance at the obsession these people had with the correct time. But every now and then, when he handled the intricate golden loz-enge, he sensed upon it a vague psychometric residue of uncleanness that repelled him, but that he could not quite place. Other things in the Schloss had it, too, odd things: the plates of a certain pattern in the big, sunny dining room in the south wing; the radio in the guards' watch room; some of the books in the library. He wasn't quite sure what was wrong with them—and indeed, it was something he sensed only intermittently. But he didn't like it.

He listened now, and the lodge was quiet.

His stockinged feet made no sound on the bare floor boards as he crossed first the darkness of his own room, then the vast, dusty spaces of the main attic. The descending stair debouched close to von Rath's study and bedroom. From the main stair to the lower floor he heard the soft crackle of the radio still. By now he knew enough German to follow the broadcast, though not most of Chancellor Hitler's speeches. Now and then a Storm Trooper's voice would speak, desultory and half asleep. In his long nights of quiet listening Rhion had learned that inside duty generally involved three sentries who made a patrol or two of the ground floor in between long periods of sitting around the watch room smoking, reading cheap tabloids like *Der Sturmer*, and comparing notes about the barmaids at the Woodsman's Horn. Sometimes one or another of the barmaids was smuggled in, to be taken by a dozen of the men in turn in the deserted kitchen or laundry in the south wing—occasionally he heard Poincelles' voice on those nights.

But tonight there was only the desultory conversation of men who have said everything they had to say months ago. He waited until he heard all three voices, then, barely daring to breathe, he stole soundlessly down the stairs and slipped like a shadow past the watch room door. There was, he knew, a backstairs leading down to the kitchen in the south wing, but its upper end was in the little dressing room attached to the empty chamber where the Dark Well had allegedly been drawn—the false Dark Well, to convince him that it had been destroyed—and that chamber was next to von Rath's. In any case he would still have had to pass the watch room door to reach his destination on the ground floor, an old ballroom in the north wing that Hagen and von Rath, upon taking possession of the Schloss the previous fall, had converted into a temple for occult rites.

Its door lay at the end of a wide oak-paneled hallway and, like all the Torweg wizards, Rhion had a key. As he relocked the door behind him Rhion could feel a sort of afterglow of power whispering around him in the utter darkness of the vast, velvet-draped room, the residue of morning after morning of ritual work and occult meditation, of painfully tiny quantities of power raised and dispersed. Beneath that, he dimly sensed the even fainter silvery tide of the ley-line that ran below.

In years past the site of the Schloss had enjoyed a peculiar reputation—it was on this spot, Rhion guessed, crossing the worn parquet floor to the altar, here where the ley-line bisected the mound, that the ancient god had originally been worshipped and the witches had later held their sabbats. He settled himself cross-legged against the altar stone, a six-foot slab of black granite draped, like the walls, in black. Upon the altar a second drape hid the ritual implements of cup, sword, dagger, and thurifer. Coming here to scry was somewhat riskier than doing it in his room, but far quicker; in his room it sometimes took him as much as an hour of intense concentration before he was able to see anything in the crystal.

He lit the stub of candle he had to force himself to remember to carry in his pocket these days—thanking all the gods of wizardry that von Rath had seen fit to board up all the windows of this room and no light would show to the guards in the compound outside—and, taking the scrying crystal from its bag, angled its facets to the light.

The Dark Well was still there, wherever "there" was. It was quiescent, no more than a half-seen shadow in the absolute blackness of that other, windowless room. Studying it with his wizard's sight through the medium of the crystal, Rhion estimated the size and proportions of that chamber: thirty feet wide and immensely long, the low ceiling propped with heavy beams, the uneven floor paved with the rough, damp stone he recalled. In fact, he reflected wryly, it was of a size and shape and composition to be directly beneath the ballroom/temple where he now sat. Ceiling, beams, and floor were as far as he could tell identical to those in the portions of the Schloss' cellars that he had entered.

"I'm probably sitting directly on top of the goddam thing," he muttered to himself, closing his hand over the crystal, the image dying in the darkness of his palm. The stairs leading down into the cellar were kept double padlocked, and it was a good guess that the only keys were in the hands of von Rath and of the SS lieutenant in charge of the guards. On one of his trips down there—unobtrusively supervised by von Rath—he had gained the impression that the portion of the cellar which should lie under the north wing was blocked off by a wall, the wall piled high with boxes. That meant a concealed door, undoubtedly locked, as well.

He cursed himself mildly for never having taken up Shavus on the old Archmage's offer to teach him to pick locks. The only way he could get into that cellar was by magic . . . and of course he would not be able to use magic until he could get into the cellar and charge the Spiracle—if his spells worked, and if the charging didn't kill him.

And unless he had another wizard to help him, it probably would.

Always, like an ox at the millstone, he came around to that again: to the Dark Well; to Poincelles . . . to trust; and to his instinct that stepping into the Void alone and unassisted would be safer than trusting the French occultist with the smallest information regarding his real intentions and abilities.

He sighed and pushed up his glasses to rub his aching eyes. Twenty days remained until the summer solstice, twenty days until he could—with luck—raise enough power from the turning point of the Universe to open a gap in the Void so Shavus and the others could pull him through . . .

If he could get in touch with them. If he could find another wizard he could trust. If . . .

He shook his head and, opening his hand, looked down into the crystal again.

In it he saw the sea. Black waves ran up onto beaches in darkness, beaches crowded with men whose faces and bodies were outlined in the sudden, terrible glare of yellow-white explosions—beaches littered with wrecked equipment, hideously strewn with tangled corpses in the shell-holed sand, and men standing knee-deep in water, or huddled in shallow holes they'd scooped out in the sand, desperate for even the illusion of shelter. A long quay extended into the sea, longer than Rhion had ever seen, even in the great harbor of Nerriok, and this, too, was jammed with men. They stood quiet, without shoving, while death spat and whistled around them, burning fragments of metal leaving red streams of fire in the dark. Men waiting. And far out over the water to the west, the gold pinprick of a ship's light gleamed suddenly in the black.

Perhaps, Rhion thought wearily, closing his hand over the crystal again, he should be glad. These men would be the spiritual brothers of those who had blinded and mutilated Jaldis, who looked with distrust upon magic and all that it stood for, who could not see beyond their own pockets and their own bellies and who wanted to turn the world into the image of their own greedy, limited minds.

Perhaps he was simply weak; between the Reich's obsessive racism, self-righteous closed-mindedness, and casual arrogance, and these corrupt and nameless servants of the mechanist English, there didn't seem to be a lot to choose. The best thing he could do, Rhion thought, would be simply to go home.

If he could.

"Useless!" Paul von Rath thrust from him the body of the dead white rat and the pan of poisoned sugar water in which a seven-carat garnet gleamed mockingly, a talisman of protection inscribed with the colored sigil of the interlaced runes of Eohl, Boerc, and Ehwis. "Nothing—it did nothing at all!"

"I d-don't understand," Baldur stammered, his weak, bulging eyes peering from rat to gem and back again with baffled outrage. "The rite we used to charge this talisman came from Johan Weyer's own private journal! There was no way he would have recorded a false rite, or—or changed details. I made every allowance, every transposition of the k-key words and phrases according to the best redaction we possess of the Dyzan manuscript . . ."

Rhion, hitching back the sleeves of the long white robe in which the wizards all worked in their meditations and occult experiments, crossed the big laboratory and picked the jewel from its glass petri dish. He wiped the poisoned solution off with a lab towel and turned the gem a few times in his palm. "It's charged, all right."

"Of c-course it's charged!" Baldur whirled to paw through the stack of notes on the nearby bench as if for documentation of the fact, nearly knocking over a beaker of the strychnine distillate they'd used to test the poison spell's effectiveness. "The formula was impeccable, the source absolutely certain!"

"Give me that." Gall, in his flowing robe and shoulder-length white hair looking very much like the ancient priests of whom he was always having visions, almost snatched the talisman from Rhion's hand. From a little labeled box on the laboratory table he removed a smooth stone tied to a silken string—this he held over the gem, watching its random movement with pale, intolerant eyes.

"No one is blaming you, Baldur," von Rath said gently.

"But nothing can have gone wrong! The p-power you raised in this morning's rite was enormous, stupendous . . ."

"It was certainly greater than it has been," Rhion remarked, retreating to the corner of the lab. Like the temple immediately below it, the room that they had fitted up as a wizards-kitchen had had all of its windows boarded over—a pointless affectation from a thaumaturgical point of view but one that had allowed Rhion to work on the Spiracle late at night unobserved by the guards in the yard. The reflections of the kerosene lamps that illuminated the room in preference to electricity gilded the young Captain's fair hair almost to the color of honey and glinted on the steel swastika he wore on a chain about his neck. On shelves around what had at one time been a drawing room on the second floor of the north wing an assortment of jars, boxes, and packets contained everything Rhion had ever heard of as necessary to the making of talismans: iron, silver, gold, and copper of various purities; salts and rare earths; every sort of herb and wood imaginable; gems, crystals, both cut and uncut; parchments and strange inks. There was a small forge, crucible, and press, even an icebox containing samples of the blood of various animals and birds. And yes, he thought, smiling to remember the first time Tally had come to the rooms he'd shared with Jaldis, even a mummified baby alligator . . .

And for all the good it had done them so far, the shelves might just as well have been stocked with twigs and pebbles, like children playing "store."

Baldur snuffled and wiped his nose on the sleeve of his robe. "Maybe the formulae are p-poison-specific? It could explain . . ."

"Nonsense," Gall retorted coldly, returning his pendulum to its box. "I have said before, it is a wizard's sublime faith in himself that conquers poison."

"It c-can't be! Then a talisman of protection wouldn't protect someone who didn't know what it was."

"Precisely. It is only the illuminatus, the initiate, the pure, who can draw upon the *vril* . . ."

They were bickering acrimoniously as they opened the door, going from the lamplit gloom of the workroom to the sun-drenched morning brilliance of the upstairs hall outside.

Von Rath sighed and rubbed a hand over his face. "I didn't truly expect it to work," he said. "And Jacobus would tell me that was why it didn't, of course. But, Rhion, we have done everything, tried everything . . . You said the ritual of meditation this morning raised more power than ever before, but you know and I know it wasn't enough, wasn't nearly enough. Not even with every allowance you made for the position of the stars, the phase of the moon . . . Nothing. And with our army going into France . . ."

He paused, seeing the flicker of expression that passed across Rhion's eyes. "Yes," he said quietly, "I know what you would be saying. But truly, war as it is fought now—as it is fought in this world—is the province of the first attacker. Had we not taken the initiative this spring—and it was they who first attacked us a year ago—we would have been driven, as we now drive them."

"Yes," Rhion lied, turning away to mop the spilled poison where it had slopped from the dish. "Yes, I understand that."

Von Rath's voice was low and urgent. "Please understand also that the war is nothing—it is, for us, only a means to an end. It is our last chance—the last chance of wizardry—to demonstrate our powers, to regain our powers with the backing of the government. That is why we *must* succeed at what we do here."

He picked up the garnet talisman and returned it to a box of failed experiments, of talismans—properly made, properly charged—that simply did not work. The lamplight flashed across the jewel's central facet and caught on a scratch on one side, as if the stone had been prised from a setting. A good-quality gem, Rhion thought, far better than most wizards in his own world could afford for talismanic work unless they had an extremely rich patron. He could understand von Rath's concern—without the support of the government, the group would never have been able to work under these ideal conditions.

But it crossed his mind to wonder, suddenly, where the Occult Bureau got the gems it sent them.

"Rhion," von Rath said, closing the box and turning with one slender hand still on its lid, "you haven't been—coming down to the laboratory to work at night, have you?"

Rhion felt himself get cold. In anything but the golden kerosene light he knew von Rath could have seen him pale. "I did once or twice when I first got back on my feet, but not lately." He could feel sweat start under his hair and beard.

Von Rath frowned. "No, this would have been the night before last. I thought the laboratory was disturbed a little yesterday morning, as if it had been used."

While part of Rhion breathed a prayer of gratitude that he'd always been meticulous about returning things to rights after his nights of work—so von Rath *did* notice things like that—another part of him was able to put genuine puzzlement in his voice as he said, "The night before last?" He'd finished the Spiracle last week and had been catching up on lost sleep ever since.

"Yes. And Baldur also seems to think that his room has been searched, though he has become . . . a little paranoid."

"I'm told cocaine does that." Rhion remembered his own conviction that his room had been searched.

Von Rath's gem-pure lips tightened; then he sighed. "He takes it to continue his researches, you know," he said quietly. "There is a truly formidable amount of material to get through—diaries, letters, court cases dating back to the fifteenth century . . . I keep a close eye on how much he takes."

If you're his only source, thought Rhion. But, anxious to turn the Captain's thoughts away from who might have been using the laboratory at night, he suggested, "Do you think the problem of raising power might be with the composition of this group?" He pushed his glasses more firmly up onto the bridge of his nose and followed von Rath as the younger wizard started moving about the laboratory, turning down the kerosene lamps until their wicks snuffed to nothing and the shadows hovered down about them like the fall of night.

"According to Gall, and to what Baldur's read to me, the old covens seem to have been much larger than ours. Five men isn't a lot, even if they are mageborn and more or less trained. Magic can be raised from the emotional or psychic or life-force energies of human beings, as Baldur pointed out last night. But blood-sacrifice, either voluntary or involuntary, isn't the only way of doing that, you know. Perhaps if you worked with twice as many men as this, and an equal number of women, you'd get better results."

Von Rath chuckled wearily and turned from replacing a lamp chimney, shadows of irony flickering in his tired eyes. "My dear Rhion, have you any concept of the contortions Eric had to undertake to gather even this group? To find men whose loyalty was as reliable as their potential for power, and who were even willing to work as a group?" He shook his head with a half-comic smile and led the way out into the sunlit upstairs hall. "And as for women . . ." The gesture of his hand, as dismissive as a shrug, raised the hackles on Rhion's neck. "Women have no place in magic."

"*WHAT?*"

"Not true magic." *Surely you must know that,* said the flex of his voice, as Rhion stared at him, too dumbfounded even to feel outrage. "Their emotions are uncontrollable—surely you've tried to have a reasonable argument with a woman? Their intellects are on the average less than men's. That's been scientifically proven. Oh, there are one or two exceptions . . ."

"I've met enough exceptions to constitute a rule, personally."

But the little smile and the small, amused shake of his head were impenetrable. It was not, Rhion saw, a matter even for serious argument, as if Rhion had suggested petitioning the help of the kitchen cat.

Von Rath gave him a boyish half grin, a man-to-man expression of complicity. "It's hard to explain, but *you* know. It's one of those things that a true man *knows* by intuition. And at bottom, magic *is* a masculine trait. A woman's emotionalism and wooly-mindedness would only delay us, always supposing we could *find* a woman with even a tenth the level of power of a man."

Given the intolerable pressures a mageborn girl would have faced in Germany, Rhion hadn't been terribly surprised that the Torweg group was entirely masculine. And yet from Poincelles he knew that there were and always had been women occultists. But not, it appeared, in Nazi Germany.

"And in any case," von Rath went on, turning down the hallway toward his rooms, "the question at the moment is an academic one. We must find a way to raise power—we must find a way to convert that power to operationality—and we must find them soon. Only through those—only through the victory that such power will bring—can magic be returned to this world."

"And did little ratty die?" Cigar in hand, Poincelles looked around from the doorway of the watch room at the foot of the stairs. Beyond him Rhion—who had changed once more into his usual fatigue pants and a brown army shirt—could see that the room had been curtained to dimness, and the portable screen set up on which cinemas were displayed; the black-and-white images of newsreels of the war in the West flickered across it like jiggling ghosts.

"Did you have money on it living?"

The Frenchman grinned broadly. After the dawn ritual of meditation to raise power he hadn't even bothered to attend the experiment with the talisman. He'd changed out of his robe back into the same loud tweed trousers and jacket he'd had on last night—the same shirt and underclothing by the smell of it. "Boche idiots," he said.

Past Poincelle's angular shoulder the fluttering images of huge war machines appeared on the screen in the gloom of the watch room, monstrous metal beetles rumbling down the cobbled streets of towns with their turret guns swinging watchfully back and forth; then, with dreamlike quickness, they were transformed to images of men— Rhion did not have enough German unassisted by spells of understanding to catch who they were—being herded out of a building somewhere, herded into boxcars with their hands above their heads. The Ministry of Propaganda sent these newsreels, these moving pictures, out regularly to the SS, even as it sent whatever American cinemas they wanted to see . . . they had taught Rhion more about the German Reich than von Rath had counted on. Most of all, they had taught him that the Reich was sufficiently proud enough of those fearsome columns of marching men, those lines of resistant "slave peoples" being shot for intransigence, to have them thus immortalized and displayed.

Baldur, clattering down the steps behind Rhion in his own ill-fitting and dirty trousers and rumpled shirt, paused and snapped spitefully, "For a man whose country will be the next to fall to the victorious German Armies you have no room to talk!" He pointed into the watch room, where columns of armored trucks and marching men flickered across the screen. "You know where they're headed now? France! Your cowardly government is on the run and they'll be in Paris before the week is out!"

Poincelles only raised the back of his fist up under one hairy nostril and snorted in a mime of inhaling cocaine. Baldur's fleshy neck turned bright red and, wheeling, the youth lumbered away to the dining room, tripping on a corner of the hall rug as he went.

"Does he think I'm going to weep when the Krauts march into La Belle Paris?" The Frenchman's skeletal face grimaced with scorn. "I am a citizen of the world, my friend, born and reborn down through generations. What is this war to me? What is France to me? I was high mage to the court of Kublai Khan, who conjured for him the eldritch secrets of the Aklo and the Hyperborean races. Before that, in the dark years of glory in the seventh century, I conjured for Pope Leo those things that would have caused his name to be stricken from the pages of history, had any known of them but I. In the black abysses of time I was High Priest of the Cult of Thoth for the Pharaoh Ptah-Hotep, who was accursed in the Red Land and the Black Land for the things that he caused to be done . . ."

He took the cigar from his mouth and blew a stinking stream of blue smoke into the sunlit air. In the watch room Rhion heard the men give a great delighted cheer; on the screen he saw a country road, jammed with people—old men pushing bicycles laden with household goods, women hurrying, stumbling, dragging frightened children by the hand, old cars maneuvering slowly through the choking throng of people fleeing with whatever they could carry . . .

And from the sky the war planes descended, lean and deadly with the twisted sun-cross emblazoned on their silver sides, opening fire with their machine guns on the fleeing civilians below. The guards in the watch room cheered and whooped at the sight of the women running for shelter, dropping all they carried and catching up their terrified children, men scrambling like scared sheep into the bushes alongside the road, faces twisted in silent cries.

Rhion felt sick and cold. Beside him, Poincelles' voice went on, "That Baldur, he puts on airs because he wants to be in the SS, to be one of Himmler's darlings. Himmler, huh! A mediocrity, a crank—using the most powerful and dangerous elite the world has ever known to serve tea in white gloves at Hitler's garden parties. It's like using a Damascus blade to cut eclairs! Himmler claims he was the Emperor Henry the Fowler in his former life—pah! I knew Henry the Fowler! I served in his court in the great days of the Dark Ages, in the wars against the Magyars and the Slavs, and Himmler is no more his reincarnation than you are. I learn from them, yes"— he waved the cigar in the direction of the sun-washed dining room, where Baldur's voice could be heard querulously demanding more sugar for his coffee, —"as I learn from you. But all this is merely a step along the way."

The black, knowing eyes gleamed and he reached out to pat Rhion's cheek, the pointed fingernails pricking through his beard like dirty claws. "I am in this for myself, my little friend. You really ought to trust me."

On the newsreel screen the war planes made another strafing run at the crowded road. A man scrambled out of one of the cars and bolted for the roadside; his foot tangled in the wheelspokes of a fallen bicycle and for a moment he tugged frantically to free it, desperate, horrified, as the double line of bullets ripsawed the road, bursting a crate of chickens ten feet from him in an explosion of blood and feathers, then swept on to cut him in half. The guards catcalled and shouted facetious advice; Horst Eisler half turned in his wooden chair, called out, "Rhion, you got to come in and see this!"

And the wizard born and reborn, mage to the court of Kublai Khan and High Priest of the gray cult of Thoth in the silent deeps of time, strolled off down the hall toward the dining room to get his breakfast, trailing a line of bluish stench in his wake.

6

From his window in the darkness, Rhion watched the cadaverous shadow of Poincelles cross the yard to the wire. The sentry had been loitering in the spot, smoking, for some minutes now—it was this which had first caught Rhion's attention. Now he saw the Frenchman hand the Storm Trooper something and, reaching out with his mageborn senses, heard him say, ". . . maybe all night. Square the next man, will you?"

"*Jawohl*, mate." The guard saluted. "Heil Hitler." And he strolled away lighting a cigarette, his shadow fawning about his feet like a cat as he passed beneath the floodlight.

Fascinating. Rhion scratched his beard and leaned an elbow on the sill. With his room unlit behind him, there was little danger of being seen as long as he kept back far enough to prevent the glare from catching on his glasses.

His first thought, that Poincelles was out to do some courting in the woods, was banished by the rather large satchel the French mage carried. Services rendered were usually paid for more neatly than that. Besides, he knew the man generally got his boots waxed, as the saying went, in the village, or had Horst Eisler bring one of the barmaids up to the Schloss itself.

When von Rath had mentioned that morning that someone had been working in the laboratory, Rhion had immediately suspected Poincelles. Deeply interested, he continued to watch as the Frenchman unshipped two short lengths of wood from the satchel's carrier straps and used them to prop up the lowest of the three electrified strands of the fence. That particular stretch, he realized, at the southeast corner of the compound, was not only hidden from the rest of the yard by the corner of the SS barracks, but was the closest the fence came to the surrounding woods. Though the fence followed the contours of the ground closely, at that point, where a little saddle of land connected the Schloss' mound with the rising ground of the hills behind it, there was a shallow dip where, with the aid of props to keep from touching the wire, a man could get under.

Poincelles removed the sticks, picked up his satchel, and, brushing dust and old pine needles from his tweed jacket, strode quickly into the woods.

The guard had not reappeared around the corner of the barracks. Rhion tucked his boots beneath his arm and padded in khaki-stockinged feet down the darkness of the attic stairs.

In the upstairs hall he turned softly left along the corridor past von Rath's study door. It was shut, and through it he could hear the murmur of von Rath's voice and Baldur's eager whine. It was only an hour or so after sunset, barely full dark, and far earlier than he would have liked to try his maiden excursion outside the wire. Beside the big chamber where the Dark Well had allegedly been drawn, there was what had once been a dressing room, with a bank of closets along one wall and a discreet door leading to the backstairs and so down to the disused kitchen on the ground floor. The backstairs was narrow, smelled powerfully of mildew and mice, and was choked with bales of old newspapers and bundled-up bank notes, several million marks that had been printed in the crazy time fifteen or twenty years ago when, according to von Rath, this world's paper money had lost its value through fiscal policies that Rhion's banker father wouldn't have countenanced on the worst day he ever had. Rhion emerged into the old kitchen, and crossed it to what had been the laundry beyond, also dusty and disused, for both cooking and washing were done for the mages in the SS barracks. He cautiously unbolted the outside door that looked out onto the deserted corner of the yard facing the hills.

It was still empty. Poincelles had paid the guards well.

Retracing his steps quickly to the kitchen, Rhion collected a couple of short logs from the bottom of the old woodbox. Then he pulled on his boots, took a deep breath, and stepped outside.

No one challenged him. There was no guard in sight. Behind him, in the shadow of the ornamental turrets, the russet curtains of von Rath's study were shut.

Rhion crossed to the fence, propped the wire as he had seen Poincelles do, and, taking meticulous care not to touch it, slithered under.

He was free.

Free of money, food, and identity papers, he reminded himself firmly as he removed the logs and carried them to the shadows of the woods, all the while suppressing the impulse to leap in the air, to shout, and to dance—without the slightest idea of where he was or any convincing account of his business. *Wonderful—I'll be shot as a British spy before von Rath has time to figure out what's taking me so long to come down to breakfast.*

But free nonetheless! The cool thin smells of pine and fern were headier than von Rath's cognac. He stashed the logs where he could easily find them again and set off after Poincelles.

Had Poincelles been able to see in the dark, as the wizards of Rhion's world could, or had he been in the slightest bit used to traveling cross-country, Rhion would never have been able to track him. But the Frenchman was a city creature, a denizen of those bizarre places of which Rhion had only heard tales—Paris, Vienna, Berlin—and moved clumsily, leaving a trail of crushed fern, broken saplings, and footprints mashed in the thick scented carpet of fallen needles underfoot that Rhion, after seven years among the island thickets of the Drowned Lands, could have followed, he thought disgustedly, if he *hadn't* been night-sighted. He overtook his quarry easily and moved along, an unobtrusive brown shadow in the denser gloom, while the gawky form plowed through pockets of waist-deep bracken and wild ivy and scrambled over fallen trunks or the granite boulders that dotted the steeply rising ground.

At length they reached the road, neglected and overgrown, but still passable through the hills. Rhion recognized the road cutting in which they'd been stopped on that first excursion to Witches Hill by the work party of slave laborers from the Kegenwald camp. Now on level ground, Poincelles strode on more swiftly, jacket flapping and the frail starlight gleaming on his greasy hair, trailing an odor of cigar smoke and sweat. Atop the cut bank in the green-black gloom beneath the trees, Rhion followed. On the other side of the hills— perhaps three miles' swift walk—Poincelles turned off to the right down a weed-choked cart track, and in time, through the straight black of the pine trunks, Rhion glimpsed stars above a cleared meadow and the dark outlines of a barn. Part of the old estate farm of Schloss Torweg, he guessed, which had fallen to ruin in the crazy-money years, as Baldur had said. The meadow, like that around Witches Hill, was thickly overgrown and mostly turned to a sour and spongy swamp as the ponds and lakelets that dotted the landscape had spread and silted. The path that led to the barn was nearly invisible under saplings of dogwood and elder, and Poincelles, burdened still with his satchel and puffing heavily now, fought his way through them like a man in a jungle, making enough noise to startle the incessant peeping of the marsh frogs to offended silence.

He was clearly headed for the barn. Arms folded, Rhion waited in the tepid shadows of a thicket of young maples on the other side of the road. In time the crickets recommenced their cries, the frogs taking up the bass line, and after a moment, a nightingale added a comment in a liquid, hesitant alto. Only after several minutes had passed and Rhion was certain he would be unobserved as he crossed the relatively open meadow did he move on.

Not a light showed from the barn; but, as he approached it, Rhion scented incense, thick and oversweet, on the warm spring air. A moment later the deep, soaring bass of Poincelles' voice sounded from within, and Rhion glimpsed a sliver of golden light high up one side of the wooden structure that told him it must be curtained within.

They all kept something back, Poincelles had said.

The Frenchman had created a second temple—a secret one, for his own use, though it was good odds he'd pilfered the incense—and whatever else had gone into its construction—from Occult Bureau supplies, even as Rhion had stolen the components of the Spiracle. That could explain, Rhion thought, the disturbance of the lab. Coming closer, Rhion heard the Frenchman's words more clearly. He was chanting in Latin, a language in which many of the ancient books at the Schloss were written, and which, like German or any other tongue, he could understand when Baldur read aloud to him from the unknown alphabets. By the rise and fall of his voice the Frenchman was clearly speaking a magical rite of some kind, not unlike the ones the Torweg wizards used to raise power for their experiments and exercises.

"... invoke and conjure thee, O Spirit Marbas ... by Baralamensis, Baldachiensis, Paumachie, Apoloresedes, and the most potent princes Genio, Liachide, Ministers of the Tartarean Seat ... forthwith appear and show thyself unto me, here before this circle ... manifest that which I desire ..."

The voice rolled impressively over the nonsense names of the invocation of demons as Rhion pressed himself to the door. Peering through the cracks he saw that heavy sheets or curtains of some dark material swathed the inside of the structure, whose rotting wooden walls were chinked everywhere with split or missing boards. Finding a thin line of light between two of these curtains, he reached through a gap in the wall and fingered them gently apart, angling his eye to the opening.

In the center of huge interior darkness Poincelles stood, naked and hands uplifted, piebald with the upside-down shadows of seven black candles arranged around him in a wide ring. With his wrinkled and sagging buttocks jiggling at every jerk of his upraised arms, his voice booming out the names of imaginary devils to re-echo in the harlequin of rafter shadows overhead and his head jerking every now and then to flip his hanging forelock out of his eyes, he should have been ridiculous, but he wasn't. "Asmodeus I conjure thee; Beelzebub I conjure thee, King of the east, a mighty King, come without tarrying, fulfill my desires ..."

Standing in the cool outer darkness, Rhion sensed a kind of power being raised, dim and inchoate as all power was in this diminished world but present nevertheless. It reminded him strongly of some of the slimier rites of the renegade sects of the Blood-Mages, with its stink of irresponsibility, of greediness, of contempt for everything but self—contempt even for the demons it purported to summon. Before Poincelles, a woman lay on the altar beneath an inverted pentacle, naked, also, with a chalice between her thighs. Her head lay pointing away from Rhion, her face obscured by the blackness of the altar's shadow, but the candlelight caught a curl of cinnabar hair lying over a breast like a rose-tipped silk pillow. Beneath the cloying incense, the muskier pong of hashish lay thick in the air.

"Give me what I ask!" Poincelles switched to French in his excitement, threw his sinewy arms wide. "Give me and me only the keys that those men are seeking! Give me influence over the wizard Rhion! Place him in my unbreakable power, bind him to me, deliver him into my hand so that he cannot do other than my bidding. Make him teach me and me alone his wisdom! Cause him to trust me, lure him into my power, blind his eyes and soothe his fears . . ."

His voice cracking with self-induced frenzy, the lean shape stepped forward between the girl's knees and lifted the chalice to the pentacle that flickered like molten silver as the vast shadow of his arms passed across it. "O Asmodeus, Lord of the Mortal Flesh! Beelzebub, Lord of this World! We offer this rite to you, this magic raised out of the flesh that You created, this sacred lingam raised in your honor . . ."

So much for Poincelles! Disgusted, Rhion stepped back and let the curtain's tiny chink fall shut. *Strictly speaking that should be a virgin, but that must be another one of those wartime shortages they keep telling us about, like ersatz coffee.* He hoped Poincelles was paying her plenty for her trouble.

But knowing Poincelles, he was sure the money was probably coming ultimately out of von Rath's pocket.

As he waded back through the damp weeds toward the road, he heard the girl cry out in rapture, but something in the timbre of that outburst of ecstasy told him it was faked. He shook his head. His father had always said you got what you paid for.

But it left him definitely back at square one, facing the prospect of stepping into the Dark Well alone. "Always supposing I can get at the damn thing," he added dryly, stepping out of the shadows of the hedges into the rough surface of the main road.

The moon was rising, edging every pine tip, every weed stem, and every sunken pond in milky silver. The night breathed with its singing.

Curious, thought Rhion, that even the spirits seemed to have deserted this world. The luminous mirrors of pond and marsh should have been alive with nixies and water goblins, the long grasses aflicker with the half-seen ectoplasmic wings of the faes and the brown, scurrying feet of lobs. He would almost have welcomed the ghost-cold shadow of an errant grim. Had those bodiless life essences, like the power in the ley-lines, sunk to hibernation in the ground?

He turned back and studied the sagging black roof line of Poin-celles' barn. Tonight's expedition was far from wasted, he thought. He'd found another place where power of a sort had been raised—enough of it would cling so that the place could serve as a beacon to Shavus, perhaps enough to give him a fighting chance of opening a gate, if coupled with the power of the upcoming solstice midnight, though he would have preferred a place situated on a ley.

But that thought led to another. It was still early, he thought, looking at the stars. Instead of turning left, up the hill toward the Schloss, he moved on down the road, following its curve back up the other side of the hills.

The moon stood clear over the distant eastern ridge when he reached Witches Hill. Soaked in the pallid light, the Dancing Stones seemed to shine with the wan limmerance of forgotten spells as Rhion waded up the hill in the dew-heavy grass. Exhausted as he had been on his first visit there with Gall and Baldur, Rhion had sensed no magic in the place. But now it seemed that for once Gall had been right. The magic that had been there once was not dead, only deeply asleep.

It was obvious to him now which of the two shapeless stones lying in the ground had been the altar of the ancient rites. Sitting on its higher end, Rhion pressed his palms to the age-pitted surface and felt it cold and wet with dew. Rain and sun had almost rinsed away whatever had been there, dimmed it beyond what could be detected when the sun was in the sky. But in the sleeping hours between midnight and dawn an echo of it whispered, like the memory of voices after the singers have gone.

Closing his eyes, he let his mind sink deep.

It had all been a long time ago. Very little was left: the faded impression of a drum tapping, the memory of other moons. There had been blood—a lot of blood, animal and human. Some of it was mixed with semen—a virgin's first experience, the psychic charge still glittering faint as pyrite crystals deep in the fabric of the stone; elsewhere lay the deeper and more terrible charges of power drawn from pain and death. Power had been raised here, again and again, from that ancient triad of sex, death, and sacrifice, sometimes unwilling and at other times freely given, the magic woven of that power now lost in the turning winds of time.

But its residue remained.

Rhion took off his glasses, bent forward until his face touched the stone. Unlike Gall—or unlike what Gall claimed—he had no visions of eldritch priests, no cinema-show reenactments of the past. But the stone now felt warm to his palms. Like unheard music, he felt the power whisper along the leys that crossed beneath the altar, drawing power from the net of silver paths that covered the earth, dispersing it back to the world's four corners again.

After a long time he came back to himself, lying facedown on the altar, all his muscles aching, his hair and the back of his khaki uniform shirt damp with sweat. He groped around for his glasses and put them on again, to see Orion's belt hanging low in the east. He muttered, *"Verflucht!"* and stumbled to his feet, knees trembling. It was an hour's walk back to the Schloss, and after last night's efforts at scrying he was achingly short of sleep.

On his way down the hill he paused and looked back at the Dancing Stones. They seemed to have sunk back in on themselves, returned to being no more than three massive, almost shapeless slabs of rock, half hidden by the long grass of the neglected hill.

If any living magic remained in them it was too dim, too deeply buried, for his own attenuated powers to raise. But at solstice-tide it would draw on the powers of the leys, and that would help. And it was bright enough to serve as a beacon, provided he could get word to Shavus about what to look for in the dark of the Void.

He turned and headed back to his prison again.

He reached it an hour before the early summer dawn. Watching from the edge of the woods, he saw no sign of a guard. "At least Poincelles got his money's worth out of *something* tonight," he muttered, as he set up his props and wriggled under the fence. On the walk back, he'd felt sick from the strain of concentration; now that had passed, and he was ravenously hungry. As he slipped through the laundry room door his mind was chiefly occupied with ways to sneak a few hours of unnoticed sleep during the day.

Then he saw that the door into the old kitchen was open. He'd closed it behind him—he knew he had. *A guard?* he wondered, and then his eye lighted on two pieces of wood, suspiciously similar to the short logs still tucked beneath his arm, lying against the wall where the shadows were thickest. If he hadn't been night-sighted he wouldn't have seen them at all.

Poincelles would have bolted the outside door when he came in. So would a guard who found it open.

God damn it.

So someone else was poking about the Schloss at night, undoubtedly the same someone who had searched Baldur's room, perhaps who had searched his own.

He set down one of his props silently and hefted the longer one clubwise in his left hand. He wondered if he should summon a guard to take care of the intruder, if there was an intruder, but realized in the next instant that it would only lead to questions about what *he* was doing wandering about at two in the morning with dew-soaked trouser legs and pine needles sticking to his boots.

Pushing his glasses firmly up onto the bridge of his nose, he tiptoed to the half-open door.

Like the disused laundry room, the old kitchen was dark and almost empty, containing little but old counters and a big stone sink. The door opened to his left. Taking a deep breath, he sprang forward and slammed it back fast and hard.

Unfortunately the unknown intruder was hiding under a counter to the right of the door, and an arm was around his neck and jerking him backward before he could react to the swish of trouser cloth and the stink of ingrained tobacco smoke behind him.

He twisted against the grip, fighting for balance. Tearing pain sliced his upper arm; he flailed with the club, wrenching and thrashing, and half felt, half heard a knife go clattering at the same moment an elbow smashed him full force across the face, sending his glasses spinning off sideways as he crashed back against the sharp edge of the sink. Before he could get his breath a fist caught him in the solar plexus with an impact like a club.

For an instant as he crumpled over, he remembered the knife and thought, *This isn't fair* . . . Then swift footfalls retreated and left him lying at the foot of the sink wondering if his lungs would ever work again. He had just come to the conclusion that they wouldn't when other footfalls, distant but purposeful in the opposite direction, warned him that the SS was on its way.

"Just what I need," he gasped, lurching painfully to his feet. "Protection." For a moment he thought he was going to vomit; the small of his back where he'd slammed into the sink hurt more than he'd thought possible, and he could feel the side of his face beginning to puff up. His right arm hurt, but he could move it, and he felt blood soaking into his shirt sleeve. It took him a nerve-wracking minute to find what was left of his glasses, twisted metal frames and shards of glass scattered broadcast over the flagstone floor. With the heavy footsteps coming nearer he swept the bits into a black corner beneath the sink; and there he found the knife, a folding pocket blade honed to a deadly edge and still bloody. He shoved it and his bent glasses frame in his pocket and, holding his bleeding arm, ducked into the nearest closet and pulled the door to.

Through the cracks he could see the beam of an electric flashlight pass to and fro, then fade as the Storm Trooper crossed the room. Cramped in the mildew-smelling darkness, Rhion considered remaining where he was until the man had checked the laundry room and departed for good, but realized that he'd find the outer door open and, if he was worth his pay—which half the SS weren't, but Rhion didn't feel like betting his liberty on it—would come back and make a thorough search.

With swift silence and an earnest prayer to whatever gods were in charge of magic in this world that he wouldn't encounter an unscheduled wall or chair in his myopic flight, Rhion slipped from the cupboard and ducked through the door into the hall. He made it back to his attic room without further mishap, trembling with nerves, shock, hunger, and exhaustion, just as the wide window was turning dove-gray with the first light of summer dawn.

"Fools." The slant of the morning sunlight, bright and hard as crystal in these high, arid foothills, splashed into the shadows of the Archmage Shavus' cloak hood and made his blue eyes glint like aquamarine. At one time the great southeastern gate of the city of Bragenmere had overlooked a wide stretch of open ground, between the walls and the broken slopes leading down to the plains and the marshes of the sluggish Kairn; but in the years of peace since Dinar of Prinagos' usurpation of the Dukedom, a cattle market had grown up there, and then a produce market for those who did not want to cart their wares through the narrow streets to the market courts within the city, and lately a number of fair new houses had been built by merchants eager for more spacious quarters than were available within the walls. Even at this hour, barely after sunrise, the gate square was bustling with drovers, butchers, and greengrocers, the warm summery air choking with yellow dust and thick with vendors' cries. "Imbeciles, both of them!"

Tallisett of Mere, every inch the Duke's daughter despite the plain green gown she'd pulled on that morning when driven from her bed by strange, craving dreams, folded her arms and looked across at the cloaked and hooded old man who had been waiting for her on the steps of the fountain by the gate. "You didn't seriously think Rhion would let poor old Jaldis walk into the Dark Well by himself, did you?"

"I seriously thought Jaldis would have had the sense not to go without my help."

"Nonsense," the Gray Lady said from her seat on the worn sandstone steps at the old man's side. She looked up at him and Tally, shaking back the long braids of her malt-brown hair. "You spoke to Jaldis—you know how he was about his dream of helping the wizards of the world without magic . . ."

"And *you're* the one who spoke to our little partridge Rhion just before they left," the Archmage countered. "You could have forbidden him to go, and without him Jaldis wouldn't have been able to."

"I think you're wrong, my friend," said the quiet voice of the third hooded form on the steps, a tall, thin man leaning on a long black bow of horn and steel—Gyzan the Archer, greatest of the Blood-Mages. "Jaldis would have gone with or without his pupil to help, and how would Rhion have stopped him? He wasn't that powerful a mage, you know . . ."

"He still should have done something," Shavus snapped irritably, and glanced back at Tally. "And *you* might have done something, missy, to keep them both out of trouble, instead of letting them lose themselves, perhaps for good, at a time when the Order of the Morkensik Wizards needs all its strength."

"And we others don't?" the Lady inquired tartly. "As I've heard it, the rumors of a conspiracy among wizards speaks now of one Order, now of another. Vyla of Wellhaven says the Earl has banished all the Hand-Prickers from the In Islands, but in Killay it was Filborglas they arrested . . ."

"Oh, Filborglas." With a scornful wave, Shavus dismissed the Archmage of the Black Ebiatics. "His creditors were behind *that* arrest, most like."

"I would not be certain of that," Gyzan said. "There has been unrest everywhere, like a pervasive malaise. In every city of the Forty Realms one sees posters and broadsides denouncing wizards and workers of magic, depicting us as seducers, liars, and thieves. Even those people who have spoken with us, who know the untruth, are uneasy."

Tally was silent, thinking about her own coming out to the market this morning. Last night at dinner in her father's hall there had been strawberries for the last course, cool and heartbreakingly sweet, and all night, it seemed to her, she had dreamed of them, dreamed of wanting more. Shortly before dawn the unreasonable conviction had grown upon her that she could find more strawberries like those in the market outside the gates—she no longer even recalled the train of reasoning that had led her to this conclusion—but the craving had grown in the predawn darkness to obsession. Perhaps had she slept in the same room with her husband, Marc of Erralswan, that lazy young nobleman would have talked her out of it, but they had never shared a bed, having married to scotch the scandal of her affair with Rhion. In any case, Marc was God knew where with God knew what woman . . .

At last, unable to stand the desperation any longer, Tally had risen, dressed in her plainest gown, and ridden down to the market by the gates, only to be met by Shavus, Gyzan, and the Gray Lady of Sligo and to come to the realization that the strawberries and the dream-inspired yearning had been part of a spell to bring her outside the gates to meet them.

And despite all the years she had known Rhion, despite her friendship for his master Jaldis and her understanding of their wizardry, her first emotion had been one of extreme resentment, of violation. They had tinkered with her freedom, tampered with the secret chambers of her dreams.

And she understood suddenly how easy it would be to fan this kind of distrust to consuming flame.

"That was why we called you here, Tally," the Gray Lady said gently, almost as if the Lady had read her mind—or at least, Tally thought wryly, her expression. "To ask you if it is safe to be seen entering Bragenmere—to ask how things stand with your father the Duke—and so that it would not be seen that you had had a message from us, if it so befell that it is not."

"Of course it's still safe," Tally said, a little uneasily. "Father has been under pressure from a number of people—merchants, the priesthood of Darova, and especially the priests of Agon—to ban wizards from the Realm, but he's never gone back from his stand that they do no more harm than apothecaries or knifesmiths or rope spinners or anyone else whose wares can cause harm . . . or, he'll add, for that matter, priests and lawyers. The rest of it he says is all silly rumors."

"Silly rumors," Gyzan murmured, his scarred hands shifting on the smooth shaft of the bow. His hairless, ugly face broke into a grin. "I like that."

"Like the silly rumor at the turn of the spring that a Blood-Mage's spells were responsible for the latest seizures suffered by the High Queen's son?" Shavus demanded, his pale eyes glinting under the coarse shelf of his brows. "That was when the Queen locked Gyzan up, though no complaint was ever made and no trial would have been held . . . nobody even knew where that rumor had started, any more than they know who'd been putting up those broadsides and posters."

"Was that what happened?" Tally remembered vividly the cold of that bitter spring night, standing in the black shadows of the gateway watching the procession of masks bob away into rain and mist, while she huddled in her ash-colored cloak, waiting for a man who never came. She still remembered the leaden awfulness of hearing the tower clock strike midnight and knowing that Rhion was gone.

Rhion was gone.

"But why would you have done such a thing?" she asked, turning to Gyzan. "That's what those rumors never say. Why! You aren't even in the employ of one of the Lords . . ."

"People believe anything of wizards," Shavus returned dourly. "The Earl of March believes I can fly—that I just travel horseback, when I can afford it, to confuse people. Silly bastard. They call the Lady Nessa 'Serpentlady' because her patron the Earl of Dun's got it through his thick skull that she has a snake with ruby eyes and couples with it to get her power. Your father's been a good friend to us, missy, but these days with rumor spreading like bindweed, it pays to take precautions, that's all."

From the gates nearby there was a sharp clattering of hooves; Tally turned, startled, to see a small group of riders emerge, bound for a day's hunting. She glimpsed her father, tall and broad-shouldered in his red leather doublet and plumed cap, and his fair, fragile, pretty second wife; saw her husband, Marc, like a bright bird of paradise in green, flirting already with one of her stepmother's ladies; and near beside them, her sister Damson, corseted brutally into yards of plum-colored brocade and plastered with jewels. With her rode her husband, Esrex, pale, cold, and slender, looking as if he detested the whole business. Of their son, Dinias, heir to the Dukedom from which her father had ousted Esrex' grandfather, there was no sign. Probably he was having another bout of chest pain and wheezing, Tally thought, trying to summon up sympathy for the boy in spite of his thoroughly unpleasant personality. She noted that her own son—Rhion's son—six years old and rosy and fierce as a lion cub, had somehow finagled his way onto the saddlebow of one of the huntsmen, and shook her head.

Beside her, she was aware of Shavus' gesture, a slight tracing of runes in the air with his fingers; though Damson turned her head their way Tally saw her sister's bulging gray eyes pass over them unseeing.

And for all she had said about her father's support of wizards, about how safe it would be for them to enter Bragenmere, she was glad the old man had surrounded them with the thin scrim of spells that had prevented Esrex and Damson from seeing her in the company of mages.

She sighed and turned back to them. "They should be back a few hours after noon—it's too hot to be hunting after that," she said. "Father put Jaldis' rooms under seal when Jaldis went away, and asked me if Rhion had gone with him—I think to make sure Jaldis hadn't gone alone. Esrex has been after him to destroy the contents of those rooms and to burn the books Jaldis left with him, but Esrex has always hated Rhion and Jaldis and is out to impress the priests of Agon."

"And as far as you know, the Dark Well's still up in that loft of his?"

"As far as I know." Tally reached forward and helped the Lady of the Moon get to her feet. The matter must be serious, she thought, for she had never heard of the Gray Lady leaving the Drowned Lands in all the years Rhion had been Scribe there. "I know Father will let you up there . . ."

"Good." The Archmage grunted. His blue eyes grew grave, losing that cynical sharpness as they met hers once more. "For I'll tell you the truth, missy—there's a smell in the air that I don't like. I tried to talk Jaldis out of going to that other world of his, saying wizardry here would need as much help as he claims it does there, and he wouldn't listen. But now I think things are serious enough— with the spies of Agon everywhere, and strange rumors going about— that it's time I contacted Jaldis and our little Rhion and brought them back, whatever they may feel about their other world. And I've a feeling we're going to need all the help we can get."

8

"I never liked the idea of you staying in the attics." Von Rath handed Rhion a chunk of raw beef and frowned down at him severely. "Now you see what happens?"

"It was my own fault." The meat was cold on the gruesomely swollen flesh. A glance at the mirror had showed him the whole area had turned purplish black. "And I'd rather fall down the stairs once than wake up every morning with a headache from the cigarette smoke in the rest of the house." Rhion leaned back against the iron spindles of the bedframe and shut his other eye, hoping his explanation had covered all the physical evidence and that the sentry hadn't seen fit to report the unlocked door of the laundry room.

"I shall speak to the men . . ."

Rhion waved his free hand irritably. "No! They think I'm a lunatic already, for Chrissake. The last thing I need is for the guards to have a grudge against me for keeping them from smoking in the lodge."

Von Rath frowned. Rhion guessed the concern in his eyes was genuine, but mixed with it was a Prussian officer's almost disbelieving indignation that his orders might not be obeyed. "They would not dare."

"They would." He cocked one nearsighted blue eye up at the tall black figure standing over him. "Ordinary Troopers have ways of getting back at people who cause them trouble. It's something I don't want to deal with. Besides, you'd have to tear out the paneling and burn every rug and curtain in the house to get rid of the smell. Don't worry about it. I'll be fine."

"You are not 'fine.' " Von Rath folded his arms and looked down at the little wizard with an expression of exasperated affection. "I have not noticed any smell of tobacco, though I am not a smoker myself, but I will take your word for it. I have sent for Dr. Weineke from the labor camp at Kegenwald. She should be here this afternoon to do something about getting you new eyeglasses. All right?"

"All right." The knife cut on the back of his right arm hurt damnably under a clumsily improvised dressing. Though shallow, it would take twice as long to heal unstitched and leave an appalling scar, but Rhion could think of no way to work that into an explanation of a fall down the stairs. Fortunately he was left-handed, and the arm's stiffness could, with luck, pass unnoticed. "Thank you."

Curious, he thought, as von Rath's footfalls retreated across the attic and creaked, with a slight vibration, down the narrow stairs, how the young SS wizard was equally capable of such consideration and charm, and of that calm arrogance, that close-minded assumption of his own rights at the expense of everyone whom he considered less than himself. It was, Rhion had found, one of the things that lay at the heart of Naziism, along with a paranoid sense of persecution by imperfectly identified forces—and one of the things that reminded him most of the masked followers of the Cult of Agon, the Eclipsed Sun.

Only here the mask that hid the follower from himself was subtler, not concealing the face, but changing it as it was perceived by others and by the face's owner. An illusion, if you would—an illusion of altered perception.

Yet another of those things, he thought wryly—like horseless vehicles and flying machines, like artificial light and the ability to talk across great distances—that was magic without magic: magic without the disciplines and limitations that all mages learned.

He shut his eyes against the thin, white afternoon light, and wondered just how much of what he had said von Rath believed, and whether he should dig his boots from their hiding place beneath the bed and clean the pine needles off them—wondered for all of five seconds before he dropped into a heavy and exhausted sleep.

He woke, late and suddenly in the afternoon, from a confused dream about the Dancing Stones. Tallisett had been there, sitting on the altar stone in the old green gown she sometimes wore, her unbraided hair a wheaten cloak stirred by the faint night winds. Though he'd been far away in the deep grass of the meadow he could somehow see her face, calm and serene and a little sad, and past her shoulder saw the looming darkness of a shape and the glint of cold starlight on a blade. The Gray Lady, he thought dimly, remembering the sacrifice of the equinox . . . the blood black upon stone in starlight, the calling down of power. Frightened, he'd started to run, weeds pulling at his knees and his boots sucking in the heavy mud, stumbling, calling out her name, knowing he must reach the place by midnight and that midnight was near.

But when he'd gotten there she was gone. Only the stones remained, and on the altar stone, like a long puddle of ink in the darkness, lay a pool of blood. His chest hurt from running and he stood over the stone, fighting for breath, while all around him the whisper of crickets and tree toads murmured in the meadow below.

A terrible sense of déjà vu overwhelmed him, as if he had been here before—as if he knew what must happen here. He could feel magic rising up through the hill, radiating from the stones, the earth, the turning wheel of the Universe, fragmenting out along the leylines to the farthest corners of this magicless earth and back again to the place where he stood at the crossing of the leys. Then faint and very close, as if the unseen musician stood at his elbow, a flute began to play. He looked around and saw no one. But in the chancy glimmer of the summer starlight, slow and ponderous and infinitely graceful, the Stones began to dance.

He woke staring at the ceiling rafters, the music of that ancient dance fading from his mind. He tried to hold it, to call back the shape of the tune, but it slipped away—in the yard below his window a sentry called out a joke to some crony about why Hitler held his hat in front of him while reviewing military parades, and the music slipped away and was gone.

Stiff and aching, Rhion rolled from the bed. Though it hurt to move, he fished out his boots and laboriously cleaned them, using rags torn from the bloodied shirt. Fortunately it was one of four or five identical Wehrmacht hand-me-downs and unlikely to be missed. He'd already torn off part of it to fashion a bandage and swabs for the alcohol he'd pilfered from the workroom downstairs; he started to rip off another piece, and, as the effort pulled agonizingly at his injured arm, he fished from his pocket the knife he'd picked up in the kitchen last night.

It was a folding clasp knife of the kind many people in his own world carried, but contained in its handle of old yellow ivory several blades instead of just one, blades of varying sizes and types. The longest had been recently sharpened to a deadly edge; the second was smaller, of a convenient size to carve feathers into pens, had these people done such a thing. Pens here were metal tubes that either held ink or more usually sputtered it broadcast over documents, hands, and shirt pockets. The third blade seemed to be a punch, the fourth a corkscrew, the fifth a short, flat-tipped slip of metal Rhion could guess no use for but that was bent and scratched as if it had, in fact, been used. He cut the shirt apart, folded it carefully, and hid it behind the loose board with his coffee beans. Then he returned to sit cross-legged on the end of the bed, back propped against the iron-barred footboard, the knife gripped lightly in his hands.

He closed his eyes and sank into meditation, feeling the smoothness and age of the ivory, the coldness of the tiny silver pins that held it to the body of the clasp, the curious, hard lightness of the steel, while his mind probed into the fabric of the tool itself, as it had probed into the stone last night.

Dimly he became aware of the smoke stench and racket of the Woodsman's Horn, the dirty songs and the stinks of tobacco, men's bodies, spilled beer. Overlying it he felt the charge of the perceptions of the one who had held the knife, bitter red rage, disgust, hatred— a poisoned hatred of men, of self, of Germany. *A woman*, he realized, a little surprised—one of the barmaids almost certainly. The pungence of sex clouded all surface impressions, messy, dirty, and dangerous, a thing to be gotten through quickly, a tool to be used as men were all tools to be used . . .

For what? He probed deeper, feeling the texture of that rage. Violent, despairing, contemptuous . . . but not hopeless. A moving anger. Moving toward a goal.

Searching. Searching this house.

Searching for what?

He slowed his breathing still more, deepening his trance. He sank past the images of greedy, fumbling hands and obscene laughter, of smutty songs and the smell of incense—*incense?*—seeking what lay in the deeper shadows beyond.

A man. Age and wisdom, or at least what were perceived as such . . . And beyond those perceptions, overlain by all else, he became aware of the man himself. Long ago this had been his knife. Then sharply, distantly, Rhion saw a gray-bearded man using this knife—yes, to carve feathers into pens like a civilized human being. To write . . . To write . . .

. . . *magic.*

??!?!!

"Rhion?"

The touch of a hand on his shoulder broke him out of his trance with a gasp and he nearly cried out as his startled jerk wrenched every bruise and ache and cut. Von Rath caught his arm—fortunately the left one—to steady him, and Rhion stared up at him, sweat springing out on his face, for a moment not recognizing who or where he was.

"Are you all right?"

"Uh—yeah," he managed to say, breathless with the shocked disorientation of being brought cold out of a deep trance. His hands were shaking as he fumbled the knife back into his pocket. "Fine. Just—just give me a minute."

Von Rath stepped back, clearly puzzled. Shutting his eyes, Rhion tried to gather what remained of the trance back into his mind to close it off, but fragments of his consciousness seemed to be floating everywhere around him in a cloud, and his head throbbed painfully. "I did knock." Von Rath's voice was apologetic and concerned, grinding disorientingly into his consciousness. "It is not the time for meditations . . ."

"Oops." Rhion grinned shakily. "I've been looking all over for the piece of paper with the meditation schedule on it . . . Never mind," he added, seeing von Rath's baffled expression. "Joke. Very small joke." And one that would be lost on a German anyway. He inhaled deeply a few more times, then gave it up as a bad job. In time his head would clear, certainly after he slept again, which didn't sound like such a bad idea. He finger-combed back the thick curls of his hair. "What is it?"

"Dr. Weineke is here. For your eyeglasses."

Dr. Weineke was a cold-faced woman of forty or so whom Rhion hated on sight. Having been startled from deep meditation, he was far more conscious than usual of the auras that clung to things and people, and in her voice and her hands when she touched his face, he felt an evil terrifying in its impersonality. The place she had come from had left a smell upon her soul, like the ubiquitous stench of cigarettes that permeated the ugly female version of the SS uniform she wore.

She examined his eyes in the dining room, a long and rather rustic hall with heavy beams and what was obviously intended to be a Gothic fireplace at one end. Wide windows looked out onto the south end of the compound yard, facing the garages. Beyond the wire, molten patches of late sunlight lay halfway up the rusty coarseness of the pine trunks and gleamed far-off on a pond away among the trees. Poincelles, Horst, and an older SS Trooper named Dieter were drinking coffee at the far end of one of the several long tables that occupied the room, Poincelles in his booming voice listing every rival magician, former in-law, and disapproving scholastic colleague he knew in Paris and just what he hoped the Gestapo—the Secret Political Police—would do to them.

"It will take at least ten days for the dispensary to fill this prescription," Dr. Weineke said as she put away the last of her small glass sample lenses and jotted a note on a piece of paper. "Perhaps much longer, with the demands of the troops in the field." She gave a cursory glance to the bruise on Rhion's face and made a small disapproving noise with her tongue. Then she turned to von Rath, who sat on the table nearby like a schoolboy with his feet on the seat of his chair. "Knowing the importance of the Professor's work, I took the liberty of bringing an assortment of eyeglasses that might serve him in the interim."

"How very clever of you!" Von Rath's smile, like his words, were something he'd obviously learned in a manners class, gracious and warm for all they weren't genuine. Weineke colored up like a girl as she reached under the table and brought up a cardboard carton, which she set on the table beside Rhion. It was half full of pairs of eyeglasses.

"Try them on," she invited in what she evidently considered a genial voice. "One will surely be close enough to allow you to continue your so-valuable labors."

Rhion put his hand into the box and nearly threw up with shock.

The psychic impact was as if he'd unsuspectingly plunged his arm into acid. Yet at the same time what was in the box—the dim miasma floating over those neat, insectile frames and dust-covered lenses— was ephemeral, gone even as he jerked his hand out, sweating and gray-lipped and sick. He glanced quickly to see if von Rath and Weineke had noticed, but they were talking together, the SS doctor dimpling under the young mage's adroit courtesy as if his words were a glass of cognac. If she'd known how she would have smiled.

Hands shaking, sweat standing cold on his face, Rhion looked back at the box. For a moment it seemed to him that those flat, folded shapes of metal and glass were the skeletons of men, stacked like cordwood for burning, sunken eyes sealed shut and mouths opened in a congealed scream of uncomprehending despair.

He blinked. The vision disappeared.

"Where did you get these?"

Weineke glanced over at him with a clinical little frown; von Rath, too, looked worried at the sudden whiteness around his mouth. The doctor said, "They were confiscated from political prisoners, criminals, enemies of the Reich. Is there something wrong?"

"Just . . . I—my head aches." He turned away quickly and, aware of their eyes upon him, put his hand into the box again.

Now that he was braced for it, the sensation was almost gone. The gold-rimmed spectacles he picked up were only spectacles. The concentration of evil, of horror, of a depth of despair unimaginable to him—of the truest touch of hell he had ever encountered—had slipped beneath the surface of reality again like a bloated corpse momentarily submerging in a pool. He could have probed into the metal and crystal to look for it, but didn't dare.

He hated the thought of putting them against his face.

They were an old man's glasses, meant to adjust farsightedness rather than myopia. He blinked and took them off. One of the most evil men he'd ever encountered, the old Earl of Belshya, had been ninety-four, and he supposed the Reich could have enemies that ancient who were dangerous enough to be locked up in the hell whose aura hurt his fingers as he reached into the carton again. He didn't believe it.

The next pair, silver-rimmed, he couldn't even touch. The boy who had worn them was dead. Through the silver, the most psychically conductive of metals, he could still feel how it had happened.

Beside him, von Rath and Weineke were engaged in soft-voiced conversation. ". . . victory slipping through our hands. Those prisoners I asked you to hold in readiness for us . . ." The primrose air smelled of cigar smoke and coffee, and across the room Horst was roaring with laughter over one of Poincelles' witticisms. Rhion barely heard. He doubted he'd have been so aware of the auras clinging to the glasses if they hadn't been all together in a box, if he hadn't just been shocked from a psychometric trance; but he realized now where he'd felt that aura before. It was the same sense that clung to the yellow-patterned dishes on which they were sometimes served lunch, to one particular chair he hated in the library, to the watch they'd given him and the books in strange tongues he found hard to touch.

Those were things that had been confiscated when their owners—those mysterious and ubiquitous "enemies of the Reich"—had been taken away to be tortured and to die for crimes, it was clear from the aura of the glasses, they for the most part did not even comprehend.

He picked a tortoiseshell pair—tortoiseshell being almost completely nonconductive—but the man who had worn them had been far more shortsighted than he, almost blind. Horst and Poincelles sauntered over, still carrying their coffee cups, the Frenchman's cigar polluting the air all around them. "Oh, not those," Poincelles objected, taking the tortoiseshells from Rhion's hand, "they make you look like a mole."

"How about these?" Horst took a pair from the box and tried them on, making faces through them; Poincelles laughed.

"Trudi will go for those. You know she loves intellectual types."

The young Storm Trooper crowed with laughter—Trudi, if Rhion recalled correctly, was the little black-haired minx at the Horn who had yet to give any evidence of literacy. Of course, in a country whose ideal woman was a devout and pregnant cook, this would scarcely be held against her.

"These are close." Rhion put on a pair of rimless glasses with fragile silver temple pieces. They weren't as close as another pair he'd tried, but the horror that clung to these was less suffocating, less terrifying, than some.

Poincelles grunted. "They make you look like a damn rabbi."

The word—not in German—came to his mind with the meaning of "teacher," but was overlain with a complex of connotations Rhion could not easily identify. Von Rath laughed gaily. "You're right! All he needs is side curls," but Dr. Weineke gave him a long, thoughtful scrutiny that turned his blood cold for reasons he couldn't guess.

"How about these?" Horst balanced a pair of gold-framed lenses without temple pieces on the high, slightly skewed bridge of his nose and assumed an exaggeratedly pedagogical air. "If the class will now come to order!" He rapped with his knuckles on the table and pinched his lips.

"You're right." Poincelles grinned. "I had a Greek teacher at Cambridge who wore some like that, the strait-laced old quean. You've captured the look of him . . ."

"Ah!" Von Rath laughed again, plucked them off the Storm Trooper's face, and adjusted them on Rhion's. "Now *that's* the thing for you. Distinguished and scholarly."

The old man. The thought came to him instantly and whole, and was as swiftly gone, a half-familiar face glimpsed while crossing a crowded street. He touched the delicate frame hesitantly—the lenses balanced by pressure alone—and, though afraid of what he might find, closed his eyes and dipped within.

It was the same old man whose personality he had felt buried in the depths of the knife. But he sensed clearly here a gray old city, a basement room of stove, table, thick-crowding shelves of worn books, and a bed behind a faded curtain of flowered calico; grimy windows afforded only the view of passing boots. He saw bony hands using the ivory clasp knife to sharpen old-fashioned quills. The smells of cabbage soup, the sound of contented laughter, constant learned argument, droning chants—a little dark-haired girl with coal-black eyes . . .

And beneath the patina of pain and shock and dread, of hunger and the ever-present stinks of filth, degradation, and death, he tasted again the elusive wisp of magic.

Beside him Horst was laughing. "No, a monocle! Hey, Doc, any of those dung-eating Communist Jews wear a monocle?"

"You don't look well." Von Rath's voice slipped softly under the younger man's coarse guffaws. He leaned one flank on the table next to Rhion, stood looking down at him, head tipped a little to one side, dark, level brows drawn in a frown of concern.

Rhion removed the pince-nez and inconspicuously slipped it into his shirt pocket, and eased the rimless glasses carefully on over the swollen left side of his face. Though he felt as guilty as if he'd erased a plea for help written in a dying man's blood, he knew he'd have to ritually cleanse them if he was going to wear them regularly.

Did von Rath know? he wondered, looking up at that beautiful face, delicate even with its sword scar—dreamer, wizard, as much an exile in this world as he was himself.

He'd been talking to Dr. Weineke with the casual intimacy of longtime partners.

He knew.

Rhion closed his eyes, fighting the tide of inchoate realization about what the Nazis did and were. "My head aches," he said truthfully. "You have no idea how stupid I feel falling down the stairs like a two-year-old, but if you don't mind, I'm going to go back up and lie down again. I'll come back in a couple of hours. Maybe you and I can work through the Dee and the Vatican letters tonight, so the day won't be a total loss."

Von Rath shook his head. "It does not matter if it is. Baldur and I will finish them. Rest if you need to rest."

Horst and Poincelles were still playing with Weineke's collection of eyeglasses as Rhion mounted the stairs to his own room.

9

"Who's the old man?"

Taken unawares by the question, the barmaid Sara turned sharply, slopping beer on the tray she had been about to lift from the bar; for a split second uncertainty and fear gleamed in those spitcat eyes before they melted into warmth as ersatz as the average cup of German coffee. Then she smiled and brushed her hip lightly against Rhion's crotch. "Don't worry about my old man, Angeldrawers. Old Pauli does the settling-up with him." But he knew she was sparring for time.

"I don't mean your pimp," Rhion said quietly and took from the breast pocket of his shabby brown shirt the gold pince-nez. "I mean the old man who wore these—the old man who used to cut quills with the knife you tried to stab me with."

Her hand shut around his wrist with the same startling strength he'd felt dragging him off-balance in the laundry room, and her eyes changed from a courtesan's to an assassin's. "Where did you get those?"

They were jammed shoulder to shoulder in a mob of black-uniformed men and locals in shabby serge around the bar; with the cessation of the newscaster's staccato voice a few moments ago, the

Woodsman's Horn had returned to a chaos more characteristic of Saturday nights than of the normally quiet Thursdays. But with the triumphs in the West, the locals had all crowded in to listen to the broadcasts. Now men slapped each other on the shoulder and laughed, congratulating and triumphant—the French falling back in utter confusion, the British ousted, helpless, waiting for the Reich's conquering armies, Belgium and Holland on their knees ... An extremely drunk man in the golden belts and brown uniform of a local Party leader was explaining at the top of his voice to a bored-looking Trudi how England's work force would be organized for the good of the Reich, and over at the piano a group of the guards from the Kegenwald labor camp were singing *"When Jewish blood spurts from the knife, things go twice as well."*

Rhion transferred the glasses to his free hand and thence to his shirt pocket again. He didn't raise his voice. "Can we go somewhere and talk?"

She drew breath to speak, not sure, he guessed, whether to try out another lie. The next instant someone grabbed Rhion roughly from behind, twisting his arm painfully as a boozy gust of breath from over his shoulder demanded, "This Jewish squirt bothering you, sweetheart?" Twisting to look back, Rhion saw two Storm Troopers, camp guards, blond, clean-shaven men with iron eyes. "You want us to give him a lesson in manners?"

Since you're so highly qualified in that field ... Rhion, panicked, had the sense not to say it; his gaze cut frantically to the smoky room, but Horst, who'd driven him into town, was nowhere in sight. *Christ, I'll report the bastard* ...

For a moment Sara considered the matter. Then she dimpled co-quettishly and shook her head. "Oh, let him go." She made bedroom eyes at the men and insinuated herself between them, and they released Rhion to make room for her. Her little hands fluttered, caressing collar flashes and sleeve bands as if in childlike admiration of the insignia. "But it's good to know German maidenhood is being so well protected."

Obviously the qualifications for maidens have been lowered for the war, Rhion thought, edging out of the crowd as quickly and incon-spicuously as possible and heading for one of the vacant tables in a shadowy corner of the room. *I wonder if Poincelles made that clear beforehand to the lords of the Tartarean Seat?* As he sat down, he found he was shaking. He hadn't counted on Sara having allies, nor considered the possibility of being beaten bloody in an alley in mistake for a Jew.

He studied her as she teased and flirted with the growing circle of Storm Troopers, always in motion, touching the wrist of one man as he lighted a cigarette for her, the arm of another as she looked up into his face with those huge black eyes. Her garish hair was sticky with the sweat that sheened her face in the frowsty heat; in her cheap, green, flowered dress, her body seemed to crackle with nervous energy and the promise of sensual outrageousness.

Though there was always one barmaid on active duty, it was never the same one—the girls appeared and disappeared regularly through the inconspicuous door near the bar. Old Johann was slumped unconscious in a corner, no more regarded tonight than a half-dead dog. Music blared forth from the radio again, soaring, passionate, incongruously beautiful—the music of this world was some of the loveliest Rhion had ever heard, totally unlike anything he had known in his former life. He wished he could write some of it down for Tally, who would be fascinated by its complexities.

"Who are you?"

Rhion looked up. Sara set two tankards of beer on the table before him. He had seen nightshade sweeter than her eyes.

"Professor Rhion Sligo." He took a sip of one of the beers. "But Auguste told you that last week." He produced the pince-nez again and held it out to her. "I found these in a box of about two hundred pairs that the doctor from Kegenwald brought for me to choose from after you broke mine the other night." Up at the bar he'd seen her take in the black eye and the bruise on the side of his face.

Her hand, which had started toward the glasses, flinched back and clenched on itself, and the red mouth, wide and generous under its paint, hardened. She blew a cloud of cigarette smoke at him and laughed. "I was pretty drunk here the other night but I think I'd remember breaking your glasses for you, Professor. Maybe it was Trudi—she's pretty much like me when the lights are out." She plucked the glasses from his hand and tucked them in the soft chasm between her breasts, and gave him a mocking smile, daring him to lay a hand on her with the men within call.

"I'm talking about three o'clock in the morning the day before yesterday," Rhion said quietly. "At Schloss Torweg, after you got done helping Poincelles raise his—ah—ritual energies. As the closest thing this country has to a professional wizard, when someone tries to kill me I can usually figure out who it is." He pulled the knife from his pocket and slid it across the table toward her.

She laughed again, shaking back her hair. "Christ Jesus, a wizard! What'd you do, cut the cards and get a number that added up to the Gematria of my name? Going to turn in your Ouija board notes as evidence to the local Gauleiter? You'd better find your keeper and head on back to the Schloss, or you *will* get a lesson in manners." With a cocky flip of her skirt she turned to go.

"Wait a minute! Don't call the Etiquette Squad!"

She turned back, irresolute, and he talked fast.

"If I'm Gestapo all I have to do is pull an i.d. and it's you they'll be taking out of here, not me. If I'm not . . ." She came back like a feral cat, ready to scratch or flee. He lowered his voice again. "If I'm not you don't have anything to lose listening to me, do you? What have you been looking for up at the Schloss?"

Her dark eyes shifted. The soft mouth flexed a little, and she brushed aside a sticky tendril of hair from her cheek. "Drugs," she said quietly. "Cocaine—Baldur keeps a stash of it under a floorboard in the corner of the workroom upstairs."

"Don't be ridiculous. Why risk being shot for spying over something you can get out of Poincelles in trade for a couple of trips up to his temple? And you know as well as I do that in this country they make arrests on a lot thinner evidence than party tricks and numerology."

Slowly, still tense and unwilling, she pulled out a chair and sat across from him, dropping her cigarette and crushing it out beneath one high red heel.

"Are you working for the old man? You've been searching the place— what are you looking for?" He leaned across to her. "I have to know." And when she didn't answer, only studied him with those wary black eyes, he added, "I haven't told von Rath. I can't—I couldn't let him know I'd been out of the compound that night. I'm more or less a prisoner there myself. The old man is a wizard, isn't he?"

She picked up the knife where he had left it on the table, turning its blunt brownish length over in her hands. The red paint on her nails was chipped and chewed, the nails themselves bitten off short. "Yes," she said, after a long time. "He's my father."

"Can you take me to him?"

Her voice was vicious. "It's word of him I'm looking for." She fumbled another cigarette from her dress pocket and flicked the wheel on a brass lighter made from a rifle bullet, but her fingers were trembling. Rhion, though he hated cigarette smoke, reached to steady the flame for her, but she jerked her hands away with a vitriol glare that made him remember how the knife had reeked with her loathing of men.

The mild narcotic of the nicotine seemed to steady her. "I've seen people do psychometry," she said after a moment. "One of the girls in my dorm at college used to do it at parties, but she had to be two drinks drunk . . ."

"College?"

Under the sweaty points of her red hair her glance was scornful. "You think I could get into every SS barracks between here and the Swiss border by waving my degree in chemistry, pal?"

"Ahh—no."

She smoked in silence, her lipstick leaving lurid stains on the white paper of the cigarette, her eyes avoiding his. As she smoked she swallowed back her rage, a little at a time, like a bile of nausea. "I heard the SS had an Occult Bureau that was holding people like him in special custody. Then I found out about your place . . ." She raised her eyes to his, and in them he saw how she hated him for having the power to tell her what he knew. "You say those came from Kegenwald. Could you tell me if he . . . if he's still alive?"

In spite of his black eye and the wound on his arm that smarted every time he moved, Rhion's heart went out to her. For all her hardness she was very young. She would, he knew, far rather have been hurt herself stealing the information, would rather have traded her favors for it, than simply ask it of a man. "He wasn't dead, or in immediate fear of dying, when they took his glasses off him," he said slowly. "But I have no way of telling how long ago that was, or what might have happened to him since. Do you know why the Occult Bureau is imprisoning wizards?"

"God knows." She shook her head wearily.

"And the magic that he uses . . ." The name of it, half-glimpsed in the deepest fabric of the penknife, returned to him. "The—the Kabbala . . ."

Her eyes, closed in momentary frustration, flicked open again, and in them he saw the bitter look of a cornered animal. "So you know," she said, and suddenly all the tautness seemed to go out of her, all the catlike readiness to scratch and flee. She sighed, her eyelids creasing with an exhausted irony. "The damned thing is that if he wasn't a Kabbalist I think he'd be dead now. Most of the people they arrested in Warsaw that first week ended up dead—not just Jews, but gypsies, teachers, priests, Communists, newspaper editors . . ." She pushed wearily at her hair. "Papa's brothers are all rabbis, they thought what he studied was crazy. But I think it's the only reason he was separated out, locked up instead of shot. I've been searching the Schloss for information, something that might tell me if he's still alive, and where, and what they want with him . . ."

"You're a Jew, then?" Rhion said, enlightened but keeping his voice as quiet as possible.

Sara rolled her eyes ceilingward. "So what are you, the flower of Aryan manhood?"

He blinked at her, startled. "I'm from another universe," he explained. "I don't even know what a Jew looks like."

"Holy Mother of . . . The boys in the barracks said you were crazy. Are you circumcised?"

"Yes," Rhion said, nonplussed by the apparent switch in topic. "What does that have to do with anything?"

She regarded him, baffled, through the bluish haze of smoke, then shook her head. "I'm beginning to *believe* you're from another universe," she said in a tone that indicated she believed no such thing. "Just don't get yourself picked up by the SS, pal. And you might remember that if you breathe one word about my own ancestry, they won't even take me outside to spare the furniture before they shoot me. All right?"

"All right," Rhion agreed, still puzzled. "How powerful a wizard is your father? I've heard von Rath mention the Kabbala, but he seemed to think it was worthless by definition, being Jewish. *Is* there power in it?"

"Is there . . ." Sara stared at him, mouth open. "It's all hooey, you poor deluded shnook! The whole goddam business is about as real as the tooth fairy! If there was anything in it, do you think they'd be *able* to round up Kabbalists and their families like sheep for the . . ."

"Sara!" a voice behind her bawled, and two Storm Troopers came swaggering up. One of them, a guard from the Schloss, saw him and muttered, "Oh, Professor . . ." but the other eyed him with utter contempt.

"C'mon, Sara, the beer don't taste as good without you to serve it."

"What you want with this little kike, anyway?" the other added, pulling her to her feet and into his arms.

Sara smiled, kittenish, her body suddenly supple again, all hips and breasts and teasing little hands. "Well, what's a poor girl to do if *real* men don't give her a cigarette now and then?" She took one from the camp guard's breast pocket and put it between soft pouty lips. The man's arm was around her, his hand cupping her buttock, as the three of them vanished into the crowd around the bar.

Rhion sipped his beer, deep in thought.

So much, he thought, for the last country in the world to believe in and support wizardry. Evidently the Reich only supported such wizards as would give it what it asked for, and somehow it made him feel better to know that other wizards had had the good taste to be "enemies of the Reich." There was a wizard as close as the Kegenwald camp, five miles at most from where he sat.

Adrenaline scalded his veins. There was, in fact, a possibility of getting out of here alive.

He thought back on what von Rath had told him of the Kabbala. It hadn't been clear because it was a field of studies rather than any specific book or rite, a tangled labyrinth of meditation and spells rooted in a central symbol called the Tree of Life and spreading in endless thickets of numerological calculation, esoteric scriptural exegesis, and six thousand years' worth of learned quibbling. Sara had taken the knife—her father's folding penknife—from the table, but he recalled vividly the sense of magic deep within it, like the lingering brightness that lay within the Dancing Stones.

Horst appeared at his side, adjusting his tie by touch and clearly unaware of the immense smear of fuschia lipstick under his left ear. The blond girl Ulrica was walking with that leggy stride back to the bar, already smiling a mechanical smile for the next man or men, and Rhion saw Sara heading toward the recently vacated back room with the two Troopers who'd taken her from him.

He glanced up at Horst. "Would you talk to whoever you have to talk to about having that Sara girl come back to the Schloss with me tonight?"

Horst's face split into a grin of complicity and delight. "Sure thing!" he said, and then added hastily, "Sir. I mean—I knew you'd like her."

He turned at once toward the bar and Rhion said quickly,"When she's not busy." No sense adding a couple of sexually frustrated drunk Nazis to his other problems.

He settled back in his chair, nursing his beer and wondering how difficult it was going to be to break Sara's father out of Kegenwald.

"And don't get any ideas, cupcake," Sara murmured, snuggling against him in the dark backseat of the open car and running a hand along his thigh. "Your chauffeur eavesdrops—he can see us in the driving mirror, too. Unless that's part of your price?" She turned her head against his shoulder, and he felt the tension in her muscles as he put his arm around that slim hard waist and drew her close.

"I have a wife and two kids at home and I never sleep with women who've tried to knife me."

"I bet there's lots of those."

The men were leaving the tavern. As Horst turned the big blue Mercedes in the yard, the yellow headlight beams splashed across the Schloss' three-ton Benz flatbed, catching a firefly glister of silver buttons and gleaming eyes beneath the rolled-up canvas cover. The gray-uniformed Kegenwald guards were mostly walking back to the camp, and as the open Mercedes passed them, striding along in threes and fours down the single narrow street of the village, one or another would wave and call out to Horst, or to Sara.

The street ran past the new church, and the old church, and so out into the dark of the endless pines.

It was thirty minutes' drive to Schloss Torweg, a walk of nearly forty kilometers. Railway trains—the primary means of long-distance transportation in this world—went faster than that, flying machines faster yet. Rhion smiled, hearing the Gray Lady's voice in his mind: *To go so far at such speed, and yet you will still arrive there with what you are inside.*

He leaned back in the soft leather of the seat, watching the stars flick in and out of the black frieze of branches. The constellations were the same ones he knew, though their names here were different.

This potential for perfection, for comfort, he thought as the wind riffled his hair, *and what are they doing? Using their airplanes to strafe fleeing civilians and their radios to incite men to hate.* He remembered what he had seen in the scrying crystal and in the Ministry of Propaganda's newsreels.

Had the world gone insane when magic had disappeared?

Not a pleasant thought.

Then they turned a corner where the road returned to its ancient, sunken track, picking up once more the line of the Kegenwald ley, and his blood turned cold.

Power was running along the ley. He could sense it like a sound, a texture in the air, and even stronger, there came to him the chill psychic stench of evil. But as he reached to touch it, to see what it was and where, it was gone. Sara felt the flinch of his body and raised her tousled head sharply from his shoulder, and he realized that quiet as she had been, she'd been waiting tensely for his slightest move.

"What is it?"

"I don't know."

But a hundred yards' distance from the Schloss he felt it again, as the harshness of the yard lights glowed between the black trees, and this time he knew.

They had raised power.

The whole lodge—even the air around it—was lambent with energy, darkly glowing with a horrible, unfocused strength. Sara asked him again softly, "What is it?" as she felt his breath catch in horror; she sat up and pushed back her ruffled curls, but by her voice he could tell she felt nothing. A guard came whistling casually to open the gates. Horst cracked a joke with him about Goering's wedding night that he'd heard at the Horn.

In the luminous square of the lodge's open door von Rath stood waiting. He still wore his white ceremonial robes, and the electric glare in the hall behind him showed his body through. It was only when Rhion got close that he saw blood spots on the hem and sleeves.

"We've done it!" Von Rath sprang down the steps to seize his arms and staggered. Even allowing for the lesser light of the floodlit yard, the younger wizard's eyes were dilated to black, and he swayed on his feet like a drunken man. His hands, gripping Rhion's shoulders, were convulsively strong. "We've done it!" The smell of his robes was horrible: fresh blood, burned flesh, incense. Past him Rhion could see the air in the hall pulsing with power, power that flowed uncontrolled down the paneling and moved like snakes of cold light on the stairs. Instinctively he balked when von Rath tried to draw him over the threshold.

"Horst," he ordered shakily, "take the girl up to my room. Sara, wait for me."

Von Rath waved impatiently. "Let the guards have her, you don't want a woman at a time like this. Come." His hand like iron on the nape of Rhion's neck, he dragged him up the steps and into the accursed house.

"Baldur was right, you see," he whispered exultantly as he pulled Rhion past the watch room and down the wide, paneled hall. His drugged eyes had a hard, terrible shine, like opals in which some evil spirit had been bound. "Gall was right. The Adepts of the Shining Crystal—they knew! They had the secret of how life force can be woven into magic! Baldur found the rites—they were coded, concealed in the Lucalli Diaries . . . How to draw forth power, all the power we need . . ."

As von Rath pulled him through that hideously vibrant house Rhion held out his hand, summoning witchlight to his palm. Nothing happened. He fumbled a match from his pocket and held it out, half afraid to call fire to the dried red sulfur-paste at its tip. He felt almost afraid to speak, for fear of waking some terrible force by the softest of words.

No fire burst onto the match, but out of an obscure fear that things were on the verge of uncontrolled chaos Rhion put the match tip into his mouth and wet it thoroughly before dropping it onto a table in the hall. "Were you able to convert it?"

"Not yet." Von Rath halted with him before the temple's doors. There were no guards in this part of the house, no lights. The temple doors stood open, and Rhion recoiled before the dark power he saw moving within, shifting and quivering in the blur of candlelight and smoke. Within the long, black-painted room he could see horribly half-familiar marks scrawled everywhere on the parquet, save around the altar, where Gall, stripped to his underwear, was engaged in washing the floor.

The smell told Rhion what had gone on that night, and the hair lifted on his neck.

"But don't you see?" von Rath giggled, shivering all over with triumph and glee. "*We won't need to.* I made Baldur see the things I wanted him to see. The three of us here in the temple, performing the blood-rites of power, and him on the other side of the house . . . I made illusions in his mind and *he saw them!*"

Rhion pulled away from the clutching hands, disgusted and horrified. "If he was as crocked as you are I'm surprised he didn't see Venus on the half shell rising out of the sink!"

"No." He caught Rhion's face between his palms, staring down into his eyes and seeing in them nothing but his own triumph, his own vindication, his own joy. "He saw nothing, no hallucination, but those that I projected into his mind. He wrote them down, with the exact times of their appearances—they were the same, Rhion!

"Don't you see? Maybe we can't convert power to physical operancy, not yet, though that will come. But once we can control illusion, *we can take out the British air cover.* And that will be enough to ensure the success of the invasion of England. And after that—" His voice sank to a whisper. "—they'll give me anything I want."

10

Sara was waiting for him when he got to his attic room. The door was barricaded; he tapped at it softly and spoke her name, and after a moment heard a chair being moved. Her hair was rumpled, half the buttons torn off her dress to show a sailor's paradise of bosom, her smile sardonic. "Big hotshot wizard and you can't levitate a little chair?" The electric bulb over the bed was on; Rhion automatically switched it off and took a match from his pocket to light the candles. In the diffuse glow of the yard lights outside Sara put her hands on her hips. "Now, look, *boychik*, I've had enough . . ."

"I hate that light," he said wearily, pushing up his glasses to rub his eyes. From his trouser pocket he took the notes he had been given—notes von Rath had insisted on going over with him, while Gall cleaned up something in the corner of the temple that clattered with soft metallic noises—and put them in the drawer with the wrist-watch he never wore these days. "Horst brought you up here?"

She sniffed, sitting back on a corner of the bed but watching him warily. "After a couple of the boys in the watch room who'd heard old Pauli declare open season got done pawing me, yeah."

He winced. "I'm sorry."

"The hell you are. You got a cigarette?"

He shook his head. "I don't smoke."

"You and Hitler." In the candlelight her eyes were dark and very angry. "You're all bastards."

"Do you want to go home?"

"Home?" She laughed bitterly. "I haven't *got* a home. You think after all this I'm gonna be able to go back to Aunt Tayta and Uncle Mel in New York and be their little girl again?" She turned her face from him, the wide mouth clenched taut under its smeared lipstick. He wanted to go to her, to comfort her as he would have comforted anyone in that much pain, but he knew if he touched her she'd break his jaw.

Then she drew a deep breath, forcing some of the tension to ease. "Oh, hell," she said in time. "I get pinched and kissed all the time at the tavern—it wasn't anything I don't do every day." Rhion thought about the two Storm Troopers and wisely said nothing. " 'Invest in good faith,' Uncle Mel is always saying—he's a tailor. 'Make them smile when they remember you.' Auntie would kill him if she knew how I was applying that particular sample of avuncular wisdom."

And still she watched him, like a cornered animal, waiting for him to make a move toward her, to prove to her that he was, in fact, like every other man. After a long minute, when he didn't, she said in a much quieter voice, "I want to see my Papa. You say you're a wizard. You show me him in that damn crystal of yours." She jerked her head toward the scrying crystal's hiding place in the rafters and he realized she must have taken some opportunity, either now or during her earlier searches of the place, to go through his room. "Then I'll go back to town."

Rhion took a deep breath, brought over a chair, and fetched the crystal down. "I can't show you him."

Her mouth twisted. "What a surprise!" she said sarcastically. "How come it's always the wizard who gets to squint into the crystal ball? It's only his word to the marks what this person or that person is doing."

"Well, it's the goddam best I can do!" Rhion flared. "Now do you want it, or do you just want to get the hell out of here and let me go to bed? Jesus, why do I always end up dealing with you at three in the morning?"

"I want to see him," Sara said, her voice suddenly small and tight, and looked away.

She had, as she'd said, slept her way through every SS barracks between here and the Swiss border to find him. Rhion felt the anger go out of him, remembering that. Of course she expected him to cheat her. Sitting on the bed with her disheveled hair and rumpled dress, she looked very young and alone. Rhion moved the chair out of the way, wincing as the cut on the back of his arm pulled, and said, "All right, give me the glasses. But I can guarantee you right now, if your father's as wise as you think he is, that what he's doing is sleeping."

He took a piece of chalk from his pocket and sketched around himself a Circle of Power. As he settled his mind, deepening it into preliminary meditation, he noted that Sara, chatty as she was with the men in the tavern, seemed to realize the need for silence. *Of course*, he thought. *She's a wizard's daughter.* Whether she thought it was hooey or not, her father had taught her the rules.

The moon stood low, a sickly scrap of itself tangled in the black of the eastern trees. Even the crickets' endless screeking in the warm spring night had fallen silent. With the moon's waning the dark field of power enveloping the house felt stronger yet. Rhion guessed he could have tapped into that field to make the scrying easier, but instead blocked it from the Circle as best he could; as a result, it took him the usual endless forty minutes to raise the strength. His head began to ache, but nothing would have induced him to partake of what had been done tonight. The pince-nez lay like an insect's cast chitin in his right hand, the crystalline lattices of the glass holding the psychic energies that had surrounded them; in his left the scrying crystal flashed sharply in the reflected candlelight. He pursued those flame reflections down into the stone's structure, sinking through the gem's familiar pathways until colors came, then darkness, then the clear gray mist that rolled aside so suddenly to reveal a tiny image, like something reflected over his shoulder or in another room.

"It's a cell about eight feet square," he murmured, and somewhere behind him the bedsprings creaked as Sara leaned forward. "Cement walls, cement floor, iron cot, bucket in one corner." A part of him whispered in relief. He had been afraid to look into the place where the glasses had come from, afraid of what he might see. "There's a window high up, floodlight outside . . . A man sitting on the edge of the cot. Tall and skinny . . ." Rhion frowned, concentrating on details. "His head's been shaved, the stubble's gray and white . . . Long eyebrows, curling—gray. There's a scar on his lip, not very old . . ."

The glasses still between his fingers, he touched the place and heard Sara's hissing intake of breath. "Bastards. *Bastards!*" Poisoned tears shook in her voice. "He had a mole there, under his beard. They shave them when they put them in the camps."

If he thought about it—if he let anger or outrage or anything else intrude on the effort of concentration—he would lose the image altogether and be unable to get it back. His training had given him discipline to exclude even the worst of horrors from his mind. But it was a near thing.

After a moment he went on, "He's wearing dark pants of some kind, patches . . . gray shirt in rags. His knees are skinny, bones sticking out through the cloth—long thin hands, brown age spots— He looks too old to be your father."

Dimly he heard her voice say, "He was forty-one when he met Mama."

"He's standing up, walking to the window, trying to look out but it's over his head. He's worried, fidgety, pacing around."

"Can you tell where the place is?" She leaned forward, her hands with their bitten red nails clasped on her knees. "Is he still at Kegenwald?"

"I don't know." He spoke dreamily, detached, struggling to keep his concentration focused on the old man's face. A curious face, beaky and strong in spite of its egglike nakedness, the dark eyes as they gazed up at the narrow window filled with horror and concern that held no trace of personal fear. Rhion felt a kind of awe, for having tasted the aura of the place, through the box of glasses and through Dr. Weineke's cold smile, he knew he himself would have been huddled in a corner puking with terror. And he knew there were still things about this that he didn't know.

"Have you seen the camp?" he asked softly. "I can go up and look through the window myself, describe what I see . . ."

Within the crystal he saw the old man look up swiftly, at some unheard sound outside. Then he pressed to the wall beneath the window, straining to hear, and Rhion concentrated on moving past him, up the wall until he was level with the opening, which, he saw now, was barred, wire laced into the glass. Through it he could see a vast, bare yard under the glare of yellow floodlights, row upon row of bleak wooden barracks beyond and, past them, a wire fence closing off the compound from the dreary, endless darkness of the pinewoods. Wooden towers stood along the fence, manned by dark shapes with glinting machine guns. Between two such towers was a wire gate, which gray-clothed sentries opened to admit the smaller of Schloss Torweg's two flatbed transport trucks.

The truck turned in the yard, pulled to a stop before a building opposite the barracks; more guards emerged from the building's lighted door into the floodlit glare. With them was Dr. Weineke, her graying fair hair pulled back tight and every button buttoned, though it must be nearing four in the morning, and another man in a more ornate black SS uniform whom Rhion guessed was the commandant of the camp. Auguste Poincelles climbed down from the truck cab, rumpled and unshaven but moving with that gawky, skeletal lightness characteristic of him. He said something to Weineke and gestured; she nodded, and the camp commandant craned his head a little to see as guards untied the canvas flaps of the truck's cover.

They brought out three stretchers, one of which they hadn't had a spare blanket to cover.

"Jesus!" Rhion shut his eyes, but not fast enough—for an instant he thought he was going to be sick. The facets of the crystal bit his palm as he clenched his hand over it, as if that could let him unsee what he had seen. "Oh, God . . ."

"What?"

He pressed his hands to his face, unable for a moment to speak.

By the face—or what was left of the face—of the woman on the stretcher, she'd been conscious for most of it.

Then anger hit him, terror laced with rage. Though violence had never been part of his nature, he'd have horsewhipped a man who'd perform such acts upon so much as a rat. Baldur had read him secondhand accounts of the accursed Shining Crystal group, but the thought of such things actually being done, no matter in what cause—the thought of the kind of power that would result and what it would do to those who summoned it—turned his stomach and brought sweat cold to his face.

"Are you all right?" Hard little hands touched his shoulders, soft breasts pressed into his back. "What did you see? What is it?"

He shook his head, and managed to whisper, "Your father's all right," knowing that would be her first concern. "It's just—I looked out through the window . . . He's at Kegenwald, all right. Weineke was there, and Poincelles—Poincelles drove the truck . . ."

"What truck?"

He shook his head again, trying to rid it of what he knew would always be there now, as if burned into his forebrain.

"What did you see?" She pulled him around to face her where she knelt on the floor. When he wouldn't answer she snagged her purse from where it lay at the foot of the bed, took out a tin flask, and pressed it into his hands. He wasn't sure whether the stuff inside was intended to be gin or vodka, but it didn't succeed at either one. Nevertheless, it helped.

After a long moment he whispered hoarsely, "Back in my world those in the Dark Traffic—the necromancers, the demon-callers—usually have trouble getting victims. I see now they just don't have the right connections."

"You mean von Rath's doing human sacrifice."

Though he knew she was only thinking in terms of throat-cutting, he nodded.

"Papa . . ."

"It's all right," he said quickly, seeing the fear in her eyes. "I'll help you get him out."

For the length of an intaken breath she was just a girl, wonder and gratitude flooding her wide dark eyes. But the next moment all that she'd done to get this far came back on her, and her body settled again, her parted lips close and wry. "And what do you get out of it?"

"I need his help. I need the help of a wizard to get me back to my own world."

He almost laughed at the speed with which she adjusted the cynical exasperation on her face to an expression of grave belief.

"All right. What do I have to do?"

"You don't believe me, do you?"

"Of course I—" She paused, regarding him for a steady moment, then shook her head. "No. But I know I can't spring him alone." For a moment they sat in silence, their knees almost touching in the smudged ruin of the chalked circle, candlelight warming the translucent pallor of her face and throwing wavery thread-lace shadows from every tangled red strand of her hair. Then she looked down at the tin flask still in her hands, and twisted and untwisted its metal top as she spoke. "That's the other reason I'd put up with Poincelles and those grunts in the barracks to get a chance to search the house. It wasn't only word of him—records and files—I was looking for, but documents, seals, signatures to fake—anything. I've been out to look at the camp—I know all the roads around here—I've got faked i.d.s, ration cards, clothes, pick locks . . . But I know that's not gonna get me spit, walking in there alone. A woman . . ." She shrugged. "I thought maybe Poincelles . . ."

Her mouth flinched with distaste at the memory of the darkness in the barn temple, and Rhion saw again the point of the downturned pentacle like a silver dagger aimed at her nude body, heard Poincelles' evil chant.

"You tell him anything?"

She shook her head. "I was always afraid to, when it came down to it. He really believes that crap . . ." She paused, her eye darting up to meet Rhion's, and then grinned apologetically. "Present company excepted. But he's . . . Some of the stuff Trudi told me about what he did with her . . . some of the stuff he asked me to do. And there was some rumor about him and one of the local League of German Maidens, a kid about twelve . . . Jesus! There was a stink about that—it was before your time. So I never had the nerve. And besides, I don't trust the momzer to keep his word."

"Don't," he said. "But you're going to have to trust me."

After Sara had left, Rhion looked over the scrawled pages of notes.

He had mastered sufficient spoken German to understand radio broadcasts, and enough of the spiky, oddly curliqued alphabet to read simple notes, though the thick tomes of histories, records, accounts of magic over the centuries still defeated him. But though Baldur's handwriting had been made no easier to decipher by the vast amount of mescaline the boy had taken, the meaning was clear.

22.17—Buzzing. Large bee in corner of ceiling near door.

22.38—Three red lights about seven inches apart on the wall behind me, four feet above floor.

23.10—Something in corner of room? fur?

23.50—Hole in floor, three feet in front of door. Twelve inches across. Can see edges of floorboards cut cleanly as with saw. No light down inside.

Below, in von Rath's neat handwriting, was appended the note: "Illusions projected for sixty seconds at a time, perceived for between five and thirty seconds."

It was dawn. The sky had been lightening when he'd walked Sara down to the waiting car, which had passed Poincelles' covered flatbed in the sunken roadway before the gates. Birds were calling their territories in the dew-soaked pockets of bracken among the pine trees, the thin warbling of the robins answering the chaffinch's sharp "pink-pink," reminding Rhion hurtfully of mornings when he'd sit in meditation on the crumbling stone terrace of the library in the Drowned Lands, listening to the marsh fowl waking in the peaceful silence.

Around him, the forces that had been raised by the blood-rite were slowly dispersing with the turn of the earth. He could feel them clinging to the fabric of the house like some kind of sticky mold—called up, incompetently tampered with, but unable to be used or converted to operancy, they lingered in shadowy corners, ugly, dirty-smelling, dark. Did the rites of the Shining Crystal even include dispersal spells? he wondered wearily. It was lunacy to suppose a group capable of raising this kind of power wouldn't have the sense to use them, but any group fool enough to raise power out of an unwilling human sacrifice, a pain sacrifice, a torture sacrifice, was probably too stupid to realize what they were tampering with in the first place. In any case that part of the ritual might have been taken for granted and not written down—they frequently weren't—or written down elsewhere and lost. He should, he thought, have gone down to the temple himself and worked what he could to neutralize the energies raised.

But there wasn't enough money in Germany to make him go into that temple tonight.

Rhion flipped to the next sheet. That was in von Rath's handwriting, neat and precise, having been written out before he'd taken the potent cocktail of mescaline, peyote, and psilocybin himself.

Bee—22.17
Triangle of red lights—22.38
Fox—23.09
Glass of beer—23.25 (That one evidently hadn't gone through at all.)
Hole in floor—23.50

In a room at most a hundred feet away, which von Rath had been in scores of times, into the mind of someone who knew him and hero-worshipped him and concentrated on his every word and expression and who was, moreover, magically trained himself and out of his skull on drugs.

But he'd done it.

Rhion folded the papers and sighed. He took off his glasses, lowered his head to his hands.

Shouldn't you do something? a part of him asked.

For instance? Every time he closed his eyes he saw the mutilated body of the woman, like some twisted shape of driftwood in the bitter electric glare, and the two other forms beneath dripping blankets. He saw the camp, the guards, Weineke, the commandant—all the structure of power that made it so easy for von Rath to order up victims as he ordered up silver or mandrake roots or anything else he wanted from the Occult Bureau; he saw, too, the fleeing women and children scattering before the diving planes, and the boxful of spectacles that turned before his eyes into neat little corpses, folded up like frozen insects awaiting disposal.

The implications were more appalling still.

He had the sensation of being trapped in a nightmare, of teetering perilously on the edge of a dragging spiral of horror incomprehensibly worse in its dark depths than it was up here at its crown.

The gray beach he'd seen in the scrying crystal came back to him, too, men standing in the sea while boats bobbed toward them—brightly painted pleasure boats, some of them, or big, strange-looking craft with unwieldy mechanical paddles on their sides and rumps, crewed by men and women too old, too soft-looking—too kind-looking—to be soldiers. English civilians, Horst Eisler had said. A stupid and decadent race, von Rath had called them, but a race nevertheless willing to brave the choppy sea in whatever craft they could find to take those men off the beaches, out from under the flaming death of the German guns. In the crystal, he'd seen the British war planes, too, searing soundlessly overhead and fighting heart-stopping midair battles with the German fliers.

We can take out the British air cover, von Rath had said. With illusion at his command, he could.

And then . . . *they'll give me anything I want.*

The thought of what that might be made him shudder.

How much command von Rath would ever gain over illusion was problematical, of course. No matter how much power he raised, unless the hallucinations could be directed consistently and accurately into the minds of large numbers of strangers it wouldn't do much good, and Rhion knew that without magical operancy such control simply wasn't possible.

But having seen the demon unleashed in von Rath's eyes, he knew also that von Rath would not hear him when he said that. From his own experience of having the long-denied magic within him released, vindicated, broken forth into the air, he knew just how strong were the forces driving the young mage—how strong they would have been even were it not for the centuries of denial and disbelief being thrown off, as well. He would continue trying, continue the hideous blood-rites, continue raising the ghastly energies and releasing them unused and without any sort of control, until . . .

Until what?

Rhion didn't know. He was wizard enough to be academically curious about the results, but every instinct he possessed told him to get out and get out fast.

For a few moments he toyed with the notion of aiding Sara and her father to escape to England, wherever the hell England was, and offering his services to the English King. But aside from the fact that once away from the Dark Well he would lose forever his chance of contacting Shavus and establishing a pickup point for his jump across the Void—in effect, exiling himself here permanently—there was no guarantee that the English King wouldn't have him imprisoned. Like the Solarists, he seemed to believe that magic not only didn't, but couldn't, exist. Moreover there was always the chance that the English King was as evil as the Chancellor of Germany, though the thought of another realm as comprehensively soulless as the German Reich was something Rhion didn't want to contemplate.

No, he thought. The best thing to do was to contact Shavus, establish a point where their power could reach out to guide him across the Void, and get the hell out of this world of luxurious insanity. And for the first time since he'd come here, that didn't look completely impossible.

11

The Duke of Mere greeted Shavus the Archmage with great cordiality when the old man appeared at the gates of Bragenmere, four nights before the last new moon of spring. For all his bluff, warrior heartiness, the Duke was a man of learning, and welcomed scholars—mageborn or otherwise—to his court. Even the most disapproving of the cult priests, the chill-eyed Archimandrite of Darova and the silent Mijac, High Priest of Agon behind his funereal veils, dared not remark. Sitting at supper the first night, Tallisett couldn't hear what the Duke and the Archmage had to say to one another; but, looking along the glitter of the high table at the two big, middle-aged men, the dark crimson velvet of the one in no way belittling the shabby brown-and-black homespun of the other, she rather thought they were comparing the finer points of shortsword technique with the salt spoons.

But on the second night, as she was hurrying down the corridor toward the vestibule where the Duke's guests assembled before walking in procession, two by two, into the state dining hall, she was stopped at the head of the stair by a pale, precise figure that materialized from between the malachite columns, and a cool voice inquiring, "Whither away, little cousin?"

It was Lord Esrex.

She curtsied politely, but her eyes were wary. She had never trusted her brother-in-law, even before his attempt seven years ago to have Rhion executed and herself disgraced—his friendliness now put her all the more on her guard. "I'm late. They'll be going in soon . . ."

"Not until I'm there." He leaned a narrow shoulder against a column drum and drew the white silk of his glove through his slender hand. "Surely you know the reason they're having a state dinner? I'm the guest of honor—your father's chosen to make me governor of the lands for which he married that brainless little slut at the turn of the spring."

Tally felt her cheeks heat with anger, for she liked her new young stepmother, but she only said calmly, "If you've received the impression she's a slut, I'm afraid the spy network of the Cult of Agon isn't as accurate as it's made out to be. Even the most careless gossip in the court could tell you Mirane of Varle is devoted to my father."

She was rewarded by the color that flamed to the tight-skinned, delicate face. He would, she knew, have been delighted to be able to prove the Duke's new wife unfaithful, even as he had sought for years to prove that Rhion of Sligo, and not her husband Marc of Erralswan, was the father of Tally's children, and for the same reason—to discredit any heirs to rival his own son's claim to the Dukedom from which his grandfather had so rudely been thrust.

But with icy and bitter precision the scion of the White Bragenmeres waved her words away. "He thinks he can make it up to me, giving me that pittance for the wrong he has done my family. And if he's deluding himself that he's still man enough to father a child on that straw-headed little lightskirt. Is that why he welcomed the Archmage to court? To get him a tincture of potency, now that his own tame conjure has disappeared?"

She realized he was baiting her, seeking information, and shook her head, reaching to straighten the pendant pearl that hung at her throat with a hand cluttered by unaccustomed rings. For the full ceremonial of a state dinner she wore her husband's colors, emerald green, ribboned and tasseled in silver, the bronze-blue eyes of a peacock's tail hanging around her half-bared shoulders in a delicate collar. "I'm not in his confidence, cousin."

"They tell me other wizards are arriving in the city now," Esrex went on softly, his pale eyes studying her face. "The Serpentlady of Dun came in last night, they say—carrying her lover in a basket, I should expect—and Harospix Harsprodin from Fell. So the ears of Agon are not as inaccurate as you might think."

"Since everyone who enters the gates, mageborn or not, is under Father's protection," Tally replied steadily, meeting his gaze, "there's no particular reason why wizards should conceal their movements. I suppose Agon's spies simply like to feel important, telling their masters at the temple what they could have learned by the asking." She tilted her head at the sound of a muted fanfare of music echoing in the deep arches of the stairwell, so close above their heads. "Shall we go down?"

The ceremony of investiture, in which Esrex was given temporary governorship of the dower territories Mirane had brought to her middle-aged husband, took place between the great course and the sweets, and Tally took her leave as soon as Esrex, Mirane, and the Duke had resumed their seats and the musicians had begun the light, flirty tunes that traditionally heralded the entry of dessert. She did not like the way Esrex's pale, heavy-lidded eyes sought out her own two sons—Kir rosy and vigorous and just turned seven, four-year-old Brenat already asleep with a chicken bone clutched in one plump hand—or the way he glanced sidelong at the Duke's fair-haired bride of ten weeks, as if trying to guess the reasons for the blooming sparkle that seemed to radiate from the core of her body.

In the deserted vestibule, the glow of the oil lamps showed Tally a piece of paper lying on one of the spindly-legged couches; she picked it up and saw it was a rough drawing of her father and a wizard. The wizard, a grotesque figure in a long robe with no effort made to distinguish which order of wizardry or who the wizard was, had removed her father's head and was replacing it with that of a sheep.

Cold went through her, cold followed at once by a hot flood of furious anger. She ripped the paper in half, turned to thrust the pieces into the bowl of the nearest lamp, when a deep voice from the shadows said softly, "Don't burn it."

Looking up swiftly, she saw Gyzan the Archer standing with arms folded in the darkness between the vestibule's many columns.

"Give it to your father. He may be able to identify who printed it, and where."

"Would it do any good?" Her hands shook, her whole body swept with shivers of anger and a curious, helpless dread. From the great hall behind her the clashing of cymbals filtered, a bright glitter of sound—dancers in red with the long noses of goons were bounding and whirling among the tables, to the ripple of laughter and applause. "They just keep appearing, just like the rumors keep spreading. You can't stop them any more than you can stop rumors."

"Perhaps not." The tall Blood-Mage came over to her and took the paper, held the pieces together to study the drawing. "But one can do what one can to find the reason behind it. Hmm. One of the milder ones, I see . . ." His hands on the cheap yellow handbill were brown and deft, and in the lamplight Tally noted how both his little fingers had been cut off just above the first knuckle in the strange rites his Order practiced and how the rest of the fingers were scarred with ritual cuts.

"The reason is because people hate the mageborn, isn't it?" Tally followed him quietly across the vestibule, past the silent guards outside the bronze doors, and over the wavery harlequin of torchlight and darkness that fell like a silken quilt across the flagstones of the great court outside. "Because they fear them? Only now the fears aren't just of a single wizard using spells to cheat honest men or seduce chaste women—they're fears that wizards will organize and take over the Forty Realms. Which is funny," she added with a sudden, shaky laugh, "when you think of it. I mean, the idea that any group of wizards *could* get together long enough to conspire in *anything* is something that could only be believed by someone who doesn't know wizards."

The sounds of argument in Jaldis' rooms at the top of the octagonal library tower were clearly audible as Tally and Gyzan climbed the final flight of stairs from the uppermost of the bookrooms below.

"Why not?" she heard the Gray Lady's soft tones, now clipped and very angry. "Because you don't want other wizards to learn how to communicate with other worlds than our own?"

"My dear lady," Shavus' gravelly bass rumbled. "It's a matter of principle. Were the case different you'd be arguing for me, not against. The magic of the Dark Wells—the knowledge of how the Cosmos is put together and what things can affect its very fabric— is a powerful and terrible lore. It cost Jaldis years of seeking and study . . . it almost cost him his life seven years ago . . ."

Gyzan opened the door and let Tally pass before him into the room, the peacock feathers of her collar and headpiece flashing strangely in the soft, blue-white witchlight that flooded the neat little chamber. The Archmage, in the act of leaning forward from Jaldis' carved chair, paused to note their entry, then turned back to the Gray Lady who stood, arms folded tight about her, in the curtained window embrasure. Near the small hearth sat Nessa of Dun—the Serpentlady, tall, heavy, and beautiful in the brown-and-black robes of the Morkensik Order—and with her the boyish, white-haired Astrologer of Fell and another brown-robed Morkensik mage whom Tally could not identify, though she knew him by sight as she knew so many of the wizards who had come visiting Jaldis over the past seven years.

"Any magic, any body of knowledge that powerful, must be kept to the smallest number of folk," the Archmage went on, his ugly face anxious and conciliating. "You know how quickly such things can be perverted to the worst uses. Remember what happened when the Blood-Mages learned the lore to summon demons . . ."

"That was the Dark Sect, the wizard Canturban's students," the Gray Lady protested.

"That's true," Gyzan added. "Even the other Blood-Mages shun them."

"Be that as it may." The Archmage waved a heavy-muscled hand. "It could as easily have been any of those splinter sects. You know no Blood-Mage has the training in balance and restraint that wizards must have—your pardon, Gyzan, but you know that's true."

"I know nothing of the kind. All Blood-Mages aren't like—"

"The wider the knowledge," Shavus went on as if his friend had not spoken, "the more chance there is for . . . accidents. Or spying."

"You're saying you don't trust us."

"I'm saying I don't trust some of the people who have access to the library on your islands. Suppose one of your Ladies takes it into her head to go over to the Earth-witches next year and takes with her whatever she may have found out? Can you guarantee *they* won't . . ."

"The Earth-witches are perfectly harmless."

"They say," Harospix of Fell remarked.

The Lady's sharp hazel gaze flicked to the Morkensiks sitting grouped by the hearth. "I am only saying that this concentration of knowledge can be taken too far." She looked back at Shavus. "From what I understand, he didn't even teach Rhion how to open a Dark Well, for fear I'd get that information out of him."

"Well, you *did* seduce him in an effort to get Jaldis' books away from him."

"That was *not* . . ." the Gray Lady began, then glanced sidelong at Tally, and fell silent.

"Oh, Shavus," Nessa chided and caught Tally's eyes mischievously. "As if she'd need a reason to try to seduce Rhion!"

Both Tally and the Gray Lady laughed, and Shavus, relieved, rose to his feet and went to clasp Tally's hands in his own. "I think you know Nessa, the Court Mage of the Earl of Dun," he said. "Harospix Harsprodin, and his student Gelpick of Wendt. They've come— and Erigalt of Pelter and Frayle the White should be here by tomorrow—to help in seeking through the Dark Well for some sign of Rhion and Jaldis and to assist in bringing them back. As you know it needs magic on both sides of the Void in order to make the jump, and since, as Jaldis says, there is no magic in that world or, if any, only a very little that can be raised at the solstices and the equinoxes, it's going to need a great deal on this side to bring them through. We're going to be watching by the Well in turns."

"And the other Morkensiks were kind enough to come and make it unnecessary to share the Well's secrets with myself or Gyzan," the Gray Lady added, turning back from the window, for all her soft stockiness moving with powerful grace. Her hands, rubbing on the plain meal-colored homespun of her sleeve, were thick with muscle from the bread bowl, the shears, and the spindle; alone among them, she did not wear the robe of a wizard, but only a simple dress, such as the peasant women of the Drowned Lands wore, with irises embroidered on its breast.

"Nay, I never said that!" Shavus protested.

"Did you think it?"

Shavus hesitated. Harospix inclined his snowy head with a courtier's grace. "There are different forms of magic, Lady," he said gently. "Different frames of reference. At the moment it is not the time to deal with the inevitable misunderstandings of trying to mesh an intellectual system like the Morkensiks' with an organic one such as your own."

The Gray Lady's lips pressed thin; Gyzan folded his arms, and within his tattooed eyelids his brown eyes were grave and sad.

"Then if you have no more need of our presence here," the Gray Lady said, "Gyzan and I will return to Sligo. No—" She raised a hand as Shavus got quickly to his feet. "I'm not angry with you. Just please let me know if you hear anything."

"Of course," the Archmage promised, glad to make whatever concessions would let him out of a fight with the Ladies of the Moon.

"The Archer may remain with us as long as he pleases," she went on, picking up her gray wool cloak from the table and swinging it over her broad, square shoulders. "Inar the Solarist has taken refuge there with us also, and we've had word that Vyla of Wellhaven is on her way, with two of the other exiled Hand-Prickers . . ."

Shavus' intolerant blue eyes widened in alarm; Tally could easily read in them his relief that the Gray Lady was carrying away no secrets to spread among that motley gang.

"You will, of course, be welcome among us at any time," the Lady added mildly, "since Rhion has taught even the most prejudiced among us that there are *some* decent Morkensiks."

"Well, thank you, my lady." The old man smiled.

She paused in the doorway. "Don't smile," she said gravely. "The day may come when you need that sanctuary. Good night."

"Damned arrogant intellectual jackanapes," she went on vi-

ciously, as soon as she and Tally had descended out of earshot—
quite a distance for wizards. They crossed through the scriptorium,
their footfalls echoing sharply in the warm, dreamy darkness where
the smells of ink and parchment lingered. Gyzan had remained for
a few moments to show the pieces of the scurrilous handbill to
Shavus; the Lady and Tally walked down the stairs in silence, not
speaking until they reached the lowest floor, the many-pillared entry
hall where the colored glow of cressets in the courtyard cast dancing
reflections on the marble walls. The Duke's guests were spilling out
of the main hall now and into the court, where the warm summer
evening breathed with the smell of jasmine and wisteria, with the
lemongrass of the torches and the thin pungence of the dust that
always seemed to hang in the dry upland air.

"Listen, Tally," the Lady said, halting in the darkness and touching the younger woman's beribboned sleeve. "What Shavus is refusing to understand is that knowledge is not simply for use. It is for
saving, for passing along, maybe to people we don't know in the
distant future. Yes, I tried, by means of spells and coercion, to get
Rhion to show me where Jaldis hid his books when they stayed
among us, though it is a lie to say that I used my body to try to
coax that knowledge out of him . . . I tried because I feared that the
knowledge would be lost."

Tally frowned. "But if you don't know who will be using it in
the future, ill could come of it."

"Ill can come of any knowledge," the Gray Lady said softly.
"There is only so much that we can control. Rhion told me that
seventeen years ago nearly all Jaldis' books were torched out of
existence by the old King's soldiers when they arrested him—when
they put out his eyes, tore out his tongue, and crippled him. There
was knowledge in those volumes that was lost forever, Rhion said.
Now something about these rumors of conspiracy troubles me, something about the fact that they seem to be centered here, in Dun, in
Fell, and wherever any of the Great Lords has a wizard in his employ. Though I've never liked the thought of a mage selling his
powers to a Lord—it is not for such that these powers were given
us by the Goddess—I will say that it does keep the Lords themselves

in balance and prevent any one of them, or any Cult, from aggrandizing too greatly. Without them . . ."

She frowned, rubbing her hands again uneasily over the coarse
wool of her cloak. "Without them it would become a contest of
strongmen." She glanced up at Tally in the woven shadows, studying
her face.

"We need Jaldis' books, Tally," she said softly. "Rhion told me
before he left that Jaldis turned them over into your father's keeping."

Tally was silent for a long time. She was remembering the handbill
she had found, remembering others that had appeared, pasted to the
walls of taverns and public baths; remembering the way Esrex had
looked at her sons, and the black-robed priests of the Hidden God
who seemed always to be about the court these days.

But they were Jaldis' books, Jaldis' secrets. He had trusted her
with them, as he trusted her father and trusted Rhion. "I—I can't,"
she said softly and wondered if the Gray Lady would put a geas of
some sort upon her, as she had put a geas upon the strawberries, to
draw her out of the city that morning. She turned away, crossing
the vestibule to the doors. The Lady walked with her, her soft-
booted feet making little sound on the speckled red terrazzo of the
floor.

"He is my friend," Tally finished simply, turning within the
shadow of the great bronze doors. "And Rhion . . ."

"I understand." And in the darkness she could hear the sadness
in the Lady's voice.

"If what Shavus says is true," Tally went on hopefully, "they'll
. . . they'll be bringing Rhion and Jaldis back through the Void at
the summer solstice, when they can raise enough power on the other
side—Nessa, Harospix, Erigalt, and the others." She shivered with
the thought, the desperate hope, of seeing Rhion alive and safe and
with her again. *Please, Goddess*, she prayed to Mhorvianne, the bright-
haired lady of illicit loves, *please bring him back safe*. "That's only a
few weeks."

But somehow she heard in her own voice the note of false heartiness she would have pitied in another, and cringed from it.

"So it is," the Lady said quietly. She drew her cloak about her, though the darkness outside, alive with torches like jeweled gold lace, was balmy with the summer's lazy warmth. "And perhaps all will be well. If it is not . . ." She reached out and touched the younger woman's hand.

Her voice sank almost to a whisper, sweet and strangely audible beneath the voices of servants and grooms, the jingling of horse gear, and the laughter of guests in the court beyond the arcade where they stood. "If it is not, remember that you and your children will always find sanctuary in the Drowned Lands."

Another shadow seemed to thicken from the general gloom behind them; Tally got a brief glimpse of Gyzan the Archer. Then the two wizards stepped back and seemed to melt into the darkness again, becoming one with the shifting reflections of torchlight beneath the arcade.

Tally straightened the collar of pearls and feathers about her neck and tucked with her fingers at the stray tendrils of her hair, preparing to return to the lights and music of the feast. Beneath the green silk of her husband's colors and the thick bullion and pearls, her heart was beating fast. Shavus had brought the others of their Order, to watch beside the Well until the turn of summer—and at the turn of summer, they would bring Rhion and Jaldis back.

If something hadn't happened in that other world.

If they could even *find* that other world in the darkness of the Void.

Mborvianne, guide them . . . Goddess of the Moon, help them . . .

Resolutely stifling the fear that had walked with her every day since the equinox of spring, she started back along the arcade toward the main palace. As she did so a moving shadow caught her eye, slipping from pillar to pillar. At first she thought it was Gyzan and the Lady, but a moment later, as the shadow stepped into the court and vanished into the crowd, she saw that it was only a servant, hastening on some errand from the empty library to the color and life of the feast.

12

"Why wasn't I told you were going to do a major ceremonial last night?"

Von Rath looked quickly up from his breakfast porridge and then away. In the buttercup brilliance of the sunlight pouring through the wide dining-room windows he looked ghastly, drawn and gray and sleepless. As if, Rhion thought, even after he had gone to bed, staggering from the drugs he had taken, he had not slept, but had only lain awake in the whispering darkness, wanting more.

"Baldur only came to me after you had left for the village." Von Rath set his spoon meticulously across the top of the bowl of barely touched oatmeal. On the other side of the room, Poincelles was consuming a hearty plate of bacon and eggs in blithe disregard of Himmler's recommendation that SS Troopers breakfast upon porridge and mineral water—Himmler owned the largest mineral water concession in Germany. On top of Rhion's memories of last night the greasy smell of the bacon was nauseating. Neither Baldur nor Gall were anywhere to be seen.

A little too airily von Rath went on, "Oh, perhaps we should have waited for you to return, but when he showed me the rite he had discovered—decoded from the Venetian Lucalli's diaries—somehow I knew we did not need to wait."

"Like hell." Rhion dropped into a chair. "It takes more than an hour and a half to push through the paperwork to get three prisoners sent over here from Kegenwald for you to disembowel. They're efficient, but they're not that efficient."

The gray eyes met his, the cold opal gaze a stranger's, and Rhion saw again the demon move in their depths. "Do you object to that?"

"I object," Rhion said slowly, picking his words with the utmost care, "to you doing a rite involving human sacrifice, especially an unwilling human sacrifice, without consulting me. The field of power raised from such a sacrifice is septic and unpredictable. Without stronger guards than you can raise in this world, you could end up killing everyone in the house. You don't know how to direct the power you raised last night—you sure as hell didn't know how to disperse it."

Von Rath frowned, genuinely puzzled. With a chill stab of shock Rhion understood then that the man had not even been aware of the horrors that had gibbered in the corners of the darkness last night.

"It was dispersed," von Rath said. "We used the usual formulae . . ."

"The usual formulae are about as effective as a traffic citation against a division of Panzers! The whole house was glowing when I got here. What you did—human sacrifice, especially a torture sacrifice—is the most dangerous way there is of raising power . . ."

"Nonsense." There wasn't even defensiveness in his voice—only a kind of brisk relief. "Human sacrifice has been practiced since the dawn of time, and the Adepts of the Shining Crystal never spoke of danger, though they regularly used this method of raising power." He spoke with the same matter-of-fact calm with which he had quoted his "scientific" statistics on the intelligence of women or the cultural superiority of the Aryan race. "And in any case," he went on, "they were not true human beings. The women were gypsies, the boy a Jew."

Rhion looked away from him, his fist clenching involuntarily with rage, fighting back words that wouldn't change the calm conviction in those opaque eyes but would only put paid to what little freedom of action he himself might still have. Von Rath had once said to him *Surely you've tried to have a reasonable argument with a woman* . . . Rhion had had plenty of those, but what he'd never had—though he'd occasionally been foolish enough to try—had been a reasonable argument with a member of either sex in the grip of an obsession that amounted to lust.

After a few moments he said quietly, "I don't care if they were Hitler's charladies and the King of Belgium; unless the victim is willing, a blood-rite with a sentient intelligence runs the risk of releasing forces that can completely distort the powers raised. You raised a hell of a lot of power last night, but without physical operancy—without technique—*you can't control it*."

Von Rath leaned forward and, with slender white fingers still stained faintly brown under the nails, moved his porridge bowl just slightly, so that the edge of the saucer lined up perfectly with the waxed oak grain of the table's wood. "And whose fault is it," he asked gently, "that we do not have physical operancy?"

Rhion experienced a sensation exactly similar to that of a man hanging by a rope above an abyss, when he feels the first strand part. *Oh, Christ.*

Von Rath went on in that soft, level voice, "You were the one who told us that the Rites of the Shining Crystal, should we decode them, would be of no use to us. Fortunately Baldur saw in them more promise than you apparently did."

"What Baldur saw in them was the possibility of power." Rhion had known that this would come, but still he felt the blood leaving his extremities. He was aware as he never had been before of his absolute isolation in this place, of von Rath's absolute power over him . . . of the beating of his own heart. "What he didn't see—what my guess is he didn't want to see—is their danger to the magician who uses them."

"And why was there no mention of this danger made by the Adepts of the Shining Crystal themselves?"

"Maybe because they were so goddam vain they wouldn't admit there might be anything wrong with what they were doing?"

"Or because their own souls were strong enough to shed the petty hates of the weak?" Von Rath broke off suddenly, dark brows flinching as if at the bite of unexpected pain. He put his hand to his smudged and sunken eyes, and shook his head.

"I—I'm sorry," he said softly. When he looked up the metallic hardness had faded momentarily from his eyes, leaving them again the eyes of the young man who had dreamed of wizardry, who had asked only to be taught. "I don't know what . . . Rhion, I respect your learning. You still have a great deal of technique to teach me, and I admit I am still a novice." He frowned, trying to collect his thoughts. "But it is plain to me that you do not understand the nature of—of heroism, for want of a better word. There comes a time when a student must realize his own truth, not his teacher's; when a man must see with his own heart and his own eyes, not through books written by other men. It is intuition and courage that lie behind great deeds, not hairsplitting pedantry for its own sake."

"In other words experience isn't valid if it isn't *your* experience?" Rhion retorted dourly, recognizing the image of the intuitive Aryan hero from the cheaper sort of pulp fiction and the more fatuous articles in *Der Sturmer* available in the watch room. He knew that at this point he should have gotten up and left, but he was angry as well as scared, angry at that arrogance, angry for the old man he had seen with the wounded lip, angry for last night's dead.

"I'm saying it is valid only up to a point. Then a man must learn, and know for himself. It isn't the first time human sacrifice has been performed in the cause of the Black Order, you know."

"No," Rhion agreed slowly. "But as I understood it, the sacrifices performed by the SS at Welwelsburg were of volunteers, SS men themselves. A willing sacrifice is an entirely different matter, a completely different way of raising power."

"Is it?" Von Rath tilted his head a little, that opaqueness, that curious opalescent quality, slowly filtering back into his fatigue-shadowed eyes. "I wonder. But in any case our needs now are different. We must obtain the wherewithal to defeat Britain and defeat her quickly. And in so doing, we will give the SS power to become the Holy Order it should be, so that it can take its rightful place in the defense of the Reich and its destiny." His cool gaze seemed distant, fixed upon some unknown point, some ancient dream. "And that power now lies in my hands."

"It doesn't," Rhion said, his voice steady but his heart beating hard. "And it won't."

The gray gaze didn't even shift, didn't acknowledge that anything could stand in its way. "It will. Given time—and correct teaching." He turned back to Rhion, studying him with glacial, objective calm. "Tell me . . . Do you object to the blood-rites on so-called human-itarian grounds, or because of the danger?"

Rhion closed his eyes, seeing again the brown gypsy woman's body, the inked blue symbols of the rites barely visible under the blood that glistened everywhere on the shredded skin. He under-stood then the black self-loathing he'd read on everything Sara had touched. "What you do with your criminals here is no concern of mine," he made himself say. "But for preference I'd rather not be in the Schloss at all while you're performing a blood-rite." Every-thing within him was screaming *Coward. Coward and whore.* And looking up, he saw the words reechoed in the contemptuous thinning of von Rath's colorless lips.

"Of course I respect your wishes," the SS wizard said. "But you will give us the benefit of your wisdom and your teaching betweentimes? Because we will master this, Rhion." His tone glinted like the blued edge of a knife. "And let us have no more—ah—judgments on your part as to what is and is not safe for us to know. Understand?"

And with a gesture infinitely graceful he drained his glass of min-eral water and, rising, walked from the room.

"In other days," Baldur read, his thin voice freed for once of its nervous stammer as it framed the sonorous Latin of the ancient text, *"a mage alone could call forth power by simple acts, or by words spoken either aloud or within the mind, as in ancient times men spoke face to face with gods."*

He paused to turn a page: a narrow book, bound in brown leather mottled and crumbling with mildew, its parchment pages hand-copied, so Baldur claimed, by a scholar in the old city of Venice three centuries ago from documents far older, documents copied in Byzantium from sources more ancient still. This was a usual claim made by occult so-cieties, in Rhion's world as in this one. Baldur, no novice at dating manuscripts, had affirmed that this copy had indeed originated in the seventeenth century—a designation that puzzled Rhion, for, though records went back over forty centuries in places, this world seemed to count their years in both directions from the middle. The seventeenth century (counting forward) had been a time of intensive occult activity just before the rise of mechanistic industrialism. Through a sentence in a papal letter and a reference in the Dee correspondence, Baldur claimed to have identified the Venetian scholar Lucalli as a possible member of the infernal Shining Crystal group, though no direct mention was made of it either in Lucalli's diary or in this *Praecepta*, which, though catalogued in his library in the 1908—counting forward— inventory, might or might not have been his. But from what he had heard of the text, Rhion thought it was a good guess.

"Now men must have resort to the wills of a great congregation of folk, joined together with one accord and stirred up by dancing and the beating of drums and by the act of generation promiscuously performed (all these methods being anciently employed to rouse up the vital flames). More and more the Adept must rely upon the turning of the stars and the taking of the Universe at its flow-tide, and upon the use of potions and salves which free the spirit and stir forth the vital flame of life from their flesh. For mark this: there is an energy, a fire, in the human flesh and the human soul, from which magic can be woven."

Lounging in his corner near the window of the dimly curtained library, Poincelles glanced up from his own book and smiled.

"All possess this flame in some measure, but to greater or lesser extent, as fire burns the more or less brightly from oil depending on the degree to which it is pure. Most brightly it burns in the True Adepts, who by means of drugs and potions can call it forth from themselves at will; but lesser men of wisdom still have great measure of this flame. Even the dross of humanity, the human cattle which eat grass and breed and exist only for the purposes of the True Adepts, possess it in some degree, and thus can be used, as the flesh of cattle is used to sustain the life of a true man. This the Indian wizards of the New World knew, when they made their sacrifices; this the devotees of the black cults of Atys and Magna Mater understood, when they performed deeds for which the Emperor Trajan had their names stricken from the records of history. And this knowledge has been handed down unto those who understand.

"And it's true, it worked," Baldur added, looking up.

In the filtered afternoon light coming through the library windows the boy looked absolutely awful, his face like putty behind the thick spectacles, his hands trembling where they lay on the stained parchment page. His repeated sniffling informed Rhion also that Baldur had fortified himself with a quick sniff of his favorite poison before leaving his room, where he'd lain in a stupor since concluding his part of last night's experiment. *No fear from this group,* Rhion thought with dour irony, settling deeper into the tapestry embrace of a worn wing chair. *They'll dope themselves to death before they can destroy the world.*

But it was what they would do in the meantime that had him worried.

"What?" he asked cautiously.

"Don't you see? Of c-course you have to see!" Baldur almost shouted at him, twitching impatiently in his chair and dragging a damp and crumpled sleeve under his raw nostrils. "Those gypsy b-b-bitches last night, and the Jew . . . Pau—er—the Captain sent for them specially. The wo-women were fortune-tellers, the brat a psychic of some kind, I forget what. The Captain was wise enough—it was his idea to have anyone with p-power be picked up. 'Sp-Specially Designated.' He knew we'd need them."

"You mean, whether they'd done anything wrong or not?"

Baldur stared at him, flaccid lips agape. "They were *Jews*," he pointed out. "And anyway the experiment worked! We were right! Thursday night—at the dark of the moon—we'll work the rite using someone of greater power, greater magic, and we'll make a talisman of p-power that'll blow the roof off the building!"

"That's exactly what I'm afraid of."

Baldur heaved a sigh and slumped back in his chair, his weak brown eyes dreamy. "What a pity they destroyed it. The Shining Crystal . . . Do you think it might have been one and the same with the Holy Grail? Wolfram von Eschenbach describes the Grail as a stone, you know. Just like the Jewish-Christian Church to have pulverized such a talisman and slaughtered its guardians!"

"Jewish-Christian Church?" Rhion was startled. "I thought the Christians spent the last ten centuries killing the Jews!"

Baldur waved an airy hand. "They all come from the same source," he declared, as if that made them a single organization.

"They hate and suppress m-magic, the same way they've tried to suppress the pure Aryan Race, whose birthright true magic is."

"And whose most sterling representative and spokesman you are?" Poincelles purred maliciously.

Baldur's pasty face blotched with red. "My family can trace its German heritage back past 1640!"

"Ah, I see—that should get you into the SS with no problem, then, shouldn't it?"

The boy jerked furiously to his feet, his pudgy hands bunching with rage, and Rhion caught his arm and pulled him back as he started toward the Frenchman. To Poincelles, Rhion snapped, "Look, if you're going to waste your time pulling the wings off flies, why don't you do it someplace where it won't waste my time, too? Christ, it's like being in a girls' school—except if Baldur were a schoolgirl, you'd be doing more to him than calling him names."

Poincelles grin widened appreciatively. *"Touché,"* he murmured, rising; book under his arm, he strolled out onto the veranda just beyond the long windows, where Gall, stripped to a loincloth, was engaged in boneless runic yoga in the pale afternoon sun.

"French-Jewish pig," Baldur gritted, bending down to scrabble for the notes he'd knocked off the table in his hysterical haste. He puffed a little as he moved; the thin bar of sunlight, penetrating from the curtain Poincelles had left open, picked out a mist of sweat on his pimpled forehead.

"Is he Jewish?" Sara hadn't mentioned it.

Baldur shrugged. "All the French are." It was a statement Rhion knew to be untrue. "They're a degenerate race—apemen, beastmen, whose only desire is genetically to pollute the Aryans, the true descendants of the Atlantean root race, through the s-sexual corruption of their wo-wo-women." He straightened up, barely missing the edge of the table with his head, his hands shaking badly as he shuffled his papers into order once again.

His pouchy eyes gazed past Rhion after the older occultist with sudden, jealous hate. In a low, furious mutter he went on, "It's against him and men like him that the SS was formed. The real SS, the inner core of the SS—the shining sword blade of the Aryan Race that will turn the tide of genetic slopwork that threatens to engulf us from the

East! We're more than just an imperial guard, you know," he went on, turning to meet Rhion's eyes. "We're a religious order, like the ancient Teutonic Knights, a sacred band of all that's best of the Aryan Race. It's only fitting that we, with our birthright of magic, of *vril*, should be doing what we're doing now—forming a point of adamant for the spear of our destiny. Paul—P-Paul understands."

He gestured angrily toward the windows, beyond which, by Gall's furious gesticulations, it was obvious Poincelles had succeeded in baiting the Austrian mage. "And Himmler uses men like *that* for his purposes! When P-Paul comes into his own, when they make him head of the SS—as they'll have to, when by magic we encompass the British defeat!—the Order will be as it should be, as it has always been destined to be, a sacred band of blood and fire and m-m-magic—"

"Baldur . . ."

The boy almost leaped out of his chair at the sound of von Rath's quiet voice. Without so much as an *Excuse me* he abandoned Rhion and hurried into the hall—from his seat in the wing chair, Rhion could see the two of them standing together, the boy clutching his notes to his sagging breasts and nodding, the man speaking softly, his head tilted a little to one side, sunlight from the hall window dappling his black shoulders, his pale hair, and the scarred left profile visible through the door with pallid gold. Von Rath said something and gestured toward the library door; Rhion thought the heard his name, but the Nazi mage made no move to greet him or to enter the room.

He understood—he had understood at breakfast—that he had placed himself outside the circle of those whom von Rath considered his own kind, placed himself, in effect, with the women and children being used for strafing practice on the road. He was now merely useful, for as long as that would last.

13

"You're crazy!"

"I thought your degree was in chemistry, not psychiatry," Rhion retorted, pulling up his feet to sit cross-legged on the lumpy bed. "You have a better suggestion?"

"Yeah," Sara said hotly. "I smuggle my father a gun instead of those silly pills and have him shoot *himself* instead of letting the guards do it."

"If you could figure out a way to smuggle your father a gun instead of the pills we wouldn't be having these problems."

"No." She sighed and shook her head, frizzy red hair catching the light of the candles in gold threads all around her square, slender shoulders as she leaned back in the room's rump-sprung stuffed chair. "If Papa tried to blast his way out, he'd just hurt himself, or get into an argument about time travel or the internal combusion engine with the guards . . . Not that he knows anything about the internal combusion engine. When Mama would go visit her sisters in Pozen, my heart was in my throat every time Papa tried to light the stove or cut up a chicken to cook. He once nearly killed himself taking the chessboard down from a shelf." She nudged the two pills—clumsy wads of gritty tallow on a twist of paper—on her knee with a fingertip, not meeting Rhion's eyes. "Maybe we'd better just forget it. Thank you for wanting to help, but . . ."

"You don't think I'm really a wizard, do you?"

She raised black-coffee eyes to his. "Oh, come on," she said gently. "You're sweet—you really are—but I was *raised* around people who thought they were wizards, you know? And about half of them claimed to be from another dimensional plane or from the future or the past, or reincarnated from being Albertus Magnus or the Dalai Lama or some kind of Inca sachem. They'd talk with Papa for *hours* about magic and spiritual forces and they'd swap spells like a couple of grannies trading recipes, and for what? I never saw Papa so much as keep the mice away, let alone make himself invisible so the Nazis wouldn't see him."

"I'm not going to make him invisible," Rhion explained patiently. "I'm just going to make the guards look the other way while he crosses from the infirmary to the fence."

"If you can do that, how come you're sneaking in and out of here under the wire like the rest of us poor mortals?"

"Because it takes about an hour and a half of intense meditation and mental exercises to do it, and it wipes me out for the rest of the night."

"Yeah," Sara said wisely, getting to her feet and taking a cigarette from the pocket of her scarlet frock, "they always had some reason why they couldn't do it either."

Down below the voices of the guards drifted faintly up through the open window, the ubiquitous stink of tobacco smoke vying with the sharp sweetness of the pines. The last of the lingering northern twilight had faded less than an hour ago. As he'd listened to Sara's high heels and Horst's escorting jackboots ascend the attic stairs, Rhion had thought about how badly he'd missed the sound of a woman's voice, surrounded as he had been for months by men.

"Sara," he said, "I know you don't believe in this. But believe that if your father doesn't escape from Kegenwald, he's going to die on the night of the twenty-first of this month in a way you don't want to know about. I need this help, and we've got damn little time. You say you can get into the camp on Sunday?"

She nodded. She'd risen from the chair and walked to the window, to let her cigarette smoke drift out into the luminous dark. Candle-light softened the sharpness of her features and sparkled on the little gold chain she wore around the slender softness of her throat.

It was Saturday night. Von Rath must have paid the owner of the tavern a hefty wad of marks to make up for her absence—beyond a doubt Sara would have to surrender some of what was given her as well. The dress she wore, bias-cut cotton crepe that clung to the curves of breast and hip, was better than her usual work clothes. It had taken Rhion awhile to get used to seeing a woman's calves and ankles so casually displayed, though Dr. Weineke's SS uniform had effectively killed whatever erotic interest he'd felt in the principle.

"They let families in, if the commandant's not being a putz that day," Sara went on. "Sometimes women wait for eight, ten hours outside to see their husbands, and then he decides there's no visiting till next week. They come from all over Germany, you know—it's a work camp, mostly for political prisoners. A lot of the town mayors and priests and union leaders from Poland are there, as well as Germans who said something Hitler or the local party leaders didn't like—or *were* something they didn't like, like Jews or gypsies or Poles. The women bring food and clothing . . ." Her red-painted mouth twisted. "The commandants budget for it in the rations. They count on the men being fed at least half by their families, whether they are or not."

"Have you gone before?"

She shook her head. "Even in different clothes with my hair dyed and those fake glasses I got, I didn't want to risk anyone recognizing me. God knows enough of the guards could." She smoked awhile in silence, dark gaze fixed on some middle distance beyond the window, lost in her own thoughts.

"It's funny," she said softly, her face half turned aside and the cold glare of the floodlights from below picking out the fragile wrinkles and the lines of dissipation around the mouth and eyes. "When I heard they'd picked up Papa—when I'd heard the SS had him in 'special custody'—I thought, Hell, I know how to find him . . . or at least how to make money and get information while I looked. I had God knows how many boyfriends in New York. I worked as an artist's model while I was in school—not that Aunt Tayta ever knew where I was always going in the evenings—and the first year I was in New York, in thirty-four, I worked as a waitress to make money to start at NYU. I used to go out to dinner with one guy, have him bring me home at eight because I said I had to study, have another guy pick me up to go to the movies, have *him* bring me home in time to go out with guy number three for the midnight set at the Cotton Club. So I thought doing what I do now wouldn't be so very different. Christ, was I naïve."

Her lips flinched suddenly, and she looked down, crushing out her cigarette on the windowsill with fingers that shook.

"You must love him a lot," Rhion said quietly. She nodded, not looking, not willing to give him even the words of a reply. The pride in her, the anger at men, and the hatred of having to depend on one, however crazy, for help, was like a wall of thorns. He drew up his knees, wrapped his sweatshirt-clad arms around them. The half-healed knife cut still hurt like hell. "How did you get into Germany?"

"Through Basle." The request for information, for the story, steadied her as he'd hoped it would. "I used to go out with a guy named Blackie Wein—he ran protection for Lepke Buchalter down in the garment district. A mobster," she added, seeing Rhion's puzzled expression. "He was tied up with Murder, Incorporated—the Ice Pick League, they were called—but Blackie was all right. He was a Yankees fan like me. When I heard Papa had been picked up—that he was in 'designated internment'—I didn't know what else to do. I went to Lepke. He put the word out and got me identity papers for two hundred dollars from the daughter of a newspaper editor from Dresden who'd just got out with his family by the skin of his teeth. There was a guy named Fish who did me up a couple more sets to use in emergencies, plus some for Papa—Fish made his living passing bad checks—and another one of Lepke's boys taught me how to pick locks. That was the biggest help when I got to searching this place." She shrugged. "So here I am."

She straightened up, and walked to the chair again, to pick up the little screw of paper with the two waxy, lumpy pills that lay upon its padded arm. For a long moment she stood looking down at them. Then her eyes moved to Rhion, still sitting curled together

on the bed. "This is crazy-stupid." The break in her voice was
infinitesimal. In spite of everything, Rhion thought, she was young
enough to grab at even crazy-stupid hope. She put the pills in her
purse.

Rhion took a deep breath. "You say you can pick locks. Will you
help me with something else?"

With an almost instinctive gesture she moved a step or two away,
putting the iron-spindled footboard of the bed between them and
folding her hands around its upper bar. "Like what?"

As Rhion had suspected, there were rooms in the cellar under
the north wing, directly beneath the temple, on the ley-line itself,
the door hidden behind the piled boxes.

"Yeah, I saw that door," Sara said, as they climbed down the
shaft of the disused kitchen dumbwaiter—an invention Rhion made
a mental note to mention to the Duke's kitchen steward when he
got back, if he got back—clinging to the old rope while their feet
sought the tiny slots let into the brick of its sides. "By the scratches
on the floor it didn't get moved back and forth a lot, so obviously
they weren't keeping anybody down there." Her voice sank from a
whisper to barely a breath as they crawled out into the damp, pitch-
black cavern of the southern part of the cellar. As they ghosted
through the huge main chamber, where the furnace slept like some
somnolent monster in its aura of oily dust, the tinny echo of the
wireless could be heard from the guards' watch room opposite the
door to the cellar stairs. "How the hell can you tell where you're
going?" Her hand pressed his shoulder from behind; without her
high-heeled shoes she was an inch shorter than his own barefoot
height.

"I told you. I'm a wizard."

"Sorry I asked."

She fished the flashlight she usually carried with her from her
purse, put her fingers over the bulb and flicked it quickly on to scan
the far wall. "There."

"Just as I thought." He glanced at the ceiling beams in the blackness.

Even through several feet of floor joists, he could feel the cold evil of the temple as they came beneath its bounds. True to his word, he had gotten Horst to take him down to the Woodsman's Horn the night before last—the night of the moon's dark—and had remained there drinking bad beer and listening to a Beethoven concert over the wireless until the place had closed. It hadn't helped. Even at a distance of twenty miles he'd fancied all evening that he felt what was happening at the Schloss, and had dreaded returning there, fearing what he would find in spite of the doubled and trebled spells of protection and dispersal he had taught von Rath. He didn't know what he'd have done if one of the chosen victims had been Sara's father, but it wasn't. They had used another gypsy woman and a noted German runeologist—Aryan to the core—whose runic system had contradicted the one favored by the Bureau. After one attempt at sleep from which he'd been jerked, sweating in horror, by his dreams, he'd spent the rest of the night staring at the rafters. It seemed to him that the screams of the victims had permeated the very fabric of the house.

That afternoon von Rath had shown to him the talismans they'd made, disks of bone and crystal and stretched skin written over with the dark sigils devised by the accursed Adepts; he had talked for hours, lovingly, eagerly, obsessively, fingering them with wonderment and not seeming to remember that they had been made of the bodies of men like himself. He had spoken of the power within them and how it could be utilized and what he would do when that power was his . . . only that. Rhion did not have to touch the things to know that the power was there, glowing in them against the workroom's lamplit dark as phosphorous glows in the heart of a rotten tree. But neither he nor von Rath could utilize that power for even the simplest of spells they'd tried.

And that, he supposed, was just as well.

The boxes in the cellar were filled with moldy books, smelling of silverfish and mice; it took him and Sara a few minutes to move them aside. Behind them, as Sara had said, was a door, new, stout, and padlocked shut. "Probably used to be a wine room," he remarked in an undervoice, holding the flashlight as the girl knelt and began probing the lock with the various wire tools she'd taken from her purse. "There's marks of an older lock here above the new hasp." Shielding the light with his body, he strained his ears to hear any creak of footfalls in the hall overhead, any sign of approaching guards on the stair, or any clue that their activities were suspected. At this point, they could never hope to get the boxes replaced in time.

"This door isn't more than a year or so old," Sara breathed. "What the hell do you think old Pauli has in here, anyway? All the booze is in the cupboard in the library—all the booze he knows about, anyway; Poincelles has a stash of his own. I don't think he knows about the coke Baldur gets from Kurt at the Horn, or those little odds and ends Gall steals from the workroom . . ."

"Gall?"

"Yeah. He's got these little sacks of seeds and herbs and crystals hidden all around his room, a couple of amulets tucked under a loose floorboard, a mortar and pestle, a set of runestones, and a crystal ball cached in the bedsprings. It was a whole education, going through this place. Bingo," she added, an expression not translatable even with the Spell of Tongues. The padlock fell open.

His heart beating fast, Rhion pushed the door inward.

The Dark Well was there. The smell of the room was the same as he remembered from those first instants of consciousness: moist earth, wet stone, power . . . the strange, ozoneous air of the Void. It was here they had gathered, not in that boarded-up chamber upstairs; it was here they had taken their drugs and reached out over the Void's darkness to guide him and Jaldis. It was here Eric Hagen had died.

The pang of remembering Jaldis again twisted in him like a turned knife. Even now in this nightmare world, he still caught himself thinking that when he returned home the old man would be there. His too-active imagination wondered for a gruesome second whether his master had actually been killed by the Void or was drifting there somewhere, still alive but unable either to escape or die . . . He pushed the thought quickly away. It was something he would never know.

Drawing a deep breath, he stepped back through the door to where Sara waited, staring behind her into the cellar's dark.

"I'm not sure how long this will take," he murmured. "Get back up to the room; if they catch you down here you might be in real trouble."

"Not as much trouble as you're gonna be if they flash a light down the stairs and find all those boxes moved and the door open," she replied, peering hard in the direction of his voice. "I'll stick around."

"Thank you." Not that a warning would do him much good, he reflected. Even if he and Sara managed to reach the dumbwaiter shaft and get out of the cellar and up the backstairs to the dressing room on the second floor, the boxes being displaced would tell von Rath everything he needed to know. At this point he was certain von Rath would dismantle the Dark Well to keep him here—and that would only be the start of his worries.

Sara closed the door, leaving him alone in darkness.

In darkness he could see the traced lines of chalk and long-dried blood that marked where the original rites of opening had been done. The ritually charged swastika that had been his beacon across the Void's darkness was still there beside the triple circle of the Well itself, the symbol of the sun-cross at which he could now barely bring himself to look. Beyond it hung the shimmering brown column of shadow that even mageborn eyes could not pierce.

His pulse thudded loud in his ears as he approached it. The Well was quiescent—he could, he supposed, have passed his hand through it with no ill effects, but nothing would have induced him to try it. And it was so tenuous, he thought—the power that held it here so ephemeral that merely the breaking of the Circles, the erasure of any of the marks upon the floor, would destroy the Well and his chances of contacting the help he needed forever.

For a long time he only stood looking at the place, trying to steady his breathing and his thoughts.

A window into the Void.

A way to get home.

The thing that had killed Eric Hagen.

He could dimly sense the ley running deep beneath his feet, like groundwater in the earth, but he could no more have used its power to open the Void than he could have washed a tent in a thimble. On the night of the solstice, he thought, the power would be there, maybe. But there had better be one hell of a lot of power concentrated at the other end.

He took a deep breath, pushed up the sleeves of his sweatshirt, and, kneeling, took chalk and Sara's clasp knife from his pocket. In the darkness he drew a Circle close to the charged sun-cross on the floor, its edge touching that of the Well itself, and cut open the vein near his right elbow, where it wouldn't show, to mark the signs of Power in his own blood. He had no sense of power in doing this— he never had, in this universe—but he followed the rites meticulously, making himself believe that the faint strength of the ley-path seeped up into the chalked lines, drawing the figures of air as precisely as if they were actually visible, glowing as they would be in his own world. Trying not to think about whether anyone over there was listening.

It had been almost three months. Of course someone would be listening. Jaldis' loft was the only place they could hear, unless Shavus had used the old man's notes to open another Well elsewhere. This close to the solstice, knowing it was the only time when enough power would be available to them here, of course he'd be listening for them . . .

But Shavus had disappeared the day before his and Jaldis' crossing—arrested, murdered, banished . . . he did not know.

Maybe no one knew.

We can think of neither the future that we go to, nor the past that we leave behind . . .

Don't do this to yourself, he commanded, feeling his resolve drain like the faint weakness and shock of opening his vein. *They may not hear you if you shout for help, but they CERTAINLY won't hear you if you don't.*

Only the long disciplines of his training made him turn his mind from the sweet quicksand of despair—of not having to try because it would do no good—and calm his thoughts, quiet his breathing, even out his heart rate again. He sank into meditation, not knowing how long it would take to raise the energies, gathering all his strength into his hands. Though the room was cold, sweat stood out on his face. Clear and hard, he focused his mind on the Dark Well, willing it to open, willing the glowing channel across the endless abyss of color without color to whisper into life.

Nothing happened. The Well did not seem to change.

Deepening his concentration, he started again from the beginning. Marking the floor, the walls; weaving signs in the air cleanly and precisely, willing himself to know that he was making them correctly—willing himself not to doubt. Willing himself not to think about Jaldis; about Tally; about his own world on the other side of the Void; about that naïve young man who'd come stumbling out of the livid darkness ten weeks ago and into the arms of the SS. Willing himself to believe that it worked.

There was still no change in the appearance of the Dark Well, but he sensed—or imagined—a minute drop in the temperature of the room, a resurgence of the queer ozoneous smell. Rising, legs weak, he stepped to the three lines of chalk, blood, and ash that circled the inner core of darkness—a darkness barely distinguishable from the darkness surrounding it—and stood, his stockinged toes just touching the outermost ring, his arms outspread.

"Shavus," he whispered desperately, clinging to the image of the big old scar-faced Archmage, "Shavus, help me. Shavus, I'm in trouble, help me, please. Get me out of here. I'm alone here, Jaldis is dead."

He was tired now and queasy from loss of blood; his head was beginning to throb, but he conjured in his mind the images of the stones on Witches Hill. Between the ancient magic of sacrifice glowing deep in the dolomite's fabric and the dim silvery limmerance of the ley, enough power clung to the Stones to serve as a beacon, if Shavus knew what to look for. At that point, provided the Spiracle would hold the Void's magic—provided he didn't kill himself charging it—he could probably collect enough energy at the turn of the solstice-tide to open the Void and jump.

"I'll be there," he whispered, perhaps aloud, perhaps only in the dark at the bottom of his mind. "At Sunstead I'll be there, waiting. Get other wizards, get as many as you can. I can open the gate, but you'll have to get me through. Help me, Shavus, please. Get me out of here. Please get me out."

He opened his eyes, staring into the heart of the Dark Well, emptying his mind and focusing it with all the strength within him, all the strength he could raise.

He saw nothing.

He closed his eyes, gathering his strength again, patiently willing himself not to think, not to feel. Then he slowly repeated all he had said, conjuring in his mind the image of himself standing on the altar of the Dancing Stones at midnight, surrounded by the Void magic of the Spiracle, the power of the solstice and the leys, arms outstretched, waiting . . .

And repeated it again, the strain of it hurting him now, grinding at his bones. And again saw nothing to tell him that he wasn't just a frightened little man standing with obsessive exactness in a scribbled network of chalked lines on the floor, praying to an empty room.

In other words, he thought, mad.

It was as if he'd stood chin-deep in the ocean and had the rock upon which he was balanced tip suddenly beneath his feet; he felt despair close over him, cold and fathoms deep. A headache clamped like a steel band around his temples, and he lowered his outstretched arms, cramped and trembling, to his sides.

He has to have heard me, he thought, sinking, exhausted, to his knees. *Shavus has to have heard.* Sitting on his heels, he carefully removed his glasses, pressed his throbbing forehead with his hands.

Tally came to his mind, lying by the fire in the green jeweled gown of the Sea-King's daughter—the animal warmth and delight of his sons' small hands pulling at his robe as they cornered him in play. For a moment he saw the matte blue silences of the Drowned Lands under the phosphorous of the rising moon. For ten weeks he had worked very hard at not feeling pain. Now, his defenses spent, the pain came, wave after wave of it, breaking him like a child's driftwood fortress under advancing tide.

He bowed down over his hands, hurting with a deep, gouged ache that was worse than any physical pain he had ever undergone. Hugging himself as if the pain were in fact physical and could be eased by physical means, he doubled over, fighting to stay silent, fighting to hold it in, a chubby, shabby little man in his worn sweatshirt and faded trousers, alone in the dark on the edge of the abyss.

After a long time the pain eased a little, and he knew then that it was close to dawn. The thought of slipping back to his room, of going on with another day, was physically repugnant to him—easier just to roll down onto his side on the stone floor and sleep. But after a few minutes he got to his feet and staggered, knees jellied, to push open the door.

Sara had made her way across the cellar to the stairs that led up to the hall above, where she stood listening, the two-foot iron rod of an old mop-bucket wringer lever in one hand. Above them the Schloss was absolutely silent now, save for the metallic whisper of a wireless turned down low. The guards would be catching a little shut-eye in the watch room. It was a dangerous time, since they'd be guilty enough to wake at a whisper. He breathed, "Sara . . ." and saw her turn sharply, straining her eyes to pierce the inky dark.

As softly as he could—warily, because of the club she held—he glided toward her over the damp stone floor. "Let's get the boxes put back," he whispered, still staying well out of range until he saw her positively identify his voice and relax. Then he took her arm and led her back to where the flashlight beam couldn't possibly be seen from above.

"You want this locked up again?" she asked softly, touching the padlock. "I can put it like this but not snib it closed. That way you can get in here again if you need to."

"I will need to," he said. "But von Rath's getting more suspicious of me every day. If he finds it open, he'll know it's me tampering and will probably destroy the Well. I'll need your help getting in here again, two, maybe three more times . . ."

She muttered something really terrible in Polish and helped him lift each box to avoid scratching the floor and put it back in the order they had been, as precisely as they could recall. As she picked up the flashlight to turn it off she looked briefly at his face in the finger-hooded glow.

"You okay?"

He nodded, turning his face from her and taking her elbow; she switched off the light and let him guide her across the cellar, through the archway, to the old dumbwaiter with its rope and its tiny set-in steps.

The candles in his room had guttered out. He reached with his mind to relight them, then fumbled tiredly in his pocket for a match, the ache of thaumaturgical impotence bringing back the hurt of all that other pain. While Sara put on her high-heeled shoes he sank down onto the bed, head pounding, struggling to keep his grief at bay until she was gone.

"First time I ever left an evening here wearing the same lipstick I came in with," she remarked, though she renewed it for good measure, the glossy red giving her thin, triangular face a pulchritudinous lushness in the candle glow. "Come down to the tavern Monday and I'll let you know how things went. I'll tell Papa not to take the pills till Monday, so we can go through with the rest of this *mishegoss* Wednesday when the shop's closed . . . Hey? You okay?"

He nodded, not looking at her. Worried, she came around the end of the bed to stand looking down at him with her arms folded beneath the soft shelf of her breasts.

"What happened in there?"

"Nothing," he whispered.

She leaned down and gently removed his glasses from his face, putting them on the shelf beside the candle. He ached to touch her— to touch someone, only for the comfort of knowing he wasn't absolutely alone. But to her a man's touch meant only one thing, and she had enough of that, so he didn't.

After a moment she pulled the thin coverlet up over him, turned and blew out the candle. He heard her high heels click away into darkness as she descended the attic stairs, and a few minutes later heard the car engine start outside and fade as it drove off into the night.

In the iron hour before dawn his dreams were evil. Perhaps it was what he had read of the rites of the Shining Crystal; perhaps the souls of the gypsy women, of the young Jewish clairvoyant, and of the elderly runemaster still lingered to vent their bitter rage on one who had acquiesced in their murders. Perhaps it was only fear. In the dream, Rhion found himself bound to one of the pillars in the black-draped temple, forced to watch the rite again and again—saw von Rath, gaunt and yellow as a man with fever in his long white robe, and Poincelles in bloodstained red. Over and over he heard the screaming, as if the sound itself were being drawn and twisted as a spinner twists wool into yarn, drawing strands of power from death and pain. He saw the power itself collecting, like dirty ectoplasmic slime, in pools on the altar, pools that moved a little when no one watched.

And in the morning, at the rites of meditation that they still performed, though to Rhion's mind they had become a travesty of the calm opening to ritual work for which they had been designed, he observed their faces, wondering if they, too, had dreamed.

Gall, it was hard to tell. There was always a weird serenity about the old man, a calm that had nothing to do with right or wrong but depended entirely on his rigid apportioning of bodily and psychic energies, as if, for him, ultimately nothing really existed beyond the bounds of his own skin. Baldur, standing under the bloodred rune of Tiwaz at the northern "watchtower," was twitchy and nervous, eyes glittering behind his thick glasses as if, between his endless quest for knowledge in the ancient books and the psychoactive drugs he was taking, cocaine was the only thing keeping him together.

Poincelles . . . If Poincelles dreamed, Rhion thought, regarding the gangling, dirty man with sudden revulsion, it was with a smile on his lips. That smile lingered now, as he made his responses with an air of amused tolerance for the peccadilloes of others. If von Rath sought the wine of power in the bloody rites of the Shining Crystal, Rhion now understood, what Poincelles enjoyed was the pressing of the grapes.

But it was von Rath who frightened Rhion most. Standing by the dark-draped altar, his hands outspread over the ritual implements there—sword and cup, book and thurifer—he was visibly thinner than he had been a week ago, as if the obsession with power—with converting power to operancy—were slowly consuming both flesh and mind.

Neitzsche, philosophical guru of the Nazi Party, had spoken of the triumph of the will, but as things were in this world it was physically impossible for von Rath's will to triumph.

And as the warm spring days crept past and the moon waxed to its first quarter and then to a bulbous distorted baroque, Rhion saw more and more frequently that icy flatness in the young wizard's eyes, and felt them on his back as he came and went.

It made things no easier that on Monday evening, in between her desultory flirting with the local Party official and a couple of guards from the Kegenwald camp—Monday was a quiet night in the tavern—Sara slipped him a note under his beer mug that simply read: *No soap*. In German the phrase indicated only that bathing would be an unsatisfactory experience, but in the parlance of American cinemas it meant a miscarriage of plans.

"Scum-sucking momzer didn't even let us in," Sara muttered savagely two nights later, when she was once again up in his room. The tavern was closed Tuesdays and Wednesdays, and she and the leggy blond Ulrica had been brought out to the Schloss at Rhion's request and Poincelles'. Her hair, dyed brown on Sunday for her visit to the camp, was now stiffer, frizzier, and redder than ever in the dim glow of the candles and the reflection of the primus stove they'd pilfered from the workroom, a scalding frame for her alabaster pallor that clashed loudly with the pink of the worn and pilled angora sweater she wore.

"We waited from seven in the morning until nine at night—some of those poor broads had been on the train since nine the night before, coming in from Berlin and Warsaw and God knows where— just sitting outside the gates of the camp on the ground, without water, without nothing." Her small, quick hands squeezed out a rag in the water she was heating; it steamed in the balmy warmth as she crossed to the bed and dabbed at the half-healed knife cut on the back of Rhion's arm.

As she worked she continued bitterly, "We were scared to walk across the road to take a squat behind a bush in the woods, for fear they'd say *okay, come on in* while we were gone, with the guards all coming around and hassling whoever they thought was worth it. And there was I, feeling like I was sitting naked in the middle of Ebbets Field, praying the ones I'd screwed wouldn't recognize me because I sure as hell wouldn't recognize them, hiding behind a pair of fake glasses and trying to look frumpy and middle age . . . Christ!"

Her hand where it steadied his bared arm squeezed tight with rage so that even the chewed-short nails bit into his flesh. "And at the end of it some tight-assed kapo comes out and says 'No visitors today. The prisoners are being punished.'"

"For what?"

"Who knows? Who cares?" She dropped the cloth on the floor, and the smell of cheap gin filled the room as she soaked a second rag—the last scrap of Rhion's old shirt. The alcohol stung his skin. "Still looks clean, but you're gonna have a bitch of a scar," she added, binding the wound up again.

"Whose fault is that?" He pulled on his sweatshirt again, though the night was warm enough to have given him no discomfort; Sara gathered the discarded rags and draped them over the edge of the table to dry, then bent to light a cigarette in the flame of the primus stove. "That pushes it till next Sunday." His eyes went involuntarily to the spot in the rafters that was the Spiracle's latest hiding place. "And that's the last Sunday before the solstice."

"You don't think I know that?" She dropped angrily back onto the bed, back propped on the iron-spindled headboard, and reached across to the tableful of bedside candles to take an angry swig from the flask of medicinal gin. "Crazy goddam witch-doctors . . ." She blew a stream of smoke.

Rhion decided not to mention that von Rath had spoken of doing another experiment—not merely the making of talismans, but an attempt to convert the power of the sacrifice into workable illusion—on the night of the full moon, six nights hence and a few days before the greater rite and talisman-making on the solstice itself. If they were lucky, Sara's father would be out of danger by that time anyway. The thought of what he'd have to do if they *didn't* succeed in freeing the old man brought the sweat cold to his face.

"What is that thing, anyway?"

He glanced across at her with a start. Sara, her knees crossed in a soft waterfall of skirt gores, was looking up at the Spiracle's hiding place. "That iron and silver gismo with the crystals in it. Do all wizards hide little *tchotchkes* around where they live? Papa did."

Rhion grinned, remembering Jaldis' propensity for secret devices. "Pretty much," he said. "It's the thing I need your father's help—and yours, since you'll have to get us into that room in the cellar again—to finish." He pushed the delicate wire frame of his spectacles more firmly up onto his nose. "The rite of charging it has to be done by the solstice," he added, more quietly. "If we can't get your father out by then . . ." He shivered at the thought of taking the thing down to the cellar and stepping into the Dark Well without another wizard present to keep him from being drawn in and destroyed.

"Then we'll get him out afterward." Sara's gaze, holding his, was flint. "Won't we?"

Rhion said nothing. If they didn't get the old man out before solstice-tide the odds were horribly good he himself would be dead afterward. If he wasn't, it would be because he'd lost his nerve at the last moment—in which case it was one *hell* of a long time to the equinox, too long to count on—or because he'd succeeded, impossibly, in charging the Spiracle himself.

And in that case, he thought, could he leave Sara to her own devices? He remembered the brief vision in the scrying crystal, the old man with the scarred lip raising his eyes to the window far above his head. He owed neither of them a thing—his arm still hurt every time he moved it and he was damn lucky, given his inability either to work healing spells or get proper attention to the wound, that it hadn't festered.

But he knew the man was a wizard. He'd seen it in his eyes. And yet it was the solstice or nothing. He hoped he wouldn't have to make that choice.

Walking to the window, he felt Sara's dark eyes follow. Out in the yard one of the floodlights had gone out, and upon the ground below him he could see the ochre smear of reflected candlelight that marked von Rath's study window. A shadow passed across it: the SS wizard pacing, restless, fevered, an animal driven by invisible goads, far into the night.

14

Sara whispered, "This had better work." Her hands, as she shoved her crazy hair up under a man's cloth cap, were steady and her white face calm, stark without its habitual disguise of lipstick and paint. But the brazen glare of the camp floodlights at the bottom of the hill caught the fine glitter of sweat on her short upper lip.

Rhion only nodded. He wanted to reassure her, but was too deep in his trance of concentration to speak. In any case they had been through it all on the drive from the crossroads near the Schloss where Sara had picked him up.

In the surrounding dark of the pinewoods a nightingale warbled. Six miles away, the Kegenwald village church clock spoke its two notes, the sound carrying clearly in the moonless hush of the night. These sounds, like Sara's voice, seemed to come to Rhion from a very great distance, clear but tiny, like images in the scrying crystal. Far more real to him were the two watchtowers of the Kegenwald camp perimeter visible from this hillside, open wooden turrets mounted on long legs like sinister spiders, each ringed in floodlights and dark within.

He stood in each of those watchtowers, a shadowy consciousness more real to him now than the body kneeling in its scratched protective circle just within the gloom of the woods' edge. He spoke to each man separately—a flaxen-haired boy in the left-hand turret, an older man, tough and scarred with a broken nose, in the right. They did not precisely hear his voice, as he whispered to them the dreamy, buzzing songs of nothingness that the Ladies of the Drowned Lands had taught him. But they listened nevertheless, gazing idly in opposite directions, outward into the night.

It was not an easy illusion to maintain. With his own awareness split into dim ectoplasmic twins, he had to keep within his mind from instant to instant the separate realities of the two watchtowers—the hollow clunk of wooden floors underfoot, the dark webwork of the struts that supported the roof and the pattern the wires stapled to them made, leading up to the lights above; the moving sharpness of the air from the bristled darkness of the woods; the murky nastiness of the men's dreams. To the older sentry Rhion breathed songs dipped from the man's cramped and limited mind, the taste of liquor and blue tobacco smoke woven into fantasies of endless, repetitive, impossible intercourse with woman after woman, and all of them alike, all gasping with delight or sobbing with grateful ecstasy. To the younger, after searching the narrow hate-stained thoughts, he wove a different dream, of assembling, disassembling, assembling again some kind of automatic weapon, polishing, cleaning, making all perfect. Oddly enough he sensed the same pleasure in the precise click and snap of metal and the neat, controlled movements as the first Trooper had in his reveries of bulling endless willing blondes.

What facets of human nature these dreams revealed he couldn't allow himself to speculate, nor upon how close this magicless magic of dream and illusion was to the very devices von Rath hoped to use against the British pilots when the invasion began. It was difficult enough to maintain them, to renew again and again the sharp sweetness of their pleasure, as if every time were the first—to inject the tiniest twinge of regret and hurt if either man turned his eyes even slightly toward the hillside between the woods and the barbed-wire fence, or thought about looking back at the stretch of open ground behind them that separated the fence, with its electrified inner pale, from the long gray building of the camp infirmary.

Fence and camp lay starkly naked beneath the floodlights' acrid glare, exactly as Sara had described them, exactly as he had glimpsed them in his crystal; the hillside was bare of cover, clothed only with a thin scrim of grass against which, now, Sara's gray trousers and pullover stood out dark and unmistakable as she crept toward the fence. She moved as he had instructed her, crouched close to the earth. A few slow steps and stillness, count ten, two more slow steps and stillness again, an even, gentle progression that would not catch the guards' dreaming attention. In a long, lumpy, muslin flour sack at her belt, she carried wire cutters, wire, and wooden props to get her under the inner electric fence. Edging forward under the barrels of the turret guns, there was nothing else she could possibly have been.

Yet neither guard moved. The slight relaxation induced by the nicotine they smoked Rhion subtly deepened, increasing with his songs the influence of the drug. To them it had never tasted so good, to them their dreams had never been so fulfilling, so hurtfully satisfying . . .

Just as Sara finished cutting a slit in the wire of the fence, the back door of the infirmary opened. Through a haze of oiled machinery and shuddering bosoms Rhion was aware of the tall, raw-boned form standing in the shadowy opening, the floodlight throwing a coarse glitter of silver on scalp and jaw as he turned his head, looking doubtfully from one tower to the other. Then he looked across the open ground.

It was nearly seventy feet from the shelter of the shadowed door to the wire. The infirmary stood a little apart from the ugly ranks of green-painted barracks, ground commanded by the wooden towers and the dark muzzles of the guns. Between the towers Sara was a sitting target, propping up the electrified wire of the inner fence with two lengths of wood. The old man shrugged and walked forward—slowly, as Rhion had hoped Sara remembered to specify in her whispered instructions of last Sunday.

. . . *red lips parted in a gasp of ecstasy, a white throat exposed by a thrown-back head . . . Oh, thank you, thank you . . . Just so much solvent on the patch . . . ram home . . .*

One of the guards shifted his weight to scratch his crotch, started

to turn toward the yard behind him. But sudden cold, sudden sorrow, overwhelmed him, an aching loneliness—and there was, after
all, no need. Everything was quiet. His daydream smiled and beckoned, a warm cocoon of virile joy. He gave a sort of sigh and settled
back as he had been before, his chin on his fist.

The old man squirmed awkwardly under the wire, sat up, looked
with a start at what he must have assumed until then to be a young
man, in her trousers and pullover, with her hat pulled down to hide
her flaming hair. Rhion saw him grasp her arm, saw her shake free
and signal for silence.

She pulled the props loose, shoved them into her bag, and took
out a bundle of short pieces of wire. The old man slipped through
the hole in the fence and waited while Sara pulled the slit shut again,
secured it with a dozen twists of wire so it wouldn't be obvious from
a distance that it had been cut. Then they moved forward gingerly,
slowly, under the dreaming eyes of the guns.

*. . . touch of gun oil in the lock, a touch in the pin housing . . . not
too much, too much is as bad as too little . . . they can never say I was
less than perfect . . . soft white hands with red nails digging into the
muscles of the back . . . The sweaty softness of those massive breasts, of
thighs clutching at his hips . . . Again, oh please, again . . .*

Sweat ran down Rhion's face, his muscles aching as if the intensity
of his concentration were a physical labor. *Dammit, come on, I can't
keep on with this . . .*

A few steps and pause. Wait. Creep-creep-pause. The floodlights
glared behind them like harsh yellow moons, throwing feeble shadows on the bare ground, like two bugs paralyzed on a kitchen floor.
The night breeze turned, and Rhion smelled a vast stench of human
filth, overcrowded quarters, and, deeper and more hideous, the stink
of death and narrow-minded evil.

They reached the trees. The old man flung his arms around Sara,
bending his tall height to clasp her close, and even in his tranced
state Rhion reflected that it was the first time he'd seen Sara respond
with uncalculated warmth to any man's touch. She reached joyfully
up to fling her arms around his neck, for that one second her father's
little girl again, happy, clean, and filled with love. His mind still on
the guards, Rhion didn't hear clearly the old man's first half-sobbing

words or what Sara replied, but he saw her place a hand on her father's arm when he turned toward where Rhion knelt and shake her head. As Rhion had instructed her beforehand, she led her father away through the bracken and impenetrable shadows, toward the road where the Mayor of Kegenwald's car was hidden.

Rhion let his mental voice die into a gentle soughing. His two dim psychic twins stepped in unison to the wide openings in the turret walls, swung themselves over the wooden rails and out into the dark air. Between the towers they met and melded into one. For a moment from that high vantage point, Rhion looked down on the camp itself, long wooden buildings already beginning to warp and split, heavier cement constructions beyond them—barracks, offices, workrooms, cells of solitary confinement or special purpose, raw-new or the older structures of the old pulp mill the place had originally been—and the pale barren rectangle of the exercise yard, all lying stark and motionless within the steel-thorned boundary of towers and fence. And because he was not within his body, he saw clearly the glow of horror that hung over the place, a sickly greenish mist, as if the very air were rotting from what was done within that place.

Turning, sickened, Rhion looked out over the woods and road in the luminous chill of the starlight. The somber pines were still and utterly dark. He saw no cars, no track of trampled bracken, and no sign that they had been pursued, observed, or detected. So far, so good.

He walked down over the air above the defoliated hillside, and in the darkness at the woods' rim saw a pudgy little form in old army trousers and a snagged white sweater, kneeling with head bowed in the dim scratchwork of a magic circle, the starlight glinting in his silver-rimmed glasses and on the sweat upon his face. He passed through the invisible door that lay between them, settling himself around the armature of those sturdy bones; then closed and sealed the door behind him.

Sickness hit him like a blow with a club. He doubled over, swearing in German as he felt the blood leave his face and extremities; though it was a mild night, he shivered with desperate chill, hair and clothing sticking to him with sweat. Knees trembling with cramp, he got somehow to his feet and staggered off through the dark woods to the disused woodsman's track where they'd hidden the car.

Sara was busy renewing the hot-wiring of the little Ford's engine when he arrived. "Christ, I don't believe it!" she breathed, as he slumped down onto the running board. "I don't effing believe it! We must have been out in the open for thirty minutes! What the hell did you do?"

"I told you I'm a wizard." He managed to grin.

"Are you all right, my son?" A long, bony hand closed around his arm, gently raising him. He looked up and met the dark eyes of the man he'd seen in the scrying crystal, the thin old man with the shaven head and the raw, new scar on his lip.

"Yeah," he whispered, but when the old man opened the door for him Rhion almost fell into the car's backseat. "I'll be fine in a minute."

The car moved off, Sara guiding it carefully down a farm track that had mostly gone back to ruts and potholes where it twisted through bracken, wild ivy, and trees. She dug in the glove box and produced a bar of American chocolate candy wrapped in paper, which she passed to them over the back of the front seat. "Give him this, Papa."

Rhion gulped down half of the bar's oily sweetness without even tasting it, then remembered Sara's father probably hadn't had anything resembling decent food for nine months and held out the rest of it to him.

The old man turned it over in long, blue-veined fingers, sniffed it interestedly, and said, "Well, according to Sylvester Graham, sugar is a pollution of the temple of the body, and I'm not sure whether chocolate is kosher or not because who knows what they put into the stuff, but as Rabbi Hillel said, it isn't what goes into a man's body that defiles it, but the words that come out of a man's mouth . . . So I think an exception is in order. Thanks be to God . . . and to you, my son." He popped the chocolate into his mouth and clasped Rhion's hand while he chewed and swallowed. "And you are? My daughter only said she had a friend who would get me out."

"Professor Rhion Sligo." The Germanized form of the name was second nature to him now.

"Isaac Leibnitz. I don't always smell like this, but I don't suppose Jonah was any bundle of roses when he came out after spending three days in the belly of a fish, either. So they teach driving cars as well as stealing them in this New York University you went to, Saraleh?"

"You'd rather I stayed in Germany and learned to cook and clean and have babies for our Führer?" she tossed back over her shoulder. In point of fact the old man smelled like an animal, his patched clothing half rotted with old sweat and crawling with fleas, his mouth, when he spoke, showing the dark gaps of missing teeth. He was pallid, emaciated, and still shaky from two days of being sick from the pills Rhion had sent to guarantee that he'd be in the poorly guarded infirmary instead of the concrete cell in which "specially designated" prisoners were kept. But for all of that, there was about him a daft and gentle charm such as Rhion had encountered in other wizards in his own world, infinitely comforting in its familiarity after the greed, fanaticism, and inhuman obsessions of the Schloss Torweg mages.

"What *did* you do?" he asked gently after a moment. "Except deliver me from out of Gehinnom, for which I will always be more in your debt than you can ever conceive. What's your birthdate, by the way?"

"Don't thank me yet." Rhion sat up and produced a handkerchief from his pocket to polish his glasses. "I'm afraid I'm going to ask you to stick around for a few days and return the favor. As for what I did, I guess it's called astral planing here. I'd meant to cast a spell of distraction on both guards, but I couldn't do it from that distance."

"No wonder you're tired," Leibnitz commented, stroking his stubbled lip in a kind of subconscious mourning for his vanished beard, while Sara made an undervoiced comment of her own in the front seat.

Rhion sighed and put his glasses back on. "It all takes so goddam much time and energy. I don't know how much Sara told you . . ."

"What could she say, with all those chaperons standing around with rifles? She said you'd get me out if I took the pills, was sick two days, and then got up at two in the morning and walked out across the back exercise yard slow enough to let the guards take real good aim at me. She said I had to have faith."

"It must have sounded pretty crazy."

He shrugged. "They say the Red Sea didn't part for the Children of Israel until the first man got his feet wet. But to get my daughter to believe you—now that's magic."

Rhion's grin was wry. "Believing crazy things seems to be what's done in this country. I'm working for the SS Occult Bureau. They're keeping me prisoner at Schloss Torweg, an old hunting lodge about forty kilometers from here. Are you familiar with the theory of multiplicity of universes, or am I going to have to go through this explanation from scratch?"

"No, no." Rebbe Leibnitz shook his head decisively. "Are you from another world on the same cosmic plane as ours—that is, Malkut, the plane of material reality—or from one of the spiritually higher planes?"

"Same plane," Rhion said, since, as far as he knew, multiplanar cosmic reality was as unprovable in his own world as it was in this. "I'm a wizard there—operative magic works there as it no longer works here. That was originally the reason my master wanted us to come here—to find out why it no longer works." He bit his lip, remembering Jaldis again with a sudden stab of unhealed loss.

"Well, my personal theory is that the roads from the spiritual Sephiroth of Tepheret to the Sephiroths of Yesod and Malkut have become blocked due to the increased influences of the elements of sulfur and fire, though that wouldn't take into account why it still works in other universes than this. Numerologically this century lies under the influence of Mars, always a bad time for those under the protection of the Beni-Elohim, the Angels of the Sephiroth of Hod. But I've heard other theories. I've met wizards from other universes before, you understand, both of the dense physical plane and those who were of a higher spiritual order, merely disguising themselves in the form of matter. There was an Englishman named Galworthy possessed by a spirit named Angarb-Koleg—and that young fellow Inglorion who stayed with me in thirty-eight—and that Theosophist woman Zelzah the Red who was traveling from dimension to dimension preaching the true path to rightness. She used to hold seances at our apartment on Gestia Ulica to contact spirits in other universes—she said the vibrations there were sympathetic—and in fact it was there she met Antonio Murillo, who it turned out had known her in a previous existence when he was a priest of the ancient Egyptian cult of Ptah and she was a temple prostitute . . ."

Rhion had heard all about ancient Egyptian cults and their reincarnated priests from Poincelles. No wonder Sara looked at him strangely. "And you?"

Leibnitz made a dismissive gesture. "Oh, I'm just a student, a scholar," he said. "All I can do is keep an open mind. All my life I've studied the Talmud and the Kabbala, searching for order in the universe, but it's a dangerous thing to translate the power one channels down from Higher Aether through the Tree of Life into magic here—"

"Aside from the fact that it can't be done, you mean?" Sara chipped in sarcastically, braking gently to ease the car into yet another rutted track.

Rhion opened his mouth to reply, but Leibnitz shook his head with a gentle smile. "Always she was like this," he said. "Well, she's a Taurus. And since she was born in the second degree of her sign, by multiplying the letters of her name by their position and adding the digits, it gives her a Tarotic key of twenty-seven, which is really nine—the Hermit, the sign of Science, but also the sign of skepticism. And added to the year of her birth this gives her a Natal Sum of one thousand nine hundred forty-four, which adds together to eighteen, the Moon, the sign of doubt . . . She has talked to wizards traveling in other bodies through the universe down from fifty thousand years in the future, and she'd say, 'It can't be done because it can't be done.' Now what kind of attitude is that?"

"The usual one, unfortunately," Rhion said, remembering with a grin his own attitude about three-quarters of the mystical gobbledygook in the Schloss library and most of what Leibnitz had just said. "You're right. Magic and those who can work it are distrusted in my own world, hated, legislated against . . ."

"It is because magic is arbitrary," Leibnitz concluded. "And so it is. And unfair, and in many cases against the Will of the Creator. It is cheating. What business is it of mine to use the powers of the universe to make myself richer, when for whatever reasons the Lord thinks that in this lifetime I could learn more as a poor man?"

"He used to give Mama that argument when there wasn't money to buy milk."

They had reached the edge of the old meadow where Poincelles' secret temple stood. Though woods crowded thickly on its higher end near the barn, down here the ground was boggy, standing water glinting between patches of rank, waist-high grass. The crying of a thousand frogs prickled the night.

"Can you walk, Papa?" Sara asked worriedly, turning in the driver's seat. "I don't dare try to take the car through this. Even if we didn't get stuck we'd leave a track they could follow from hell to Detroit. Besides, I have to get the car back to the Mayor's . . ."

"She not only steals cars, she steals the Mayor's car," Leibnitz informed—presumably—God, looking skyward as he clambered out.

"He was the only one who had a gas ration."

"I'll take him up to the barn." Rhion slid along the seat and scrambled out the same door Leibnitz had, for the lane was narrow, and tangled ditches filled with stagnant water and blackberry brambles flanked it on either side. As he put his hands on the doorpost to pull himself out, Sara caught his wrist, dragging him back. Her whisper was carbon steel in the darkness.

"You tell him anything about how I'm living now and, so help me God, I'll kill you."

Shocked that she'd even think of it, Rhion started to demand *What the hell do you think I am?* But the vicious glitter in her eyes told him what she thought he was—a man, coarse, careless, and stupid. He shook his head, an infinitesimally small gesture that her father, standing by the corner of the car staring raptly around him at the milky darkness, would not see. "I promise."

She threw his hand from her grip, despising his touch, and turned her face away to put the car in gear. Its rear wheel nearly ran over Rhion's foot as she popped the clutch and drove off without a word.

"Poincelles, feh." Leibnitz picked his way through the long weeds that surrounded the barn and its three crumbling sheds, disregarding, as Rhion did, the black and terrible Seals of the demons Andras, Flauros, and Orobas written in secret places to defend against intrusion. "A *paskudnyak* out for what he can get. I knew him when he was still with the Order of the Golden Dawn, and even then I didn't trust him. What can you expect of a man whose numerological key works out to be sixteen? And if you trace out his name on the number grid of the geometric square of Saturn . . ."

"In here." Rhion pushed aside a plank on the back of the barn, slipped through the crack, and edged along between the splintery boards of the wall and the tarpaulin that hung inside until he found the opening between two tarps. Behind him, he heard Leibnitz's breath hiss sharply, though it was pitch-dark in the barn until he drew from his pocket a match and the stub of a candle. The tiny light spread gradually outward but did no more than hint at the dark shapes of the draped altar, the black candlesticks, and the shadowy gleam of the inverted pentagram beneath which Sara had lain. The smell of old tar and dust was almost drowned by an ugly medley of dried blood, snuffed incense, the thick choke of burned wood.

"*Chas vesholem,*" the old man whispered, looking around him in the dark.

Hating the place himself, Rhion moved swiftly to the far wall, where, behind another join in the tarps, he found the tin box of food and the bundle of clothes and blankets Sara had left there the day before. Rebbe Leibnitz did not move from where he stood; when Rhion returned to him, the box and bundles under his arm, he turned firmly and, slipping through the tarps again, went out the way they had come.

"Poincelles has already bribed the Troopers at the Schloss to stay away from this place," Rhion said, as they settled down in the darkness of one of the sheds and, after a muttered prayer, the old Kabbalist set to the bread and cheese and apples in the box like a starving wolf. "When he hears about the hue and cry for you, it's a good bet he'll take steps to keep the camp guards away, as well. My guess is von Rath knows about the place already but I suspect Poincelles doesn't think so—and anyhow he's stolen too much of the Occult Bureau's property to furnish it to want anyone looking too closely."

"The *tzadik* Akiba ben Joseph, the greatest of the rabbis, says that it is no sin to eat food that is unclean to save one's life, for your life is the Lord's property, which it is incumbent upon you to preserve . . . and by extension I suppose that it is also permissible to hide behind the demon Lilith's skirts in there." The old man jerked one greasy thumb at the dark bulk of the barn against the star-powdered sky. "But that place makes me want to wash more than nine months in the pigsty of their camp."

"Amen," Rhion muttered, drawing his knees up and wrapping his arms around them. Poincelles' spells, curses, and protective demon seals might have no power in them, but the dirty magics done in the barn clung to the place like a stench. "It's only for a couple of nights."

The old man grunted, wrapped what was left of the food again in its papers, and replaced it in the box. "There. If I eat more I'll be sick. Now—what are they doing in that place? That Schloss, that lodge of theirs . . . I saw the truck go out last week, and twice the week before, taking people they've been keeping, like me, apart from the others, people they don't put onto the lumber gangs or send to the mills to work. And the ones who work in the crematoria whisper about how they came back . . ."

"Have you ever heard of a group called the Adepts of the Shining Crystal?"

Cocking his head, Leibnitz thought about it for a moment, then frowned. "No. And I've heard of most, at least in Europe, though in America . . ." He shrugged resignedly, leading Rhion to wonder what this America, whose participation in the war von Rath seemed to fear, was really like. "They're crazy over there."

Sitting in the blackness of the shed, his back to one of its splintery doorposts, Rhion spoke of all that had befallen him since he had received, in the rainy solitudes of the Drowned Lands, word that Jaldis had wanted to see him in Bragenmere. He had meant to give a swift and concise encapsulation, but it didn't turn out that way.

"We have the night before us," the old man said gently, and, for the first time in three months, Rhion found himself able to talk—about the Nazis, about his unhealed grief for his old master, and about his loneliness and his growing fears. Sometimes he touched back on his original topics—the Spiracle, the Dark Well, the need to be at the stones on Witches Hill at the maximum pull of the sun-tides—but more frequently, as the Dog Star rose burning above the eastern trees and the birds woke and cried their territories, each to each, in the hushed dark of early summer predawn, he found himself talking about Tallisett and his sons, about the Ladies of the Moon, about wizardry, and about magic.

"As far as I can tell magic just—just *isn't* in this world anymore," he said, turning his head a little to look down the slope at the meadow, spread out in a shimmering of water and weeds and a thin white ground mist. In the stillness and utter peace it seemed impossible that such a place as Kegenwald existed. "From what I can tell, nobody did anything to cause this, any more than human malice causes the fall of night. It happened. Even the faes are gone, the faërie-folk—water goblins, pookas, lobs, grims. It might change some day, but there's nothing I or anyone can do to change it."

He sighed. "I'm not even sure if the damn Spiracle will work, you know? They work on little things, but something like this . . . It's never been tried. I thought of rigging up a Talismanic Resonator, which would draw on the Void itself . . ." He shook his head. "But aside from the fact that it would create a field anyone could use, including von Rath, it just needs too much power. So it has to be a Spiracle."

He looked back, aware that the old scholar was regarding him quietly in the darkness.

"What you are doing," Leibnitz said slowly. "It is irresponsible, you know."

Rhion closed his eyes. From the first that knowledge had murmured in his heart, try as he would to turn his mind away from it, he knew that the old man was right. "It's my only chance."

"That does not matter. If for whatever reasons the Lord saw fit to withdraw operant magic from this world—if that is what happened—it says much for your opinion of your own judgment that you want to bring it back for your own convenience."

"I'm not talking about my convenience, dammit!" Rhion said passionately. "I'm talking about my life! I wasn't the first one who circumvented the rules; I shouldn't even *be* here!" But he knew that any of the mages of his own world—Shavus, Jaldis, the Lady—would have told him that it didn't matter. And in his heart he knew it didn't.

But in his heart he could not bear the knowledge that he would never see Tally again, never see his sons. That he would be trapped in this hellish place, a prisoner of the Reich, for what remained of his life.

"*Tzadik*, please," he whispered. "There's only one place they know where to look for me now and only one time when I'll be able to raise enough power to open the Void. Part of it's that I think I really would rather die trying to escape than stay here, but as things are I think it's only a matter of time before von Rath kills me anyway. With or without your help, I'm going to have to try."

"There." The old man's hand was warm and strong on his wrist. The first nacreous grayness of dawn showed him the hooked nose, the long brows curling down over shadowed eyes, the strong lips with the shameful stubble of a convict and the red, raw circle of the scar. "You deliver me from hell and three hours later I'm coming on you like the *balabos* . . . You have given me my life, and you have found and taken care of my Sara. For that I owe you. And I can't let you remain in this world long enough for these evildoers to figure out some way of bending your knowledge to their wills. So I will do what I can, and let the Lord of Hosts—Who knows more about the whole thing anyway—handle the rest."

15

"He's sending me away!" Tallisett paced angrily to the long windows of her sister's room, the dark-green wool of her skirt sweeping across the tufted green-and-purple rugs, her hair catching a wheaten gleam as she passed through the windows' latticed light. Her sister Damson, seated beside the cold fireplace in the long brocade gown she favored in her rooms because it hid her partridge plumpness, didn't look up.

"He wouldn't even see me!" Tally continued passionately. "He said he was ill, but he was out hunting yesterday . . . He sent his *chamberlain* to tell me!"

"Father is ill," Damson replied, her voice low. Her short, stubby fingers continued to move over the lace ruffle she was making, crossing and recrossing the glass bobbins over one another on the pillow with a faint, musical clinking as she worked, the sunlight sparkling on the jeweled galaxy of her rings. "It's the summer heat, you know. It brings on the flux unexpectedly. He was taken ill last night. So were Esrex and Elucia, a little."

"But *why?*"

Damson was silent for a few moments more, her hands like stout little overdecorated spiders spinning a web. In this room the strong summer sunlight was broken into harlequin shards by the window grilles and softened by the moiré shadows of the trees in the water garden outside; beyond Damson's shoulder, Tally could see into the small room that had been fitted up as a private chapel to Agon, the Hidden One, Lord of the Eclipsed Sun. The smell of incense lay thick upon the air.

"Father thought it would be best." She sounded maddeningly like Esrex. Tally sometimes tried to remember whether her older sister had been that secretive, that calculating, that single-minded, before she'd married their cousin. But it had been twelve years, and her recollections of that time were little more than a child's, passionately worshipful of everything her sister said and did. In those days she had also had nothing to hide herself.

"We've heard that the Serpentlady of Dun is in the town," Damson went on, her owlish, protuberant eyes still fixed upon the twinkling bobbins. "And Erigalt of Pelter. With the Archmage still here, there are those who say it's scandalous for the Duke's daughter to be spending her time—"

"Who says?" Tally demanded, and this time Damson looked up at her, mildly blinking, her face a careful blank.

"It is nearly the summer solstice," she said. "With what the mages do at that time, Father thinks it would be better if you were somewhere else."

"*What* do they do?" Tally strode back, to stand over the shorter woman, hands on her hips. "Don't tell me *you* believe the mages hold orgies at midnight . . ."

"You know they do."

"Some sects do. Not the Morkensiks, or the Selarnists, or . . ."

"You're arguing semantics now," her sister said placidly, and went back to her lacemaking. "I know what Father told me, about why he thinks it better that you leave. Is Jaldis returning then, too?" And without appearing to, she watched her sister's face from beneath straight little bronze lashes.

Tally bit her lip and looked away. A week's custom hadn't dulled the hurt of what Shavus Ciarnin had told her he had heard, in the dark of a dream, sleeping beside the Well.

In a gentler voice, Damson asked, "You've heard something, then?"

Tally shook her head and turned away. Damson, with remarkable quickness for one of her soft bulk, set aside the pillow and got to her feet, catching her sister's slim brown wrist in her hand. "Please," she said, her voice low now as they stood in the chapel door. "This is for your own good, Tally. You may not think they commit abominations at the turning of the year's tides, but—"

"Who told you they were coming here?" Tally countered softly. "The priests of Agon?"

Damson's round gray eyes shifted. "Don't mock at Agon's Cult." She glanced into the close, tiny room beside them, as if behind the stone doors of the shrine, smooth and featureless like everything about that Cult, the Veiled God listened to all they said. "Yes, his devotees are everywhere. Since Esrex has become one of the inner circle of initiates he has learned a great deal; many things are now possible for our House. The influence of the High Priest Mijac may very well end in Elucia marrying the Heir."

"The Heir?" For a moment Tally thought she meant Dinias. "You mean the *Queen's* Heir? He's only a toddler!"

"He's turned four," Damson pointed out reasonably. "And the Queen has miscarried twice, it isn't likely now she'll give him a rival. What's six years, when he's fourteen and she twenty? It isn't as if she has a—romantic disposition, as you did."

She was watching Tally closely now. Rhion's name hung unspoken between them, fraught with a shaky tangle of joy to know he was alive and terror of the unknown dangers in which he stood. *I'm in trouble, help me, please,* Shavus had reported he had said. *Get me out of here . . . Get me out . . .* Tally said nothing.

"Tally," Damson said slowly. "I don't know whether you've done—anything foolish—since you married Marc. Esrex . . ." There was long silence, the old scandal and blackmail and coercion conjured for a moment, like the heart-twisting smell of a remembered perfume. Since the night it had happened—Rhion's arrest, Tally's imprisonment, the terror of not knowing what would meet her when she was finally sent for—neither sister had spoken of it—of it, or of anything else they thought or felt. They had become strangers, except for the knowledge that bound them at their roots.

After a moment Damson went on, with a certain amount of

difficulty, "I'm telling you now, that kind of thing isn't possible, if Elucia does in fact marry the Queen's son. There must be no breath of scandal. Stop being naïve. If Father found out, he would never permit it."

"You mean Esrex would never permit it," Tally replied, her voice low and perfectly level now. "For whom do you think your husband is doing this, Damson? Uniting the realm of Varle with the Bragenmere lands by becoming governor, making advantageous alliances that will put the lord of those joint realms on any royal Council, putting out of commission *anyone who might be able to use other than military power against him?* You think your husband is doing that to help Father? To help the man who ousted Esrex' family from the Ducal Seat? Who's being naïve? Or is that something you'd just rather not know about?"

She pulled her hand away from her sister's moist grasp and stood for a moment considering her, the cold weariness in her heart that comes with the final realization that the one you have loved has not existed for a good many years. It was a woman of thirty-five she saw, finally, and no longer the unconscious image of a plump, witty, brilliant girl of eighteen. She felt tired, and just a little sick—not like a child who has lost a cherished toy, but who has discovered in that toy a breeding place of maggots and grubs. "I suppose the real question," she finished quietly, "is whether you're a fool or Esrex' whore."

And turning, she left the vestibule and strode down the corridor, her long green skirts billowing in her wake. For a long time Damson stood without moving, round face irresolute, upon the threshold of the Shadowed God.

16

The girl didn't look to be more than sixteen. She'd probably been pretty once, in a haunting wildcat way, before they'd shaved her head, and even now, after months of starvation and ill usage in the Kegenwald camp, some of that beauty remained. In bistered pits, her eyes seemed huge; the bones of her wrists and hands appeared grotesque as she rubbed her bare arms for warmth. The unfurnished chamber in the south wing—the great master bedchamber in which the Dark Well had supposedly been drawn—never really got warm. From his post behind a one-way mirror in the adjacent dressing room Rhion could see the girl's pelvic bones outlined under the worn fabric of her ragged and dirty gray dress as she paced back and forth, barefoot on the uncarpeted oak planks.

When they had first brought her into the room she had huddled unmoving in a corner, like a partridge freezing into stillness in a hopeless hope that the hawk will pass it by. Having talked to Rebbe Leibnitz and the guards in the watch room and having seen the Kegenwald camp, Rhion understood this. Only an hour ago had she begun, cautiously, to move about, first doggedly examining every corner of the room, trying its three locked doors and its boarded-up windows, peering curiously into the the dark sheet of the one-way mirror on the wall. These explorations had taken her rather less than two minutes, for the room was empty save for a latrine bucket in one corner. After that, she had simply paced, hugging herself for warmth and staring nervously all around her with huge, obsidian eyes.

Rhion wondered whether her fear stemmed wholly from being in the power of the Nazis—a condition that scared him sick—or whether, animallike, she sensed what was going on in the house tonight.

He glanced down at the watch that lay on the padded leather arm of his comfortable chair. Eight-thirty. The sun would have set by this time, though twilight would linger till after nine. He found himself listening intently, though he knew that both these rooms and the temple downstairs on the other side of the house were quite soundproof.

Nevertheless, he felt it when they started, as he had felt it when the sun had dipped behind the somber black pickets of the hills. His scalp prickled and he felt the sweat start on his face; if he closed his eyes he could see von Rath lying upon the naked black stone of the altar, like a sleeping god in the thin white robe—*"vestis albus pristinissimus et lanae virginis"*—save for the febrile tension of his muscles and the tautness of eyelids bruised with stress and lack of sleep. Rhion knew the horrors of the opening rites, for he had seen them again and again in tormented dreams: Poincelles pacing out the bounds of the temple, a white puppy held aloft by its hind legs in one massive hand, its dying struggles splattering his crimson robe with blood; Gall and Baldur like strange angels in black, merged with the greater shadows that followed their movements back and forth across the velvet-draped wall; the reflection of candlelight in the eyes of the victims. Bound at the foot of the altar, they would know, as occultists themselves, what would come next.

"I told you I didn't want to have anything to do with it," he'd said to von Rath that morning. They had finished the early ritual work—for which Rhion had barely made it back from bidding farewell to Rebbe Leibnitz—and had been on their way out of the temple's small robing room: Rhion, exhausted and ravenous, to a breakfast he felt he had heartily earned; von Rath upstairs to his study. "I don't even want to be in the Schloss when it's going on."

"You disapprove of what I do?" The German tilted his head a little on one side, eyes cold and flat, like frozen quicksilver, voice gentle but perilous.

"If I wrote it on ancient parchment in Latin with illuminated capitals would you believe it?" Rhion retorted, covering his outrage, his anger, his panic with sarcasm. "*What you are doing is dangerous. It's always dangerous to do a blood-rite—it's always dangerous to do any rite drugged* . . ." And within him another voice, made furious by everything he had learned from Leibnitz, everything he had seen and sensed of the camp—by the scenes in the crystal and the laughter of the guards—screamed *How dare you—How DARE you—murder human beings, men and women, for ANY reason* . . . while fear of von Rath and guilt at his own cowardice nearly stifled his breath. Sara would have spat in von Rath's face and died.

He took a deep breath. "You don't have the control over the forces you're releasing. Without a conversion to physical operancy, you can't."

"So." Von Rath's bloodless mouth tightened. "I find it curious," he went on, after long silence, "that of the two reasons you gave that deny me my power, one has already been proven a lie. Is the other a lie, as well?" He placed a hand on the nape of Rhion's neck, slim fingers cold as steel and terrifyingly strong, and looked down into his eyes. Against a feverish flush the old dueling scar on his cheek stood out cold and white. "Are you lying to me, Rhion? Is this world truly bereft of the point of conversion, the crossover between will and matter?" His thumb moved around, to press like a rod of steel into the soft flesh under Rhion's jaw. "Or is that merely your final secret, the thing that in your opinion should not be shared with those whose destiny it is?"

Backed to the wall at the foot of the dim stairs, Rhion felt the tension of that powerful hand that could, he guessed, snap his spine with a madman's strength; in von Rath's eyes he saw nothing human at all.

"It's my final secret," he said. "I just thought I'd hang around until you got tired of waiting and started sticking hot wires under my fingernails before I disappeared in a puff of smoke." He pulled away from the thoroughly nonplussed wizard's grip. "You brought me here as an advisor, all right? And I'm stuck in this world—for the duration of the war, considering the risk of someone else dying to open another Dark Well. That might be years. I'm not happy about that, but do you think I'm going to trade decent food and a comfortable place to live for a permanent berth in an English insane asylum? If I understood how to convert to physical operancy, you think I wouldn't better my own position here by telling you?"

Von Rath flinched, as if from the blow that could break the self-perpetuating cycle of hysterics, and shook his head like a man waking from a dream. "No—I don't know." He passed his hand across his face, and for a moment his eyes were the eyes of the man Rhion had first known, the young man whose dreams had not yet become obsessions. There was even something like pain there, the pain of puzzlement, of knowing he was becoming something else and not quite knowing if he wanted it or not. "And yet for one second— Eric did. I know he did."

He frowned and shook his head. "That's odd, you know, it's been weeks since I've even thought of him . . . He was my friend . . ." He rubbed his sunken, discolored eyes. From the half-open door of the watch room across the hall came a guard's laughter and the nauseating gust of cigarette fumes. "But without operant magic we could never have brought you here."

"You don't think I've been living on that knowledge, that hope, for the past three months?" Rhion put his hand on the sinewy arm in its clay-colored shirt sleeve, led the way down the shadowy blueness of the hall. "I'm still trying to figure that one out. I keep telling you, I was only brought along to wash out the bottles. Jaldis was the one who knew what the Void is and how the Dark Wells work. Look," he added more gently, "when did you last get any sleep? Or have anything decent to eat? And I'm not talking about that lousy porridge. If Poincelles can get eggs and sausage out of the cook, you sure as hell should be able to."

The younger man pulled his arm away impatiently and stepped back toward the stair. "Later, maybe," he said in his quiet voice. "There is too much for me to do now. Perhaps other rites of the

Shining Crystal have survived, either in code as something else, or in fragments in letters—I haven't yet found their correspondence with St. Germain or Jean Bodin, and I know there must have been some—that can be pieced together. With our position in France solidified we must be able to deal with Britain. Time is of the essence now."

He passed his hand over his face again, and when he looked up his eyes had changed, as the hard edge of his desires crept slowly back into command. In the golden bar of light that streamed down the hall from the open door of the dining room, he looked, with his immaculate black uniform and electrum hair, like a daemon roused, blinking, from the dark of its cave.

"We aren't asking you to be part of the ceremony, you know." The voice was gentle, but inflexible as steel again. "Only to observe the subject and to take notes. We will be working on a naïve subject tonight, one whose mind I have never encountered. It will take all the energy the four of us can raise, but it is something in which no outsider should be allowed to meddle. Will you do that much?"

Reluctantly, Rhion had agreed.

Wearied with her pacing, the girl—a gypsy, von Rath had said, a race traditionally reputed to number a large percentage of psychics—sat again on the floor in the corner and lowered her head to her folded hands, rocking her body like a whipped child. Rhion glanced automatically at his watch. Six minutes after ten. He could feel the power growing in the house, a whispering behind him that seemed to be lodged within the walls, a terrible vibration in his bones. The bank of closed cupboard doors at his back made him nervous, as did the small, shut door of the backstairs to the kitchen, which led down from this little room. Part of him wanted to slip down that way and out of this accursed house before something happened, but terror of what might be waiting in that dark and cluttered stair stopped him. He wanted to open the main door into the hall, but feared what he might hear—or see—in its empty shadows.

A chill shook him, as if the air in the room had grown colder, and he had the uneasy sense of things taking place beyond the boundaries of human perceptions. He glanced at the watch again and wrote down the time: 10:23. The girl seemed to notice nothing.

At ten minutes after eleven, she got to her feet again and began

to pace once more, endlessly rubbing her skinny brown arms. There
was nothing in the room, no food, no water, no blanket or source
of heat. Rhion wondered whether that was a condition of the experiment or whether they had simply not thought about it.

Power was everywhere around him now, creeping like thin lines
of phosphorous along the paneling, dripping down the grain of the
cupboard doors at his back, crawling along door sills and floorboards. A kind of mottling had appeared on the wall to his left, near
the backstairs door, as if light were buried deep within it, and he
had the sensation of something moving behind him, near or perhaps
in the cupboards, almost—but not quite—visible from the tail of his
eye. He was too experienced to turn and look. He knew he'd see
nothing. One never did. Sweat stood out on his face and crawled
slowly down his beard. Sometimes he thought he heard voices speaking, not shouting in agony, but simply muttering with angry, formless
rage. It was the third blood-rite, the third sacrifice, of men and
women chosen for psychic power or occult knowledge. Their curses
would linger.

I'm sorry, he wanted to cry to the cold, beating air. *Nothing I
could have said would have saved you!* But the rage of the dead was
not selective. It did not hear.

They're fools . . . God, get me out of here! But he knew he was as
much a prisoner as the girl in the other room.

At 11:24 she stopped in her pacing, her shaved head jerking up
suddenly, as if seeing or hearing something that startled her. Rhion
noted it, and the time. But she shook her head and paced on, back
and forth, endlessly, tirelessly, not seeing the yellowish ooze of cold
light that had begun to drip down the walls, not sensing the freezing
iron tightness of the air, not hearing the formless whisper, in Yiddish
and German and Romany, that seemed always to growl on the other
side of the air. Agony, horror, despair, and a gloating sexual delight
filled the air, poisoned ectoplasmic wool from which von Rath's
mescaline-saturated mind was endeavoring to spin its magic strands.
Sick and wretched, hands shaking and breath coming shallow and
fast, Rhion tried vainly to stop his ears and to wall his mind against
it, wanting nothing but to get out, to escape this place and never
come back . . .

At thirty-five minutes after midnight, the girl wedged herself into a corner of the room again, wrapped her thin arms around her bony knees, and stared into the room dully, her fear at last blunted by exhaustion. She moved as if startled once more, at five of one, but by the way she looked around the room she saw nothing.

At quarter to three, just when Rhion could smell the beginnings of dawn in the lapis infinity of the world outside, Gall knocked on the door to tell him that the experiment was over.

11:00—cat
11:24—face on wall   11:24—Stopped pacing as if
                                         startled, resumed
                                         immediately
12:10—glass of water
12:45—spider

                                   12:55—Raised head and
                                         looked around room
                                         as if checking for
                                         something, settled
                                         down almost at once.

"Promising." Von Rath laid the two sets of notes on the library table before him, aligned their edges with his habitual neatness, and surveyed his fellow mages with eyes like glacier ice. "Your impressions?"

"It was—astounding," Baldur whispered reverently, black-rimmed nails picking at the edge of a nearby book. "I c-could feel the power flowing into you, you blazed like a torch with it."

"You were losing twenty-nine thirtieths of it." Rhion leaned back in his chair. His whole body ached from lack of sleep, the few hours of dream-tortured slumber he'd fallen into that morning doing nothing to make up for two nights without and his exertions on the astral plane on top of that. The splinters of sunlight forcing their way between the library's snuff-colored curtains were agonizingly bright in the room's brownish twilight; Poincelles and Baldur both squinted and winced whenever they turned that way. Gall, as usual, sat stoically in a corner. From his window during one bout of sleep-

lessness Rhion had seen him at dawn, walking calmly nude down
the path beyond the wire to Round Pond for his morning swim.

"There was power in the room," von Rath insisted doggedly. "I
know it. I felt it."

"Some of the Shining Crystal texts mention a Talismanic Resonator," Baldur put in diffidently. "They do not say what it is, but
they speak of it as establishing a field of power."

"As the Holy Grail did," Gall said, shifting his slender form in
his chair, the harsh afternoon sunlight making of his long white
hair a glowing halo. "And as certain other sacred relics could. The
crystal tip of the golden pyramidion atop the ancient Pyramid of
Khufu . . ."

"Which you were privileged to buy from a trusted antiquities
dealer in Cairo?" Poincelles inquired sarcastically, glancing up from
filing a broken fingernail back into a neat point.

"A Talismanic Resonator will work only if there's something for
it to resonate with," Rhion said, firmly cutting off Gall's indignant
rejoinder. "And in this universe you'd kill yourself raising a field as
little as a mile across."

"Perhaps a stronger drug? Or another type of drug?"

"Be my guest," Rhion retorted sourly. "Only don't ask me to
take any—or to be in the building when you start screwing around
with power while under the influence." He took off his glasses to
rub his red and aching eyes. Von Rath looked far worse than he had
yesterday morning when they had spoken outside the temple, as if
he had not slept at all. Good, thought Rhion. It meant he'd sleep
soundly tonight.

Hurting for sleep himself, Rhion considered putting off breaking into
the Dark Well and activating the Spiracle for another twenty-four hours.
He needed rest desperately—Rebbe Leibnitz probably did, too—and
there seemed little chance of getting any during the remainder of the
day. He didn't relish the thought of trying to manipulate the power of
the Void, even at his most alert.

But some obscure instinct prickled at him, like a damp wind ruf-
fling at his hair; an awareness that tonight would, for a dozen half-
sensed reasons, be better than waiting for tomorrow. Tonight was
Wednesday. If they put things off until tomorrow night Sara would

have to find an excuse not to be at the tavern, and too many of those would begin to make someone suspicious. Tonight the moon would be at its full—a slender source of power, but one the Lady had taught him to use. Tonight von Rath was likelier to be asleep, and tomorrow might see some kind of preparation for the solstice sacrifice itself afoot. He groaned inwardly and wondered if he could manage to steal a nap during the afternoon.

The others were still arguing. He should have been keeping his mind on them but couldn't.

"There are other d-drugs listed in the Anascopic Texts—"

"That are pharmacologically absurd."

"Not to mention that the body ought to be purified, rather than polluted, before the working of magic."

"Nonsense." Baldur pushed back his lifeless dark hair with one twitching hand and sniffled. "The potion Major Hagen used in the D-Dark Well ceremony—"

"Which killed him."

"We don't know what killed him. It was the same potion P-P-Paul—Captain von Rath—used last night, and at the rites before, and it elevated him, exalted him."

"He could have been flying in circles around the chandelier," Rhion spoke up wearily, "and it wouldn't have done him any good. Without the ability to convert power to physical operancy, you can disembowel every Jew in Germany, and it's not going to buy you one damn thing."

"Then I will disembowel them." Von Rath looked up, his face a skull's face in the gloom. "Every occultist, every medium, every psychic—every child whose house was visited by the *poltergeisten*—every source of personal *manna*, of the inner power, the *vril*, of magic, that we can lay our hands on, will be sacrificed. If we can raise enough power it *must* convert, it *must* answer to my bidding. And for that we will sacrifice every one."

He was looking at Rhion as he spoke, and Rhion felt the blood drain from his face as he understood.

The soft voice sank still further, like the murmur of the angry ghosts whose power whispered still in the colder corners of the house. "Every one. You say there is no physical operancy in this

world. So. Yet one of the so-called Jew wizards incarcerated at the
Kegenwald labor camp escaped only the night before last, escaped
across an open yard under plain sight of the guard towers without
being seen."

Dear God, no, not when I'm so close . . . "That's possible with
illusion."

"And illusion is what we are trying to raise against the RAF. The
thing that you say cannot be done."

Poincelles laughed. "Escaping from a prison doesn't need illusion.
Just a little . . ." And he rubbed his fingers together suggestively.

"In France, perhaps," Gall replied coldly.

"This is the real world, my dear Jacobus."

To von Rath Rhion said quietly, "It isn't the same." His lips felt
numb.

"So you say." Von Rath stood up, for an instant in the shadows
seeming to be a skeleton in his black uniform, with his wasted face
and frostburn eyes. His voice was the dry stir of demon-wings. "We
have trusted you, Rhion. We have believed your assurances that you
have made with us—with the Holy Order of the SS—with the destiny of the German Reich—a common cause."

He tipped his head to one side and regarded Rhion, not even as
a friend once trusted and trusted no longer, but as a stranger as
unknown to him as the men he had killed last night.

"The summer solstice is coming—a time of power. The Universe
is moving to its balance point, when its powers can be turned by a
single hand. On that day we will make a talisman of power, a battery,
against the day later in summer when we can give our abilities to
the assistance of our Fatherland in the breaking of our enemies'
stronghold. We depend upon the aid you have professed yourself
willing to offer us. And if we find that you have lied to us in your
assurances and betrayed our trust, I tell you now that it would be
better for you if you had never been born."

Sara and her father were waiting for him in the redolent darkness
of the trees beyond the Schloss' yard lights. The full moon rode
high, limpid and regal; a whispered catch of the hymn the Ladies
sang to her floated through Rhion's head as he stood motionless in

the shadows of the old kitchen door, watching Poincelles stride like
a lean and feral tomcat from the direction of the guards' barracks, a
couple of props under his arm.

> *I left the house of the Sun,*
> *I left the houses of light,*
> *To walk in the lands of the stars,*
>   *in the lands of the rain.*
> *Children living in darkness,*
>   *I give you what I can.*
> *Children of the earth,*
>   *I give you what I can.*
> *Children of magic,*
>   *I give you what I can . . .*

By the drenched quicksilver light, the Frenchman set the props
up—Rhion thought wryly that the ground in that little gully must
be getting pretty well grooved—shoved his little bundle of implements under the wire, and then followed with that curious, gawky
agility that seemed almost spiderlike in the dark.

Rhion hated him. Early in their friendship, Sara had shown him
the place where Poincelles had taken up the threshold-board at the
entrance to the attic to put a talisman of badly cured lambskin
where Rhion would cross it a dozen times a day, a talisman, she
informed him, consecrated to bringing him under Poincelles' influence—"Bastard paid me twenty marks to help him raise 'sex mag-
ick' to charge it," she'd remarked, screwing the board down again
above the rotting, mouse-eaten thing. "I should have charged him
fifty." Having no power, it didn't trouble him. But in dreams, again
and again, he had unwillingly witnessed the torture rituals of the
Shining Adepts and had seen how they were accomplished; he
knew who had laughed when the knife went in.

As Poincelles approached the shadowy verge of the trees, a figure
appeared. For an instant Rhion's heart stood still—then he saw that
the waiting girl was smaller than Sara and the pale blonde of the
most Teutonic type. Long braids hung down over the white uniform
blouse of the League of German Maidens, framing a face at once

pretty and sensual, with a lush mouth and discontented eyes. When Poincelles put a hand upon her waist she raised her arms to circle his neck. Scarcely louder than the rustle of the pines, Rhion heard his throaty chuckle.

Then they were gone.

"If he thinks he's gonna deceive Asmodeus with that little *tchotchke* he's out of luck," Rebbe Leibnitz remarked dryly, when Rhion had reached the lichen-blotched granite boulder behind which the old man and his daughter waited. The old scholar had traded his camp rags for an ill-fitting utility suit of the kind a workman might wear on his day off; his hands were shoved deep in the shabby jacket's pockets; under the bill of the cap that hid his shorn head, his dark eyes gleamed with amusement. Beside him, Sara was dressed as she had been two nights ago in a man's trousers and pullover, with only a frizzed red tangle sticking stiffly out from beneath a cap of her own. Close to, her clothes smelled of smoke, but she hadn't lit a cigarette for fear of the smell or the pinpoint of its light alerting the guard. Her pockets bulged with her housebreaking tools.

"He doesn't seem to have much luck getting virgins, that's for damn sure," Sara sighed, with a shake of her head. "But you'd think he'd have more sense than to go looking for them in the League of German Mattresses." She glanced over at Rhion, her dark eyes, like her father's, a gleam in the shadow of her capbill. "Even money he's going to ask those demons of his to bring you under his power again."

"Doesn't matter." Rhion put aside the brief memory of Sara's nude body stretched on the altar beneath the downturned point of the inverted pentacle, candle flame like honeyed gold on the spread legs and perfect breasts. "What matters is, he's paid the guards to look the other way between here and the house."

Rhion crossed the open ground first, setting up his props, slipping under the wire, and returning to the darkness of the old laundry room that he had so recently left. He sank his mind down through the stillness of the black house, picking out the dim chatter of the wireless in the watch room and the creak of a lazy body shifting in a chair. Mice scratched behind the dining room wainscot and in the stuffy backstairs, beetles ticked like watches, timing the coming of the summer-tide. The very air of the house felt uneasy, filled with angry dark things that waited behind some sightless angle invisible to human eyes, hunting for a way out into the world of men. When his fingers brushed the wood of the wall, it felt warmer than it should have, charged with unholy power. The whole house was turning into a giant battery, a hideous talisman of the forces released there.

He turned his mind quickly from it and sought in the thick dark air of those turning corridors, those closed-in rooms, for other sounds. He heard the slow, untroubled draw of breath from Gall's room—a panting, adenoidal snuffle from Baldur's. Then soft, shallow, and even, the breathing of von Rath sounded in a closed and seemly sleep.

At his low whistle Leibnitz and Sara left the shelter of the woods, crossed to the fence, set props, slithered under, took the props and moved across the yard to join him with surprising agility and speed. Rhion pulled the door shut; his pulse was hammering and a cold tightness in his chest had driven out all tiredness or thought of sleep. There was no turning back now. The only way out was through.

"Here." By the reflected glow of the yard lights beyond the windows, Sara led the way to the old dumbwaiter shaft. "Can you manage, Papa?"

"Fifty years I am learning the wisdom of great men, the Torah and the Talmud and the names of the angels of each sphere of the world and the numbers by which the Lord rules the universe, and now at my age I find I should have studied to be Tarzan instead." He glanced at the neat footholds recessed into the shaft wall and the rope hanging down into darkness. "How many steps are those?"

Sara shrugged. "I don't know. Twelve or thirteen, I think."

He waved his hands and addressed the ceiling. "She doesn't know. If it's twelve it computes to three, which is fulfillment and the realization of goals, but if it is thirteen it computes to four, an astronomic squaring that implies legally constituted authority which around here is not something we want to be dealing with . . ." His voice faded into a mutter as he climbed gingerly down the shaft. "I should have known that when the sum of my birth's Gematria computed with this year's date to give me 3,255, I should have known then to watch out . . ."

Sara rolled her eyes ceilingward, and followed.

The cellar was pitch black. Sara fumbled her flashlight from the deep pocket of her trousers, but Rhion caught her hand and shook his head, then, remembering she couldn't see the gesture, breathed, "No."

"A light's not gonna call more attention than the sound of us tripping over boxes."

"I'll guide you." Their voices were barely a flicker of sound in the stillness, but nonetheless made him uneasy. They were close, so close. It seemed to him now that in the silence von Rath must hear, even in sleep, the thudding of his heart.

A rat skittered through the dusty coal bin as they passed it; ghostly sheets of spider floss lifted from the old drying racks with the breeze stirred by their passing. Rhion led them down the long abyss of the cellar, past the crouching, crusted iron monster of the sleeping furnace, his ears straining for the faintest sound from above.

But there was nothing. Only the faint underwhisper that had begun to grow in the house itself, the angry, buzzing murmur of its restless ghosts.

This has to work, he thought desperately, his hands cold in the warm strong grip of Leibnitz' fingers, the hard little clutch of Sara's. *This is our last chance. Please, God, let it work.*

But the gods of his own universe and of this one hated wizards. *It figures.*

They shifted the boxes as quietly as they could, and while Rhion and Leibnitz stood between the flashlight glare and the stairs that led up into the main part of the house, Sara went to work on the lock.

"This also you learn in America?"

Sara opened her mouth to retort and Rhion cut her off hastily with a whispered "Will you stand guard?"

"What, you're not going to give her a tommy gun?"

"Papa, I'm telling you I'd trade Mama's silver candlesticks for one right now."

Rhion pulled the scandalized scholar through the door before he could reply, and closed it behind him. For a moment they stood, sealed into the darkness; then Rhion took a stub of candle from his pocket and, with a guard's steel lighter with its Deaths-Head engraving, called flame to its wick.

Beside him, Leibnitz breathed, *"Kayn aynhoreh . . ."*

The dim patterns of protective circles drawn upon the floor, the marks of old blood and ashes, lay undisturbed in the darkness. In their center was nothing to be seen, even with a wizard's sight, yet somehow, though its light touched the dirt-crusted stone of the opposite wall, the candle flame did not penetrate that inner dark. The air here seemed colder than in the cellar outside; the silence had the anechoic quality of unseen infinity.

"What . . . is it?"

"Can you see it?" Rhion nodded toward the circles.

The old man's grizzled eyebrows knotted, and the dark eyes beneath them were suddenly the eyes of a mage. "Not *see*."

Rhion took from his pocket the other candle stubs he had brought. Doubled and trebled, the soft glow filled the room with a wavering underwater light. Around him he sensed the heavy calm of the earth that grounded away the horrors that had been raised in the house; for a second he seemed to hear the stirring of the night breeze through the long grass of the meadow beneath Witches Hill, and see the glimmer of the full moon in the round pond near the ruins of the old Kegenwald church. Far-off he sensed other things, long lines of stones in the molten glow of the moon, earthen mounds shaped like serpents among summer trees at dawn, stone crosses, many-roofed shrines gleaming like gold on distant hills in dry afternoon sun. Beneath his feet he was aware of the slow pulse of the ley that joined that dim net of power overlying all the earth.

He set the candles down. His shaking fingers fumbled at the buttons of his shirt, and drew from under it, on its string around his neck, the Spiracle of iron and silver and salt, each of its five crystals seeming to speak one glinting, unknown word as the lights touched them. The candle glow slid along the silver in a running flow of amber runes.

"This is not a good thing that you do," the old man whispered. "But you must be got away from this—this abomination of a place, to let these men here destroy themselves as they will." He stood stroking the round, ragged scar on his stubbled lip, gazing with a kind of reverie into the dark colors of the circle's heart. The wistfulness Rhion remembered in von Rath's eyes from the early days, the yearning to know only that it was true, shone briefly on his face. "I am glad that the Lord let me see this," he added simply. "Tell me what you need me to do."

As when he had worked with the Dark Well just after the new moon, once Rhion entered the trance state necessary to raise power he had only the vaguest idea of time. For awhile he and Leibnitz worked together, drawing out signs of protection and concentration, he in his own blood, the Kabbalist in the ochre chalk he'd instructed Rhion to procure from the wizards-kitchen above. In the candles they burned a tiny pinch of the dittany the old man had insisted was proper for such spells; as a background to his own meditations, Rhion heard the murmur of that deep old voice framing one by one the names of the angels of the Sephiroth of Malkut, the protectors of the material world, but, oddly enough, the sound was soothing rather than distracting, a familiar mantra of magic, no matter what form it took. From the Circle of Power they drew a corridor to the edge of the Dark Well, and for a long time Rhion stood on the brink of the abyss, staring into a cold darkness of colors he could not consciously see.

But it was there. Endless, lightless, it yawned just—and only just— beyond the perception of his mind, a column of nothing into which it would be perilously easy to step. An angle of perception . . . a degree of difference from the sane and material earth . . . The twisted metal of the Spiracle seemed cold and dense in his hand, and through the concentration of his spells he wondered if he shouldn't have taken the safer route and set up a simple resonator after all.

But it was far too late. The spells of charging coiled like smoke through his exhausted brain, spells he had learned in the Drowned Lands, in the octagonal library tower in Bragenmere, and in Shavus' strange stone house; he had no notion of whether they would work or not.

He twisted his fingers through the string that had held the Spiracle around his neck; the crystals bit deep in the soft flesh of his left palm as he grasped it tight. Leibnitz' bony grip closed firm around his right. This had killed Eric Hagen, they had said . . . Taking a deep breath, he stepped into the Well.

Though the Well itself was only half awakened, he could feel its pull on him immediately through his trance state, the cold pressure on his solar plexus, at the base of his skull, in his eyes. His mind held hard to the spells of protection Jaldis had taught him the night before they'd entered the Void together, and felt the strength of the Void overwhelming him.

But there was magic there. The taste of it, the touch, was unmistakable; he raised the Spiracle in his left hand and saw the blue light that ran round the iron ring, springing in tiny serpents from crystal to crystal, flickering down his fingers like electrical bug feet, to lift the hair on the back of his arm. The Void was drawing at him—drawing him in and drowning him—but he held the ensorcelled circle high and whispered the words he had learned and used when it had only been a question of making devices that would let him breathe underwater, or keep him warm in places of lightless cold. He could see the dark of the Void now, a colored abyss without light in which burned not one distant gleam to show him the way through.

And that dark he wove to the Spiracle, like a man tying floating strands of silver spider thread one by one into a basket's rim, binding the wild magic to follow him like a banner into the magicless world outside. The Void pressed on him, dragged at him. It was becoming difficult to breathe and he had to call on all his strength merely to remain conscious, but he barely noticed. When he moved the Spiracle in the throbbing darkness, he saw how each separate crystal of the ring left a track of shuddering silver light.

Magic was his again.

Eric Hagen must have felt it, bursting on him like argent lightning in the dark—joy like the shattering of a star.

Blackness rushed through the split defenses of his mind, sweeping him away. His sight went dark, and he fell.

A hand clutched his, the jerk of its strength nearly dislocating his shoulder. A voice cried his name. Drowning in freezing blackness, Rhion could see nothing—darkness, ghost shapes that tore at him in swirling wind—bitter cold. Then tight and hard, a beam of what looked like brilliant yellow light stabbed through the murk, and he thought he heard names being called upon, syllables of power, like falling sparks of fire, a resonant vibration in his bones. Fighting back a wave of faintness, lungs hurting as they sucked vainly at airless void, he tried to make his way along that light, tried to see its end.

Numb with cold and nearly unconscious, still he could feel the hand holding his. He grabbed at the sinewy wrist with both his hands, fumbling desperately, and for an instant blacked out completely.

Then he was on his knees on the cold stone floor, gasping at the moldy air with its faint whiff of ozone, shaking desperately and clutching the tall skeletal body that held him close against it. Though the room was cold and damp, it felt warm by comparison. For a moment the lenses of his glasses misted. Groggily he was aware of a name being called.

"Rhion . . . Rhion . . ."

His hands tightened over the smelly wool of Leibnitz' shirt. Both hands . . . He gasped, "Oh, Christ, no . . ." and then saw the Spiracle hanging by its string, where the string was tangled tight around his nerveless fingers.

"Rhion . . ."

"Rhion, goddammit!" A blast of air struck his face as the door was opened suddenly; he got his feet under him and stood as Leibnitz turned. The new voice was Sara's.

"Get the hell out of there, both of you! All the guards in the goddam world are coming down the stairs!"

17

"This way!"

"The door . . ." Rhion whispered, his mind still cloudy, his numb hands fumbling with the Spiracle as Sara and her father dragged him away into the dark of the cellar. "Cover it back—"

"Screw that! Come *on!*"

A second's thought told him she was right. The jackboots of Storm Troopers thundered in the hall above, the locks rattled open . . . He was a fool not to have realized that von Rath, even in his dreams, would know that magic had entered this world.

They were beyond the shadowy tower of the furnace before the yellow blast of flashlight beams stabbed down into the room, focusing on the open door, the scattered boxes. Leaning heavily on Leibnitz—though he was six inches shorter than the old Kabbalist, Rhion outweighed him by a good forty pounds—he cast a quick glance behind them, and saw von Rath himself, naked beneath a red silk bedgown, among his black-clothed guards, standing in the black door that led to the Well. Then Sara was shoving him ahead of her into the dumbwaiter shaft.

By the time he'd climbed to the old kitchen, Rhion knew there was no hope of escape across the yard. A chaos of shouts and drum-

ming boots was rising like a storm outside, where dark forms raced
back and forth in the chilly arclight. As she swung herself across the
dumbwaiter counter, Sara whispered hoarsely, "Up the backstairs
. . . fast . . ."

Neither Rhion nor her father questioned that she had a plan. She
had been over the house enough times to know its every trapdoor
and closet. Rhion could hear the guards from the watch room
searching the cellar in groups of three and four while those in the
barracks combed the yard outside. They had a few moments. Flashlight shielded by her palm, Sara led the way up the old servants'
stair, cursing as she banged her shins on the mold-furred bales of
worthless currency. They emerged into the old dressing room with
its one-way mirror, where Rhion had watched the gypsy girl last
night.

"There's a trapdoor in the ceiling of the cupboard," Sara panted,
pointing to the dark line of doors that had made him so nervous
last night. "It leads up to the crawlspace above this wing. You have
to go first, Papa . . . you're tall, you can pull me up. Rhion, you get
your *tochis* back to your attic and get in your jammies. There's still
time to come down rubbing your eyes and asking what the fuss is
about."

"No," Rhion said softly. He did not look at her—he stood, instead, with his hand on the wing of the leather armchair, gazing
transfixed into the gleaming black rectangle of the one-way glass.

"God damn it, we've got no time." Her hard little hand jerked
at his sleeve, and he shook it off. He felt chilled all over, as if out
of nowhere he'd felt the whistling descent of a sword blade pass
within centimeters of his face, as the implications of what he saw
beyond the dark glass sank in.

"Help me up there." He turned abruptly and dove into the closet,
where Leibnitz' kicking feet were just vanishing through an inconspicuous square hole in the ceiling. Below, he could hear the voices
of the guards as they emerged from the cellar to search the house.

"For Chrissakes . . ." Sara began, and he caught her waist, lifted
her toward her father's reaching hands.

"Get me up there!" He shut the closet door behind him and reached
up. Leibnitz caught one of his wrists in both big bony hands, and

after a second, Sara caught the other. In the low, cramped space between the ceiling and the rafters of this wing, a dead lift wasn't easy, but they managed to get his shoulders up to the level of the rafters on which they crouched; after a certain amount of puffing and kicking, he pulled himself through the hole and fitted the neat plank trap over it behind him.

"Well, you sure put your foot in it now." Sara switched off her flashlight, leaving them in pitchy dark. "Old Pauli has no proof who was potchkeying around in there."

"No." Bent nearly double, he edged around behind Sara where she sat balanced on one rafter and stretched himself out on the one beyond. The crawlspace rose to a peak of about four and a half feet above either of the lodge's two wings—only in the center block was there a half-story for attic rooms. Away in the darkness he could see—and smell—the nests of the rodents that lived there, and catch a glimpse of their angry eyes. *Sorry about violating your* Lebensraum, he thought wryly. *Into every life a little* Anschluss *must fall.*

"There's no reason for him to guess it was you," Sara went on. "Personally, I'd love to see that momzer Poincelles sashay in here an hour from now and try to explain where he'd been."

Rhion shook his head, though Sara saw nothing of the gesture in the dark. "No," he said again. "They changed that room, the one where they put the people on the receiving end of their experiments . . . the room on the other side of the glass."

"Huh?"

"It's a one-way mirror." He felt carefully in his trouser pocket where he'd shoved the Spiracle in his haste. "I could see into that room."

"Oh, come on, it's pitch dark in there."

"I saw," he insisted quietly. "They've put furniture in there in the last twenty-four hours—a bed, a chair, a desk—and they've unbolted the door into the washroom on the other side."

Footsteps thudded in the hall below, and though they had been barely whispering before, all three fugitives fell silent. A thready line of diffused light briefly outlined the square of the trapdoor in the dark, but by its angle the guards didn't even aim their beams at the ceiling. In a guttural murmur of curses they were gone. Rhion laid his head down on his folded arms and breathed again.

For nearly an hour none of them spoke. Closing his eyes, stretching out his hyperacute wizard senses in the dense and stuffy blackness, Rhion found he could track the men back and forth, not only on this floor, but on the one below and in the central block and north wing of the house. He heard their voices and the thick uneasy drag of their breath as they moved from room to silent, haunted room; he felt the zapping tingle of electricity as they switched on light after light, unwilling—ignorant though they were of the inchoate powers lurking there—to be moving through the place in the dark. He heard a sergeant curse, and the opening and shutting of closet doors. Then far off, dim and deep, a voice came to him, chanting spells of breaking, of dissolution, and he heard the distant scrape of metal and soap and brickbats on stone.

Von Rath was dismembering the Dark Well.

Rhion shut his eyes, a shudder going through him at this last severing of any means of communicating through the Void. He fumbled in his trouser pocket again for the Spiracle. *This has to have worked*, he thought despairingly. *Don't tell me I'm really stranded.*

His fingers touched the twisted iron, and he knew.

Magic was in it. The cold of the Void whispered in his mind as he drew out the braided circlet. It seemed to him a faint spark glinted deep in the heart of each of the five stones. Holding it up, he could see through it down the length of the crawlspace—rafters, dust-clotted cobwebs, the accumulated nastiness of a century of mice—to the narrow black louvers at the end. Yet as if he looked through a smoked mirror, he knew.

Down below he heard the moist pat of von Rath's bare feet, ascending the chipped stone steps to the downstairs hall. Baldur's anxious, stammering voice demanded if he was all right and what he had done. Then he heard Poincelles' deep tones and caught the sound of his own name. Rhion wondered fleetingly just what account the French wizard was giving of his evening, but, satisfied that von Rath's mind was temporarily distracted, he risked one of the lowest level spells he knew and summoned a tiny ball of blue light to his cupped palm.

It lay there glowing, the size of his little fingernail, a luminous edge of cerulean along his fingers, a chill spark in the scratched glass of his spectacle lenses and the deep blue of his eyes.

"Jesus H. Christ," Sara muttered, sitting up and stretching the kinks from her back. "All right, Merlin, what do we do now? Poincelles has got to be back by this time, so you've blown your chance of pretending it wasn't you."

Pallid dawnlight had begun to thin the gloom under the roof, and in the yard the muffled gunning of engines sounded, the clatter of metal, belt leather, boots. A man cursed.

"He is." Rhion closed his hand, killing the light that Sara had not seen. "And it wouldn't be safe for me to go back even if they didn't think it was me. The bed they've put in the other room . . ."

"Yeah, what was the deal with that?" Sara asked. Beyond her, on the other side of the trapdoor, her father continued to lie full length on the beam, only turning slightly to prop himself up on one bony elbow to watch them with dark eyes under the brim of his grubby cap. "The room's got locks on the doors and no windows, it's the logical place if they're gonna hold a prisoner. If you say they're going to be making a big sacrifice on the solstice . . ."

"If they unbolted the washroom that connects to that room," Rhion said quietly, "it argues for longer than a day. And that bed not only had blankets, it had pillows. There's only one prisoner in this place I can think of who rates a pillow and an easy chair. That room was fixed up for me. They planned to lock me up the day before the solstice, just in case."

"So, you think they don't trust you?" Leibnitz inquired, and Rhion grinned.

"As for what we do now . . . We lie low." He replaced the Spiracle on its string in the open neck of his shirt, the jewels gleaming softly in the dark tangle of chest hair. "Here, for twenty-four hours, while they're out searching the woods. Tomorrow morning, just before dawn, we slip out and hide in the woods."

"Great," Sara muttered savagely. She pulled off her cap and shook out her hair with an impatient gesture, the grimy light catching metallic splinters of brass in the red. "You get the whole countryside up in arms—it's gonna be a real trick for me to get back to town

long enough to collect the food and clothes and money I've got
stashed in my room, let alone getting the three of us to the Swiss
border." Her voice was soft—they were all whispering barely louder
than breath—but dripped with sarcasm. "Not to mention the fact
that we don't even *have* identity cards for you, and on the run we
sure as hell won't have a chance to get them."

"Don't worry about me," Rhion said softly. "I'm not coming with
you. And once the solstice is over—after midnight Friday—von Rath
won't be searching nearly as intently for me. He knows he has to
catch me before the solstice, before the pull of the sun-tide gives me
the power I need to open the gate in the Void and make the crossing
to my own universe. That's why he's turning out his entire force
now."

"Fair enough," Rebbe Leibnitz agreed and, rolling over onto both
elbows, pulled a stub of pencil and his pince-nez from his pocket
and began making a numerological calculation of the most auspicious
hour and minute to leave the attic on the dusty plaster beneath the
beam where he lay.

"I hate to break this to you, cupcake," Sara whispered dourly,
"but there ain't no Santa Claus. Von Rath has mobilized the goon
squad because he's afraid you're going to hightail it to England and
spill your guts to Winnie Churchill. Within a week, this search is
going to be nationwide." She sat up tailor fashion, slim and straight,
with her red hair hanging down over her square, thin shoulders and
jutting breasts beneath the grimy shirt. Some of the acid left her
voice, and there was concern in her dark eyes. "You poor deluded
boob, what do you think's going to happen to you tomorrow night?
You'll just go 'poof' and disappear?"

"Yes," Rhion said simply. "I hope so."

"*Oy gevalt* . . . We *all* hope so, but it doesn't work that way."
She started to pull up her shirt to get at the money belt Rhion knew
she habitually wore underneath, then paused, cast a quick glance at
her father—obliviously working out some kind of calculation from a
vesica piscis drawn over the Square of Mercury—and turned her back
on both men. Rhion looked away from the girl's slender rib cage
visible beneath a bizarre strapwork of lace and elastic underpinnings,
and tried with indifferent success to think of other things.

She turned back, shirt tail hanging out and a creased wad of papers and marks in her hand. "These might do us in an emergency, if I can't get to the rest of my stuff," she said. "And I might not. They know I'm your—ah—friend . . ." She cast another quick glance at her father, as if she feared that he had somehow, within the camp, heard rumors about the redheaded bar girl at the Woodsman's Horn and intuitively connected them with his only child. "Once we get on the road it's gonna be a trick to hide Papa's head till his hair grows out a little."

She transferred the papers to her pocket, withdrew from the same pocket a pack of filthy cards and shuffled them deftly, quietly, in the half light. In the yard below, the sounds of departure had died. The smell of dust was fading. A woodpecker's hammering clattered unwontedly loud in the silence. Deep in his marrow, like a whispering of the leys that netted the earth, Rhion felt the stirring of the suntide begin.

"Rhion . . ." Sara looked up from the hand of gin she'd automatically laid out for the two of them between the rafters. "Why don't you come with us? Forget the goddam summer solstice. We'll get you out of this *versbluggene* country somehow."

He smiled and shook his head, touched by her concern. "I know you don't believe me," he said, "but tomorrow midnight really is my only chance to get home. It's the only time the wizards of my world will know where to look for me, and the only time I'll have enough power."

For a long moment she studied him, worry softening the brittle cynicism of her eyes. Without her customary coating of lip rouge and makeup, she looked far younger than usual, exhaustion and stress darkening the lids of her eyes and sharpening cruelly the tiny lines of dissipation already printed in the tender flesh. Then she shook her head. "I wish to hell I knew where they got you," she said softly. "Or where your home really is."

"I've told you and you don't believe me." He smiled.

"I know," she sighed. "Munchkinland."

"So what's not to believe?" Rebbe Leibnitz raised his head and adjusted his pince-nez reading glasses with long, bony fingers. "You remember Horus the Invincible, Saraleh, who stayed with us back in twenty-eight when *he* was an exile from his own dimension . . ."

"I remember he never returned the money he borrowed from you."

Leibnitz shrugged. "So if he had, would we be hiding in a better class of attic today? He needed the money to continue his search for the Lost Jewels of Power that would open the Dimensional Gates . . ."

Sara rolled her eyes. "I give up. Give my regards to the Witch of the West."

The day passed, oppressive and stifling. In the cramped, dark space beneath the roof tiles, the heat grew quickly intolerable; the inability to move about became torment in itself. In spite of it all, Rhion slept for hours, a breathless uncomfortable sleep on the eight-inch beam, tormented by cloudy dreams, while, unable to smoke, unable to pace, Sara fidgeted her way through endless games of solitaire and her father covered all the plaster within his considerable arm reach in a scrawled carpet of numerological abracadabra. Now and then Rhion opened his eyes to see the three hard splinters of brazen light that crawled along the slant of the struts overhead or Sara's face, sweat-beaded and intent with her dark lashes turned to ginger by the sun. Then he would slide back into a gluey abyss of dreams.

He dreamed of Tallisett, riding in a swaying litter up the coiled road that led away from Bragenmere's yellow sandstone walls and into the dry hills of the Lady Range . . . dreamed of the Duke, white-faced and ill, raising his head from the pillows of his sickbed to accept the cup Lord Esrex handed him with an encouraging smile, while in the background a dark, veiled shape stirred a little in the shadows . . . dreamed of the octagonal library tower against a robin's-egg evening sky, its windows rosy with lights that gleamed on the steel helmets of armed men slowly gathering in the court below.

The dreams faded, turned cloudy and strange. Dimly, through his sleep, he felt the turning of the universe as the sun-tide strengthened and the year approached its pivot point, where its forces could be seized and swung by a man who knew its laws. Even those who knew nothing of magic felt it somehow, that at those two points—

midsummer and midwinter—the doors that separated the mortal from the uncanny stood open, to admit sometimes fairies, sometimes the ghosts of the dead, and sometimes God. And even in his sleep, his hand, which lay curled around his glasses upon his chest, moved to touch the Spiracle, to feel there the whispered magic of the Void.

Then he dreamed, much more clearly, of Paul von Rath, sitting in his own study, that dark, vast room choked with stolen books, unkempt, unshaven for the first time since Rhion had known him, gaunt cheeks spotted with the dry fever of his obsession and gray eyes chilled and narrowed to cold silver-white as he bent over his books, reading . . . He wore no uniform, only the dressing gown of thick, dark silk he'd had on in the cellar, his naked chest visible beneath it and the steel swastika on its chain at his throat catching the light in a flat, hard flash. Like something scried at a distance, Rhion saw him raise his head as the study door opened and saw Poincelles there, dark face flushed with spite . . .

Then he woke, gasping, the heat pressing upon him like a slow ruthless vampire, and sweat running down his face, matting clothes and beard and hair. The sun was sinking. The three splinters of light from the louvered vent had stretched to arrows, then to attenuated javelins, and now were fading altogether; in the yard were the sounds of truck engines and the dulled, angry grate of men, foul-mouthed with disappointment and fatigue.

"They sound beat," Sara whispered, her lips twisting in a grin as she flipped over a card. "Good—by two in the morning, we'd be able to take a steam calliope and horses out of here without them noticing."

The sentries around the perimeter of the house had been doubled, but the men were, as Sara had said, exhausted from a day of combing the woods, and it was a simple matter to create an illusion near the fence in a spot just out of view of the gully under the wire. It was a fairly ordinary illusion—two dogs copulating—but of sufficient interest to the type of men who made up the SS to hold their attention. Rhion, Sara, and Rebbe Leibnitz crossed the yard together and slipped under the fence and so into the woods.

Rhion and Leibnitz spent the following day hiding in the woods on the slopes behind Witches Hill. The guards from the Schloss,

fortified with Waffen divisions from Kegenwald and even from Gross
Rosen, were still searching, though not very energetically, Rhion
thought, scrying for them in a pool of standing water. Still, the
danger from them was real enough to prevent him from sleeping
much or from sinking for long at a time into the meditation he knew
he'd need to gather his strength for tonight.

He attempted to scry for the SS wizards both in water and in his
crystal and, not much to his surprise, could not. At another time of
year, perhaps, with greater concentration . . . But for them, too, the
sun-tide held some little power; their seal after all was the sun-wheel,
turning in reverse. He did manage to see the Schloss from far off, a
tiny image in the pond, and as the afternoon lengthened and the
shadows began to cool he saw the gray truck with its black swastikas
creeping like a poisonous beetle on the straight track that ran from
the Schloss' gates away toward Round Pond and thence to the Kegenwald road. *I will disembowel them*, von Rath had said, leaning
forward in the stifling gloom of the Schloss library. *Every one . . .
Every one . . .*

They would be saving the most powerful wizard they had for
tonight's sacrifice, Rhion thought, and shivered. More than one,
probably, to draw out their souls, the essences of the lives, their
torment, and their pain, focusing them by those ancient rituals
through von Rath's drugged mind to make talismans of power in the
vain hope that quantity might somehow make a qualitative difference.

If they caught him between now and midnight, Rhion had a
horrible certainty about what his own fate as well as Leibnitz' would
be.

At sunset, Sara returned. Rhion had scried for her half a dozen
times during the day, at intervals in a thoroughly enjoyable argument
with Leibnitz about the multiplicity of God, not because he thought
he could help her at this distance but because he could not do
otherwise. But her errand had been uneventful, and she came up the
path to the clearing where they were to meet, pushing a stolen
bicycle before her with a cardboard suitcase of clothes strapped to
its handlebars. "I got train tickets," she said briefly, opening her
handbag—a considerably older and more conservative one than she

usually carried—to hand Rhion a bar of black-market chocolate and extract a cigarette for herself. She wore a sternly tailored brown dress and low-heeled walking shoes, in keeping with the persona on her identity papers, an assistant bookseller's clerk traveling with her boss on a buying tour. To her father she tossed, from the suitcase, a shabby tweed jacket, a clean shirt, and a better-looking cap. "I also got you a razor, Papa—you don't have enough beard yet to look like anything but an escapee from a camp, and if you shave, it'll look like you've got more hair than you do."

Leibnitz put a defensive hand over the half-inch of grizzled stubble that covered his jaw. "The Rabbi Isaac ben Solomon Luria says—"

"Well, Isaac ben Solomon Luria didn't ever have to pass himself off as a *goyische* bookseller on the way to Switzerland, so shave! Papa, please."

"The child is a staff for the hand, the Yebamoth says," the old man muttered, turning back toward the pool that still reflected the sweet silver green of the sky, "and a hoe for the grave. 'Even a child is known by his doings . . .' "

Sara turned back to Rhion and, for the first time, reached out and took his hand. "Please come with us."

He smiled and shook his head. Hate himself though he might for the selfish cowardice of it, with the dipping of the sun behind the black hackles of the hills, he had felt himself relax. Von Rath and the others would be beginning their ceremony. He knew where they were, knew that the SS mage's attention would be fully occupied until after midnight. And in spite of his horror at what he knew would be going on, in spite of his loathing for what they did and were trying to do, what he felt was relief. He was safe. It wouldn't be he who lay on the black granite of the altar under Poincelles' knives; it wouldn't be his pain, his magic, his death, that they wove into their unholy power.

It occurred to him that he perhaps owed it to this world to return to the Schloss and burn the place and its books to the ground. But even the ability to convert what energy he could raise to physical operancy wouldn't help him against several dozen Deaths-Head Troopers. He could not risk even the chance of delay, and his own reserves of strength were perilously low. With the power of the solstice behind him, it was still going to take everything he had and everything he could summon from the lambent magic of the stones even to open the Void; Shavus, back at the Duke's palace in Bragenmere, had better be on the other side with one hell of a lot of magic to get him through.

"I'll be all right."

"You don't even have a goddam identity card!" Her hands, small and delicate and hard, tightened over his and she shook him, as if this would somehow make him understand.

"I keep telling you I won't need one."

She stared into his eyes for a long minute, then shook her head and turned away. "Okay," she sighed. "You win. Papa, you stay here. Rhion, I'll go with you to these rocks of yours. If you go poof and disappear, I'll admit I was wrong. If you don't . . . You come out of the country with us, because you're gonna need all the help you can get. Deal?"

It might have been the turning of the earth toward the darkness, the lengthening of the shadows of the black ridge of hills, but it seemed that cold came over him, the leaden taste of defeat and death. He shivered. "It might be better if you got away while you can," he said quietly. "Von Rath's . . . busy . . . tonight; I don't think the search will be heavy between now and midnight."

"The hell with that, we can take the seven A.M. train as easy as the eleven P.M. Papa, if I don't come back . . ."

"Then I won't come back," he said placidly, returning from the pool with a nicked and dripping face, tying his tie. "I'm coming with you. This," he added, with wistful eagerness, "I want to see."

Light lingered in the midsummer sky as they made their way down the mountain. During the long afternoon Rhion had cut an elder sapling with Leibnitz' clasp knife, the only weapon or tool either of them possessed, to make a staff, on which he mounted the Spiracle as a headpiece. Now, as they walked, the last glow of the day flickered along the rune-scribbled silver, and it seemed to him that the five crystals knotted within it whispered to one another in some unknown speech. On the western side of the hills, power was rising, power called from pain and savagery and the black crevices of the human soul, but here in the hill's long shadow the night was untouched. Among the dark pines and bracken, the cool air whispered of old enchantments. Rhion could feel a second ley when they crossed it, wan and attenuated but living with the life buried deep in the ground, pointing straight and glowing to the crossing at the Dancing Stones. Sunk in a half trance as he walked, Rhion sensed the lift and swell of the solstice power, as sun, stars, moon, and time drifted to their balance point, and it was as if every leaf, every fern, every mushroom, needle, and fallen fir cone gave forth a faint silvery shine.

The Stones, when he reached them, seemed to glow with it in the dark.

All gates stood open tonight. As he walked toward those two lumpish guardians and the broken altar between them, he felt as if he had been here on other solstice eves. His fear of pursuit, the sick terror he felt at what he guessed would happen to him if they were caught, eased and fell away. He sensed the whisper everywhere of freely given death and ecstatic mating, as if hundreds of bare feet all around him even yet swished the deep grass that washed the Stones' sides.

He had reached the Stones by midnight. He could escape. Jaldis . . .

He wasn't sure why he thought of the old man just then—perhaps out of sorrow that for him there would be no returning, perhaps only some echo of a dream that he couldn't recall.

Sara and her father stopped just beyond the edge of the trees that ringed the meadow. Rhion, his mind already settled into the rhythm of the triumphant sun, walked on alone.

The power of the ancient stone rose to meet him as he touched it. Every breath he drew drank light from the murmuring air. Overhead the moon stood, a day past full and half risen to its zenith, like the sweet swell of summer music drowning the stars. As he invoked the four corners of the earth, Rhion touched, like a ghastly shudder in the air, a fragment of the power that was being raised to the west, a stench of burned flesh and agony, and felt along the network of the leys that elsewhere it was the same, rites of hate being performed in ancient places of power whose names were only names to him: Nuremburg, Welwelsburg, Munich. The dread of pursuit touched him again, and with it the strange sense of *déjà vu*, but with the drawing of the Circle around the Stones he cut out both the thin psychic clamor and the evil power raised.

By the stars it was after eleven, though he did not need to see the sky's great clock to know that midnight was near. Through a deepening trance he called the last remnants of his own power from his exhausted flesh, linking it with the altar stone and the turning firmament above, and he knew that no matter how many wizards Shavus had called in to help him on the other side, the jump was going to be bad.

A bluish haze of light trailed from his fingers as they brushed the altar stone, and everything that had been written there over the course of millennia seemed to swim to the surface: ancient runes; spells of light; handprints with fingers cut away in sacrifice; and the names of gods that went back to the name of the single power, the oldest names of the Mother and the Sky.

He stepped up onto the altar stone, barely aware of the world outside the Circle he had drawn and of the two dark forms of the only people he had cared for in this world watching from the edge of the trees. Raising the Spiracle on its staff he summoned, and seemed to see, far off and mere inches from his feet, a column of smoky darkness, stirring nameless colors, an abyss without light. All that was within him called forth the power of the Void, of the stone of sacrifice on which he stood, and of the turning stars.

He waited.

He knew when midnight came. The whole universe whispered a single word. Somewhere, dimly, there were shrieks, but the Circle he had drawn around the place held them out. The dark field of the Void's magic enveloped him, and he reached out into it, seeking . . .

And found nothing.

No light, no sign, no answering call.

He deepened his concentration, forced his aching mind to focus more sharply, more clearly, searching that darkness, waiting, reaching, not thinking about what it meant that they were late.

If late was all they were.

He thought, *No. Please, no.*

In his trance state, time was not the same, but he knew when a half-hour passed, and then an hour. The wheel of the stars moved slightly overhead; the moon climbed, unconcerned, toward her shining zenith.

Please?

The power of the ancient stone, pouring up through him toward the balanced stars, began to fade at three. He clung to it for as long as he could, but felt it go, as the swinging momentum of the Universe slid away and its vast, lazy turning resumed its wonted course. Still Rhion remained, standing upright on the stone, the staff upraised in his hands, until his knees shook with the exhaustion of forty-eight hours of fatigue and dread, and the world lapsed back from its waking dream of magic into its accustomed sleep.

They hadn't heard or couldn't come—or had decided, for reasons best known to them, to leave him where he was.

Or it might just be that Sara was right. He had only dreamed of Tally and Jaldis, of his sons and his parents and the world in which he had grown up, dreamed while incarcerated in a madhouse somewhere. Perhaps the truth—the real truth—was merely something he had forgotten.

He closed his eyes, fighting to believe this was not the case. For a moment it seemed that everything within him ripped and gave, and inner darkness poured into the hollow that was left. Opening them, he called the last fragments of strength, or hallucination, to stare into the darkness—if it was darkness—seeking some tiny splinter of light, a mark, a rune, a thread of magic to guide him through . . .

But there was nothing. Only the slow growing of a pallid dawnlight and the death, each by each, of the stars before the prosaic white of day.

He lowered his arms, letting the field of Void magic around him die. His back and shoulders ached and his knees and hands were trembling, pains scarcely noticed and nothing beside the hurt that consumed him and left only hollowness behind. Tears tracked down his face, salty on his lips and wet in his beard. He bowed his head.

Then a quiet voice broke the dawn stillness. "Give me what you have in your hand."

He turned on the worn stone altar.

Twenty Storm Troopers were ranged in a semicircle behind him, rifles and submachine guns trained. At the center of the arc stood Paul von Rath, seared and haggard face somehow shocking in the nacreous morning light. "I see Poincelles was quite right about where he guessed you would be—he had been watching you for weeks, you know—and what you would attempt. A worthy wizard, if spiteful as a woman. Worthy indeed to have been the sacrifice for our solstice power. I think when we came for him he was surprised. Now give me what you have in your hand."

He did not raise his voice. It was soft and balanced, like the way he stood, tense in his black uniform and polished boots, eyes gray and cold as glacier ice. Sara stood beside him, his arm locked around her neck, the silver blade of his SS dagger pressed to her throat.

Equinox

18

The house identified by Intelligence as Von Rath's Berlin headquarters stood isolated in the colorless autumn 300wasteland of empty fields, scrubby birch and pinewoods and nodding weed stems that stretched along the Spandau canal north and west of the city, a wasteland Berliners called the Jungfern Heide. Limping awkwardly down the long drive that connected it to the tramline of the Alt-Moabitstrasse, Captain Thomas Saltwood studied what could be seen of the building above its gray stone wall. The steep roof had shingles cut out in coy Victorian half circles like a fish's scales, a bit of rusted iron gingerbread along its ridge crest, and two rounded dormers that spoke of attics above the second floor. *Or first floor, as the Britsish would have it,* Tom thought with a wry grin. In Barcelona he'd nearly gotten himself killed by climbing one flight of stairs too few to meet a local Communist leader in what ultimately turned out to be the wrong flat. He still remembered the disgusted lecture Hillyard had given him on the King's English, once the shooting was done.

As the long-delayed Intelligence reports had indicated, the nearest house—another middle-class Victorian villa—was boarded up and deserted, over a half mile away, and the isolation of the SS house was further emphasized by the wire fence enclosing nearly an acre of ground outside its already forbidding stone wall.

"But it beats hell out of that lodge in the forest they were in all summer," Tom murmured to himself, as he let himself through the unlocked, unguarded chain-link gate where the drive entered this outer perimeter. He said it in German. He had been speaking in German, even to himself, since he'd paddled ashore the night before last in Hamburg.

The villa wall was eight feet high, blocks of the same dreary gray granite from which most of Berlin's overpoweringly heavy public buildings were made. The wrought-iron gate had recently been backed by sheet steel; on either side of it, cut stumps and a litter of twigs, chips, and rotting berries marked where two beautiful old rowan trees had flourished. *Blocked the field of fire from the gate,* Tom thought, looking regretfully down at the raw, foot-wide stumps. *Damn Nazis.*

In a way he was a little surprised actually to be here. The confusion of an impending invasion that had followed Dunkirk had put off his errand; the chaos of German bombs hammering London—invariably pulping those East End neighborhoods whose inhabitants were only trying to make ends meet on two pounds a week, he added to himself—had put it off again. Hillyard had departed for a Commando base in Scotland, taking Tom with him, and though Tom had ultimately spent an energetic summer, he hadn't really expected to get any closer to the SS's tame magicians than Boulogne.

He scratched his unshaven jaw, checked his watch, and turned back to survey the line of telephone poles that ran from the villa back to the drive's junction with the main road. Acid-drip devices were accurate to within ten minutes or so. He was burdened with a heavy tool kit and a massive orthopedic boot that not only made him limp whether he remembered to or not but that provided—along with the patch over his left eye—a visible reason why a man of good health and military age was wearing no uniform more formidable than that of the telephone company. It had taken him at least that long to walk this far.

He rang the bell by the gate. "Telephone company," he said to the young Storm Trooper who appeared, speaking in the slangy

Berlin dialect he'd picked up from old Stegler in the Wobblies. "We had half a dozen complaints this morning; we're tryin' to trace a fault in the line. You having trouble?"

"No," the young man said, regarding the orthopedic boot with unconcealed distaste and starting to shut the gate again.

Tom pulled out two cigarettes and offered one to the sentry, who hesitated, then pushed the heavy gate back. " 'Preciate it if you'd check," Tom said, ignoring as best as he could the derision in the young man's eye. "We're short on petrol this month and it's a bitch of a hike."

"Do you good," the guard said coolly, taking a lungful of smoke. "It is better to strengthen feeble muscles than to pamper them."

Saltwood made himself laugh heartily. "I keep tellin' myself that." He grinned, thinking, *I hope you draw guard duty tonight, creep.*

But the guard, clearly mollified by this gesture of submissiveness, stepped back and opened the gate. Mentally thanking the encyclopedia salesman he'd once ridden the rails with, who'd taught him the value of agreeing with insults, Saltwood limped in, gazing around him incuriously at the house and outbuildings while the young man went into a small wooden gate lodge and picked up the telephone. By the way he slammed it down again Tom knew the acid drip he'd rigged in the main junction box had worked.

The Storm Trooper emerged from the lodge looking at Saltwood as if the crippled telephone repairman had been personally responsible for the nuisance—which was, in fact, the case—and said, "I'll take you in."

Saltwood shook his head sympathetically and stubbed his cigarette out against the granite of the gatepost, carefully stowing the butt behind one ear. "Bitched-up Jew wiring, that's what it is." He followed the young man across the yard.

From atop the telephone pole while installing the drip, Tom had gotten a fair look at the house already. In a way, he was glad of the summer's delays—it would be a hell of a lot easier to disappear into Berlin once the job was done than to escape the hue and cry in the wilds of the Prussian woods. He guessed this house at ten rooms exclusive of attics, completely surrounded by the wall. The old coach house and a servants' cottage had been converted to quarters for half a dozen guards, Deaths-Head SS, not Wehrmacht—not an army project, then. The shrubbery all around the inside of the wall was badly overgrown, an easy sneak-up. While the sentry knocked diffidently on the door of the downstairs study, Saltwood observed the catches on the windows, easy enough to trip with a knife blade.

"I hope for your sake the matter is critical, Trooper Weber," said a voice as soft as a thug's silk scarf. Turning, Saltwood saw in the study doorway the man who must be Captain von Rath.

Saltwood shifted his eyes away immediately, knowing he must not stare. But the man who stood framed in the umber gloom was only superficially recognizable as the one whose picture he had seen in London. The man in the picture he'd been shown in London—a picture taken in Prussia in the spring—had had the look of a man dying, burning up inside. This man . . .

For some reason, Saltwood, schooling his features into casual respect that had no trace of recognition as he looked back, was reminded more than anything else of a wealthy and well-cared-for woman in the fourth month of a pregnancy that pleases her. Von Rath had that same glow, that same sense of beauty fulfilled and radiant . . . that same very slight air of smugness. The gauntness had filled out without losing the shape of those splendid cheekbones, and even the man's hair seemed thicker, brighter, stronger despite its close military cut. Yet there was something else, something that the picture had entirely failed to convey, though Saltwood was damned if he could figure out what. Strong as a physical impact, he had a sense of evil, of wrongness—of darkness masquerading as triumphant light.

Oh, come on! he chided himself, disgusted. *I thought you got over that good guys/bad guys stuff in Spain!*

But when von Rath's frost-silver gaze touched him, he shivered and came at the major's beckoning with an unwillingness that went to the bone.

"Short in the wiring someplace," Tom explained, his ingratiating grin feeling like a badly made denture. "Buggered up half the lines around here. We need to check whether it was in a phone here, either one that's still in use or an outlet that was taken out, see." Von Rath made no response, and Tom felt the sweat start under his cheap billed cap.

He had talked strike in mines and on factory floors, never knowing which of those scared and angry men were the management
bulls, but he'd never in his life had this sense of irrational terror of
another man. As he spoke, he noticed small details: the almost metallic quality of the pale gaze; the short saber scar on the cheek; and
the white slimness of the hands. Of course with a "von" hanging off
the front of his name, he'd never done a day's manual work in his
life. Like Marvello the Magnificent and every other carney magician
Tom had ever met, von Rath wore hoodoo amulets around his neck—
twenty or more circles made of jewels and glass and what looked
like animal bone on one necklace, and on another a single uneven
ring of woven silver, crystal, and iron. This medicine-show fooferaw
should have been funny, like Hitler wearing *lederhosen*, but it wasn't.
Tom couldn't tell why.

"There is a telephone in my study," von Rath said at last, "and
another upstairs in my room. A third is in the guards' lodge out
back. Those are all that have ever been in this house. Take him
around, Weber, and see that I am not disturbed again."

While Saltwood opened up the bottom of the study telephone
and poked around inside, von Rath returned to his bulbous Beider-
meyer desk and his book, but Tom was nerve-wrackingly conscious
of the man's presence in the room. *Get a hold of yourself,* he thought
irritably, trying not to run out of the room when he was done; but
by the gleam of sweat on Trooper Weber's upper lip when that
young man met him in the hall again, he saw that von Rath had
that effect on others, as well.

And why not? he thought, disgusted with himself as he followed
Weber upstairs. *He looks like a dangerous hombre to cross, even if he
does wear Woolworth's Finest strung around his neck. HE's the one I
ought to kill.*

But ten years of bar fights, of tangles with management stooges
on picket lines and occasional pop-skulled crazies in hobo jungles
made him think uneasily, *I'd sure hate to try.*

"Chilly bugger," he volunteered, pulling apart the phone in von
Rath's Spartan bedroom and giving it, and the skirting boards, a
cursory once-over. Trooper Weber, his arrogance still cowed by the
encounter with von Rath, nodded. Von Rath's chamber was by no

means the original master bedroom of the house—either Sligo had that one or they were using it as a workroom. "Any chance of getting a quick look at the other rooms in case there's a dead lead? It'll take just a glance around the skirting and save me a trip back here if we *still* can't find the short. That way we won't have to disturb His Nibs again."

Weber hesitated, then nodded, and gave Tom a tour of three other bedrooms on the upper floor, during which Tom was able to orient himself mentally and establish entries and possible escape routes. Only at the far end of the passage, where the two major bedrooms stood opposite one another, did Weber demur. "It is forbidden to go into either of those."

"What's in there? Secret plans?" The locks on both were new.

Trooper Weber gave him a fishy stare. "There is nothing in there." He was a lousy liar.

Tom shrugged. "No old phone leads? It'd be a wire about so long sticking out of the skirting . . ."

"There is nothing like that."

"Thank Christ for that." He turned and limped back down the hall, deliberately slowing his pace to irritate his guard, who had to keep stride with him. To the right of the stairs as he emerged on the ground floor was a sliding door of polished mahogany, also recently decorated with a brand-new lock, but as he limped over to investigate, the door was shoved open from within and a young man poked his head out.

"Who are you? What do you want? What is this man doing here, Trooper?" The boy was short, fat, and coked stupid—past him Tom had an impression of black tapestries and some sort of altar, candles, chalked circles on the bare floorboards, and a stink like a San Francisco joss house.

Trooper Weber saluted smartly. "A man from the Fernsprechamt, Herr Twisselpeck. He wants to know if there was at any time a telephone in that room that might be causing a short in the lines in the neighborhood."

Herr Twisselpeck—the boy couldn't have been over eighteen—swiveled weak tea-colored eyes up to Saltwood; beneath thick glasses and enough dope to raise the dead, Tom could see the jealousy in them at his height and the breadth of his shoulders. "So they're hiring c-cripples these days, are they?" he demanded nastily. "No, there isn't a telephone in here. There never was a telephone in that room. You should know we'd never have ch-chosen it for the temple, the Holy Place of Power, if there had been any kind of electrical wiring in its walls." He jerked back into the darkness of the temple and tried to slam the doors—the heavy, sliding mahogany slipped out of his jittering hand on the first try and he heaved and fussed at it for a moment to coax it closed. A moment later the lock clicked.

Tom shook his head. "Takes all kinds."

As he was limping after his escort toward the guards' station— once the old carriage house—and taking more accurate note of the wilderness of overgrown shrubbery that should conceal very nicely his appearance over the wall, he espied an old man, clothed in nothing but a loincloth despite the autumn chill of the day, standing rigidly on a little terrace at one corner of the house, his left arm held to his side, his right crooked out before him, elbow bent so that his fingers pointed back at his abdomen, right knee bent up to rest his foot on his left knee, for all the world as if he endeavored to mold his body into an approximation of the letter B. As they passed the old man began to yodel, a long, undulating, full-throated howl in which the drawn-out sounds "Booo-o-o-o-e-r-r-r-c-cccccc . . ." could be barely distinguished.

Tom had seen weirder things in California.

He came back later that night.

He'd repaired the junction box, lest the inconvenience drive von Rath to contact the real Fernsprechamt. It was an easy matter to disconnect the entire box again at two A.M. With luck no one would know of Sligo's death until morning, but if there was a slip-up and the alarm was raised, they would be that much later getting the dogs after him. With even a few hours' start he'd be well on his way back to Hamburg.

He approached the house from behind, sliding under the wire and crawling through the scrubby sedges of the enclosed field, his black SS uniform hidden under a ragged gray blanket. The field, unlike much of the wasteland of the Jungfern Heide, had been recently mowed; in places, the bare ground showed signs of fire. The moon was a few days past full, bright as a beacon in an almost cloudless midheaven. A bomber's moon, they were already calling such conditions in London.

At Commando headquarters in Lochailort they'd given him a collapsible ladder, a lightweight steel alpinstock with rungs folded into it on either side. The wall was higher than the ladder's six-foot length, but not by more than a yard. He'd picked his spot carefully that afternoon, where the bulk of the old coach house would screen him from the sentry who would in all probability be stationed by the kitchen door. Once he was over, his uniform would almost guarantee anonymity—he'd thankfully disposed of the eyepatch, boot, and four-day beard that had constituted his disguise—and he made the jump down, taking the stock with him and stowing it out of sight in the bushes, without a sound.

The house was dark. There was a tiny chink of light around a blackout curtain in the front hall, where a guard would probably be dozing; another guard stood by the back door. Like a specter Saltwood glided through the dark laurels, forced open a dining-room window, and stood listening for a moment to the silence of the house. A chair creaked in the front hall. Looking through the dining-room door, he saw a Storm Trooper sitting in a hard-backed chair beside a lamp in the front hall, reading a lurid-covered paperback novel and moving his lips slightly with the effort. Tom slipped the garrote from his pocket, disposed of the man without trouble, took his keys, and manhandled the limp body into the bottom cabinet of a built-in china hutch where nobody was likely to look. Folding the wire garrote back around its wooden handles, he stepped quickly over to the "temple" doors and, with his pocket flashlight shielded behind his hand, had a quick look around to make sure it was no more than it seemed.

It wasn't. A black-draped inner sanctum straight out of the Benevolent Protective Association of the Rhinoceros Lodge, a Rosicrucian's lobster-supper dream complete with a closetful of white, black, and scarlet robes and a louring stench of old blood and charred meat that even the whorehouse incense couldn't conceal. He wondered what they'd sacrified. Jemal Nightshade, a slow-spoken Negro who'd worked beside him in the West Virginia mines, had confessed one

night over a couple of drinks to offering chickens to the *loa* back in
Port au Prince—a goat, if the family could afford it.

Did they really believe this stuff?

Saltwood remembered those bone amulets and shriveled little skin
bags hanging around von Rath's neck, and shivered unaccountably.
Evidently twelve years of being force-fed the opium of the masses in
Lutheran Sunday school hadn't been completely eradicated by the
big doses of Voltaire, Marx, and Hobbes he'd had since, he thought,
hugging the wall as he climbed the stairs to keep his weight from
creaking the risers. The lab, at a guess, would be in one of those
two locked bedrooms upstairs, or in one of the attics . . .

In the darkness, the sense of the infernal in the place was stronger,
revolting him as none of Jemal Nightshade's talk of *veves* and *legba*
ever had. When it came right down to it, Nightshade's voodoo had
never struck him as being that different from old Tommy Wu's
ginseng Buddhism or the sight of those old Spanish women in Sar-
agosa, crawling over cobblestones with bleeding knees to kiss a pillar
in a church. *Come on!* he told himself. *All this is just to make people
think they're crazy . . . And anyway, let's not talk about evil after you've
just added that Storm Trooper—not to mention that Merced County
"special deputy" the orange growers hired to bash the migrants—to your
body count in Spain.*

You're here to do a job.

A wavery thread of candlelight marked the bottom of one of the
locked upstairs doors; the other room was dark. Tom entered that
one first, gingerly trying key after key in hair-prickling silence, then
stepping cautiously inside and flashing the light quickly around. It
was a laboratory, all right—an absurd wizards-kitchen straight out of
L. Frank Baum, stocked with everything from mandrake roots (in a
wooden box labeled with Teutonic thoroughness) to a collection of
revolting mummy fragments, undoubtedly looted from every mu-
seum from Paris to Warsaw. There was not a shred of wire, not a
radio tube, not a soldering iron to be seen, even in the drawers and
cabinets.

Saltwood smiled inwardly. *What a collection! Old Marvello would
swap his firstborn child for a crystal ball that size!*

That means the real lab must be across the hall, or in one of the attics upstairs. But the lab itself was of only secondary importance.

He looked back at the thread of light under the door. *Not strong enough for a working light . . .*

A bedroom, then. And he'd seen von Rath and Twisselpeck, and the old geezer on the terrace that afternoon fit the description Mayfair had given him of the third member of this particular cell of the Occult Bureau, Jacobus Gall . . .

At a guess, this room would be Sligo's.

Of the three new keys on the ring, he'd already eliminated one as belonging to the lab door; the first of the remaining two he tried fitted. He had a story ready that his uniform would have backed up; but when he stepped silently through the door, he found he didn't need it. The man sitting perched on a laboratory stool at the table had his back to the door, and was far too absorbed in what he was doing to look around or even, evidently, notice that someone had entered. Even in the dim glow of a single candle, which was all the illumination the room could boast, Saltwood recognized him: Professor Rhion Sligo, self-styled wizard and pet mad scientist of the SS, a broad-shouldered bearded little man clothed in a hand-me-down Wehrmacht sweatshirt and patched fatigue pants, bent over a weird construction of braided metal wires, small glass spheres, and the biggest hunk of rock crystal Saltwood had ever seen.

Both Sligo's chubby hands rested on the twisted wire base of the thing—crude and lumpy iron wound around with something that looked like gold but was probably brass. His head was bowed, his eyes shut and his breathing slow, as if in sleep or deep meditation. Saltwood took the garrote from his pocket and silently unwound it, wrapping the handles tight in his hands.

He really does believe it . . .

His face still turned away from Saltwood, the Professor straightened up a little on his backless stool and raised his head, but the candlelight showed his open eyes focused inward, devoid of any awareness of his surroundings. It seemed to Tom, standing behind him, that a faint secondary glow seemed to be coming from the crystalline gizmo on the table, shining faint bluish white, like distant stars, in the lenses of Sligo's glasses.

Sligo stretched out one hand, keeping the other on the gizmo's base.

It has to be a reflection. An optical illusion . . . But it seemed to Tom that in Sligo's cupped hand a seed of blue-white light blossomed, cold St. Elmo's Fire that threw a ghostly radiance on every line and ridge of his fingers without appearing to burn the flesh. *But if it's a reflection of the candle flame, shouldn't it be orange?*

Tom stepped nearer. Sligo stretched out his hand, and the ball of light drifted upward like an ascending balloon. He raised his head to follow it with his eyes. Fascinated as Saltwood was by the trick, the trained assassin in him said *Now.*

Tom stepped soundlessly forward and crossed his arms; Sligo never knew what hit him until the garrote pulled tight. With the dancer's grace that an Italian thug had taught them all at Lochailort, Tom turned his body, hooked his shoulder under the taut wires and dragged the little man off his stool and up onto his back. He felt the futile twist of Sligo's body, the slapping, desperate grope of his hands as he tried franticly to find something to grab or strike. But in this position there was nothing, no purchase possible, no way to make contact with anything but the strangler's back and sides. Thirty, forty seconds at most . . .

But with a final convulsion, Professor Sligo hooked one foot in the stool on which he'd been sitting and kicked it as hard as he could against the wall. In the dead silence of the night it made a noise like the house falling down, and von Rath's room, Saltwood knew, was immediately next door.

Cursing, he threw Sligo's limp body to the floor and whipped out the dagger that was part of the SS uniform, jerked his victim's head back by the hair, and slashed at the exposed throat. For one split second he found himself looking into Sligo's wide, terrified blue eyes . . .

And the next instant light exploded, blinding as the glare of a welder's torch, inches in front of his nose. Taken totally by surprise, Tom flinched back from it and felt the body pinned beneath him twist free. Blinded by the aftermath of the glare, he made one flailing cut at where he thought Sligo would be as he tried to get to his feet, and, a split second too late, thought, *That stool . . .*

Somewhere behind him Tom heard the sobbing gasp of Sligo's breath—then the lab stool connected full force with his head and shoulders.

Saltwood couldn't have been unconscious for more than a few seconds. Electric light flooded the room as he came to; yells, curses drifted into his awareness, and a black ring of shapes swimming like sharks through his returning vision. He curled instinctively as a boot crashed into his belly; a second one exploded against the back of his head . . .

And then silence.

Swamped in pain and half stunned, still he knew what that silence meant.

"Stand up," said the voice like the whisper of silk over the point of a knife.

It wasn't easy to do so without retching. Groping at the table for support, Saltwood noticed the lumpy gizmo of iron and crystal was gone. Professor Sligo stood next to the door, green with shock except for the livid red bruise of the garrote across his throat.

"Lay him on the bed," von Rath instructed quietly, not moving from the doorway where he stood. "Get him brandy." Over the dark-red silk of his dressing gown, the double chain of amulets gleamed faintly, the small circles of bone clinking against one another and against the twisted ring of silver and iron. His face was calm, impersonal, but Saltwood knew that with him in charge of it, whatever would happen next was going to be bad.

"Who sent you?"

"He's one of ours!" Baldur Twisselpeck gasped, stumbling belatedly through the door and shoving his smudged glasses onto his face as one of the half-dozen Storm Troopers pulled the forged SS i.d. from Saltwood's pocket.

"Don't be stupider than you are." Von Rath barely glanced at the young man. "Papers can be faked—as can a patched eye, a limp, and a telephone repair kit."

"You mean that was him today?" Baldur gaped, blinking. He was shouldered out of the doorway by Jacobus Gall, barefooted and, like von Rath, evidently naked under his dressing gown, and like von Rath also seemingly indifferent to cold. Gall went to where Sligo lay, eyes shut now under a tangle of hair that was almost black against his waxy skin, on the bed that occupied most of the narrow room's western wall. Looking around him, Saltwood saw in the better light that the room was, in fact, Sligo's bedroom. Its windows were boarded up; the door had no handle on the inside.

Tom realized that Sligo was a prisoner, and not a free agent as Mayfair had believed.

"He should have a doctor," Gall stated, examining the bruises left by the garrote. "If he is to assist in the demonstration Monday . . ."

"The phones are dead again, Captain," an SS Sergeant reported, entering from the lights of the hall. "We could send Reinholt to the Lebensborn in the Grünewald—that's the nearest doctor—and from there he could phone the Gestapo . . ."

"I expect you put the telephone out again before entering this house." Von Rath's ice-gray eyes returned to Saltwood's face. "Didn't you?"

Saltwood said nothing.

Without looking back at them, von Rath added, "As for the Gestapo, I think not." Head tilted a little to one side, he continued to study Saltwood with disquietingly impersonal interest. "He is of a higher type, isn't he, than the Jew and Slavic swine they've been sending us from the camps?" he went on softly. "A finer body, certainly, and therefore a stronger and fitter mind."

Saltwood felt his stomach curl with dread. *Oh, Christ . . .*

"Shameful, isn't it?" Baldur Twisselpeck said sententiously, crowding back to van Rath's side. "The orphans of the race, betraying the heritage of their Fatherland to breed with the corrupt apemen of Jewish-dominated countries like—"

"Oh, I think not," von Rath purred, with a dreaminess in his level voice that was almost pleasure, though his eyes remained chill, almost blank, as if whatever dwelled inside were wholly occupied with itself and itself alone. "If that is the case—if his blood is corrupt—he is certainly a throwback to the original root race, and that's all we need. It is all that the best of the British will be. Gall, be sure to take his cranial index and other physical data tomorrow.

Himmler will want to see them." He signed with his finger to the sergeant.

Two Storm Troopers closed in on Tom from either side, hand-cuffing his wrists behind him and shoving him before them out of the room. Behind him, he heard von Rath say, "Take him to the house on Teglerstrasse for tonight and tomorrow. We'll need him there for the demonstration in any case. See that he comes to no harm."

Looking back over his shoulder, Saltwood saw von Rath step through the door of the bedroom, switching off the lights so that only the candle's feeble gleam illuminated the boarded-up chamber. Taking a key from his dressing-gown pocket, he locked Sligo in. As Saltwood's guards pushed him down the stair, the murmur of von Rath's voice drifted behind him, with Gall's crisp Viennese tones and Baldur's adolescent adenoidal whine.

"Should we send for a doctor?"

"I don't think it will be necessary. I've mastered all he can teach me."

"Then after the demonstration, Himmler can have him? I'm sure Himmler's right—I'm sure there's some kind of physical difference that gives him his powers. Mengele should be able to make some-thing of it . . ."

"Nonsense! Proper purification of the body, proper nutrition and mental attitude is all that is needed for the working of magic."

"Scarcely," von Rath purred. "Nevertheless, I don't think we need share with Herr Himmler what can be learned from—ah—experimentation. And after Monday's demonstration we may not need to deal with Himmler again. For you see, providence has been kind. We needed a higher type of subject for our final demonstration, the type of trained warrior with whom our invading forces will ac-tually have to contend. And now we have him."

19

The solar at Erralswan was a small room, situated in the stumpy tower at the southwest corner of the rambling sandstone manor house, the windows that on three sides overlooked the walled-in orchards and gardens making it, on these cold autumn afternoons, the warmest and sunniest place in the house. Even so, fires had been kindled in the braziers of beaten copper; the sun that strewed an intricate lacework of bare tree shadows through the latticed window-panes had lost its power to warm.

Tallisett of Erralswan stood for a long time in that bright, chilly drench of light, looking down at the locked doors of the cupboard-desk that stood between the windows, her arms folded, almost literally shivering, not with cold, but with a gust of irrational rage.

The cupboard-desk was of the old-fashioned, simple kind frequently found in the seats of country lords like this one, made of pickled pearwood, simply and cleanly carved. The pale wood showed up admirably the half-dozen small, oval splotches of indigo that dotted the edges of the tall, narrow, enclosing doors—when Tally took the desk's small key from her belt and opened those doors, she had to do so carefully, so exactly did those telltale smudges coincide with where it was easiest to place her hands.

She already knew what she'd see when she opened the desk, but at the sight of her letters, in their neat pigeonholes, all daubed and thumbed with more spots of indigo, renewed anger swept her, so that for a moment she felt she could scarcely breathe. The top sheet of the little pile of half-written stationery on the minuscule writing surface was smeared, not only with those grubby blue thumbprints, but with a very fine white powder that in places had begun, itself, to turn a faint blue. This sheet she lifted carefully, holding it by the very tips of her fingernails, and carried it to the brazier in the corner; the two silky red bird dogs sleeping in front of it in the scattered glory of the autumn sunlight raised sleepy, hopeful heads as her skirt hem brushed their fur, but for once she had no greeting for them. She placed the sheet on the blaze and waited until it caught.

After it had completely burned she turned away, to descend the stone stairway to the gardens, and seek her husband.

"It's Neela, it has to be," she said.

Marc frowned irritably, though whether it was because she'd interrupted him while he was working one of his new horses, or because he resented an accusation against the pretty black-haired housemaid whom Tally knew he was planning to bed—if he hadn't done so already—she wasn't sure. From this, the largest of the paddock yards, one could look down the length of the narrow, upland vale nestled between the shouldering walls of the Lady Range and the granite cliff of the main mass of the Mountains of the Sun: sheep country, green and empty of trees, crisscrossed with low stone fences and crystal-cold despite the deceitful brilliance of the sun. Tally pulled the long featherwork shawl more closely about her shoulders and shivered.

She went on, "I've thought before this that my desk was being searched, my letters read. Last week when I went into Yekkan I bought a powder from a Hand-Pricker, which will cling to a human hand and leave purple stains on whatever it touches, stains that appear only hours later. I found such stains not only on the papers of my desk, but on the sheets of my bed, and around the fireplace, and on brooms and rags in the servants' hall . . ."

"You went to a *Hand-Pricker*?" Marc caught her by the arm in a crushing grip, and she saw, not anger, but fear in his dark eyes. Then he cast a swift look behind him, at his stablemaster who was training another of his dark, thick-necked two-year-old colts in the first of the elaborate carousel figures that would be required in the mounted fêtes of the capital that winter, and drew Tally closer to the yellow sandstone wall that flanked the paddock on that side, so that his horse stood between them and any possibility of being seen from the yard. "My lady . . ." he said warningly.

She shook her head, baffled by how much he was making of it. "Everyone goes to Hand-Prickers."

"*Not* everyone," he whispered hoarsely. "In fact it's far fewer than most people believe."

"That's nonsense," she said, still puzzled at the look in his eyes. "If nobody goes how do they make the kind of living they do—and what does it matter anyway? What matters is that one of my servants is searching my rooms . . ."

"Hand-Prickers make their living as poisoners, as abortionists, as everyone knows—by transmuting base metals into gold . . ."

"*Marc.*" Tally pulled a little away from him, shocked at hearing this kind of thing from him. From Damson, last June, it was to have been expected—she was close to the inner circles of Agon's cult and would promulgate their oversimplifications whether she believed them or not. But with all the years Marc had been at her father's court he had to have known better. "You know as well as I do that they can't make base metals into gold without expending more energy than it's possibly worth."

Marc shook his head. "They only say that." He placed his big hands on her shoulders and looked gravely down into her eyes. Out of court costume, in the plain green tunic and close-fitting sleeves of a country squire and with his hair braided back, he seemed both older and more approachable than he did in Bragenmere, where the ceremonial of her father's household gave them the ability to distance themselves from one another. Here at Erralswan, though the summer had not been an easy one, she had remembered why she had always liked the big, easygoing young man whom she had part bullied, part bribed, part begged to marry her seven years ago.

"It's only a story they put around," Marc said, in a still lower whisper, as if he feared that some wizard would overhear, "to keep the secret of their wealth to themselves—so they can buy the influence of powerful nobles. My lady, these days it doesn't pay to be seen having anything to do with people like that, particularly for you."

Behind them the horse, bored, tossed its head. Past the low sandstone wall of the paddock Kir's voice could be heard, raised in a joyous shout as he led a pack of the half-dozen pages of the household in a charge down one of the long arbored walks that connected the main house with its several attendant pavilions. Tally caught a glimpse of them through the latticework of the vines, now nearly bare of their summer leaves, and felt a cold little dart of fear.

Carefully she said, "Why 'particularly' for me?"

"My lady," her husband said quietly, using the honorific in which he had always addressed her, "the days are past when you, or anyone, could be seen associating with . . . well, with just anyone. They're finding out things about wizards, and how they work . . ."

"*Who* is finding out 'things'?" Tally insisted warily. "What kind of 'things'?"

"About what they do to people who come within their power." Marc glanced around him again, though there was no one in the yard but the stablemaster and he was fussing lovingly over the colt's feet. "Now, I know you—and in fact anyone who knows you can attest that you haven't had your soul stolen, or your will taken over, by wizards . . ."

"That's ridicu—"

He put a finger to her lips. "They do it, my lady," he said softly. "They do it. We're only just finding out how frequently. And they turn such people into their servants, to get them still other slaves."

For a moment she could only stand openmouthed with shock at the enormity of this lie. The sheer scope of it took her breath away almost as much as the fact that it was coming to her from Marc, Marc who had always been cheerfully friendly to the wizards at her father's court, who had bought Mhorvianne only knew how many love philters from Jaldis and Rhion over the years . . . "That's the most absurd thing I've ever heard!"

He bit his lip, hesitating for a long moment—Tally felt almost that he was waiting for the groom to get out of earshot before he spoke again. "I see I'm going to have to tell you," he said softly. "I didn't want to, because I know you liked old Jaldis and Rhion, and I swear to you I've never heard a thing against either one of them, even if they did . . . Well, everyone says their disappearance was opportune."

He lifted his hand to silence her as she opened her mouth again, but the gesture was needless—Tally was outraged beyond speech.

He went on, "They arrested a conspiracy of wizards the night you left Bragenmere, in your father's very palace, in Jaldis' rooms. I'd like to assume that with his disappearance they were trying to take your father's library for whatever knowledge it contained, and not that Jaldis himself had summoned them."

Tally closed her mouth, stood for a time looking up into the handsome, healthy tanned face bent so gravely above her own. All these endless summer months she had suspected something had happened after her departure, though out here in the deeps of Marc's countrified fief there had been no way of knowing for certain, and she had feared to write to anyone she knew at court. Damson's words to her before she had left had frightened her; she knew how easily letters could be intercepted and read. So she had waited, knowing that if Rhion had indeed been brought back with the turning of the summer-tide she would eventually hear of it . . . someone would get word to her . . .

And so she had waited, through the nerve-racking weeks.

Marc went on in almost a whisper, "So you see, they have this information from the wizards themselves. From their confessions."

"Under torture." Her heart was beating heavily, hurtingly in her chest. *Shavus* . . . she thought. The old man was vain, arrogant, maddening, but never did he deserve that. *The Serpentlady, Harospix . . . Dear Goddess, did the Gray Lady get away safely? Did Gyzan?*

Marc nodded. "Of course. The things they've confessed to aren't anything you would learn of without torture. But that doesn't mean they aren't true."

Of course, she thought bitterly. *I chose Marc for my husband partly because he was easily led—because he'd believe what I told him and not ask questions. Why be surprised that I'm not the only one he'll believe?*

"And Father let them?" Her mouth felt dry. She remembered her father and the gruff old Archmage dueling with the salt spoons.

"Your father's been very ill," Marc said. "You know that, Damson's been writing all his letters for him, with only his signature . . .

but yes, his signature was on the orders. He must protect his realm—
and not only his own realm, but humankind.''

Tally was silent. A part of her felt very still and cool, detachedly
contemplating pieces of a puzzle fitting together. She didn't even feel
anger—at Damson, or at Marc—only a sort of clarity, as if she were
seeing them for the first time in decent lighting. For no reason, she
remembered the tiny, crystalline clinking of her sister's lace spindles
and the breath of incense that moved about the shrine of the Veiled
God. A cold mountain wind breathed down across the stable yard,
stirring her heavy skirts and making the feathers of her shawl ripple
in the light like a meadow of iridescent, red-bronze grass.

But part of her remembered Gyzan, Shavus, and the other mages
who'd been in Jaldis' tower that night, remembered Jaldis' sunken,
empty eyepits and limping step, and she felt her breath thicken and
heard the dizzying roar of blood sounding in her ears. It seemed
to take her forever to collect her thoughts. "Do you know . . . who
was among those arrested?"

"The Archmage," Marc said quietly. "The Harospix Harsprodin,
who had been one of the Queen's advisors. The Queen was deeply
shocked at his betrayal, and by his confession that it was he who'd
been causing her little boy's seizures, and even more shocked when
it became obvious that your father's illness was almost certainly the
result of the Archmage's spells.''

"Shavus wouldn't—"

Marc shook his head. "According to his own confession, he cast
the illness upon your father when your father began to suspect him
of trying to steal his soul, of trying to rule the country through him.
Tally," he insisted, as she shook her head, refusing to believe, "it
was written in his confession! It was what he told Mijac—the doctors
sent to your father's bedside by the priests of Agon can't make head
nor tail of his illness! He betrayed your father. The wizards he has
sheltered for so long, befriended for so long, were only using him!
Don't you understand?''

With a feverish shiver Tally remembered the letters she'd had all
summer from her father, written in Damson's neat, secretarial hand—
the wording had been frequently reminiscent of Damson, as well.
She wondered if the signature on the orders for arrest had been the

same as on her letters: unsteady, mechanical, like a man gravely ill—
or a man deeply drugged.

"Do you know," she faltered, "what time that night the wizards
were arrested? Whether it was before or after midnight?"

And Marc shook his head.

They will have destroyed the Dark Well, Tally thought, crossing
the paddock quietly and turning toward the villa, almost shocked at
her own ability to appear calm. Her heart pounded sickeningly in
her breast, and her belly turned cold every time she thought about
how confession was extracted—about what Rhion had told her of
his own brush with the priests of Agon.

Was he one of the ones they took? She thought about it for a moment and found it unlikely. *Even if he had* . . . Her mind shied from
the thought of what Esrex would have done to force a confession
from Rhion as to the paternity of her sons. *Even if he had withstood
it and died, Esrex wouldn't have passed up the chance to let me know.*

*But if he didn't make the crossing before the arrest—if he didn't come
stumbling out of the Dark Well right into the arms of Esrex and the
masked servants of the Hidden God—that means he's still stranded
wherever he is, with Jaldis dead, without magic, in trouble,* he said.

And there was no one of sufficient power to bring him home.

She paused at the rear door of the house, hating the thought of
returning to her rooms. The purple handprints would be fading by
this time, as they did after a few hours, though the Hand-Pricker in
the village had assured her that at a word from him they would
return. *For all the good that would do,* she thought bitterly. *Marc
would never consent to bringing him here—and as things are, if he has
any sense of self-preservation he won't come.*

And in any case, disposing of one spy would only mean there'd
soon be another one that she didn't know about. *His devotees are
everywhere,* Damson had said.

With sudden resolution, Tally turned her steps left, crossing behind
the rustic sandstone of the stable's east wall and thence around to the
long, sloppy succession of sheds and huts that housed the kennels and
the mews. At this time of the day the dog boy was in the rough brick
kitchen, preparing the mulch of chopped mutton and grain the dogs
were fed on those days when they weren't hunting; the pack bounded

happily to the low fence to greet her, swarming around her skirts, tails lashing furiously as she climbed over the stile and hopped down among them. Despite her fears, despite her dread, she had to laugh at the earnest joy in those furry unhuman faces, and clucked to them, calling them the love names that always made Marc roll up his eyes: "My rosy peaches, my angelmuffins, my little wuzzlepoufkins . . ." The big staghounds and mastiffs, the rangy wolf killers whose shoulders came up to her waist rolled ecstatically on the ground, long legs waving in the air, for her to scratch their bellies.

In time she made her way into the first of the half-dozen huts where the dogs slept, raised a little off the ground for ventilation, low-roofed and smelling of the old blankets on which they slept and the herbs hung from the rafters to freshen the air. Tucking up her skirts, Tally knelt in the sun-splintered shade at the back, surrounded by a sniffing congregation of interested wolfhounds, pulled aside the mass of blankets, and lifted the floorboard beneath.

Barely visible in the gloom below the floor, she could make out the shape of a large square bundle, wrapped in waxed leather; under the leather, she knew, for she was the one who had wrapped it and the four others like it hidden in other holes and corners of the kennel, was oiled silk, and then the spell-woven cloth they'd been swathed in when she'd first smuggled them out of her father's strong room. All summer she had been waiting for a question from someone—her father, Shavus, *someone*—about where they were.

Now she knew the question wouldn't come.

No one but her father knew where Jaldis' books had been bestowed—her father, the wizards, and she.

I feared that the knowledge would be lost, the Gray Lady had said. And, speaking of the wizards, *Without them it would become a contest of strongmen.*

And very calmly, she wondered where it would be best to hide her children, when she fled from Erralswan and made her way to the Ladies of the Moon.

20

The room was small, smaller than the attic cell in which Saltwood had spent last night and the long, nerve-racking day before, and empty save for the wooden chair in which he sat and the mirror on the wall. Its windows, like the ones of the cell, were boarded over, the boards not hastily nailed but screwed down with proper Teutonic thoroughness and the screwheads countersunk. Since the Storm Troopers who'd searched him—none too gently—had taken his watch, he could only estimate the passage of time, but in the locked attic room with its iron military cot he'd been fed three times, and by the raw cold—what? twelve hours ago? Anyway between meal #2 and meal #3—he'd assumed it was night. At least the bed had had blankets.

And that made today Monday, the twenty-second of September.
The day of von Rath's "demonstration."

Restless, he rose from the hard-backed chair and prowled the room again, as if he hadn't done so immediately upon being locked in. It told him nothing he didn't already know with dreary intimacy—that the room was ten feet by ten, that the bare walls had been papered once and later thickly painted in yellowish white, that the naked floorboards were stained and dirty and that at one point whoever had owned the house had possessed a small dog, imperfectly trained. A wire screen protected the mirror, clearly a one-way window. *Spying bastards.*

He'd been here nearly an hour already, to the best of his estimation, and wondered how long it would be before anyone came. Boredom and tension had long ago erased most of his fear of the Nazis, even some of his dread of von Rath, and he would have welcomed almost anything as an alternative to this hideous combination of inaction and surmise.

Yesterday, as von Rath had instructed, the magician Gall and a gray-haired female SS doctor with a face like the sole of a boot had come to his cell, backed up by four Storm Troopers. They'd ordered him to strip at gunpoint and conducted a physical examination in eerie silence, never asking him a question, never even giving him a verbal order after the first, as if he were a beast whose docility was assured. And with four automatics pointed at him, he reflected wryly, it sure as hell was. In the event it hadn't been nearly as bad as being gone over by Franco's boys.

The really unpleasant part of all this, he figured, was only a matter of time.

A sharp, whining buzz made his head jerk up, while his hackles prickled with loathing at the unmistakable quality of the sound. *Hornet!* There'd been nests of them in the tangled creek bottoms where cows habitually got themselves hung up, and over the years he'd been stung enough to give him a healthy loathing of all insects that flew with their feet hanging down.

Black and ill-tempered, it was banging against the ceiling over his head, wings roaring in a fashion reminiscent of the Heinkels over London.

They should be nesting in September, dammit, he thought, and then, *How the hell did it get in here?* Then it buzzed him with a strafing run like a Messerschmitt's and he backed away, ducking and swatting with his hand. There had to be a nest in the rafters above the ceiling panels, though how it had gotten into the room was a mystery.

The hornet, fully aroused now, dove at his face, and he swatted at it again, cursing the Nazis for taking away his belt, his cap, and anything that might be used to protect his hand. He crowded into a corner as the insect whirred up against the ceiling again, where it droned in furious, thwarted circles, banging against the plaster in its rage. Finally it lighted, crawling discontentedly around like a huge, obscene fly.

Saltwood didn't budge. It buzzed and circled a time or two more, then lighted on the wall.

Cautiously Tom edged forward, flattening and stiffening the muscles of his hand. The hornet remained where it was. A quick glance around the room revealed no way it could have gotten in, no crack or chink, but the concern was academic at the moment. He moved out of his corner, more slowly, more carefully than he had stalked the guard he'd killed last night, more delicately than he had entered that poor wretch Sligo's little cell. He needed all the experience he'd picked up in Spain and all the training Hillyard had beaten and cursed into him at the Commando base at Lochailort—if he missed now he was in for a hell of a stinging.

The insect heard him and was in flight when he struck it. It made a satisfying crunch and splat on the wall.

Great, he thought, wiping his ichorous palm on his thigh. *You're looking at torture by the Gestapo and what really scares you? Two inches of black bug.*

But at least he could fight back against the bug.

Slowly he walked around the room again. *Dammit, the bastard had to have gotten in somehow. If there was access to a crawlspace . . .* The thought of wriggling out through a crawlspace filled with hornets wasn't particularly appealing, but neither was the alternative. And in any case he'd *been* over the place . . .

He stopped, staring up at the ceiling. How he'd missed it before he couldn't imagine, but there it was—the faint, unmistakable outline of a trapdoor. It fit flush. Nailholes marked where a molding had been pulled off and painted over . . . *Painted over? So how had the hornet got into the room?*

He couldn't imagine, but didn't particularly care. The ceiling was high, higher than he could reach even at nearly six feet with long arms. He cast a wary glance at the mirror—Who knew when they'd come into that side of it to watch him get the third degree?—and fetched the chair. It wouldn't buy him much time, but anything would help.

With a roar like a thunderclap the chair burst into flames.

He flung it from him, flattening back against the wall in shock. The chair bounced against the opposite wall near the door, the fire spreading across the dry wood of the floor in greedy amber trails. *Diversion?* he thought, ripping off his clay-colored uniform shirt to wad over his mouth and nose against the smoke. *Maybe. It'll weaken the door, if the smoke doesn't get me first.* A firefighter in Tulsa had told him once that most victims of fire weren't burned but smothered. The flames were spreading fast, but he pushed back his panic at being locked in with the blaze and crouched low to the floor where the air would be better. The fire was around the door, but it was eating its way across the planks toward him as well. In the midst of it the chair was beginning to fall apart, smoke streaks crawling up to blacken the walls. He shrank back as the fire's heat seared his bare arms and chest. The blaze was all around the door—if he miscalculated his timing, flung himself at the door and it *didn't* give, he'd burn.

Then, abruptly as it had begun, the fire began to sink. Before Saltwood's startled eyes the flames ceased their advance, flickering down into fingerlets and then tiny tongues no bigger than two-penny nails that guttered out one by one. Within minutes, the only things left of the blaze were a huge patch of charred floor, the still-guttering chair, the suffocating heat, and the upside-down waterfall of smoke stains around the door.

What the HELL?!?

He crossed swiftly to the door, pulling his shirt hastily on without bothering to button it, and tried body-slamming the door. It didn't give, though it was roasting-hot to the touch. He kicked it, hoping the wood had weakened. It hadn't.

Puzzled, shaken, he turned back to stare at the flame still flickering over what was left of the chair. He'd seen a dozen fires in his year in the Tulsa oil fields, but *nothing* like that. Doubtfully he took a step toward it.

What happened then took him so completely by surprise that his mind barely registered the impossibility of it, only reacted in terror and shock. *SOMETHING* came at him, from out of where he couldn't imagine—something round and small and bristling with dripping scales, something with huge jaws and tiny black hands like a monkey's, something that whizzed through the air like a thrown baseball straight at his face.

With a yell of horror he struck at it, dodging back. It zigzagged crazily after him, chisel teeth snapping in a spray of sulfur-smelling slime. He retreated across the room, slapping at it in growing panic, his mind stalled with fear; his back hit the wall and the thing dove in under his block, the claws of its little hands ripping and digging in the flesh of his arm. He yelled again as it began to climb toward his shoulder, and smashed it against the wall. It bounced squishily and continued fighting its way up, its round mouth tearing tablespoon-size chunks of his flesh, its slobber and the ooze that dripped from its smashed head burning the ripped muscle like lye. He beat it again and again on the wall, shoulder numb from the impact, and still it came on. It was making for his face, his eyes . . .

In panic, he dove for the burning chair and shoved his arm, the thing still clinging greedily, into the center of the sinking blaze.

His shirt caught immediately, but the creature fell off, wriggling and twisting like a lizard with a broken back. Saltwood stripped off his shirt, flung it away to burn itself out in a corner, arm seared and blistered and throbbing with pain, flesh hanging in gory flaps and blood dripping from his fingers. Staggering, he fell back against the rear wall of the room, watching the creature's death agonies in the fire until it was still. A stench like burning rubber filled the room, with the hideous smell of his own charred flesh.

The secret weapon, he thought, gripping his burned arm tight against him, fighting the nauseating wash of shock and pain. *Damn Sligo, damn that crazy little bastard* . . . His breath came in ragged sobs, sweat burning his eyes, the agony in his arm making him dizzy. He had no idea how the Nazis would use this secret, these hideous things, but whatever he had experienced here, he wouldn't wish on Hitler.

Well, he thought, *maybe* . . .

And then he blinked. The pain in his arm was gone.

The burned patches on the floor were gone.

The chair was whole, lying on its side near the door where he'd thrown it.

There was no dead creature, no ashes, no little trapdoor in the ceiling . . . not even the smashed remains of a hornet on the wall.

The room was precisely as it had been when he'd been brought here. His shirt, unburned, lay crumpled on the floor. He looked at his left arm, and saw the skin whole with its dusting of sunburn over the thick core of muscle and bone.

He went and got his shirt, because even the heat of the fire had died out of the room and it was unpleasantly chilly, but, as he put it on, he wedged himself in the far corner and waited without moving until an hour later, when the door opened and von Rath came in.

"You were apprehended in the uniform of a Storm Trooper, bearing Schutzstaffel identification papers." Von Rath folded his arms and tipped his head a little to one side. "It makes no difference to me or to our experiment whether you are English or German, but as Reichsführer-SS Himmler will point out, the penalties attached to espionage are far less exacting than those for treason to the Black Order and to the Reich." As he spoke von Rath nodded toward the two men who had entered the room in the wake of his little knot of guards. One was a golden giant of a man, like an overweight Norse god, with the left breast of his white uniform jacket plastered in medals—Saltwood knew his face from the newspaper photograph he and other members of the Lincoln Brigade had thrown darts at in their quarters in Madrid. It was Hermann Goering. Had it not been for the military gingerbread decorating the other man's black SS uniform, Saltwood would have taken him for somebody's clerk— small, mild, bespectacled, and self-effacing, clutching his clipboard with a slightly apologetic air and completely overshadowed by the splendid commander of the Luftwaffe. With a shock, Saltwood realized that was Heinrich Himmler, head of the SS and the Gestapo.

After a moment he said quietly, "Captain Thomas Saltwood, Eleventh Independent Battalion." He'd been promoted after the big raid on Boulogne.

"The Commandos," von Rath said, and nodded as if pleased. "Not only the highest racial type, but trained."

The air of smugness clung to him, radiated from him; Saltwood could see by the slight dampening of his ivory-fair hair that he had gone through some exertion, but there was no sign of it in the glowing pinkness of his face. Over his black uniform jacket he still wore his hoodoo beads. Looking at them more closely—for they were almost on level with his eyes where he sat handcuffed to the same chair that had appeared to burst into flames an hour ago— Saltwood realized with a shock of revulsion that several of the disks were made of human skin stretched over what must have been human bone. They were wrapped and trimmed in gold, and written over with the kind of weird magic signs with which Marvello had decorated his blue stage robe and pointed hat, a horrible juxtaposition of the gruesome and the absurd.

Oddly enough, even those didn't trouble him as much as the iron circle, hanging alone upon its silver chain. There was some kind of disturbing optical effect connected with it, a sort of blurring, as if it were impossible to see it directly. And yet, when he looked again, he could see the buttons of the man's uniform clearly through its ring, the texture of the jacket wool, and the links of the chain beneath.

"And yet he is an American," Goering said thoughtfully.

Saltwood looked across at him. "Some of us don't need an Anschluss to tell us who our brothers are."

The big man's eyes gleamed approvingly at this show of defiance, but von Rath said, "It makes no difference. Our purpose is not to gather intelligence but to conduct a psychological test. If you do not give us accurate answers about what you experienced we have thiopental available, but we would prefer an undrugged subject, as much as you, I am sure, would prefer to avoid being drugged."

Saltwood glanced up at him. "You realize using prisoners of war for tests of any kind is against the Geneva accord?"

The cold face twitched in a smile that looked strangely automatic. "You are not a prisoner of war," he pointed out gently. "You are a spy. If you prefer, we will turn you over to the Gestapo, whose methods, as you will learn, are also against the Geneva accords."

No way out, Saltwood thought. He might as well find out what the hell had been going on here. If Himmler and Goering—the second and third honchos of the Reich—had shown up to watch, this device of Sligo's, whatever it was or did, was big stuff. He shivered, remembering the slashing, clawing thing chewing its way up his arm, and looked again down at the uncharred shirt sleeve, the uninjured flesh beneath, and the unburned wood of the chair in which he sat. His arm still hurt like hell. Impossible to believe it hadn't been real.

"Fair enough."

The door opened quietly, and the fat boy Baldur Twisselpeck entered, followed by white-bearded Jacobus Gall, both carrying clipboards similar to those held by the two Nazi bigwigs. Von Rath gave them an inquiring glance; Gall nodded and said, "You may question her after you are done with him."

Von Rath turned back to Saltwood. He, too, held a clipboard, but didn't bother to look at it; he spoke as if he knew it all by heart. "At ten forty-five today you looked up at the ceiling of this room, started striking at something in the air. What was it?"

"A—a hornet," Saltwood said, after a moment of fishing the German word—*eine Hornisse*—from the disused memories of the high plains. "It struck at my face. I don't know how it got into the room. I waited till it lighted, then crushed it."

"Have you been stung by a hornet before, Captain Saltwood?"

"Yes."

"And you suffered no extraordinary adverse effects?"

"I puff up and hurt like hell; I don't know if you Aryans do it differently."

"You are obviously of Aryan stock yourself, Captain," Himmler said in his soft voice, looking up from his clipboard and blinking behind his round spectacles. "It grieves me to hear such treason to your birthright."

"I'll tell that to my Sioux grandmother," Saltwood retorted. "She'll be flattered."

Very calmly von Rath struck him, an open-handed blow across the face that wrenched his head on his neck and brought blood from his lip. Saltwood jerked angrily against the handcuffs that held him to the chair and heard the guards behind him move, ready for trouble, but nothing came of it. He settled back, blue eyes glittering dangerously. After a moment's silence, von Rath went on, "Then at ten fifty-two you started looking around the room. What did you seek?"

"The place where the hornet got in. I can't swear to the exact time because your little cherubs lifted my watch . . . I wanted to know if there were going to be more of them, or if it might lead to some way out."

"And did you find the place?"

"There was—" He paused, glancing up at the corner of the ceiling where the trapdoor had been—*It really had, dammit!*—and wondering how stupid this was going to sound. "I thought I saw a kind of trapdoor up there, the kind that gives access to . . ." He didn't know the German for crawlspace, so finished with ". . . attics."

Goering and Himmler looked quickly at one another. Himmler asked, "What part of the ceiling? What corner of the room?"

"Left-hand rear corner as you come in the door. It was about two feet square, painted over white. I know I didn't see it when I came in."

"And when did you first see it?" Himmler asked, leaning forward, fascinated.

"Only when I killed the hornet. In fact, I was looking at the ceiling when the damn bug was flying around up there, wondering how it had got in. I'm sure—I'm *almost* sure—there was no trapdoor then."

Von Rath went on, "And you brought the chair over directly underneath the trapdoor as soon as you noticed it, presumably to attempt an escape."

"To see if I could get out that way, yes."

"This chair you're sitting on now?"

"Yes."

Goering was staring at von Rath with unbelieving awe; Himmler's attention was fastened on Saltwood, his moist little lips parted with eagerness, his dark eyes bright.

"And what happened?"

Saltwood took a deep breath. "I— The chair caught fire."

If von Rath had been a cat he would have purred and washed himself the way cats did when they knew they were being admired. "Did it?"

Hell, Saltwood thought, *dammit, it did!* "Yeah. I don't understand . . . I felt the heat. I threw it away—it hit the wall over by the door. The fire spread . . ." Once in Tulsa, Saltwood had had his boss' car stolen from him by a troop of Cherokee teenagers on bicycles. He recited his story as he'd recited his explanation then, keeping his eyes straight forward and simply recounting the events as they'd happened, ridiculous and unbelievable as they sounded, but he was conscious of the two Reichsministers whispering together, comparing notes on their clipboards, gesturing with covert amazement.

"It is incredible," Goering whispered, when Saltwood had finished. He was looking stunned. Himmler, throughout the narrative, had been gradually puffing himself up with the same kind of gratified smugness that characterized von Rath, and now looked so pleased Saltwood wished the bigger man would swat him. "Absolutely unbelievable. And the other subject . . ."

"I have no doubt," Himmler purred, "that the results will be exactly the same."

"Bring her in," von Rath said, and Gall and Baldur, who had been standing listening, turned and left. To the SS guards von Rath said, "Take this man into the other room." As Saltwood's hands were unmanacled and he stood up, von Rath continued to his two distinguished visitors, "Other experiments can be devised, of course, using more subjects simultaneously, but I'm sure this proves . . ."

The closing of the door shut out the sound of his voice—the room was soundproofed.

Like the house out in the Jungfern Heide, this place—the house on Teglerstrasse, von Rath had called it—was a modestly isolated villa set in its own wide grounds, which were also walled; though, as far as Saltwood could tell from the glimpse he'd gotten by the combined moonlight and headlamps when they'd brought him here, without the fortresslike quality of the house where they were keeping Sligo. The district, where middle-class suburban villas had begun to encroach on country cottages, lay well to the northeast of Berlin's sea of industrial slums, but it was more heavily built up than the Jungfern Heide. During the day, listening against the slant of the attic ceiling, he'd been able to make out occasional sounds of traffic on Teglerstrasse itself. He wondered why von Rath had wanted separate establishments. As part of this "demonstration" of theirs?

The place was smaller than von Rath's headquarters, having, Saltwood guessed, four rooms downstairs and four, maybe six, up. His guards now escorted him to what had been an upstairs parlor, rugless, cold, and containing a plain wooden table and three more hard kitchen chairs of the pattern already familiar to him. Evidently all the better pieces of furniture had found their way into some Party official's residence. Its window wasn't covered, but it *was* barred; as soon as the guards had recuffed his hands in front of him and locked the door, leaving him alone, he strode over and looked out. Treetops were visible over a buff sandstone wall more decorative than functional, and the roofs of neighboring "villas." On the gravel drive below were parked two large Mercedes staff cars, a three-ton Benz LG.-3000 transport with a tie-down canvas cover, and a number of motorcycles. Storm Troopers and two minor officers in the uniforms of the Luftwaffe stood by them, smoking. Beyond, he could see iron gates, backed with sheet metal, as were those of the house in the Jungfern Heide on the other side of town. It was broad daylight, by the angle of the cloud-filtered sun shortly after noon.

Escaping over the wall with six-guns blazing didn't look like a real promising bet.

Nevertheless Tom began a meticulous examination of the room.

There were two doors—one into the hallway, the other, presumably, into another room. Both were locked—new locks, as in the Jungfern Heide house, set in the old oak of the doors. At a guess, he thought, looking at the scratches on the bare floorboards beneath the three chairs and the way they were grouped around the table, prisoners were interviewed here. A Gestapo safe house? God knew how many of those there were around the outskirts of Berlin. Easy enough for the Gestapo, or the SS, to acquire from those "enemies of the Reich" who disappeared into concentration camps. *Real nice property*, his mind framed an advertisement, *comfortable, detached, suburban villa; privacy, security, all the modern conveniences, and a place to put the kiddies when they're bad . . .*

He thought, as he had many times during last night's interminable incarceration in the attic cell, about poor Professor Sligo, locked in his windowless room and completely at the mercy of a fruitcake like von Rath. No improvement over whatever insane asylum they'd gotten him from.

But he'd sure as hell come up with something. Possibly not of his own free will, but SOMETHING.

He shivered again and rubbed his arm. Hallucinogenic gas? *Never spend your hard-earned cash on liquor again, folks—skip all that time-consuming drinking and go straight to the D.T.s!* As he never had before, he pitied old Charlie the wino who'd hung around the West Virginia mines, screaming as he tore imaginary snakes from his clothing. *Christ, if that's what it's like I'm going teetotal.*

And he grinned mirthlessly. *Right—you'll turn down the glass of brandy von Rath's going to offer you before he shoots you as a spy.*

He had to get out. If he'd been shocked enough, panicked enough, to shove his own arm into what he thought was a fire to get rid of that thing eating its way up toward his face, God knew what havoc Sligo's invention would work in the forces defending the roads up from the English beaches against the first Panzer divisions, the RAF boys going against the Luftwaffe in the Sussex skies.

No wonder Mayfair wanted Sligo destroyed—and no wonder Intelligence wouldn't believe the rumors they'd heard.

Having made a circuit of the room, he went back to the second, inner door. Hinges on the other side, dammit—in any case he didn't have so much as a belt buckle to pry them out with. He didn't have a cigarette, either, and was feeling the need of one badly. As he knelt to examine the lock he became aware of voices in the other room, the faint creak of footsteps, and the dim, protesting groan of an overburdened chair.

"Damn it, Captain, it's unbelievable!" came a booming voice he recognized as Goering's. "I wrote out those instructions myself! Even Himmler didn't know what they were going to be until I made them up! And you on the other side of Berlin, miles away . . . For him to see them in that kind of detail . . ."

"It is . . . quite commonplace," von Rath's soft voice said.

"I only wish you'd had this perfected a month ago! Because of the damned British air cover, Hitler's been vacillating on the invasion plans for weeks! We're down to the last possible days—and if he puts them off again we might as well forget it until next spring! Dammit, I keep telling him I only need four clear days . . ."

"You shall have them now." Von Rath's voice was clearer, then softer as if he were pacing; Saltwood bent his head, listening, knowing if he could only get this information back to Mayfair somehow . . . "And as you see, you will no longer be troubled by the RAF. I am sorry about the delay—it was a question of accumulating—ah—sufficient strength. We came to Berlin as soon as we could. If the invasion itself can be launched on the twenty-fourth—"

"The day after tomorrow?"

Holy Christ! He wondered if he could make it to Hamburg, get in touch with the radioman there—to hell with getting himself taken off, if he could just warn them . . .

"Is it possible? Is that time enough?"

There was a long pause. "Just," Goering said at last. "The forces are assembled, the landing barges are ready . . . We've been on standby, then standdown, then standby again since July. All we need is to convince our Führer that such an enterprise will, in fact, succeed."

"After the demonstration you will have this afternoon, believe me, you need have no fear."

"Damn it, Captain . . ." The chair creaked again, and Goering's voice got louder. Saltwood could almost see them standing together, overweight Thor and darkly shining Loki.

"You will have your four days of clear weather," von Rath promised again, his voice sinking low, "and the wherewithal to blast the RAF from the sky. And in return . . ."

Boots thudded in the hall. Saltwood was on his feet and over to the window in one swift move as a key rattled in the lock. He had a brief glimpse of three Storm Troopers, guns pointed, in the hall as the door was opened and a woman shoved unceremoniously in. Then the door banged, and the lock snapped again.

Not a woman, he thought, taking another look—*a girl.*

She looked about twenty-two, her pointy white face framed in hair that was frizzed electric from her red ears to her slender shoulders, and above that, along the part, dark and luxurious brown-black with highlights of mahogany. Her eyes, taking in the black uniform pants and boots he wore, the clay-colored regulation shirt with its Deaths-Head emblems, were soot-dark and filled with spit-cat hate.

"Don't jump to conclusions," Saltwood said. "I'm an American— a Captain in the MO9."

In English she said, "Oh, yeah?"

"Yeah," he replied in the same language with as flat a midwestern accent as he could still conjure to his tongue. With a shock he realized she was American, too.

"So who pitched for Cincinnati in 'thirty-eight?"

Saltwood stared at her, appalled. "I don't know, I always thought baseball was a Christly dumb game! I mean, Jesus, paying two bits to watch a bunch of guys in knickers stand around in the sun all day and scratch and spit?"

She perched one slim haunch on the corner of the table and shook back her particolored hair. "Some American!" But the hate was gone from her eyes.

She dug in her pocket for cigarettes and a lighter—she wore some kind of ill-fitting uniform, short-sleeved white blouse, gray skirt, and sensible shoes wildly at odds with the voluptuous figure beneath. As he took the smoke she offered him he saw her nails were bitten to the quick.

"You have any idea what's going on around here?" he asked, raising his manacled hands to take a thankful drag. "Those hallucinations . . . That—that hornet, and the fire . . . that thing that flew at me through the air . . ."

"What?" She blew a line of smoke. "You missed the trapdoor?"

21

"You gotta remember I grew up with this stuff." Sara crossed one knee over the other—she had beautiful legs, shapely, strong, and slim-ankled, and to hell with the black stubble that sprinkled them and the white ankle socks of the League of German Maidens—and drew on her cigarette while Saltwood prowled, for the fifth time, from the window to the inner door to the outer door, checking, testing, trying to put something together before it was too late. The guards were always there outside.

"I don't know *how* many reincarnated ancient Egyptian priests I met when I was a little girl, or travelers from other dimensions or other astral planes, and they were *all* wizards or used to be, but they couldn't practice in this dimension for one reason or another. You might as well sit down and take a break, cowboy. I've been over this room half a dozen times in the past week or so. You could fill it up with water and it wouldn't leak."

"That's how long you've been here?" After one final glance out the windows at the guards standing around the vehicles, he came back to her, but remained on his feet beside the table where she sat, unable to conquer his restlessness.

She nodded, setting her cigarette to burn itself out on the table's edge. "Eleven days—I kept count, scratching marks on the inside of the dresser drawer in my cell."

Tom had seen the marks when he'd gone over the room where he'd been kept. "Why inside the drawer?"

She shrugged, long black lashes veiling her eyes as if embarrassed at the childishness of her impulse. "If they knew I was keeping track they'd erase them, add to them, or change them when they searched the room, just to make me crazy—to make me—I don't know, feel helpless, feel off guard, like nothing was my own. Papa says they did that a lot in the camp."

"Hell," Tom said, feeling the old anger heat in him. "And I thought the special deputies were bad, the ones the fruit growers hired to chouse the migrants from camp to camp." He settled on the edge of the table, his handcuffed hands folded on his thigh. "Your father's here, too?"

"Yeah. I bunked in his room last night, sleeping on the floor." She glanced up at him, and he saw, in spite of the cynical toughness in her eyes, how close she was to tears of sheer exhaustion, worn down by the bitter grindstone of being always watched, always helpless, and of never knowing what would happen next. Her brows, heavy and unplucked, grew together in a dark down over the bridge of her nose; there was a fine little pen-scratch line on either side of her mobile red mouth that emphasized each wry twist and each smile.

She shrugged again and made her voice offhand. "One more strike against that momzer von Rath. They kept us in the solitary cells at Kegenwald when Rhion was still at Schloss Torweg. They'd bring him in once a week to talk to us, once he was on his feet again. They—hurt him pretty bad after they caught him," she added slowly. "There was a limit to what they could do if they wanted him to go on working for them, but I don't think he ever really got over it. But he insisted on seeing us, talking to us, to make sure we were all right and hadn't been taken away." Her gaze returned to her lap, where her small, hard fingers traced over and over again a seam of her skirt.

Great, Saltwood thought. *And after all that, I come along and try to assassinate the poor stiff for being a Nazi. And I may have to yet,* he reflected. "So what is it he's doing?" he asked gently. "What is it he's made?"

Her mouth twisted, and the old gleam of ironic humor came back to her eyes. "Like I said." She grinned up at him. "I've met *dozens* of wizards in my life, and they were *all* working on some kind of *shmegegeleh* that let them do magic—or would, once they got it perfected, usually out of the damnedest stuff—cardboard pyramids, 'sympathetic vibrating generators' made out of old colanders and copper wire, hoodoo amulets with stuff I didn't want to know about wadded up and stinking to high heaven inside. But none of them gave me the creeps the way that Spiracle does. Old Pauli'll stand there fingering it, either on the chain around his neck with all his other damn filthy *tchotchkes* or fixed on the head of a wooden staff, and the look in his eyes is the same as I'd see in the eyes of the real crazy ones, the ones who claimed to hear God or the Devil whispering at them."

She shook her head again, her dark brows pinching together; then she dismissed the fear with a dry chuckle. "Rhion—and Papa, who's just as bad—claims it gives von Rath magic powers."

"Great!" He made a gesture of disgust with his manacled hands. "That gets us exactly nowhere."

"You've got to remember Rhion believes it himself." She swung around at the sudden throb of engines in the driveway below. Tom was already halfway to the window to look—she scrambled leggily down and followed. Shoulder to shoulder, they watched through the bars as Storm Troopers and Luftwaffe bodyguards clambered into cars and truck and mounted the phalanx of motorcycles. Foreshortened almost directly below them, von-Rath exchanged crisp Heil Hitlers with Goering and Himmler on the gravel of the drive.

"You heard about the new system of National Socialist weights and measurements?" Sara asked absently. "A 'goering' is the maximum amount of tin a man can pin to his chest without falling over on his face. God knows what's really going on." She turned her head to look up at Saltwood, pale noon sunlight glinting in her coffee-black eyes. "What happened to us could have been nothing more than posthypnotic suggestion . . ."

"I was never hypnotized!"

"The hell you weren't." She stepped back a pace from the glass and regarded him, hands on hips. "They could have hypnotized you and told you not to remember it—that's one of the oldest ones in the book."

Tom was silent a moment, considering that. He could remember everything clearly, except for a certain patchiness in his recollections immediately preceding Rhion smashing him over the head with the lab stool. At least he *thought* he could remember everything. "Maybe," he said slowly. "If von Rath was supposedly sending those—those hallucinations—from his h.q. on the other side of town, I suppose Goering's instructions could have been transmitted here by some kind of code words over the phone, the way the carney magicians do. But what would be the point, if they couldn't repeat it in a combat situation? And that invasion starts Wednesday—the day after tomorrow . . . ."

Sara swore in Polish. "You sure?"

"I heard Goering talking about it in the next room. He and von Rath are cutting a deal of some kind. Von Rath claims he can give Goering four days' clear weather, which is a hell of a promise over the English Channel this time of year, plus this hallucination thing, and God knows what else. You don't . . ." He paused, uncertain. "This is going to sound stupid, but you don't think there's some kind of—of thought-amplification device involved, do you?"

"What the hell do you think magic is supposed to be, if not the action of thought waves on the material world? But I'm here to tell you, cowboy, in four years of analytical chemistry, I have yet to see anybody circumvent the law of conservation of energy, or make two things like hydrogen and ethylene combine without throwing in some platinum as a catalyst. It just doesn't work that way." She frowned. "What scares me is that there obviously *is* something going on. It doesn't hook up with any of the stuff Heisenberg and Einstein have been doing—or at least not with anything they've published—but once you get unpicking atomic structure, who knows? But there's got to be instrumentality of some kind. Anything else is like trying to change gears without a clutch. And whatever the hell Rhion *did* come up with—whatever he *thought* he was doing—von Rath's going to be able to use it."

"I was with the Eleventh Commandos when they hit Boulogne in July," Saltwood said quietly. "I saw the landing barges the Germans have ready. And whatever's going on, I have to get the hell out of here and let London know the balloon's about to go up."

Sara started to reply, but before she could, boots thudded outside the door. Another woman might have edged closer to him, for the illusion of protection if for nothing else; she only set her fragile jaw, but he saw the fear in her eyes.

The door banged open. Von Rath stood framed against a black wall of Storm Troopers, gun muzzles bristling around him. A moment later, guards entered the room, keeping the two prisoners covered. As Sara had said, the German was fingering the Spiracle on its silver chain, absently and yet lovingly, his head tilted a little as if listening for sounds no human should hear. "It is time," he said, "for the second part of our—ah—psychological tests."

Sara folded her arms. "Does that mean I get my room back?"

The opal glance touched her without a shred of humanity. "You are welcome to it for the remainder of the day," he said in his soft, well-bred voice. "But by tonight the question will be academic."

Saltwood saw the impact of that widen her eyes as he was pushed through the door.

Soldiers were everywhere in the wide wire-fenced enclosure that encircled the house in the Jungfern Heide when von Rath's little cavalcade rumbled carefully through the opened wire gate and off the drive. Sitting with half a dozen Storm Troopers in the back of the covered transport, Saltwood got a glimpse through its canvas curtains of the men who closed the gate behind them. They turned to look at him with stony hatred in their blue eyes. *Must have found the body of their pal in the downstairs hall.* A bad lookout when von Rath was done with him—always provided he survived this round of "psychological tests."

As the truck pulled around he could see Goering, with his gray mob of Luftwaffe bodyguards, walking slowly back and forth across the flat, weedy ground of the field, pausing now and then to stamp the hard-packed earth. "Absolutely no hidden wires, ladies and gentlemen," Saltwood said wryly to no one in particular in the voice of W. C. Fields. "You will observe that there is nothing up my sleeve but my arm." Closer to, Himmler was making a much more cursory examination, which he broke off when von Rath's car braked to a halt and came hurrying to its side.

"It was astounding, Captain," Saltwood heard the little Reichsführer-SS say. "You have completely vindicated the Occult Bureau! Completely vindicated the true purposes of the SS as the spearhead of our Race's destiny. And if you have, as you say, found a method to release the *vril*, the sacred power bequeathed to the Aryan Race from the root race of Atlantis, we will indeed have nothing further to fear from those who oppose us. I have already put you in for promotion to full Colonel and a position as First Assistant to the head of the Occult Bureau . . ."

"I am honored," Von Rath inclined his head respectfully to the nervous, bespectacled bureaucrat before him. But by the steely edge of his soft reply, Saltwood guessed that Sara had been right. *Completely vindicated Himmler's pet bureau and all he gets out of it is full Colonel? First Assistant?* He'd heard Himmler was stingy and jealous of his influence and power. How long would it be, he wondered, before the Reichsführer-SS went diving out a window for fear of something he thought he saw in the middle of the night, leaving the power of the SS like a honed dagger in von Rath's patrician hands?

Did von Rath believe it was magic? Or were the chain of faintly clinking amulets and the concealment of the control mechanism of Sligo's hellish device as an iron circle that, sure enough, he now carried on the head of a bona fide wizard's staff merely cover, a ruse to approach that clever, sneaky, powerful little man on his credulous blind side?

Sara was right about the Spiracle, too. It *did* give him a faint creeping sensation. Not when he looked at it straight, but a moment ago, glimpsing it from the corner of his eye, he'd seen—he didn't know what he'd seen—a darkness that wasn't really darkness radiating around it, a sense of spider strands of something too fine to see floating in all directions, webbing the air . . .

A fragmented picture flashed through Saltwood's mind, something driven from his memory by the blow that had knocked him out—maybe only a hallucination itself . . . Rhion Sligo had been perched in the darkness on his tall-legged stool, watching raptly as a ball of bluish light drifted slowly up from his hand . . .

But before he could think about it, he was being shoved over the lowered tailgate and walked between four guards to where Paul von Rath, accompanied now by Himmler and Goering as well as the inevitable swarm of bodyguards, stood beside a slightly smaller—maybe two-ton—covered flatbed transport truck.

A man in the clay-colored uniform of the motor pool was holding the hood propped open, and a Luftwaffe Captain reverently held Goering's white gloves as the big Reichsmarshall poked around the engine.

"It hasn't been out of my sight all day, Herr Reichsmarshall," the driver was saying. "You can see yourself there's nothing in the engine . . ."

The huge man grunted and straightened up, chest ribbons flashing like an unimaginative rainbow in the pale sunlight. Saltwood remembered Sara's joke and grinned. "I'm more familiar with a plane's engine than a car's," Goering said, as the driver shut and latched the hood, "but I'll swear he's right. Very well, then." He slapped the fender. "Let him drive this."

Himmler said nothing, but his dark eyes blazed with suppressed excitement, like a child about to see a show. Saltwood felt his flesh crawl.

Von Rath turned to him, his voice soft and polite, as if he barely remembered striking him—barely remembered, except in a cursory way, who he was. "You will drive the truck around the course marked by those orange flags." They were only scraps of cloth tied to weeds and brambles, and here and there to a stake where the ground was bare. "You may drive inside or outside of them, but if you attempt to crash the fence I can assure you that you will be killed instantly."

There were no guards on the perimeter of the field. Looking back at von Rath's calm smile, Saltwood knew that their absence was not an oversight.

"May I walk the course?"

The Captain—*oops, sorry, Colonel now, thank you, Mr. Himmler*—considered it for a moment, one hand idly fingering the pale staff of stripped, close-grained greenish wood on which the iron Spiracle was mounted. Then he shook his head. "I assure you it has been examined for hidden devices by men at least as skeptical as yourself."

Saltwood almost asked, *Who, for instance?*—Himmler and Goering both seemed to have swallowed the whole malarkey hook, line, and sinker. But he knew that particular piece of smartassery would only get him another smack in the mouth. So he shrugged and said in English, "It's your ball game." He turned to the cab of the truck.

The blood pounded in his ears as they handcuffed his left wrist to the steering wheel, leaving his right hand free to work the ignition and gears. Were they counting on him to make a run for it? It would be child's play to crash the fence, a jolting dash to the driveway or, if necessary, cross-country to the Alt-Moabitstrasse—he was pretty sure of his way back to the house on Teglerstrasse where Sara and her father were . . .

The house on Teglerstrasse? he demanded, aghast at himself. *What the hell are you thinking? You'd be GUARANTEEING your capture by going back there. Your first duty is to get your arse to Hamburg and get London word of the invasion. Sara knows that, if anyone does.*

And what makes you think you're coming out of this alive anyway?

Dammit, he thought, studying those beautifully smiling lips, those weirdly empty gray eyes, *what the hell has he got? Does he believe this crap himself?*

"Drive three times around the course," von Rath said, as Tom turned the key in the ignition, "and then return here."

And disregard any fire-breathing monsters that get in your way. He pressed the accelerator, let out the clutch, and jolted toward the first of the orange flags.

On the first half of the circuit he was taken up with getting the feel of the truck over the bumpy, unpaved ground and with scanning the earth all around him, particularly around the stakes and flags for signs that it had been dug up or tampered with. Though of course Goering had had a much better view . . . At the far end of the field he had a panicky impulse to crash the fence, head like hell toward the Spandau canal, but a second later cold feet overcame him. There was something wrong with the setup. He knew it, smelled it, as he had smelled thunderstorms when he was a kid riding herd and as he had smelled ambush in the dry canyons of the Meseta. He had no doubt that if he tried it, somehow, von Rath would kill him. Or were they counting on that fear?

Rounding the far turn he saw them standing like an official photograph in *Das Reich*: Goering in white and Himmler in black, with von Rath holding his iron-headed staff like some strange, glittering angel between them. Around the cars and back toward the house a shifting mill of men formed an obscuring backdrop from which an occasional face emerged—he thought he saw the pale flutter of Gall's long beard, the glint of glasses that had to be Baldur's. But he sensed all eyes on him, all attention on the gray truck as it moved and jerked over the rutted ground.

Then Himmler, his glasses gleaming in the wan light, leaned over and said something to von Rath, and the SS Captain lifted his hand, the crystals in the staff-head flashing . . .

The explosion of light nearly blinded Saltwood, the roaring blast deafening, and for one second he thought, *That's it* . . . But with almost comic simultaneity he realized he was still alive and that the only jarring came from the truck bouncing over the field. *No blast effect*, but only light that turned his vision to a whirling mass of purple spots and a noise like the German ammo dumps at Boulogne going up.

The next second the shooting and yelling started, as if all spectators from Goering on down had simultaneously discovered that their hair was on fire. As Saltwood's vision cleared a little, he saw Storm Troopers dashing from all corners of the field toward the place where the two Reichshonchos were staggering about, half doubled over and holding their eyes. Lights ripped the afternoon brightness like flashbulbs at a Hollywood premiere and someone was running toward the truck, desperately waving the iron-circled magic staff and yelling for him to stop.

He recognized Rhion Sligo.

The truck fishtailed in a cloud of thrown dirt as he hit the brake. Bullets had begun to spatter, but because of the lights still popping with gut-tearing intensity all around them, nobody could aim. Rhion flung himself up on the off-side running board and hooked one arm in a death grip through the frame of the open window—the other hand still firmly hanging onto the staff—and yelled, "Get us out of here FAST!"

Saltwood was already in gear and heading for the fence.

"You know the city?" the little professor panted, as bullets rip-sawed the ground a dozen feet away and a few strays pinged off the hood of the truck. "Seven twenty-three Teglerstrasse—it's out past the Weisensee. Don't pay any attention to anything you see or hear . . ."

Seven twenty-three Teglerstrasse was the Gestapo safe house where Sara and her father were kept.

Wire whipped and sang around the radiator, then ground lumpily under the tires. Saltwood pointed to the right. "Blow the top off that pole."

Rhion shook his head, too out of breath to explain.

"Catch it on fire, then—it's the phone junction." *What the hell am I saying? This isn't even REAL.*

The pole was in flames as Rhion scrambled through the door and dragged it shut after him, awkwardly because he would not release his hold on von Rath's infernal stick. Things were not helped by the fact that Saltwood had begun to veer and swerve to avoid the hail of bullets now spattering all around them.

"And get down on the floor. I'm Tom Saltwood, American vol-unteer—British Special Forces."

"Rhion Sligo." He raised his hand in an unsteady Nazi salute and added politely, "Heil Roosevelt."

And at that moment, far off, barely to be heard above the chaos of submachine guns, shouting, and revving engines, rose the long, undulating wail of air-raid sirens. Tom twisted in his seat, scanning the colorless sky. Through the window of the cab he saw them, the black silhouettes of the escorting Hurricanes, the heavier, blunter lines of a phalanx of Wellingtons and Whitleys, swinging in from the northwest.

"It's a raid!" He let out a long rebel yell of delight. "It's a . . ."

There had been sporadic raids on Berlin for nearly a month, but if Mayfair had known one was due to coincide with his own project, he hadn't said anything about it. Though the main bomber group was still far off, there must have been one overhead he hadn't seen—

hadn't heard, either, when he thought of it—for as the first of the swastika-marked cars swung onto the drive to pursue the escaping truck there was a groundshaking roar and every vehicle in the field behind them went up in flames.

"Fast," Rhion whispered, slumped gray-faced and sweating against the grimy cloth of the seat. "For God's sake, get out of here fast."

Like a cow climbing free of a mudhole, the truck heaved itself onto the Alt-Moabitstrasse and ran before the bombers like a stampede before summer lightning.

The first bombs started falling as Saltwood and Sligo hit the outskirts of Berlin. As their truck cut onto See Strasse to avoid the thicker traffic of the city center, a half-dozen yellow-white flares sprang up, dazzling in the waning afternoon light, ahead of them and to their right. "They're going for the railroads," Saltwood guessed, veering sharply around a panicked flock of women dragging children across the road to a shelter. "That'll be the Settiner Station. Those off to the far right will be the Anhalter goods yards . . . Dammit, lady, look where you're going!" he yelled as a young blond woman, eyes blank with terror, came pelting out of an apartment house with her arms full of something lumpy wrapped in a blanket and dashed almost under his wheels. He missed her with a screeching of tires and, in the rearview mirror, saw two gold-rimmed Meissen teacups fall out of the blanket and shatter on the tarmac of the road.

Another explosion went off close enough to make the ground shudder. "For Chrissake, they're not anywhere *near* you yet," he muttered, slamming on the horn, then the brakes, and swerving around a panic-stricken elderly couple in the road. "Worse than the goddam Londoners."

The Berliners, of course, were not nearly as used to air raids— *yet*, he thought grimly—as Londoners. And it was obviously the first time for Sligo, though, locked up in the Jungfern Heide, he might have heard the sound of far-off bombs. The little professor's face was gray with shock, appalled horror in his blue eyes behind their rimless specs as he looked around him at the panic and the rising flames.

"This is . . . how you people fight wars."

"You oughta see London if you think this is good," Tom muttered savagely, slewing through the intersection of Turm Strasse, the steely waters of the Landwehr Canal winking bleakly through brown and yellow trees. "Or Rotterdam—what the Luftwaffe left of it. Or Guernica and Madrid, for that matter." An explosion to their left jerked the vehicle almost off its wheels. Saltwood flinched at the roar of the blast, the shattering storm of fragments of brick, window glass, and filth that came spitting from the mouth of one of those narrow gray working-class streets that surrounded the canal locks. For a moment, the cloud of plaster dust and dirt was a yellow-gray fog through which nothing was visible, and Tom slowed as much as he dared, knowing by the droning buzz that the Wellies were directly overhead now. "I'm just hoping to hell the bridge across the locks is still standing when we get there—it'll be one of their main targets."

"It will be," Rhion said softly. His hands, chubby, yet curiously skilled-looking, moved along the rune-scratched wood of the staff. His eyes were shut.

"Right," Saltwood muttered, gunning again through the clearing fog of debris, the wheels jerking and bumping over the edge of a vast talus slope of loose bricks, broken lath, twisted pipe, and shattered glass that lay half across the road.

And by some miracle, the bridge over the Landwehr Canal still stood, though the locks themselves were a shambles of burning weirs and floating debris. Looking across that vast span of unguarded concrete, Saltwood felt his stomach curl in on itself. Buildings were burning on all sides here, the heavy gray nineteenth-century warehouses and the massive, six-story tenement warrens of the working-class districts all around. He slowed, feeling safer in the shadows of the buildings.

"There's got to be a tool kit in this thing," he said, twisting his body to grope with his free hand behind the seat. "I want you to hunt for a hacksaw, get me out of this damn handcuff."

"Later!" Rhion said urgently. "After we get across the bridge!"

"Yeah? You're not the one who's gonna be handcuffed to four thousand pounds of internal combustion engine if that bridge takes a hit when we're in the middle of it."

"It won't," Rhion insisted, fixing Tom with a desperate blue stare.

"Believe me, it won't! We have to get across now—it could be destroyed while we're trying to get the cuffs off . . ."

"So we just backtrack to the Turm Strasse and go around. Christ knows the streets are clear." Another blast, very close this time, and both men ducked involuntarily as brick and glass spattered on the side of the cab like a shotgun blast.

"No! Please believe me, I know what I'm talking about, we've got to get across it, put as much distance between ourselves and that house as soon as possible."

Through the clearing dust, Saltwood saw that the bridge still stood. Would it ten minutes from now, always supposing they could *find* the goddam hacksaw and the blade didn't break?

He let out the clutch. "If we go down I'm taking you with me, pal."

He hit the bridge at fifty and accelerating. Concrete abutments flashed past, a glimpse of fires roaring up out of oil spilled on roiled brown water and of metal snags and cables floating like water weeds. Once clear of the buildings, he saw how many bombers were overhead—the whole sky was crossed with the smoke of rising fires. Like a bird laying eggs on the wing, he saw a Wellington directly above them drop its load, black teardrop shapes drifting leisurely down.

Though Tom would have taken oath the bombs were dead on target, the nearest hit the water thirty yards away. The blast nearly swept the truck off the bridge—he felt the tooth-jarring clatter of the speeding vehicle's door bouncing on the railings and veered, blinded, into the tidal wave of brown water hurled up by the blast. He cut in the windscreen wipers and through a grimy blur glimpsed—impossibly—the concrete span still arrowing before them, and hit the gas as hard as he could. At the same time he screamed, "You crazy Jew!"

A second stick of bombs took out the bridge as the truck slewed onto See Strasse and away through the burning town.

"Right," Tom whispered, braking to a halt. They had passed the big intersection of Müller Chausse and the main force of the bombing lay behind them now, though the streets were still empty as if in a city of the dead. "Now you dig out that tool kit and cut me the hell out of this!"

"How far have we come?" Rhion asked, not moving, though he cast a panicked glance at the streets behind them.

"Six or seven miles, and what the hell difference—"

"More than you think." He fumblingly unfixed the Spiracle from the head of the staff—it was held on with a wrapped iron wire—his hands shaking so he could barely manage it, and shoved the iron circlet into his shirt pocket before he'd set the staff aside and get out of the cab. Bombs were still falling as close as a half mile away in the cramped, sprawling labyrinths of the nineteenth-century factory districts around the canals, and, though Rhion flinched at the sound, he moved swiftly, decisively, as he came around the cab and dug behind the seat for the gray-painted tin box. "I don't know how far the Talismanic Resonator's field extends, for one thing. For another, von Rath's bound to search the house . . ."

"How the hell did you get out of your cell anyway?" Saltwood looked up from pawing, one-handed, through the tool kit. "I thought they locked you in."

"They did." Rhion grinned shakily. "But you left the key in the lock when you—ah—"

"Uh—yeah," Tom finished. In brief silence they regarded one another. There was a shiny patch of red scar tissue on the inside of the bridge of Rhion's nose, close to his left eye— circular, almost half an inch across, the size of the end of a cigarette. The burn was only a few months old; Saltwood could see another one in the pit of Rhion's throat through the open collar of his shirt. *They hurt him pretty bad,* Sara had said. The bruise of the garrote was still purple-red and angry under the clipped line of his beard.

"Look," Rhion said awkwardly, starting to saw inexpertly at the handcuff chain. "I'm sorry I knocked you out. I didn't know . . . I hope they didn't . . ."

"Nah. They needed me in one piece to blow me up. Here, be careful—there's no replacement blade in that kit. You ever used one of these things before? Put your strength in the pull, and keep it straight . . ."

"I could have used the power of the Resonator itself to open the lock," Rhion went on matter-of-factly, bending over his work, "but even that little—comparatively little—might not have left me enough power of my own to put on the lightshow that blinded von Rath and his guards long enough to let me grab the Spiracle itself, and Baldur or Gall might have sensed something. Frankly, I don't know whether they could or not. So the keys helped. Surprise was the only edge I had . . . I was hoping you'd figure out what was going on and pick me up, since I'm not sure I could drive one of these things and I had to get enough distance between the Spiracle and the Resonator to break up the field before von Rath figured out what I'd done."

"Uh-huh," Tom said soothingly, as Rhion glanced behind him again—Tom had seen him look in the truck's side and rearview mirrors a dozen times on the hellish dash along See Strasse. Not surprisingly, of course. Bombs were still falling to the south and west of them, close enough for the ground to shudder under the nearer blasts. It was typical of the way things were done, Saltwood thought dourly, that it would be these sprawling slums, where two and three families shared windowless and crowded flats, to get the pulping, and the millionaires' houses over in the Grunewald to go untouched. In that way it was London all over again.

"The problem is," Rhion went on, "I don't know how far the field extends, or how far away I have to be to be safe."

"Huh?" said Tom. "What field?"

The Professor raised his head again; behind the rimless glasses, his blue eyes were filled with a growing fear. "Magic field."

Oh, Christ, Sara warned me. "Well," Tom said, "I think we're probably pretty safe."

"The hell we are." For a moment their eyes met, and there was something in the older man's that made Saltwood pause. When he spoke again his voice was low and deadly earnest. "I had to set up a Talismanic Resonator in the temple in that house, it was the only place where there was any kind of stored power at all. It drew on the Void energies coming through the Spiracle. At the level of power available in the temple, you'll get a field if they're within, oh, maybe a mile, two miles of each other . . ."

Oh, Hillyard's gonna love this. That the crazy little coot had something there, Tom didn't doubt—enough to startle and blind von Rath and his minions sufficiently for Rhion to seize the control mechanism concealed in the Spiracle, at any rate. And it was abundantly clear to him by the Professor's taut voice and desperate eyes that he whole-heartedly believed everything he said.

"But they're not," he pointed out, latching onto the one element of Professor Sligo's discourse he felt he could answer intelligently. "We've got to be five, six miles from the house by this time." The chain was cut almost through. Saltwood took the hacksaw from Rhion, who had begun to shiver with shock and reaction, and worked and twisted at the half-sawn link with a screwdriver from the kit until the chain broke with a loud snap. "Besides, even if von Rath has got some kind of transport by this time, the raid's still going on, and the bridge is out." And by the sound of it, he thought uneasily, the second wave of Wellies was on the way.

"We can't risk it." Rhion hurried around the other side of the cab again and scrambled in as the boom of explosions resumed over the long, shuddering siren wails. "Don't you understand? If von Rath gets within two miles of us—of the Spiracle . . ." He touched his pocket, where the thing's lumpy outline stood out against the cloth. ". . . or if he manages to find some kind of power source to increase the potential of the Talismanic Resonator—he's going to be able to use magic."

22

Whew, Saltwood thought, as he dropped the truck into gear again and jerked into motion, *for a minute there he had me worried.*

In the empty streets—the panic-stricken populace not yet having acquired the casual attitude the Madrilenos had eventually achieved about bombing not in their immediate neighborhood—and away from the danger of any but stray drops, Saltwood was able to make good speed. They left the sea of crowded gray monoliths of the working-class districts gradually behind them, the heavy developments giving place first to two-story shops and shabby, semidetached houses, then to trees, free-standing *Biergartens*, petty-bourgeoisie villas, and open fields. Here an occasional car passed them, driving fast without headlights in the slow-gathering twilight; an occasional family could be seen, crowding near a garden wall, staring southwestward toward the burning center of Berlin with horrified eyes. *Get used to it,* Tom thought savagely, remembering the motionless red-blanketed lumps carried away by the Air Raid Wardens from collapsed piles of London tenements, the overcrowded school buildings filled with homeless people and the stench of fear and excrement, and the middle-aged men and women picking through the piles of smoking brick for something salvageable from the only homes they'd ever known. *It's going to be bad*, Hillyard had said, back in the pub before this had ever started, little knowing how bad it would get. *Here's a little greeting from your brothers and sisters in London.*

It was clear the guards of 723 Teglerstrasse weren't going to be crouched conveniently in the cellar.

"When they bring me here they hoot one long, two short," Rhion said quietly, as the dented and mud-covered truck pulled up before the iron-sheeted gate. He'd replaced the Spiracle on von Rath's magic staff and was again clutching it like a child hanging on to a favorite toy.

"Be ready," Saltwood muttered, hooting out the code. He slipped the truck into first again and prepared himself for a frenzy of strong arm. "With luck they won't see that half those dents are bullet holes till it's too late."

Only one Storm Trooper opened the gate. He stepped back to let the truck pull in, then stepped casually close, his Schmeisser dangling at his back.

Saltwood slammed the door open into the man's face, threw himself out before the guard had regained either his balance or his wits, pulled the Schmeisser from him with one hand, and slugged him hard and clean across the chin with the other. The Storm Trooper staggered and Saltwood shot him with a fast burst of shells, ripped the sidearm from the bloody corpse's holster as Rhion was springing down from the cab on the other side. He grabbed the Professor's arm and the two of them pelted up the gravel drive at a weaving run.

Bullets spattered from the open door. Saltwood returned fire and the guard there fell out forward, sprawling at the top of the steps with blood trickling down the worn marble in the dove-gray evening light. Without letting go of his staff, Rhion bent and pulled the man's weapons free: automatic, submachine gun, and the silver-mounted dagger of the SS. "Search him," Saltwood yelled, ducking into the door and covering the downstairs hall. "Get his identity papers, any money you can . . ."

A head appeared around a door and Saltwood fired at it with the automatic, ducked back at a returning shot and flung himself down with a long, low roll to catch the guard as he leaned around the door for a second try. Weaving from side to side, Rhion darted into the shadows of the hall and stopped to relieve Saltwood's newest victim of his weapons, as well.

"You ever fired one of those things?"

The Professor shook his head as he followed Saltwood up the stairs at a run.

"Stand guard here. Tuck it into your arm like this, arm *tight* to the body, pull the trigger—it'll fire a burst as long as you hold the trigger down. Aim *low*. The kick'll pull the gun up. And put down that goddam stick."

Rhion's hand tightened stubbornly around the smooth wood as Tom yanked on it, his eyes suddenly blazing. There was no time to argue so Tom let the matter drop, muttering, "Crazy bastard . . ." to himself as he dashed up the attic stairs to the room where he himself had been kept.

The doors up there were bolted, not locked with keys. He slammed the bolts back and threw the door open; only a residual burst of caution, like a sixth sense, stopped him on the threshold when he saw the room empty. The next second a chair swooshed down hard enough to have broken his shoulder—Sara had been hiding next to the door.

"Christ almighty . . ."

She saw who it was—she already had the chair coming up for another swipe—and her pointed pale face burst into a smile that stopped Saltwood dead in his tracks, as if he'd seen a striking snake unfurl butterfly wings. "Tom!" And, a second later, the child-nymph turned lynx again. "There's five, six guards in the house . . . I heard shooting . . ."

On the other side of a narrow hall was another locked door. Throwing it open, he saw a mirror image of the room where he'd been kept two nights and a day—like a cheap hotel with cot, chair, a few books and magazines, and a copy of *Mein Kampf* instead of a Gideon Society Bible. For a moment he saw no one. Then Sara yelled "Papa!" and a tall, gangly, bearded old man emerged from crouching behind the door of the tiny washroom.

"So is this the cavalry or the Indians?" he demanded in German with a thick Yiddish accent, cocking one wise dark eye at Saltwood.

"Cavalry," Sara said briefly, already helping herself to the spare pistol and SS dagger Saltwood had stuck through his belt. "There's a shed out back, I didn't hear them take out the staff car today."

A shot rang out somewhere below as they were racing down the attic stairs. Rhion was flattened behind the corner at the top of the next flight, the Schmeisser in one hand and his magic wand tucked awkwardly under his arm. Keeping his grip on the staff, he stepped quickly around the corner and let fly a burst from the submachine gun that knocked him staggering and ripped holes in every direction in the wall panels and ceiling before the gun juddered itself completely out of his hands.

Sara scooped it from the floor with a blistering oath in Polish and fired down the stairwell, ducked a returning burst, then fired again, her grip steady as if on a range. There was the sound of something falling at the bottom, then silence and the stench of cordite. She started to move, and Rhion shook his head violently, waving her back. Distantly, over the long, continuous ululation of the air-raid sirens, another siren could be heard, the grating two-note seesaw of the police.

Rhion made a gesture with his fingers.

There was a clattering below and Saltwood saw, past Sara's shoulder and down the stairs, a Storm Trooper leap out of hiding behind a door in the hall, spinning to point his gun away from them, toward the front door, as if startled by something there. Sara fired. The man flung out his arms as the bullets smashed through his rib cage, and went sprawling. The four of them barreled down the stairs. Oddly enough, Saltwood could see nothing in the downstairs hall that might have startled that last Trooper into exposing himself to Sara's fire.

"Check the shed out back for a car," he ordered, and Sara vanished through the rear door under the stairs while Saltwood methodically stripped every body he could find of weapons, spare clips, money, and papers. The police sirens were getting closer. Von Rath must have got to a phone. Rhion and Sara appeared at the back door again at the same moment Sara's father emerged from another door, carrying the sort of string shopping bag German housewives took to market, bulging with bread, cheese, bottled water, and beer.

"Car out back," Sara yelled. "We threw two spare gas cans in the trunk."

Tires crunched in the gravel out front. Saltwood made a dash for the back, hoping against hope they'd make it out of the alley before the inevitable flanking parties blocked both ends. Rhion paused in the doorway and made a gesture of some kind with his staff. From the front drive there was a shattering explosion, yellow and white light stabbing through the gathering twilight.

So there was some kind of radio-controlled bomb in the truck after all, Saltwood thought, as the Professor dashed to join them, the crystals in the staff head winking sharply in the reflected light of the fires. *So much for Goering's expertise.*

The car was an open staff Mercedes, gray, sleek, and well cared for. Despite the fact there were no keys in the fascia board, it was running. Somehow it was no surprise to Saltwood to learn that Sara could hot-wire cars. The fugitives piled in over the doors with their gear, guns, magic wand, and picnic lunch. Then Tom had it in motion, roaring out into the narrow, moss-cobbled alley in time to see two motorcyclists and half a dozen running Storm Troopers appear around the corner to their left and a carful of machine-gun-brandishing Luftwaffe to their right.

"Right!" Rhion yelled, half standing in the front seat and raising the gleaming Spiracle against the evening light.

"We'll have a better chance—" began Saltwood, jamming into first.

"RIGHT, goddammit!"

Not quite knowing why, but figuring the odds were really pretty much the same, Saltwood swung the wheel right and floored it.

For a second Tom thought the bang he heard was a bullet—single-shot auto—but then realized it had been the sound of the oncoming Luftwaffemobile's right front tire blowing out. The big car jumped, swerved frenziedly, then slewed sidelong into the brick wall of the alley. Saltwood scraped paint from his own right-hand door on the stone alley wall as he barely avoided the still-bounding vehicle and gunned on up the alleyway while the other car caromed into the foremost of the motorcycle's brigade, coming to a stop with one bumper against the alley wall and the other braced on the corner of the shed, effectively blocking all further pursuit from that direction.

"Well, I'll be—go to hell," Tom said, his eyes on the rearview mirror.

The flames rising from the front courtyard seemed awfully comprehensive for just one car, and there was no pursuit from that direction, either. If the pursuit cars were parked close around the truck, a spark could have jumped . . .

"We've got to switch cars." Sara leaned forward over the back of the seat. "They'll know we've got a staff Mercedes. Turn that way, down that alley . . ."

"You know Berlin?" Tom demanded, obeying.

"Don't you?"

"Just the main streets, from the maps."

In the gathering twilight it was growing hard to see, for every house was blacked out, every street lamp in this quiet suburb unlit, and Tom kept the Mercedes' lights off. No sense getting stopped for violating blackout regulations. Overhead, the droning of the bombers still filled the sky; the far-off thunder of explosions and glare of fire to the southwest marked where the RAF was still taking its revenge.

"I don't need a map to tell me this is a neighborhood where people can afford cars," Sara returned, gesturing to the monotonous brick villas, the occasional cottages, and countrified houses whose rooflines loomed against the flame-lit sky. "Most people put their cars up on blocks because of the gas rationing . . . We've got ten gallons in back and whatever I can siphon out of the tank, and I hope to hell you got ration cards."

"Do I look like an idiot?" Tom retorted.

She poked him in the back. "You're wearing an SS uniform, cowboy—what do you think?"

Then she leaned over to Rhion, put her arms around his neck, and kissed him a little awkwardly on his untidy brown curls. "God, am I glad to see you safe." She turned back to Tom. "Thank you." The gruff uncertainty in her voice was odd, considering her earlier sophisticated calm. "I—I don't know how the hell you managed to escape and get Rhion out of there, but thank you."

"It was an allied effort," Tom replied with a grin. "The Prof managed to break up their demo, and after that they were too busy dodging the bombs to follow us too hard. Once we switch cars we can head for Hamburg. There's enough farm tracks and country roads that run parallel to the autobahn that we shouldn't get too lost."

"As long as we don't get too found, we'll be fine. Down that alley there . . ." She nodded toward a deep gap between two gray-stuccoed walls—a line of sheds and garages loomed dimly out of the darkness as they turned, and beyond them were the roofs of a line of semiattached houses, eloquent of the hopes of real-estate developers, the pretentions of well-to-do shopowners, and the managers of banks. "That looks promising."

Several of the doors stood agape, revealing an assortment of garden tools and broken furniture—one or two were locked.

"My daughter the car thief," Rebbe Leibnitz sighed, as Sara crowbarred the padlock hasp free of the nearest door's brittle wood with a screwdriver from the Mercedes' tool kit and, a moment later, pushed it back to reveal a massive green American Packard saloon.

"Better your daughter the car thief than your daughter the deceased former hostage of the Reich," she muttered, opening the car door and perching on the seat with one graceful white leg dangling out the door for Saltwood to admire. "This heap still got its batteries or are we gonna have to jump it?" A moment later the engine coughed into life. The leg retreated into the car, and the Packard itself grumbled out into the narrow lane, shuddering with the effort of its long-silenced motor to stay awake. "Got a piece of tubing? Some hose?" She leaned out the door again. "What is this, the minor leagues?" she added, getting out and leaving the car to idle as she darted back into the utter blackness of the garage.

She emerged a moment later with her stolen SS dagger in one hand and a piece of rubber garden hose in the other, with which she siphoned most of the gasoline from the gray car's tank to the green's. "Which way are we heading?" she asked as she worked. "I'll drive ahead and you follow me for a couple miles, so they won't connect finding this buggy—" She kicked the Mercedes' tire. "—with the report of a stolen car and know what to start looking for."

"You used to do this for a living or something?" Tom inquired, closing the door once more and maneuvering the lock back into a semblance of its former appearance, while Rhion and Rebbe Leibnitz transferred their belongings from one vehicle to the other.

"Just brains, cowboy."

"And dating every gangster on the East Side," her father added glumly. " 'A tree shall be known by the fruit it bears . . .' And what's the date of your birth, by the way, Captain Saltwood?"

"Down this alley," Saltwood replied to Sara's earlier question, "two rights should get us back onto See Strasse. We can cut back to the Alt-Moabitstrasse and head for Hamburg that way."

"No!" Rhion said sharply.

The others looked at him, baffled.

"We can't go back the way we came! I left the Resonator in the temple at von Rath's headquarters. If we get too close, we risk it picking up the Void energies of the Spiracle and reestablishing the field."

"Dammit," Saltwood snapped, "I'm not taking a fifteen-mile detour around the other side of Berlin because you don't want to step on the cracks of the sidewalk! They're gonna have the dogs on us fast enough! Now get in the car!"

Rhion balked. "You don't understand."

"I understand we haven't got the time or the gas to waste. We've only got a couple hours' lead, if that, before they figure out where we're headed and get the whole SS on our butts, and I for one would rather risk all the wicked wizards in the world than half a squad of sore-assed Deaths-Heads, so get in the car and quit arguing!"

Rhion opened his mouth to protest further, but Sara reached out, grabbed the Professor by the arm, and dragged him into the Packard with her and set off down the lane. Muttering to himself, Saltwood slammed into the Mercedes and followed, hoping they wouldn't encounter any unscheduled pedestrians in the utter darkness to complicate matters still further. As they neared Berlin again the red light of fires illuminated their way, burning out of control among the endless blocks of workers' flats. Smoke stung Saltwood's eyes as he drove.

"Friggin' crazy—loony," he muttered to Leibnitz, who sat in the backseat of the open Mercedes like a king en route to his coronation. "When I tried to get him to let go of that silly stick I thought he was going to tear into me! He may be some kind of genius, but . . ."

"He surrendered it once three months ago," the old scholar said softly, "and has regretted it since. I think he would die rather than let von Rath have it again." The wind flicked back his silky white hair and the ragged strands of his grizzled beard. In spite of the plain gray Labor Service uniform he wore—like Sara's and Rhion's, stripped of all its emblems—he reminded Tom strongly of the old Jewish men who'd argue *pilpul* and politics on the stoops of Yorkville, thrashing the easy theories of communism and socialism and the Industrial Workers of the World into their component atoms and examining them one by one, as was the fashion of Talmudic scholars everywhere. "So what did he mean, field? What Resonator was he talking about?"

"Christ knows." Saltwood frowned, concentrating on keeping the Packard in sight. Its taillights had been removed to comply with blackout regulations, and, in blocks where intact buildings shielded them from the glare of the fires, it was difficult to see anything at all. The night was getting cold, too. In spite of having stripped a uniform jacket from one of the less gory corpses Saltwood felt chilled, driving in the open car. "He made this widget out of wire and glass and claims it lets him do magic if it gets within a couple miles of that—that Spiracle of von Rath's."

He heard Leibnitz gasp. The old man leaned forward sharply, white hair fluttering back over his shoulders. "Did he say how?"

The desperate earnestness in his voice made Tom remember Sara had described her father as being as crazy as Sligo. *Just what I need— TWO of them!* "I don't know. Some *boruyo* about drawing energy through the Spiracle and setting up a resonating field."

"*Kayn aynhoreh,*" Leibnitz whispered in horror. "*Chas vesholem,* he can't have."

"He sure as hell thinks he has." And yet, unbidden, there rose again to his mind that half-obliterated fragment of memory: Rhion Sligo with one hand on that tangle of wire and crystal in the dim candlelight of his prison room, and the bluish drift of ball lightning floating upward from his other—empty—palm.

Hallucination, he thought, made uncomfortable at some deep level by the thought, as if, back in his socialist days, he'd stumbled across conclusive evidence that it was not economics but women's fashions—or sunspots—or maybe even God—that ruled history. *Maybe some kind of electrical byproduct of the device, whatever it is, like the St. Elmo's Fire that burned on the horns of the cattle on the nights of thunderstorms, when they were thinking about stampeding . . .*

"Stop them," Leibnitz ordered. His long, blue-veined hands, resting on the seat back beside Tom's head, were shaking. "He's right, we'll have to detour through the center of the city."

"Down Prinzalbertstrasse past SS headquarters? Don't you start!"

"You don't understand! We can't risk . . ."

They rounded a corner, and Saltwood jammed on the brakes just in time to prevent a collision with the Packard in front of him. They were in among the narrow streets of tenement warrens now, pitch dark save where they were lit by the yellow glare of fires. A bombed building had disgorged a vast talus spill of debris across the road before them. Beyond, the street was a chaos of flames, of firemen and tangled hoses, of brown water trickling down the broken asphalt glittering hotly in the reflections of the blaze. Men and women crowded around them, dazed and quiet. A little boy in the brown uniform of the Hitler Youth stood alone, sobbing in helpless pain and terror with blood running down the side of his face from a huge cut in his scalp. Above them loomed what was left of the tenement, the rooms ripped open as if by a giant knife, shabby wallpaper, dirty old furniture, and cramped, tiny chambers laid bare to the glaring orange inferno.

Saltwood set the brake and got out of the car. Rhion and Sara had already debarked. For a few moments the four of them stood together on the fringe of the ruin, unnoticed by the people coming dazedly from the shelter across the road or stumbling, bleeding and covered with filth and a hundred years' worth of coal and plaster dust, from the cellars of the buildings all around.

Aside from the boy, who couldn't have been more than seven— God knew where his parents were, or if they'd survived—there wasn't a Nazi uniform in sight but Saltwood's own.

Rhion whispered, "And I wondered why magic had been taken from this world."

Around them there was a mutter of voices: "The English . . . The English . . ." "Everything we saved . . ." "Maybe we can sleep at Aunt Berthe's . . . But she was down in Tempelhof, they were hit, too . . ." "Has anyone seen a little girl? Six years old—her name is Anna, she has brown hair . . ." "He won't let this go unavenged. Our Führer won't let them get away with this . . ."

Rhion's hands closed tight over the staff he held, the crystals of its iron head glinting softly, as if with a light of their own, in the leap and jitter of the shadows. "Christ, what would they do if they had it?"

Over the city, the sirens were sounding the all-clear.

As they drove south again through the Moabit district, avoiding the fires and ruins and tangled traffic of the industrial targets, Rhion was silent, sitting beside Saltwood with closed eyes, head bowed and hands folded tight around the smooth, rune-scrawled wood of the staff. Leibnitz, leaning forward from the backseat of the Packard, was speaking to him in low, passionate German that lapsed frequently into Yiddish: ". . . Already you have endangered all the world in making the Spiracle . . . given them a chance to use magic, to call up the forces of the Universe . . . open the windows to let through the energies of the Void into this world, where only the Most High knows what they will do . . ."

"I had to do something," Rhion whispered. "I had to get it back."

"At the cost of bringing to life again the magic they seek? And if he takes the Spiracle from you this time . . ."

"He won't." The little man did not open his eyes, but Saltwood could feel him shiver as if, beneath that quiet, the tension of fear, of dread, of grief were nearly unbearable. "He won't."

"And you grew up with this going on?" Tom threw a glance back to the seat behind him, where Sara was half turned around, watching through the small oval of the rear window for signs of pursuit.

She half laughed. "This and worse. We'd always have somebody staying with us: Kabbalists arguing until four in the morning whether the path between the Cosmic Spheres of Yesod and Netzach was represented by the Star or the Emperor; white witches cussing like fishwives at the Adepts of the Golden Dawn; pyramidiots and menhir-hunters pulling each other's hair about how many inches are in a megalithic foot and whether Easter Island lies on a ley . . . *oy gevalt!* And Papa making his little number squares and adding up the letters of everybody's names and birth planets while Mama hunted through all the pockets of all the coats in the house for enough kopecks to buy bread for the next day. And then like as not Papa would give whatever was in the cupboards to some crazy Rosicrucian who needed it to get to France where, he'd been 'directed in meditation,' he'd find the clues that would lead to the rediscovery of Atlantis . . . not that there was ever very much," she added, her voice turning small. "In the cupboard, I mean."

Tom was silent, remembering the pinched gray look on his own mother's face those nights after an oatmeal supper when she'd sit working on the bills. Though there'd always been food of some kind on the table, he'd always been hungry—especially in the spring, when they simply couldn't afford to lose what one steer would bring them toward the mortgage and the costs. Toward the end it had been the worst. "What happened to her?" he asked quietly. "Your mother?"

"She died." The words were like the chop of a kindling ax. In the dark of the backseat she turned her face away, a delicate shadow profiled against the blackness of the city, the occasional flare where a far-off blaze burned near a warehouse or factory. There were few of those here in the Charlottenburg district, amid the blocks of expensive flats with their pseudo-Assyrian cornices and their Hollywood-Gothic turrets and pillars. Every window was blacked out, but the very air around those eyeless monoliths seemed to seethe with suppressed life.

After a moment, Sara added quietly, "While I was in America. Of influenza. I should have gone back to Warsaw then and tried to make Papa come with me, but there just wasn't the money. I could barely make my school expenses, much less get passage for one over and two back. And anyhow the immigration quotas for Jews were jammed, and nobody was gonna let an extra one through."

He wondered how she'd gotten the passage money when she'd heard her father had been interned—much less the dough it would cost for the black-market identity cards she'd mentioned—but didn't ask. The lines around her mouth and in the corners of those coal-black eyes said things about where she'd been and what she'd passed through on her way, and he knew better than to touch those open wounds. He found her beautiful, with her dark, hard eyes and her crazy particolored hair, in the way he'd found the Spanish girls beautiful, who'd fought beside him in the hills, a beauty of voice and inflection, a beauty of toughness, like cats who fend for themselves and can only occasionally be coaxed to curl purring on a man's knee.

Beside him, Rhion seemed to have revived a little, eating bread and cheese out of Leibnitz' little string shopping bag and gesturing with it as he said, ". . . and in any case I had no choice. I could never have gotten the edge over him, even for the second I did, without magic of some kind, and by myself I didn't have the power to keep the field going. Everything here requires such a *hell* of a lot of power. The temple there was the only place to get it. There any fruit in there? Or chocolate?"

"Chocolate, ha! They all trade it for cigarettes, the Nazi *chozzers* . . . You still shouldn't have left it."

"As long as we stay away from that house we're safe. Outside the range of a couple of miles from the Spiracle the Resonator's inert. The way it draws power, it should be even less than that, by this time. We should be far enough away to be safe. By the way . . ." He turned to Saltwood, glasses flashing dimly in the darkness. "Where are we headed?"

But even as he spoke Tom was hitting the brakes, cursing, his stomach sinking within him. "Gestapo headquarters, it looks like," he said grimly, shifting gears and starting up again slowly, knowing there was no escape, no evasion. "Or hell. So hang onto your hats."

Ahead of them, in a line of flashing red lights, dark forms, and bobbing electric torches, stretched an SS roadblock.

23

In the throat of the Pass of God's Ax, Tally drew rein and rose in her stirrups for the tenth time that day, turning her head and listening. The wind keened thinly along the high stone faces of the cliffs that lined the way, whined among the boulders that strewed their feet, and roared with a soughing like the sea in the pines that formed a spiky black rampart along their brows, a hundred and twenty feet above. But when it eased for a moment the sound came again, unmistakable, and then Tally knew.

She was being followed.

Wind caught at her hair and whipped it in her eyes as she scanned the pass behind her. The earthquake that had twisted the foundations of the world six hundred years ago had changed the shape of this pass; steep and jagged now, it ran straight for barely a hundred yards at any one time, winding back and forth through the fractured bones of the Mountains of the Sun; only in the thirty years of her father's rule in Mere had it been possible for a lone rider to pass through without fear of being robbed, not once, but several times.

Worriedly she reached inside her grimy sheepskin jacket, to touch the amulet she wore.

This is the only road down to the Drowned Lands, she told herself firmly. *It's logical I'd be taking it; logical they'd guess where I'd be going. The fact that they're coming doesn't mean I was betrayed.*

Her horse jittered uneasily, and the spare mount, burdened with food and the leather-wrapped bundles of Jaldis' books, flicked its ears and snuffed at the wind. Tally gauged the length of this particular reach of the pass, calculated in her mind how many more miles of narrow canyon, hemmed in by unscalable cliffs, lay between her and the wet, cloud-scarved woods of the downward slopes beyond.

A burst of speed . . .

But no burst of speed would take her beyond the sight of the riders in the pass behind her, and the clatter of her horses' hooves would carry. Then they'd know she was there, and the amulet she wore would not hide her from their eyes.

But if that old Hand-Pricker told them to look twice at any sloppy-looking man in an old sheepskin coat, she thought, panic rising in her chest, *it won't hide me anyway . . .*

Whatever happened, she knew she must not let herself be caught. Not in flight from Erralswan. Not with Jaldis' books.

In a scattered few seconds the whole scene in the Hand-Pricker's hut returned to her, and with it the memory of the smell of the place, the reek of filth, old blood, dirty bedding, and cats. The Hand-Pricker himself had shrunk blinking from her, an emaciated man of middle age whose light-brown hair and beard had both been crusted stiff at the ends with the blood of sacrifices made years ago; bloodstains had shown up even on the faded black of his robe. He'd stammered, "T-the woman who wanted the powder," and in his watery yellow eyes was the fear that more trouble was coming to him.

"I need an amulet," Tally had said, setting down a small bag of money among the litter of herbs and sticks and crumbling fragments of half-mummified toads on the table. She'd already cropped her hair short like an urchin boy's, and wore a boy's breeches, shirt, and dirty sheepskin jacket. "An amulet that will turn aside men's eyes, make them believe that they see a man in these clothes, fat and harmless and bearded; and I need it quickly."

"Who—whom do you flee?"

In his eyes she saw that he'd already half guessed. *The eyes of Agon are everywhere* . . .

"Isn't it enough to know," she had asked softly, "that I fear for my life and the lives of those I love?"

Fumblingly, he had made the amulet, pulling at the cords that passed through his fingers and palms and earlobes until the blood came, rocking and whispering above the flat rock in the corner of his hut, stretching forth his bleeding hands to murmur the name of the familiar spirit that gave him—so the Hand-Prickers believed—his power. And Tally, sitting at the table with the Hand-Pricker's cats purring around her boots and sleeping on her lap, had strained her ears for sounds in the village back lane outside, praying that no one had yet marked her lateness in returning to her husband's house.

She had already left Kir and Brenat, in the charge of their nurse, with the local physician. That worthy had been sufficiently puzzled by Kir's symptoms—hallucinations, convulsions, and pains in the joints unaccompanied by any fever or inflammation (Kir was an enthusiastic actor but Tally had drawn the line at drugs that might do him real harm)—to recommend sending him immediately to a more skilled practitioner in Brottin, far down the mountain and, she hoped, out of harm's way. But there was always a chance that their nurse was one of Agon's spies. Or one of the grooms. Or . . .

Or anyone.

That was the worst, the nightmare of all this. Not knowing whom to trust.

Those who did not serve Agon through hate, like Mijac, or cynicism, like Esrex, might just as easily do the Veiled God's bidding through fear.

"I'm sorry to have brought this upon you," she said, reaching out to take the dirty little bolus of wax, blood, sticks, and feathers that the wizard held out to her in his sticky hands. "But truly, even if I hadn't come here, trouble would come upon you. The men who hate magic are moving—the men who seek to remove magic from the world, so that no one may challenge their power or see their doings and expose them for the lies they are."

"But I—I'm not one of the great ones, you know," the mage had whispered. "I stay out of the way—I don't make trouble—the Lord of Erralswan has never . . ."

"The Lord of Erralswan has never thought of you one way or the other," Tally said sadly. "And now people are making him think. If you can use a scrying crystal to see the movements of armies—if you can cast a spell of darkness, confusion, or illness against an enemy's troops—if you have the slightest ability to read the winds or the signs of the bones that would tell of treachery and ambush— people will make the Lord of Erralswan think that you are his en- emy, you are a traitor, you are not deserving of even a hearing because you are who and what you are. It needs no magic to cast an illusion like that."

The man had only looked at her, holding his big gray cat in his arms, his eyes stupid with fear and the hope that she wasn't right.

Tally looped the amulet's cord about her neck and slipped the blob of gritty wax into her jacket. "Flee, if you can," she said, her voice quiet and her eyes holding his. "The Lady of the Drowned Lands is gathering mages on her islands; you will be safe there. She needs the help of everyone who can do magic, everyone who was born with that seed in his blood . . ."

"Is that where you are going?"

She hesitated, but knew the man would guess it; then nodded.

He'd swallowed hard, his thin fingers, pierced through with bits of twine and string for the small blood-sacrifices of his system of power, stroking the soft, thick fur of his cat's head while the animal rubbed its cheek against the tattered black sleeve. "I—I've lived here all my life," he'd said uncertainly. "The people here know me . . ."

But as Tally turned to go he'd stepped quickly forward, to touch her sleeve.

"That amulet . . ." he said. "It won't . . . My power, the power of my blood, of my familiar spirits, isn't—isn't great. The amulet will keep you cloaked from the eyes of your foes, only as long as you don't draw attention to yourself. If they know you're there, if they've noticed you, or are looking for you, it won't help you. You must keep still."

You must keep still.

Rhion had said something of the kind to her, also, when he'd given her similar talismans to keep the neighbors from seeing her, all that long summer she'd first known him, when he and Jaldis had been living in the Lower Town. But listening to the jingle of harness, the strike of hooves, clear and sharp now in the stony pass behind her, she knew that if these riders had visited the Hand-Pricker in Yekkan and had forced from him that the woman they sought was going disguised as a man, the amulet would do her no good.

Even as the scene had returned to her—whole and complete in seconds—she had been scanning the pass, seeking cover in the rocks, looking for anything, a stand of trees, a boulder large enough to conceal a woman and two horses . . .

But there was nothing, only a few scrubby knots of mountain laurel halfway up the gray-yellow shale of the cliffs, a low-growing tangle of heather among the rocks . . .

Her gloved hands, aching from the unaccustomed work of making and striking camp, of caring for the horses, and loading the packs, felt cold on the reins. She must either sit in full sight of the riders when they came into view and pray that the Hand-Pricker hadn't told them who to look for . . . or flee.

If she fled they would certainly see her. And she wasn't at all sure she could outrun riders in the rocky tangle of the pass.

Panic pounded at her, flapping like a bird against the cage of her ribs. Every second lost made it increasingly unlikely she could escape if she bolted.

It would be a long way down the damp gray forests of the north side of the mountains, misty country among the clouds, and then the rainy lower slopes leading down to the Drowned Lands below. She could never do it with the riders of Esrex' household, the riders of the White Bragenmeres, on her heels. Not traveling alone.

What it came to, she thought, was trust. Trust in that scabby, frightened man in Yekkan; trust in his not-very-strong amulet; trust in the strength of his heart against the fear of the Veiled God. She drew her horse a little out of the main road and bowed her head, feeling as if she were drawing in upon herself, making herself invisible in spirit and hoping that Shilmarglinda, Goddess of Beasts, Fruit, and Birth, would keep the horses from snorting or neighing.

And waited.

From the misty shadows of the pass the masked riders of Agon appeared, anonymous, dark-clothed, empty-eyed, and at least thirty strong, and swept down the road beside which she sat, their hoof-beats ringing in the narrow way.

24

"Right," Tom said grimly, slowing and downshifting. "Rabbi, Sara, down on the floor. Rhion, get one of those guns and get ready. We're going to crash it."

"No!" Rhion said sharply.

At the same moment Sara added, "If you give Rhion a gun we're *all* gonna be killed," a judgment call with which Saltwood had to agree, though he wanted to point out that the chances that they would all be killed in the next five minutes were astronomically high as things stood.

While the car slowed Rhion busily unwrapped the iron wire that held the circlet to the staff. Concentrating on the barricade, Saltwood was conscious again of a strange and disturbing optical effect connected with the Spiracle whose nature he couldn't quite define. In the dim flare of the approaching flashlights he had an evanescent sense once more of seeing something floating around the twined iron loop, something that wasn't precisely a webby cloud of spider strands, but that made him think of one for reasons he couldn't guess.

Yet when he turned his head he saw nothing strange and, in fact, wondered why he had thought he had. It was only a ring of twisted iron and silver, scratched with odd little marks and holding five crystals in a pattern not symmetrical, but certainly definite, a pattern governed by what he dimly guessed to be the proportions of some non-Euclidean geometry. He noticed how gingerly the Professor cupped the Spiracle in his hand, framing it with thumb and middle finger and never allowing his fingers to pass through its rim.

Rhion's voice was very calm. "Lie on the floor over the guns and gear," he instructed, handing the decapitated staff back over the seat. He glanced at Tom. "You have a pass?"

"Yeah, but they're looking into the cars with flashlights, in case you didn't notice." Slowing down, he had to talk fast—in another few seconds he'd have to decide whether to hit the gas or the brake. "If we stop long enough for that . . ."

"Don't worry about it." Rhion settled himself back into the seat, folded his arms with the circlet concealed in his hand, and bowed his head, his eyes slipping shut.

"*Don't worry about it?* Are you out of your frigging mind? You think they're not going to notice two people crouching down on the floor . . . ? Not to mention you sitting there looking like a picture on a wanted poster . . ."

"I said don't worry about it! Tell them you're transporting the car through to somebody important at Ostend! Don't mention us at all."

"You're nuts!"

"Do it, Tom!" Rhion's head came up, his eyes blazing behind the glasses that flashed redly in the lights of the barrier. "There are about forty soldiers on the other side of that barrier with guns. You crash it and we're Swiss cheese!"

Saltwood wasn't sure how he'd deduced that, for beyond the lights of the barrier he himself could see only darkness. "Dead is one thing! Trying out the electrical fittings at Gestapo headquarters is another!"

"Don't you think I know that?" Rhion demanded, his voice shaking, the burn scars on his face and throat shiny in the moving glare. "Do it. They won't see us."

The barrier was twenty feet away—yellow-and-black-striped sawbucks stretched between a couple of trucks parked across the road, around which hooded lights threw a feeble blur of illumination. Beyond that the blackout made anything further impossible to determine. At least a dozen Storm Troopers were in evidence, plus one or two civilians—Gestapo. He threw a fast glance at Rhion, who had subsided again into his attitude of meditative stillness. Did he only guess there were more men waiting in the darkness, or could the man really somehow see without light?

Muffled from the floor behind him, Sara's voice said, "Trust him, cowboy. He got Papa out of the camp at Kegenwald in the weirdest cockamamie way I've ever seen."

After one last agonizing waver Tom eased on the brake. "If this goes wrong I'll kill you."

"You do that," Rhion mumbled. He sounded half asleep.

A flashlight slammed its beam into Saltwood's eyes, and he squinted against it and wondered if they noticed the sweat that prickled his hair and every inch of his backbone. "Name?" a voice demanded from behind the light.

"Deitmarr, and get that bloody light out of my eyes!" Saltwood snapped furiously.

The light moved aside as he thrust the late Corporal Deitmarr's identity card up at the SS lieutenant in charge of the barrier. "I'm taking this heap through to Kesselring at Ostend," he added, jerking his hand to indicate the shiny length of the Packard. "And a damned cow it is, too, but he says he wants it."

The flashlight beam flicked over Rhion's still, dozing form, swished the backseat mechanically while the lieutenant was still studying Saltwood's pass. "You seen any sign of a gray open Mercedes, four passengers, bearded man, red-haired girl, blond man in part of an SS uniform . . ." He rattled the words off mechanically, as if his mind were on something else.

"Crucifix, no! I've spent all afternoon in the damn garage trying to get this expletive deleted bastard of a bloody car to start." *Aren't you going to ask me about those people crouched down in the backseat? Or this handcuff manacle on my left wrist?*

"You taking it all the way to Ostend?"

"If the thing doesn't effing die on me on the way." It was impossible that the man didn't hear the slamming of Saltwood's heart.

"Good luck, then."

He thumped the roof of the car. Saltwood drove on, wondering if he'd somehow been shot without noticing it and this was delirium.

He forced himself not to pat the dried blood on his uniform jacket, the bullet holes that had finished off its last occupant. *Dammit, they HAVE to have shown up that close, the guard HAS to have seen them!* The headlights flashed across lines of armed shadows, massed in the darkness behind the trucks. Tom wondered how Rhion had known that.

"Nobody get up," Rhion mumbled into his beard, the iron circlet still cradled between thumb and middle finger, almost out of sight against his side. "There'll be more. Tell me when the next one's coming up, please, Tom."

Saltwood swore, quietly but with considerable feeling, through the next three miles of street, pausing only long enough to repeat the entire performance at the next roadblock. When he glanced beside him he could see in the gleam of the receding flashlights that sweat trickled down the sides of the Professor's forehead and matted the long strings of his hair. As they drove on into the blackness of the countryside, Saltwood was quiet for a long time.

"He did that getting Papa out of the camp." Sara fished in the pocket of the SS field jacket she wore over her somewhat grubby BDM uniform and produced a couple of cigarettes that she must have looted from the dead guards on Teglerstrasse. Crouched by the dim glow of the hooded headlight with a local map, Saltwood grinned—he hadn't thought of looking for cigarettes himself, but the woman didn't miss a trick.

Behind them, above the dark blur of half-naked trees, Berlin was a smear of smoke, lit from beneath by the fevered glare of fires still burning out of control in every industrial district in the city and from above by ice-hard diamond stars. Sara's breath puffed in the deepening cold as she went on, "He told me to go up and cut my way through the wire in full sight of two guard towers, with every floodlight in the place on . . . He'd told Papa just to walk out the door and over to the fence to meet me. And all the time he just sat there at the edge of the woods, like he did in the car tonight, with his eyes shut, meditating." She pulled a lighter out of another pocket, steel with the wreathed Deaths-Head of the SS embossed upon it. The bright leaf of flame called reddish echoes from even the dusky hair that framed her face and picked sharp little shadows from the corners of her eyes. In the car behind her the Professor and Rebbe Leibnitz were conferring quietly, heads together. She glanced back at the two shadowy forms and her dark brows pulled down over her nose. "Sometimes it's like he's just another of Papa's harmless lunatics," she said softly. "Other times . . ."

She held out the lighter. When Saltwood touched her hand to steady it, she flinched very slightly, but consciousness of her fingers' touch went through him like a swig of brandy, warming even when he took his hand away.

It seemed impossible to him that, when he'd waked up that morning, he hadn't known her. In a way he had, he thought . . . He'd seen the scratches she'd made on the inside of the dresser drawer, marking off days in defiance of captivity, in defiance of helplessness. And he grinned to himself. *Now there's a step better than those heroes of legend who fall in love with a lady's portrait . . .*

And now it was as if he'd known her for years.

"You figured out where we are?" she asked, her scratchy Brooklyn accent breaking into reveries he knew he had no business having until they were safely back in England—or at least safe on the submarine.

"Uh—I think so." There had been half a dozen maps in the glove box, but only this one had shown the countryside around Berlin in any kind of detail. "That T-fork we just passed must be this one here." He pointed on the map. Around them the thin woods of birch and elm were silent, save where, not too far in the distance— probably at the end of this twisting, weed-choked lane—a wireless chattered in some farmhouse in the cold stillness of the night. "Which means that has to be the road to Rathenow. Even if we keep to the side roads, we can make Hamburg easy by midnight. The people I know can get in touch with the patrol boat . . ."

"That's in the wrong direction."

Saltwood looked up, startled. Rhion and Rebbe Leibnitz had gotten quietly out of the car and were standing behind him in the deep, dew-soaked grass that clogged the lane. Rhion wore the black greatcoat of an SS officer that reached nearly to his ankles, starshine glimmering faintly in the round lenses of his glasses and in the irregular pentangle of crystals on the head of his staff. Leibnitz, still in shirt sleeves, was hugging himself and shivering with cold.

"Papa, for Chrissake put on a jacket . . ." Sara began, exasperated, and Leibnitz shook his head stubbornly.

"I wear what they give me because I will not go naked like Noah before the eyes of the Lord, but before I put on their damn *Todten Kopf* uniform I will freeze."

"What do you mean," Saltwood asked wearily, "the wrong direction?" He stood up out of the dingy pool of headlight glow, a powerful bulk towering over the smaller Professor. Weariness, hunger, and the exertions of the day were catching up with him. His left arm still hurt damnably, as if the monster head that had ripped his flesh and the fire that had seared it had been real, and the manacle of the sawed-off handcuff chafed painfully at the wristbones. The last thing he needed, he reflected irritably, was another of Rhion's meaningless quibbles about where they should and shouldn't go. "It's the only direction there is, pal, if we want to get to England."

"But I don't," Rhion said. "Where the hell *is* England, anyway?"

He really IS nuts, Saltwood thought, exhaling a thin trail of cigarette smoke that shimmered white in the icy dark. *Not that I had any question about it before* . . . "You want to stay in Germany, maybe? I guarantee you won't like it."

The Professor shook his head. Starlight caught the silver bevel of his spectacle edge, the cold double-Sieg-rune on the collar of his coat. He gestured with the staff he held, and the Spiracle's crystals winked frostily, an all-seeing, faceted eye. "I didn't take this back from von Rath—I didn't risk what's going to happen to me if he catches me this time—to go to work for the people who were dropping those bombs this afternoon." He nodded back toward the glowing red stain in the sky.

Saltwood began, outraged, "Do you know what the Nazi bombers have been doing to London . . . ?"

"And what would *you* people do if you had magic?" Rhion asked quietly. "If you could use the powers channeled through the Spiracle? Pulp Berlin, maybe, to convince Hitler to withdraw from the war?"

Saltwood hesitated. Later he supposed he shouldn't have. But he remembered Spain—that war of freedom against fascism in which the "free" countries of the world had declined to participate—and he knew full well how the military mind worked. He should, he supposed, have denied the possibility utterly. Maybe if he'd been a real soldier he would have.

"I don't know."

"Nor do I." A skiff of wind moved the skirts of Rhion's great-coat like a dark wing. "And I don't want to find out. Or what you'd do with it after that. I never wanted to come to your world, or to have anything to do with your *verkakte* war. In any case, my only way out of Germany—my only way out of your world—lies at the Dancing Stones near Schloss Torweg. That's the only place the wizards in my world will know where to look for me, and tomorrow night, the night of the autumn equinox, is the only time when I'll be able to raise enough power to reach out to them and make the crossing. And that's where I'm going."

"The hell you are," Tom said, his voice now equally soft.

"Rhion," Sara said quietly, "you did that at the summer solstice. Nothing happened. Except that you got caught."

The Professor flinched at her words, averting his face; his pudgy hands tightened around the pale wood of the witch staff. "I don't know why it didn't work last time," he said, keeping his voice level with audible effort. "Anything could have gone wrong. The political situation there was unstable when I left . . ." He shook his head, as if trying to clear some cloudy image there, some half-remembered dream. "But I do know it's my only chance. My last chance. I have to believe they'll try again, at least this once. I have to be there."

Kindness, pity, and compassion deepened Sara's voice. "And if it doesn't work?"

There was a long silence, broken only by the distant hooting of an owl in the frost-thick silence of the starlight. Then Rhion whispered, "I can't think about that."

She moved toward him, hand outstretched, but he stepped back abruptly, dark against the starry darkness, the light catching in his glasses and the crystals of the ring. Looking at him, Saltwood had the curious impression that the night sky seen through the Spiracle was different. Perhaps it was only the way the crystals caught the light . . . but it seemed to him for a split second that half a galaxy of brightness, of tiny pinlights infinitely far away, seemed caught within that loop, an alternate firmament that had nothing to do with the one overhead.

"Tom," the soft voice came from the compact silhouette, "if you could get Sara and her father to England I'd appreciate it. Von Rath planned to use the magic of the Spiracle to take out the RAF. Without it they've got no illusion, they've got no weather-witching—they've got no more than they had in June. By the time they can reformulate a plan—any plan—it'll be winter. Tomorrow and the next few days are really their last chance this year. Just by escaping, just by taking this, I've put a hole in their plans, and von Rath knows it."

"That doesn't mean they couldn't make another one, or use that Resonator thing."

"If they made one they couldn't charge it," Rhion argued in the self-evident tone of a medium explaining why the lights have to be turned down before George Washington's spirit will tip tables. "The Resonator's useless away from the Spiracle. Believe me, once the Spiracle is gone there'll be no way they can convert psychic energy to magic."

"Not so fast." Saltwood dropped his cigarette end and stepped clear of Sara, his automatic now in his hand, leveled at Sligo's chest. "I don't want to take you to England at gunpoint, Professor, but I'll do it. We need you and we need that widget of yours, whatever the hell it really is and whatever it really does. And don't think I won't pull the trigger," he added quietly, as Rhion made a move to step past him, "because I will."

Behind him he heard the whisper of Sara's indrawn breath, but, after all, she said nothing. She understood.

"Now, I was sent here to kill you. I'd rather take you back alive—I'd rather you *came* back with me willingly—but I'll kill you rather than let you fall into Nazi hands again, which is exactly what you'll do if you pull this dumb routine because you think the fairies are gonna come take you away if you stand in the right place. So sit down . . . Sara, there's a couple pairs of handcuffs in the gear we took from Teglerstrasse. Get me one."

Sara stepped toward the car.

* * *

Saltwood remembered her doing that. She was still standing a few feet from him, her hand on the car door, moments—*but how many moments?*—later, when he realized that Rhion Sligo was gone.

Stunned—more than stunned—he shook his head. He hadn't—he COULDN'T have—fallen asleep on his feet.

He looked down at his hands. He still held the gun, but the map of the area he'd shoved into his pants pocket was gone.

Sara whispered, *"Mah nishtanna,"* and staggered. Saltwood sprang to steady her. She pushed him away in swift revulsion. "All right already, I'm fine . . ." In the reflected glare of the headlights she was white. "What the *hell* did he do? He was just standing there one second . . ."

In the long weeds of the road bank, Rhion's track was starkly clear where he'd waded through the powder of glittering dew.

"He has the Spiracle," Leibnitz's voice said, deep and quiet, out of the darkness. "He can do pretty much whatever he can conjure up the strength within him to do—whatever he dares do." In the starlight his white hair and beard glittered as if they, like the grass, were touched with frost, his eyes, pits of shadow under the long jut of brows. "I only hope—and you should hope, too, Captain Salt-wood—that he makes it back to those stones okay, and that his friends really do pick him up at midnight tomorrow night." His breath was steam as he spoke, his long hands, wrapped around his arms, colorless as a mummy's against the gray cloth.

"Because if he doesn't—if Paul von Rath gets his hands on that Spiracle again—I'm telling you now the Nazis invading England are going to be the least of everybody's problems."

"Goddam crazy little bastard." Saltwood eased the car through the long weeds, overgrown branches of elder and hawthorn slapping wetly against the windscreen, wishing to hell he dared uncover the headlights enough to get a good view of the potholes of the farm track that led back to the main road. But the risk of being stopped was great enough without tampering with blackout regulations, and without Rhion and the Spiracle—whatever it really was—there was

little chance a questioner wouldn't notice the bulletholes in Salt-wood's uniform jacket, the pile of gear in the backseat, his lack of true resemblance to any of the various i.d. papers he carried, or the startling similarity of all the car's passengers to the descriptions of fugitives undoubtedly being circulated by this time to every corner of the Third Reich.

In addition to the map it rapidly became clear that Rhion seemed to have taken a third of their money and food, and assorted ration books and identity papers, as well. Those last had been stowed in the car. Thinking about that made the hair creep on Saltwood's scalp. How the hell long had he been standing there, gun pointing at nothing, unaware of anything taking place around him?

"Where the *hell* did they dig him out of?"

"I been trying to figure that out for months." Sara pulled her knees up under a second field jacket she'd put over them like a blanket, and huddled tighter into the one over her shoulders. Her father, on her other side, still sat ramrod-straight and shivering in his shirts sleeves, his dark gaze turned worriedly out into the frost and blackness of the night.

"My *guess*," she went on slowly, "is that who he thinks he is is based on some kind of distorted reality, though it's hard to tell what that originally was. And he believes in it one hundred percent him-self."

Saltwood glanced curiously sidelong at her as the car emerged onto the Rathenow road. Instead of turning left, which would have taken them eventually to the Elbe and thence to the Hamburg au-tobahn, he turned right, eyes straining in the darkness for the cross-road where he'd turn off toward Brandenburg and then swing south of Berlin and head east. *Thank God the Germans can't stand anything that isn't neatly labeled.* He recalled only too clearly trying to get around in London after its inhabitants—expecting an invasion any hour—had taken down every street and road sign in the city, not that London was ever oversupplied with such things.

"So he told you?"

She nodded and brushed back a tendril of the dark hair which framed her face. "Three, four days after they took us prisoner last June, that bodyguard of his, Horst Eisler, showed up at Kegenwald one night and drove me back to the Schloss. Rhion was still laid up—I don't think he'd have told me some of the things he did if he hadn't been doped up and hurting and scared. He . . ." She paused, and Saltwood felt, rather than saw, the change in the way she sat, the lessening of the reflex tension of her muscles as she forgot where she was, remembering only the darkened room, the pudgy hand desperately gripping her own.

Then she shrugged, rearranging the first thoughts to cut less close to her own heart. "He talked to me then about his woman and his kids back in Oz or wherever the hell he thinks he comes from. About his old master who was supposed to come here with him but died or disappeared on the way through this Void thing he talks about, and about how his parents wrote down in the family Bible that he'd died the day he told them he was going to be a wizard. The whole setup—he claims his woman's father is a Duke or something—makes me think he might be a Hungarian or Austrian Jew from one of the old university towns, except that, when I met him, he claimed he didn't even know what a Jew was. A Freudian would say that's significant in itself.

"But you know," she went on softly, "he didn't have to do what he did. He didn't have to give von Rath that Spiracle in the first place, or let them make him teach them how to use the device it's a control to, if there is one. I mean, Papa and I had no claim on him. He'd only met me about three weeks before, only broke Papa out of the camp because of some magic ceremony he claimed he needed to work down in the cellars under Schloss Torweg."

"Then he isn't . . ." Tom began, with elaborate casualness, swinging the car to the right and heading down the two-lane strip of asphalt through the dark, tree-sprinkled fields that would eventually lead to the old Prussian capital. "You and he aren't . . ."

He hadn't thought so, watching them together—the physical stiffness, so at odds with the sensuality of her face, was noticeable with him, as well. But though the affection between them seemed casual, it clearly ran very deep. His impression was that she regarded the Professor as an uncle or an older brother . . . only not quite. And in the panic confusion of flight from Berlin, of the bombing and getting through the blockades and out into the open darkness of the countryside, there had been no time for unnecessary words, no way to tell for sure. He felt more relief than he'd have cared to admit when she laughed, startled and tickled, and said "RHION? Oh, Christ . . ." and laughed again.

Good, he thought.

"But you know," she added more quietly, switching to English with a quick glance at her father, who was deep in trying to calculate, with a pencil stub on the back of a ration book, some elaborate *kamea* regarding the superimposition of the number keys of all of their names over the Seal of Mars, "if I ever *do* get interested in a man again, it'll be because . . ." Then she shied away from that train of thought, too. "Well . . . Rhion was the first man I've met in— oh, years—who wasn't a bastard." She spoke a little defensively, seeming to retreat in on herself again, and Tom felt a flash of anger at them, whoever they were: the man or men who had put that wariness in his dark-haired girl's eyes.

She'd been a hostage, a prisoner of the SS—the way she watched him, the way she'd pulled away from the touch of his hand, the grim set to her mouth as she'd gotten back in the car, might, he had thought, have stemmed from that. But now he wasn't so sure. Very carefully, he said, "Be that as it may—whatever happens, I promise you I'm not a bastard."

Their eyes met, and held; then Tom flicked his gaze back to the dark road unwinding before them. The sinking glow of the fires in Berlin was to their left now and farther off in the darkness. Overhead, the gypsy moon did a fan dance with the clouds.

"Thank you," Sara said softly, and after that was silent for some time.

It was a hundred and sixty miles to Kegenwald, eastward toward the Polish border. Beyond that, according to Sara, it was another fifteen or twenty to Schloss Torweg itself. "These stones he's heading for are in a kind of overgrown meadow the other side of the hills from the Schloss—which is just an old hunting lodge from back in Bismarck's time. There's a farm track through the hills . . . Let me borrow the pencil, Papa."

The old man sniffed and relinquished it. He'd outgrown the back of the ration book and was currently filling up both sides of an

envelope he'd unearthed from beneath the seat with abstruse nu-
merical calculations, magical squares, and jotted transliterations between Hebrew and Greek. "Those stones probably started life as an
observatory of some kind," he remarked, angling the envelope to
what little moonlight filtered through the window. "They're a hundred and fifty kilometers east of the easternmost examples of cham-
bered barrows, let alone stone circle or alignments. I'll have to write
my friend Dr. Etheridge in Florida about this . . . We've been cor-
responding now fifteen years . . ."

"I don't think there was anybody who published anything in an
anthropology or linguistics or archaeology journal in the last thirty
years Papa *didn't* correspond with," Sara explained. "Not that he
ever got them before they were at least six and usually ten years out
of date."

"If it was real knowledge it never goes out of date."

"Tell that to all those Newtonian physicists."

"So Newton wasn't wrong. Gravity still works, *nu?*"

"Here." Sara held up the map she'd drawn—Tom risked a glance
at it, then went back to concentrating on the road. "That noise
better be the tappets knocking," she added after a moment, cocking
an ear at the dry rattle the engine had developed.

"Doesn't sound like a valve," Tom replied. "Though God knows
how long this baby was driven after grease and oil got scarce . . .
Thanks," he added. "If it wasn't for you coming with me, I'd have
hell's own time catching up with our Professor. It looks as if he
could have picked up a train in any of three places that would get
him to Kegenwald by tomorrow afternoon. At least I'll know where
to intercept him."

Sara didn't answer, and he felt her silence, as surely as he felt the
vibration of the road through the tires and the engine's choking clink.
Her father had gone back to making sigils and demon keys on the
back of the envelope.

Hesitantly Saltwood asked, "You do understand that's my first
duty, don't you? To find him. To bring him back with me, if I can,
but . . . to make sure the Nazis don't get him or his device again,
one way or the other."

She sighed deeply, as if giving up something she knew she never could have. "I understand. It's what you came here to do—I know that. But I think after midnight tomorrow he'll come. He'll have no place else to go. You think I'm riding along just to act as your guide?"

"I hoped it was because you'd fallen desperately in love with me," he said, and she flashed him a wicked grin. "But I still think we should have found a hiding place to leave your father."

"If you think I'm going to let my daughter go hotzenplotzing around the countryside with some Amerikanischer shaygets, you have another think coming," Leibnitz said resignedly. "And besides, according to these calculations . . ."

"By the way," Tom asked Sara, anxious to avert another spate of numerological abracadabra, "have you ever heard Rhion speak anything other than German?"

"N-no," said Sara. "That is . . ." She hesitated, and a glance sideways in the muted lights of a passing military convoy showed him a look of bafflement, as if she had suddenly been faced with a memory that did not fit. He eyebrowed for amplification, but after a moment she shook her head, dismissing something for which she could find no words. "No."

They met no opposition as they drove on eastward in the cold Prussian pines. All the roadblocks, Saltwood guessed, had been set with the assumption that they'd take the westward road: *To England, home, and glory*, as Hillyard would have said. Obviously no one was counting on the fact that their mad Professor was even madder than they'd thought.

They stopped at eleven in Custrin, the little town sunk in darkness and sleep. While Sara "laid chick," as they said on the East Side, watching out for the local bulls, Saltwood broke the lock on the gas pump in front of the general store, filled the Packard's tank and the jerry cans, then raided the store itself for several quarts of oil and as much bread, cheese, mineral water, and bottled beer as he could cram into his pockets. He left the late Corporal Deitmarr's money in a pile on the counter and, as an afterthought, helped himself to a cheap cloth laborer's cap, which he presented to Rebbe Leibnitz on his return to the car. There was nothing resembling a blanket or jacket in the ranks of tinned food, cheap galoshes, and clothespins, or he would have taken that, too, but the old man greeted the gift of the cap with startled joy, and with thanks and a murmured benediction immediately put it on.

There were, of course, a number of SS uniform caps in the back of the car—Saltwood had needed one, as well as a tie and a belt and various odds and ends to complete his disguise—but he'd guessed the old Jew would rather go bareheaded and disrespectful in the eyes of the Lord than wear one, and no wonder. "I didn't think you cowboys knew about things like that," Sara said softly in English as they pulled away from the darkened store and once more into the sandy pine barrens.

"What's not to know?" Tom shrugged. "Half the agitators in the union were Jewish. We had this Trotskyite Chassidic rabbi who used to come in to play chess with me and argue politics with old Stegler every Saturday as soon as it got dark enough so you couldn't tell a black thread from a white one. He told me that a man of your people would no more walk around without his head covered than he'd walk around without pants." And, seeing how she still looked at him, half unbelieving, like men he'd seen when a woman turned out to know what a manifold was, he added with a grin, "You been hanging around with Nazis too long."

She smiled back slowly. "I guess I have."

"Chas vesholem."

Even asleep—if the restless doze in which he drifted could be so termed—Saltwood heard the shock in the old man's voice and felt him startle through the worn leather of the Packard's lumpy seats. He came awake at once. Dark pines still flashed past the car's windows, as they had when he'd given the wheel to Sara and tried to get some rest. The rattle in the engine was worse—*Just what we need. A ring job in the middle of Germany.* The windows were fogged with the outer cold, save for long smears on the front where Sara had wiped them with her sleeve. It was too dark to see his watch—or, more accurately, the late Corporal Dietmarr's watch.

"What's up?"

Leibnitz shook his head. He, too, had clearly been asleep, blinking and startled, like a man waked by an evil dream. "I don't know."

He lifted his cap enough to smooth his rumpled hair and replaced it, looking around him, disoriented, shaken. "Something—some feel in the air. Can't you feel?"

Saltwood shook his head but said softly, "Pull over, Sara, and cut the lights."

She obeyed. They all had far too much respect for instinct to quibble over the delay. Without asking she got out, and Tom behind her. For a moment they stood listening, the air like bitter steel on their faces, their breath a steam of diamonds in the moonlight filtering down through the black pine branches above. The weeds on the banks above the road were stiff with frost like a white salt rime that would show the smallest track. On such a night noise would carry. But Saltwood heard nothing: no rustle of bracken in the woods all around, no crunch of tires on the ill-tended asphalt. He checked his watch by the moonlight—quarter past two.

Uneasily he got back into the car, taking the wheel once more. Irritated as he had once been by the hooded headlights that kept their speed down in the flat stretches, now they made him feel safer.

"Where are we?" he asked quietly.

"About twenty miles from Kegenwald."

"We pass anyone?"

"Not since that motorcyclist an hour ago . . . What's that?" He felt the jerk of her body as she slewed around in the seat. At the same moment light flicked in the corner of his vision and, a second later, gleamed in his rearview mirror. Leibnitz and Sara were both pressed to the side window, their breath misting it again, peering tensely into the dark. "Cut the lights," Sara ordered hoarsely, and Tom obeyed. With the strength of the moonlight there wasn't much difference, except where the pines overgrew the road in pockets of inky shadow. "There," she breathed. "See?"

Blue lights were moving among the pines along the side of the road. Saltwood felt the hair lift on his neck.

They were not lanterns. They were moving too fast, for one thing; for another, some of them floated far too high for a man to be holding. By the eerie glow in the bracken, others were rolling along the ground, though the undergrowth, stiff and brittle with frost, did not rustle, only shone with that skeletal light. It was hard to tell how many of them there were, weaving in and the trees, but they were definitely following the course of ι.

Saltwood turned on the headlamps and pressed the accel thankful that these Prussian roads ran straight and flat as a Ka. highway and to hell with the ruts and potholes and teeth-rattlin, jolts of the chewed and broken paving. Whatever was happening, he wanted no part of it.

In the rearview mirror he saw the lights swirl down the bank onto the road, then pour after the car like bubbles on a river. He pressed the pedal harder, and the lights followed in a bobbing swarm; Saltwood thought they were growing brighter. The car bucked and pitched over the broken road, and he veered, trying to avoid the worst of it. But his eyes kept returning to the mirrors as he sped faster and faster, fear growing within him at what he saw—or thought he saw—or almost saw—behind the lights. Something dark and large, something that ran silent, vibrationless, with a faint glint of metal. Something that moved with level and deadly speed.

He pushed the car for more jolting speed, Sara and her father clinging to the interior straps for all they were worth, knowing to the marrow of his bones that whatever was back there, its black shiny smoothness catching the blue gleams of the lights, he must not let it overtake them. Peripherally he was aware of other lights, a bluish glow powdering the frost-stiff bracken and thin blue discharges like tiny lightning sparking down the trunks of the pines. The granite faces of the old glacial boulders by the road glittered as if laced with diamonds. He barely saw them, his eyes glued now to the mirror.

Why did he have the impression that whatever moved behind those blue lights, metallic, shining, mechanical though it seemed, was alive? More speed, the Packard's old motor clanking hideously . . .

"TOM!"

His eyes flashed back in time to take in a blurred impression of the road's sudden curve, the black masses of boulders looming directly ahead. He hit clutch and brake, the heavy car fishtailing wildly—they should have plowed straight into those boulders but somehow didn't, and he felt the wheels leave the ground.

rolled at least once—Tom wasn't sure—and struck some-
.ch a glancing blow before it came to a rocking halt on its
ⲟara twisted on top of him, her flat-heeled shoes digging into
thigh as she wrenched her door open like a hatch. Tom remem-
ⲟered the three five-gallon cans of gas in the trunk and was halfway
out of the door after Sara before it occurred to him to wonder if
the pain in his legs was because one of them might have been broken.
Together they dragged open the rear door, in crammed black panic
during which his mind registered nothing but the seconds ticking by
until the car would go up like a bomb, and dragged the stunned
Leibnitz out of the tangled welter of guns, groceries, and papers in
the back. Dragging the old man between them, they ran.

The Packard blew up in a fireball of red light, Tom and Sara
falling flat with Leibnitz between them, while fragments of metal
and stray bullets from all the spare clips exploded like shrapnel and
hissed on the frosted ground. Frozen pine needles jabbed Saltwood's
stubbled cheeks like splintered glass as he buried his face in his arms.
Maybe it'll think we died in the crash.

It?

The blackness moving behind the blue lights, implacable and
deadly and . . . real?

As real as the flying demon head that had ripped his arm?

He sat up slowly, his legs stabbing with pain. Now that the fluid
in his veins was turning from adrenaline back to blood again, the
pain was starting, in his legs, in his back, in his thigh where Sara
had stepped on him getting out of the car, and in a dozen other
places where he'd hit the framis in the crash or where flying clips of
ammo or miscellaneous junk had hit him . . .

Sara, too, was sitting up, shuddering with cold and shock, pine
needles sticking in her hair.

The blue lights were gone. Beyond the glare of the burning car,
which lay on its side with its front end twisted where it had struck
a tree, the road ran straight as an arrow out of sight in both directions under pine-shrouded blackness. Tom could see the black tire
lines where he'd hit the brakes and the swerve and jag marking the
skid where he'd tried to turn to avoid rocks that weren't there.

Around them in the dark, boots crunched shrilly on the frost.

Tom scrambled to his knees, gun in hand, as metal glintc dark of the trees all around. *Dozens of them, Jesus* . . .

The flames on the car leaped suddenly higher, outlining a sir shape before him, thick ivory hair and the face of a scarred angel.

With a dozen guns leveled on him, Saltwood pulled the trigger. The gun clicked harmlessly.

Automatics *did* jam, of course.

"Throw it down." Von Rath's voice was still that same soft level, as calm as if he had known all along that it would misfire. They might have been back at the house in the Jungfern Heide—Jesus, had it just been that morning?—getting ready for another "psychological test." Yet there was a difference. The cold angel face almost glowed, coruscating with a kaleidoscope of emotion—fever, hate, and triumph like the crack of lightning that could burst planets asunder; in the red reflection of the flames, the amulets of bone and jewel seemed to bleed glowing blood.

More Storm Troopers materialized from the woods, fire glinting on the muzzles of their guns. To fight would be hopeless, suicidal . . . Tom wondered how they'd known where the car would go off the road.

"Throw it down," von Rath repeated. "I'm going to give you a demonstration and you might not wish to lose your hand just yet."

"Throw it down already!" Leibnitz breathed, using his daughter's shoulder to haul himself painfully to his feet.

Though it went violently against the grain to do so, Saltwood obeyed, tossing the weapon onto the frozen pine straw between them and standing up carefully, keeping his hands raised and in view. Von Rath looked down at the gun for a moment and moved his fingers.

With a rending bark, the clip blew up.

Von Rath smiled, and one fine, slender hand came up to stroke the talisman's that rattled and whispered around his neck. "So," he said softly. "I was correct in my guess. Rhion Sligo has come east, bringing the Spiracle with him. The invasion will not have to be postponed after all. I should hate to disappoint Reichsmarshall Goering, after all of this." The cold gray eyes, no more human now

nake's, passed over Tom and touched Sara briefly, then came
st upon her father.

"Very good," he murmured. Two men came up behind him, the
bearded wizard Gall and a tall fair Storm Trooper of unbelievable
beauty whom Saltwood had the dim impression he'd seen before,
but knew he never had. "Just in time for the sacrifice of power, to
raise the forces of the equinox to help the invasion of England. There
will be, of course, another sacrifice later . . ." His lips stretched a
little, as if part of him still remembered about smiling without remembering why, and he spoke to the beautiful youth who came
crowding close to his side. "And that, my Baldur, though a little
late for the equinox, will, I'm sure, give us no less of a yield of
talismanic power—and no less gratification in the making of it. Take
them away."

25

"You brought the Resonator here, didn't you?" Rebbe Leibnitz spoke so calmly, so conversationally, that for a moment Saltwood thought von Rath was going to be surprised into answering him man to man. The SS wizard paused on the threshold of the great, grim old stone lodge on its flattened hill, startled, and looked back at the elderly Jew in the glow of the hall lights as they passed inside; he even opened his mouth to reply. Then he seemed to settle back a little— Tom had seen the same effect when an Alabama bigot was addressed from behind by an educated black man—and cold superiority returned to his eyes. He had, after all, been addressed not by a real man, but by only a whatever "only" was in these parts.

His smile was that same flat stretching of the lips. "He was a fool to have left it," he said softly. "Did he think I would bow meekly to that imbecile Himmler's insistence that you were headed west to England? That I couldn't come up with enough of my own men to follow him to the ends of the earth to recover the Spiracle and avenge its theft?"

"I thought you made it to begin with," Tom said, and the frosted quicksilver gaze turned upon him.

"The Spiracle is the property of the Reich's destiny, the tool of its ultimate triumph. As I am its tool." Saltwood wasn't fooled by the well-bred calm of his voice: it was the voice of a man insane with jealousy, quietly citing every rational reason why his woman had no right to leave him—to leave HIM. He could see von Rath almost visibly trembling with hate.

"We are all its tools," said that shiningly beautiful youth—whose name was apparently Baldur, too—who dogged at his elbow in the same fashion Baldur Twisselpeck had back in Berlin. And where was Twisselpeck, anyway? Saltwood wondered obliquely.

The young man sniffled and put a hand on von Rath's elbow, then went on in a curiously familiar whining voice, "And he'll pay for it, P-Pauli. Don't worry. Let me do it this time instead of Gall— I'll see to it . . ."

"Indeed." This time von Rath's smile was genuine. "And the Resonator can run for years, I expect, on the power we will raise from that—payment. The soul of a wizard, trained and empowered . . ."

Madre de Dios! Saltwood thought, shaken by what he saw in that dreamy smile. *He really BELIEVES it!*

"A pity we won't be able to take him until nearly midnight," Gall said, coming up to join the other two, like a demented patriarch with his flowing locks and silver beard. "Between the old Jew and the forces of the equinox itself I should be able to raise the energies to make quite a tolerable talisman of power—although not as much as if you yourself were to be officiating—but it does seem a waste."

But if von Rath believes it's magic, Saltwood thought, groping in confusion for some thread of rationality in all this, *and Rhion believes it, and evidently Gall and Twisselpeck and this other Baldur, whoever HE is . . . Then who IS the scientific brains behind this—this device, whatever it is? How can they make it work if they're ALL nuts?*

Von Rath turned and studied them by the dreary glow of the hallway lamps. The fading of the smile he'd worn when contemplating Rhion's death under the knife—and Sara had told Saltwood during the drive of how these self-styled mages "raised power"—left his face completely inhuman again, as if the only emotions of which he was capable were inseparably connected to the Spiracle—as if to him, only the Spiracle and the powers it gave him were real.

He reached out and cupped Sara's chin with his hand. "Where will he be?"

She pulled back angrily and the gloved black grip tightened, the guard who held her handcuffed wrists behind her shoving her forward again. Saltwood was aware that any struggle on his part would be useless, for there were two guards holding his arms, besides the dozen or so ranged around the wood-paneled hallway with guns. But he was aware of an overwhelming desire to smash in that scarred, godlike face.

Sara said, "I don't know, goy."

As calmly as he had struck Saltwood for mouthing off at Himmler, von Rath slapped her, keeping hold of her chin with his other hand to prevent her head from giving with the blow. Tom gritted his teeth and looked away, knowing a struggle wouldn't help Sara and might get him hurt badly enough to prevent later escape. When he looked back, he saw the red welt puffing up on the girl's cheekbone and the involuntary tears of pain in her eyes.

"I know he's in the neighborhood by the fact that the Resonator has come to life," von Rath went on softly. "Ironic, isn't it? Had he not been approaching—though to be sure, with the power from the temple *here* the field of magic is nearly eighty kilometers wide—I would not have been able to use my powers to capture you with such ease. I shall have to tell him that, as he watches you die. And having captured you, I think taking him will be an easy matter. Surely he isn't fool enough to come here with any kind of silly notion of reopening the Dark Well—I'm sure he knows as well as I do that it cannot be done. Will it be the Dancing Stones again? Or that barn Poincelles used? I never was certain how much power that French *untermensch* was able to raise with those degenerate rites he practiced, and our little friend may know some way to utilize it . . . Was that why he wanted you?"

Her voice shook slightly. "He never laid a hand on me."

The golden Baldur giggled like a schoolboy. "Didn't want a dose of the clap, I expect."

"Be still." The inflection was that of a man ordering a dog to sit, and Baldur's square, noble mouth puckered in a pout. "Where will he be?"

"He didn't say."

Von Rath shrugged and nodded to his men. "Take her into the dining room. Gall, get the tools . . ."

"This is stupid!" Saltwood raged, yanking against the grip of the men who held him, and at the same moment Leibnitz spoke quickly. "Don't tell him anything."

"For Chrissake!"

All trace of the old man's slightly comic air of resignation was gone. His dark eyes flashed with calm authority. "Better she should die than the Spiracle fall into their hands again," he said quietly. "She knows it." He turned back to his daughter. "Don't you, Saraleh?"

Sara hesitated, mouth taut and eyes darting, suddenly huge in a face white as chalk. *She doesn't know THAT,* Tom thought, *but she sure as hell knows what von Rath will do to Rhion when he catches him.*

"To hell with that," he said sharply, his eyes going to von Rath. "He's heading for the standing stones."

Von Rath's cold glance went immediately to Leibnitz, who had turned his face away, then to Sara's tear-brimming eyes and the relaxed slump of her shoulders. "So," he said quietly. "Baldur, see them locked up. Jacobus, come with me. If the two of you are going to be performing the sacrifice without me tomorrow night . . ." His voice faded as he climbed the stairs, the white-haired crackpot and two stone-faced guards in his wake.

Baldur signaled the other guards with a jerk of his hand, a weirdly schoolboyish gesture for an officer of the SS, and started after his master toward the stairs. Leibnitz turned to the young man as if they had been alone in the dingy hallway and said quietly, "He's mageborn, Baldur. You think he doesn't see you as you are?"

The young man stopped, his ridiculously crestfallen expression wildly inappropriate on that beautiful face. "I—" he stammered, halting, and the guards, too, stopped. He sniffled and wiped his nose on his sleeve. "Of—of c-course he sees everything. But one has one's p-pride, and—and there are the others . . . And after all these years . . ."

What the HELL are they talking about?

The beautiful youth shuffled his feet, sniffled again, and ran a nervous hand through the tawny splendor of his hair. "It—it came to me tonight, when Paul's power . . . That is—I realized I c-could be however I chose, look however I willed. With the field of the Resonator I have power! For the first time in my life, it is as I have always dreamed it would be! Would you like to see it?" There was suddenly an ugly glitter in his eyes. "You'll see it tomorrow night anyway, Jew."

"Yes," Leibnitz said gently. "Yes, I would."

Baldur snapped his fingers at the guards like the Crown Prince of Ruritania in an MGM musical. "Bring them."

To do him credit, the sergeant hesitated, but apparently thought better of any remark containing the words *ought not*. In any case, Saltwood thought, there were enough and more than enough guards to subdue the three of them, and more yet visible through the door of the watch room which led off the hall. Led by Baldur, the squad escorted them down a short corridor to a locked door, Saltwood wondering how much more insane things would get. There had to be reality *somewhere* under this increasingly baffling layer cake of fantasy, reality that could be used to escape, at least to get word to England . . .

As he unlocked the double mahogany doors Baldur said, quite seriously, to the sergeant, "Kill them if they attempt to cross the threshold. Beyond it is holy ground."

Oh, boy!

For the first moment Saltwood had a vague impression of darkness, of black walls on which silver hoodoo signs gleamed softly in the reflection of the dim corridor light, of a faint smell that must have been much worse closer up, for the old rabbi drew back with an expression of revulsion and horror, as if the door had been opened to a charnel house.

And with Leibnitz out of the doorway, Saltwood could peer inside.

There still wasn't much to see. Marvello the Magnificent had put up a better front in a canvas tent. By comparison with the Meditation Chamber of the Swami of the Celestial Realms, the place was stark and the decorations amateurish. There wasn't even the inevitable portrait of

Hitler on the wall—only a crimson swastika, seeming to burn somberly against the darkness. And yet . . . and yet . . .

The place raised the hackles on Tom's neck.

On the black altar in the center stood the widget he'd last seen by candlelight in the locked bedroom in Berlin, the device he hadn't paid much attention to, being in the process of getting ready to strangle its inventor. The grimy light from the hall must have caught odd reflections in those spheres of glass wound like bubbles in kelp among the strips of iron, for they had an odd glow that seemed to be answered from one portion of the heart of that fist-size lump of raw crystal. Even the rough iron and the other metal—brass or gold, though surely it couldn't be gold—had a glitter that, through a trick of the shadows—maybe one of the guards behind him was moving— seemed to pulse like the beat of a heart.

Whatever was going on, Saltwood thought uneasily, backing away, it might not be magic, but it was pretty damn weird. Just what *had* he seen in his rearview mirror? How *had* von Rath been so sure his gun would jam?

Magnetic field? he wondered, trying to separate what little he knew of actual science from Einstein's speculations and Flash Gordon serials. *Something under the altar, maybe? It's one for Mayfair's boffins, if I can even get word of it back to them . . . Christ, they're starting the invasion the day after tomorrow!*

Leibnitz' deep voice interrupted his thoughts. "I wonder how long it's going to take Himmler—and Hitler, for that matter—to realize they're playing Frankenstein to von Rath's Adam."

"And why not?" Baldur retorted hotly, his voice scaling up nearly an octave with excitement, his blue eyes glittering as if drugged. "Not the Adam of that stupid fable, not a monster against nature, but the culmination of nature, the New Adam of the Reich's destiny. Why shouldn't it be P-P-Paul? He can raise power! He can store it in talismans! And when he achieves the Spiracle Rhion stole from him, he'll be able to use it against his enemies, outside the Reich and within it. The SS has always known the virtue of magic, so what better glory can they ask than magic itself? . . ."

The boy was working himself into a frenzy. Saltwood, feverishly calculating ways and means of escaping at least long enough to get hold of a radio and warn England, barely listened. But as Baldur turned to close and lock the "temple" doors and the guards led their prisoners away, he cast one glance back, and wondered why he had the impression, even as the shadows fell across it, that Rhion's Resonator glowed more brightly in the dark.

"Now would you mind telling me," Saltwood asked, crossing the bedroom to make sure the window bars were as firmly embedded in the concrete of the sill as they looked, "what the *hell* that was all about? You sounded like you knew that kid." The bars were solid. They were lucky, he supposed, that the window wasn't boarded over, as it had been quite recently by the look of the woodwork around it. It would have been nice had the heat in the rest of the house penetrated to this room, but one couldn't expect everything.

The salt-white glare of the arclights in the yard—they were far out of range of even the most stray British bomber—turned Leibnitz' long hair to silver as he sat wearily down on the bare mattress of the bed. "Oh, I do. Baldur Twisselpeck, one of von Rath's tame wizards."

"Baldur Twisselpeck?"

At the same time Sara, halting in her examination of the wooden walls, the floorboards, the ceiling for possible means of egress, turned to stare at her father. "That's crazy! Baldur is that poor greasy *shmendrik* who followed von Rath everyplace . . ."

"That was him," Leibnitz said and, when Sara stared at him in the dense pewter-colored gloom, "Wasn't that his voice?"

She hesitated, thinking back. Then she shook her head, the tangle of her red-and-black hair swirling. "Papa, that's insane! Baldur was a geek, a *nuchshlepper*! It couldn't be a disguise; that kid's six inches taller, the eyes weren't the same color, and the face . . ." She hesitated again.

"It is illusion." Leibnitz drew up his long legs to sit tailor-fashion on the end of the iron-framed cot. "Like the illusions of the lights that pursued us on the road, the illusions you both saw in their little tests . . . Like half those guards downstairs were illusions. Von Rath hasn't got twenty men in this house. How could he have got more than that away when Himmler wanted them all on the westward roads?"

"Thanks for not telling me that downstairs," Saltwood grumbled, prowling back to the door to verify that the hinges were, in fact, on the outside. "I'd have had a nervous breakdown trying to figure out which ones to watch out for." What *would* he have done, he wondered, if Leibnitz had said down there, *Hey, pal, half those guys aren't real.* Like Rhion, the old man could be weirdly authoritative. *If I stay here much longer, I'm going to be as crazy as the rest of them.*

But from what von Rath had said, a long association didn't look at all likely.

"Don't you understand?" The old man leaned forward, his brown-spotted hands curiously graceful in the bars of bitter light. "The Resonator that didn't work two miles from the Spiracle back at that little *pishke* temple in Berlin has all the power, everything, they raised here all summer. It's pulling the energies of the Void through it and feeding them back into one hell of a field, and in that field von Rath, and Gall, and that poor *doppess* Baldur can do as they please . . . What have you there, Saraleh?"

While he'd been speaking Sara had been testing the floorboards under the bed, and had found a loose one. But when she crawled out of the leaden bar of shadow Saltwood saw only a few bits of chalk in her hand and the glinting flash of a piece of broken mirror. She shook her head, her shoulders slumped under the baggy and bullet-holed black jacket she still wore. "Nothing, Papa. Just chalk."

"Nothing is nothing," Leibnitz said, and rose stiffly. Saltwood, his own bruises seizing up, hated to think how a sixty-five-year-old man's brittle bones and unworked muscles were handling that kind of maltreatment.

He was sore enough to be sarcastic, however. "There's a piece of wisdom for you."

"Good," Leibnitz approved, nodding. "Your *shaygets* does recognize wisdom when it comes up and bites his ankle. There's hope for the *goyim* yet." He took the odd collection of fragments from Sara's hand and carried them back to the wan stripes of the window-light.

"Some kid's collection, it looks like—"

"No," her father corrected, stirring them with his fingers. It really was only a few pieces of odd trash. His breath made a smoke against the sharp chiaroscuro of the floodlights, for it was icy cold in the room. Outside, frost glimmered silver upon the ground, the guards' tracks leaving a ragged streak of black along the perimeter fence. "This was the room where they kept Rhion after they caught him, wasn't it? I think they were his things."

While the old man muttered and poked at the bits of glass and chalk, Sara walked back to where Saltwood stood next to the rump-sprung plush easy chair that, with the bed and a broken-down dresser, was all the furniture that the room contained. Her arms were folded as if for protection across her breasts, her face drawn and waxy with strain and tiredness. It was close to dawn. Half hidden by that weirdly particolored hair, the bruise on her cheek from von Rath's slap was darkening; by the way she walked, the wreck had left a couple of doozies on her shoulder and hip.

"Thank you," she said softly, not looking up at Tom for a moment, speaking English so her father would not hear. "I—I didn't know what to say. To von Rath, I mean. I didn't want to tell them—I know what they'll do to him—but . . ."

"Did your father really mean that?" he asked, still more softly, as if speaking English were not sufficient to exclude the old man from their conversation. "That he'd expect you to die—to let them torture you—before you'd let them get hold of that stupid magic wand Rhion's so crazy over?"

She sighed, still hugging herself, a small, compact dark figure, save for those splendid white legs and that pointed little face. "Papa . . . Yes, he meant it. And he would die over those crazy magic games he plays. I used to think I was tough enough to die before I'd rat on a friend, on someone I cared as much about as I care about poor old Rhion. And I'd like to think I am that tough. But still . . ." She looked up at him through the tangles of her black hair, and there was a tiny gleam of self-deprecating humor in her eyes. "Does it sound as awful to you as it does to me to say I'm glad you told him?"

"Yep," he said and, reaching out, gently took her hand, drawing her down into the chair with him. It was almost big enough for them both to sit comfortably—he felt her shy from the touch of his arm around her, his shoulder against hers. Then she relaxed, a wordless *Oh, what the hell* that went from her body to his like a sigh of relief; he'd been afraid she'd pull away, and lie the night in uncompromising loneliness and pain. After forty-eight hours of physical and mental strain, of which the last twenty-four had been without sleep, culminating in violent physical exertion, a drive halfway across Germany, and an automobile accident, he couldn't get interested in much more, even if she'd let him.

But though he felt her uncertainty still, her hesitance and reflex caution, it was a start—the start of something he wanted more, and differently, than anything he could remember wanting since he'd gone back to Detroit from a year in the oil fields to discover his mother and sisters were gone, no one knew where.

Things took time. He sensed that time was what he would need with this woman, this girl. To gain her trust, her—*Go on, say it, Tom!*—love, he was willing to put in all the time he had.

Which was, at a rough guess, about twenty hours. But they drifted to sleep together in the armchair as if world enough and time lay before them like a warm English summer, back in the days before the sun-cross was anything more than a good-luck symbol superstitious women stitched into baby quilts.

In the hard electric glare of a corner of the Kegenwald train station, Rhion of Sligo, wizard, mad professor, exile from another universe, and fugitive-at-large, sat huddled in a black SS greatcoat with his staff propped at his side, staring down at the broken fragment of mirror in his hand. He couldn't see clearly, for even the little effort involved in scrying tired him, and he was exhausted already from the thin cloak of look-over-there and who-me? that he'd held about him for the past eight hours—the spells that had let ticket sellers be distracted as they glanced not-quite-at the identity cards of men seven inches taller than he with blond hair, the spells that had caused pretty girls to walk past or minor fights to break out as the police or the SS came near him in train stations, and the spells that had given people the impression he was a smelly old derelict like Johann at the Woodsman's Horn, a presence to be noted very briefly and then resolutely ignored.

But he was very tired now. He was freezing cold, for the night ticket seller and the single police guard on duty at the station were sitting next to the electric stove at the far end of the bare little room—men who had not seen him get off the train and would not see him leave. He was worn out physically with the sustained effort of magic-working in a world where the energy levels of air and earth were so low, despite the coming equinox, his body hurting for sleep that he knew would be far too dangerous a luxury. Food helped, though it was difficult to get the sweets he chiefly craved—he'd scored some black-market chocolate on the train but that hadn't lasted long—and what passed for coffee in stations along the route didn't have nearly the kick of the rations the SS got.

So his vision in the fragment of mirror was at first only shapes against darkness. He had, of course, used a shard of mirror to keep tabs on Sara and her father while they were at Kegenwald, to make sure von Rath didn't move them elsewhere, or hurt them . . . though there was nothing he could have done if von Rath had.

Then the vision cleared a little, and he felt a pang go through him as he realized what he saw.

Sara and Saltwood.

Well, that was logical, he thought, seeing how dark the girl's hair was, pressed to Saltwood's shoulder, only flaming into its old crazy, frizzed red down at the level of her ears. There was the peace of friendship in the way they held one another—the way he'd never dared touch her, had always been too cautious to touch her, too careful of those old wounds, old hurts.

He ought simply to be glad she was on her way to healing.

And there was Tallisett.

The hurt inside him crushed tighter at the thought of her, the slowly growing knowledge that he would never see her or his sons again—the loneliness he had endured for six endless months in hell.

He realized that what he grudged was the easing of that loneliness. In his hornier moments he had considered going to bed with Sara, but only with part of his heart. What he had really wanted was to be held, to be loved, and to know he wasn't so goddam alone.

He was very tired of being alone.

Or just very tired. He shook his head. It was nearly dawn outside. It was an all-day walk to Witches Hill if he was going to reach the standing stones well before midnight tonight, and he'd have to find food and, he hoped, someplace to rest between here and there.

The worst of it was wondering whether he was, in fact, insane. It had occurred to him before this, jostling in the crowded trains, shoulder to shoulder with old women, fretful children, and unshaven men nervous with the nervousness of the unemployed in a land where unemployment was a crime—it had occurred to him again and again in his months of captivity, when the only faces he had seen, the only voices he had heard, had been von Rath, Baldur, Gall, and the guards.

It was a very real possibility that he was a lunatic who had dreamed all the complexities of his former life—dreamed of Tally, and his children, and the calm peace of the Drowned Lands—while incarcerated in a madhouse somewhere. Then Tom and Sara were right, and he was only imagining that he could see his friends in this fragment of glass he'd picked up in a corner of the washroom in the Frankfurt-am-Oder station, and that he only believed he was in control of the actions of others when they did not pay attention to him.

It certainly made more sense than his own version of events.

Yet try as he would, he could conjure no picture of a former life, no rational explanation for his escape save cause and effect, no reason why von Rath and the SS would be so interested in the madness of one patently Jewish lunatic. But if he was mad, perhaps the pursuit was as illusory as the rest of it?

He shook his head, exhausted and eroded and cold to the marrow of his bones.

If he was mad, he was left with nothing—only this bleak train station, with its clean-painted white walls and its posters of noble Aryan manhood in uniform performing feats of heroism under the dingy electric glare.

If he was sane, he was left with only the standing stones and the hope that Shavus had somehow heard his cry three months ago—the hope that it had only been some unforeseen hitch which had prevented the Archmage from gathering the requisite congregation of wizards to reach across the Void and bring him back, the hope that, in the precarious moments of the Universe's balance at midnight of the equinox, he could somehow raise enough power to open a gate in the fabric of Being.

And beyond the standing stones there was nothing. Exile from Germany—exile from his own world forever—at the rosiest stretch of hysterical optimism. Or death. He'd been around the SS long enough—he knew von Rath well enough—to know that a bullet in the back of the neck was another exercise in rosy optimism.

He closed his eyes, not wanting to think about the endless walk from Kegenwald to Torweg, while the sun-tides gathered, and he waited for the night.

Twenty-four hours, he thought. In twenty-four hours it would all be over, one way or the other. He would be at the stones at midnight . . . It was his final chance.

Outside the church clock struck four. By the electric stove at the far end of the room the guard rustled a newspaper, and the station attendant asked whether it looked like there'd be war with Russia.

Rhion opened his eyes and looked again at the glass.

He realized where Tom and Sara were.

The dark bulk behind them was the bed where he himself had slept during most of three months. The white glow of the floodlights lay in cross-barred patches over the beaky dark shape of Rebbe Leibnitz' forehead and nose. The chair where Saltwood and Sara curled together in a tight knot of trust was the one where he'd sat endless hours, peering at his broken piece of scrying glass alone.

They were at Schloss Torweg.

Rhion lowered his forehead to his hand and thought, *No. PLEASE, no.*

They must have come after him.

And they'd somehow stumbled into Nazi hands. Evidently von Rath hadn't completely shut up the Schloss when they'd come to Berlin for the demonstration.

If they were there, the place would be guarded. He thought about what it would take, the strength it would need to work the requisite spells, the drain on the last thin reserve he was keeping to catch the momentum of the Universe, to fling across the Void in the hopes of reaching the farthest extent of Shavus' power . . .

He couldn't do it.

His power was exhausted.

In any case he doubted he could do it before midnight. And if he wasn't at the stones at midnight . . .

Sitting slumped on the bench, shivering in his long black coat, Rhion cursed for several minutes in German, in Polish, in Yiddish, and in his own rich, half-forgotten tongue. Then he got to his feet, stiff and aching and leaning on his crystal-headed staff, and wondered where in Kegenwald it would be possible to buy black-market chocolate.

26

It was afternoon when Saltwood woke up, feeling worse than he'd felt since his teenage bar-fighting days in Tulsa. There were other similarities to those days, too, besides the general sensation of having gone to sleep wadded up in the bottom of a clothes hamper after having been thoroughly beaten with a chair: the gluey stickiness in his mouth, the feeling that his eyeballs had been deep-fried, and the sleeping presence in his arms of a woman whose existence he hadn't even suspected forty-eight hours ago.

The differences were that he was starving hungry instead of nauseated by the mere mention of food, that he felt awe and admiration as well as tenderness for the woman curled up against his chest, and that her father was sitting on the floor six feet away, rocking back and forth whispering Hebrew magic to himself.

It was the day of the autumn equinox. The twenty-third of September. Tomorrow—unless by some miracle Rhion Sligo could avoid capture—the invasion of England was going to start, spearheaded by Paul von Rath and whatever infernal device was controlled by the iron Spiracle. That the device in some fashion caused the most believable hallucinations this side of the soft room was beyond question. Whether it could or couldn't affect the weather or blow things up at a distance was undecided, but that first effect would be enough to give the Luftwaffe the edge they needed over the RAF. Hell, he thought, they might be able to use it to fox that secret early-warning system the Brits were said to be using—who knew?

He knew already that with von Rath and his men waiting for Sligo on Witches Hill tonight, both rescue and assassination were out of the question. There were simply too many of them—in the face of those odds his own recapture would be a foregone conclusion. Everything within him might revolt at the thought of leaving the device and its hapless inventor in the hands of the Nazis, but at the moment, the thing of paramount importance was to get word back to England somehow and warn them at least what to expect.

And here he was, the only man who might possibly be able to save England, locked up in a Gothic mansion in Prussia with a woman he suspected he was falling in love with and a lunatic rabbi.

Cautiously so as not to wake Sara, he wormed his way out of the worn plush chair, gritting his teeth at the thought of what straightening his back was going to be like. Bar fights with the oil company goons, he decided, had nothing on explosions and car crashes. Clutching at furniture and cursing all the way, he stumbled into the little washroom—barred and secured as tight as the main bedroom—that adjoined it.

After dashing cold water on his face—which didn't help—he studied himself for a moment in the mirror. No wonder Sara'd had second thoughts about sitting on his knee. There was a cut on his forehead and a blackening bruise on his cheek he hadn't even noticed from the crash last night, as well as an itchy pyrite glitter of stubble. There was no razor, of course. Considering the amount of time the Professor must have spent in places where they wouldn't give him a razor, it was no wonder he wore a beard.

When he came out, finger-combing his short fair hair back from his face, Sara was awake, and her smile when she saw him reduced Hitler, the war, von Rath, the invasion of England, and the fact that he was surrounded by candidates for the funny farm and stood in immediate danger of being killed to inconsequential sidelights.

"You look awful," he said conversationally, and Sara grinned back, shoving the red-streaked raven tangle of hair back from her bruised face.

"Well, your resemblance to Clark Gable at the moment isn't strong enough to knock me down. I feel like I fell down a flight of stairs."

He nodded toward her father. "What's he up to?"

"About the eighth Sephiroth." The old man had chalked a giant diagram on the floor before him, three interlocked lines of circles connected by trails of Hebrew letters and surrounded by a cloud of jotted notes in the same writing. "It's the Tree of Life, supposedly the diagram of the way the Universe works. Meditating on it and calling on the names of the angels of each Sephiroth—each of those little circles—you're supposed to be able to summon sparks of holy fire down from the Outer Aether to help you out with your spells."

He leaned his shoulders against the wall, hands hooked in his pockets, and studied the complicated maze of abracadabra scribbled across the gray floorboards. "He know any?"

"Sure." She got to her feet and began gingerly twisting her back and shoulders, her black brows pulled together in pain. "Call up fabulous wealth, yes; fame and fortune, yes; the wisdom of Solomon, yes; avert an evil eye the size of Ebbets Field, yes; but unlock the door? Nah!" She winced at an incautious movement of her neck and added, "Ow! Aunt Tayta always told me never to go driving with American boys and by damn she was right. Those *chozzers* took my cigarettes, too."

She padded over to him in her stockinged feet, the SS jacket still wrapped stolewise around her shoulders and the sunlight from the window calling electric gleams of copper and cinnabar from the red portion of her hair as she looked out at the men moving in the yard below. By the light, Tom calculated it was just past one o'clock, and more or less warm.

"They all look pretty real to me," he commented, and Sara gave a wry chuckle.

"He must have called in reinforcements from Kegenwald," she said after a moment. "The ones in the gray field dress are Waffen from the camp—I recognize a couple of them. The ones in black must be those Pauli brought with him from Berlin."

Tom frowned. There were, in fact, not very many of those, not nearly as many as he'd seen when they were taken last night.

"Look," he said quietly, still keeping to English. "They were serious about your father, weren't they?"

She nodded.

"When will they come for him?"

"A little before sundown. They have to—to make certain preparations in the temple."

"They'll probably take you away then, too, if they're going to use you as a hostage when they wait for Rhion up on Witches Hill. Since they haven't tried to feed us so far, we'd better not count on anyone coming in before that." He took a deep breath, knowing what he had to say next and hating the expediency of it, hating those dry odds of life and death. "You know if we do manage to get out of here, we can't stick around to save him."

Her mouth compressed hard, but she said nothing.

"The only place we know where to find him, they'll be there, too. And right now the thing that has to be done is to get word back to England. With luck we might—just—make it to Danzig by morning. That's the bottom line, Sara. I'm sorry."

For a moment he was afraid she'd suggest that she remain and attempt the rescue, but she didn't. Her square, thin shoulders relaxed; her breath blew in a soft sigh of defeat. "I know. I probably couldn't make it through to Danzig by myself and, anyhow, I wouldn't know who to get in contact with—I could be Gestapo for all your contacts know . . ."

And if you were killed I don't think I could stand it. He bit his tongue on the words, a little surprised even at himself. But there was something inside him that had lost one too many things, one too many people, in the course of his life. The thought of losing her before they'd even properly begun was a darkness he couldn't bear to face.

". . . and anyhow," she finished, her face still turned away, "I couldn't leave Papa. No." Then she shrugged and chuckled grimly, looking up at him with bitter amusement in her eyes. "What the hell are we talking about anyway? We're never gonna get out of here."

His voice was very quiet. "I'll be fast." Their eyes met, and he saw the fear in hers.

"You'll still be . . ."

"Rhion?"

Leibnitz' whisper brought both their heads around sharply. The old man was bent over the fragment of mirror glass he held cupped in his palm, his open eyes fixed upon it with an odd, glazed expression. In German he said, "Rhion, is this you, can you hear me?" And he leaned down toward the glass, a listening expression on his face.

Saltwood tiptoed soundlessly up behind him, Sara close at his side. Looking down over the old man's shoulder, he could see only a broken triangle of Leibnitz' lined face reflected in the glass.

"Rhion," the old man breathed, "a door-unlocker spell I need, fast, and whatever you do to make them not see you."

They traded glances. Sara's expression was one of deep concern and pity, but Saltwood felt the hairs creep on the back of his neck as Leibnitz added querulously, "No, I don't know what kind of locks they are!" His exasperated tone was exactly that of a man having an argument on the telephone. "They're the locks on your room at the Schloss!"

There was a long silence. Baffled, Saltwood stepped around in front of him to watch his eyes. At the move the old man's head jerked up. "Don't step on the . . ."

Saltwood looked down at the lines of chalk under his feet.

Leibnitz relaxed in disgust, straightening his bowed back, and finished, ". . . Tree. And now we have lost him." He held out his other hand to Sara, and she had to almost lift him to his feet.

"Papa . . ." she began worriedly.

"Come," he cut her off, staggering as he turned toward the door so that she had to catch him again. Saltwood realized the old scholar had been sitting in meditation all night. The room had been far from warm, and his injuries had stiffened; he was lucky he could stand. It didn't seem to have affected the calm serenity of his madness. "We got no time to lose."

"Papa, for crying out loud . . ."

"You got a better way to spend the afternoon waiting for them to come kill us?"

Pretty inarguable. Saltwood hid a grin and turned back to the window, rubbing absently where the manacle of the cut-off handcuff still chafed his left wrist and studying the yard once more. There was the electrified fence, though that wouldn't be on during the day when the main gate was open. The Schloss stood on high ground, sloping down on three sides outside the perimeter of the fence. All the land around the bottom of its little rise was clear. Only on the side toward the hills did the pines crowd in close on the fence, though there was still a gap of thirty feet. He couldn't see any vehicles from here, though the guards last night had had an LG-3000 and the Waffen Troopers had to have gotten here somehow from Kegenwald. Stealing something from Kegenwald village looked more promising, though it would be a hell of a hike. They could get food there, too, and be on the main road east to Danzig.

But, as Sara had said, what the hell was he talking about? They still had to get out of the room.

He turned around to study the layout of the place once more just in time to see Leibnitz open the door.

"We've got to destroy the Resonator!" Leibnitz whispered urgently. "At the cost of our own lives the thing has got to be destroyed!"

"The hell it has," Saltwood muttered back, keeping a firm grip on the old man's skinny arm. There was no guard in the upstairs hall, but he could hear them below, lots of them, as they slipped into the little dressing room next door and down the old backstairs. "If they're getting ready for some kind of fandango at sunset, that temple's gonna be crawling. What we've got to do is get the hell out of here."

In broad daylight? demanded the part of his mind that still didn't believe Leibnitz had picked the lock on the door. It had to have been jammed, or not caught in the first place—Jesus, what an idiot he'd been for testing all the window bars six times and not thinking to check whether the lock on the door had really caught! But he was positive he *had* checked. Anyway, they could have been in Danzig by this time.

Across—what?—thirty feet of open ground and under the wire?

The insanity around here must be contagious. Rebbe Leibnitz certainly seemed to believe he'd received instructions for invisibility through a two-by-three-inch chunk of broken mirror, but Saltwood was still wondering how he'd gotten talked into making a break for it under those circumstances.

Perhaps, he thought, as Sara opened the door to the lightless and mildew-stinking pit of the backstairs, because they had no choice. If they stuck around they were dead meat anyway, and being the only three people in the history of Naziism who actually *were* shot while trying to escape beat hell out of getting asked questions by the Gestapo. So in the long run it probably didn't matter.

And just as they reached the end door of the old service wing, a fight broke out on the other side of the Schloss.

The noise was unmistakable—from the Tulsa oil fields to the West Virginia mines, in the migrant camps of California and every dockside bar from New York to San Francisco, it was the same—the way every Storm Trooper, whether von Rath's black-uniformed goons or the gray-clothed stooges from Kegenwald, dropped whatever they were doing and ran around the corner of the building. God knew what it was about, Saltwood thought—*Cigarettes, at a guess, since there're no women around.*

It's damn convenient, he reflected as the three of them walked rapidly across to the wire and Tom held it up for Sara and her father to slip under, then rolled through the little gully himself. *But it ain't magic.*

They crossed the open ground and disappeared into the woods beyond.

"There's a big farm about three miles this side of Kegenwald where they've got a Hillman Minx up on blocks," Sara panted, striding as rapidly as she could under the added burden of helping her father. "The owner's one of the local Party bosses. He used to see me when I was—ah—tending bar in town . . ."

"*Kayn aynhoreh*," Leibnitz groaned. "You lay on top of the piano and sang songs, too?"

"Don't gripe, Papa, it's how I found you. Anyhow," she went on hastily, "once they find out we're gone, they'll sure as hell guard the camp and may be able to spare a patrol or two in town, but they can't cover all the farms."

"A Minx is a trashcan!"

"It's the newest car in the neighborhood—besides, the Nazi *chozzer's* got a tractor, too, we can steal the battery out of, and there'll be petrol. He wangles the rationing."

"Let's hope he wangles oil and grease, as well," Tom grumbled, wading ahead through a waist-deep pocket of soft autumn bracken. "Minxes *eat* grease—if we can't get some we're gonna be walking to Danzig."

"Danzig, shmanzig," Leibnitz muttered, balking as his daughter tried to hurry him over the uneven ground. "If we don't go back and destroy that Resonator this whole thing is pointless."

"When we radio for a pickup in Danzig, I'll ask for an air strike, how's that?" Saltwood said, more to pacify him than because he had any intention of demanding bombers that would, he suspected, be desperately needed on the southern beaches by morning.

"And what makes you think they'll be able to find it?" the rabbi demanded, limping heavily, his dark eyes grim in the shadow of his billed cap. "What makes you think they won't crash on the way, the same way they're going to crash when they come against the Luftwaffe over the Channel?"

"Oh, hell, Papa, if they've got the device out at the Channel they can't use it to guard the Resonator here, can they?" added Sara.

"You don't understand! The Resonator—"

"Don't worry about it," Saltwood snapped, feeling like he was in an argument with a six-year-old about where the Lone Ranger got his silver bullets from. "Let's take first things first."

"The car," Sara said.

"No—food."

"Destroying the Resonator should be the first thing."

Saltwood sighed. It was going to be a long, long way to Tipperary.

It had been a number of years since Saltwood had had occasion to live entirely off the countryside. In Spain he and his mates had usually been able to scrounge a meal out of Republican partisans, even if it had only been bread and goat cheese. But the memories of his hobo days, of riding the rails in search of work or traveling to organize for the union, stood him in good stead now.

Sara, a denizen of the streets, first of Warsaw, then of New York, looked askance at the berries he gathered from the hedges and stared at him in disbelief when he offered her a handful of rosehips. "You sure they're not poison?"

At the far end of the pasture he cut a milk cow out of a small herd—"This was easier when I had a horse"—and improvised a pail from a tin can found in a ditch and washed out in one of the ponds that dotted the countryside. "For somebody who looks like a big dumb farmboy you know a lot."

"For a Yankees fan," he replied with a grin, "you're not too bad yourself."

She stuck out her tongue at him and handed the improvised cup on to her father. It was good to be in the open air again. Purely aside from the swarms of SS goons, lunatics, and self-proclaimed wizards that had thronged it, there was something Tom had definitely not liked about that house. The rough country of sandy pine hills and isolated farmsteads through which they traveled, swinging wide to avoid the roads whenever they could, slowed them down but kept them out of sight of whatever authorities might be around; it also impressed on Saltwood the impossibility of intercepting Rhion before the Professor walked into von Rath's trap.

"Poor little bastard," he remarked, keeping a weather eye down the farm track beside whose weed-grown ditch they had paused to rest. The sun was touching the tips of the pine-cloaked hills to the west, gilding the throw-pillow clouds heaped around it and covering all the eastward lands in a pall of cold blue shadow. "I wish there was something we could do for him. I wouldn't leave a dog to the SS, but he's the one who ducked out on us."

And if it wasn't for him and his stubbornness about returning to those damn stones we wouldn't even BE in this mess.

As if she read his mind Sara sighed and shook her head. She'd grown quieter during the day's long hike, exhaustion and hunger slowing her down more than she'd counted on, though up until an hour or so ago, she'd still frothed every time Saltwood had insisted they take a rest. "I felt terrible, you know, watching him standing there on that stupid stone with his hands upraised, waiting. Like watching—I don't know. Some poor *goyische* kid on Christmas Eve waiting for Santa Claus." Sitting on a felled and rotting fence post, she pitched a pebble across the narrow road into the thickets of brown sedge and fireweed. She glanced up at Tom. "You ever have Santa not show up, cowboy?"

He shook his head, remembering paper chains and popcorn strings, and the line of shabby stockings pinned to the wall near the belly-stove—Tom-John-Kathy-Helen-Shanna-Ma'n'Pa. He still rattled off the family names as they all had, as a single word, and smiled a little at the memory. He'd spent a year searching for Ma and the girls, and still wondered what had become of them, and if there was something else he should have done.

"Nope. Sometimes he didn't bring a whole lot, but he always showed." He glanced at the sky. "It'll be dark in an hour," he said quietly. "We've got to stick closer to the roads if we're not going to get lost."

"They'll know we're gone now." She pulled the scuffed jacket closer around her and rubbed her hands. The evening was cold already and, from the feel of the air, by morning there would be hard frost. "They'll be hunting."

"They'll be sore as wet cats," Tom said, "but as bad as they want Sligo and that patented whizzbang of his, most of their men will be up at Witches Hill. There's just too much territory for them to cover to find us." He held a hand down and helped Sara and her father, who had sat silent, numbed with exhaustion, to their feet. If they didn't get a vehicle soon, the old man wouldn't be able to go on, and Saltwood didn't like to think about what might happen in that event. Sara might realize the impossibility of risking England's defeat to go back for Rhion, but she'd never leave her father. And in that case . . .

He pushed the thought of that decision away. *First things first.* He shrugged his shoulders deeper into his scarred and bullet-holed jacket and revised his estimate of times again to allow for a slower pace.

It was an hour after full dark, and icily cold, when they saw the first of the lights.

A bluish ghost-flicker of ball lightning shown far to their right in the trees; catching a glimpse from the corner of his eye, Tom halted in his tracks; but when he scanned the rustling darkness, it was gone. "What is it?" Sara asked quickly, looking up at him in the gloom, and her father, taking advantage of the halt, leaned against a pine trunk, his hand pressed, as it had been more and more frequently, to his chest.

Saltwood shivered, wondering just what kind of powers the Resonator—whatever it did—gave to von Rath, and at how great a distance. *"Nada,"* he breathed. "Let's get moving."

The second light flickered a hundred yards ahead of them ten minutes later, and this time they saw it clearly. Over head-high—ten, twelve feet above the tips of the bracken and weeds—it bathed the delicate fans of dry foliage around it with cold dim light for a few seconds, then vanished as inexplicably as it had come. Distantly, Saltwood thought he heard a truck pass on the road that their course had paralleled since dark. It was hardly unusual for a rural district on a clear autumn evening, but something inside him prickled a warning. "Move back into the woods."

The third light flickered into being closer still and to their left a few minutes later and, after a short time, appeared again, near enough to shine on their upturned faces. It was small, the size of a child's hand, a round blue-white bubble like the glow around some innermost seed of brightness. The chilly light reminded Saltwood of something . . . candlelit darkness . . . the phosphor reflection in upturned glasses . . . They pressed on, both of them supporting Leibnitz now, deeper into the blackness between the trees. Increasing cold made their breath steam and stung the inside of his nostrils. The old man, who still adamantly refused to wear any part of the SS uniform, had begun to shiver.

Then that glowworm brightness glimmered into being directly over their heads, and somewhere not too far behind them he heard the muffled confusion of men's voices.

"Christ, they're trackers!"

"Can you kill it?" Saltwood whispered, turning to Leibnitz and not even thinking about what that question implied. "Or send it someplace else?"

"I . . . I think . . ." The old scholar frowned, his high forehead corrugating into thick lines of concentration as he held onto the younger man's broad shoulder. Above their heads the light faded, wavered a little where it hung, then slowly began to drift away.

Mental powers, Saltwood decided. *A brain-wave amplification device and to hell with your ethylene and platinum, Saraleb.* Unless it was sheer coincidence . . . He tightened his grip around the old man's rib cage and headed up the rising ground. Glancing back, he saw the light bobble uncertainly and go out.

"I—Rhion said . . ." The old man spoke with difficulty, his eyes shut, still concentrating hard. "He said a wizard . . . cannot scry the presence of another wizard . . . The Resonator field . . ."

They were right at the feet of a line of low moraine hills, nearly invisible above them in a vast looming bulk of pine trees, and the countryside here was littered with granite boulders half buried in weeds and sedge. Saltwood left father and daughter in the dark blot of one such outcrop's shadow and moved softly back toward the oncoming swish of boots in bracken, flexing his hands. In the shadows of the trees it was almost impossible to see, save where the starlight caught on silver and on the blued gleam of a rifle barrel. A nervous guttural voice whispered something about *"die Hexenlichte . . ."*

Tom rose out of the bracken almost under the Trooper's feet. It was very fast—grab, strangle, twist, and then the man's body was inking down into the deep pocket of brown fern, and Tom was moving off, dagger, sidearm, rifle in his hands. He supposed he should have stopped to strip the coat, but it would have occupied dangerous seconds—the man's companions weren't fifty feet away among the pitchy shadows of the trees—and Leibnitz would have put up a fight about wearing it anyway.

The old man was shuddering, his eyes pressed shut, his breathing the rasp of a saw, when Saltwood reached their hiding place again. Without looking up Leibnitz whispered, "I can't . . . He is stronger than I. I feel his will pressing on me . . . his strength . . . The talismans he has made . . . Ach, that strength . . ."

Dimly, blue lights began to flicker and weave among the black pine needles overhead.

Saltwood handed Sara the rifle and dragged Leibnitz to his feet. "Move!"

Behind them someone yelled.

Lights were bobbing everywhere now, the yellow lances of flashlight beams springing on, zagging wildly among the trees. Tiny balls of witchlight, purplish flecks of St. Elmo's Fire, swirled like fireflies overhead, and against him Saltwood could feel Leibnitz sobbing for breath as they ran. The lights broke and scattered, but it was like trying to elude a swarm of softly shining hornets—they reformed, drifted, darting here and there in a numinous cloud. Had Sara been Saltwood's only companion he would have told her to head in another direction to split the pursuit, but he knew she was as exhausted as he and unable to manage her father's unwieldy bulk alone.

Leave her. He could just hear Hillyard saying it. *It's your duty to warn England, your duty not to be taken, no matter what the cost . . .*

Stick my bloody duty. He shoved aside the image of the RAF Spitfires crashing on the Sussex beaches in flames. Rhion had said, *I didn't risk what's going to happen to me to work for the people who were dropping those bombs . . .*

The words echoed in his mind. *What the hell's the point of defeating the Nazis if you become one inside?* "There anyplace to go?" he gasped, as they thrashed their way up the high ground, dodging trees and flashlights, stumbling over rocks half buried in the pine mast and ferns. "Cover, anything?"

"Not with those frigging lights overhead there's not!" In the blue glow, the sweat made points of her dark hair around that pale triangular face, moisture gleaming on her cheeks in spite of the cold that turned their breath to steam.

Creepers, wild ivy and morning glory, snagged at their feet, branches slashed their faces as they stumbled on. Leibnitz gasped ". . . strength is growing . . . talismans . . . all those deaths . . . He can use it . . . equinox . . . midnight . . ."

Midnight! It must be close to that. Rhion would walk slap into the ring of SS troopers on Witches Hill . . . von Rath would head for Ostend in the morning with the Spiracle to take part in the invasion . . . The British wouldn't get so much as a warning as to what was coming up the beaches, out of the skies . . . until their pilots bailed out because of imaginary cockpit fires or imaginary monsters chewing on the wings. The lights poured around them in a bluish cloud. Stumbling under Leibnitz' weight, Saltwood couldn't imagine why they hadn't been shot yet.

The ground fell out from under them so abruptly it was only Saltwood's hair-trigger reflexes that kept them from going over. He felt the gravelly clay crumble under his boots before he actually saw anything but darkness ahead, and flung himself back, catching Sara and her father. Beyond the last overhanging thickets of dead and dying undergrowth the road lay at the bottom of a twelve-foot bank where it cut through the saddle of land between the hills. Blue light flooded them as they skidded to a halt on its brink, searchlight-bright, only it blazed from over their heads: the glow of witchfire, of magelight . . . of magic.

There were two covered trucks and an open Mercedes down on the road below, with half a dozen Storm Troopers grouped around them. Baldur—the godlike golden SS Baldur, not the podgy, bespectacled Baldur Twisselpeck from Berlin—was at the wheel of the car, and as the guards leveled their submachine guns on the fugitives, Paul von Rath stood up in the backseat, Lucifer ascendant in fire and shadow and rage.

27

"Bring them down."

Saltwood had already heard the men come up behind him, crowding out of the shadows of the trees. With a bitter oath Sara turned, bringing up her rifle, but the range was already too close. A Trooper tore it out of her hand and shoved her backward over the edge of the bank. Saltwood, hampered by Leibnitz' full weight, was only starting to turn when three rifle barrels thrust into his back and then he was falling, too, rolling down a slide of desiccated ivy and fern in a tangle of arms and legs.

He landed hard in a cold puddle of water, started to rise, and was struck over the back of the head by somebody's gun butt, driving him to his hands and knees. Gun and dagger were ripped from his belt before he recovered enough to think about committing suicide by putting up a fight.

"Put the Jew in the truck," went on that calm, soft voice, shaking now with an inner core of blinding rage. "Bind him, gag him, blindfold him. Baldur, remain with him, since he seems to be able to twist the powers we have released to his own corrupt and dirty spells."

Raising his head, Tom could see the golden youth and three or four Storm Troopers cross to where Leibnitz lay facedown in the wet yellow leaves of the roadside ditch. They picked the old man up, a broken scarecrow with his patched gray clothing and emaciated limbs. Only when they were halfway to one of the covered trucks did Leibnitz show by the feeble, disoriented movements of returning consciousness that he was still alive. Baldur struck him.

"You goddam Nazi coward!" Sara flung herself toward them but was caught, easily, by two Storm Troopers—Saltwood lunged to his feet more to protect her than to go after Baldur, and the men behind him had been waiting for that. The struggle wasn't long.

"Bind the whore and put her in the other truck," von Rath said calmly, still standing in the backseat of the open Mercedes, Satan in uniform, the thick chain of talismans lying like a hellish emblem of office over shoulders and breast. Those that had been made of jewels seemed to burn in the shadowless blue magelight that flickered all around him, and even those wrought of bone and skin and twisted hair pulsed in that strange radiance, with something that might have been a kind of light but was more probably, Saltwood thought distractedly, a reflection sparked from the jewels, or the silver on his uniform, or something . . . some rational explanation . . . In some odd way those dead and mounted mementos of past sacrifices seemed more living than von Rath's eyes.

The wizard went on, "We have just time to reach Witches Hill, if we drive fast. Gall is waiting there already, but, with our hostage guaranteed, now we should have no trouble. So the night will not be totally lost. But you . . ." He turned to Saltwood, and a spiteful vindictiveness crept into his voice. "By leading this escape you have cost me the power I could have raised through an equinox sacrifice. You have almost cost me what I could have gotten from a second sacrifice, the sacrifice of a wizard, for without his Jewish whore as hostage, he would not have let himself be taken alive. You will pay for that."

Saltwood felt something twist inside of him, a sharp stab of pain in his entrails, like the appendicitis he'd had as a kid. He bit his lip, gasping, trying not to cry out, but the pain grew, turning his knees to water. For a moment the men who were holding him took his weight; then they dropped him to the icy and broken pavement of the road.

Christ, he thought, *what is this?* all the while curling tighter over himself, tighter, retching as red claws ripped at him inside, like taking a bayonet in the gut, worse . . . He heard Sara cursing, was dimly aware of her fighting like a wildcat against the men who held her, men who were staring from him to von Rath's cool face and back with growing uneasy horror. He tasted blood and bile in his mouth, blood trickling from his nose, and his teeth shut on a scream, fighting to keep himself from screaming *Stop it! STOP IT! PLEASE!!* and thinking *Bastard, I won't give that to you.* Powder trails of pain and fire ignited along every nerve, burning up his flesh. It was all he could do not to scream, and he could feel that, too, coming . . .

Then the pain was over and he was lying on the wet gravel, weak and shaking and scared as he had never been scared before. Cloudily he was aware of a man swearing, "Bite me, you Jew bitch!" and von Rath's voice, querulous and peremptory, commanding, "NO!"

Looking up, Tom saw one of the guards who'd been holding Sara shaking his bloodied hand, the other still gripping her, his fist frozen in middraw.

Von Rath shook his head, his brows pulling slightly together, the expression of a man puzzled by something he has done flickering, very briefly, to life in his inhuman eyes. His soft voice had a halting note. "We—we have no time for this." He passed his hand across his eyes and then the expression was gone, but for a moment Tom had the impression the SS wizard had been too involved in his own display of power to remember even the necessity of capturing Sligo alive. As if, for the moment of the exercise of his power, he had forgotten, literally, everything.

Then he looked back at Saltwood, the inhuman calm returning to his eyes. "I must . . ." A last fragment of uncertainty flawed his voice, then was gone. "I must try this again with someone of equal strength." His glance shifted to the guards. "Kill him."

Saltwood felt the barrel of an automatic press the back of his neck and heard the trigger pull.

Only the silence after Sara's scream "TOM!" made it possible to hear the flat click of the hammer coming down.

As if he didn't quite believe that nothing had happened, the guard pulled the trigger twice more, the clicks very loud now in the growing silence that spread among the men gathered beneath the cold umbrella of phosphor light, and all heads turned, not to von Rath, but to the dark of the road beyond.

Beyond the range of the corpse-candle glow, feral starlight caught in the lenses of glasses, in the five crystals of the Spiracle at the head of a staff. Then darkness fell, blinding and total, and Saltwood whipped one leg behind him and jerked down the guard with the gun, smashing the man's head on the pavement and ripping the dagger from his belt while noise erupted all around him, a chaos of shouts, curses, the crunch of boots, and the slap of bodies running head-foremost into the sides of trucks.

Then the darkness split, lightning tearing down in splattering flame as the bolts hit the road where Rhion had stood. In the white-purple glare, Tom saw Sara standing still a foot or so away and grabbed her wrist as darkness slammed down on them again, some instinct telling him to pull her away from the truck behind her. An instant later the vehicle burst into flames that illuminated a milling chaos of black- and gray-uniformed men surging all around them.

"Papa!" Sara yelled as the bushes on both sides of the road went up, and lunged for the second truck. For the first time Saltwood noticed that she, too, had acquired a dagger. At the same moment he almost tripped over the body of the Storm Trooper whom von Rath had stopped in the act of striking her. The beautiful Baldur met her in the dark arch of the truck's canvas cover, his own dagger held point-down for the overhead stab favored by Hollywood directors—Saltwood hurled him easily aside into the path of another advancing Trooper. Sara was already dragging her stunned father from the back of the truck; Tom kicked another attacker in the groin, grabbed the old man's arm, and, as the second truck burst into flames, bolted for the dark of the road cut where Rhion had last been seen.

Underfoot the potholed pavement heaved and split, hurling the three of them to their knees. Its center buckled upward, pulling apart to spew forth what seemed, for a hideous second in the holocaust of shadows, to be black things, shining, living, glittering, and crawling among a sticky ooze of glowing greenish slime. The next instant fire swept across it and the things were still—pebbles, Saltwood thought dimly, scrambling back into the shelter of a granite boulder that projected from the tall road bank—only pebbles and water after all, but burning, burning in impossible flame . . .

Lightning struck the bracken of the opposite bank, the dry brush roaring up in a screen of incandescent gold. A dark figure broke from it a second before it flared, darting across the lowering flames that still flickered on the pavement as if every crack and pothole were filled with gasoline. Another levin bolt cracked, tearing the road to pieces behind them, and then Rhion rolled into the shelter of the boulder, face streaming sweat as if he'd plunged it into a sink.

"They took that Resonator you made to the Schloss," Saltwood gasped. "Whatever the hell it does . . ."

"He still thinks it's a Flash Gordon deathray," Leibnitz chipped in, as were-light exploded around them and Rhion flinched and gasped.

"Yeah, I figured that out." He was holding himself upright on the staff, his face drawn with pain—Saltwood remembered as if from a nightmare the gut-rending agony von Rath had . . . *willed on him? But that was impossible.* Then Rhion drew a deep breath, and the pain seemed to ease. But in his blue eyes the haunted look of darkness remained, of grief and hopeless loss.

It was, Saltwood realized, only minutes short of midnight. Quite quietly, he said, "Sorry we made you miss your bus."

"Not your fault." Lightning flashed again, striking at the boulder behind which they crouched and seeming to shatter off it, splattering in all directions and running down the stone in lapis rivulets of fire.

"Gall's waiting for you up there, you know—or at least he was. He's probably hot-footing it back here as fast as he can to cut us off."

Rhion nodded. Beneath the brown tangle of his beard his face was ashy and taut with pain, his breathing a ragged gasp.

"We couldn't warn you . . ."

"This flat-footed, goyischer *shlemiel* stepped on the Tree of Life before I could tell you . . ."

"It's all right. I'd hoped . . ." He gasped, averting his face for a moment, his whole body shuddering under the renewed onslaught of pain. Leibnitz reached quickly up, his bony, age-spotted hands folding over the smooth pudgy ones where they clung to the wood of the staff. For an instant Saltwood felt a burn of heat on his back, smelled scorching wool—then with a cry he saw spots of flame spring up on the back of Sara's jacket. He struck them out, panicked and disoriented, feeling heat breathe on his face, his hair . . .

Then it was gone, and Rhion was straightening up again, shaking, as if his strength had gone with it. "I can't . . ." he whispered. "He has the talismans . . . all their power, drawn into himself . . . Poincelles and the strength of the summer solstice. All the sacrifices they did . . ." He shook his head. In a small voice he added, "And he was stronger than me from the start."

Slowly, between the surface of the rock and Sara's shoulder, Leibnitz levered himself to his feet. "It will be midnight soon," he said softly, and Rhion nodded. Under the scratched spectacles and the sweaty points of his hair his eyes were shut. Sara's image sprang to Saltwood's mind again, the mad Professor standing on his magic stones, arms outspread, waiting to be taken away by wizards and enchantments that never came.

Dimly, from down the road beyond them, the growl of truck motors could be heard. A moment later hooded headlights flashed into view, and standing up in the lead truck's open cab Saltwood made out the long white mane and silvery beard of the wizard Gall, cutting them off from any hope of flight.

On their other side von Rath had stepped forth into the roadway. The blazes that still flickered, impossibly, on the riven asphalt sank; the ranks of Storm Troopers formed up behind him like a wing of darkness and steel. A nimbus of shadow seemed to surround the Nazi wizard himself, that queer, eldritch, spider-shot aura that Saltwood had once or twice thought he'd seen from the corner of his eye floating near the Spiracle. But this darkness was growing, spreading, lifting like a column of smoke around a core of lightless flame.

"Can you run for it?" Rhion asked quietly.

"Are you kidding? With Gall and his stooges behind us and von Rath able to zap us the minute we . . ."

Rhion shook his head, and for an instant, from the corner of his eye, Saltwood had the same strange sense he'd had before about the Spiracle—that the shadow-twin of the darkness which surrounded von Rath gathered there like a veil of impossibly fine black silk, shot through with invisible silver. Its crystals seemed to have caught the cold glitter of the stars, but no stars at all could be seen now, through the center of its iron ring. Saltwood wasn't sure what it was that he *did* see there, in that terrible, shining abyss.

"No." Rhion's voice was barely audible, his eyes not on Saltwood, but on von Rath's advancing form. "No. It will be all right. It was my fault—my doing . . . But it will be all right."

His face like chalk, Rhion stepped from cover and walked to the center of the charred and rutted ruin of the road. Gall called out something and men sprang down from the truck and started to run forward, but something about that solitary brown figure made them hesitate and stumble to a halt.

In the silence of midnight, Rhion held up the staff in both his hands.

It seemed to Saltwood that the lightning came down from five separate points of the heavens—heavens deep and star-powdered and impossibly clear. They hit the head of the staff and for one second he thought the darkness—the veil—the whatever-it-was that had always seemed to hang there invisibly—was illuminated with a horrible electric limmerance that speared out in all directions along those silver spider strands.

Von Rath shouted "No!" in a voice of rage and disbelief and inhuman despair.

And the very air seemed to explode.

Von Rath screamed.

It was like twenty men screaming, a hundred—dunked into acid, eaten by rats, rolled in fire that wouldn't die. The chain of amulets around his neck burst simultaneously into—not flame, but something else, something worse, something Saltwood had never seen before—something that sheathed the Nazi wizard in searing brightness even as it sank into his flesh, eating into him as fire streamed back out of every orifice of his body, as if he had been ignited by that lightning from within. The screaming seemed to go on for minutes but couldn't have lasted for more than twenty seconds or so, while Rhion stood braced, the glare of the lightning that never ceased to pour like water down into the head of the staff blazing off his glasses, and von Rath screaming, screaming like the damned in their long plunge to hell.

Then silence, and the dying crackle of flame. The Spiracle at the head of the staff was gone, the staff itself burned down to within inches of Rhion's hands. The troops on both sides stood back in frozen horror, staring at the crumbling, burning thing in the SS uniform slowly folding itself down to the blackened ground.

A voice shrieked *"Pauli, NO!"* There was the flat crack of an automatic, and Rhion twisted, his body buckling over, and fell without a cry.

Baldur Twisselpeck, short and fat—*And where the hell did he come from?*—stood in front of von Rath's Mercedes, clothed in a straining SS uniform to which he couldn't possibly have had any right and clutching an automatic, tears pouring down his pimply cheeks.

Ashen-faced, the men started to move forward in the sinking illumination that came from the fires along the roadbed and the two burning trucks, toward Rhion's body and what was left of Paul von Rath. None of them seemed to notice Baldur, who had fallen to his knees, sobbing hysterically, clutching his gun to him and groaning "Paul . . . Paul . . ."

"Let's go," Saltwood breathed, turning to Sara—and found her gone.

The first spattering burst of machine-gun fire from the abandoned Mercedes cut Baldur nearly in half. The second sustained volley took out both Gall and the gas tank of the truck in which he stood, and as men scattered in all directions the Mercedes jumped forward, bounding like a stallion over the chewed-up pavement to screech to a stop a few feet from the boulder where Saltwood and Rebbe Leibnitz still crouched.

Sara yelled "Get in, goddammit!" from behind the wheel.

Saltwood heaved Leibnitz into the backseat, which contained all the guns Sara could collect, grabbed a Schmeisser, and sent raking bursts in both directions at the men who were already starting to run towards them. Bullets panged noisily off the fenders and hood, and Saltwood felt one of them sting the back of his calf as he bent down to haul Rhion's body out of the way of the wheels.

How much of that HAD been real? he wondered, looking down at the slack face, the broken glasses, the black bruise of the garrote across the throat. If they got out of this alive, there'd be time to mourn. But he was acutely aware that Rhion had done what he himself had refused, for expediency's sake, to do: he'd come back for them, and to hell with what it cost.

Then he saw Rhion's eyelids flinch. One of those chubby hands tried to close around his wrist, then loosened again, but by that time Saltwood was hauling him into the backseat of the Mercedes, heedless of the rifle bullets whining like angry flies around him. "Drive like hell!" he yelled as Sara hit the gas. "He's still with us!"

"How bad?" she yelled back, as Storm Troopers scattered before the big car's radiator like leaves in a gutter. The burning truck with Gall's half-roasted body still hanging out of it flashed past; a last bullet sang off the fender and Sara swore. Then there was darkness, and the remote white light of the cold half-moon.

There was an entry wound between the two middle ribs; the exit wound, gaping and messy with splintered bone, was just under the shoulder blade, and hissed faintly with every gasping breath. Behind the rimless glasses Rhion's eyes were open now, staring with a curious, terrible bitterness into the midnight sky. "Bad."

With a small sigh that broke off sharply in a wince of pain Rhion turned his head, beard and eyebrows standing out blackly with shock in the moonlight. "Can you get me to the Stones?" His voice sounded normal but very quiet.

"Oh, for Chrissake!" Sara groaned, exasperated. "We've got enough of a head start to make it to Danzig."

"Please."

"It's too goddam late! You said midnight, and midnight is over! Do we need to keep on with this?"

"Saraleh," Leibnitz said gently, "the reason it's too late is because he came back to help us."

The fires had vanished into the darkness behind them. On the other side of the hills another glare of orange flame and rising smoke marked where Schloss Torweg would be, and Saltwood was so numbed, so exhausted, so shaken that he didn't bother trying to think up a reasonable explanation for that.

The big car rocked and jolted over the sorry road, and, beyond the spiky black of the pines, the wheel of the stars moved calmly past its point of balance, down the long road to the next solstice at the dead heart of winter, three months away. The cinnamon tips of her hair flicking back under the fingers of the night wind, Sara continued to expostulate, "We're gonna get frigging caught! This is our chance, our last chance . . . There'll be search parties all over the goddam countryside . . ."

Rhion, teeth shut hard now, said nothing, but Saltwood said, "Get us there, Sara, okay?" and felt Rhion's hand tighten on his own.

"He's not gonna make it," Sara said softly, "is he?"

Around them, the countryside was deeply silent. They had found the Stones deserted, though ringed with plentiful evidence of Gall's earlier ambuscade—cigarette butts, tramplings in the wet grass, and an occasional puddle of urine behind a tree. That no one had been there since they'd departed shortly before midnight was obvious; dew had formed already on the grass, and would hold the slightest mark. In the deepening cold it was already turning to frost.

Saltwood looked back at the form lying on the fallen stone in the cold starlight, which picked out in chilly relief the lenses of his glasses, the silver swastikas and buttons of the SS greatcoat they'd put over him. "Not the way we'd have to be traveling."

Like a bent, gray stork in the wavery shadows, Rebbe Leibnitz sat on the edge of the stone at Rhion's side, sketching the arcane circles of the Sephiroth and writing all the Angelic Names he knew in the last crumbling fragments of the chalk he'd had in his pockets. The Hebrew letters formed a pale shroud of spiderweb, draped over the ancient stone of sacrifice and trailing away into shadow. In its center Rhion lay without moving, his breathing agonizing to hear.

Hesitantly Sara said, "The Nazis would probably patch him up if they found him. With von Rath gone they're going to need him . . ."

"No!" Rhion half raised himself from where he lay on the stone, then sank back with a gasp, his hand pressed to the makeshift bandages on his side. As they strode back to him Saltwood could see the track of blood glittering in his beard, and the dark seep dripping through his fingers. "Don't let them . . ." Then his eyes met Saltwood's, and he managed a faint grin. "Oh, hell, it's your job not to let them, isn't it?"

" 'Fraid so," His voice was gentle.

Rhion coughed, fighting hard not to. When he was twelve, Saltwood remembered, he'd been chousing cows out of the edges of the badlands twenty miles from the ranch when his horse Mickey had broken a leg. He'd known that to leave the animal alive would be to condemn it to being brought down and torn to pieces by coyotes. The hurt had lasted in him till he'd left the ranch completely . . . and enough of it remained even now to make him remember as he unholstered his gun.

Glancing up, he could see the echo of his thoughts in Sara's eyes. It was after three in the morning of the first day of the long slide of autumn to winter. It would be a cold drive to Danzig.

Hesitantly Sara said, "We—we don't need to travel that fast. I mean, with von Rath dead and the Spiracle gone, that puts the kibosh on whatever secret plan they had for the invasion of England. As Rhion said, even a week's delay to figure out something else is going to put them into winter. We could keep ahead of them . . ."

"It wouldn't do us any good," Saltwood said gently. "He needs a doctor, and he needs care; long before we could get him either of those, he'd be dead in a lot of pain and we'd have put ourselves in a concentration camp for nothing."

He looked back at the stone, where Leibnitz, draped like a Roman patriarch in the carriage rug that had been in the back of the Mercedes, was inscribing the pyramids of power over the numerological squares of the planets, scribbling the Names of the 1,746 Angels in charge of the Cosmos and all its myriad doings. Saltwood still wasn't entirely certain what had gone on back there on the road. Whatever the device had been— radio-controlled explosives or clairvoyant hallucinogens or whatever—Rhion had somehow caused it to backfire on itself badly, that was clear. That he'd done so under the impression that he was destroying his only means of returning to his fantasy home lent a quixotic heroism to the little madman that dragged on some corner of Tom's heart he thought he'd left in a Spanish prison.

And Rhion had saved their lives—and bought England and the world time—at the cost of his own.

Sara walked back to the altar stone, her Schmeisser tucked under one arm. Her breath was a ghostly cloud in the moonlight as she said, "Papa, you should be back in the car." The open vehicle wouldn't be much warmer, but Leibnitz was clearly at the end of his strength. "You can't do anything further here."

Saltwood half expected the old man to protest, but he didn't. He stepped back, holding the blanket around his skinny shoulders with one hand.

"No," the old scholar said softly, and the moonlight glimmered on the steam of his breath, the silky stiffness of his ragged beard, like quicksilver frost. "I have summoned it back, all the power that went forth from their meeting; summoned it back from the energy tracks along which it dispersed to all the corners of this sorry earth."

He turned his head to look down at the still, dark shape lying upon the altar, and in the emaciated wrinkles of his face Saltwood could see the glint of tears. "It is sacrifice that gives power, you see, Saraleh," the old man whispered. "Not death, but the willingness to give up everything, to burn the future to ashes, and all that it could have been, and to let it go. That is what they did not and could not understand, wanting power only for what it could give to them. That is what raises the great power from the earth and the air and the leys beneath the ground, that thunderclap of power that went forth; that is why he conquered."

His hand sketched a magic sign in the air; then, bending, he kissed the tangled hair that lay over Rhion's forehead. "The Lord go with you, my friend—to wherever it is that you will go."

Rhion made no response. Sara stepped forward and kissed him in her turn. Then she turned quickly away, hitching the machine gun under her arm. Taking her father's elbow, she walked slowly back toward the car, the tracks of their footprints dark and broken in the first glitter of the frost.

Saltwood walked over to the Stone. In the moonlight the chalked Kabbalistic symbols seemed to glimmer on the close-grained dolomite of the ancient altar. The night was still, but with the passage of shadows across their ice-powdered faces the other two Stones did, in fact, seem ready to begin dancing, as soon as no one remained to see.

His automatic felt like lead in his hand.

Rhion raised his head a little, propping himself on one elbow. His hand, pressed to his side, was black with blood. "I know you have to get moving if you're going to make it to Danzig ahead of the pursuit," he said, his breath a blur of whiteness in the freezing air, slow and ragged as if he fought for every lift of his ribs. His eyes were sunk back into hollows of shadow behind the broken spectacles, his forehead creased with pain. "But can you give me till dawn?"

For what? Saltwood thought. *For your magic friends to get their act together and show up with the fiery chariot after all?*

But something told him Rhion didn't really expect that to happen anymore. A rime of frost glittered already on the coarse wool of the greatcoat draped over him—its hems and sleeves, even, scribbled with the Seals of Solomon, the Tetragrammaton and the Angelic Names—and turned the weeds around the stone to a frail lace of ice, and the night promised colder yet.

With any luck, Saltwood thought, cold as it was, by dawn Rhion would be dead.

He put the automatic back in its holster. "Hell," he said softly, "you gave us till spring."

Rhion shook his head, his strength leaving him as he sank back down onto the bloody stone. "When I came here," he said quietly, "it was because I couldn't imagine anything worse than a world where magic no longer existed. But I've seen . . ." He coughed again, pressing his hand to his side. "I've seen what is worse—a world where even the concept that other human beings are as human as you are is disappearing . . . and I see now, too, that this—this kind of lie—is what was starting in my own world, was being used like a weapon for whoever cared to wield it. That is how it starts . . ." He was silent for a moment, his face tense with the struggle against agony, and Tom saw the dark threads of blood creep from beneath him to mingle with the pale signs of the chalk.

Then he whispered, "I couldn't let them have it. But when I went back . . . it wasn't for that."

"I know," Saltwood said.

"Take care of her."

He grinned wryly. "You think she'll let me?"

A sharp spatter of gunfire crackled on the edge of the woods. Saltwood ducked instinctively, turned and ran back along the black track of footprints in the palely shining grass toward the red flash of

Sara's gun barrel. It was a party of Storm Troopers from Kegenwald. The whole countryside was probably alive with them, either seeking vengeance for the somewhat confused events of the night or still hunting for Rhion, unaware of what had gone on in the road cut. It really didn't matter. The results would be the same.

The skirmish was sharp but protracted, a cat-and-mouse game of quick firefights and long waiting in the deepening cold, of slipping and stalking painstakingly through the absolute darkness of the pine woods, of waiting for a whisper, a breath, the movement of a shape against the slightly paler gleam of the frozen pine mast. Saltwood had done it a hundred times over the last few years, in the mountains of Spain and in training in the hills of Scotland, and upon occasion, more recently, in the wet fields of France. He had fought colder, fought hungrier, fought in worse physical shape, but when he came back to the car with the thin dawnlight streaking the sky above the trees he didn't remember ever being this tired, this bone-weary of fighting, this fed up with the expediency of killing men to make the world a better place.

Since he'd gotten into the unions in his early twenties, it seemed to him that he'd always been fighting *somebody* to make the world a better place to live in. One day, he thought, if he survived the war, it would be good simply to live in it for a change.

Like Rhion, he wanted to go home.

Sara came out of the woods, an officer's greatcoat slung over one arm and three more submachine guns hanging by their straps from her other shoulder. With characteristic practicality she had been looting the bodies of the slain. In the frame of her dark hair, her face was gray with strain and exhaustion, and blood smeared her hands and her knees, and tipped the ends of her hair. She stood for a long moment in the deep, frozen grass looking at Tom, and in her face, in the tired stoop of her body, he saw the sickness of utter weariness, of nausea with everything she had done from the day she had set out for Germany to rescue her father. She did not move toward him, but when he crossed to her, his feet crunching in the brittle weeds, she held out her arms, and they stood pressed together, locked in each other's warmth for a long time while she wept.

"I'm sorry," she whispered finally, scrubbing at her eyes with the back of her sleeve, a schoolgirl gesture that touched his heart. "I don't . . . I'm not usually this stupid . . ." Her arms tightened around his waist, and he felt her shivering. "I'm really not—not like you've seen me at all. It's just . . ."

"I hope you're not too different when things are quiet," Tom said, and kissed her gently on the lips.

She shook her head, holding him closer, her face pressed to the old, dry bullet holes and bloodstains of his jacket. "I don't know what I'm like anymore. Like I've been torn apart and haven't been put back together yet. That's—that's the worst of this."

"Well," he said softly, "I'll be there, if you want me to stick around, while you're figuring it out. There's no hurry. Warm up the car." From the tail of his eye he could see her father crawling stiffly out from under the Mercedes where he'd taken refuge during the shooting, picking frozen weed stems out of his car rug and beard. "I'll be back," Tom promised gently. "And then I'll take you home."

He climbed the sloping meadow in the pewter twilight of dawn, the frost-thick grass crunching under his boots, his automatic in his hand. He'd been afraid the Storm Troopers had gotten to Rhion, but a glance at the stiffened carpet of the grass told him otherwise—it would have held the mark of a butterfly's foot. It shimmered eerily, like powdered silver, in the light of the moon that hung like a baroque pearl above the hill where the old holy place had been. The frost there was thicker, all but covering the tracks he, Sara, and her father had left a few hours ago. It furred the ancient altar of sacrifice, half obscuring the crooked abracadabra that Leibnitz had written there in the hopeless hope of attracting the attention of some mythical convocation of wizards gathered in the Emerald City of Rhion's deranged dreams.

But the odd thing was that it seemed to have worked.

The black greatcoat lay flung back, stiff with rime and patched with blood, and blood lay in congealing puddles on the age-pitted surface of the enchanted stone itself, mixing with the Kabbalistic nonsense of signs. But of Rhion himself there was no trace, nor did any track but Saltwood's own cut the frost that glittered in a carpet of fragile ice in every direction.

28

"D'you think he made it?"

The drone of the DC-3's engines steadied as they reached cruising speed; Tom Saltwood turned away from the icy window glass through which could be seen a fumy, tossing ocean of cloud, ink and pewter meringued with the icy white of the late-rising moon. Pillars and columns of vapor loomed around them, solid-seeming as the mountains of some fantastic landscape. Tom hoped the gangly Yorkshireman in the cockpit knew what the hell he was doing, because at black and freezing three A.M., he wasn't even sure he himself could have said which way England lay under all that cloud cover, much less how to get there without crashing. He also hoped the Freedom Fighters in Danzig had gotten their radio message through to England, and that they weren't going to be met by a squad of Spitfires, after all the long, exhausting journey to Danzig and two days of hiding out in the radio man's cellar, living on canned beans.

But at the moment, he scarcely cared. They were airborne. The Luftwaffe, being largely occupied elsewhere, hadn't sent a plane after them beyond one or two cursory shots as they'd passed over Danzig.

It was over.

He felt as he had felt jammed in a corner of the destroyer *Cod-*

rington's gun deck, grimy and exhausted, amid stinks of oil and cordite, sweat and vomit, and feeling glad to be there with all of his soul that was still awake enough to feel anything . . .

It was over. He was heading home.

The DC-3 had been stripped for conversion to a cargo carrier, and rattled like an empty boxcar. Curled on the cleated wood decking at his side, Sara lay wrapped in a couple of gray Army blankets, her crazy red-and-black hair glinting every now and then when the jogging gleams of the dim cockpit lights struck it. Other than that, the narrow hold was in darkness, Rebbe Leibnitz's hawklike face no more than a pale blur and a liquid gleam of eyes.

"Made it?" the old man asked, the lift of his eyebrow audible as a note in his voice.

Shadow blotted the dim glow of the cockpit lights; a voice with a soft Somersetshire burr said, "We're leveled off—will you have a cigarette, Captain?"

"Yes—thanks," Tom said, and the copilot leaned in to extend a pack. "Mind if I take another for Miss Leibnitz when she wakes up? She'll kill me if I don't ask."

The man laughed. "By all means. By the way, we got word just before we left England, a message for you from a Mr. Mayfair. He said he'd put through special immigration papers for Mr. Leibnitz— as a former prisoner of the SS there'll be no problem."

"When I was just somebody Hitler wanted to have starved and beaten to death it was 'Well, everybody's got their troubles,' " Leibnitz muttered under his breath as the copilot's dark form vanished once more behind the cockpit curtain. "But let them think I can be of some use to them, and they're baking me a cake. Made it where?"

Tom glanced down at Sara's sleeping form, tucked one cigarette behind his ear, and busied himself with lighting the other. The gold glow of the match outlined his cupped hands in light, sparkled in the silky whiteness of Leibnitz' beard. He lowered his voice, as if fearful that even in her sleep, Sara would sigh and roll her eyes in disgust. "Made it back to where he came from."

The smell of burnt sulfur whiffed a little in the cold air of the cabin, then a draft dispersed the thin ribbon of smoke to nothing again.

Leibnitz' voice spoke out of the dark. "There was a lot of power released that night—in the battle, in the destruction of the Spiracle, in the implosion of the field and the rising-up in rage of all those talismans von Rath had made for himself . . . All that power channeled to magic, picked up by the net of the leys, spread out to the corners of the world and brought back again. Power far beyond the power of the equinoxes, the power of the heavens . . . power such as this world has not known in a long time."

By daylight, Tom thought—when they stumbled off this flying sardine can onto the tarmac of Coventry Field in the gray fog of an English morning—he wouldn't believe this anymore, either. He knew he'd start to wonder if he'd looked closely enough at the frost around the standing stones, or if Rhion had been less badly wounded than he'd seemed. But now he remembered only the glint of the five jewels in that last pouring stream of lightning, and the way Rhion's upturned glasses had picked up the glare of it, and the dark blood mingling with the scribbled spiderweb of chalk upon the stone, with no body in the center where a body had lain before.

Months later, long after it had become obvious that the cross-Channel invasion had, in fact, been canceled for that year, on one of his trips down to London, he was to stop in at the Red Cow again and encounter Alec Mayfair, grizzled and slow and cautious as ever . . .

And because of their conversation on that occasion Mayfair lent him a copy of a dossier, a folder filled with copies of Intelligence reports not considered secret enough or important enough to rate special classification. The reports spoke of a massive series of escapes from concentration camps and labor camps throughout Germany: during an outbreak of inexplicable fires at Dachau that kept the guards too busy to notice the departure of eighty-seven Jews led by three of von Rath's "specially designated" Kabbalists; unexplained quarrels among the guards at Buchenwald that amounted to a camp-wide riot during which fifty-four Polish, Jewish, and gypsy children vanished from the camp along with a "specially designated" gypsy witch; the execution of three guards at Gross Rosen for neglect of duty in allowing twelve Jewish and Polish occultists apparently to cut the wires literally under their noses and walk out; and others;

many others . . . all, apparently, at or about midnight on the night of September 23.

There were other matters in the file, too: notes of a British coven raising a visible cone of white light that was seen by a number of witnesses to stretch eastward through the black overcast of the skies toward Germany; a copy of a Gestapo report of the collapse of scaffolding supporting landing barges destined for the invasion at Brest pinned to a local newspaper clipping from the village of Carnac on the Quiburon Peninsula forty miles to the south telling of "lights" seen among the long rows of standing stones at the very hour of the scaffolding's collapse—midnight of the twenty-third—and of the strange things found in the morning among cold ashes at the foot of a menhir known as Le Manio.

An article from the Indian Hill, Massachusetts, *Intelligencer* describing the onstage heart attack of a vaudeville magician during the six P.M. show on the twenty-third, when, as he later said, he'd looked out over the audience and actually seen around each patron a halo of colors, filled with pictures of their pasts, their hopes, their dreams . . .

An article from the *Sentinel* of Rattlesnake Mound, Mississippi, was about a sixteen-year-old Negro girl who'd found $8,000 worth of long-buried Indian artifacts by placing three pieces of brass in her hand and walking along the ridge where pirate treasure was said to be buried, late in the afternoon of that same day.

There was an account of a near-riot at the *San Francisco Chronicle* when representatives of eight prominent Chinatown families came demanding information on an alleged Japanese dawn offensive against Chinese nationalist forces around the Szechwan village of Weihsien in western China, about which they had heard from a geomancer making feng-shui calculations on Mt. Diablo in Berkeley . . . and an intelligence report, dated two weeks later, regarding such an offensive at dawn of the twenty-fourth—or two in the afternoon on the twenty-third in Berkeley—or midnight in Germany . . .

There were other reports: the death of a planter in Haiti when he inexplicably swerved his car into one of his own gateposts while going down his drive; rumors of werewolves among the Navajo and rumors of shamanic activity in Siberia against the marching Japanese;

an unexplained fire in the barracks of occupying German forces in Denmark, and the discovery the following morning of a horse's skull, inscribed with runes of hatred and defiance, close by.

And annotated in a woman's hand, calculations backward and forward through time zones: all of these incidents had taken place at, or about, the twenty-third of September, at the hour when it was midnight on the sunken backroad in Germany that led to Witches Hill.

There was no explanation appended to any of them. Nor did Mayfair offer any, when he took the folder back.

But that lay in the future. Now Tom only sat, weary in all his bones with Sara's head pillowed against his thigh, tasting the welcome bitterness of nicotine and watching the unsteady movement of the chill edge of starlight on Leibnitz' face as he spoke.

"Oh, he made it, all right," Leibnitz said softly. "But as to what his stay in this world made of him—as to what power will cling to him from the magic of sacrifice—it is hard to say. And those wizards who brought him back—I don't think they quite know what they have."

It will be all right, Rhion had said. *It will be all right.*

Tom blew a stream of smoke and reached down with his free hand to touch Sara's hair. It was far from over yet . . .

Due to Mayfair's good offices he knew Sara would be staying in London with her father, while he himself would be going back to the Commandos at Lochailort . . . But London wasn't so far.

He glanced back up at the old man, already feeling that he'd known him and his daughter half his life and rather looking forward to knowing them for the other half. "We'll never know."

And in the faint gleam of the cockpit light he saw the old scholar smile as he folded bony hands about his knee. "And what makes you think one day we won't?"

"Will he live?"

Rhion heard the words from deep in darkness—a darkness that flashed with pain at every breath he drew despite the cloudy blur of what he dimly recognized as poppy syrup and spells, a darkness safe and warm after the soul-fraying chaotic night of the Void. A darkness that beckoned deeper, and to which he wanted, more than anything, to retreat forever.

The Gray Lady's voice said, "I don't know."

No, thought Rhion, drawing further back into that darkness. He didn't know.

Soul and body he felt empty and broken, as he had when von Rath's men had finished with him. The sweetness of the Lady's voice-spells, like the scent of roses carried over water in the night, had drawn his spirit back to his shattered flesh, had given him something to hold to . . . if he chose to hold.

But he had had enough. And the voices he heard around him in that darkness, drifting nearer and then away again, were not encouraging.

"The Cult of Agon has to have wizards of its own in its employ," someone said at one point, a young man's voice that Rhion dimly recognized as belonging to one of the Ebiatic novices he'd occasionally met at the Duke's court. "Powerful wizards . . ."

"It would explain how the Town Council of Imber was able to enter our House to make its arrests," someone else agreed, and in a half-forgotten chamber of Rhion's mind the ghost of a former self smiled, for it was Chelfrednig of Imber, who'd once had him and Jaldis run out of town for practicing magic in the territory of the Selarnist wizards. "I was only fortunate that I was gathering herbs that evening . . ."

"It explains the arrests of Mernac and Agacinthos in Nerriok, and the Blood-Mages in the In Islands last week," added Cuffy Rifkin, an Earth-witch from up the Marshes whom Rhion knew well.

"And it *certainly* makes clear how they managed to get the better of Shavus and the other Morkensiks at the turning of summer."

So that's what happened . . .

But it was still apart from him, still distant. More near, more important, were the smells of peat smoke, herbs, and water, the smells of the Drowned Lands: wet fern, mossed stone, and bread. The gray curtain of sound that rustled like silk in a darkened room was the stirring of rain on the ivy of the walls of his own house and in the long cattail beds below the terrace.

He was home.

Something would have stirred within him at that, he thought, only it had not the strength.

"What I'm saying," the witch Cuffy's voice went on, "is that, though he's the only Morkensik we've got, he's not what you'd call a powerful mage."

"I don't know," the Gray Lady said softly. "The magic that carried him across the Void—the strength I felt out there on the Holy Isle—was not the magic of sun-tide or star-tide or anything else I have felt. I don't know what he is now, what he has become."

Lying in darkness, Rhion knew. Beneath the drugs, beneath the drained exhaustion left by the traversing of the Void, beneath the agony of splintered ribs and torn flesh, he knew. Power lay in him like a fist of light, sleeping in the core of pain that lay at the center of his being. He could open that fist, and the power would radiate forth from his hands . . .

If he was willing to do it. But he knew what it would mean.

It would mean taking responsibility for this ragtag of mages who had gathered here. It would mean putting himself against the might of the Cult of the Veiled God, and against the men who found it increasingly convenient to use its lies. It would mean enduring what that responsibility, that leadership, would cost.

The power was in him, willed to him by those murdered Kabbalists, by the gypsy woman whose body he'd seen, by the old runemasters and young psychics, and even by the darkly grinning Poincelles—fragments of power that could never have been power in the world to which it had been born, fused now in darkness and in light.

But to use that power . . .

Dying would be easier. And no one could say he hadn't earned that right.

A hand brushed his hair, touched his beard, and his hands. Someone whispered, "Rhion?"

And it wasn't any thought of power, or responsibility, of sacrificial shoulds or future ifs that made him open his eyes. Only that hearing her voice, he couldn't do otherwise—couldn't imagine doing otherwise, though he knew that the choice was between that sweet, dark peace and going through all that he had gone through again . . .

But this time he would go through it with her beside him.

Tally had cut her hair. Without the sugar-brown silk cloak of it, her head looked small and delicate, like a bird's.

He wondered how he could ever possibly have considered dying. "The boys?" he asked, after their mouths parted again. His voice was inaudible and the two words left him as breathless as if he'd lifted them, like huge rocks. She had to bend close to hear.

"They're safe. The Lady's keeping an eye on them through her Mirror—we're bringing them here as soon as we can figure out how to do it safely."

The mages gathered round: the Lady, with her long hair graying where it hung over the lilies embroidered on her dress; Gyzan, touching his forehead with spells of healing and ease in his mutilated hand; Cuffy Rifkin in rags and necklaces of spell-bones; Chelfrednig and his Selarnist companion Niane, their white robes stained and patched; a couple of Ebiatics in black; a scrawny, chinless Hand-Pricker with a big gray cat in his arms; and others.

Rhion thought that, if there'd been a concerted roundup of wizards by the authorities, it had clearly gone after the powerful ones—aside from the Lady and Gyzan there was no one here of any great strength. It was the first time he'd seen mages of so many different orders working together, something that probably wouldn't have happened, he thought, if any of them had been very powerful alone.

He whispered, "Thank you," and the effort of it took all he had. He closed his eyes and for a time heard nothing but the voice of the rain.

"Rhion, I'm sorry."

He looked up again. The room was empty but for Tally, still sitting on the low stool at the side of his bed. The single candle made a halo of her short-cropped hair. He moved his hand a little to touch it, then whispered in mock severity, "I won't beat you this time, but you'd better grow it back," and it surprised her into laughing, as he'd hoped it would.

"No," she said, her gray eyes growing somber again. "I'm sorry that after all you've been through to come home, home isn't . . . isn't . . ."

"Isn't what I left?" He looked around him, at the age-bleached stone of the walls, dyed amber where the candle flame touched, and at the half-opened shutters and the glisten of green-black ivy in the rain beyond. Her fingers over his were cool, as they always had been; he knew that his own hands had lost the chill of death.

"But it is, you know," he said. "I just didn't know it at the time. What did Jaldis say? *We can afford to think neither of the future nor of the past we leave behind* . . . He was wrong." He sighed. "He was wrong."

"Tally?" The door curtain at the far end of the room moved aside; framed in the darkness were two dark blurs of shadow, one his own height, the other tall. "Vyla of Wellhaven says she has seen in her crystal the armies of Bragenmere moving down the passes toward Fel," Gyzan's voice said. "They will be besieging that city in the morning."

The Gray Lady added, "If the worshippers of Agon don't open the gates to them, under the impression that doing so would please the Veiled God."

"So," Rhion said, as Tally's fingers closed involuntarily tighter over his. "It's started here." As if at a great distance, he thought he saw peace and darkness beckon to him, like a tiny figure at the crown of a far-off hill. But he turned from it, as he had turned from the Dancing Stones, and said softly, "There's work to do."

"Now?" Tally looked down at him worriedly, as the dark figures melted back into the shadow of the door, leaving the whispering, rainy stillness of the night to close them round.

Rhion smiled and drew her down to him. "In the morning." And he fell asleep with his head on her arm.

Author's Note

This was an extremely difficult book to write for a number of reasons, chief among them being the number of books that *could* have been written. But I did *not* want to write a book about the Holocaust, I did *not* want to write a history of the SS, or an examination of the Occult Bureau, or an account of occultism in general, or the Blitz, or Operation Sea Lion. All of those books have been written, by people more qualified than I.

What I *did* want to do was to do justice to those topics where they touched upon my own piece of magical fantasy, without being led too far astray. This I hope I have accomplished—I certainly did the best I could. World War II is an area awkwardly placed historically as far as I am concerned. It lies beyond the scope of my own memories, but it is close enough in time to the present to be massively documented, and I frequently found myself swimming in a morass of details, trying to decide which to include and which would only bog down the storyline in endless sidetracks.

I know that I got many things wrong. To the best of what I could learn, there was a distinction between the smaller labor camps and concentration camps per se, and everything I have read indicates that the systematic construction of death camps for the stated purpose of exterminating Jews, Poles, gypsies, and other "undesireable races" did not begin until early in 1941, though the intention and the plans predated that time. I have tried to be accurate about vehicles, weaponry, and technology, and about the major events of the war insofar as occasionally conflicting accounts would let me. I have stuck to the attitudes expressed in Nazi literature as closely as I could—certainly no modern parallels of events, personalities, or groups are intended, either in the historical or the fantasy components of my tale.

To those who lost family and loved ones in the disasters of those years, who might feel that I have trivialized of their deaths by turning the whole thing into a background for what is, basically, entertainment, I apologize sincerely. I lost no one—my mother's family left Poland years before, and it could be justly argued that I operate from a position of ignorance.

My intention is, as it has always been, strictly to entertain—but in doing so, at least I have tried not to gloss over facts, or do violence to the truth as I could learn it. I hope that I have succeeded on both counts.

About the Author

At various times in her life, Barbara Hambly has been a high school teacher, a model, a waitress, a technical editor, a professional graduate student, an all-night clerk at a liquor store, and a karate instructor. Born in San Diego, she grew up in Southern California, with the exception of one high-school semester spent in New South Wales, Australia. Her interest in fantasy began with reading *The Wizard of Oz* at an early age and has continued ever since.

She attended the University of California, Riverside, specializing in medieval history. In connection with this, she spent a year at the University of Bordeaux in the south of France and worked as a teaching and research assistant at UC Riverside, eventually earning a Master's Degree in the subject. At the university, she also became involved in karate, making Black Belt in 1978 and competing in several national-level tournaments. She now lives in Los Angeles.